CAMORRA CHRONICLES

Collection Volume I

TWISTED LOYALTIES

TWISTED EMOTIONS

TWISTED PRIDE

Cora Reilly

TWISTED LOYALTIES

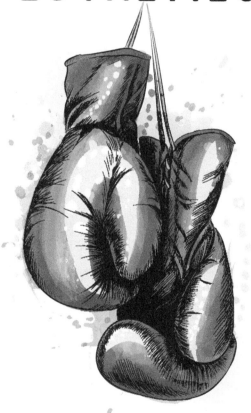

Book One
The Camorra Chronicles

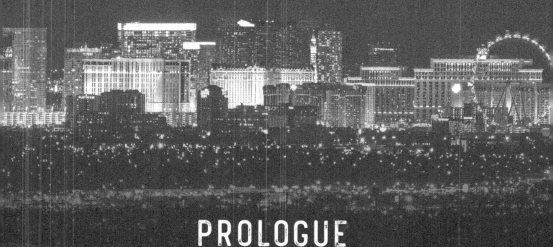

PROLOGUE

NEW YORK—*Famiglia territory*

Luca had been Capo for more than ten years, but things had never been this fucked up. Perched on the edge of the wide mahogany desk, Luca scanned the crinkled map showing the borders of their territory. His Famiglia still controlled the entire length of the East Coast, from Maine to Georgia. Nothing had changed in decades. The Camorra, however, had extended their territory far beyond Las Vegas into the east, having acquired Kansas City from the Russians only recently. Their Capo, Remo Falcone, was starting to get too confident. Luca had a fucking inkling that his next move would be attack either Outfit or Famiglia territory. Luca had to make sure Falcone set his sights on Dante Cavallaro's cities and not his own. Enough of his men had already died in the war between the Famiglia and the Outfit. Another war with the Camorra would tear them apart.

"I know you don't like the idea," he muttered to his soldier.

Growl nodded. "I don't, but I'm in no position to tell you what to do. You are Capo. I can only tell you what I know about the Camorra, and it's not good."

"So what?" Matteo, Luca's brother and right hand man, said with a shrug, spinning his knife between his fingers. "We can handle them."

A knock sounded and Aria entered the office, which was in the basement of Luca's club, the Sphere. She curiously raised her blond eyebrows, wondering why her husband had called her. He usually handled business on his own. Matteo and Growl were already inside. Luca leaned against the desk and unfolded his tall frame when she stepped into the room. She went over to him and kissed his lips lovingly then asked, "What's wrong?"

"Nothing," Luca said matter-of-factly, his lips set tight, eyes holding a wary glint. Something was off. "But we've contacted the Camorra for negotiations."

Aria glanced at Growl. He had fled Las Vegas six years ago after he'd killed the Camorra's Capo, Benedetto Falcone. From what he'd told them, the Camorra was much worse than the Outfit or the Famiglia. Besides the usual business of drugs, casinos, and prostitution, they also dealt in sex slavery and kidnapping. In the mafia world, the Camorra was considered bad news. "You did?"

"The fight with the Outfit is weakening us. With the Bratva already breaching our territory, we have to be careful. We can't risk the Outfit forging a deal with the Camorra before we get the chance. If they fight us together, we'll be in trouble."

Guilt filled Aria. She and her sisters were the reason why the truce between the Chicago Outfit and the New York Famiglia had dissolved. Her marriage to Luca was supposed to create a bond between the two families, but when her youngest sister, Liliana, fled Chicago to marry Luca's soldier, Romero, the Outfit's boss, Dante Cavallaro, declared war on them; he couldn't have reacted any other way.

"Do you think they will even consider talking to us?" Aria asked. She still wasn't sure why she was here in the first place. She didn't have any useful information about the Camorra.

Luca nodded. "They sent one of their own to talk to us. He'll be here soon." Something in his voice, an undercurrent of tension and worry, raised the little hairs on her neck.

"They're taking a huge risk by sending someone. They can't know if he's going to return alive," Aria said in surprise.

"One life is nothing to them," Growl murmured. "And the Capo didn't send one of his brothers. He sent his new enforcer."

Aria didn't like the way Luca, Matteo, and Growl were looking at her.

"They think he'll be safe," Luca said and after a long pause added, "because it's your brother."

The ground dropped away from Aria's feet, and she gripped the edge of the desk. "Fabi?" she whispered.

She hadn't seen or talked to him in many years. Since they declared war, she wasn't allowed to contact her brother. Her father, the Consigliere of the Outfit, had made sure of it.

She paused in her thoughts. "What's Fabi doing with the Camorra? He is a member of the Outfit. He was supposed to follow my father as Consigliere one day."

"He was supposed to, yes," Luca said, exchanging a look with the other men. "But your father's got two younger sons with his new wife, and apparently one of them will become Consigliere. We don't know what went down, but for some reason Fabiano defected to the Camorra, and for some reason they took him in. It's difficult to get accurate information on the matter."

"I can't believe it. I'm going to see my brother again. When?" she asked eagerly. Fabiano was almost nine years younger than Aria, and she'd practically raised him until she had to leave Chicago to marry Luca.

Growl shook his head with a frown.

Luca touched Aria's shoulder. "Aria, your brother is the new Enforcer of the Camorra."

It took a few seconds for the information to sink in. Aria's eyes darted over to Growl. His tattoos and scars, and the darkness lingering in his eyes, scared her. And being married to Luca, she wasn't easily scared anymore.

Growl had been the Enforcer of the Camorra when Benettone Falcone had been Capo. And now that Falcone's son had seized power, Fabi had taken over the role. She swallowed. *Enforcer.* They did the dirty work. The bloody work. They made sure people obeyed, and if they didn't obey, Enforcers made sure their fate was a warning to anyone considering the same.

"No," she said softly. "Not Fabi. He's not capable of that kind of thing." He had been a caring, gentle boy and had always tried to protect his sisters.

Matteo gave her a look that told her she was being naïve. She didn't care as long as it kept the memory of her kind, funny little brother alive. She didn't want to imagine him as anything else.

"The brother you knew won't be the brother you'll see today. He'll be someone completely different. That boy you knew … he's dead. He has to be. Enforcement isn't a job for the kindhearted. It's cruel and dirty work. And the Camorra doesn't show mercy toward women like is habit for New York or Chicago. I doubt that's changed. Falcone is a twisted fucker like his father," Growl said in his raspy voice.

Aria looked at Luca, hoping he'd contradict his soldier. He didn't. Something in Aria cracked. "I can't believe it. I don't want to," she said. "How could he have changed so much?"

"He's here," one of Luca's men informed them, walking into the office. "But he refuses to hand over his weapons."

Luca nodded. "It doesn't matter. We outnumber him. Let him through." Then he turned to Aria. "Perhaps we'll find out today."

Aria tensed with the sound of steps approaching. A tall man stepped through the open office door. He was almost as tall as Luca. Not quite as broad, but muscled.

A Tattoo peeked out under his rolled-up shirtsleeves. His dark blond hair was buzzed on the sides and slightly longer on top, and his ice-blue eyes …

Cold. Calculating. Cautious.

Aria wasn't sure she would have recognized him in the street. No longer a boy, he was a man—and not just judging by his age. His eyes settled on her. The smile of the past didn't come, even though recognition flashed in his eyes. God, there really was nothing left of the lighthearted boy she remembered. But he was still her brother. He would always be. It was foolish, but she rushed toward him, ignoring Luca's growled warning.

Her brother grew tense as she threw her arms around him. She could feel the knives strapped to his back, the guns in his chest holster. She was confident there were more weapons on his body. He didn't hug her back, but one of his hands cupped her neck. Aria looked up at him then. She hadn't expected to see the anger in his eyes as he returned his focus to Luca and the other men in the room.

"No need for drawn weapons," he said with a hint of cold amusement. "I haven't traveled all the way to hurt my sister."

His touch on her neck seemed more like a threat and less like a gesture of familiarity.

Luca's fingers closed around her upper arm, and he pulled her back. Fabiano followed the scene with dark humor in his eyes, remaining stock-still.

"My God," Aria whispered in a voice thick with tears. "What happened to you, Fabi?"

A predator grin curled his lips.

Not Fabi anymore, she thought. That man in front of her … he was someone to be afraid of.

Fabiano Scuderi.

Enforcer of the Camorra.

ONE

The past:

Fabiano

I CURLED INTO MYSELF AND DIDN'T FIGHT BACK. I NEVER DID.

Father grunted from the effort of beating me. Punch after punch—my back, my head, my stomach—creating new bruises and awakening old bruises. I gasped when he shoved the toe of his shoe into my stomach, swallowing down bile. If I threw up, he'd only beat me worse. Or use the knife. I shuddered.

Then the hits stopped, and I dared to look up, blinking to clear my vision. Sweat and blood dripped down my face.

Breathing hard, Father glowered at me. He wiped his hands on a towel that his soldier, Alfonso, had handed him. Perhaps this was the last test to prove my worth. Maybe I'd finally become an official part of the Outfit. A Made Man.

"Do I get my tattoo?" I rasped.

Father's lip curled. "Your tattoo? You won't be part of the Outfit."

"But—" He kicked me again, and I fell back to my side. I pressed on, not caring about the consequences. "But I will be Consigliere when you retire." *When you die.*

He gripped my collar and pulled me to my feet. My legs ached as I tried to stand. "You are a fucking waste of my blood. You and your sisters share your mother's tainted genes. One disappointment after another. All of you. Your sisters are whores, and you are weak. I'm done with you. Your brother will become Consigliere."

"But he's a baby. I'm your oldest son." Since Father had married his second wife, he'd treated me like dirt. I thought it was to make me strong for my future tasks, so I'd done everything I could to prove my worth to him.

"You are a disappointment like your sisters. I won't allow you to bring shame down on me." He let go of me and my legs finally gave out.

More pain.

"But, Father," I whispered. "It's tradition."

Rage twisted his facial features. "Then, we'll just have to make sure that your brother is my oldest son." He nodded at Alfonso, who rolled up his sleeves.

Alfonso landed the first punch in my stomach then my ribs. My eyes remained on my father as blow after blow shook my body, until my vision finally turned black. My own father would have me killed.

"Make sure he won't be found, Alfonso."

Pain. Bone deep.

I groaned. Vibrations sent a twinge through my ribs. I tried to open my eyes and sit up, but my lids were crusted shut. I groaned again.

I wasn't dead.

Why wasn't I dead?

Hope flared up inside me.

"Father?" I croaked.

"Shut up and sleep, boy. We'll arrive soon."

That was Alfonso's voice.

I struggled into a sitting position and peeled my eyes open. Through blurry vision, I could see I was sitting in the back of a car.

Alfonso turned to me. "You're stronger than I thought. Good for you."

"Where?" I coughed then winced. "Where are we?"

"Kansas City." Alfonso steered the car onto an empty parking lot. "Final stop."

He got out, opened the back door, and pulled me out. I gasped in pain, holding my ribs, then staggered against the car. Alfonso flipped open his wallet and handed me a twenty-dollar note. I took it, confused.

"Perhaps you'll survive. Perhaps you won't. I suppose it's up to fate now. But I won't kill a fourteen-year-old kid." He grasped my throat, forcing me to meet his eyes. "Your father thinks you're dead, boy, so make sure you stay away from our territory."

Their territory? It was my territory. The Outfit was my destiny. I didn't have anything else.

"Please," I whispered.

He shook his head then walked around the car and got in. I took a step back when he drove off, sinking down to my knees. My clothes were covered in blood. I clutched the money in my hand. This was all I had. Slowly, I stretched out on the cool asphalt. Pressure against my calf reminded me of my favorite knife, strapped to a holster there. Twenty dollars and a knife. My body ached. I never wanted to get up again. There was no sense in doing anything. I was nothing. I wished Alfonso had done as my father ordered and just killed me.

I coughed and tasted blood. I'll probably die anyway. My eyes flitted around. Graffiti covered the wall of a building to my right: a snarling wolf in front of swords.

The sign of the Bratva.

Alfonso couldn't kill me himself.

This place surely would. Kansas City belonged to the Russians.

Fear urged me to get to my feet and leave. I wasn't sure where to go or what to do. I hurt all over. At least it wasn't too cold. I began walking, looking for a place to spend the night. Eventually, I settled for the entrance of a coffee shop. I'd never been alone, never had to live on the streets. I pulled my legs against my chest and swallowed a whimper. My ribs. They hurt fiercely. I couldn't return to the Outfit. Father would make sure I was dead this time. Perhaps I could try to contact Dante Cavallaro. He and Father had worked together for a long time, and I'd look like a fucking rat. A coward and weakling.

Aria would help. My stomach clenched. Her helping Lily and Gianna was the reason why Father hated me in the first place. Running to New York with my tail between my legs, begging Luca to make me part of the Famiglia, wasn't going to happen. Everyone would know I had been taken in out of pity, not because I was a worthy asset.

Worthless.

This was it. I was alone.

Four days later. Only four days. I was out of money and hope. Every night I returned to the parking lot, hoping, wishing that Alfonso would return, that Father had changed his mind, that his last pitiless, hateful look had been my imagination. I was a fucking idiot. And hungry.

No food in two days. I'd wasted the whole twenty bucks on burgers, fries, and Dr. Pepper the first day.

I held my ribs. The pain had gotten worse. I'd tried to get money by pick-pocketing today. Chose the wrong guy and he beat up. I didn't know how to survive on the street. I wasn't sure I wanted to keep trying.

What was I going to do? No Outfit. No future. No honor.

I sank down on the ground of the parking lot, in plain view of the Bratva graffiti. I lay back. The door opened as men left the building, walking away. Bratva territory.

I was so fucking tired.

My death wouldn't be slow. They would take their time. The pain in my limbs and hopelessness kept me in place. I stared up at the night sky and began reciting the oath I'd memorized months ago, in preparation for the day of my induction. The Italian words flowing from my mouth filled me with loss and despair. I repeated the oath over and over again. It had been my destiny to become a made man.

There were voices to my right. Male voices in a foreign language.

Suddenly a black-haired guy stared down at me. He was bruised, though not as badly as me, and dressed in fight shorts. "They say there's a crazy Italian fucker outside, spouting Omertà. I guess they meant you."

I fell silent. He'd said 'Omertà' like I would say it, like it meant something. He was covered in scars. Probably a few years older than me. Eighteen, perhaps.

"Talking that kind of shit in this area means you've got a death wish or are bat-shit crazy. Probably both."

"That oath was my life," I said.

He shrugged then looked over his shoulder before turning back with a twisted smile. "Now it's going to be your death."

I sat up. Three men in fight shorts, bodies covered in tattoos of wolves and Kalashnikovs and heads clean shaven, stepped out of a door next to the Bratva building.

I considered lying back and letting them finish what Alfonso couldn't.

"What family?" The black-haired guy asked.

"Outfit," I replied, even as the word ripped a hole in my heart.

He nodded. "Suppose they got rid of you. No balls to do what it takes to be a made man?"

Who was he? "I got what it takes," I hissed. "But my father wants me dead."

"Then prove it. Get the fuck up from the ground and fight." He narrowed his eyes when I didn't move. "Get. The. Fuck. Up."

And I did, even though my world spun and I had to hold on to my ribs. His black eyes took in my injuries. "Suppose I will have to do most of the fighting. Got any weapons?"

I pulled my Karambit knife from the holster around my calf.

"I hope you can handle that thing."

Then the Russians were upon us. The guy began some martial arts shit that kept two of the Russians busy. The third headed my way. I swiped my knife at him and missed. He landed a few hits that had my chest screaming with agony, and I dropped to my knees. With my body battered and bruised, I had no chance against a trained fighter like him. His fists rained down on me, hard, fast, merciless. *Pain.*

The black-haired guy lunged at my attacker, ramming his knee into his stomach. The Russian fell forward, and I raised my knife, which buried itself in his abdomen. Blood trickled down my fingers, and I released the handle like it burned me as the Russian toppled to his side, dead.

I stared at my knife sticking out of his belly. The black-haired guy pulled it out, cleaned the blade on the dead man's shorts, then handed it to me. "First kill?"

I nodded, my fingers shaking as I took it from him.

"There will be more."

The two other Russians were dead as well. Their necks had been broken. He held out his hand, which I grabbed as he pulled me to my feet. "We should leave. More Russian fuckers will be here soon. Come on."

He led me toward a beat-up truck. "Noticed you slinking around the parking lot the last two nights when I was here to fight."

"Why did you help me?"

There was that twisted smile again. "Because I like to fight … and kill. Because I hate the fucking Bratva. Because my family wants me dead too. But most importantly, because I need loyal soldiers who will help me take back what's mine."

"Who are you?"

"Remo Falcone. And I will be Capo of the Camorra soon." He opened the door to his truck and was halfway in when he added, "You can help me or you can wait for the Bratva to get you."

I got in. Not because of the Bratva.

Because Remo had shown me a new purpose, a new destiny.

A new family.

TWO

Leona

THE WINDOW OF THE GREYHOUND BUS FELT STICKY HOT, OR MAYBE IT was my face. The infant in the row behind me had stopped wailing ten minutes ago—finally, after almost two hours. I peeled my cheek from the glass, feeling sluggish and tired. Squeezed into the stuffy seat for hours, I couldn't wait to get out. Las Vegas' posh suburbs rolled past me, their immaculate landscaping sufficiently watered by sprinklers. Surrounded by desert, that must be the ultimate showcase of having money. Elaborate Christmas decorations adorned the porches and the fronts of freshly painted houses.

Despite how beautiful, that wouldn't be my stop.

The bus trudged on, the floor vibrating under my bare feet, until finally it arrived in that part of town where no tourist ever dared set foot in. The all-you-can-eat buffets cost only $9.99 around here, not $59; I could afford neither. Not that I minded. I'd grown up in areas like these. In Phoenix, Houston, Dallas, Austin, and more other places than I cared to count. I slipped into my flip-flops, swung my backpack over my shoulder, getting ready to depart the bus.

Out of habit, I reached into my pocket for a cell phone that was no longer there. Mother had sold it for her last dose of crystal meth. The twenty dollars she got for it had been out of pity, no doubt.

I waited until most of the other people had left before I stepped off the bus, releasing a long breath as I stood under the sun. The air was drier than in Austin, and it was a few degrees colder, but still not wintery cold. Somehow, I already felt freer being away from my mother. This was her last shot at therapy. She needed to make it a success. I was stupid for hoping she could.

"Leona?" came a deep voice from somewhere to the right.

I turned, surprised. My father stood a few feet from me, with about thirty more pounds on his hips and less hair on his head. I hadn't expected him to pick me up. He'd promised to do it, but I knew what promises from him and my mother were worth. Less than the dirt under my shoes. Perhaps he'd really changed like he'd claimed.

He quickly stubbed out his cigarette under his worn loafers. The short-sleeved shirt stretched over his paunch. There was a disheveled air about him that had me worried.

I smiled. "The one and only."

I wasn't surprised he'd had to ask. The last time I'd seen him had been on my fourteenth birthday, more than five years ago. I hadn't exactly missed him. I'd missed the idea of having a father—one he could never be. Still, it was nice to see him again. Maybe we could start anew.

He came over and pulled me into an awkward hug. I wrapped my arms around him despite the lingering stench of sweat and smoke. It had been a while since someone had hugged me. Standing back, he scanned me from head to toe. "You've grown." His eyes paused on my smile. "And your pimples are gone."

Have been for three years. "Thank God," I said instead.

My father pushed his hands into his pockets, as if he was suddenly unsure of what to do with me. "I was surprised when you called."

I tucked a strand of hair behind my ear, unsure where he was going with this. "You never did," I said before soon regretting it. I hadn't come to Vegas to dish out guilt. Dad had never been a good father, but he'd tried occasionally … even if he always failed. Mom and him … They were both fucked up in their own ways. Addiction had always been the thing that got in the way of caring for me the way they should have.

He gave me an appraising look. "Are you sure you want to stay with me?"

My smile wavered. Was that what his hesitation was all about? He didn't want me around? I really wished he mentioned that before I'd paid for a bus ticket that took me through half the states. He'd said he beat his addiction, that he had a decent job and a normal life. I wanted to believe him.

"It's not that I'm not happy to have you with me. I missed you," he said quickly. Too quickly. Lies.

"Then what?" I asked, trying but failing to hide my hurt.

"It's not a good place for a nice girl like you, Leona."

I laughed. "I've never exactly lived in the nice parts of town," I told him. "I can handle myself."

"No. It's different here. Believe me."

"Don't worry. I'm good at staying out of trouble." I'd had years of practice.

With a meth-addicted mother who sold anything, even her body, for her next fix, you had to learn to duck your head and mind your own business.

"Sometimes trouble finds you. It happens around here more often than you'd believe." The way he said it, I worried that trouble was a constant guest in his life.

I sighed. "Honestly, Dad, I've lived with a mother who spent most of her days in a drug haze. You never worried enough to take me away from her. Now that I'm grown up, you're worried I can't handle living in the City of Sin?"

He looked at me as if he was going to say more but then finally took my backpack from me before I could tighten my hold on the strap. "You're right."

"And I'm only going to stay here until I've earned enough money for college. There are enough places around here where I can make decent money with tips."

He looked relieved that I wanted to work. Had he thought I was going to live off him?

"There are more than enough places, but few that are fit for a girl like you."

I shook my head, smiling. "Don't worry. I can handle drunkards."

"I'm not worried about them," he said nervously.

Fabiano

"Are you really thinking about working with the Famiglia?" I managed to pant as I dodged a kick aimed at my head. "I told you how they fucked with the Outfit."

I thrust my bandaged fist into Remo's side then tried a kick at his legs, but he landed a fist into my stomach instead. I jumped back, out of Remo's reach, and feigned an attack to the left and instead kicked with my right leg. Remo's arm shot up, protecting his head, taking the full force of my kick. He didn't fall. "I don't want to work with them. Not with Luca fucking Vitiello nor with Dante fucking Cavallaro. We don't need them."

"Then why send me to New York?" I asked.

Remo got two quick blows to my left side. I sucked in a breath and rammed my elbow down on his shoulder. He hissed and darted away, but I got him. His arm was hanging low. I'd dislocated his shoulder. My favorite move.

"Open refusal?" he asked half in jest, giving no indication that he was in agony.

"You wish."

Remo liked to break things. There wasn't anything he liked better. Sometimes I thought he wanted me to revolt so he could try breaking me because I'd be his biggest challenge. I had no intention of giving him the chance. Not that he'd succeed.

He glared and lunged at me. I barely dodged his first two kicks; the third hit my chest. I was thrown into the boxing ring and almost lost my balance but caught myself by gripping the rope. I quickly straightened and raised my fists.

"Oh fuck this shit," Remo snarled. He grabbed his arm and tried to reposition his shoulder. "I can't fight with this fucking useless limb."

I lowered my hands. "So you give up?"

"No," he said. "Tie."

"Tie," I agreed. There had never been anything but ties in our fights, except for the very first year when I'd been a scrawny kid without a clue how to fight. We were both strong fighters, used to pain and indifferent about whether we lived or died. If we ever fought it out till the end, we'd both end up in body bags. No doubt about it.

I snatched a towel from the floor and wiped the blood and sweat from my chest and arms.

With a grunt, Remo finally managed to set his arm. It would have been quicker and less painful if I'd help, but he'd never let me. Pain meant nothing to him. Nor to me.

I threw a clean towel at him. He caught it with his injured arm just to prove a point. Attempting to dry his hair, he only managed to spread the blood from a cut on his head all over his black hair. He dropped the towel unceremoniously. The scar running from his left temple down to his left cheek was an angry red from fighting.

"So why?" I asked, removing the red-tinged bandages around my fingers and wrist.

"I want to see how things are going over there. I'm curious. That's all. And I like to know my enemies. You will be able to gather more information than any of us just by watching them interact. Most of all, I want to send them a clear message." His dark eyes became hard. "You aren't thinking about playing happy family with your sisters and becoming one of Vitiello's lapdogs, are you?"

I cocked one eyebrow. More than five years and he really had to ask? I swung myself over the boxing ring and light on my feet, I landed on the floor on the other side with close to no sound. "I belong to the Camorra. When they all abandoned me, you took me in. You made me who I am today, Remo. You should know better than to accuse me of being a traitor. I will put my life down for you. And if I must, I will take the Outfit and the Famiglia to hell with me."

"One day you will get your chance," he said.

To lay down my life for him or to take down the other families?

"I have another task for you."

I nodded, expecting it. He held my eyes. "You are the only one who can get close to Aria. She is Vitiello's weakness."

I kept my expression impassive.

"Bring her to me, Fabiano."

"Dead or alive?"

He smiled. "Alive. If you kill her, Vitiello will go on a rampage, but if we have his wife, he'll be our puppet."

I didn't have to ask why he had an interest in tearing down the Famiglia. We didn't need their territory, and it wasn't worth much as long as Dante owned everything in the middle. We were making enough money in the west as it was. Remo was out for revenge. Luca had made a mistake when he'd taken in the former Enforcer of the Camorra, and he'd made an even bigger mistake when he'd sent the man back to kill many high-ranking Camorrista while Las Vegas was without a strong Capo to lead the city. Before Remo, that is.

"Consider it done."

Remo inclined his head. "Your father was a fucking fool for overlooking your worth. But that's how fathers are. Mine would have never allowed me to become Capo. It's a pity I didn't get to kill him myself."

Remo envied me for that. I could still kill my father, and one day I would.

It had been years since I'd last treaded New York ground. I'd never liked the city much. It represented nothing but loss to me.

The bouncer in front of the Sphere gave me the once-over as I approached. I detected another guard on the roof. The street was deserted except for us. That wasn't going to change until much later when the first partygoers would try to get into the popular club.

I stopped in front of the bouncer. He rested his hand on the gun at his hip. He wouldn't be quick enough. "Fabiano Scuderi," I said simply. Of course he knew. They all knew. Without a word, he let me walk into the waiting room. Two men barred my way.

"Weapons," one of them ordered, pointing at a table.

"No," I said.

The taller of the two, several inches shorter than me, brought his face close to mine. "What was that?"

"That was a no. If you're too deaf or stupid to understand me, get someone who can. I'm losing my patience."

The man's face turned red. It would take three moves to sever his head from his body. "Tell the Capo he's here and refuses to put down his weapons."

If he thought he could intimidate me mentioning Luca, he was mistaken. The times when I'd feared and admired him had long since passed. He was dangerous, no doubt, but so was I.

Eventually, he returned and I was finally allowed to pass through the blue-lit lobby and dance floor then down to the basement. It was a good place if someone wanted to stop outsiders from hearing the screaming. That didn't manage to unnerve me either. The Famiglia didn't know the Camorra very well. They didn't know me very well. We'd never been worth their attention until our power had grown too strong for them to ignore.

The moment I stepped into the office, I scanned my surroundings. Growl stood off to the left side. *Traitor.* Remo would love to have his head delivered to him in a plastic bag. Not because the man had killed his father, but because he'd betrayed the Camorra. That was a crime worthy of a painful death.

Luca and Matteo, were in the middle of the room, both tall and dark. My sister, Aria, with her blond hair was like a beacon of light.

I remembered her to be taller, but then again, I was a kid when I'd last seen her. The shock on her face was obvious. She still wore her emotions on the sleeve. Even her marriage to Luca hadn't changed that. You'd think he'd have broken her spirit by now. Strange that she was the same as I remembered though I had become someone new.

She rushed toward me. Luca reached for her, but she was too quick. He and his men drew their weapons the moment Aria collided with me. My hand came up to her neck momentarily. She hugged me, her hands splayed out on my back where I had my knives. She was too trusting. I could have killed her in a heartbeat. Breaking her neck would have taken little effort. I'd killed like that before, in fights to the death. Luca's bullet would have been too late. She looked up at me hopefully. Then, slowly, realization and fear set in. Yes, Aria. I'm not a little boy anymore.

I looked back at the men. "No need for drawn weapons," I said to Luca. His cautious gaze flitted between my fingers positioned perfectly on her neck and my eyes. He recognized the danger his little wife was in, even if she didn't. "I haven't traveled all the way to hurt my sister."

It was the truth. I had no intention of hurting her, even though I could have. What Remo had in mind for her, I couldn't say. I slipped a note into the pocket of her jeans.

Luca lunged toward us and pulled her away from me, warning clear in his eyes.

"My God," Aria whispered, tears filling her eyes. "What happened to you?"

Did she really have to ask? Had she been so busy saving my sisters that she hadn't considered what that would mean for me?

"You, Gianna, and Liliana happened."

Confusion filled her face. She really didn't get it. Cold fury shot through me, but I pushed it down. Every horror of my past had made me into who I was today.

"I don't understand."

"After Liliana ran off as well, Father decided that something must be wrong with all of us. That perhaps Mother's blood running through our veins was the problem. He thought I was another mistake in the making. He tried to beat it out of me. Maybe he thought if I bled often enough, I'd be rid of any trace of that weakness. The moment his whore of a second wife gave birth to a boy, he decided I was no longer of use. He ordered one of his men to kill me. The man took pity on me and drove me to some shithole in Kansas City so the Bratva could kill me instead. I had twenty dollars and a knife." I paused. "And I put that knife to good use."

I could see the words sink in. She shook her head. "We didn't want to hurt you. We just wanted to save Liliana from a horrible marriage. We didn't think you'd need saving. You were a boy. You were on your way to becoming a soldier for the Outfit. We would have saved you if you'd asked."

"I saved myself," I said simply.

"You could still … leave Las Vegas," Aria said carefully. Luca sent her a glare.

I laughed darkly. "Are you suggesting I'll leave the Camorra and join the Famiglia?"

Wincing, she seemed taken aback by the harshness of my tone. "It's an option."

I turned my gaze toward Luca. "Is she Capo or you? I came here to talk to the man leading the show, but now I think it might be a woman after all."

Luca didn't seem fazed by my words, at least not openly. "She is your sister. She does the talking because I allowed her to do so. Don't worry, Fabi, if I had anything to say to you, I'd say it."

Fabi. The nickname didn't provoke me the way it was supposed to. I'd grown out of it. Nobody knew me by that name in Vegas, and even if they did, they wouldn't dare use it.

"We are not your enemy, Fabi," Aria said. And I knew she meant it. She was the Capo's vice, and yet she knew nothing. Her husband saw me as I saw him: an opponent to watch. A predator intruding on his territory.

"I'm a member of the Camorra. You *are* my enemies." If this journey had been good for anything, it proved to myself that there was truly nothing left of that stupid, weak boy I'd been. That had been beaten out of me, first by my father, and later in the street and in the fighting cages as I fought for a place in this world.

Aria shook her head, refusing to believe it. She hadn't abandoned me on purpose, hadn't sealed my fate by helping my sisters run away, but sometimes the things we caused by accident were the worst.

"I have a message from Remo for you," I told Luca, ignoring my sister. I'd deal with her later. She wasn't the only reason why I had come to New York. "You have nothing to offer Remo or the Camorra, unless perhaps you send him your wife for a joy ride." The words left a bitter taste in my mouth, if only because she was my sister.

Luca was halfway across the room before Aria stepped in his way. I had my gun out and one of my knives. "Calm down, Luca," Aria begged.

He glared at me. Oh, he wanted to rip me to shreds, and I wanted to see him try. He'd be a challenging opponent. Instead, he let my sister talk him down, but his eyes held a promise: *You are dead.*

Remo would have never listened to a woman, would have never shown that kind of weakness in front of anyone. Neither would I. The Outfit and the Famiglia both had grown weak over the years. They weren't a threat to us. If we handled the situation with cleverness, soon their territories would be ours.

I performed a mock bow. "I assume that's all."

"Don't you want to know how Lilly and Gianna are doing?" Aria asked hopefully, still looking for a sign of the boy she used to know. I wondered when she'd realize that he was gone for good. Perhaps when the Camorra took over someday, I'd ram my knife into her husband's heart.

"They mean nothing to me. The day you left for your pampered life in New York, you ceased existing for me."

I turned. Presenting my back to the enemy wasn't something I usually did, but I knew Aria, with her puppy dog eyes, would stop Luca from killing me. I wanted to show him and his brother, Matteo, that I didn't fear them. I hadn't feared anyone in a long time.

It was almost two o'clock in the morning. It had begun snowing a while ago, and a fine layer of white powder covered my jacket and the ground. I'd been waiting for more than one hour. Perhaps Aria had more sense than I gave her credit for.

Soft steps crunched near my right. I pushed off the wall, drawing my gun but lowering it when Aria, wrapped in a thick wool coat and scarf, came into view. She stopped across from me. "Hello, Fabi." She held out the paper that I'd shoved into her pocket. "You said you wanted to talk to me alone because you needed my help?"

Her need to help others—first Gianna, then Lily, and now me—was her greatest weakness. I really wished she'd stayed home. I moved closer.

She regarded me with sad eyes. "But you were lying, weren't you?" she whispered. If we weren't standing so close, I wouldn't have understood her. "You were trying to get me alone."

If she knew, why had she come?

Did she hope for mercy? Then, I realized why she'd whispered. I tightened my hold on my gun. My eyes searched the darkness until I found Luca leaning against a wall to the far left, his gun pointed at my head.

I smiled because I'd underestimated her. A small, weak part of me was relieved. "Finally being sensible, Aria."

"I know a thing or two about mob life."

Only the things Luca allowed her to see, no doubt.

"Aren't you worried for your life?" she asked curiously.

"Why would I be?"

She sighed. "Did the Camorra want to kidnap me?" Again, a whisper, obviously not meant for Luca's ears. Was she trying to save me from his wrath? She shouldn't.

I didn't say anything. Unlike Luca, I didn't divulge information because she batted her eyelashes at me. The time when she'd held power over me as my older sister had long since passed. My silence seemed all the answer she needed.

She lifted one arm and I followed the movement cautiously. With her other hand, she removed a piece of jewelry from her wrist and held it out to me.

"It was Mother's. She gave it to me shortly before her death. I want you to have it."

"Why?" I asked as I peered down at the gold bracelet with sapphires. I didn't remember our mother wearing it, but I was twelve when she'd died and on the brink of starting the induction process to the Outfit. I had other things on my mind than expensive jewelry.

"Because I want you to remember."

"The family that abandoned me?"

"No, the boy you used to be and the man you can still become."

"Who says I want to remember?" I said in a low voice, leaning down to her so she could look into my eyes despite the darkness surrounding us. I heard the soft click of Luca releasing the safety of his gun. I smirked. "You want me to be a better man. Why don't you start with the man who's pointing a gun at my head?"

She pushed the bracelet against my chest, and I took it reluctantly.

"Perhaps one day you'll find someone who will love you despite what you've become, and she will make you want to be better." She stepped away. "Goodbye, Fabiano. Luca wants you to know that next time you come to New York, you will pay with your life."

My fingers tightened around the bracelet. I had no intention of returning to this godforsaken city for any other reason than to rip New York from Luca's bleeding hands.

THREE

Fabiano

RETURNING TO VEGAS ALWAYS FELT LIKE RETURNING HOME. I'D BEEN IN Nevada for almost five years. When I first arrived, I didn't think I'd last that long. Five years. So much had changed since Father had wanted me dead. The past was the past, but sometimes the memories came back. They were a good reminder why I owed Remo my loyalty and my life. Without him, I'd be dead.

Perhaps I should have seen it coming after I messed up my first job as an initiate of the Chicago Outfit. I'd been honored with the task of patrolling the corridors on the wedding day of my youngest sister, Liliana. I was excited … until I came across my sisters, Aria and Gianna, with their husbands, Matteo and Luca, as well as Liliana and someone who *definitely* wasn't the man she'd married.

I knew immediately that they were taking Liliana to New York with them, and I also knew that as a member of the Outfit, I was supposed to stop them. I didn't have my tattoo yet, since my initiation wasn't completed, but I'd already been sworn into the Outfit. I was only thirteen. I was weak and stupid back then and had allowed Aria to talk me into letting them go. I'd even let them shoot me in my arm so it would look convincing to everyone. To make it look as if I'd *tried* to stop them. Dante Cavallaro didn't punished me. He believed my story, but Father wrote me off that day like he'd written off the daughters he couldn't control. And that's when it all started. Things were set in motion that led to a member of the Outfit becoming part of the Camorra.

After my messed up first job, I was only allowed to watch from the sidelines, deemed too young to be a real part of the Outfit. I was still eager to please Dante and my father but failing miserably.

I should have died after Alfonso had left me in Bratva territory. The Russians would have beaten me to death; if not them, then someone else. I had no clue how to survive on the street or on my own. But Remo knew. He had been born a fighter. It was in his blood, and he showed me how to fight, how to survive, how to kill.

He let me live in the shabby apartment he shared with his three brothers. He put food on our table with money he won in the fighting cages, and I paid him back with loyalty and the fierce determination to become the soldier he needed at his side to help him kill the fuckers laying claim on a territory that was rightfully his.

Almost four months later, I wasn't the pampered Outfit boy anymore when we arrived in Reno, part of the Camorra territory. Remo and Nino had beaten it out of me in training fights and had taught me how to fight dirty. More importantly, Remo had showed me my worth. I didn't need the Outfit, didn't need a position handed to me on a silver platter. Remo and I, we had to fight for what we wanted. That was all I needed: a purpose and someone who saw my worth when no one else could.

When we first set foot on Camorra ground, they were still in turmoil since their Capo had been killed by a man called Growl. Without a new Capo, there was a lot of fighting over the position.

Remo, Nino, and I spent the next few months in Reno, earning money by fighting and eventually winning every match until even the newest Capo in Las Vegas started to notice. We went there together to kill everyone who was against Remo. And when he finally took over as Capo, I became his enforcer, a rank I hadn't inherited—a rank I'd paid in blood and scars for. A rank I was proud of and would defend till my death, just like I would defend Remo.

The tattoo on my forearm marking me as a made man of the Las Vegas Camorra went deeper than my skin. Nothing and nobody would ever make me break the oath I'd given to my Capo.

I drew in a deep breath. The smell of tar and burnt rubber hung in the air. Familiar. Exhilarating. The flashy lights of Las Vegas burned in the distance. A sight I'd grown used to. *Home.*

The glamor of the Strip was missing in this part of town, just off Sierra Vista Drive. Violence, my favorite language, was spoken fluently around here.

A long row of race cars lined the parking lot of the closed Boulevard Mall. It was the starting point of the illegal street race going down tonight. Some of the drivers nodded a greeting in my direction, while others pretended not to notice me. Most of them still had debts to pay, but tonight I hadn't come for them. They didn't have to worry.

I headed toward Cane, one of the organizers of the race. He hadn't yet paid what he owed us. It was a sum that couldn't be ignored, even though he was a profitable asset.

Most of the money we made with illegal street races came from bets. We had a camera team that filmed the races and put them in a locked forum on the Darknet; everyone with the log-in code could watch. This part of the business was pretty new. Remo had established the races when he seized power. He didn't hang on to the old-fashioned rules that bound the Outfit and the Famiglia—rules that made them slow to adapt. He was always on the lookout for new ways to make the Camorra more money, and he was successful in his endeavors.

A few engines roared, saturating the air with gasoline vapors. The start was only a couple of minutes away, but I hadn't come to watch the race. I was here on business.

I spotted my target next to our bookie, Griffin—a short guy, almost wider than he was tall. Cane's pockmarked face twisted when he saw me coming his way. His eyes searched the parking lot and it looked like he considered running.

"Cane," I said pleasantly as I stopped before him. "Remo is missing some money."

He took a step back and raised his hands. "I will pay him soon. I promise."

I promise. I swear. Tomorrow. Please. Words I'd heard too often.

"Hmm," I murmured. "Soon wasn't your due date."

Griffin shut off his iPad and excused himself. The dirty work in our business drove him away. He was only interested in the financial aspects.

I took Cane by the collar of his shirt and dragged him off to the side, farther away from the starting line. Not that I cared if anyone watched what I was doing, but I wasn't keen on eating smoke and dirt once the cars raced off.

I pushed Cane away from me. He lost his balance and fell on his backside. His eyes darted left and right, as if he was searching for something to defend himself with. I grabbed his hand, twisted it all the way back, and broke his wrist. He howled, cradling his injured hand against his chest. Nobody came to help him. They knew how things worked. People who didn't pay their debts got a visit from me. A broken wrist was one of the kinder outcomes.

"Tomorrow, I'll be back," I told him. I pointed at his knee. He knew what I meant.

Over to the left side, near the starting line, I noticed a familiar face with black curls. Adamo, Remo's youngest brother. This was definitely not where he was supposed to be at this time of the night. He was only thirteen and had been caught racing before. Apparently, Remo losing his shit on him hadn't made him see reason. I jogged over to him and the two older guys beside him, who looked like they were up to no good. The moment they spotted me, they dashed off, but Adamo knew better than to try that.

"What are you doing here? Shouldn't you be in bed? You've got school in the morning."

He gave a bored shrug. Too cool for a proper reply.

I grabbed his collar, forcing his eyes to finally meet mine. "It's not like I need an education. I'll become a made man and earn money with illegal shit."

I released him. "Can't hurt to use your brain so the illegal shit won't send you to jail." I nodded toward my car. "I'll take you to Remo."

"You didn't finish school. And Remo and Nino didn't either. Why do I have to do this shit?"

I slapped the back of his head lightly. "Because we were busy taking Las Vegas back. You are only busy getting yourself in trouble. Now move."

He grimaced, rubbing the back of his head. "I can go home by myself. I don't need a ride."

"So you can try to sneak in without him noticing?" I nodded toward my car again. "Not going to happen. Now move. I have better things to do than to babysit you."

"Like what? Beating up other debtors?"

"Among other things."

He trudged toward the car and practically flung himself into the passenger seat then closed the door with so much force I feared he'd damaged the soft close mechanism. Since he'd hit puberty, he was completely intolerable, and he had been difficult even before that.

The moment I set foot in the gaming room of the abandoned casino that functioned as our gym, I heard the gasps. I placed my palm against Adamo's chest, stopping him. I should have known Remo wasn't alone. Bad news always drove him to the gym.

"You will wait here."

Adamo crossed his arms. "It's not the first time I've seen Remo beating someone up."

The youngest Falcone brother had witnessed violence over the years. It was impossible to shelter him from the cruel realities of it all, but Remo didn't want Adamo to start the induction process before his fourteenth birthday. Until then, he wouldn't see the worst of our business.

"You will wait." I said firmly before I walked over to Remo. Adamo skulked over to the broken Champagne bar and began smashing a few glasses.

When I stepped into the second gaming room that we used for kickboxing training, Remo was kicking the living daylights out of some poor fucker I didn't know. He was probably still furious with me because I hadn't been successful in bringing Aria back to him. Or maybe he was mad because of my earlier phone call telling him about his brother being out in the middle of the night. Again.

He stopped when he spotted me, wiping some sweat and blood from his forehead with the back of his hand. He hadn't even bothered wrapping his hands with tape, too eager to let off some steam.

"I took that one off your hands. Sometimes I need to get down to business myself," he said. He looked back down at the bloody heap of a man curled into himself, moaning, his gray hair matted with blood.

I chuckled as I jumped up onto the platform of the kickboxing ring. "I don't mind."

"Where is he?"

"I made him wait in the entry."

He nodded. "And?" Remo came toward me, letting his victim lie in his own blood. The scar over Remo's eye was slightly redder than usual, as it always was when he overexerted himself. "How did it go in New York? Your message wasn't very enlightening."

"I failed, as you can see. Luca didn't let Aria out of his sight."

"I figured as much. How did he react to my message?"

"He wanted to tear out my throat."

An excited gleam filled his eyes. "I wish I could have seen Vitiello's face." One of Remo's wet dreams included a cage fight against Luca. Tearing apart the Capo of the Famiglia will be his ultimate triumph. Remo was a cruel, ruthless, deadly fighter. He could beat almost anyone, but Luca Vitiello was a giant with hands built to crush a man's throat. No doubt, it would be a fight that made history.

"He was pissed. He wanted to kill me," I told him.

Remo gave me the once-over. "And yet there isn't a scratch on you."

"My sister held him back. She's got him in the palm of her hand."

Remo's lips curled in disgust. "To think that people on the East Coast still fear him like he's the Devil."

"He's a huge, brutal fucker when my sister isn't around to keep him in check."

"I'd really love to meet her. Vitiello would lose his fucking mind."

Luca would tear down Las Vegas for Aria—or at least he'd try. I was uneasy discussing the topic of Aria. Despite my indifference toward her, I didn't like the idea of her being in Remo's hands.

Remo looked down at my hand. I followed his gaze and realized I was twirling the bracelet around my fingers.

"When I told you to bring me Luca's treasure, I meant something else," he said darkly.

I shoved the bracelet back into my pocket. "Aria thought she could soften my heart with it because it belonged to our mother."

"And did she?" Remo asked, something dangerous lurking in his dark eyes.

I laughed. "I've been your enforcer for years now. Do you really think I still have a heart?"

Remo chuckled. "Black as tar."

"What about that guy?" I nodded toward the whimpering man, wanting to distract Remo. "Are you done with him?"

Remo seemed to consider the man for a moment, and the man quieted immediately. Finally, Remo nodded. "It's no fun if they're already broken and weak. It's only fun to break the strong." He jumped over the ropes of the ring and landed beside me. Clapping my shoulder, he said, "Let's grab something to eat. I have organized some entertainment for us. Nino and Savio will join us too." Then he sighed. "But first I'll have to have a talk with Adamo. Why does that kid have to get in trouble all the time?"

Adamo was lucky his oldest brother was Capo or he would have ended up dead in a dark alley by now. Remo and I went back into the entry area. Adamo was leaning against the bar counter, typing something on his phone. When he spotted us, he quickly slipped it into his back pocket.

Remo held out his hand. "Mobile."

Adamo jutted out his chin. "I have a right to some privacy."

Few people dared to disobey Remo. Even fewer survived when they did.

"One of these days, I'll lose my fucking patience with you." He grabbed Adamo's arm and turned him around, motioning for me to grab the mobile and I did.

"Hey," Adamo protested, trying to reach for it. I blocked him, and Remo pushed him against the wall.

"What's the fucking matter with you? I'll tell you again, don't test my fucking patience," Remo muttered.

"I'm sick of you telling me to go to school and be home by ten when you, Fabiano, Nino, and Savio spend the night doing all kind of fun stuff."

Fun stuff. He'd see how fun most of the things were once he was inducted next year.

"So you want to play with the big boys?"

Adamo nodded.

"Then why don't you stay here? A few girls are coming over in a bit. I'm sure we'll find one who will make you a fucking man."

Adamo flushed red then shook his head.

"Yeah, that's what I thought," Remo said grimly. "Now wait here while I call Don to pick you up and take you home."

"What about my phone?"

"That's mine for now."

Adamo glowered but didn't say anything. Ten minutes later, Don, one of the oldest soldiers in Remo's service, picked up the youngest Falcone.

Remo sighed. "When I was his age, I didn't say no to a free piece of ass."

"Your father set you up with your first hooker when you were twelve. Adamo probably hasn't even gotten to second base yet."

"Perhaps I should push him more."

"He'll be like us soon enough." This life wouldn't leave him with a choice.

Soon, the first girls from one of Remo's strip clubs arrived. They were eager to please, as always. Not that I minded, I'd had a long day and could use a good blowjob to get rid of some of the tension. I watched through half-closed eyes as one of the girls got down on her knees in front of me. I leaned back in the chair. This was why the Camorra would overrun the Outfit first and then the Famiglia. We didn't let women meddle in our business. We only used them for our needs. And that was something that would never change. Remo would never allow it. And I didn't give a fuck. I jerked my hips toward the willing mouth. Feelings had no place in my life.

FOUR

Leona

D AD LIVED IN A SMALL, RUN-DOWN APARTMENT IN A DESOLATE CORNER
of the city. The Strip seemed far away—and so did the beautiful hotels
with their generous customers. He showed me to a small room. It smelled
of cat piss, like the rest of the apartment, even though I hadn't seen one. The
only furniture was a mattress on the ground. One wall was packed almost to the
ceiling with old moving boxes stuffed with God knew what. He hadn't even put
sheets on the mattress, nor did I see any kind of bedding.

"It's not much, I know," he said, rubbing the back of his head. "I don't have a
second set of bed linen. Perhaps you can go out and buy some today?"

My mouth almost fell to the floor. I had to pause to compose myself. I'd
spent almost all of my money on the bus ticket. What I had left was supposed to
buy me a nice dress for potential job interviews in decent restaurants and cocktail
bars near the Strip, but I could hardly sleep on an old mattress that had sweat
stains on it … or worse.

"Do you at least have a pillow and a spare blanket?"

He placed my backpack beside the mattress, grimacing. "I think I have an
old wool blanket somewhere. Let me check." He hurried off to who knew where.

Slowly, I sank down on the mattress. It was saggy and a plume of dust rose
into the stale air. My eyes traveled over to the mountain of boxes threatening to
crush me beneath them. The window hadn't been cleaned in a while, if ever, and
only let dim light in. There wasn't even a dresser where I could put my clothes. I
dragged my backpack over to me. Good thing I hardly owned anything. I didn't
need much. Everything I ever held dear, my mother had sold at some point for
her next hit of crystal meth. That taught me not to cling to physical things.

Dad returned with a heap of black rags. Could that be the source of the cat smell? He handed the pile over to me, and I realized that it was the wool blanket he'd mentioned. It was moth eaten and smelled of smoke and something else I couldn't place—but definitely not cat. I set it down on the mattress. I had no choice but to buy bed linen. I stared down at my flip-flops. Right now they were my only shoes. The soles of my favorite pair of Converse sneakers had fallen off two days ago. I thought I'd be able to get new shoes as soon as I arrived in Vegas.

I pulled thirty dollars from my backpack. Dad eyed the money in a strange way. Desperate and hungry.

"I don't suppose you have some spare change for me? Business is slow right now, and I need to buy some food for us."

I hadn't asked what exactly his business was; I learned that asking too many questions often led to unpleasant answers.

I handed him ten dollars. "I need the rest for bedding."

He looked disappointed but then nodded. "Sure. I'll go get us something to eat for tonight. Why don't you go to Target and see if you can get a comforter and some sheets?"

It almost seemed as if he wanted to get me out of the apartment. I nodded. I really wanted to get out of my sweaty pair of jeans and T-shirt, but I grabbed my backpack and got ready to leave.

"You can leave that here."

I smiled. "Oh … no. I'll need it to carry whatever I buy," I lied. I learned to never leave my stuff lying around with my mother or she would pawn it. Not that I had anything of worth, but I hated people rummaging through my underwear. And I knew that look Dad had when he'd seen my money. I was fairly certain he'd been lying when he said his addiction was a thing of the past. There was nothing I could do about that. I couldn't fight that battle for him.

I trudged out of the apartment, Las Vegas' dry air hitting me once again. Despite the cold, a few guys were swimming in the community pool, doing dives and shouting. The pool area looked like it could use a good cleaning as well. One of the guys spotted me and let out a whistle. I picked up my pace to avoid a confrontation.

Sheets, a comforter, and a pillow cost me $19.99, leaving me with exactly one cent. No pretty dress or shoes for me. I doubted a restaurant would hire me in my secondhand clothes.

When I returned home, Dad wasn't there … and neither was any food. I searched the fridge but found only a few cans of beer and a jar of mayonnaise. I sank down on the chair, resigning myself to wait for my father.

When he came home, it was dark outside. I'd fallen asleep at the table, my forehead pressed up against my forearms. I scanned his empty arms and miserable expression.

"No food?" I asked.

He froze, his eyes flitting around nervously, searching for a good lie.

I didn't give him the chance to lie to me and rose to my feet. "It's okay. I'm not hungry. I'm going to bed."

I was starving. I hadn't had a morsel to eat since the donut I'd treated myself to in the morning. I kissed Dad's cheek, smelling alcohol and smoke on his breath. He avoided my eyes. As I headed out of the kitchen with my backpack, I saw him taking a beer out of the fridge—his dinner, I assumed.

I put the new sheets on the mattress then dropped the comforter and pillow on top. I didn't even have nightclothes. Instead, I took out a T-shirt and a fresh pair of panties before lying down on the mattress. The new linen, with its chemical scent, masked the stale stench of the mattress. I hadn't seen a washing machine in the apartment, so I'd have to earn some money before I could have my stuff washed in a laundromat.

I closed my eyes, hoping I could fall asleep despite the rumbling of my stomach.

When I got up the next morning, I showered, trying not to look at anything too closely. I would have to give the bathroom and the rest of the apartment a good clean once I found a job. That had to be my top priority for now. I changed into the nicest things I owned, a flowery summer dress that reached my knees. Then I slipped on my flip-flops. It wasn't an outfit that would get me any bonus points at a job interview, but I didn't have a choice. Dad was sleeping on the sofa, in yesterday's clothes. When I tried sneaking past him, he sat up.

"Where are you going?"

"To look for a job."

He shook his head, not looking very hungover. Alcohol was the least of his problems. "There aren't any respectable places around here."

I didn't bother telling him no respectable places would ever hire me looking the way I did.

"If you get the chance, maybe you can buy some food?" Dad said after a moment.

I nodded without saying a word. Swinging my backpack over my shoulder, I left the apartment. Unfortunately, Las Vegas' winter decided to rear its ugly head today. In my summer clothes, it was bitterly cold, and the promise of rain lay in the air. Dark clouds hung heavy in the sky.

I strode through the neighborhood for a while, taking in the shabby exteriors and homeless people. I walked for ten minutes, heading toward downtown Las Vegas, when the first bar came into view. I quickly realized that for a girl to work there, she had to be willing to get rid of her clothes. The next two bars hadn't even opened yet and looked so run-down that I doubted there was any money to be made working there. A wave of resentment washed over me. If Dad hadn't made me spend all my money on bedding, I could have bought nice clothes and gone looking for a job closer to the Strip and not around here, where the worth of a woman was linked to the way she could dance on a pole.

I knew strippers earned good money. My mom had been friends with dancers, before she'd started selling her body to truck drivers and worse for a quick buck.

Losing hope, my head started to swim from lack of food. The cold air wasn't helping either. It was already one in the afternoon and things didn't look good. Then the sky opened up and it began raining. One fat drop after another plopped down on me. Of course, the one day in December it rained in Nevada I was wearing sandals. I closed my eyes for a moment. I didn't really believe in a higher power, but if someone or something was up there, it didn't think too fondly of me.

The cold became more prominent as my dress stuck to my body. I shivered and rubbed my arms. I wasn't sure how far from home I was, but I had a feeling that I'd be down for the count with a cold tomorrow, if I didn't find shelter soon. The low hum of an engine drew my attention back to the street and to the car coming my way. It was an expensive German car, a Mercedes of some sort, with tinted windows and matte black varnish. It was sleek and almost daunting.

My mother hadn't been the kind of mother that warned me of getting into strangers' cars. She was the kind of mother who brought creepy strangers home because they paid her for sex. I was cold and hungry and just over this city already. I wanted to get back into the warmth. I hesitated then held out my arm and raised my thumb. The car slowed and came to a stop beside me. The way I looked, I assumed he would have driven right past me.

Surprise rushed through me when I saw who sat behind the wheel. A guy, early twenties maybe, dressed in a black suit and black shirt. No tie. His blue eyes settled on me and heat crawled up my neck from the intensity of his gaze. Strong jaw, dark blond hair, shaved on the sides but longer on top. He was immaculate, except for a small scar on his chin—and I looked like I'd crawled out of the gutter. Wonderful.

Fabiano

The girl, dressed for anything but this weather, caught my attention from afar. Her wet dress was plastered to her thin body and her hair to her face. She had her arms wrapped around her stomach and an ugly backpack hanging off her right shoulder. I slowed considerably as I approached her, curious. She didn't look like one of our girls, nor did she strike me as someone who knew the first thing about selling her body. Maybe she'd only just arrived in Vegas and didn't know that these streets belonged to us and she would have to ask if she wanted to hit them.

I expected her to scuttle off when I came closer. My car was easily recognizable. She surprised me when she held out her hand for me to pick her up. I pulled up beside her. If she tried to offer me her body, she was in for a nasty surprise. And if this was some insane robbery scheme, with her accomplices waiting to catch me by surprise, they'd be in for an even nastier surprise. I put my hand down on my gun before I slid my window down. She bent over to look inside my car.

She smiled in embarrassment. "I got lost. Can you take me home perhaps?"

Not a hooker.

I leaned over and pushed the door open. She slipped in then closed the door. She put her backpack on her lap and rubbed her arms. My eyes fell to her feet. She was wearing only sandals and dripping water on my seats and the floor.

She noticed my gaze and blushed. "I didn't expect rain."

I nodded, still curious. She definitely didn't know me. She was pale and trembled ... but not from fear. "Where do you need to go?"

She hesitated before letting out an embarrassed laugh. "I don't know the address."

I raised my eyebrows.

"I only arrived yesterday. I live with my father."

"How old are you?"

She blinked. "Nineteen?"

"Is that the answer or a question?"

"Sorry. I'm out of it today. It's the answer." Again with the embarrassed, shy smile.

I nodded. "But you know the direction to your father's place?"

"There was a sort of campground nearby. It isn't very nice there."

I pulled away from the curb then sped up. She clutched her backpack.

"Are there any markers you remember?"

"There was strip club nearby," she said, a deep blush tingeing her wet cheeks. Definitely not a hooker.

I humored her and drove in the general direction she'd described. It wasn't like I needed to be anywhere else. Her ignorance of my position was almost amusing. She looked like a drowned cat with her dark hair plastered to her head and her dress clinging to her shivering body. I could hear her stomach rumble.

"I wish I knew the name of the club, but I was only paying attention to bars I could work in … and that definitely wasn't one of them," she said quickly.

"Work?" I echoed, cautious again. "What kind of work?"

"As a waitress. I need to earn money for college," she said then fell silent, biting her lip.

I considered her again. "About a mile from here is a bar called Roger's Arena. I know the owner. He's looking for a new waitress. The tips are good … from what I hear."

"Roger's Arena," she echoed. "Strange name for a bar."

"It's a strange place," I told her. It was an understatement, of course. "But they don't have high standards when it comes to their personnel."

Her eyes widened then she flushed with embarrassment. "Do I look that bad?"

My gaze traveled from her slender calves over her narrow waist up to her fine-boned face. She didn't look bad, quite the opposite. But her clothes and wet hair and those worn sandals … they didn't really help matters. "No."

She didn't seem to believe me and tightened her grip on her backpack. Why was she clinging to it so tightly? Did she have a weapon inside? That would explain why she'd risked getting into a stranger's car. Maybe she thought she'd be able to defend herself. Her stomach growled again.

"You're hungry."

She tensed, which was more than the simple question called for. "I'm okay." Determined and stubborn, her eyes remained glued to the windshield.

"When was the last time you've eaten?"

A quick glance my way then her eyes fell down to her backpack.

"When?" I pressed.

She looked out the passenger window. "Yesterday."

I narrowed my eyes at her. "You should consider eating every day."

"We had no food in the fridge."

Didn't she say she lived with her father? What kind of parent was he? From the way she looked, probably as caring as my own father had been.

I steered the car toward a KFC drive-in.

She shook her head. "No, don't. I forgot to take money with me."

I could tell she was lying.

I ordered a box of wings and fries and then handed them to her.

"I can't accept this," she said quietly.

"It's chicken and fries, not a Rolex."

Her eyes darted to the watch on my wrist. Not a Rolex, but not any less expensive. She didn't put up much of a fight, her resolve quickly dissipating. Soon, she tore into the food as if her last decent meal had been a lot longer than just yesterday. I watched her from the corner of my eye as my car glided through traffic. Her nails were cut short, not the long red fake nails I was used to.

"What do you do? You look young for a businessman or lawyer," she said when she was done eating.

"Businessman? Lawyer?"

She shrugged. "Because of the suit and the car."

"Nothing like that ... no."

Her eyes lingered on the scars covering my knuckles, and she didn't say anything anymore. She sat up suddenly. "I recognize the street. Turn left here."

I did and slowed when she pointed at an apartment complex. The place seemed distantly familiar. She opened the door then turned to me. "Thank you for the ride. I doubt anyone else would have picked me up with the way I look. They probably would have thought I wanted to rob them. Good thing you aren't scared of girls in flip-flops."

My lips twitched at her joke. "No. I'm not scared of anything."

She laughed then quieted as her blue eyes traced my face. "I should go."

She got out and closed the door, quickly running for cover. I watched her fumble with the keys for a while before she disappeared from view. Strange girl.

Leona

I glanced back out the window as the Mercedes sped off. I couldn't believe I let a total stranger drive me home. And I couldn't believe I let him buy me food. I thought I'd outgrown that kind of thing. Back when I was a little girl, strangers had occasionally bought me food because they pitied me. But this guy ... he hadn't showed any signs of pity. He didn't watch me with his mouth hanging open, only to tear his eyes away the moment I noticed his gaze, and he definitely didn't look ashamed for his own wealth. And the suit ... somehow it seemed out of place on him.

He hadn't revealed what he did for a living. Not a lawyer or businessman, then what? Maybe his parents were rich ... but he didn't seem like the trust fund type.

Not that it mattered. I'd never see him again. A man like him, with a car like that, he must spend his days on golf courses and in fancy restaurants, not in the places where I could work.

Dad wasn't home. Considering the force of the rainfall, I'd be stuck in the apartment for a while. I walked into the kitchen, checked the fridge, but found it as empty as it was this morning. Then I sank into a chair. I was cold and tired. If I wanted to wear these clothes tomorrow, I'd have to hang them so they could dry. The dress was the nicest piece of clothing I owned. If I had any chance securing a job at this arena, I needed to wear it.

So far, this new beginning wasn't very promising.

The next day I went in search for Roger's Arena. It took me a while, and eventually I had to ask passersby for the way. They looked at me like I had lost my mind, asking for a place like that. What kind of place had Mercedes guy suggested to me?

When I finally found Roger's Arena, a nondescript building with a small red neon sign with its name beside the steel entrance door, I stepped inside. Now I understood why people had reacted the way they had.

The bar wasn't exactly a cocktail bar or night club; it was a huge hall that looked like it had once been a storage facility. There was a bar on the right side, but my eyes were drawn to the huge fighting cage in the center of the large room. Tables were arranged all around it with a few red leather booths against the walls for the VIP customers.

The floor was cement and so were the walls, but they were covered with wire mesh fence. Woven into the wire were neon tubes that formed words like honor, pain, blood, victory, and strength.

I hesitated in the front, half a mind to turn around and leave, but then a black-haired woman headed my way. She must have been thirty, thirty-one. Her eyes were heavily lined and her lips were a bright pink. It clashed with the red glow of the neon lights. She didn't smile but didn't exactly look unfriendly either.

"Are you new? You're late. In thirty minutes, the first customers will be here, and I haven't even cleaned the tables or the changing rooms yet."

"I'm not really working here," I said slowly. And I wasn't sure it was a place I should consider working.

"You aren't?" Her shoulders slumped, one of the thin spaghetti straps sliding off and giving me a glimpse of the strapless pink bra beneath her top. "Oh damn. I can't do this alone tonight. Mel called in sick, and I …." She trailed off. "You could work here, you know?"

"That's why I'm here," I said, even though the fighting cage freaked me out. *Beggars can't be choosers, Leona.*

"Perfect. Then come on. Let's find Roger. I'm Cheryl, by the way."

She gripped my forearm and pulled me along. "Is the pay bad? Is that why are you having trouble finding staff?" I asked as I hurried after her, my sandals smacking against the concrete floor.

"Oh, it's the fighting. Most girls are squeamish," she said offhandedly, but I had a feeling there was more she wasn't telling me.

We walked through a black swinging door behind the bar counter, along a narrow corridor with bare walls and more doors, toward another massive wooden door at the end. She knocked.

"Come in," said a deep voice. Cheryl opened the door to a large office that was foggy from cigarette smoke. Inside, a middle-aged man, built like a bull, sat behind a desk. He flashed his teeth at Cheryl, his double chin becoming more prominent. Then his eyes settled on me.

"I got us a new waitress," Cheryl said, the hint of flirtation in her voice.

"Roger," the man introduced himself, stubbing out a cigarette on the ketch-up-smeared plate in front of him. "You can start working right away."

I opened my mouth in surprise.

"That's why you're here, right? Five dollars an hour, plus everything you make from tips."

"Okay?" I said uncertainly.

"Dressed like that you won't earn many tips." He picked up his cell phone and gestured for us to leave. "Get something that shows off your ass or tits. This isn't a nunnery."

When the door had closed, I gave Cheryl a questioning look. "Does it always go like that?"

She shrugged, but again I got the impression that she was keeping something from me. "He's just really desperate right now. Tonight's an important fight, and he doesn't want things to get messy because we're low on staff."

"Why does it matter how I'm dressed?" Worry overcame me. "We don't have to do anything with guests, right?"

She shook her head. "We don't have to, no, but we have a few rich customers that spend good money … especially if you give them some special attention."

I shook my head. "No, no. That's not going to happen."

She nodded, leading me out back. "It's up to you. You can leave your back-pack here." She pointed toward the floor behind the bar. I reluctantly set it down.

I couldn't keep it on me when I worked. She rummaged through a small closet to the left of the bar and appeared with a mop and a bucket. "You can start by cleaning the changing room. The first fighters arrive in about two hours, until then clean everything."

I hesitated and she frowned. "What? Too good for cleaning?"

"No," I said quickly. I wasn't too good for anything. And I'd cleaned up every possible disgusting thing in my life. "It's just that I haven't eaten anything since last night and I feel a bit faint."

The fridge was still empty, and I was still out of money. Dad didn't seem concerned about food at all. Either he ate wherever he was at night or he lived on air alone. Pity crossed her face, making me regret my words. Pity had been something I had been subjected to far too often, and it had always made me feel small and worthless. Having a mother who sold her body on the street, my teachers and social workers had showered me with their pity—but never with a way out of the mess. When the guy from yesterday bought me food, it hadn't felt like an act of charity.

Cheryl set down the mop and bucket and grabbed something from a fridge behind the bar. She set down a coke in front of me then turned and went back through the swinging door. She showed up a minute later with a grilled cheese sandwich and fries, both cold.

"They're from last night. The kitchen isn't open yet."

I didn't care. I scarfed everything within a few minutes and washed it down with the cold coke. "Thanks," I said with a big smile.

She searched my face then shook her head. "I probably shouldn't ask, but how old are you?"

"I'm old enough to work here," I said. I knew I needed to be twenty-one to work in a place like this, so I didn't mention that I'd just finished high school this year.

She looked doubtful. "Be careful, chick," she said simply and pushed the mop into my arms. I took it, picked up the bucket, and headed for the door with the red neon sign reading, "Changing Room." I wedged it open with my elbow and slipped in.

There were several open shower stalls, a wall of lockers, and a few benches inside. The white-tiled floor was covered with bloodstains and dirty towels. Great. They'd probably been there for days. The smell of beer and sweat hung in the air. Good thing I learned to deal with stuff like that, thanks to my mother. I began mopping and was still at it when the door opened again. Two middle-aged men tattooed from head to toe stepped inside. I paused.

Their eyes wandered over me, settling on my flip-flops and dress. I smiled anyway. I'd quickly learned that it was easier to disarm people with a smile than with anger or fear, especially if you were a small woman. They nodded at me, disinterested. When the first began to tug at his shirt, I quickly excused myself and headed out of the room. I didn't want to watch them undressing. They might get the wrong idea.

A few guests were already mingling around the now red-lit bar, obviously impatient for drinks. Cheryl was nowhere in sight. I set down the bucket and the mop and hurried toward the counter. Once behind it, I faced the group of thirsty men, smiling.

"So what can I get you?"

Relief flooded me as beer seemed to be the only thing they wanted. That request was one I could handle. If they asked for cocktails, I'd be lost. Half of them wanted draft beer. I handed them their full glasses and the other half got bottles. I quickly scanned the fridge. There were only three bottles of beer left, and I doubted they would last long. These guys looked like a case of beer would be a good appetizer.

Where was Cheryl?

When I was starting to get nervous, she finally walked through the door, looking slightly disheveled. Her skirt was askew, her top put on the wrong way, and her lipstick was gone. I didn't say anything. Had she already earned some extra money with a customer? I glanced around toward the few men gathered at the tables and the bar. Some of them were throwing me curious glances, but none of them looked like they were about to offer me money for having sex. I relaxed slightly. It was a touchy subject for me because of my mom. The moment one of them put money in front of me for sex, whether I was desperate for money or not, I'd be out of this bar so fast. There was a strange atmosphere in the bar; people exchanged money, talking in hushed voices. Someone sat in the corner, typing into his iPad, as customers approached him and handed him money. He was a very round, very short man with a mousy face. He must be taking bets. I didn't know anything about the laws in Nevada, but this didn't look legal.

None of my business.

"Doll? Give me a beer, would you?" a man in his sixties said.

I flushed then quickly reached for a glass. It started to feel like this place might be prone to trouble.

FIVE

Fabiano

PULLED UP INTO THE PARKING LOT OF ROGER'S ARENA, KILLING THE engine. My muscles were already taut with eagerness. The thrill of fighting still got me after all these years. In the cage, it didn't matter if your father was Consigliere or construction worker. It didn't matter what people thought of you. All that mattered was the moment, your fighting skills, and your ability to read the enemy. It was one against one. Life was seldom as fair as that.

I stepped into Roger's Arena. It was already crowded. The stench of old sweat and smoke clung to the air. It wasn't an inviting place. People didn't come here for the atmosphere or good food. They came for money and blood.

The first fight was about to start. The two opponents were already facing each other in the cage in the center. They weren't the main attraction. All eyes turned to me then quickly avoided my steely glare as I strode past the rows of tables filled with spectators. My fight was last. I'd fight the poor sucker who had proven to be the best over the last few weeks. Remo thought it was good to have me beat the strongest fighters to a bloody pulp in a cage to show everyone what kind of enforcer the Camorra had. And I didn't mind. It helped me remember the beginning, helped me stay grounded and vicious. Once you allowed yourself to get used to the easy life, you set yourself up for attack and for failure.

My eyes were drawn to the bar. It took me a moment to recognize her, since she wasn't shivering and dripping wet like yesterday. She had long amber curls, sharp yet elegant features. She was serving drinks to the men gathered at the bar, men with eyes like hungry wolves. She was focused on the task, oblivious to their staring. Taking too long pouring a simple beer, it was clear she did not have any experience working in a bar. To be honest, I hadn't expected her to start working here. That she had taken the job after seeing the cage told me one of two things: she was desperate or she'd seen worse in her life.

She glanced up, noticing my attention. I waited for her inevitable reaction, but it didn't come. She smiled shyly, her eyes lingering on my clothes. No suit today. Black jeans and a black long sleeved shirt, my preferred style, but sometimes the suit was necessary. She hesitated then quickly returned to the task of serving beer to an old fucker.

Who was this girl? And why wasn't she scared?

Tearing my eyes away from her, I headed toward Roger, who was talking to our bookie, Griffin. I shook hands with both men. Then I nodded toward the bar. "New girl?"

Roger shrugged. "She showed up in my office today, looking for a job. I need new staff." He narrowed his eyes, regarding me with uncertainty. "Do you want me to alert Stefano?"

Stefano was our romancer. He preyed on women, pretended to be in love with them, and eventually forced them to work in one of the Camorra's whorehouses.

I didn't get along with him and gruffly shook my head. "She doesn't fit the profile."

I didn't know how Stefano chose the girls he pursued, and I didn't give a fuck.

"So how's it going?" I nodded toward Griffin's iPad, where he managed all of the incoming bets.

"Good. The few idiots who have bet against you will bring us a lot of money."

I nodded, but my eyes found the bar counter again. I wasn't even sure why. I had driven the girl home last night on a whim and that was it. "I'm grabbing something to drink."

Not waiting for either of them to reply, I made my way toward the bar. People chanced looks at me before sheepishly averting their gazes. It was annoying as fuck, but I'd worked hard to earn their fear.

I stopped in front of the counter and put my gym bag down beside me then sat on a stool. The men at the other end of the bar threw uneasy glances my way. I recognized one of them as someone I'd recently paid a visit to over three grand. His arm was still in a cast.

The girl I'd picked up on the street came over to me. Her skin was slightly tanned but didn't have the unnatural orange tinge of someone who went to the tanning beds like most of the women who worked in our establishments.

"I didn't expect to see you so soon," she said, smiling that shy smile that reminded me of days long gone. Days I wanted to forget most of the time. She had a light sprinkle of freckles on her nose and cheeks and cornflower blue eyes with a darker ring around the irises. Now that her hair wasn't dripping wet, I noticed it wasn't black but a dark auburn with natural golden highlights.

I rested my forearms on the counter, glad my long sleeves covered my tattoo. There would be time for the big reveal later. "I told you I frequented this place."

"No suit but still all black. I take it you like it dark," she teased.

I smirked. "You have no idea."

Her brows drew together then the smile returned. "What can I do for you?"

"A glass of water."

"Water," she repeated doubtfully, the corners of her mouth twitching. "That's a first." She let out a soft laugh.

I hadn't changed into my fighting trunks yet. I didn't tell her that I had a fight scheduled that evening, which was one reason why I couldn't drink or that I had to break some legs in the morning, which was the other.

She handed me a glass of water. "There you go," she said, walking around the bar and wiping a table next to me. I let my eyes trail over her body. Yesterday I hadn't paid nearly enough attention to the details. She was thin and small, like someone who never knew if there would be food on the table. But she managed to carry herself with a certain air of grace, despite her baggy clothes that hid the shape of her body. She wore the same dress from yesterday and those horrible flip-flops … still completely wrong for the temperatures.

"What brought you here?" I asked.

Her father lived in a bad part of town. I couldn't believe that she didn't have anywhere else she could stay. Anything would have been an improvement. With her freckles, shy smile, and elegant features, she belonged in a nice suburb, not a fucked up neighborhood, and definitely not working at a fight club in mob territory. The latter was my fault of course.

"I had to move in with my father because my mother is back in rehab," she said without hesitation. There was no reservation, no caution. Easy prey in this world.

"Do I know your father?" I asked.

Her brows puckered. "Why would you?"

"I know a lot of people. And even more people know me," I said with a shrug.

"If you're famous, you should tell me so I don't embarrass myself with my ignorance," she joked easily.

"Not famous," I told her. Notorious was more like it.

She waved a hand at me. "You don't look like a lawyer or businessman today, by the way."

"What do I look like, then?"

A light blush traveled up her throat. She gave a delicate shrug before she headed back behind the bar, hesitating again as she eyed my arms that I had propped up on the bar.

"Could you help me get a few beer cases from the basement? I doubt Roger wants to do it, and I don't think I'm strong enough. You look like you can carry two or three without breaking a sweat."

She turned and walked over to the swinging door leading to the back then looked over her shoulder to see if I was following.

I set down my glass on the counter and stood from the barstool, curious. She seemed completely unaware of *what* I was. And I didn't mean my rank in the mob. People were usually uneasy around me, even without seeing my tattoo. She wasn't a good actress, and I would have sensed fear had she harbored any. I followed her to the back and then down the long staircase into the storage area. I knew exactly where we were. I'd used it for a couple intense conversations with debtors. The door shut behind us. A flicker of suspicion shot through me. Nobody could be that trusting. Was this a setup? That would have been equally stupid.

She searched the back of the room, never once looking over her shoulder to see what I was doing. Too trusting. Too innocent.

"Ah, here they are," she said, pointing at a couple of beer cases. She looked over at me then frowned. "Is something wrong?"

She sounded concerned. For fuck's sake, she sounded concerned *for me*. Every other girl in Vegas, and every man as well, would have shit themselves if they were in a soundproof basement … alone with me. I wanted to shake some sense into her.

I strode toward her and picked up three cases. As I straightened, I caught a whiff of her sweet scent. *Fuck.*

She smiled up at me. She wore close to no makeup, only enough to highlight her natural beauty. Touching the soft dusting of freckles on her cheek, she sheepishly asked, "Do I have something on my face?" finishing with an embarrassed laugh. I could tell she was self-conscious about her freckles, but fuck me, I liked them.

"No," I said.

"Oh, okay." She searched my eyes, her brows drawing together. *Don't try to look behind that mask, girl. You won't like it.* "We should probably go back upstairs. I'm not supposed to leave the bar unattended for too long."

Had she seen something in my gaze that finally gave her a healthy dose of fear? The way she held the door open for me with that same unsuspecting expression, I guessed not.

I nodded toward the stairs. "Go ahead."

She hesitated then walked in front of me. Maybe she thought I wanted to get a good look at her ass, but her dress made that impossible. The truth was I hated having people behind me.

We strode through the narrow corridor, when the door to the main area opened revealing Roger and Stefano.

Both of them looked dismayed, seeing me with the girl. Her face shifted into one of unease at the sight of Stefano, which made me curious. He looked like any mother-in-law's dream, and his charm was the Camorra's best weapon when it came to luring women into our whorehouses.

"Fabiano, can I have a word with you?" Roger asked, his eyes scanning the girl, probably looking for a sign that I'd assaulted her in the storage room. Stefano, too, gave me a contemplating look. "Go back to work, Leona."

Leona. So that was her name. She hadn't struck me as a lioness as her namesake insinuated. Perhaps there was more to her.

She hadn't moved, despite Roger's order. Her eyes were on me. I nodded. "Go ahead," I told her. "I'll be there in a minute."

She left and to my utter annoyance, Stefano decided to go after her. *Back off, fucker.*

He'd definitely set his sights on her. Why was he even considering her for one of our whorehouses? She really didn't look the type.

"I know you handle things however you want, but recently I've lost too many waitresses to the Camorra's whorehouses … or unfortunate accidents."

Those accidents were mostly related to Remo's soldiers acting out of turn.

"I'm glad to have that new girl. The customers seem to like her, and she actually knows how to behave herself. I'd appreciate it if she could stay in my service for more than a couple of weeks."

"We handle things however we want. You just said it, Roger," I said in warning. "If we decide to put her to use in one of our other establishments, we don't ask you."

He nodded, but a vein in his forehead swelled with suppressed anger. He didn't like it. That made two of us.

I walked past him and pushed the door open with my elbow then stepped behind the bar.

Leona was busy chatting to two ancient customers, laughing at something they had said. Stefano sat at the other end of the bar, watching her like a hawk.

His brown hair was immaculately slicked back. I bet the asshole spent hours in front of the mirror. As Leona continued to chat with the older men, it seemed she was determined to ignore Stefano. I set down the cases, and Leona shot me a grateful look with those baby blues. When the men at the bar saw me, they quickly focused on their beer.

I walked around the bar and picked up my gym bag where I'd left it, stopping beside Stefano. He glanced up at me from his sitting position. He was below me in ranks, so the challenging glint in his eyes made me consider sticking my knife into them. "You think about making a move on her?"

"I'm considering it," he said. "She looks like she would respond well to the slightest sign of kindness. Makes her easy to manipulate." Would that sick as fuck leer still be on his face if I cut his throat?

"She doesn't seem interested in your advances."

"That'll change," he said smugly.

"Has Remo seen her?" That was the only thing that mattered.

"No. I only just found her, but I'm sure he'll approve."

I had a feeling Stefano was right. "Don't waste your time. She's already taken."

"By whom?"

"Me," I growled.

He frowned at me but then shrugged, emptied his beer, and left. I watched his back as he disappeared through the door. Stefano was someone to watch. He and I had never gotten along, and I had a feeling that wouldn't change anytime soon. Stefano knew better than to make a move on someone I wanted.

My eyes found Leona again. She'd been watching my exchange with Stefano with a confused expression. With the background noise of the bar, there was no way she could have heard anything. She was so different from the women that usually frequented the places I spent time in. There were women who were unable to hide their fear and then ones that hoped to gain something from being close to me. She didn't know who I was. It was strange being treated like someone ... normal. I'd fought hard to receive the respect and fear everyone showed me, but it hadn't bothered me that she was unaware of my status. I wondered how long it would be before someone told her and how she'd look at me then.

"I know that look," Remo said, sneaking up beside me. I should have realized he'd entered the scene. People were even more uneasy than they were when it was only me in the room. He nodded toward Leona. "Take her if you want. She's yours. She's nobody. It's not like we need her anyway. She doesn't look like much entertainment, though."

I glanced over to Leona. She was wiping the counter, unaware of the lewd looks she was drawing from some of the men around her.

"I don't want to take her," I said then amended when I saw Remo's bewildered expression. "I won't."

"Why not?" Remo asked curiously.

Danger. "You said it yourself, she doesn't look like much entertainment."

"Perhaps she's more exciting when she's trying to fight you off. Might be worth a try. Some women turn into feral cats when they're cornered." He clapped my shoulder.

I didn't say anything.

Remo shrugged. "But if you don't want her …"

"I do," I said quickly. "I'd appreciate if word got around that I have my eyes set on her. Just in case. I don't want Stefano messing with her."

Remo chuckled. "Sure. Put your claim on her, Fabiano."

That was the advantage of being on his good side. Remo allowed me things his other soldiers couldn't even dream of. With that, he left and went to a table with some of the high rollers from one of our premium casinos. I returned to the bar. There would be time to change into my fighting trunks later.

The other men excused themselves, and Leona came over to me, her brows drawn together. "Am I missing something?"

I shrugged. "I'm the reason why some of them lost money." *And limbs.*

She opened her mouth to say something, but the sound of a body smashing against the cage silenced her, followed by a round of ecstatic applause. She clapped a hand over her lips, eyes widened with shock. I glanced over my shoulder. One of the fighters was lying on the ground, unconscious. The other was standing over him, arms raised, doing some sort of weak-ass victory dance. Perhaps he'd be my next opponent in a couple of weeks … if he won a few more times. I'd have to break his knees to prevent future dancing.

"It's horrible," Leona whispered, her voice clogged with compassion, as if she could feel their pain.

I turned to her.

"Why does anyone want to watch something that brutal?"

Brutal? She hadn't seen brutal yet. If she was lucky, she never would. "It's in our nature," I said. "Survival of the fittest. Power struggles. Blood thirst. That's all still ingrained in our DNA."

"I don't think that's true," she argued. "I think we've moved on, but sometimes we fall back into old habits."

"Then why do people still look up to the strong? Why do women prefer the alpha males?"

She snorted. "That's a myth."

I cocked one eyebrow and leaned closer, catching a glimpse down her dress. White cotton. Of course. "Is it?" I asked.

She scanned my face, red creeping up her throat and settling on cheeks.

I stifled a laugh and got up before she could say anything. It was time to change. "I'll be back in a moment," I told her.

When I entered the changing room, the other fighters fell silent. A couple of them returned my stare; one openly challenged me with his eyes. I assumed he'd be my opponent tonight. He was around six-four, one inch taller than me. Good. Maybe this would be a longer fight.

I got undressed then pulled up my shorts. Hopefully they saw all my scars. They knew nothing of pain. I smirked at my opponent. Maybe he'd live to see tomorrow.

I left the changing room and walked back to the bar. Leona was frozen as her eyes trailed from my bare feet up to my shorts and my naked chest. The glass she was cleaning fell from her hands and landed with a plop into the dishwater. A myriad of emotions flashed across her face. Shock. Confusion. Fascination. Appreciation. That last one I could feel in my dick. I'd worked hard for my body.

I grabbed my glass sitting on the bar and downed the rest of my water. Then I took the tape out of my bag and began wrapping my hands, feeling her curious gaze on me the entire time.

"You're one of them?"

I tilted my head, not sure what she was referring to. A fighter? A member of the Camorra? A killer? Yes, yes, and yes.

There was no fear in her eyes, so I said, "A cage fighter? Yes."

She licked her lips. Those damn pink lips gave my cock ideas I didn't need before a fight.

"I hope I didn't offend you earlier."

"Because you think it's too brutal? No. It's what it is."

Her eyes kept tracing my tattoo and the scars—and occasionally my six pack. I leaned over the bar, bringing our faces closer. I knew everyone was watching us, even if they tried to be discreet.

"Are you still certain women aren't into alpha males?" I murmured.

She swallowed but didn't say anything. I took a step back. Everyone in the room should have got the message. My balls tightened with the look she gave me. Something about that girl drew me in. I couldn't say what it was, but I'd figure it out.

"It's my turn," I told her when I was done taping my hands.

"Don't get hurt," she said simply.

The men near the bar exchanged looks, snickering, but Leona was unaware of their reaction.

"I won't," I said then turned and made my way past the tables, toward the fighting cage.

I stepped into the cage under the yowling and thunderous applause of the crowd. How many had bet against me? If I lost, they'd be rich. Unfortunately for them, I never lose.

I caught Leona watching me from behind the bar counter, eyes still wide in surprise. Yes, I was a fighter, and that was the least dangerous part of me. She stopped what she was doing and came around the counter. She climbed on a barstool, shook off her flip-flops, and brought her legs up until she sat cross-legged, the skirt of her dress carefully draped over her thighs. This girl. She didn't belong here.

My opponent entered the cage. He called himself Snake. He even had snakes tattooed to his throat; they rose up over his ears and bared their fangs on both sides of his head. Snake. What a fucking stupid name to give yourself. I didn't know why people thought a scary name would make them seem scary. I'd never had to call myself anything but Fabiano. It was enough.

The ref closed the door and explained the rules to us. There were none—except that this wasn't a fight to the death, so Snake would likely live.

Snake hit his chest with his flat hands, letting out a battle cry. Whatever got his courage up.

I lifted a hand and beckoned him forward. I wanted to get this fight going. With a roar, he charged at me like a bull. I dodged him, grabbed his shoulder, and rammed my knee into his left side three times in quick succession. The air left his lungs, but he didn't fall. He swung a fist at me and got my chin. I jumped back, aimed a hard kick at his head, and despite his quick reaction, my heel caught his ear. He staggered into the cage, shook his head, and attacked again. This would be fun.

He lasted longer than the last, but eventually my kicks to his head got him. His eyes went out of focus more and more. I grabbed him by the back of his head, brought up my knee at the same time I thrust it into his face. I could feel the crunch of his nose and cheekbone as they broke against my knee. He yowled hoarsely and toppled backwards. I went after him. I jump-kicked him into the cage, and when he hit the ground with a resounding thud, I crouched over him and rammed my elbow into his stomach. Once. Twice. He weakly patted the floor, face swollen, breathing labored. Giving up.

"Surrender!" cried the ref.

I never understood men like him. I'd die before I surrendered. There was honor in death but not in begging for mercy. I rose to my feet. The crowd cheered.

Remo gave me the thumbs-up from his spot at the table with the high rollers. I could tell from the excited gleam in his eyes that he wanted to get into the cage again and soon. Schmoozing the high rollers was high up on his hate list, but someone had to do it. Nino was eloquent and sophisticated, but after a while, he forgot to plaster emotions on his face; once people realized he didn't have any, they ran as fast they could. Savio was a teen and capricious, and Adamo … Adamo was a kid.

I turned around. Leona was still sitting on the stool in front of the bar, watching me, horrified. That was a look that was closer to the ones I was used to getting from people. Seeing me like this, covered in blood and sweat, maybe she finally understood why she should be terrified of me.

She untangled her legs from her dress, hopped down from the stool, and disappeared through the swinging door.

I climbed out of the cage, dripping blood and sweat on the floor. I'd need to stitch myself up.

I occasionally heard, "Good fight," from someone as I walked by. I shook a few congratulating hands then retreated into the changing room. Seeing that my fight had been the last of the night, and my opponent was on his way to the hospital, the room was empty. I opened my locker when a knock sounded. I grabbed one of my guns and held it behind my back as I turned. "Come in."

The door opened a crack before Leona poked her head in, her eyes closed. "Are you decent?"

I put my gun back into my gym bag. "I'm the least decent guy in this city." Except for Remo and his brothers, perhaps.

She opened her eyes cautiously, searching the room until they settled on me. Relief flooded her face, and she slipped into the room before closing the door behind her.

My eyebrows shot up. "Are you here to give me a victory present?" I asked, leaning against the lockers. My cock thought of all kind of presents she could give. And all of them involved her perfect mouth and her undoubtedly perfect pussy.

"Oh … I only have a bottle of water and clean towels." She showed me what she held in her hands, smiling apologetically.

I shook my head, chuckling. God, this girl.

Realization flooded her face. "Oh, you meant …" She gestured in the general direction of her body. "Oh, no. No. Sorry."

I closed my eyes, fighting the urge to laugh. It had been a while since a woman had made me laugh. Most of the time, they just made me fuck them senseless.

"I hope you can live with a bottle of cold water," she said in a teasing voice.

When I opened my eyes, she was in front of me, holding out the bottle. She was more than a head shorter than me and less than an arm's length away. Stupid girl. She needed to learn self-preservation. I took the bottle and emptied it in a few gulps.

She scanned my body. "There's so much blood."

I chanced a look. There was a small cut over my ribs where the sharp edge of the cage had grazed me. Bruises were forming over my left kidney and on my right thigh. The majority of blood wasn't mine. "It's nothing. I've had worse."

Her eyes lingered on my forehead. "You've got a cut that needs to be treated. Is there a doctor around I should get?"

"No. I don't need a doctor."

She opened her mouth to argue but then seemed to think better of it. She paused.

"You looked so ..." She shook her head, her nose puckering in the most fucking adorable way possible. Fuck, those damn freckles. "I don't know how to describe it. *Fierce*."

I straightened, surprised. She sounded almost fascinated. "You weren't disgusted? I thought it's too 'brutal.'"

She shrugged, one delicate motion. "I was disgusted. It's such a savage sport. I don't even know if you can call it that. It's all about beating each other up."

"It's also about reading your opponent, about seeing his weaknesses and using them against him. It's about speed and control." I scanned her again, reading her like I did all my opponents. It wasn't difficult to guess why Stefano would have chosen her if allowed. It was obvious that she'd had a difficult life, that that there was nobody to take care of her. It was obvious that she wanted more, that she wanted someone to take care of her, someone who was kind to her, someone to love. Stefano was good at pretending he was someone like that. Soon she'd learn that it was best to rely only on yourself. Love and kindness were rare, not only in the mob world.

"I don't understand why people watch others hurt each other for sport. Why do people enjoy inflicting pain on somebody?"

I was the last person she should ask. She had never seen me hurt people. That fight was a joke in comparison to my jobs as an Enforcer of the Camorra. I liked to hurt people. I was good at it and had learned to be good at it.

SIX

Leona

HIS EYES WERE UNREADABLE. WHAT WAS HE THINKING? IT DAWNED ON me that I was starting to annoy him with my constant talk about the brutality of fighting.

Cage fighting was obviously important to him. I was still trying to understand the three sides of him I'd seen so far: the businessman, the guy next door, and the fighter. Though, I now realized that only the latter had seemed natural … like it was the only one where he didn't feel he was pretending.

"I should probably leave," I said. It wasn't the best idea to be in the changing room with him. People might get ideas and start talking, and that was something I really didn't want.

He nodded. The way he was watching me sent a shiver down my spine. His eyes, always so keen and cautious, and blue like the sky over Texas in spring, kept me frozen in place. *Get a grip.* I turned and strode toward the door. Before I walked out, I risked one more glance over my shoulder. "I don't even know your name," I said.

"Fabiano," he said. The name seemed too normal, too gentle for a man like him, who was now covered in blood.

"I'm Leona," I told him. I wasn't even sure why, but for some reason he made me curious.

He hooked his fingers in his shorts, and I quickly left, but before I closed the door, I caught a glimpse of his backside as he headed for the shower. His muscles flexed with every step. Oh hell. I tore my gaze from his perfect butt. There were scars all over his back, but they didn't look like flaws on him. Heat shot straight to my head, and I quickly turned around, only to stare at Cheryl's face. "Hon, don't play with the big boys. They don't play nicely," she said cryptically.

"I'm not playing with anyone," I said, embarrassed that she had caught me spying on Fabiano.

She patted my shoulder. "Just stay away from the likes of him."

I didn't get the chance to ask her what she meant. Roger shouted for her to come into his office. She thrust the mop at me. "Here, you have to clean the cage." Then she rushed off.

It was already two in the morning, and I was incredibly tired. Only a few guests remained scattered around tables, drinking their last beer. Most people had left after Fabiano's fight. I shuddered when my eyes took in the bloody mess that was the fighting cage. I'd never had trouble with blood, but this was more than I'd seen in a long time. The last time I'd had to clean up such a mess was when my mother had hit her head on the bathtub in a crystal meth rage.

I sighed. There was no use in postponing the inevitable. I climbed through the cage doors and began mopping. The last guests gathered their things, and I waved at them when they called out to me, wishing me a good night.

I kept my eyes open for Roger, hoping he'd give me some cash for today's work. I really needed a few bucks to buy food and perhaps another pair of shoes. I grimaced when I saw a few drops of blood had gotten on my naked toes. Sandals definitely weren't a wise shoe choice for a job like this.

Occasionally, I allowed myself to glance in the direction of the changing room door, but Fabiano seemed to be taking his time showering. An image of him naked under a water stream came to my mind. I quickly wiped the last blood-stain away and got out of the cage. I was too tired to think straight. I needed to get home, though the idea of walking home in the dark for over a mile didn't sit well with me. I wasn't easily scared, but I had a healthy sense of self-preservation.

After I'd put the mop and bucket away, I continued into the corridor that led to Roger's office, but I hesitated halfway through it. A woman was screaming. I shivered. Then I heard Roger's voice. "Yes, you like it up your ass, you slut. Yes, just like that."

Cheryl was the one who'd screamed, but apparently it was in pleasure. This was too disturbing. I desperately needed the money Roger owed me, but there was no way I was going to interrupt whatever they had going on. I backed away and straight into a strong body. Opening my mouth, I was about the release a startled scream when a hand clamped down over my lips. Fear shot through me and instinct took over. I shoved my elbow back as hard as I could and collided with a rock-hard stomach. My opponent didn't even wince, but he tightened his fingers around my waist.

"Shhh. It's me."

I relaxed, and he dropped his hand from my lips. I twisted in his hold, tilting my head back. Fabiano. He was dressed in his black shirt and jeans, and he was clean. The wound at his hairline was stitched up. So that was what had taken so long! I couldn't imagine fixing myself with a needle, but as a cage fighter he probably had to suffer through worse pain than a few needle pokes.

"You scared me."

There was a hint of amusement in his eyes.

Fabiano

I scared her? If this was the first time I'd scared her, then she was as crazy as she was beautiful.

"I didn't want you to interrupt Roger with your scream," I said. Nobody wanted to see Roger with his pants down.

Her eyes skittered to the door and she shuddered. "I didn't know they were a couple. They didn't act like one."

"They aren't," I said. "They fuck."

"Oh." A tantalizing blush colored her cheeks. "I should be going."

"Do you want me to drive you?" I wasn't sure why the hell I was offering her a ride again. After all, she didn't exactly live around the corner from my apartment.

She paused, conflict dancing in her eyes. Finally some distrust. Perhaps seeing me fight had made her realize that she should have never gotten in my car in the first place. It was funny how differently people reacted to someone, depending on the outfit they wore. Suit? Trustworthy.

"I can't let you do that again."

"Then call a taxi. You shouldn't be walking in this area alone at night." I could name all the reasons why she shouldn't.

"I don't have any money," she said then looked like she wanted to swallow her tongue.

I reached into my bag and pulled out a roll of fifty-dollar bills.

Leona's eyes grew wide. "Where do you get so much money?"

She didn't look impressed, only wary. Good. There was nothing worse than women who decided you were only worth their attention after they saw you had money.

"Money for winning my fight." Which was almost the truth.

I untangled a fifty-dollar bill and held it out to her.

She shook her head vehemently. "No. I really can't take it."

"You can give it back when Roger's paid you."

She shook her head again but with less conviction this time. She was tired. I could tell. "Take it," I ordered.

She blinked up at me, stunned by the command but unable to resist, so she finally took the note. "Thank you. I'll pay you back soon."

People always said that to me.

She hoisted her backpack up on her shoulder. "I need to go," she said apologetically.

I walked her outside. My car was right in front of the door. She glanced at it. "Do you earn that much money cage fighting?"

"It's not my job. It's a hobby."

More curiosity on her part. No questions. A girl who had learned that curiosity killed the cat.

"Call a taxi," I told her.

She smiled. "Don't worry, I will. You don't have to wait."

She wouldn't call a taxi. I could tell. I waited patiently. If she thought she could drive me off like that, she was mistaken.

"I don't have a phone," she reluctantly admitted.

No money, no phone. I reached for mine in the pocket of my jeans when she sighed and shook her head.

"No, don't. I really want to walk. I can't afford to waste money on a taxi," she said with blatant discomfort.

It was obvious she was poor, so it was futile of her to try to hide it from me. Stefano wouldn't have seen her as the perfect prey if she wasn't an easy target. And hell, with this shabby dress, shabbier sandals, and the fucking shabbiest backpack on the planet, it took no fucking genius to see how poor she was.

"Then let me at least walk with you," I told her to my own surprise.

I didn't want Stefano to give her another go or have one of the thugs put a hand on her. Something about her trustful innocence drew me in like a moth to the flame. It was the thrill of the hunt, no doubt. I'd never hunted someone like that.

"But you could drive. You don't have to walk."

"You can't walk alone at night, believe me."

Her shoulders slumped and her eyes darted to my car. "Then I'll ride with you. I can't let you walk with me and then back to the bar again to get your car."

I held the door open for her, and she slipped in. Too trusting. I slid into the seat beside her. She sank into the leather seat, yawning, her arms wrapping tightly around her old backpack.

I doubted she had any treasures hidden in its depths. Perhaps she really had some sort of weapon inside to defend herself.

Knife? Pepper spray? Gun?

Nothing would have saved her if I had any intention of having my way with her. I started the engine, which came to life with a roar, and pulled out of the parking lot. In a confined space like this, she wouldn't be able to get in a good shot. I would have no trouble disarming her, and then she'd be defenseless. Women often carried weapons because they thought they would protect them, but without the knowledge of how to use them, they were only an additional risk.

She told me her address again.

"I remember, don't worry."

She ran her fingertips along the black leather of her seat. "Are you from a rich family?"

I was, but that wasn't why I had the car and everything else. "No," I told her.

She fell silent. She was brimming with more questions. It was written all over her face.

When I pulled up in front of the apartment complex, the door on the second floor opened. I immediately recognized the man—moderately tall, half bald, paunch drooping over his belt, all over pathetic—as one of the gambling addicts who frequented one of our casinos. I hadn't handled him yet. He wasn't important enough and had never owed us enough money to warrant my attention. Soto had dealt with him once. He took care of the lowlife scum our business attracted. After that one time, he'd always been on time with his payments. He was a looser who always chased the next dollar to spend it on gambling.

"That's my dad," Leona said. There was a hint of tenderness in her voice. Tenderness that he sure as hell didn't deserve. "Thanks for the ride."

Her father was heading down the walkway toward us then froze when he recognized me behind the steering wheel. Leona and I got out.

"Leona!" he croaked. His eyes did a quick scan of her body. "Are you okay? Did he …?" He cleared his throat at the look I gave him. I hadn't expected that kind of worry from him. From what I'd seen of him so far, he only gave a fuck about himself. People like him always did. That was why I enjoyed dealing with them.

Leona blinked. "What's going on? I'm fine. Why are you acting so strange?"

"Are you okay?" he asked again.

I strode over to them. Immediately, the smell of cheap spirits wafted into my nose. Gambling and alcohol were a thunderous combination, one that eventually led to an early grave. Either by the Camorra, or by Mother Nature.

She nodded, then gestured toward me. "Fabiano was nice enough to drive me home."

I was many things, but nice wasn't one of them. Her father looked like he was going to blow a gasket. "Haven't I told you to be careful around here? You can't just go around talking to …" He fell silent, saving his own sorry ass.

I gave him a cold smile. "I really enjoyed *talking* to your daughter."

He nervously rubbed his palms over his faded jeans.

"Leona, go ahead. I need to have a talk with your father," I said.

Leona's eyes darted between her father and me. "You know each other?"

"We have a mutual friend."

"Okay." She gave me an uncertain smile. "See you soon?" It was half a question, half a statement.

"You bet," I said quietly.

Her father clutched my arm the moment she was gone.

"Please," he begged. "Is this because of the money I haven't paid? I will pay it soon. Just don't—"

I let my gaze fall to his fingers grabbing my arm, and he let go like he'd been burned. "Don't what?" I asked dangerously.

He stepped back, shaking his head. He was worried for himself. He'd thought I had come to deal with him.

"I would be sad to see her leave," I said casually. "I suppose she's going to stay for a while?"

He stared at me.

"I'd really hate for her to hear the wrong things about me. Understood?"

Slowly he nodded.

I returned to my car. His fearful gaze followed me as I drove off. I wasn't even sure what exactly made me want to make her mine. Her father knew there was nothing he could do to stop me, not that he was the type to try. The only thing that could have stopped me from pursuing her, now that my interest had been stirred, was Remo, and he had no reason to interfere.

SEVEN

Leona

I SLEPT LATE THE NEXT DAY. I DIDN'T HAVE TO WORK UNTIL THREE IN THE afternoon and needed to get some rest. When I walked into the kitchen, a box of donuts sat on the table. Dad was clutching a coffee cup.

"Morning," I said, even though it was almost twelve o'clock. I poured some coffee for myself before I sank down into the chair across from him.

"You got us breakfast," I said, and helped myself to a donut. I knew better than to expect pleasant surprises to occur on a daily basis.

"I asked a neighbor for some money until I get paid tomorrow." He was some sort of courier, from what I'd gathered. I wondered how he could keep the job, considering that his breath always stunk of alcohol.

"I could give you fifty dollars," I said, pulling out the money from the waistband of my shorts. I'd learned to hide money close to my body. "Then you could pay him back and get us food for the next few days."

He eyed the money as if it was something dirty. "Where did you get it?"

"I found a job," I said with a smile.

He didn't look happy. "And they paid you fifty dollars on your first day?"

He made it sound like I had been doing something forbidden, *something dirty.*

"No, not yet. I will get paid today, though." That was what I hoped at least. I wasn't sure how Roger handled things, but since he didn't ask for my social security number or any other relevant information, I assumed that it wasn't a regular paycheck.

"Then where did you get that money?"

He looked angry. What was the matter with him? He and Mom had definitely never asked many questions when it came to money. "Fabiano gave it to me."

He jumped up, his chair toppling to the ground with a bang. I flinched in my seat. Distant memories of him fighting with my mother as he raised his fist and she clawed at him filled my mind.

"You borrowed money from … him?"

"What's wrong?" I asked.

"You can't go around borrowing money from people like him. We don't need any more attention from him."

"People like him," I repeated. "What kind of people exactly?"

He looked torn. I wasn't sure who or what he was trying to protect, but it certainly wasn't me. He had never been the protective father figure.

"I know he's a cage fighter, Dad. I saw him fight, okay? So please mind your own business." Like you've done the last five years.

"You did? Why?" Then something seemed to click in his mind, and he closed his eyes. "Don't tell me you're working in Roger's Arena."

"I do."

He picked up the chair and straightened it before falling into it, as if his legs were too weak to carry him. "You should have never come here. I shouldn't have let you. You're going to get us both in trouble. I really can't use this kind of baggage right now."

I frowned at my coffee. "I'm a grown up. I can handle myself. I can't be picky with the jobs I get. It's not like I have much of a choice."

"Give him that money back today. Don't use it for anything. And—"

"Stay away from him?" I interrupted. It was too late for Dad talk.

"No," he said quietly. "Be careful. I don't need you to mess things up. It's too late for me to tell you to stay away."

I got the feeling that he meant it in a different way than I had. "I could stay away. It's not like I'm bound to him."

Dad shook his head. "No, you can't stay away, because that's no longer up to you. He'll decide from now on, and he won't let you stay away until he gets whatever it is that he wants from you." His lips curled, like he knew exactly what that was.

I hated how he could make me feel dirty with that one expression. Like he had any right to judge me when he gladly let my mom sell her body so he could pay his gambling debt.

"We're not living in the Middle Ages, Dad. It's not like he holds any power over me." I wasn't even sure why we were discussing this. Fabiano and I had done nothing but talk, and so far he'd been the perfect gentleman. Perhaps Dad's drinking problem was worse than I thought. Or maybe he was into harder drugs. Mom had been paranoid too.

He pulled a cigarette—his last one—from a battered packet before lighting it and taking a deep pull. "The Camorra owns the city and its people. And now *he* owns you." He released the smoke from his lungs, cloaking us in it. I coughed.

"Camorra?" I had heard the term in a report about Italy on television a while back. They were a branch of the mob, but this was Las Vegas not Naples. "You mean the mob?"

Dad got up. "I said too much already," he said regretfully, taking another drag. His fingers that held the cigarette shook. "I can't help you. You're in too deep already."

In too deep? I'd been in Las Vegas for three days and worked at Roger's bar for only one day. How could I be in too deep? And what exactly did that mean?

Dad didn't give me the chance to ask more questions. He rushed out of the kitchen, and a few seconds later, I heard the entrance door slam shut.

If he insisted on beating around the bush, I'd have to pepper Cheryl with questions. If her cryptic warnings from yesterday were any indication, she definitely knew more. I wasn't going to ask Fabiano directly about it unless I had no other option. He'd probably laugh in my face if I asked him about the mafia.

Cheryl was putting glasses onto the shelves attached to the wall behind the bar when I walked in. The red neon lamps were still off, and without their glow, the area looked dull. There was also another woman wiping the leather of the booths. She nodded in my direction when she caught me staring. Her hair was a nice shade of light brown, but her face looked long in the tooth, used up. Hard drugs. It made her age difficult to guess. She could have been forty or thirty. There was no telling.

I headed straight toward Cheryl and put my backpack down behind the bar. When our eyes met, my cheeks grew hot at the memory of what I'd overheard her do with Roger last night. Luckily, she didn't seem to notice.

"You're late," she said, a bit on edge.

I glanced at the clock on the wall. Actually, I was right on time, but I decided not to say anything. After all, I needed to pump Cheryl for information.

"Sorry," I said as I grabbed two glasses and helped her fill the shelves.

"You could clean up the changing room or Roger's office. I've got this."

Roger's office was the last place I wanted to clean. "I'll clean the changing rooms," I said, turning to her.

She returned my gaze questioningly. "What's up?"

"You know I'm new in town, so I'm not in on what's going on around here," I began and could see her defenses on alert. Perhaps getting answers from her wouldn't be as easy as I'd hoped.

"But people are acting strange around Fabiano ... You know, the guy who fought the last battle?"

She laughed bitterly. "Oh, I know him."

I was taken aback. "Oh, okay. So what's the matter with him? My father freaked out when Fabiano gave a ride home last night."

"*He* gave you a ride home?"

Okay. This was really starting to grate on my nerves. Why couldn't she just spill it?

"He did. It was late and he didn't want me to walk by myself. He seemed worried." I decided not to mention that he'd picked me up the night before too.

Cheryl gave me a look like I'd completely lost my mind. "Trust me, he wasn't. I don't know why he took you home, but it sure as hell wasn't out of the kindness of his heart. You are lucky nothing happened."

I moved closer to her until we were almost touching. "Cheryl, just tell me what's going on. This bar, Fabiano ... everything is off."

"This is Camorra territory, chick. Everything belongs to them—and your Fabiano—to some degree."

He wasn't my Fabiano, but I didn't want to interrupt her, fearing she would change her mind about giving me an honest answer.

"He's Falcone's right hand."

"Falcone?"

The name didn't ring a bell, but it sounded Italian. She cursed under her breath. "It's not my business. I don't want to get in trouble."

"So is Falcone some kind of mobster?" I'd seen movies about the mafia, and I knew they were the bad guys, but was that even reality? This was the twenty-first century. The mafia seemed like something out of the roaring twenties, old men smoking cigars in fedoras. Fabiano was someone who instilled respect in others, I could see that, but did that stem from him being a mobster or the fact that he looked intimidating? Anyone who'd seen him in the fighting cages would think twice about a confrontation with him.

"Some kind of mobster," she murmured like I had committed blasphemy. "You say it like it's a normal job, chick. It's not, trust me. The things the

Camorra does, the things your Fabiano does, they ..." Her eyes went to something behind me, and she fell silent.

"Go clean the changing rooms," she muttered.

I turned, spotting Roger a few feet from us, a disapproving expression on his face. He wasn't looking at me, only Cheryl, and a silent conversation I wasn't privy to seemed to take place between them.

Taking the mop and bucket, I hurried past him. I was used to being the new girl in town. I'd moved about a dozen times in the last ten years and had always felt like I was on the sidelines of life because of it. I never got the inside jokes.

I knew being a mobster wasn't a normal job. These people were bad news. But Fabiano hadn't seemed bad. Something about him made me curious, made me want to catch a glimpse behind that cautious mask he wore. Who knew why he'd become a mobster? Sometimes life just left you with no choice.

I was glad that cleaning the changing room required no concentration at all, because my mind was occupied processing the news. I wasn't sure what to think because I didn't know enough. The Camorra, Falcone, mobsters ... the words held no meaning for me. But for my father and Cheryl, they did. For them, they instilled fear.

My train of thought was interrupted when the first fighters entered the changing room. Apparently, there were fights scheduled every evening. I wondered where Roger found all these guys eager to beat each other up. Many of them had as little choice as I did when it came to finding a job.

One of them, the youngest of the lot—around my age—sauntered closer. I lifted the bucket from the white-tiled floor, ready to leave them alone. He gave me a flirtatious smile, which died when one of the other guys whispered something in his ear. After that, I might as well have been invisible. Confused, I left the room. Was I some kind of pariah? The untouchable cleaning lady?

Not that I had any interest in flirting with that guy, but his change in demeanor was a slight blow to my confidence. I didn't kid myself into thinking I was a stunner like some other girls, certainly not wearing the same flowery dress as I did yesterday.

At least I didn't smell. Yet.

I faltered in my steps when I saw a familiar face enter the bar. Fabiano was dressed in black slacks and a white dress shirt with the sleeves rolled up. The white contrasted nicely with his tan. He was a sight to behold. Tall and handsome, aloof and cool, he exuded power and control. He held himself with natural grace that mesmerized me. It was like watching a lion on the prowl. There was almost too much of him to take in. His words about alpha males flashed through my mind, followed by the fact that he was a member of the Camorra. People had warned me to stay away from him.

My mother had always said I was a fixer. I needed something broken so I could see if I was capable of mending it. Injured animals, sick people, broken-down cars. *Her.* She'd said it would get me in trouble one day. Because people couldn't be fixed, and one day I'd find someone so broken, he'd break me before I could mend him.

Was that what had drawn me to Fabiano from that very first second? Had I sensed that something about him was broken and I needed to fix it?

Fabiano

Something in her expression was different. She was a bit more hesitant than before. I watched her carry the bucket and mop behind the bar then busy herself taking stock of the fridge, with her back turned to me.

I had a feeling she didn't want me to see her face. Perhaps she thought she could disguise her emotions from me. *Like that was going to work.* A look at her body told me everything I needed to know. She was tense and her breathing was too controlled, as if she was trying to appear unaffected but failing miserably.

I leaned against the counter, resting on my elbows, watching her silently. She wore the same dress again and the same sandals. It was starting to drive me crazy. Couldn't her father stop gambling for one fucking day so she could buy herself some decent clothes? Rage rose up inside me at the obvious neglect she'd probably been suffering all her life. Neglect was something I knew all too well. It came in different shapes and forms.

I waited patiently until she could no longer pretend that there was anything remotely interesting inside the fridge. She squared her shoulders and turned to face me. Her smile was all wrong. Tense and unsure. On the verge of being fake. There was a flicker of caution in her eyes but still no fear.

"Water?" she guessed, already reaching for a glass.

I shook my head. "No fight tonight. Give me a scotch."

"Right," she said. "Are you going out? You look nice."

"Nice, hmm …" She didn't need to know that Remo and I would be checking out one of our strip clubs tonight. There had been some inconsistencies with the books, which we needed to investigate. And after that, we'd have a long talk with the sluts working there.

A blush spread over her cheeks, making me want to reach over the bar and brush my fingers over them to feel her heated skin and those damn freckles. The innocent act usually wasn't something that got to me, because it usually was just that … an act. With Leona I could tell she wasn't acting.

"All business, no fun," I told her.

Her smile faltered again. She reached for the cheapest bottle of scotch. I shook my head. "Not that one. Give me the Johnnie Walker Blue Label over there." It was the most expensive scotch Roger's Arena offered. It wasn't really an establishment for fine tastes. The guys around here liked their drinks how they liked their women: cheap.

"That's thirty dollars a glass," she said.

"I know," I said when she slid the glass over to me. I downed a long sip of the amber liquid, enjoying the burn. I didn't drink often and had only been drunk twice in my life. There were other ways to get a high … fucking and fighting, my favorites.

I pushed a fifty-dollar note over to her. "Keep the rest."

Her eyes grew wide, and she gave a small shake of her head. "That's too much."

She fumbled in the cash register and pushed the twenty dollars over to me. Then she bent down for a moment to retrieve another fifty-dollar bill and put that down in front of me as well.

"I told you I don't want that money back, and that twenty dollars is your tip."

"I can't accept either. It's not right."

"Who told you?" I asked.

She blinked, then averted her eyes. "Who told me what?" She was a horrible liar and an even worse actress.

"Don't lie to me," I said, a hint of impatience creeping into my tone.

Her blue eyes met mine. She hesitated. "I overheard a few people talking."

I didn't believe that shit for a second.

She scanned my face. "So is it true?"

"Is what true?" I challenged.

"That you are part of the Camorra?"

She said it like the word meant nothing to her. She didn't know what we stood for, didn't know how powerful we were. For most people, the mere word fostered fear, but not for her. I hoped it would stay that way, but I knew it couldn't. Living in this part of town, working for Roger, she'd soon see or hear things that would make her realize just who the Camorra was and what they did.

"I am," I said, emptying the rest of my scotch.

Her eyes widened in surprise. "Aren't you supposed to keep it a secret?"

"It's difficult to keep a secret that isn't one." The Camorra was Las Vegas. We controlled the night clubs and bars, restaurants and casinos. We organized the cage fights and street races. We gave the poor fuckers bread and games, and they greedily accepted any distraction from their miserable lives. People knew of us, recognized us. There was no sense in trying to pretend we were something else.

"But what about the police?" she asked.

A few other customers tossed glances her way, their glasses empty, but none of them would dare come over to interrupt us.

"Don't worry," I said simply. I couldn't tell her about our association with the sheriff of Clark County or even our connection to some of the judges. That wasn't something she needed to know.

Seventy dollars sat on the bar between us. I picked it up and stalked around the bar. Leona's gaze was a mixture of caution and curiosity. I took her wrist. She didn't resist, only watched me intently. I fought the urge to back her up against the wall and get a taste of her. Fuck, I really wanted that taste.

I turned her hand and put the money into her palm. She opened her mouth, but I shook my head. "I don't want that money back. You will buy yourself a nice dress and wear it tomorrow. And do me a favor, get rid of those fucking sandals. Then our debt is settled."

Embarrassment filled her face as she looked down at herself. "Do I look that bad that you feel the need to buy me clothes?"

"I'm not buying you anything. I'm just giving you the money."

"I'm sure it's a big no-no to take money from someone like you," she said quietly. I still held her hand, and I could feel her pulse speeding up under my fingertips.

I leaned down to her ear. "It's an even bigger no-no to refuse a gift from someone like me."

She shuddered but still didn't pull back. When I released her, she stayed close to me. "Then I have no choice, I suppose," she said.

"You don't," I agreed.

People were watching our exchange with poorly hidden curiosity. A glance at the clock revealed I needed to get going. I didn't want to make Remo wait.

"Tomorrow I expect to see you in your new clothes," I told her.

She nodded then finally took a step back. Her expression was torn.

"So you'll be back tomorrow?" she asked.

I walked back around the bar then turned to her once more. "Yes."

Leona

I watched Fabiano's retreating back. Now that he wasn't there to distract me anymore, I realized how many customers were sitting in front of empty glasses.

Cheryl and the waitress of unidentifiable age were at the other end of the room and only now began to make their way over to me. I quickly hid the money in my backpack before I rushed toward the first table to take their orders. I could tell that people were eyeing me curiously. The conversation with Fabiano had drawn more attention to me than I enjoyed.

I could still feel the remnants of shame when I thought of his demand. I needed to buy a new dress for myself. I knew my clothes had seen better days. And my flip-flops … I stifled a sigh.

Perhaps I should have stood my ground and refused the money. Owing the mafia money was bad news, but Fabiano had gifted me the money not as a mobster but as a … what exactly? We weren't friends. Barely knew each other. Was I in his debt … or worse in the Camorra's? Did he expect something in return?

The idea was terrifying and exciting all at the same time. Not that I would ever give him any kind of physical closeness in return for money, but the idea that he might be interested in me filled me with a giddy kind of excitement.

"So staying away from him isn't going so well, huh?" Cheryl said as she came to a stop beside me, carrying a tray stacked with beer bottles.

"I can't stop him from having a drink in the bar," I said with a small shrug.

"He isn't coming for the drinks. Before you started working here, he was hardly around, and to be honest, I preferred it that way." She sauntered off, her hips swaying from side to side as she expertly maneuvered past tables on her high heels.

I sighed. My mother's knack for troublesome men had obviously been handed down to me. Perhaps there was a way for me to shirk Fabiano's attention. The problem was part of me didn't want him to lose interest in me. Some twisted, idiotic part was eager for his attention. That a man like him had even a flicker of interest in me boosted my meager self-esteem. Back in school, boys had only showed me attention because they thought I'd give it up easy being the daughter of a whore. They weren't interested in me because I was pretty or clever but because they thought I was easy. Fabiano didn't know about my mother, and with the way he looked, he certainly had no trouble finding willing women.

Cheryl shot me a glare across the room. I'd been lost in my thoughts and ceased working again. I pushed Fabiano out of my head. If I didn't want to lose this job, I'd have to get a grip.

That night after work, Fabiano wasn't there to drive me home. And I realized I'd been secretly hoping that he'd come in after he handled business … whatever that meant.

I swung my backpack over my shoulder and gripped the straps tightly as I began my walk home. Few people were around at this time, and those that were made me want to run. I quickened my pace, checking my surroundings. Nobody was following me, and yet I felt as if I was being hunted. All this talk about the Camorra had been fuel for my imagination.

It was ridiculous. I was used to walking on my own. My mom had never picked me up from anywhere back home, not that we even had a car. I had been the one who had to search for her on more than one occasion when she didn't return home. Often, I'd find her passed out in one of her favorite bars or in an alley.

When I finally made it to my dad's, I released a relieved breath. The lights were still on in the living room.

"Leona? Is that you?"

Dad sounded drunk. I hesitated. I remembered the last time I'd seen him drunk when I was twelve. He'd had a huge fight with my mother and hit her so hard she lost consciousness. She left him after that. Not that the men got better. For my mom, life was a downward spiral that never stopped. Perhaps she'd put a stop to it now, her last chance rehab.

I stopped in the doorway of the living room. Dad was sitting on the sofa, the table in front of him covered with beer bottles and papers. They looked like betting slips. I doubted he was celebrating his luck.

"You are late," he said, a slight slur in his voice.

"I had to work. The bar is open late," I said, wanting nothing more than to go into my bedroom and let him sleep off his intoxication. He pushed off the sofa and came around it, closer to me.

"I thought you weren't drinking anymore."

"I'm not," he said. "Most of the time. Today wasn't a good day."

I had a feeling the good days were few and far between. "I'm sorry," I said automatically.

He waved it off, taking another step in my direction, almost losing his balance. Memories of all the fights between him and my mother that I'd witnessed resurfaced, one after the other. I didn't have the energy for them now. "I should probably go to bed. Tomorrow will be another long day."

I turned when I heard his uncoordinated steps and then his hand clamped around my wrist. I jumped in surprise.

"Wait," he slurred. "You have to give me some money, Leona. Roger must have paid you by now."

I tried to slip out of his grip, but it was too tight—and painful. "You're hurting me," I said through gritted teeth.

He didn't seem to listen. "I need money. I need to pay off my betting debts or we'll be in trouble."

Why would *we* be in trouble if he didn't pay *his* betting debts?

"How much do you need?" I asked.

"Just give me all you have," he said, his fingers on my wrist as much a way to keep me from leaving as it was to keep himself upright.

I knew how it was going to go; Mom was the same way with her addiction. She stole every penny she found in my room, until I had no choice but to carry it on my body at all times. Not that I was able to fend her off on her more desperate days.

"I need to save money for college and we need food." I didn't hold much hope that he'd use his own money for grocery shopping. The donuts had been a one-time exception.

"Stop thinking about college. Girls like you don't go to college."

I finally managed to free myself of his crushing grip. Rubbing my wrist, I took a step back from him.

"Leona, this is serious. I need money," he said.

The despair on his face made me reach into my backpack. I took the fifty-dollar note and handed it to him. That left me with a little over one hundred dollars after Roger had paid me today. Tips were decent in the arena.

"That's all?"

I didn't get the chance to reply. He staggered forward, catching me by surprise. He ripped my backpack out of my hand, shoved his arm inside, and began rummaging through my belongings. I tried to get it back, but he pushed me away. I collided with the wall. When he found the rest of the money, he dropped the backpack and pushed the notes into his jeans pocket.

"A good daughter wouldn't lie to her father," he said angrily.

And a good father wouldn't steal from his daughter. I picked my backpack off the ground. One of the straps had now ripped. Fighting tears, I rushed into the bedroom and closed the door.

Tired and shaken, I sank down onto the mattress. Of course, nothing had changed. I'd lost count of the times my mother had promised me she'd start anew. The drugs had been stronger than her willpower and her love for me. And here I was with my father, who battled his own addiction, and I was stuck with him. Why did people in my life always break their promises?

I had no money to leave Las Vegas, and even if I did, where would I go? I couldn't afford an apartment anywhere, and I had no friends or family I could turn to.

I undressed, putting the dress carefully on the ground. Without money, I wouldn't be able to buy new clothes, but there was no way I could wear my dress again. It smelled of sweat and had a ketchup stain on the skirt. I took jeans shorts and a plain white shirt out of my backpack. They were crumpled from Dad rummaging through my bag, but they'd have to do.

Tired, I lay back on the mattress.

College isn't for girls like you.

Perhaps I was silly for dreaming about it, but my dreams were the only thing that kept me going. I wanted to get a law degree. Help people who couldn't afford a good lawyer. I closed my eyes. An image of Fabiano popped into my head. Nobody would ever take money from him. He was strong. He knew how to get what he wanted. I wished I were like that. Strong. Respected.

Early the next morning, I washed my summer dress then hung it over the shower stall to dry. Even though I still had a few hours until work, I left the apartment. I didn't feel comfortable there after the incident with Dad yesterday. He hadn't scared me. Too often, I had been confronted with the same blatant despair from my mother.

Luckily, I'd found a few dollars in coins that I'd gotten as tips yesterday at the bottom of my backpack. I wanted to grab breakfast for myself.

With my coffee to-go and a Danish, I strode through the streets without any real purpose. When I noticed the bus, which was heading toward the Strip, I used the last of my money to buy a ticket. I wasn't even sure why. It wasn't as if I could ask for a job anywhere there. They would laugh in my face.

I got off near the Venetian and just kept walking, marveling at the splendor of the hotels, at the lightheartedness of the tourists. This was a different Las Vegas than the one I'd experienced so far. I eventually stopped in front of the fountains of the Bellagio. I closed my eyes. How was I ever going to get a good job around here when I couldn't even buy myself a decent dress?

I had seen the security guards keep an eye on me when I'd wandered through the hotels. They had me pegged as a thief from just one look.

Dad would keep taking my money, unless he suddenly stopped losing his bets, which was highly unlikely. The house always won.

I asked a passerby for the time since I had no watch or phone. I had only thirty minutes until I had to be at work. There was no way I was going to be on time, considering that I'd given my last cent for the bus ticket to the Strip and would have to walk back. That would take at least one hour, probably longer. With my luck, it would probably start raining again.

Walking away from the luxury of the Bellagio, I felt more and more out of

TWISTED LOYALTIES | 67

place on the Strip, with my wrinkly white shirt and secondhand jeans shorts. To top it off, I was freezing my butt off. Perhaps Dad had been right and I didn't belong in college; I'd still be working in Roger's bar when I was old and bitter. I almost laughed then shook my head. If I stopped believing in my future, it was lost, but days like yesterday made it hard to stay hopeful.

Fabiano

I spotted Leona the moment I stepped out of the Bellagio. The doorman handed me the key to my car, and I slipped in, never taking my eyes off the girl. The engine came to life with its familiar roar, and I pulled out of the driveway, heading down the street toward Leona.

She didn't notice me until I pulled up beside her and rolled down the window. My eyes traveled down to her fucking flip-flops. "Shouldn't you be wearing your new dress today?" I shouted over the noise of the engine and the traffic driving past us as I leaned over the passenger seat to get a good look at her.

Leona was dressed in a wrinkly white shirt that was stuffed into old jeans shorts. Though I appreciated the first glimpse of her lean, toned thighs, I was annoyed that she hadn't bought a new dress for herself. I wasn't used to people ignoring my wishes like that.

She shrugged, though looked obviously uncomfortable. I pushed the passenger door open. "Get in," I ordered, trying to rein in my annoyance.

For a moment, I was sure she'd say no, but then she dropped her backpack from her shoulder and sank down on the seat. She closed the door and put the seat belt on before finally meeting my gaze, almost defiantly.

I let my eyes wander over her body, coming to rest on the faint bruises on her left wrist. I took her hand and inspected the bruise. She pulled away and hid her wrist beneath her other hand.

"I lost my balance in the shower this morning," she lied easily.

"Are you sure you didn't fall down the stairs?" I asked in a low voice. Anger began to simmer under my skin. I knew bruises. And I knew the lies women told to hide they were being abused. My father had hit my sisters and me almost every day, especially Gianna and myself. We were the ones he couldn't control, the ones always doing wrong in his eyes. I'd lost count of the times I'd seen my mother cover up her bruises with makeup.

The bruise around Leona's wrist was from a grip that was too tight.

She gave me a look, but her expression faltered and she shook her head. "It's nothing."

"Who did this?"

"It's nothing. It doesn't hurt or anything."

"Your father."

"What makes you think that?" she asked, her voice a bit higher than before.

"Because he's the only one you have reason to protect."

She licked her lips. "He didn't mean to hurt me. He was drunk. He didn't notice how tightly he was holding me."

Did she really believe that? Or was she scared of what I'd do to him? And by God, I wanted to tear into him like a starved bloodhound.

It wasn't like it was my business what her father did to her. It shouldn't be. But the mere idea that he was hurting her made me want to pay him a visit and give him a taste of what I was capable of.

"Is that why you're dressed like that?" I asked with a wave at her clothes. I pulled the car away from the curb, crossed four lanes to reach the turning lane, then did a U-turn, which was followed by a cacophony of car horns and raised middle fingers from drivers on both sides of the street.

"What are you doing?" Leona asked, gripping the sides of the seat. "That's the wrong way."

"It's not. We're buying you a dress and fucking new shoes. If I have to see you in those fucking flip-flops one more time, I'll go on a rampage."

"What?" Her eyes widened. "Don't be ridiculous. I need to get to work. I don't have time to go shopping."

"Don't worry. Roger will understand."

"Fabiano," she said pleadingly. "Why are you doing this? If you expect anything in return, I'm not that kind of girl. I'm poor, but that doesn't mean I can be bought."

"I have no intention of buying you," I told her. And it was true. Something about Leona made me want to protect her. It was a new experience for me. Not that I didn't want her in my bed, but I wanted to make her want it too. I'd never had to pay for sex, and never would. The whores in Vegas were on the Camorra's payroll anyway.

She watched me for a long time. "Then why?"

"Because I can and because I want to."

The answer didn't seem to satisfy her, but I focused on the street, and she didn't ask more questions, which was a fucking good thing, because I really didn't want to analyze my fascination with her. She reminded me of my sisters. Not in a kinky way. More like she reminded me of a longing I'd buried deep in my chest. Fuck me.

"So your father stole the money I gave you?" I asked eventually, my fingers bearing down on the wheel wishing it were his fucking throat.

She nodded. "He seems to be in trouble."

If he were in real trouble, I'd know it. The money he owed us, it couldn't be much. If Soto still handled him, he was a lucky man.

"Men like him are always in trouble," I told her. "You should get away from him."

"He's my father."

"Sometimes we have to let go of our family if we want to amount to anything in life."

Surprise and curiosity registered on her face. I gritted my teeth, annoyed at myself for my words.

I parked at the curb in front of one of the high-class boutiques that the It-Girls I occasionally fucked—when they felt they needed to add a thrill to their pampered life—frequented.

Leona looked toward the storefront then back at me, her lips parting in disbelief. A small crease formed between her brows. "Don't tell me you want me to go in there. They won't even let me inside looking the way I do. They'll just think that I've come to steal their clothes."

Would they? We'd see about that. I got out of the car, walked around the hood, and opened the door for her. She stepped out then reached for her backpack. I stopped her. "You can leave it in my car."

She hesitated but stepped back so I could shut the door. She looked around nervously, feeling fucking uncomfortable. I held out my hand for her. "Come," I said firmly.

She put her palm in mine, and I closed my fingers around her hand. That Leona trusted me despite what she knew about me made me want to be good to her, which was surprising. I rarely wanted to be good to anyone. I had enough money so one dress wasn't going to kill me. And new shoes were really more for my own sanity than anything else. These flip-flops had to go.

I led her toward the store. The shop window was decorated with silver and golden Christmas decorations. The security guard, a tall, dark-skinned fucker, gave her the once-over but let us enter when he registered my face. The saleswoman couldn't hide her disdain at Leona's appearance. Her red painted lips twisted, and Leona's hand in mine tensed. My eyes slanted to Leona. Her free hand fidgeted with her wrinkly white shirt; shame washed over her face and her freckles disappeared among her blush.

Leona shifted closer to me, seeking safety. She sought fucking safety with a man like me. I doubted Leona noticed, *but I had*—so I raised my eyes to the saleswoman's face, letting her glimpse behind the mask I wore so she could see why I was the Enforcer of the Camorra. Why some people begged me before my knife was ever against their skin. She stiffened and recoiled.

I smiled coldly. "I assume you can help us."

She nodded quickly. "What is it you're looking for?" she asked me.

"You should ask her," I said in a low voice, nodding toward Leona.

"A dress," Leona said quickly then added, "And shoes."

The saleswoman took in Leona's flip-flops, but this time her expression didn't betray her disdain. Good for her.

"What kind of dress?"

Leona sought my gaze, helpless. I gestured for the woman to give us a moment. She scurried off to the back of the store, where another saleswoman stood behind the cash register.

"I never got to choose. I don't know anything about dresses or shoes. I got whatever fit me from Goodwill."

"You never had a new piece of clothing?" I asked.

She looked away. "Clothing wasn't a priority. I had to put food on the table." Her eyes were drawn to the rack of dresses to our right.

"Try on whatever catches your eye."

It became obvious pretty quickly that she wasn't going to touch any of the dresses, so I pulled out a dark green dress with long sleeves and held it out to her. She took it and followed the saleswoman toward the changing rooms in back. I leaned against the wall, keeping my eyes on the curtain hiding Leona from view. It was taking longer than it should for her to get changed.

"You okay in there?"

She came out, grimacing. I straightened. The dress hugged her body in all the right places and flared out until it reached her knees. The back dipped low, revealing her delicate shoulder blades and spine. She looked completely different. She regarded herself in the mirror and shook her head, her lips setting in a tight line. "This feels like a costume," she said quietly. "As if I'm pretending to be someone I'm not."

I moved closer. "And who is it you're pretending to be?"

She glared. "More than *white trash*."

"White trash," I repeated in as calm a voice as my anger allowed. "Who called you that?"

"I'm the daughter of a junkie and a gambling addict. I am white trash. I'm not this." She gestured at her reflection.

"Nobody will ever call you white trash again, you hear? And if they do, you will tell me and I will rip their throats out. How about that?"

She tilted her head, again trying to read me ... to understand. "You can't change my past. You can't change who I am."

"No," I said with a shrug, my finger trailing down her throat. She wasn't breathing, and I, too, held my breath at the feel of her soft skin. "But you can. I can only force people to treat you as you want to be treated."

She tore her gaze away from mine and took a step back. I dropped my hand then went back out and selected another dress. She took it without a word and slipped back into the dressing room.

I sank down onto one of the armchairs that was way too soft. Leona looked fucking good in every dress she tried on. Nobody would take her for white trash dressed like that. Nobody should take her for white trash dressed in her fucking secondhand clothes either. "Buy them all," I told her, but she shook her head firmly.

"One," she said, raising a single finger. "I'll get one because I promised you, but no more." She lifted her chin and straightened her spine. Stubborn and brave, despite what she knew of me.

"Then take that one." I pointed at the dark green dress that she'd put on first.

"Isn't it too revealing?" she whispered.

"You have the body for it."

A pleased blush spread across her freckled cheeks, but she still hesitated. "I don't want people to get the wrong impression."

I tilted my head. "What kind of impression?"

She looked away, fumbling with the fabric of the dress. When the saleswoman was out of sight, she said quietly, "That I'm selling more than drinks. Cheryl mentioned that a few customers pay her to do *other things*."

I rose from the armchair and moved closer. She peered up at me. "Nobody will try anything, Leona. They know you are off limits."

Her brows drew together. "Why?"

"Take the dress," I ordered.

She stiffened her spine again. Stubborn. I softened my next words. "You promised."

She nodded slowly. "Okay."

I turned to the saleswoman, who was hovering outside the changing rooms. "She's going to put it on right away. We still need shoes."

She hurried off and came back with matching flats in dark green leather. I'd hoped for stilettos but doubted Leona could walk in them anyway. I nodded my approval, and she handed them to Leona. Her eyes met mine, filled with question, before she disappeared behind the curtain once more.

Leona came back out of the changing room, dressed in her new dress and shoes, looking fucking amazing. I let my eyes wander over her slender shoulders, her narrow waist, and lean legs. The dress ended a couple of inches above her knees and dipped low on her back, revealing inch by inch of immaculate skin.

She carried her old clothes. I wanted to tell her to throw them away, but I had a feeling she didn't have any clothes to spare. Instead, I went over to the cashier and paid for the dress and shoes.

Leona's eyes grew wide when she saw the sum.

"I can't believe how much you paid! I could have bought ten dresses at Walmart for that much money," she whispered as I led her out of the shop.

I pressed my palm against the naked skin between her shoulder blades, relishing in her small shiver and the way goose bumps rose on her skin. The familiar blush spread over her cheeks. Before I opened the door, I leaned down to her, my lips brushing her ear. "It's worth every penny, trust me."

She released a small, shaky breath and quickly got into my Mercedes, as if she needed to put some space between us. There was no way I'd let her get away from me.

EIGHT

Leona

SMOOTHED MY FINGERS DOWN THE SOFT MATERIAL OF THE DRESS. IT WAS made from silk and cotton, something I'd never worn before. It felt almost too good for me. I never could have afforded this kind of dress, nor would I have ever paid that much money for a piece of clothing. And the shoes. I didn't know leather this soft existed. For Fabiano, it was nothing.

"Thank you," I said eventually. We'd been driving in silence for a while. The surroundings that flew past us were becoming shabbier. It wouldn't be long before we arrived at Roger's Arena.

Fabiano nodded his head as he drove. I wished I knew what was going on in there, why he was really doing this. My eyes lingered on his strong jaw, the dark blond stubble, the way his mouth was set in a determined line. He always seemed in control. Even during his fight, he never gave up control. He had dominated his opponent with little effort. Was there a time when he ever lost it?

As I watched him drive, I got my first good look at the tattoo on the inside of his right forearm. It was a long knife with an eye on the top of the blade, near the hilt, with words written in intricate letters. It looked like Italian and was too small for me to read.

Fabiano pulled into the parking lot of Roger's Arena and turned off the engine. He purposely held out his forearm so I could take a closer look. Had I been staring that openly?

"What does it say?" I touched my fingertip to his skin, tracing every single letter and marveling at how soft his skin felt. He was all hard lines and muscle, power and danger, but his skin betrayed that when I touched him, he was only human.

"Temere me, perché sono l'occhio e la spada," Fabiano said in flawless Italian, from what I could tell. He caressed the words with his tongue, almost as if he was their lover. A shiver raced down my back. I couldn't help but wonder how it would feel if he whispered words of passion into my ear in that same voice. "What…" I cleared my throat, hoping he couldn't tell how his closeness and voice affected me "…what does it mean?"

"Fear me cause I'm the eye and the blade."

A lover's voice delivering such harsh words. "Do all mobsters have this tattoo?" I asked.

He smirked. "Made men or Camorrista, as we like to call ourselves, but yes, members of the Camorra all have the same tattoo. It's a way to recognize each other."

"The eye and the blade," I repeated. "What does it mean? What do you have to do to bear that tattoo?"

He leaned over and for a moment. I was sure he would kiss me—and worse that I would have let him. Instead, he ran a finger down the length of my arm, a dark look in his eyes. "That's something you don't want to know," he murmured.

I nodded. With him being so close, it was hard to concentrate. I needed to get out of this car.

"Go out with me."

"I have to work," came my dumb reply.

He smiled a knowing smile. "Not every day. When's your next day off?"

I hadn't talked to Roger about that, and with the way my financial situation was, I couldn't afford to take a day off.

"It doesn't matter. Let's say Wednesday."

That was only two days away. I didn't come to Vegas for a date. I swore to myself that I'd keep my head down and stay out of trouble. Going on a date with a member of the mob wasn't exactly doing that.

"I can't. I …" I couldn't come up with an excuse, and Fabiano's eyes spoke a clear meaning. Any answer other than yes was unacceptable.

"I don't know if I can get that day off."

"You will."

Did the bar belong to the Camorra? Or was Roger too scared to refuse Fabiano's request?

All my life people had trampled over me. Nothing had ever come easy. I'd had to fight for everything I had, and suddenly here was Fabiano, who got what he wanted and could handle things for me with a few simple words. It shouldn't have felt good, but I'd always been on my own. My mother hadn't been in any state to take care of me, and my father was hundreds of miles away and just as incapable. Now there was someone taking care of me, and I liked it, liked handing over some of the burden of always having to fend for myself, having to make every decision. I liked it too much.

Men like Fabiano were used to controlling others. If I let him, he'd take total control of my life, *of me*: body and soul. I needed to be careful.

I tore my gaze away from his face. A trickle of sweat trailed down my back. The air was too stuffy in his car. I got out, glad for more space between me and Fabiano.

He followed me, of course. *More like prowled after me.*

"Are you coming in for a drink?" I asked, torn between wanting him to and wanting him to leave.

"Not today, but I'll have a quick talk with Roger about Wednesday."

His hand touched my back as he led me inside. The heat of his palm on my skin was way more distracting than it should have been.

The moment we entered the bar, Cheryl's angry eyes zoomed in on me, then on Fabiano, before she whirled around and headed through the door behind the bar. Most of the tables were still empty. The first fight hadn't begun yet, but a look at the clock revealed I was almost one hour late. Guilt overcame me. I hated disappointing people who relied on me. Roger was certainly furious.

His reddened face as he stalked into the bar confirmed my worry. He stopped in his tracks when he saw me standing beside Fabiano.

Fabiano stroked my skin lightly with his thumb. I had to resist leaning into his touch. Instead, I gave him a quick smile then rushed off toward the bar. Roger didn't spare me a glance, but I could tell that he was seething. I watched as Roger walked toward Fabiano and listened to him, eventually nodding, but he didn't look happy about it.

Cheryl slid up to my side. "New dress?" she asked suggestively.

I flushed, though I had nothing to be embarrassed about. I removed a few of the empty bottles lined up next to the sink and stashed them in the crates below the bar.

"Chick, I know you're new here, but don't think he's buying you stuff because he feels sorry for you. That man isn't capable of feeling sorry."

Annoyance rushed through me. She pretended like she knew all about him. How could she say that he had no feelings? Just because he didn't show them didn't mean he didn't have them.

"Cheryl, I know what I'm doing. There's nothing to worry about, trust me."

She pointed at my bruised wrist. "That's only the beginning."

"He didn't do that." Cheryl rolled her eyes. Men sitting at a table had tried to catch our attention, so I went over to them. This conversation with Cheryl was leading nowhere.

Fabiano came over to me. The men at the table fell silent as he stopped beside me. He touched my naked back again, and I saw the look he gave the other men. Was he being possessive? He leaned down. "Wednesday, I'll pick you up at six on your street." He straightened and stalked off, leaving me with the searing imprint of his touch on my back.

"So, two lagers and three pale ales?" I repeated their order.

They nodded but didn't say another word.

When I returned home that night, the apartment was dark and quiet. The door to Dad's bedroom was ajar. He wasn't there. I really hoped he wasn't gambling again.

I slipped out of the dress and carefully laid it on one of the moving boxes. Tomorrow I'd wash it so I could wear it again for my date with Fabiano on Wednesday. My stomach tightened with nerves and excitement. When I finally lay down and closed my eyes, I could feel his hand on my back again and smell his musky scent. My hand found its way between my legs, remembering the way he looked half-naked, the lithe way he'd moved during his fight, the strength he oozed so easily. I'd never felt so drawn to someone before. I moved my fingers at a quick pace, imagining it was Fabiano.

After I finished, I felt even more nervous about our date. I never had trouble refusing guys; none were ever remotely interesting enough for me to risk my reputation. But refusing Fabiano ... that would prove to be more difficult.

Fabiano

Remo was lounging on the sofa, watching the latest race on his enormous TV. The races were getting more and more popular by the day. If we could operate the races in all of the states and Canada, we'd be swimming in money. With the Outfit and the Famiglia in the U.S. and the fucking Corsican Union in Canada in our way, that wasn't going to happen any time soon. Not to mention the Bratva and the Cartel. Everyone wanted to have a fat piece of the cake.

"What's going on between you and that new girl at Roger's?" Remo asked, sending my body into high alert.

My face remained blank as I took a sip from my drink then leaned back on the couch.

Remo seemed focused on the race, but that could easily have been a way to make me lower my guard.

"Nothing's going on," I told him offhandedly.

His eyes met mine. "You're buying her things and you're taking her out. That's nothing?"

I let out a dark laugh. "Are you spying on me, Remo? Since when do you care about the girls I'm fucking?"

"I don't. She seems a strange choice. Not your usual style. And I don't need to spy on you. You know how it is."

Oh, I knew. People were always eager to talk shit about me behind my back, hoping they could rat me out to Remo and earn a reward. If they thought he'd be impressed by them acting like a stinking rat, they didn't know shit about him. Remo would remember their names, but definitely not in a way they'd appreciate.

"She's a welcome distraction. The other girls ... they're all the same. They are starting to bore me."

The women laughed because they had to, smiled their fake smiles. They regarded me like an opportunity. And I never cared. They were good for fucking and sucking.

"The thrill of the chase," Remo mused.

I smirked. "Perhaps. Let me have some fun. It won't interfere with my duties."

Remo nodded, but there was a look in his eyes I didn't like. "Have fun." He returned his attention to the bar. "She might be more skilled than she looks. Her mother is a cheap street hooker in Austin."

What the fuck? I tensed. Her mother was a whore? Was he fucking shitting me? That Remo had done a background check on Leona unsettled me even more. It was never a good thing when something caught Remo's attention. I shrugged, trying to appear nonchalant, though I had a feeling Remo had picked up on my shock. He was too damn observant. That was why he was Capo.

"I don't give a fuck who her mother is."

Remo's eyes bored a hole into my fucking skull, never halting his relentless stare. I stood from the sofa. "I'm going to work out for a while."

I needed to blow off some steam before I went to get Leona. I was *on edge*. I'd have to spend the next hour kicking the hell out of a heavy bag if I wanted to keep my cool with her.

Leona

Dad had avoided me since the incident. I heard him return home early in the morning, bump against walls, and smash his door shut in a drunken stupor. He was still hidden away in his room when I left for work.

On Wednesday I had my day off, and he couldn't avoid me. When he stepped out of his bedroom and shuffled into the kitchen, dressed in only faded gray boxers and a yellowed wife beater, he froze in the doorway after spotting me. He obviously expected me to be at work.

"Did they fire you?" he asked uncertainly. It almost looked like there was guilt on his face. The bruises on my wrist were already faded, so he was probably feeling guilty about the money he had taken from me.

I shook my head as I sipped my coffee. I had hardly eaten anything, even though the fridge was stashed with food for once after I'd gone to the grocery store. "No, it's my day off."

"On a day of a big fight?" he asked. "One of the Falcone brothers is in the cage tonight."

Surprise filled me. "I can't work all the time."

Dad sat down across from me. Under his eyes were dark circles, and he looked like he could use a long shower.

I waited for him to ask me for more money. He must have been thinking about it. He stared down at his hands then sighed. "I never wanted this kind of life for you. When you were born, I thought everything would change. I thought I could give you a good life."

"I know," I said simply. Mom and Dad both had wanted to be good parents, and for a while they had tried.

"Are you going to be home tonight?" he asked. "You could watch the cage fight with me. They're showing it on the big screen at a bar around the corner from here."

I wasn't really in the mood to watch another cage fight, but I was touched that he wanted to spend time with me, even if part of me couldn't help but be wary. And I hated it, hated that I had to be cautious when my parents showed any interest in me.

"I'm already going out," I said carefully.

"You are?" Curiosity flashed in his eyes.

I nodded and stood quickly. I placed my cup in the sink, deciding to clean it later when Dad wasn't breathing down my neck. "I should probably start to get ready." It was still two hours until Fabiano would pick me up, but I wanted to avoid a confrontation with my father.

I'd be rattled me even more, and I was already on edge because of my date. It seemed less and less like a good idea, but I couldn't back out now. Perhaps Fabiano would lose interest after tonight. It wasn't like I had anything remotely interesting to say, and I definitely wasn't going to talk about my mother. If he knew about her, he'd look at me in a different way.

I dressed in the dark green dress again. I shouldn't have let Fabiano buy me anything. All my life, I'd had to work hard for what I wanted. Having something gifted to me like that had felt amazing. Now I couldn't help but think of Fabiano's intentions. Nothing in life was for free. That was a lesson I learned early.

I checked my reflection in the mirror. It was finally possible to get a good look, after I'd cleaned the thing and the rest of the apartment yesterday. I was never into heavy makeup, even for the date, so I decided to keep it to a minimum. I didn't want it to look like I was making a huge effort, so I put on some foundation with just a hint of blush and then brushed my eyelashes with mascara. I reached for my only lipstick, a berry tone that complimented my hair color and complexion perfectly. With it almost touching my lips, I paused. What if Fabiano tried to kiss me tonight? Would lipstick get in the way?

I flushed. No kissing. I had no intention of kissing anyone, least of all Fabiano. But a treacherous part of my body tingled with excitement at the idea. Sighing, I lowered the lipstick and tossed it aside.

When six rolled around, I was nearly trembling with nerves. Luckily, Dad had left the apartment ten minutes ago, so I didn't have to worry about a confrontation between Fabiano and him.

I risked a peek out the window when I heard the sound of a car pulling up. Fabiano was already getting out and a lump formed in my throat at the sight of him. He looked marvelous, not like someone who would date white trash like me. I didn't kid myself into thinking I was anything else. A dress and nice shoes wouldn't change that.

Grabbing my backpack, I quickly left the apartment. I didn't want him to glimpse inside and see how little we had. I closed the door. Fabiano was already waiting at the bottom of the stairs, intense blue eyes scanning my body.

I descended the stairs slowly, my hand on the rail like an anchor. He was dressed in a white button down shirt that hugged his muscular form. His sleeves were rolled up again, revealing strong, tanned forearms and the tattoo of the Camorra. He'd left the upper two buttons of his shirt unbuttoned, showing off a hint of his perfect chest. Somehow knowing what was beneath his shirt, how he looked wearing only his fighting gear made this even harder. When I reached the second to last step and was eyelevel with him, a shiver ripped through my body. He looked like he wanted to devour me. I thought of something sophisticated to say, anything that would stop him from giving me that hungry look.

"Hi," was all I got out, and even that one word sounded hushed.

His mouth twitched, and he slid his hand behind my back, his palm finding the same spot of naked skin where it had rested the last time. My body came alive with a tingling, but I didn't let it show. I needed to stay in control of this evening, and most of all myself.

He led me toward his car and then we were off. It was hard not to fidget as we drove in silence. He looked perfectly at ease, as usual, long fingers curled loosely around the wheel. The tiny hairs on his hand glistened and I wondered if he was possibly still wet from a shower? *Don't go there, Leona.*

My nerves grew as the city lights thinned out and we left them behind completely. "Where are we going?"

I tried to mask the apprehension in my voice. The stupid stories I'd read about the mafia came uninvited into my mind, and I envisioned myself being buried under the desert sand. Not that the mafia had any interest in me.

He steered the car up a steep road then stopped it on a plateau. "Here."

I followed his gaze out the windshield and released a surprised breath, leaning forward for a better view. We overlooked Las Vegas from our spot. It was an incredible sight. Against the night sky, the colored flashing lights seemed even brighter. A promise of excitement and money. Despite the miles between the Strip and me, I could almost taste the endless opportunities. I wished that only once in my life I would be offered the same opportunities so many people had.

It seemed like such a romantic location for a first date. I hadn't pegged Fabiano as the romantic type, and perhaps he wasn't. Perhaps he wanted to take me somewhere remote so we could be alone. My heart thumped in my throat at the idea. His warm, musky scent filled the car, and my body reacted to it in a way I'd never experienced. He was watching me intently as I watched the Las Vegas skyline. I wished there was something I could say to break the tension, but my mind drew a blank. He reached up and stroked a finger down my neck, further down along my spine, leaving goose bumps on his way. The sensation tingled all the way down to my toes. I marveled at the gentleness of his touch, still remembering how these same hands had broken his opponent's bones with little effort. I wondered how the same hands would feel on other parts of my body. *Stop it, Leona.* If I started thinking like that, it was only a small leap before I acted upon it.

"Let's get out," he said in a low voice that left my mouth dry and my nerves on edge. When he exited the car and closed the door, my breath whooshed out of me. I tried to steal myself for his closeness, but I knew the moment I got near him again, my body would be a melting pot of conflicting feelings.

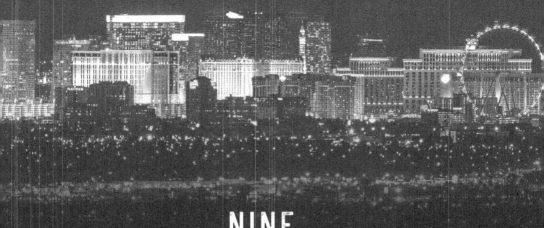

NINE

Fabiano

T HE COOL NIGHT AIR FILLED MY LUNGS. I WAS GLAD FOR THE REPRIEVE
from Leona's tantalizing scent. I wanted to bend her over the hood of my
car and bury myself to the hilt inside of her. Fuck, I wanted to do it over
and over again. I wasn't sure why these damn freckles and cornflower blue eyes
got to me, but they fucking did. She must have seen it in my expression, because
I'd never seen her more uneasy in my company than in that car.

I ran a hand through my hair, which was still damp from my earlier
shower. I'd pummeled the fucking heavy bag for too long and was almost late
for our date. In the last couple of years, I mainly dealt with whores or pole
dancers. Their intentions were always clear from the start. They either wanted
money, drugs, or a favor. They weren't shy. They wanted something *from me*, so
they showed me what they could offer. The sex had been a satisfying joyride, but
Leona was different. Her shyness irritated and fascinated me at the same time.
She was a challenge like I'd never had, and my body was eager to conquer it. Too
fucking eager.

Leona stepped out of the car, looking almost flustered. She kept her
eyes trained on the sight below us as she came around to meet me. Her hands
clutched that tacky, old backpack.

"You are obsessed with that thing," I said, feeling the irritating urge to
lighten the mood and set her at ease.

She let out a small laugh, her eyes crinkling. "I thought it went well with
my shoes." She lifted her foot a couple of inches.

My gaze went to her dark green leather flats then up to the backpack of
an unidentifiable color. Perhaps it had been beige a long time ago. She was

definitely the first woman that came on a date with me, holding a fucking back-pack. I chuckled.

"Remind me next time we go shopping to buy you one of those fancy purses girls go crazy over."

Her eyebrows shot up then knit together. "You can't keep buying things for me."

I swiveled my body around so we were standing even closer, leveling my gaze on her. She didn't back off, but I could see goose bumps form along her slender arms. "Who's going to stop me?"

Remo couldn't care less if I spent my money on women, cars, or property, as long as I didn't start betting or gambling or worse ... neglect my duties.

"I will ...?" It sounded more a question than a statement.

"Are you asking me or telling me?"

Her frown deepened, and she sighed. "I'm no good at playing these power games."

"Who said this is a power game?"

"Isn't it always? With men, it's always about exerting dominance. And you ..." She shook her head.

"And I ...?"

"Everything you do is a sign of dominance. When I saw you in the fighting cage that was perhaps the most relaxed I've ever seen you act. Outside of it you act like a hunter, always looking for someone who might dare to challenge your status."

I smiled. She seemed to think she knew me. I got that she'd seen a lot in her life, but the world I grew up in was a very different kind of shark tank. "In our world, you are either hunter or prey, Leona. I know what I am. What are *you?*"

Pressing my palms against her bare shoulders, I started to slide them lower, watching her reaction. She shivered but didn't push me away, though I could tell that she was thinking about it.

"Prey," she admitted reluctantly. "I will always be." She gazed past me, to-ward Las Vegas, looking lost and resigned.

My hands stilled on her back. This unguarded admission did something strange to me. It unleashed a protective, fierce side I hadn't experienced toward a woman since I'd been a scrawny kid and tried to defend my sisters. The soft breeze tugged at her brown curls as she lost herself in the sight of the city.

I bent down and kissed her ear. She released a shuddering breath. "Perhaps you need a protector so you stop being easy prey."

"Am I easy prey?" she asked quietly.

I didn't bother replying. We both knew how it was. And in a city like this, a city ruled by us, a girl like her was lost. "Do you want a protector?"

She closed her eyes as I kissed the skin below her ear. For once it was hard to read her. "And you think you can be my protector?"

I could protect her against almost any threat. Not against the Camorra. And not against myself. But that wasn't something I wanted to consider. "You saw me fight. Do you doubt it?"

She opened her eyes and tilted her head up toward me, blue eyes soft and probing. "No," she said. "But I think you and your way of life are threats too."

I didn't deny it.

"Why do you even want to protect me?"

To be honest, I didn't know. Perhaps Aria had somehow managed to get through to me. It made me fucking furious to think about it. That fucking bracelet. I shouldn't have accepted it.

"There's nothing I could give you in return." Her expression became more determined. "I don't have any money to spare, but I don't think you'd want it. You certainly don't need it. If there's something else you want, I'm not that kind of girl."

Not that kind of girl. Remo's words about her mother flashed through my mind. Was this an act after all?

There was an easy way to find out, of course. I gripped her hips. Her lips parted in surprise, but I didn't give her the chance to voice her protest.

I kissed her and after a moment of hesitation she kissed me back.

I could tell she didn't have much experience kissing. Fuck. That knowledge was the last straw. I had to have her. Every little inch of her. Every goose bump. Every freckle. Every fucking shy smile. All for myself.

And I had to protect her from all the wolves she believed were sheep. My fingers tangled in her curls, angling her head to the side to give me better access to that sweet mouth of hers.

I slid my hands from her waist to her bare back again then lower. Her hands came up against my chest. I savored the taste of her for a few seconds more before I allowed her to push me away.

Her dark lashes fluttered as her eyes found mine. In the dim light, I couldn't see if her cheeks were as flushed as I expected them to be. I brought my hand up and brushed my knuckles along her high cheekbones. Her skin was practically burning up with embarrassment and want. My cock twitched in my pants.

She tore herself away from me, walked to the edge of the hill we were on, and looked out toward the bright city lights.

I let my eyes take in her silhouette for a couple of moments, allowing her to gather herself before I approached. I came to a stop right behind her. She didn't acknowledge my presence, except for the slight tensing of her shoulders. Her sweet, flowery perfume drifted into my nose. I traced the line of her spine with my knuckles, needing to feel her silky skin.

Leona

That touch ignited desires I'd suppressed for a long time. Fabiano always touched me in a way that never gave me any real relief. Did he know the effect he had on me?

"Why did you bring me here?" I asked.

"Because I thought you'd appreciate the sight. You haven't been in Las Vegas for very long."

"Wouldn't the Strip be a better place to show someone the city?"

Fabiano stepped up to my side, and I was glad to be able to see him again. Having him so close behind me, his fingers running down my spine, was too distracting.

He pushed his hands into the pockets of his slacks, his blue eyes scanning over the city below us. And for the first time I caught the briefest glimpse behind his mask. This was a place he came often. I could tell. This city, it was important to him. It was his home.

I'd never had a place to call home. How would it be to look at something or someone and feel at home?

"There are too many people around who don't get the city. Up here, I have the city to myself."

"So you don't like to share?" I said teasingly.

He turned his gaze to me. "Never. Not even my city."

I shivered. Nodding, I quickly looked back to the skyline. "Were you born here?"

I wasn't very perceptive but the stiffening of his shoulders told me he didn't like where our conversation was heading.

"No. Not in the sense that you mean," he said quietly. "But I was reborn here."

I searched his face, but he wasn't giving anything away. It was all hard lines as the silence stretched between us.

"I thought this could be a new start for me as well," I said eventually.

"Why would you need a new start?"

"All my life I've been judged by the actions of my mother. I want to be judged for my own doing."

"Being in the shadow of your family isn't easy," he said, meeting my gaze. Another small crack in his mask. "But being judged for your own wrongdoings can be hard as well."

"Do you think I've done too many wrong things?"

He smirked. "You are here with me. I'd say you have a strong penchant for doing wrong things."

I feared he was right. "Because you're in the mafia."

"Because I am part of the *Camorra*." I loved the way he rolled the r's when he said the word. I could almost feel the vibrations all the way in the pit of my stomach. I wondered why he insisted there was a difference between the Camorra and the mafia.

"Because I am their *enforcer*."

"Enforcer," I said, furrowing my brows. I'd never heard that term before. "So you're enforcing their laws like some kind of mob police."

He chuckled. "Something like that," he said darkly. My gut tightened at the dark undercurrent in his voice.

I waited for him to elaborate, but he seemed content to leave me guessing, so I decided to ask Cheryl about it later. If I had a cell phone, or if my dad had a working computer, I would have Googled the term. As it was, I needed to rely on old-fashioned channels to get information. Fabiano was obviously unwilling to reveal any more about what his mafia title entailed.

"I thought you'd be eager to see tonight's fight. I hear it's a big one."

Fabiano shrugged. "It is, but I have watched thousands of fights in my life and have fought hundreds. I don't care if I miss one." His eyes settled on me. "And I wanted you for myself."

Was he embarrassed of being seen with me? The poor little waitress and the big deal mobster.

I rubbed my arms, the night's cold air catching up with me. Fabiano pressed up behind me and began stroking my arms through the thin fabric of my dress. Always close, always touching. His spicy aftershave engulfed me like his arms did.

"What do you want from me?" I whispered.

"Everything."

Everything.

That word still made my breathing hitch as I lay awake later that night after our date. There was no way I could fall asleep.

I don't like to share.

Everything.

I was attracted to Fabiano and was curious, but curiosity killed the cat. I feared that being close to Fabiano would put an end to all the plans I'd so carefully made for my future, but I wanted to see him again. I wanted to kiss him again. I knew it wasn't a good idea, and I wasn't sure what to do.

Just let it happen.

Being with him made me feel good. Very few things in my life did. Why not allow myself this small sin? Because that's what he was … sin.

The next day I made sure to be at work early so I would have time for a conversation with Cheryl. That other waitress, who I still didn't know how old she was, was there as well. Her name was Mel. I had to wait until she was finally out of earshot, off cleaning the changing rooms, before I could confront Cheryl. A few of our regular customers were already sitting at their favorite table, but they could wait a couple of minutes. The bar wasn't even officially open yet. It wasn't like they came here for the extraordinary service.

"You had the evening off," was the first thing out of Cheryl's mouth when Mel had disappeared through the back door. "On the night of a big fight."

"I had a date with Fabiano."

She shook her head, her mouth puckering. "God, chick, don't you know what's good for you?"

"What's an enforcer?"

She sighed, nodding toward the table with the early customers. "See Eddie over there?"

I nodded.

"His arm is in a cast because of your Fabiano. First warning as they call it."

My eyes grew wide. Fabiano beat people up? "First warning," I said carefully. "What's the second and third warning?"

She smiled sympathetically. "That depends how much money you owe and what kind of mood Falcone and Fabiano are in. Smashed knee cap? Cut off finger? Having the living daylights beaten out of you?" She paused for effect, gauging my reaction. "Third warning will make you wish for death."

"And if people still don't pay?" What if people weren't ever able to pay? It could happen. I lost count of the number of times my mother had been broke. A beating wouldn't have changed that. And even if she came into money, she would probably have used it for meth.

Cheryl ran a finger over her throat.

I looked down at my hands clutching the bar counter. It would have been a lie if I'd said I couldn't imagine Fabiano capable of something like that. I'd seen him fight, had seen the darkness in his eyes.

"Now you're having second thoughts," she said. "Maybe you'll get lucky and he'll lose interest in you soon. It's not like these men would ever consider having a serious relationship with someone like us."

I stiffened. "What do you mean?"

"They are Italian mobsters. They like to play with normal women, but they'll marry Italian virgins from noble upbringing. It's always been like that. I don't think a new Capo will change that."

"This is the twenty-first century, and we're not in Italy."

"Might as well be because their traditions and rules are from there."

Everything.

In my silly mind I'd construed the word to mean body and mind, but now I wondered if Fabiano was on the lookout for a few nights of fun before he moved on to the next woman. This was all too much baggage for me to handle: Fabiano being an enforcer and the mafia with their old-fashioned rules. My life had always been a mess—and was still messed up enough without him adding any fuel to the fire. Even if my body ached for his touch, and even if some stupid part of me wanted to get to know him—the real him—I had to stay away from him. Maybe I was a fixer, but I had to fix my own life before I could consider fixing someone else.

Business was slow that evening. Most customers had lost considerable amounts of money the night before, during the big fight, and stayed away from the bar. I wouldn't have minded a busy day; it would have distracted me from my wandering thoughts. When I walked past a table occupied with two older men, who'd been drinking the same beer for almost one hour, I overheard a snippet of their conversation that caught my attention.

"Killed him. Just like that. Twisted his head, broke his neck. But the old guy knew what was coming. Shouldn't have tried to run away without paying his debt. Falcone don't like that. I always pay. Even if it means no food for days. Better hungry than dead."

"You got it," rasped the other man, who then fell into a coughing fit. I busied myself wiping the table next to them, hoping to find out who had broken someone's neck. The mere idea sent a shiver down my back. Sadly, the men seemed to have caught on to my presence and switched their conversation to the upcoming fights. Had Fabiano been the one to kill a man?

When I left the bar at quarter after two that night, Fabiano's car was parked in front of the entrance.

I froze mid-step, half hoping it was a coincidence. He shoved open the passenger door. "Get in. Can't let you walk on your own at night."

One look at his handsome face, I wasn't sure I could end things between us. I wasn't even sure I wanted to anymore. People had seldom kept their promises to me. I learned to expect disappointment, but here he was, keeping his promise to protect me. For the first time in my life, there was someone who could protect me. My mother had never been capable of protecting me from her mood swings or the beatings of her disgusting boyfriends. And she certainly could not protect me from the insults other kids hurled at me.

Fabiano was dangerous. He wasn't someone to be close to, but having someone in my life that could keep me safe was too enticing.

Fabiano

I caught her hesitation when she'd spotted me. Like a mouse in front of the trap, torn between tasting the cheese and running off.

"What are you doing here?" she asked, arms wrapped around her old backpack, like she needed another barrier between us.

"I told you I would protect you, and that's what I'm doing. I don't want you to walk around alone at night."

She stared out of the passenger window, hiding her face in the shadows. My grip on the steering wheel tightened. "You can't drive me home every night. I'm sure you've got *work* to do."

Her lips pinched together and her fingers dug into her backpack. What had she heard? There were always rumors about me. The worst were usually true.

"Don't worry. I can make time for important things."

The Camorra was important. Remo and his brothers were important. She wasn't supposed to be.

She turned, brows furrowing. "Important? Am I?"

She wasn't. She was … I wasn't sure what she was to me. I kept thinking about her when she wasn't around. About those damn freckles and her shy smiles. About how she was alone, had been alone even when she'd still lived with her mother. I knew how it was to be alone while living in a house with other people. My father. His second wife. The maids.

I ignored her question. "If I'm not in the parking lot after work, then wait in the bar for me until I pick you up."

"I'm not in kindergarten. I don't need someone to pick me up. Not even you, Fabiano. There's no reason for you to do this. I can protect myself."

I pulled up to her street.

Once I'd shut off the engine, I turned to face her. "How?"

"I just can," she said defensively.

I nodded toward her backpack. "With what's in there."

"How do you …" Her eyes widened a fraction before she caught herself. "It's my problem, isn't it?"

"It was before. Now it is mine. I don't like the idea of someone getting their filthy hands on you."

She shook her head. "We're not together, are we? I can't see how it's your business."

I leaned over but she backed up against the passenger door. So that's how it was going to be? "The kiss we shared means it is my business."

"We won't kiss again," she said firmly, determined.

I smirked. "We'll see." I knew she was attracted to me. I'd sensed how strongly the kiss had affected her, how her eyes had dilated with lust. Perhaps her mind was telling her to stay away, but her body wanted to get much closer, and I would make her give in to that desire. Even now, as I leaned close to her, I could see the conflict in her body language, the way her eyes darted to my lips and her fingers clutched her backpack at the same time.

"You can't force me," she said then bit her lip, reconsidering.

"I could," I said with a shrug, leaning back in my seat to give her space. "But I won't." There was no fun in using my power to get what I wanted. Not with Leona. I wanted to conquer her. I wanted many things.

She gripped the door handle, but I put a hand down on her knee. She shivered under my touch but didn't pull away. Her skin was warm and soft, and I had to suppress the urge to trail my hand up under her skirt and between her legs. "What do you have to defend yourself?"

She hesitated.

"Believe me, Leona, it doesn't matter if it's a knife, gun, or Taser. Against me, it won't do any good."

"A butterfly knife."

I'd have guessed Taser. Women usually preferred them or pepper spray because it was less personal than having to ram a blade into someone's flesh. "Have you ever used it?"

"You mean on someone?"

"Of course. I don't care if you can make a sandwich with it."

Anger flared in her blue eyes, and I had to admit I enjoyed seeing that kind of fire in them, especially when she'd seemed so docile and sweet the first time I talked to her. It was promise she was more fun in other areas too.

"*Of course not.* Unlike you and your mob friends, I don't enjoy killing people."

Friends? The mob wasn't about friendship. It was about dedication and loyalty. It was about honor and commitment. I didn't have friends. Remo and his brothers were the closest thing to friends I had, but what connected us was stronger. They were family. My chosen family. I didn't bother explaining all this to Leona. She wouldn't have understood. For an outsider, this world wasn't easy to understand.

"You don't have to enjoy killing to be good at it. But I doubt that you'll ever get the chance to kill someone. You'd be disarmed in no time and probably get a taste of your own blade. You have to learn how to handle a knife, how to hold it and where to aim."

"You didn't deny it," she whispered.

"Deny what?"

"That you've killed people ... that you enjoyed it."

I didn't tell her that with some people there had been quite a bit of joy ending their fucking lives. And I knew that killing my father one day would outshine every other kill so far. Leona looked honestly puzzled by my reaction. Had she still not grasped the concept of being a made man?

Instead of replying, I tapped the tattoo on my forearm.

She reached out, fingertips gracing the black lines of ink. Her touch was always so careful. I had never been touched like that by a woman. They usually raked their fake fingernails over my back, clutching and stroking. Nothing careful about these encounters. I enjoyed it, but this ... Fuck, this I enjoyed more.

"Could you get it removed? Could you stop being what you are?"

I didn't know any other life. The few days when I hadn't been part of the Outfit and not yet part of the Camorra, before I'd found Remo or rather before he'd found me, I had been like driftwood caught up in the tide, no destination to my journey. Days that had felt like eternity. I'd been adrift. "I could. But I won't." Remo, of course, wouldn't allow me to quit. This wasn't a fucking job where you could give two-weeks' notice. This was for life. "You said it ... it's who I am."

She nodded. Perhaps it had finally sunk in.

"I will teach you how to use that knife and how to defend yourself."

She looked tired, which was probably why she didn't try to argue even if I could tell that she wanted to. She opened the door and got out but turned to me. "Sleep tight, Fabiano … if your conscience lets you." She closed the door and headed toward the apartment building.

When I'd started my induction process in the Outfit, I felt guilt over what I'd seen others doing. And even later, when I first started to fight at Remo's side, I felt bad for some of the things I'd done. But now …? Not anymore. After being an enforcer for years, I didn't feel anything anymore. No regret or guilt. People knew what they were getting into when they owed us money. No one got into this without a fault of their own. And most of these guys would sell their own mother if it meant money to gamble or bet or buy shit.

I'd never had to kill an innocent person. There were no innocents that frequented our bars and casinos. They were lost souls. Stupid fuckers who lost their family's home because they spent their nights gambling.

Leona was innocent. Despair had driven her to work at Roger's bar. I hoped she'd never get caught in the crossfire. I didn't like the idea of having to hurt her.

TEN

Leona

THERE HAD BEEN MANY SLEEPLESS NIGHTS BECAUSE OF THE NOISE coming from my mother's room. Either because she was at it with a john or because she was having a drug-induced fit. Now it was the noise in my head that kept me awake.

Fabiano's blue eyes flashed before me. Cold and calculating. Attentive and alert. Seldom anything else, except for when we'd kissed. There had been a warmer emotion in them. Perhaps only desire or lust, but I wanted to think it could have been something else as well.

I pressed my palms against my face. *Stop it.*

I needed to stop imagining there was something in him. I needed to stop wanting his touch when the same hands did horrible things to others. Things I couldn't even imagine. Things I didn't even want to know.

There was a sick fascination I couldn't deny nor suppress. The mafia had always been something mysterious. I just thought it only existed in the movies. But this was real life, not a Hollywood movie with a happy ending. In real life, mobsters weren't misunderstood antiheroes. They were the bad guys, the ones you didn't want to encounter.

Bad. It was such a difficult term to quantify. What was bad? I was trying to sugarcoat this whole situation, something I had a lot of practice doing. I twisted and turned then eventually sat up on my mattress and reached for my backpack in the dark.

I shoved my hand in the bag and found my knife. I yanked it out then pressed the button that made the blade shoot out with a soft click. The steel of the blade gleamed in the dim moonlight streaming in through the dust-covered windows. I'd never used it, not really. I pointed it at someone once, the same guy I'd stolen it from. He was one of my mother's johns, the worse kind. The kind that liked to beat and insult women like my mother. The kind that enjoyed making them feel even more like crap than they already did. The kind that liked to haggle over the price after the deed was done and often refused to pay. If my mother hadn't been desperate, she probably wouldn't have done him more than once, not after he barely paid her for sucking his disgusting dick and doing other disgusting things.

I was locked in my room when I heard them argue. Despite my mother's warnings to keep my room locked at all times when she had clients, the fight drew me out.

His trousers were on the couch, so I decided to check them for money. Instead, I found the knife. I hid it behind my back when he and my mother stormed out of her bedroom. Mom had been half-naked, and he was wearing only his socks and underpants.

"You're not worth thirty bucks."

"You asshole, I let you come in my mouth without a condom."

"As if your dirty mouth is worth anything."

He stopped when he spotted me. A sick grin curled his lips. "For her ... I'd pay thirty."

I was only fifteen.

He took a step in my direction. My mother's gaze had darted from me to him. Her eyes had been hazy and unfocused. She needed a fix.

I jerked the knife forward and released the blade.

"That little shit stole my knife," he snarled.

"Don't move ... or I'll stab you."

I'd wanted to, and I probably would have without remorse, if my mother hadn't started pummeling him with her fists, shrieking. "Get out! Get out, you sick fuck! Get away from us!"

He'd left without his pants, muttering curses and leaving us with sixty bucks and a knife.

I moved the knife from side to side, considering it in the moonlight. I knew I was capable of using it if need be. I wasn't as innocent as Fabiano perhaps thought I was. I knew there were people out there who deserved to die. I slid the blade back in place then shoved it under my pillow. Fabiano called to a side of me I didn't like, a side that survived under the harsh years of growing up with a whore for a mother and a gambling, addict father. Maybe that was why Fabiano's closeness scared me.

I worried he'd bring out my dark parts. I was my parents' daughter, after all, and they both were not good people. I went out of my way to be nice and not to suspect the worst in people. Over the years, I learned to smile … even when it was hard.

I wasn't sure where this thing between Fabiano and me was going, but fighting it cost too much energy and head space, both of which I needed if I wanted to build a new life. If I kept my focus on working and finding a new job, I'd be leaving Vegas in a couple of months, and then Fabiano would be a thing of the past.

The banging on my door startled me. I looked around with bleary eyes. The sun was low in the sky. As the door swung open, Dad stumbled into my room.

I sat up sleepily. "What's wrong? What time is it?"

"You need to give me some money. I know you must have gotten paid for working this week."

I had gotten money, but apart from getting us food, I set the rest aside to finally buy another less expensive dress. I rubbed my eyes, trying to get rid of the brain fog. "I thought you were working too."

He didn't say anything for a while. "They fired me."

"Before I came here?"

He sighed then nodded. So he'd lied to me. "Leona, I really need that money."

"Who is it you owe money to? The Camorra?"

"It doesn't matter."

"It does. I could talk to Fabiano—"

"Are you stupid? Just because he's fucking you doesn't mean he's going to listen to anything you say."

I screwed my lips shut, suddenly wide awake. Had he really said that?

"Don't give me that look. People are talking. You've been seen riding around in his car. They call you his whore."

My stomach tightened at the insult. I fought so hard so that label would never be put on me, and now, far away from my mother in Las Vegas, people actually called me whore.

"That's none of your business," I gritted out, anger filling my veins. I didn't want to lash out at him, even if he deserved it for lying to me constantly. "I don't have money for you."

"I let you live here and this is what I get for it?"

He was drunk. It became more and more obvious. "I pay for our food. I clean the apartment, and you already took money from me."

Even though he'd hurt me with his insults, I still felt guilty for refusing him.

Without a word, he barged in and grabbed my backpack. He rifled through it, but I'd learned from last time. He made me jump when he grabbed my wrist, dragging me to my feet. "Tell me where it is."

I smelled tequila on his breath. It had always been his favorite and my mother's.

His grip was even harder than last time. Tears burned in my eyes as I ground out, "Let me go. You're hurting me."

"Tell. Me. Where. It. Is." He shook me with every word he said.

Fury, hot and blinding, burned through me. "That's why mom left you. Because you always lost it and beat her. You haven't changed a bit. You disgust me."

He shoved me away, and I fell back on the mattress. He whirled around to leave the room, and I heard another male voice. I stiffened as steps came closer. I quickly got to my feet and pulled my jeans short over my panties.

Dad came back in, saying, "She's nice to look at. Have a go at her. That should pay my debt."

I sucked in a breath. Addiction turned even the kindest people into ruthless criminals, and my father wasn't even all that kind. Still, I never thought he'd do something like this to me. I'd always suspected he was the reason why my mother had sold her body in the first place.

Dad pointed in my direction. A man with dark hair with gray streaks came into my room. He seemed distantly familiar. One glance at his forearm showed me that he was part of the Camorra. My chest constricted with terror. I squared my shoulders, my eyes darting to my backpack that was on the ground between them and me. I wished Fabiano was here and that realization scared me shitless.

The dark eyes of the man scanned my face. Then he shook his head. "No can do, Greg. She belongs to Scuderi."

What? I stopped myself from contradicting him. If being Fabiano's meant I was safe from my father selling me off like cattle, then I was gladly his ... for the time being.

Dad sputtered and opened his mouth to argue, but the mobster turned on him and smashed his fist into Dad's face. Blood shot out of his nose, and he dropped to his knees. "Soto," Dad gasped.

Soto hit him again and again. I jumped over the mattress and grabbed the man's arm, trying to pull him off my father. Maybe Dad deserved it, but I couldn't bear seeing it. I couldn't stand back and watch him be beaten to death.

Soto pushed me aside, so I stumbled backwards and landed with my butt on the mattress. He finally let up. "Two hours," he told Dad. "Then I'll be back."

"No wait," I called when he was halfway out the door. Dad sat with his head between his knees, blood dripping onto the floor from his nose and lip. I went over to the moving boxes stacked up against the wall and reached behind the one on the ground, pulling out all my money. Two hundred dollars. I handed it to Soto. He counted the money without a word. He gave a nod and just disappeared.

"How much did you owe him?" I asked.

"150," Dad rasped.

"But he took two hundred."

"That's for his trouble of paying me a visit," Dad said bitterly. He pushed himself to his feet, one bloody palm against the wall. "If you'd given me the money right away, this wouldn't have happened. It's your fault."

He stumbled out of my room, leaving only the bloody imprint of his palm on the gray wall. I sank down on the mattress, completely drained—of my money and fight.

Fabiano

I kicked the heavy bag once again. I really needed another fight soon.

Soto strode through the training hall toward me. His expression was a bit too triumphant for my taste. That was never a good thing with the idiot. "Hall offered me his daughter as a way to pay off his debt," Soto said, stopping beside me.

"Hall?" I asked. The name was ringing a bell somewhere. He wasn't someone who owed us big money or else I'd have to take care of him. Not important.

"Leona Hall."

He didn't get the chance to say another word. I thrust him against the wall and dug my elbow into his throat. His head was turning red, then purple, before I let up slightly. "If you touched as much as a hair on her body, I'll rip you to shreds."

He coughed, glaring daggers at me. "What the fuck? I didn't do anything."

Remo strode in, glancing between me and Soto, still pressed up against the wall. I released Soto and took a step back. He rubbed his throat. "Next time I won't tell you shit about that girl of yours." He reached into his pocket and tossed a heap of bills to the ground. "There. That's what she gave me." With a nod toward Remo, he staggered off.

Remo perched on the edge of the boxing ring, elbows on his thighs, dark eyes watchful. "What was that about?"

"Nothing important."

Remo tilted his head to the side, studying me. I hated when he did that. "I don't suppose it had something to do with *that girl of yours.*"

How long had he been listening to the conversation? Damn it.

"I don't like to share my spoils," I said angrily.

"Who does?" Remo said. "If she's gets your blood pumping like that, perhaps I should have given her a try before I allowed you to claim her for yourself."

My blood boiled, but I kept my mask of indifference in place. Remo was baiting me. He would never take a woman from me nor I from him. That would be the ultimate betrayal.

"You missed a spectacular fight. Savio destroyed his opponent."

"Good for him. People will stop thinking you favor him because he's your brother. They'll see he can handle himself."

Remo nodded. "You worked a lot with him."

I was glad he didn't press the matter with Leona.

We kept discussing the upcoming fights as well as Remo's plans for an expansion of the illegal races, but my mind kept returning to what Soto had said. I needed to have a word with Leona's father.

He reminded me of my own bastard of a father, who would have sold me off too if it had meant gaining an advantage. After all, he basically sold off my sisters to their husbands. Long buried anger resurfaced. It caught me off guard.

After I left the abandoned casino, I went to Leona's apartment, but nobody was home. I hadn't ever dealt with her father. After questioning a few of my contacts, I found out where he usually spent his day, losing money and drinking himself into a stupor.

It was one of the smaller and definitely dingier casinos we owned. The navy blue carpet had faded to a worn slate blue in many places, and the cigarette burns and unidentifiable stains just added to the overall filth of the joint. I let my gaze stray through the long room with a low ceiling that was filled with slot machines as well as machines for black jack, poker and roulette. This place wasn't profitable enough to invest in actual roulette or poker tables. The guys frequenting this casino didn't have high standards anyway. Savio's fight, as well as the latest street race, was shown on the television screens in the back. I had to admit that Savio had shaped up nicely. At only sixteen, he had taken out a much older and more experienced opponent. Arrogant as he was, he didn't shy away from hard work.

Dick, the casino manager, rushed toward me the moment he noticed me. I

hadn't been here before. This was usually a casino one of the low soldiers handled if there was a problem.

"Mr. Scuderi," he said with a small tilt of his dead. "What can I do for you?"

That name always reminded me of my father. Being compared to him was
the last thing I wanted. My mood faltered, but I kept my anger in check. Dick
wasn't the target of my anger.

"You can tell me where Greg Hall is," I said.

He didn't ask why, just pointed to the far right.

Leona's father was sitting at a black jack machine. He just forced his
daughter to pay his debts and he was already gambling away money he probably
borrowed from one of our loan sharks. If I killed him now, I'd be doing Leona a
favor, but she probably wouldn't see it that way.

I tilted my head in acknowledgement, leaving him standing there as I made
my way toward the despicable coward.

I was still a few steps away when Leona's father spotted me. He dropped
the plastic cup holding chips and leaped off the stool, making a beeline for the
exit. I gave a sign to the security guard at the door, who body-checked Hall. I
wasn't going to run after that fucker. He wasn't even worth that much effort.
Hall tried to get back to his feet but the guard shoved him back down and kept
him in place until I arrived at their side.

"I'll take it from here," I told him then grabbed Hall by the collar of his
shirt and dragged him outside toward the parking lot, around the corner to
where the dumpsters were. He was making choked sounds, which I enjoyed very
fucking much.

I let go of him and he scrambled back. "I paid!"

"Do you think I'm making my way over to this shithole because of a few
fucking hundred dollars?"

That silenced him. His dull blue eyes were nothing like Leona's. That
someone like him could have ever fathered someone like her, it didn't seem
possible.

"And your debt isn't settled. Soto may have accepted your daughter's
money, but I won't. That money, you owe it to me now, and I won't be very patient with you."

"But ..." he sputtered.

"But?" I snarled and punched him hard in the stomach. "And how dare you
try to sell off something that's mine?"

Hall's eyes were wide like saucers.

"Your daughter. She belongs to me. So you think you can offer her to other
men?"

He shook his head. "It was a misunderstanding. I didn't know she was yours."

My lip curled in disgust at his fucking cowardice. I grabbed him and rolled him over so he was sprawled out on his stomach. Then I lifted his sweaty shirt and pulled my knife from the sheath at my leg. He began fighting against my hold, but I didn't ease up. I dug the tip of the knife into his skin. Blood welled to the surface. A fucking marvelous sight. He screamed like a little girl as I cut a C into his skin. "C stands for coward. Next time I'll finish the word. Got it?"

He nodded weakly against the asphalt, panting.

I pushed to my feet. He peed his fucking pants. Fucking waste of air and space. With one last glance at the pathetic man on the ground, I got into my car. I needed to see Leona.

ELEVEN

Leona

D ESPITE MY LACK OF SLEEP AFTER MY FATHER'S RUDE AWAKENING, I WAS full of energy all day. My pulse still thumped with anger and disappointment over what had happened. I wasn't sure why it still threw me off balance when one of my parents messed up. They had a habit of doing so … but offering me to his debtor like a whore …? That was low, even for my father. Desperation wasn't an excuse for everything.

"You've been cleaning the same glass for fifteen minutes. I think it's as clean as it's gonna get," Fabiano drawled.

I jumped, my eyes zeroing in on him. He leaned against the bar, elbows propped up on the smooth wood, a piercing look on his face. It was only eight o'clock. I still had almost six hours of work ahead of me. What was he doing here now?

I put the glass aside and Fabiano snatched my forearm to pull me closer. He scanned the new fingerprint-shaped bruises on my wrist. I had forgotten about them.

His eyes narrowed, his mouth setting in a hard line. He stroked his thumb lightly over the bruise before he let go. "Tomorrow I'll pick you up at home around ten o'clock. I'll teach you how to defend yourself."

It surprised me that he didn't ask who had hurt me. Unless of course he somehow found out what had happened. He confirmed my suspicions when he slid two hundred dollars over to me. I quickly glanced around to make sure no one was watching. I didn't need people to speculate the reason for the money exchange. "Here's your money back."

"My father …" I swallowed. "Is he okay?" I couldn't believe I even had to ask.

"He's fine."

I nodded and glanced at the money. "But I paid his debt. If you give me the money back, he'll be in trouble."

"That's not your fight, Leona," Fabiano muttered. "Your father will keep losing money, and eventually he'll die because of it. Don't let him drag you down with him. I won't allow it."

I knew he was right. Dad was probably already losing money he didn't have right as we spoke. He couldn't act any other way. He let his addiction rule his life. I doubted he even considered going to rehab. Rehab wouldn't save you if you didn't have the willpower to go through with it.

"Take your money…" Fabiano pushed the notes farther in my direction "… and use it for yourself, for fuck's sake."

I picked up the money and stashed it in my backpack. "Do you want something to drink while you're here?" I grabbed the Johnnie Walker Blue Label from the shelf.

"You remember," he said with a smirk.

"Of course," I said simply. I remembered every moment of our encounters. They were the bright light of my time in Las Vegas so far, as ridiculous as it may sound. I poured him a generous amount. It wasn't as if Roger would care. The Camorra owned everything anyway.

Fabiano took a large gulp then held the glass in my direction. "Want a taste?"

It sounded dirty the way he said it. "No. I don't drink. Ever."

He nodded as if he understood. Then he downed the rest of his scotch and pushed back from the bar. "I still need to do some business. See you in a few hours."

So he really intended to drive me home every night. I watched his broad back as he made his way through the hall, his gait elegant and lithe like that of a predator.

Sometimes I wondered if I was his prey, if this was an amusing chase for him that he'd soon get bored with. I wasn't sure if that was something I should be hoping for.

He didn't try to kiss me again when he drove me home that night and hadn't since our first kiss. Maybe he sensed that I would have pushed him away.

"Tomorrow morning, I'll pick you up. Dress in something you can work out with."

I got out of the car. Fabiano waited until I was inside before he drove off.

The lights were out in the apartment when I entered. I turned one on and was heading to my room when I noticed movement on the couch in the living room. Dad was sitting with his head bowed, moaning. I approached him slowly.

First I noticed the empty beer bottles on the table. If he stopped throwing away money on alcohol, he'd be better off. Then my eyes focused on his naked back and a glaring red mark.

I turned on the lights in the living room. Someone had cut a C into his back. Blood had dried around the wound. It didn't look as if Dad had treated it in any way, except for numbing the pain with alcohol, of course.

Dad didn't acknowledge my presence. He kept his face buried in his palms and let out a low moan.

"Dad?"

He grunted.

"Who did this?" I knew the answer of course.

Dad didn't reply. He was probably too drunk, considering the number of empty bottles that littered the ground. I turned and headed for the bathroom to grab a washcloth. I soaked it with cold water then searched the cabinets for something to put on the wound. Except for expired Tylenol and a few dirty Band-Aids, the shelves were empty.

I returned to the living room and touched Dad's shoulder to alert him of my presence. "I'm going to clean up your wound," I warned him. When he didn't react, I gently pressed the cold washcloth to the cut.

He hissed and lashed out at me. I avoided being hit by his elbow. "Shhh. I'm trying to help you, Dad."

"You've done enough. Leave me alone!"

His bloodshot eyes flashed with anger when he looked up at me.

"You should go to a doctor," I said quietly then put the wet washcloth down on the table in front of him in case he decided to clean his wound on his own.

He returned to his bowed position, ignoring me.

I went to my bedroom and closed the door, bone tired from a long day at work and what I'd seen. Fabiano had cut my father as punishment for what he'd done. I didn't kid myself into thinking that this small wound was the full extent of what Fabiano would do to my father if he messed up again.

I wasn't sure if I could stop Fabiano, and I wasn't sure I had the energy to try. I was sick of solving other people's problems, when I had enough of my own.

I was dressed in my jeans shorts and a loose T-shirt when Fabiano picked me up at ten o'clock.

His eyebrows climbed high along his forehead when he saw my clothes. "That's not what I meant when I told you to wear comfortable clothes."

"I don't own any workout clothes. And to be honest, this is one of three outfits I own in total, including the dress you bought for me," I said snidely.

Fabiano looked at me for a long time before he set the car in motion.

"I saw what you did to my father," I told him.

No sign of guilt on his face. "He got what he deserved. If he wasn't your father, he would have gotten worse."

"This is you being lenient?" I asked incredulously.

"If that's what you want to call it."

It wasn't the first time my father got into trouble like that. When I was around ten and lived with my parents in Dallas, he owed money to some biker group. The guys had almost beaten him and my mother to death over it. It didn't stop my father from borrowing money again.

I leaned back against the seat, my head tilted toward Fabiano. He was steering the car with one hand, the other resting on the center console. I wondered if his cool demeanor reflected his insides. Could he really be that at ease with his life?

My eyes lingered on the dark blond five-o'clock shadow. It was the first time I saw him with anything but a perfectly shaved face, and it made me want to rake my fingers over the short stubble.

Sin. That was what he was.

He glanced at me, his lips curling up, and I tore my gaze away. Playing with fire had never been part of my plan. Then why couldn't I stop thinking about the man beside me?

He pulled up in front of an opulent white concrete building, at least ten stories high with a curved driveway, shielded by a long roof with thousands of light bulbs in multiple colors, most of them broken. An abandoned casino building, I realized as we stepped through the glass revolving door into the game room. Silence had replaced the sound of the roulette wheels and slot machines. The red and gold chandelier was covered in dust. An air of forlornness lay over the empty poker tables and Champagne bar. Broken Champagne flutes littered the black countertop. This was where we would train?

"Come on," Fabiano said and continued past the deserted cashier booth.

The red and blue carpet was worn out from thousands of feet. I followed him, breathing in the old, musty smell. Fabiano wasn't impressed by our surroundings. He was in his zone. I could already see a change in his demeanor, as if he was eager for the fight. Perhaps the thrill of it was his addiction. Perhaps everyone had an addiction.

We left the first game room and stepped into the next, this one even more splendid than the first. Crystal chandeliers hung from high-arched ceilings above our heads, and the fluffy carpet softened our steps as my eyes took in the black marble columns and gold ornamental wallpaper. Most of the roulette tables had been removed, but a few remained. They were no longer the main attraction.

A fighting cage and a boxing ring dominated the center of the room, their stark brutality a shocking contrast to the luxury from the past. Randomly positioned among the remaining roulette tables were bench presses, punching bags, and other weightlifting equipment. Heavy burgundy drapes covered the shell-shaped windows. The sun shone bright, through the gap between them. Fabiano flipped a switch, and the chandeliers cast us in their splintered golden glow. This wasn't what I'd expected.

"So this is where you come to fight?"

Fabiano smirked. "This is where I come to train and occasionally fight ... yes."

"Is it always this empty?"

"Depends. It's mainly for my boss, his brothers, and me. Few other people ever come here."

"And I'm allowed here?" I asked.

He didn't say anything, only led me to a dark mahogany door, then along a hallway with peeling paint and torn carpet, around a corner and through another door. Suddenly, we were in a pool area. This room had been renovated recently. I didn't get the chance to register more than the large swimming pool made from stainless steel and the Jacuzzi sitting on an elevated platform to the right.

"We need to find you some decent training shorts," Fabiano said as he pulled me into the adjoining locker room.

It was functional like the pool area, nothing fancy or splendid.

"Why this place?"

Fabiano shrugged as he rummaged in a basket with clothes. "Remo wanted it, so he got it."

"But isn't it expensive to keep the place from falling apart? It's a huge building."

"Parts of it are falling apart, yes, but it costs us more money than a standard gym would. Still ... what's life without the occasional irrational decision?"

His blue eyes held mine, and the nerves I'd managed to calm returned full force. Fabiano yanked red shorts out of the basket. "The youngest brother of my Capo uses these. Maybe they will fit you."

I took them from him. "Capo?" I asked curiously. I had heard the term, of course, but Fabiano had said it with so much respect it surprised me.

"Remo Falcone, he is my Capo. My boss if you will."

"You think highly of him."

He nodded once. "Of course."

I had a feeling he wasn't just saying it because he had to. Cheryl had sounded terrified when she'd uttered Falcone's name, but there was no fear in Fabiano's voice.

"We didn't come here to chitchat, remember?" he said with a grin. "Now let's get changed."

Without a warning, he unbuckled his belt.

I turned around with a surprised gasp. "You could have warned me."

"I could have, but I didn't want to. I intend for you to see much more of me."

I glanced around for some privacy, but the room didn't provide any. There weren't any stalls, only lockers and an open shower area. Oh, damn it. I pulled down my jeans shorts and quickly slipped on the boxing shorts then faced him. Fabiano's full attention was on me as he leaned against the wall with his arms crossed over his bare chest. I'd forgotten about that little detail; he didn't wear a shirt when he was in the cage. My eyes trailed down to his dark blue boxers that hugged his narrow hips with the delicious V disappearing in his waistband.

"And?" he asked.

I blinked at him, tearing my eyes away from his chest. "And?" I repeated.

"Does it fit?"

How could anything not fit that body?

I realized he meant *me*. "Oh, the shorts, you mean? They are a bit loose, but it should be fine."

"You look sexy in them," he said in a low voice.

My face blazed with heat.

"Don't forget your knife. I want to see you use it."

I bent over my backpack, glad my hair hid my blush, but he probably already saw it. I grabbed the knife and straightened. He opened the door and waited for me to go through. His warm scent wafted into my nose as I passed him. I had to get a grip. We headed back to the beautiful game room, and I continued toward the boxing ring, glad to focus on something other than the dangerous, muscled man behind me.

"Not that way," Fabiano said, a smirk in his voice. I turned, and he pointed at the fighting cage to the right.

"In the cage?" I asked, horrified.

He jumped up on the elevated platform of the cage, grinning like a shark. "Of course. I want to see how you deal with stress."

"Great," I muttered. "As if fighting with you wasn't stressful enough."

He held out a hand to me. I slipped mine into his, and his fingers closed around me, warm and strong. He pulled me up. I bumped against his chest, and he held me there for a moment. I peered up at his face. The glow of the chandelier above our heads making his hair appear golden.

But a golden boy? No, he definitely wasn't that.

"I thought we were going to fight," I whispered.

His lip curled. "Just seeing how much more uncomfortable I can make you," he said.

I glared. "What makes you think this makes me uncomfortable?"

His smile widened. "It doesn't?"

I untangled myself from his hold and pointed at the cage door. "How does this thing open?"

He pressed down the handle, looking way too full of himself.

I stepped inside and goose bumps formed on my skin. I could smell stale blood beneath the prominent smell of disinfectant and steel. Fabiano closed the cage with a quiet click.

"I don't get the appeal," I said, looking around the cage. "Why do people enjoy being locked in a cage like animals?"

"It's the added thrill of not having an escape. The cage is unrelenting."

I nodded, fumbling with the knife in my hand. The biggest chandelier dangling from the ceiling right above my head was more daunting than decorative.

"I want to see you handle it."

I pressed the button that released the blade. It gleamed in the golden light. I held the knife out.

Fabiano hooked his finger, invitingly. "Do what you would do to an attacker."

I held the knife a bit higher, my palm closing tightly around the handle.

Fabiano stifled a smile. For him this was probably more than a little entertaining.

"Attack."

I took a step forward but he bridged the remaining distance between us and feigned an attack. "Try not to lose your knife."

I tightened my hold further, even though it seemed impossible. Before I knew it, Fabiano was there in front of me, tall and imposing and muscled and so at ease with what he was doing. With painful pressure to my wrist, the knife clattered to the ground. I reached for it, but Fabiano was quicker. He twisted the knife in his hand, admiring the blade.

I glared. "It's not fair. You are much stronger and more experienced." I rubbed my wrist. I hadn't even seen what Fabiano had done.

Fabiano shook his head. "Life isn't fair, Leona. You should know. Your attacker won't be a one-hundred pound female with delicate feelings. He will be a two-hundred pound fucker who likes to hurt females with delicate feelings." And then he towered over me again, and I wanted to kiss him, not fight him.

"That knife," he said in a low, threatening voice as he held out the blade between us, "it can be your salvation or your downfall." He gripped my arm and whirled me around. My back collided with his chest as he pressed me against him. I was frozen with shock. He touched the tip of the blade to the skin between my breasts then slowly trailed it down to my stomach. The pressure wasn't enough to leave a mark but my stomach turned at the thought of how it would feel if it were. "That knife can give your opponent another advantage over you. If you can't handle the knife, you shouldn't use it." He let go of me, and I staggered forward, out of his embrace. My heart pounded in my chest as I looked down at myself. I could still feel the steel on my skin. I closed my eyes, trying to stop my rising panic and worse … arousal.

Fabiano was right. If my attacker got hold of my knife, he'd use it against me. The knife had given me a sense of security, but now even that was gone. I faced Fabiano, who was watching me intently. He held the knife out to me, and I approached him slowly and took it.

"Cut me," he said.

"Excuse me?" I asked.

"Cut me. I want to see if you have what it takes to hurt someone. Cut me."

I shook my head, taking a step back. "I won't. This is stupid."

Fabiano shook his head in obvious annoyance then snatched the knife from my grip. His eyes held mine as he pressed the blade against his palm and slashed. I staggered back, not from the sight of blood, but from his actions. He dropped the knife to the ground. Blood dripped down onto the gray flooring. He squeezed his bleeding hand into a fist and more blood coated his knuckles.

"I can see that you are scared. Fear is never a good companion in a fight," Fabiano said, looking completely at ease in the fighting cage. No sign of pain either.

This was familiar ground for him, a place he felt at home in. For me, the cage seemed to tower over me menacingly. Even its luxurious surroundings couldn't change that. And it wasn't really helping that I was supposed to fight Fabiano. With his rock-hard stomach, muscled arms, and keen eyes, he already looked like a fighter. I had seen him fight. There was nothing I could compare it to. His speed. His strength. His determination.

I, however, felt out of place.

Fabiano opened his arms, palms outward. My eyes lingered on the gash in his palm. "Hit me. That's something you can do, right?"

I took a step toward him.

"Curl your hands into fists. Don't even think about hitting me with your open palm. You're not swatting at a fly."

He was making fun of me. I clenched my fists just as he ordered and took another step toward him. I wasn't even sure where to hit him. He took a sudden step toward me, startling me, and I backed off.

"Hit me," he ordered again.

I propelled my fist forward and rammed it into his stomach. A second before impact, his six pack became an eight pack as he tightened his muscles.

My knuckles collided with his hard stomach, and I winced. I pulled back immediately.

"Was that your hardest hit?" he asked.

I frowned. "Yes. Was it that bad?"

His expression gave me an unmistakable answer. "Now kick me as hard as you can and aim as high as possible."

Hitting had already felt strange, but kicking someone was completely out of my comfort zone. I swung my leg and landed a kick against his ribs. He shook his head. I might as well have batted at him with a feather boa.

"That's not good. I'm not even moving and your aim and force are already bad."

Did he have anything nice to say? I was starting to get annoyed.

He got into a fighting stance and turned away from me. Then he did a high kick against the cage. The crash made me jump and the ground vibrated under my bare feet from the force of Fabiano's kick. It was still hard to believe how high he could raise his leg and how hard he could kick with it. My leg would have fallen off if I tried to get it that high.

"Perhaps you don't have the right incentive. Most women only ever dare to hit hard when they're cornered. Let's pretend I'm attacking you."

The thought thrilled and terrified me. I nodded, trying to look like I was ready for this.

His blue eyes slid over my body. "Do what you must to escape my grip. Hurt me."

As if there was the slightest chance that I could. Without a warning he lunged forward, grabbed my shoulders, and pressed me up against the cage. Caught between the cold metal and his warm muscled chest, there was no way I could hit him. I twisted, but his hold on me didn't waver.

"Fight, Leona. Imagine I was out to hurt you, to rape you, to kill you," he said in a dark whisper that raised the hairs on my neck.

I tried to push away from the cage again, but there was no way Fabiano was budging. He was as unmovable as the steel of the cage.

"You need to do better than that," he murmured against my ear then licked a trickle of sweat from my throat. It sent a tingle down my spine. Without warning, he released me, and I quickly faced him, hoping he couldn't see what the gesture had done to my body.

He pushed his hair back, a self-satisfied smile on his face. "Brace yourself. I expect you to do better this time."

I was on the verge of protesting when he jumped forward. Before I knew what was happening, he kicked my legs out under me. I gasped as I fell backwards, bracing myself for the impact. But it never came. Instead, Fabiano's arm snaked around my waist and he lowered me to the ground. Of course that wasn't the end of it. He knelt over me and pressed my wrists into the floor above my head. His palm was slippery against my skin. Blood. One of his knees wedged between my legs, forcing them apart.

My heart galloped in my chest as I stared up at his face. Was this still a game? He looked so focused and … eager. But then a slow smile spread across his face and breathing became easier. "I hope this wasn't you really trying," he said. "An attacker could have his way with you now. It wouldn't be very difficult to rip your clothes off and force myself on you."

"You would kill anyone who did," I said. It was a horrible thing to say. And I didn't know why I had said it. I didn't know if Fabiano would go that far.

He lowered himself completely on top of me, and somehow his warm weight felt perfect. "You think?" he murmured. "Why would I do such a thing?"

His eyes immobilized me. I couldn't say anything for a while.

Suddenly I felt foolishly daring. "Because you don't like to share."

Possessiveness filled his face. He bucked his hips against my crotch, and my eyes shot open. He was hard. Heat flooded me. I should have pushed him away, but I was too surprised and fascinated.

He bent down and licked my collarbone. "I want nothing more than to fuck you right here, in the middle of this cage."

My muscles tensed. This was too fast. I still wasn't sure if I should keep this thing going between me and Fabiano. And I definitely didn't want to be fucked in a cage like an animal, even if a tiny part of my body disagreed.

I didn't get the chance to push him away, though, because he shoved himself off the ground and landed on his feet in one graceful move.

Fabiano

I crouched in front of her, taking in the sight of her widened eyes and disheveled locks. She propped herself up on her elbows but made no move to stand.

Her eyes went to my boxer before she quickly looked away. I knew she'd be blushing if her face weren't already red from exertion. A thrill went through me, as it always did when her innocence shone through. I straightened, and slowly she stumbled to her feet as well.

She was a horrible fighter. It wasn't in her nature to hurt people. Perhaps I could have pushed her into hitting harder if I actually hurt her. Pain was a strong catalyst, but hurting her wasn't something I had in mind. I wanted to make her scream but not from agony.

She balled her hands into fists. Her wrists were covered in bloody fingerprints, but the gash in my palm was only a dull throb.

"Are we going to try again?"

I smirked. She was trying to escape the situation. I inclined my head then feigned an attack. She raised her arms protectively and closed her eyes. "Don't ever close your eyes in front of an enemy."

She glared at me and tried to land a hit against my stomach. I sidestepped her futile attempt and grabbed her from behind. I locked her arms under mine and pressed my hips against her butt. I moved her forward until she was pressed up against the cage and my erection was pressed up against her firm ass. She made a sound of protest.

"Fabiano," she wheezed, anger seeping through. "Stop it."

"Make me," I challenged then lightly bit the crook of her neck, sucking the skin into my mouth. She let out a moan, stilled, and began squirming. When I released her soft skin, I'd left my mark. She tried a backwards kick but only lightly grazed my shin. "You can do better," I said.

She tried to push back, but again had no chance against me. Perhaps it was unfair. Even the best fighters didn't last long in a fight against me. What I was doing with Leona didn't even come close to fighting. Playing was more like it.

Suddenly she became slack under my touch and pressed her butt against my erection. If she thought that would throw me off, she was sorely mistaken. Unlike her, I had more than enough experience and wasn't unnerved by an ass against my cock. The only bothersome thing was the clothes separating her from my cock.

"Playing with fire?" I asked quietly.

"You started it," she muttered, indignation flashing in her eyes. There was finally some fight in them.

"And I'm willing to play it to the end," I said suggestively. "Are you?" I ground my erection against her butt once more.

She became still. "No. I'm not." Her voice was no longer playful or angry.

I peered down at the soft freckles of her nose and cheek. Her eyes met mine. She was uneasy and nervous, but not scared. She trusted me to respect her boundaries. Leona might be my undoing. I loosened my hold on her arms, allowing her to turn around. She tilted her head up, searching my face. I wondered when she'd stop looking for something that wasn't there. I pressed my palms into the cage beside her head, letting my head fall forward until our lips were less than an inch apart. Her eyes darted down, and she surprised me when she rose on her tiptoes and closed the gap. Her kiss was soft and restrained. My body screamed for something else. I deepened the kiss then grabbed her ass and lifted her until her legs wrapped around my waist. Her back pressed up against the cage, I ravished her mouth. She clung to my shoulders, her nails digging into my skin and her heels into my butt. When she pulled back, she was breathless and dazed.

"You're not good at setting boundaries," I told her.

She leaned her head back against the cage. "I know," she said guiltily.

"So that's what you call fighting?" Nino drawled as he walked in, a sport bag slung over his shoulder. His attentive gaze stopped on Leona. Every muscle in me tensed.

I lowered Leona then put my hand on her back.

Nino followed the gesture. His expression didn't change. Unlike Remo, he wasn't prone to emotional outbursts. It made him harder to read, but definitely not less dangerous. Tall, lean, immaculate beard, and dark hair pulled into a short ponytail, Nino looked like a runway model. Women fell hard for him … until they realized that his emotionless expression wasn't a mask. Nino didn't have to hide his emotions. He had none.

"We're done here," I said. I nudged Leona toward the cage door, opened it, then climbed out first before I lifted Leona down. She stood close beside me. She was wary of Nino, as she should be. Her instincts couldn't be completely off if she recognized him as a threat.

I greeted him with a short embrace and a clap on the shoulder. "Who are you training with?"

"Adamo, if he decides to show up."

I rolled my eyes. "Good luck." His eyes slid behind me to Leona. And something protective and fierce swelled in my chest. He didn't say anymore. I doubted he was really interested in her. He was curious because I showed interest in her.

I led Leona toward the changing room but only grabbed our bags.

"Aren't we going to change?" she asked.

I shook my head. I wanted to get her away from Nino. It was safer if Remo and his brothers didn't see Leona too often. I led her outside toward my car. Some of the tension dissipated as we added some distance between us and Nino.

Remo and his brothers were like family to me, but I knew better than to trust them with Leona.

Leona gave me a sideways glance. "Who was he?"

"Nino. One of Remo's brothers."

"You didn't like being around him," she said.

If she'd picked up on it, Nino would have too. That wasn't good. "I practically grew up with him. He's like my brother, but I don't like you around him. It's better if you don't get involved in that part of my life."

"Okay," she said simply.

When we arrived in front of her apartment, I turned toward her, wanting to fucking kiss her again. I played it cool since our first kiss, but I was tired of holding back, especially after what happened in the cage.

"Are you celebrating Christmas with Remo and his brothers?" she asked.

I stiffened. I hadn't expected that question. "I don't really celebrate Christmas." I hadn't in several years. Not since my sisters left for New York. I didn't care for the holidays, but now that she'd mentioned it, I realized that Christmas was only a week away.

"Me neither. I'll probably work," she said with a small shrug.

"You won't celebrate with your father or your mother?"

She stared out of the windshield, fidgeting with her shorts. "I used to. A long time ago. When I was little, we managed two or three nice Christmas evenings. The rest were a mess." She sighed. "After my dad abandoned us, my mother was busy working all the time to get money for meth. She forgot things like Christmas and my birthday. They weren't important to her. And my dad…" she shrugged "…I suppose he was glad to be away from us and the responsibility."

She still hadn't mentioned her mother being a whore, but I allowed her that small reprieve. "That's why you shouldn't feel responsible for your father. He isn't an honorable man. He should protect his own flesh and blood and not offer it to someone in exchange for a debt."

She flushed. "You know about that?"

"Soto told me."

"It's not easy to abandon him. I still love him, despite his flaws. I can't help it."

I grimaced. "Love is a weakness, a sickness. You'll see where it gets you."

Her blue eyes searched mine, still looking, still hoping. "You can't mean that. Love is what makes us human, what makes life worth living. Love is unconditional."

She said it with so much fervor that I knew she was trying to convince herself as much as me. "Do you really believe that? Do you think it turned you into the person you are today? Because love definitely didn't make me who I am. Blood and hate and thirst for revenge kept me going. They still do, and so do honor, pride, and loyalty. So tell me, Leona, did love form you?"

Leona clutched her backpack against her chest. "Not me. But nobody ever loved me like that," she said quietly. "My parents always loved their addiction more than me, and there was never anyone else. So I suppose love didn't form me." She looked me square in the eyes, a challenge. Did she expect pity? She needn't worry. Pity was an emotion I'd given up a long time ago. I was furious. Furious on her behalf.

"Then what did?" I asked.

TWELVE

Leona

"**T**HEN WHAT DID?"

That question threatened to unravel me. "I don't know," I admitted. I looked down at the scars on Fabiano's chest, at the tattoo on his wrist, appraised the confident way he held himself. Pride and honor. He oozed it. His body was a testament to his convictions … to how far he'd come. And me?

I let out a small, empty laugh. "Hope for the future kept me going. I was a good student, and I worked hard. I thought I'd have a bright future after high school. I thought I'd go to college, get a law degree, and become something more than the daughter of a…" I swallowed the word whore, not able to admit the truth to Fabiano "…drug addict, but I'm failing."

Fabiano's face still showed no pity, and I was glad for it. There was something dark and fierce in his eyes. "If you don't fight for what you want, you won't get it. People like us don't get their wishes handed to them on a platter."

How could he compare us? He was strong and successful, admittedly not in the conventional sense, but he had what he longed for. The Camorra was his passion. "You are a born fighter. I am not."

"I wasn't born a fighter. I was formed into one by the shit thrown my way over the years, Leona."

I wanted to ask him about his past, but he was always so cautious when he mentioned anything related to it. I let out a breath. He leaned over, cupped the back of my head, and kissed me. I sank into the kiss. I needed it now, needed to feel something other than desperation. His tongue danced with mine, and his scent engulfed me. I closed my eyes, allowing my body to relax.

He pulled back. "I will fight your battles for you now, Leona. I told you I'd protect you."

I nodded, as if my approval meant anything. Fabiano's overwhelming presence, his unrelenting possessiveness, they were something I never encountered before. My parents had never displayed any kind of emotion toward me. I had been an afterthought for them—sometimes useful, sometimes bothersome, never something to waste too much energy on.

Deep down, I knew Fabiano's attention would come with a price. I'd pay for surrendering to him in one way or another. But right in this moment I couldn't care less.

I got out of the car, my legs shaky. I could feel Fabiano's gaze on me all the way into the apartment. I leaned back against the door and released a breath. It felt as if he'd laid me bare without touching me, as if he knew my deepest desires, my darkest fears.

I functioned on autopilot that day. Cheryl didn't say anything, but I could tell that she wanted to.

Fabiano was waiting for me when I got off at two-thirty. He didn't start the car right away. His eyes darted down to the modest black heels I was wearing then over the blue dress. Both weren't anything special and had been on sale, but they were new. I bought them this afternoon before work to cheer myself up.

"I want to show you where I live," Fabiano said simply.

The tiredness melted away. "Okay."

I wasn't sure what else to say. This seemed like a very personal thing, like another level in our … what? Relationship? It was difficult to put a label on it. I had a feeling Fabiano didn't take many people to his apartment. He seemed like someone who kept his private space well protected. Like he'd said, he didn't like to share, and that he wanted to share his apartment with me, if only for a few hours, made me happy. At the same time, however, I knew that being alone in his apartment, with a bedroom at our disposal, opened up new possibilities I wasn't sure I was ready for … mentally. My body was a different matter.

His blue eyes regarded me for a few heartbeats, perhaps reconsidering his decision.

As we drove, we passed familiar sites like the Venetian and the Bellagio, and I wondered if I'd ever manage to get a job in a place that was even half as good. Maybe Fabiano could help me. He knew more than enough people in Las Vegas, and I didn't even want to know how many good hotels and restaurants were owned or controlled by the Camorra. I also didn't want to ask him for that kind of favor. I could only imagine how many people tried to gain something just from knowing him. I didn't want to be like that.

Silence filled the space between us. The soft hum of the engine lulled me to sleep, and I wondered if agreeing to go to his apartment this late at night was a mistake. Did Fabiano expect me to spend the night with him?

My thoughts were cut short when we pulled up in front of a sleek skyscraper and drove down into an underground parking garage.

"No villa in the suburbs with a park-like garden for you?" I asked, hoping my voice didn't give away my nerves.

He grimaced. "I prefer to live in the center of life. The suburbs are for families."

We got out of his car. The clean, new smell of the parking garage filled with dozens of luxury cars already made me feel out of place. Even new clothes wouldn't change that. My heels clicked on the white marble of the elevator as we got in. Fabiano's hand on my lower back was already oddly familiar. He pressed the button for the top floor, and the elevator began its silent ascension. Fabiano didn't say anything. Perhaps he was having second thoughts about bringing me to his home.

The elevator came to a stop, and the doors glided open without a sound. A long corridor with a plush beige carpet and cream-colored walls with golden accents stretched before us. Fabiano led me toward a dark wooden door at the end of it, which seemed to be the only door on this floor, except for the emergency exit.

My stomach fluttered with nerves when he opened the door wide for me. I stepped past him into his apartment, and the moment the light came on, I froze.

I'd never seen luxury like this before. We stood in the entrance area, which was on a higher level than the living area. Vaulted ceilings were supported by marble columns. I stepped down the three steps, my heels clacking loudly on the smooth marble. I wished I'd worn the shoes Fabiano had bought for me and not the ones I got for half-price at Target today.

The marble floor was black and white and laid out in geometrical design. Four white couches surrounded an enormous low, black marble table. Above the seating area, a huge lamp that looked like a ginormous silver ball of wool hung from the two-story-high ceiling. To the left was a dining table that could seat at least sixteen people. Like the floor, it was also made of black marble. Further to the left was the open kitchen with its white appliances. My eyes were drawn back to the living area and the floor-to-ceiling windows. A huge terrace with white columns overlooked the Strip with its illuminated skyscrapers and flashing lights.

I hesitated, not sure if I was allowed to wander around.

Fabiano made an inviting gesture, and I walked toward the windows and looked out. Now I could see that the white columns surrounded a long square pool that glowed with turquoise light in the dark.

Fabiano opened the terrace door for me, and I stepped out. Walking past the pool, I stopped at the balustrade. Down below, I could see the Strip with the Eiffel Tower. I breathed in deeply, stunned by the sight and the apartment. I didn't dare ask what it had cost. Crime paid off, if done right. My parents had never figured the right way to do it, though.

Fabiano came up behind me, his arms wrapping around my waist. He kissed my shoulder then up to my ear. A familiar tingling filled my body as I leaned into him. I didn't want to push him back, didn't want to consider how it looked being alone in an apartment with him at night. I just wanted to be, wanted to relish in the most beautiful sight I'd ever seen.

"This is incredible," I whispered. I could imagine living here, could easily imagine enjoying it. I never considered myself a girl who longed for these kinds of things, but I'd never been surrounded by it before.

He hummed his approval then nudged my hair away from my throat. He kissed the skin over my pulse point then gently bit down. I shivered at the possessive gesture. His mouth moved lower, and he licked my collarbone. His hands moved from my waist up to my ribcage, the pressure light and yet almost overwhelming. His presence, our surroundings, the possibilities of what might happen next were a tidal wave tossing me around.

"Fabiano," I said, uncertain, but my voice died in my throat when his hands cupped my breasts through the fabric of my dress. Only once had a guy groped at my breast, and it had been painful and disgusting; I had pushed him off and thrown up afterward.

Fabiano's touch was soft and yet sent spikes of pleasure through the rest of my body. I could feel my nipples harden, and I knew he would feel it against his palms. Embarrassment fought with need. I never wanted to be intimate with someone. Physical closeness had always been associated with bad things for me. Watching my mother sell her body had made me wary of allowing a man to get physical with me. I dreamed of falling in love and eventually making love with a man someday, but Fabiano didn't believe in love, and I wasn't sure if I did anymore either. Perhaps I'd have to settle for less. It wasn't the first time in my life. Being with Fabiano made me feel seen and protected. That was more than I'd had in a long time. And God did it scare me, because I knew how easily it could be taken from me.

His palms slid up to my shoulders, and he began pushing my dress down. My stomach tightened with anticipation and fear when the fabric gave way and pooled around my waist. The cool breeze touched my skin, and my thin bra didn't protect me—neither from the night's cold nor from Fabiano's hungry gaze. No one had ever looked at me like that. I closed my eyes.

Fabiano

Goose bumps flashed across Leona's smooth skin, and the outline of her erect nipples strained against the thin fabric of her bra. My cock hardened at the tantalizing sight. Fuck. I wanted her, wanted to possess her. I ran my fingers over her ribcage then up to the edge of her bra. It wasn't spectacular, nothing pricy like lace or silk, and yet she made it seem like the sexiest garment in the world. Her body tensed under my touch, but not with eagerness. I regarded her face, her closed eyes, the way she was biting down on her lower lip and her lashes that fluttered. She was nervous and scared. I wondered what had her feeling that way. I definitely hadn't given her reason to be scared of me, which was surprising in itself.

I leaned down to her ear. "Have you ever been with a man?"

I knew the answer. I was too good at reading body language and people in general not to know, but I wanted to hear it from her lips. I was fucking eager to have her admit it.

She shuddered and gave a small shake of her head.

"Say it," I ordered.

Her eyelashes fluttered open. "No, I haven't been with a man."

I kissed her throat. "So I will be your first." My cock twitched with eagerness.

"I won't sleep with you tonight, Fabiano," she whispered.

I straightened, stunned by the words. Her expression showed mostly resolve, but there was a flicker of uncertainty as well. "I'm not used to waiting. For anything."

She didn't move away from me, her back still pressed against my chest, my fingers still on her ribcage. It heaved under my touch. One deep breath and her spine straightened. "Some things are worth waiting for."

"And you are one of them?" I asked.

She looked away, out toward the city lights. Her lashes fluttered again, but this time it was to keep the tears contained. "I don't know."

The words were so quiet, the wind almost carried them off before they reached my ears.

For a moment I felt like smashing the world, like burning down everything. I wanted to go after her father and see the life drain from his eyes slowly. I wanted to find her mother and cut her throat, see her sputter on her own blood. These emotions were foreign, not because of their brutality or fierceness, but because they were on behalf of a woman. I'd had bouts of protectiveness when I was younger, over my sisters—before they left me and before I became the man I was today.

I traced my fingers down her ribs then slid my arms around her stomach. She shivered. "Let's go inside. You're cold."

Her eyes searched mine, curiously, hopefully. When she didn't find what she was looking for, she nodded slowly and let me lead her inside. The wonder returned to her expression as she took in the living area. I'd spent most of my life in luxury, had taken it for granted most of the time until it had been ripped from me. Leona had never had anything close to it. I pulled her against me, her hard nipples pressing up against my ribs.

"Stay with me tonight."

Her eyes widened. Then she gave one frantic shake of her head. "I told you, I won't sleep with you."

Not tonight, but soon. Leona might still believe she could evade me, but she was mine.

"I know," I said in a low voice then slid my hands over her back.

She relaxed then tensed as if remembering herself. "Then why? Why have me spend the night if there's nothing in it for you?"

Fuck, if I knew.

"Stay," I said again, an order this time. She looked up at me, fearful for all the wrong reasons.

"Okay," she breathed, resigned and tired.

She'd had a long day. Working at Roger's Arena wasn't easy. I lifted her into my arms. She didn't protest, as if she realized it was a losing battle. I carried her toward the stairs.

Leaning her cheek against my chest, she whispered, "Please don't hurt me. I don't think I can handle it."

I paused with my foot on the first step, glancing down at her crown of amber curls. It wasn't meant the way people usually meant it when they begged me not to hurt them. It would have been easier if it were. I wasn't sure I could stop myself from hurting her. I was dragging her into a world where the things she longed for were even less attainable than in the hopeless life she was used to.

Her breathing had flattened. Had she fallen asleep?

She shouldn't have, not in the arms of a man like me. Her trust was foolish and completely unfounded. I ascended the stairs and entered my bedroom. I never brought anyone here. I put Leona down on my bed, and she didn't wake. I allowed myself to regard her. Her narrow hips, her round breasts barely hidden from view by the sheer fabric of her bra, the outline of her pussy underneath her panties. I raked a hand through my hair. Women were supposed to be entertainment and a pleasant distraction. So far Leona was neither of those things, but I couldn't allow her to be anything else. My life was dedicated to the Camorra, my loyalties belonged only to them. It couldn't be any other way. I got out of my clothes and stretched out beside Leona in my briefs. I watched her as she slept beside me peacefully. Never had a woman slept in my bed. I never saw the appeal. I still thought of many more entertaining things to do with Leona than sleep, but watching her peaceful expression gave me a sense of calm I hadn't felt in a long time, perhaps if ever.

I curled my arm over her hip protectively and allowed myself to close my eyes. As I listened to her rhythmic breathing, I began to drift off.

I woke with Leona's body curled into me, one of her legs intertwined with mine, her breathing fluttering against my bare chest. I'd never woken up beside a woman, let alone allowed that kind of physical closeness. Sex was a different kind of closeness and all I would permit.

I carefully untangled myself from her. She turned onto her back, the blankets pooling at her hips. Her face was relaxed, no sign that she was going to wake any time soon.

She was supposed to be fun.

That was all Remo would ever allow.

Fun.

I brushed my thumb over the small nub straining against her bra. It pebbled under my touch. Leona's lips parted, but she didn't wake. I wasn't a good man, nothing close to it, and it was time I stopped acting like I was … like I could be. The bracelet Aria had given me was stuffed inside my sock drawer and it would stay there.

I trapped her nipple between my thumb and forefinger and began moving it back and forth slowly, feeling it harden even more. Leona shifted her legs. Was she feeling it between her perfect thighs? I tugged, and she let out a low moan. Her eyelids fluttered then opened sleepily before finding me. Surprise and shock flashed across her face. I tugged at her nipple once more, and her lips fell open with a gasp. My eyes on her face, daring her to stop me, I lowered my mouth to her breast and tugged her nipple with my lips, sucking it lightly through the fabric. That stopped any protest she might have had in mind. I watched her hooded eyes as I sucked harder.

I slid a finger over the edge of her bra and tugged it down, revealing the pink nub. "Fabiano," she said hesitantly, but I didn't allow her time for more words. I swirled my tongue around her nipple then pulled back to watch Leona press her legs together. She tasted amazing, like clean sweat and something sweeter. I lowered my mouth again, traced the tip of my tongue around the edge of her nipple, then slid to the peak and flicked it, licking her with languid strokes of my tongue. I sucked the small pink nipple into my mouth, relishing in the taste and Leona's shivers. She moaned again.

If playing with her tits made her come undone, I couldn't wait to dip my tongue between her silky folds.

I took my time with her nipple, wanting her to beg me for release. She ground her hips into the mattress in obvious need but didn't say the words I wanted to hear. My erection was rubbing painfully against the fabric of my briefs, driving me insane.

Done with being patient, I brushed my palm up her inner thigh. Her muscles tensed under my touch, but she didn't stop me. I held her gaze as my fingers brushed the crook between her thigh and pussy. Still no sign of protest. Instead, she opened her legs a bit wider, trust in her eyes.

Damn it, Leona.

I claimed her mouth for a fierce kiss and slipped my fingers under her panties and over her soft folds. She was so fucking aroused, so fucking ready to have me take her. Her body was practically begging for it, but that fucking trusting look in her eyes ruined it all. I ran my thumb up slowly until I brushed her clit. She bit her lip, hips rising up from the bed. I kept my eyes on her face, relishing in the twitches of pleasure, the wonder at how I could make her feel with just a simple touch of my thumb. The trust in her eyes anchored me, and I needed it to, because my body wanted more than she was willing to give, and the darkest parts of me knew nothing would stop me. And those dark parts were almost all that was left of me. Those parts of me had run the show for years. My thumb moved in slow circles over her wet flesh, and her gasps and moans were less controlled. She clutched my arm, and I kissed her hard, swallowing her cry as she tumbled over the edge. Her eyes fell shut as she shuddered, and for the briefest moment, I considered breaking my promise and breaking whatever dangerous bond was forming between us. Then she looked up at me, shy and embarrassed and guilty, and I knew it was too fucking late for that.

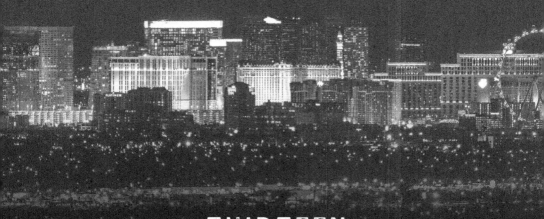

THIRTEEN

Leona

MY HEART RACED IN MY CHEST AS THE LAST WAVES OF PLEASURE EBBED away. Embarrassment slowly banished the thrilling euphoria. Fabiano didn't say anything, and I wasn't really sure what to say either. I hadn't meant for things to progress this fast. To sleep in Fabiano's bed, to have him touch me. The sensations had been wondrous, unlike anything I'd ever been capable of eliciting with my own fingers.

He peered down at me, a dark expression on his face, as if what had just happened was a mistake. I felt self-conscious under his scrutiny. It didn't make sense why he'd be unhappy about it. He hadn't gone against his own convictions, but perhaps he had come to the realization that I wasn't worth his attention. Maybe I did something wrong, though I couldn't really see how that was possible seeing as I hadn't done anything but let him touch me.

Worry filled me. Perhaps that was the problem.

I sat up. Sunlight filtered through the gap in the white curtains and past it I caught a glimpse of the Strip. I didn't belong here. I wasn't an Italian girl from noble upbringing.

"I should get going," I said lightly.

Fabiano didn't say anything, but behind his blue eyes was some kind of inner conflict raging on.

I was about to slip out of bed, when he placed his hand on my shoulder, stopping me. He leaned over to me for a gentle kiss that left me breathless then

This is only the beginning. I couldn't decide if it was promise or threat.

I slipped into Dad's apartment, closing the door with a soft click, not wanting to wake him. Seconds after the roar of Fabiano's engine had faded, Dad slunk out of the kitchen. He looked worse than the last time I'd seen him, like he needed a long shower and a few days of sleep.

His bloodshot eyes regarded me with silent judgment. They lingered on a spot above my pulse point, and the memory of Fabiano leaving his mark resurfaced. I placed my palm over the tender spot.

Dad shook his head. "You should have stayed with your mother." I didn't argue. Part of me knew he was right. I walked past him toward my bedroom. The space felt even less like home after my night in Fabiano's apartment. I knew I couldn't allow myself to grow accustomed to the luxury he had at his disposal. It wasn't something I could ever hope to have, and until now it never had been, but it was hard not to want something that beautiful once you experienced it firsthand. And his tenderness, his closeness ... that was the most beautiful thing of all. Something I needed, something I was scared to lose.

The memory of Fabiano's mouth and hands on me sent a pleasant shiver through my body. That, too, was an experience I never thought I would want and now I worried I wouldn't stop wanting it.

I changed out of yesterday's clothes and into shorts and a shirt, swung my backpack over my shoulder, and left. Until I had to start work, I stayed elsewhere. And I already had an idea where. Now that things with Fabiano were getting more serious, I needed to find out more about his past.

The library was quiet as I took my seat at one of the computers. I typed Fabiano Scuderi into the search engine and hit enter. There were a few entries about Remo Falcone from recent years, especially regarding his fighting, which included the occasional photo of Fabiano with beautiful girls that sent my stomach plummeting. Over all, he seemed to keep out of the public eye. Then I found older articles, from more than eight years ago, which surprised me.

The articles weren't from Las Vegas. They were from Chicago. Some of them mentioned a man called Rocco Scuderi, who was Fabiano's father and supposedly the Consigliere of the Chicago Outfit. I still wasn't very well informed about the mob and its terms, but even I knew that Fabiano's father was a big deal in Chicago. From what I'd gathered, the Las Vegas Camorra wasn't getting along with the other mob families in the country. Why was Fabiano here and not in Chicago? One photo of him and his family caught my eye. It showed Fabiano with his parents and three older sisters, all three of them so beautiful and elegant it hurt looking at them. This was what Cheryl meant when she said Italian virgins from noble upbringing.

I was nothing like them.

Only one of them, the youngest, shared his dark blond hair, while the eldest was almost golden and the one in the middle a redhead. They were a striking family. I kept scrolling for more results and soon found articles about his sisters as well, especially the oldest sister, Aria, with her husband, the head of the New York mafia.

I wondered why he never talked about them. Of course, I didn't talk about my mother either, but she was a crystal meth addict and a whore. The only thing that was remotely embarrassing about his family was that they were gangsters, and that definitely wasn't the reason why Fabiano had kept them a secret. If I had siblings, I'd want to stay in contact with them. I'd always wanted a brother or sister at my side for support during the many nights I was left alone when my mother was out looking for johns or other ways to get money.

At last, there was one article from a small Las Vegas newspaper about Fabiano titled "The Renegade son," which speculated about him joining the Las Vegas Camorra to become Capo. Apparently there had been a falling-out with his father that made him leave Chicago and help Remo Falcone. Overall, the information was sparse. It didn't give me what I really wanted, a glimpse behind the mask Fabiano displayed to the public.

The next day was Christmas Eve, and I went to work as if it was a day like any other. I tried to call the rehab center but hadn't reached anyone. Dad hadn't left his room before I had to leave the bar. Merry Christmas to me. Not that I had any intention of celebrating. The bar was deserted, only a few lonely souls crouched over their drinks.

"Why don't you go early?" Cheryl asked around eight o'clock. "I can handle our two customers."

I shook my head. "Don't you have family to celebrate with?"

Her lips tightened. "No. Roger will grab me around midnight for a Christmas quickie though."

I tried to hide my pity. I knew how it infuriated me when people gave me pitying looks. And it wasn't as if my Christmas was much better. "Where is he anyway? This is the first time he isn't in the bar."

"He's at home, celebrating Christmas with his daughter."

"Daughter?" I echoed in disbelief.

Cheryl nodded. "His wife died a few years ago and he's raising her alone."

"Oh." For some reason I had thought Roger didn't have a life outside of the bar.

"Just go, chick."

I sighed. Dad probably wasn't home. He'd mentioned an important race he had to watch. I grabbed my backpack then took out the cell phone Fabiano had given me yesterday so I could contact him. The only person I could think of calling was Fabiano, but would he even want to spend Christmas Eve with me? He was busy yesterday and only dropped me off at home after work … without mentioning Christmas at all. I clicked his name and quickly typed a message.

Got off early. You don't have to pick me up if you're busy. It's not too late for me to walk home.

I wasn't even out of the bar when Fabiano replied.

Wait for me.

I couldn't help the smile.

Cheryl watched me from across the room, shaking her head, and I quickly walked out into the parking lot. I knew she wouldn't be happy if she knew how much time I was spending with Fabiano. I was happy, despite everything.

Ten minutes later, his Mercedes pulled to a stop beside me.

I got in and took my seat beside him as if it had always been like this. He didn't move to kiss me, never had while we could be watched, but he put a hand on my knee.

"I didn't think you'd really go through with driving me home every night," I said, trying to ignore the way my body warmed at his touch.

Fabiano steered the car with one hand. "I'm a man of honor. I keep my promises."

Honor. A word that had played little to no role in my life so far. My parents were unfamiliar with the concept. Honor would have gotten in the way of their addiction.

My eyes traveled to the Camorra tattoo again. It scared people. Fabiano scared people. I hadn't realized it at first, but now that I looked for the little details in people's demeanor around him, it was impossible to miss.

Perhaps I didn't know enough about the Camorra and Fabiano to be scared. Maybe I was foolish not to be scared.

"I thought perhaps tonight you wanted to celebrate Christmas Eve with the Falcones." They were like his family, after all.

His fingers on my knee tightened. "Remo and his brothers don't celebrate Christmas Eve."

"But what about your real family? You never mention them."

Fabiano's lips thinned for the briefest instant before he schooled his expression into one of usual calm. "The Camorra is my family. Remo is like my brother. I don't need any other family than that."

I'd hoped he'd tell me more about his real family. I hesitated, unsure if I should mention that I'd found articles about them. I didn't want to appear as if I stalked him, even though that was the case.

"Ask," Fabiano said with a shrug, as usual able to read my face and the questions there.

"I found something about your family on the internet. There was a picture of you with them and a few articles about your sisters. One of them called you 'the renegade son.'"

His lips pulled into a sardonic smile. "Interesting twist on events they construed in that article," he said.

"So, you didn't leave for Las Vegas because you wanted to become Capo here?"

"I would have been happy becoming Consigliere for Dante Cavallaro and the Outfit. Back when I didn't know anything, I thought it was the ultimate honor to follow in my father's footsteps. Now I know that there's no honor in inheriting your position. The only way to deserve a position of power is if you fight for it, if you bleed and suffer for it."

"And you did," I said. I'd seen the scars. And even without them, you didn't become like Fabiano if life hadn't forged you in fire.

"I did, and so did Remo. He tore his position as Capo from the bleeding hands of the man who deemed himself capable of the job."

"And his brothers? What about them? Is that why they all have to fight? To prove their worth."

"That's one reason, yes."

It was strange that humankind thought it had come so far that humans considered themselves superior to animals, when we, too, still followed our base instincts. We looked up to the strong for a true leader, an alpha to guide our way, to take away the difficult decisions. The thrill of power struggles still captivated us. Why else were sports like cage fighting or boxing so popular?

I realized we weren't heading for my father's apartment nor to Fabiano's place.

"Hungry?" he asked, nodding toward the KFC drive-thru, the corner of his mouth twitching.

I nodded, wondering what he was up to.

"How about chicken for dinner and Las Vegas to ourselves?" he asked.

I smiled. "Sounds perfect."

The car smelled of the fried chicken and fries as Fabiano drove us up to the hill he had taken me for our first date. We were probably the only people who celebrated Christmas Eve with a KFC meal, but I didn't care. It wasn't like I'd had better Christmas dinners in the previous years. I was glad that Fabiano wasn't trying to imitate a traditional celebration. We parked at the very edge of the hill and stared out toward the bright city lights as we ate. "I think this is the best Christmas of my life," I said between bites of chicken.

"I wished it weren't," Fabiano murmured.

I shrugged. "So you had good Christmases with your family?"

His walls came up, but he gave me a reply. "When I was young, five or six, before my oldest sister left. After that, things quickly went downhill."

He fell silent and put down his half-eaten drumstick.

I licked sauce off my fingers then dropped them self-consciously when I noticed Fabiano watching me. He reached for my throat and brushed over my pulse point where he'd left a mark two days ago, his blue eyes possessive and ... something gentler.

"Let's go out for a bit. I have a blanket in the trunk."

Fabiano got out of the car and picked up the blanket. I walked up to the hood of the car and let my eyes take in the skyline. Las Vegas looked like it always did. It was flashy and colorful and bright. It could have been any evening other than Christmas, and I was glad for it. Fabiano came up beside me and handed me the wool blanket. I wrapped it around myself. It was soft and smelled of lavender. Fabiano's body was taut with tension, and he was looking—no, *glaring*—down at a small package in his hands.

A dark blue box with a silver ribbon. Oh, no. Was this for me? My stomach plummeted. I didn't have anything for him. I hadn't even thought about it. It had been so long since I'd celebrated Christmas that I hadn't even considered buying him a present. And what could I have gotten him anyway? He had every luxury possible.

I looked up from the box to find Fabiano now regarding me as if he was trying to make up his mind. Eventually he held out his hand with the present.

I didn't take it. "You don't have to give me anything."

His grip on the parcel tightened. "I want it gone."

Okay. I blinked.

I took the box hesitantly. "I don't have anything for you."

He didn't look surprised. "You don't have to, Leona. It's nothing."

"No, it's not. Nobody has given me a Christmas present in years," I admitted and felt raw because of it.

Fabiano's expression softened for the briefest moment. I opened the box with shaking fingers. Inside was a gold bracelet with small blue stones decorating it. "It's beautiful."

"Put it on," he said as he sank down on the hood of his car. He had a very strange look in his eyes as he regarded the bracelet, almost as if the piece of jewelry had come to haunt him.

I held my arm out for him, and he fastened the bracelet around my wrist. The stones flashed in the headlights. I'd have to keep it hidden from my father and in the bar as well. It was pathetic to think that I would rarely have an opportunity to wear it openly.

I searched Fabiano's eyes. They gave nothing away. Part of me was scared of what I wanted. Part of me was scared he'd grow tired of me the moment I gave him what he *wanted*. I knew how things could turn out.

His hand found mine, linking our fingers, and I stared down at our hands then slowly back up because I wasn't sure if he was doing this because he knew how it affected me or if he was being real. If this … whatever it was … was even real.

He cupped my face and pulled me toward him. My knees hit the bumper between his legs as our bodies molded together. He kissed me, slow and languid. I pressed my palms against his firm chest, feeling his calm heartbeat. His lips trailed over my cheek then brushed my ear.

"I can think of something you could give me as a present."

I stilled against him, my gaze seeking his. In the near dark it was difficult to read him. Sometimes it felt like he was doing it on purpose, saying something to break the moment, to destroy what could amount to something beautiful.

I cleared my throat. "I told you—"

"You won't sleep with me, I know."

I raised the wrist with the bracelet. "Is that why you bought this?"

His eyes narrowed. "So you would sleep with me?" He let out a dark laugh. "To be honest, I'd hoped you would want to do it without the help of fancy jewelry."

I flushed. "I do."

His eyes became eager, his body alert. "You do?" he asked in a low voice.

"But not today and not tomorrow. I need to get to know you better."

His face was very close to mine, and he shook his head. "You know everything there is to know. And everything you don't know yet is for your own good."

"I want to know everything, not just the good things."

"There are no good things, Leona. You know the bad things, and there are only worse things lurking behind that."

"I don't believe you," I whispered, leaning close and kissing him lightly.

"You should. I'm everything people warn you about. I'm every despicable thing they tell you and worse."

"Then why do I feel safe when I'm with you?"

He shook his head, his face almost angry. "Because you don't know what's good for you, and because you only see what you want to see."

"You are kind to me."

That seemed to be the last straw. He stood, his hands clutching my upper arms. "I'm not kind, Leona. Never have been. To anyone."

"To me you are," I said stubbornly. Why couldn't he see it?

He glared down at me then raised his eyes to the city behind my back. His grip on my arms loosened. What was he thinking?

He sank back down on the hood before he turned me around and pulled me against him so my back was pressed up against his chest.

"Tell me something about your family," I whispered. "Anything."

For a long time he didn't react. "My sisters raised me more than my mother or father did."

I held my breath, hoping he'd say more. Eventually, I risked another question. "How were they?"

Fabiano rested his head lightly on the top of my head. "Aria was protective and caring. Gianna loyal and fierce. Lily hopeful and lighthearted." I tried to picture them together, trying to bring together Fabiano's description with the press photo I'd found with their fake smiles.

"And you? How were you as a boy?"

His grip on my hips became painful, and I knew he was slipping away. "I was weak."

"You were a child." I felt him shake his head. Then he pulled back. I didn't want him to and put my hands over his to keep them in place. "What happened?"

"They left. Because they left, my father wanted me dead. And the boy he wanted dead … *died*."

What? His father had wanted him dead?

His breath was hot against my throat when he murmured, "I want to see you naked."

I tensed then tried to turn around to look at him, but he wouldn't let me see his face. His hands on my waist kept me in place. His sudden change of topic *and mood* disturbed me.

"You said you felt safe with me. Then prove it. I want to see every inch of you."

"It's not fair that you're using it against me," I said quietly. My mind was whirring with what he'd told me.

"If you feel safe, then you trust me."

Did I trust him? I wasn't sure. I hadn't trusted anyone in a very long time, if ever. I didn't even trust myself half the time.

"Or perhaps deep down you know that you can't trust a man like me. Perhaps deep down you know I'm not safe." He sounded triumphant.

I reached for the zipper on the side of my dress and slowly began moving it down. Fabiano released me so I could stand and lower the zipper completely. I reached for the hem of the dress, but Fabiano's hands were there to stop me.

"Let me."

I raised my arms despite my nerves, and he pulled the garment over my head. I shivered against the cold. He had seen me in my underwear before, yet this felt different, more exposing. I met his gaze. He sat on the edge of the hood, body taut with anticipation, like a jaguar on the verge of jumping its prey.

"Come," he said quietly, and I stepped between his legs. He unhooked my bra and let it drop to the ground between us. Then his fingers hooked in the hem of my panties. Slowly, he raked them down my hips until they pooled at my feet. His eyes took in my body unabashedly. His gaze lingered on my most private part, and I had to fight the urge to cover myself. He regarded me as if I was special and it made my breath catch in my throat. "See," I said eventually. "I do feel safe with you."

He wrapped his arms around me, pulling me close. My nipples rubbed against his dress shirt and a sweet tingle formed in my belly. "You shouldn't." His voice was rough and deep. His hands came down on my hips, then one began its slow ascend until he cupped my breast. The coldness of my surroundings became a distant memory as he tugged at my nipple, rolling it between his thumb and forefinger. I could feel myself growing wet from his touch. Slowly, his other hand slid down from my waist to my butt. He cupped my cheek and squeezed then moved lower, to the back of my upper thigh, before he slid his fingers between my legs. His fingertips brushed over me, and I released a long shuddering breath. In the dim light, I caught sight of his erection straining against his pants.

What was I doing?

Whenever I lay awake at night, listening to my mother with her customers, I imagined my future with a straight-laced husband. A man who worked nine-to-five, a man who was safe and boring, yet here I was with Fabiano, a man who was anything but. He didn't fit with the future I imagined, didn't fit into the life I'd so carefully planned out for myself. But who ever said he'd be a part of my future? He definitely never gave any indication that he wanted a forever, that he even wanted a relationship. And what did I want? I wasn't sure anymore. As his fingers worked my heated flesh and I clung to him, I decided to let go of my worries for now. My body surrendered to the feelings coiling in the pit of my stomach, and I gasped as his fingers stroked me. It was exhilarating. Alive. I felt alive. He moved faster, and I cried out, my head falling back as currents of pleasure shot through me.

The sky above us was infinite, filled with possibilities and hope. Foolish hope.

Oh God. I was falling for him.

I pressed my forehead against Fabiano's shoulder, trying to catch my breath. He took my hand and rested it against the bulge in his pants. "That's what you do to me, Leona," he growled.

Was that all I did to him?

A mix of triumph and need filled me. Need for more than what his body could give, but I reached for his zipper and pulled it down. *Settle for what you can get, Leona.*

My fingers halted. I raised my eyes to his and there was that same flicker of need. Did he feel it too? Fabiano rose from the hood, breaking the moment, and freed his erection from his pants. His eyes made me shiver, cold and hungry.

"I want you on your knees, Leona. I want my cock in your mouth."

I froze, my defenses shooting up. Another moment ruined. He was so damn good at it.

Me on my knees? That was something I swore I'd never do. Not with anyone. My mother's johns had always wanted her mouth on them, had felt powerful when she knelt before them, had enjoyed degrading her like that. Sometimes when she was high, she told me about it, about her revulsion, about the disgusting taste, about choking when they fucked her mouth without mercy. I would never allow that to happen to me. Least of all like this. I wasn't sure what Fabiano saw in me, if he cared for me or if him wanting to be in my mouth was his way of possessing me a bit more.

I took a step back, shaking my head. "No," I said. Fabiano's eyes flashed with an emotion I couldn't read.

"I'm not your whore, Fabiano. I don't like you ordering me around."

He smiled darkly. "That wasn't an order, Leona. Believe me, it sounds very different when I give an order."

Dangerous. That was what he was. Sometimes I caught glimpses of it beneath his mask, and I always tried to forget.

"And I don't like you teasing me. You keep flirting with me, letting me touch you, and you think I won't want more? Even a normal guy would want to get in your pants, and I'm a fucking *killer*. You expect me to sit back and wait patiently for you to make your mind up."

A killer. He never admitted it, but I never asked him—because deep down I didn't want to know. Even still, the concept of him ending someone's life was too abstract to grasp. It seemed like something distant, something not of this world.

A sharp comment died on my lips when I caught the hint of wariness in Fabiano's eyes. He was wary of me, thought I was playing with him, perhaps using him like the other women who'd only seen his power and the possibilities it meant for them. Fabiano and I had a hard time trusting others.

"I'm not teasing you," I said quietly. I touched his chest, feeling his heat even through the shirt. His muscles flexed under my touch, but he didn't soften, his body nor expression. He regarded me like a snake does a mouse. I sighed, not wanting to explain my reaction to him because I couldn't tell him about my mother, not without him looking at me differently. "I want to touch you," I said, and it was true. "But I won't put my mouth on you. I think it's degrading. My mother always had bad taste in men, and they all liked to put her down like that."

His eyes were too assertive, like he knew more than I was willing to share. I looked away, worried he knew exactly what I was hiding, not only about my mother.

"I have no intention of degrading you," he said. I tentatively reached for him, my fingers brushing over his silkiness. He hardened immediately, but no sound left his lips as he watched me. For once, I didn't want to know what was going on in his head, too frightened that it would tell me more about myself than about him. His hand closed around my fingers, showing me exactly how he liked to be touched.

My own breathing quickened as I stroked him harder and faster. He never took his eyes off me, and there it was again … that flicker of emotion. I tightened my grip even more, made him growl low in his throat and replaced the tender emotion in his eyes with lust. Better. *Safer.* I could break the moment too—had to break it if I wanted to come out of this unscathed.

Fabiano tensed, control finally slipping, and he released himself with a shudder. The revulsion I expected never came. I wanted to touch him, and it felt amazing to watch him like that. I wanted more of it and more than just that.

When our breathing finally calmed, Fabiano took the wool blanket from the ground and wrapped it around us, his body warm against mine. I leaned back, closing my eyes. Despite the beauty of the city below, nothing could compare to the feel of our bodies pressed against each other. I'd been alone for so long. Perhaps all my life. And now there was someone whose closeness gave me a sense of belonging I hadn't thought possible. Fabiano was a danger to anyone around him, but to my heart he posed the greatest danger of all.

FOURTEEN

Leona

CHRISTMAS MORNING. MY FATHER WOLFED DOWN THE FRENCH TOAST I prepared then got up. "One of the biggest races of the year goes down on Christmas. I need to place my bet."

Of course he had to. It was always about betting and gambling. About races and fights. How could I expect my father to want to spend Christmas with me? I nodded, swallowing the bitter words that wanted to spill from my mouth. He left the kitchen, leaving me alone with the dirty dishes. I waited for him to leave the apartment before I took the folded piece of paper with the number of the rehab center from my backpack and dialed it with my new phone. After two rings, a clipped female voice answered. "I'm calling for Melissa Hall, I'm her daughter." Guilt filled me. This was only the second time I'd tried to call since I was in Las Vegas, but the doctors had told me that it was better to give my mother time to settle in before she was confronted with influences from the outside world. And secretly I'd been relieved to be away from her troubles for a while.

There was silence on the other end except for the click-click of someone typing something into a keyboard. "She left two days ago."

"Left?" I repeated, my stomach clenching tightly.

"Relapse." The woman was silent on the other end, waiting for me to say something. When I didn't, she added, "Do you want me to get one of her attending doctors so he can explain the details to you?"

"No," I said angrily then hung up. I knew everything. My mother had given up again. I wasn't sure why I had expected anything else from her. And now she was out there alone, without me. Fear jabbed at my insides. This had been her last chance. She'd overdosed twice in the past, and I had been the one to save her, but now I was too far away. She couldn't be on her own. She forgot to eat, and she got sad after the stimulating effect of meth wore off, too sad, especially after a john treated her like shit. She needed me.

I stared bleakly at the plates in front of me, listened to the deafening silence of the apartment. Tears blurred my vision. I needed to find her before it was too late. I had always been the caretaker in our relationship. My mother was like a child in so many ways. I should have never listened to the doctors. I'd known from the start that my mother was a lost cause. There was only one person I could turn to.

I typed '**I need your help, Fabiano. Please.**' into my mobile and pressed send.

Fabiano

"Today is going to bring us millions," Nino said.

I tore my gaze away from the TV screen that showed the warm-up race. Nino was staring down at the iPad in his lap.

Remo shook his head at his brother, annoyed. "Watch the race for fuck's sake. We have a bookie for the numbers. Enjoy yourself for once. Stop acting like a fucking math nerd."

Nino shrugged. "I don't trust our bookies to do a better job than I can. Why settle for a lesser option?"

Savio snorted. "You are so fucking full of yourself."

If Nino wasn't Remo's brother, he would have studied math or some shit like that. He was a genius, which made him twice as lethal.

Remo slid his knife out of the holster across his chest then threw it with a flick of his wrist. The sharp blade pierced the soft brown leather beside Nino's left thigh. Nino glanced up from the iPad then down at the knife protruding from the sofa. "Good thing the races bring us so much money ... You keep destroying our furniture," he drawled.

Remo waved him off.

Nino put the iPad down on the table beside him then pulled out the knife. He began twisting it between his fingers.

"So how's it going with your waitress?" Remo asked. "Not bored of her yet?"

I shrugged. "She's entertaining enough."

Nino's assertive eyes regarded me above his toying with the knife. I wasn't sure what his twisted brain had gathered from the one time he saw me with Leona. He didn't understand emotions. That was my salvation.

"Good fuck?" Savio asked, grinning.

I wasn't happy about the turn our conversation had taken.

"What the fuck?" Savio exclaimed, pointing at the TV. "Adamo is driving one of the race cars."

We all turned to the screen. Adamo was overtaking two cars at once; their drivers hadn't seen him coming up behind them. "Good driving skills for a thirteen-year-old," I said.

Remo scowled. "One of these days I'm going to kill him, brother or not."

My mobile vibrated in my jeans pocket. I took it out then glanced at the screen. Leona.

I need your help, Fabiano. Please.

Feeling Remo's eyes on me, I slid the phone back into my pocket.

"Your waitress," he said.

I crossed my arms behind my head. "She can wait."

"Why would you waste your day with us if you can have a nice fuck?" Savio asked before standing. "Actually, why didn't you organize some kind of entertainment, Remo?"

Remo reached for his mobile. "Obviously family time is over." Then he laughed at his own joke before his eyes slid over to me. "Go to her. Then we won't have to share the girls with you."

I got up with a shrug, as if I couldn't care less if I stayed or left, but my mind was reeling. What was going on? Leona sounded desperate.

"Don't overexert yourself with that girl of yours," Remo said with a shark smile. "It wouldn't look good if my enforcer lost a fight."

I rolled my eyes. My next fight was in six days, on New Year's Eve. "Don't worry."

The streets were deserted as I drove to Leona's. People were celebrating Christmas with their families. I caught the occasional glimpse through windows where people exchanged presents or shared a family meal. I knew most of it was a façade. My family had always made a big show out of celebrating Christmas together as well, but behind closed doors we had been as far from a happy family as you could get. Our father had always made sure that we were miserable.

Last night was the first Christmas Eve I'd enjoyed in a long time. Because of Leona. My hands clenched. I shouldn't have given her the bracelet. I wasn't sure what had gotten into me.

Nothing. I wanted to get rid of the fucking thing. That was all. And why not give it to Leona?

I parked in Leona's street and got out of the car. I hadn't bothered texting her.

I rang the bell and moments later Leona opened the door, looking surprised and relieved. Her eyes were red from crying. I chose not to comment. Consoling others wasn't my forte, and I had a feeling she preferred me ignoring her emotionality.

Behind her I saw the small apartment she and her father shared, with the worn-out carpet and the smoke-yellowed wallpaper. She followed my gaze and flushed. "I didn't think you'd come," she said quietly.

"I'm here."

She nodded slowly then opened the door wide. "Do you want to come in?"

The apartment was a far cry from being inviting, but I stepped inside. Leona closed the door and then her arms were around my waist in a tight grip. She shuddered. I hesitated then raised my hand to her head and touched her lightly.

"Leona, what's going on?" Had someone hurt her? When could that have happened? I brought her home around four in the morning. It was only twelve now.

She raised her head. "Please help me find my mother."

"Your mother?"

"She left rehab. She can't take care of herself without me. I have always been the one who made sure she ate and didn't overdose. I should have never left her, but I thought she was safe in rehab."

"Shhh," I said, touching her cheek. She was shaking. "I'm sure your mother is fine."

"No, she isn't. She can't deal with life." She closed her eyes, and I knew what was coming. "She sells her body for crystal meth. And sometimes it makes her feel so dirty and horrible that she just wants to give up. I won't be there to stop her next time that happens."

After all the neglect Leona had suffered, she shouldn't be worrying about her mother like that. That she did stirred some part of me I thought was dead. "I will find her for you," I told her. "Where was she last seen?"

"Austin."

That was a bit of a problem. The Mexican cartels and local MCs were in control of Texas. Remo wanted to change it, eventually, but right now the Camorra had little power there. Remo had his contacts, of course—people who'd rather see us in power than the Mexicans. Perhaps one of them could help. But that would require that *I ask* Remo for help.

"Are you sure your mother won't come to find you?"

Leona gave a miserable shrug. "I don't know. She might. If she remembers where I went. She doesn't always remember. Her brain is a mess because of all the drugs." She closed her eyes. "If something happens to her, I'll never forgive myself."

"Nothing will happen to her," I said firmly. I stroked her cheek, and she gave me a teary smile. "Thank you, Fabiano." I lowered my head and kissed her lips. The kiss was sweet. I'd never had a fucking sweet kiss in my life.

When I returned to the Falcone mansion, I heard the moans. I made my way into the entertainment room with the pool tables, couches, TVs, and boxing ring. Savio was bent over a naked woman sprawled out on the pool table, thrusting into her. Another woman fingered herself on the same table.

She sat up when she spotted me then hopped off. I fucked her before, but I didn't remember her name. She sauntered over to me, but I shook my head, narrowing my eyes at her. She froze, eyes darting with unease.

"Where is he?" I asked.

Remo never took these women into his bedroom.

"Outside," Savio muttered then kept fucking the whore.

I strode out toward the living area and onto the terrace. Remo was there, naked, his hand fisting a woman's hair while fucking her mouth hard. He was glaring down at her as if he'd rather slice her open than shoot his cum down her throat.

His eyes shot up to meet mine, and he stopped thrusting but held the woman in place with his fist, his cock deep inside her mouth.

"I need your help," I said. He had already gathered information about Leona's mother, so I knew he'd find her.

Remo's black brows drew together. He shoved the woman away, and she landed on her ass then quickly scurried off. He didn't bother covering himself.

"I need to find someone. Leona's mother."

"You do?" he said quietly, suspicion tightening his eyes. "Why do *you* need to find the crack-whore?"

If he thought Leona was becoming too important to me, which she wasn't, he might take actions into his hands and get rid of her. "Because Leona got it in her head that the crack-whore will die without her help."

Remo came closer. I couldn't tell his mood. He was … tense. "And you are helping her because …?"

That was the fucking question, wasn't it?

"Because I want to." It was a dangerous admittance. I had to hope that the years we'd spent like brothers protected me.

"That got something to do with your sisters and how you were abandoned and that shit?"

"You saved me when I needed saving."

"I wasn't being heroic, Fabiano. I did it because I knew you were worthy to become what you are today."

"I'm not being heroic either. Will you help me?"

Remo shook his head. "Don't start going soft on me, Fabiano." He didn't sound angry or threatening.

I relaxed my stance. "I'm not, trust me."

Remo ran a hand through his hair. "You are a cock-blocking asshole."

"You probably would have killed her before you shot your cum down her throat."

"I would have killed her while shooting my cum down her throat," Remo said with a twisted grin. He grabbed his pants and pulled them on. "I assume the whore is somewhere in Texas, selling her worn-out pussy to any asshole with a few bucks?"

"Probably."

"Good opportunity to piss off the Mexicans, I suppose. Perhaps I can call in a favor with the Tartarus MC."

I didn't thank him. He wouldn't appreciate it.

FIFTEEN

Fabiano

SOMETHING HAD REMO EXCITED. I CHECKED HIS FACE OCCASIONALLY, knowing things that excited Remo usually involved blood and destruction.

Soto entered the room, dragging a woman in by her arm.

I stifled a sigh. Women weren't in my scope of work. Remo knew I preferred to handle men, and in the last couple of years, he allowed me that leniency. I doubted he understood, nor approved of my reluctance to deal with women, but hurting them had never given me the same thrill punishing men did. Soto, on the other hand, got off on degrading the weaker sex … in more than just the literal sense.

Degrading. Leona's expression when I'd asked her to give me a blow job flashed in my mind, but I banished any thought of her.

I threw Remo a questioning look. Why was I supposed to watch him dish out punishment to some run-down crack-whore?

Soto shoved the woman in our direction. She teetered on her too-high, red patent leather heels and eventually tumbled to her knees. She got back up, revealing ripped fishnet stockings. The tight red pleather dress hung off her emaciated body. When she lifted her face to stare fearfully at us, a jolt of recognition went through me. I masked my shock before Remo could pick up on it. He had been watching me closely in the last few days since I'd asked him for help.

Dazed eyes, cornflower blue like Leona's, darted from me to Remo to Soto. There was a distant resemblance. Perhaps in younger years, Leona's mother looked even more like her daughter—before the drugs and the alcohol and the constant beatings from johns.

She wobbled on her high heels, fingers trembling, and there was a fine sheen of sweat on her leathery skin. She needed her next fix.

"Found her," Remo said, an excited gleam in his eyes that told me this was about more than just helping me. More than once, I'd regretted my decision of approaching him. Leona was no longer one among many to him. She was someone with a name and a face, someone to be wary of.

"Had to hand over a few thousand in cash to the *president* of the fucking MC for this worthless whore because she worked his streets. I wonder what part of her is supposed to be worth five thousand dollars. Just look at her."

I didn't have to. She wasn't worth that much money.

Five thousand dollars.

Fuck.

Tartarus had ripped us off. And Remo let them. Not good.

"What do you say, whore? Are you worth that much money?" His voice was dangerously pleasant. People who didn't know him might have mistaken it for kindness.

She quickly shook her head, obviously knowing how to handle dangerous men. With a past like hers, it shouldn't have come as a surprise. "Wh-where am I?"

"Las Vegas, *my property*, and now you are too."

She nodded slowly, dazed, then her expression shifted. "My daughter Leona is here."

Shut the fuck up. I didn't want Leona's name spoken in this room. I needed to figure out a way to get my girl out of Remo's head.

"That she is," Remo said, eyes slithering over to me, his lips tightening. "Now back to that five thousand dollars you owe me."

Damn it. It would have been easy for me to pay the money, but I wasn't out of my mind.

She smiled crookedly. "I earn good money. I know what men want."

Remo's dark eyes traveled over her body. "I doubt any man would want to get his cock dirty like that."

She didn't even flinch at his words. She'd heard worse. Whatever pride she once had was gone. She had no honor. She had nothing. That was why Leona clung to her virginity like it was her only salvation. And even knowing that, I still wanted to take it from her.

From his pocket, Remo pulled out a small see-through bag with two meth cubes and let it dangle from his fingertips. Leona's mother sucked in her breath, a sharp, raspy sound. Her body became taut, eyes keen and eager. For him it was nothing. Our storage was full of meth and heroin and ecstasy, full of money too.

She took a step toward him, licking her cracked lips.

"You want this, hmm?" he asked in a low voice. She gave a jerky nod.

"What would you do to get it?"

"Anything," she said quickly. "I'll suck your cock and you can have my ass. No condom."

As if Remo would settle for someone like her. He *was* Las Vegas. He could have anyone. Remo's mouth tightened with disgust. "There isn't enough bleach in the world to clean you."

"Then perhaps him?" she nodded toward me.

Remo's eyes turned on me. "I think he prefers a younger version of you. Less used up."

Leona wasn't used up in any way. She was pure and innocent. She was *mine.*

Leona's mother looked at Soto. Even he didn't look remotely close to being excited about the prospect of fucking her. He usually wasn't choosy over where he put his ugly cock, but that woman was too wasted even for him.

"I'm good, Boss," he said, waving her off like a bothersome fly.

Remo closed his fingers around the bag. "Perhaps you have something else you can offer us. Or perhaps someone else?" He tilted his head with a dangerous smile. "Perhaps that daughter of yours will take it up her ass in your stead. She might even be worth five thousand dollars."

My fingers twitched for my gun, but I stilled. This was crazy. I'd sworn loyalty to Remo and the Camorra. This wasn't about the woman in front of us. Remo was testing me. That he felt the need to do so unsettled me. Leona was a distraction. She wasn't a threat to the Camorra in any way.

"She's not like that. Do not touch her," Leona's mother said fiercely. I re-garded her anew. Little was left of her. She had no pride, no honor, nothing, but despite her need for the drugs in Remo's hands, the part of her that cared for her daughter—no matter how little was left of it—won out. That was more than one could say about Leona's father.

Remo threw the bag on the ground. "You're not worth my time."

She scrambled forward and took the bag, cradling it like a child. "You are my property as long you owe me money. Hit the streets. You're too used up, even for our whorehouses." She wasn't listening. She was rummaging in her purse. Eventually her hand emerged with a syringe crusted with old blood. Of course, she didn't snort or smoke the shit. Shooting it into a vein boosted its stimulating effects.

Remo's face contorted with rage. "Not here!"

She reared back. I moved over to her, gripped her upper arm, and hoisted her to her feet. I dragged her out, Remo's eyes burning through my back as I did. "Five thousand plus interest, Fabiano. Tell Leona too."

I shoved Leona's mother onto the backseat of my Mercedes then got behind the wheel. "Don't even think about shooting up in my car," I snarled, angry at her, at Leona, and most of all myself.

Leona's mother cowered against the seat. She didn't move the entire ride, except for her eyes, which watched me like I was about to pounce on her. She was already broken. I sighed and left her in the car as I set out toward Roger's Arena.

The moment Leona saw me, she dropped everything and rushed toward me.

"I found her. She's in my car."

Leona's eyes widened, and she hugged me. Fucking hugged me in the middle of Roger's Arena, under the eyes of dozens of customers. I gripped her arms and pushed her away.

Leona

My arms fell, realizing what I'd done. Fabiano looked pissed. And I got it. Not only did he have to keep up appearances, but people weren't supposed to know about us.

"How is she?" I asked as I followed him outside. I could barely keep up with his pace. He seemed desperate to get away.

He yanked open the door and Mom stumbled out. She looked a mess, as if she'd been found with a john and didn't have time to clean herself properly. I'd seen her worse off, so I moved forward and wrapped my arms around her. She hugged me back briefly then dropped her arms, trembling. When I saw the syringe and plastic bag in her left hand, I knew why. "I need …" she whispered.

I nodded. I knew she needed a hit. I stepped back and she fell to her knees, nervously fumbling with the plastic bag.

Fabiano stood close behind me. I could feel his presence like a disapproving shadow. The smell of melting crystal meth filled my nose as Mom held the spoon over her lighter. She let out a small moan when the needle finally pierced her bruised skin.

I cast a glance over my shoulder. Fabiano's expression was stone. Hard, unrelenting, cold. "Thank you."

Blue eyes narrowed a fraction. "Five thousand, that's what Remo had to pay for her. Until she can pay it off, she belongs to the Camorra."

"That's too much money. She'll never be able to pay it off. She was barely able to pay for meth and food before."

He looked away and headed for the driver's side. "She's sold her body for years, she'll have to keep doing it. We'll send her the johns who don't have enough money for the whorehouses and she'll give them what they want."

I stared at his back because he wouldn't show me his face. "But those men are always the worst. They like to beat and humiliate women."

He stopped with his hand on the car door. His shoulders sagged. His eyes were cold as a glacial lake as he turned his head. "I can't do anything. I did too much already. You don't know how much I'm risking for you. Your mother is lost, Leona. She has been for a long time. Save yourself and let her handle her shit alone."

"I can't," I told him. He got into the car and drove off without another word. *You don't know how much I'm risking for you.*

"Why? Why are you risking so much," I wanted to ask, but he was gone. And he wouldn't reply anyway.

Mom curled into herself, a blissful expression on her face. It wouldn't last long. Her breathing quickened, and she rolled on her back, chest heaving, eyes wide, pupils dilated.

"Who's that?" Cheryl's voice made me jump. She appeared beside me.

"My mother," I admitted.

Cheryl didn't say anything as we both watched my mother get lost in her drug haze. Over the years it got worse. Meth destroyed her piece by piece. "She can't stay here. Roger will lose his shit if he sees a junky in his parking lot."

"I know," I said. "But I don't have a car, and there's no way a cab will give us a ride with her like that."

Cheryl sighed. "I hate to say it, chick, but you are more trouble than you look." She pulled car keys from her back pocket then pointed at an old, rusty Toyota. "Get in. I'll give you a quick ride. Mel can handle the bar."

"Thank you," I whispered.

She waved me off and helped me lead my mother to her car, positioning her on the backseat. She also helped me get my mother into the apartment, even as my father raged around us. I had paid for food and had given him more than enough money in the last few weeks. He would have to deal with Mom sleeping on the couch for now.

"You will end up just like her!" he shouted as he stormed out. Cheryl was already gone.

I perched on the edge of the couch beside my mother, who was mumbling in her drug-induced daze. Her eyes twitched around as she trembled with nervous energy. Mom being in Vegas meant more trouble for me. I didn't want her to work the streets again, but I didn't have nearly enough money to pay off her debt to the Camorra.

My mobile beeped. I removed it from my backpack.

It was a message from Fabiano.

Do you need me to pick you up from work tonight?

Even though he was pissed about the situation, he honored his promise to protect me. I smiled down at my phone.

No. I'm home with my mother. Thank you.

"That look," Mom croaked, startling me. "Who is he?"

"No one. There's no one, Mom. Sleep."

She rocked back and forth, the drugs beckoning to her. "I hope he's good to you."

"He's good to me," I said. Good *for* me ... that was a different matter.

"Does he love you like you him?"

My throat closed. "Sleep, Mom." I knew her body was torn between the stimulating effect of the meth and utter exhaustion from lack of sleep and food. And finally her eyes closed, but she didn't lie down. Soon she'd go looking for johns.

Love broke people. It had broken Mom before, and the drugs did the rest.

I didn't love Fabiano. I ... I was falling for him. Falling deeper and deeper every day. Into his darkness and what lay beneath it.

Fabiano didn't want love. He didn't believe in it.

I couldn't love him.

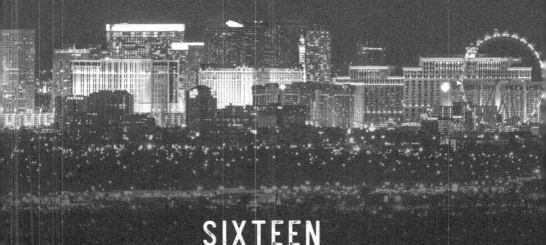

SIXTEEN

Leona

MY STOMACH FLUTTERED WITH NERVES, AS IF I WAS THE ONE WHO HAD to fight in a cage. I glanced at the changing room doors, waiting for Fabiano to emerge. This was his second fight that I got to watch, but this time I was worried. Worried for Fabiano, worried he'd get hurt … or worse. In the last few weeks of me working in Roger's Arena, I'd seen how brutal cage fighting could be. Several men had died in the hospital afterward. What if something happened to Fabiano?

I hadn't seen him since he'd dropped off my mother in the parking lot yesterday. I was in the storage area when he came in, and it drove me crazy that I couldn't tell him again how much I appreciated his help. Mom had been sleeping when I left, and I made her promise me she wouldn't leave the apartment alone. We'd figure out a way to get the money she owed later, until then my savings would have to do. My father wasn't going to help, that much was clear.

The door of the changing room opened, and Fabiano stepped out, tall and muscled. I smiled. He looked invincible. Fabiano was grace and fierceness and power as he strode toward the center of the room under the cheers of the crowd. His eyes were the scariest thing I'd ever seen. He was furious. Because of me, because of my mother. Perhaps his opponent, who waiting for him, saw it too, because for a moment he looked like he wanted to cancel the fight.

Fabiano leaped into the cage, catlike and breathtaking. His eyes sought mine and for a split second he looked at peace.

I had stopped washing the glasses, stopped listening to the customers. There was only him. The crowd erupted with a new wave of cheers. That *man*. He was mine. I had never been worth anything, but one look from him made me feel like the center of the world.

His opponent hopped from one foot to the other, balled fists raised, trying to goad Fabiano into action. One last glance at me, and Fabiano leaped toward his opponent.

His punches were hard. There was no hesitation in his hits and kicks. His eyes were keen and attentive, reading his opponent and using his weakness. Everything about this sport was brutal and hard. Relentless. But Fabiano's movements boasted grace and control. The crowd yowled and applauded every time he landed a hit. Blood soon covered Fabiano's hands and arms. He was harder and crueler on this opponent than last time.

Cheryl leaned in close as she put dirty glasses in the wash water. "I hope that puts some sense in you. If that doesn't scare you shitless, nothing will."

Fear was the last thing on my mind as I watched Fabiano. Cheryl regarded me then shook her head. "Oh, chick, and here I thought Stefano was the Camorra's romancer. Who would have thought that their monster would break your heart?"

"He isn't a monster. And he's not breaking anything," I murmured.

She loaded her tray with beer bottles for the next table. "He will break *something*. If it's only your heart, you're lucky. And if you haven't seen his monster until now, you might be in more trouble than I thought. Don't come running to me when you encounter it."

She knew nothing. "Don't worry."

Soon the man was lying on the ground. Fabiano crouched over him, punching him over and over again.

I shivered and felt relieved when the man finally patted the ground in surrender. The referee entered the cage and raised Fabiano's arm into the air. Fabiano looked my way, his body covered in blood.

He looked magnificent. His words about alpha males and their appeal from our first meeting came back to me, and I had to admit that he had been right as far as I was concerned. Fighting never mesmerized me before but watching Fabiano was something else entirely.

He climbed out of the cage and accepted the congratulating hands of several customers, but his eyes kept returning to me. I put down the dishtowel then grabbed a bottle of water.

"Where are you going, chick? Right into the lion's den?" Cheryl shook her head and took my place behind the bar. "Go ahead. Everyone has to dig their own grave, I suppose."

I sent her a grateful smile despite her annoying words and slunk toward the changing room. People were still too focused on the fighting cage, where the Camorra's bookie was stationed.

I didn't bother knocking before I entered the changing room. Fabiano saw me following him. I doubted anyone ever managed to sneak up on him. My clothes stuck to my skin from working all day and it should have made me self-conscious. I needed a shower, but my need for something else was even stronger. Fabiano wiped the remaining traces of blood from his body. Now his chest only glistened with sweat, the sheen accentuating every hard ridge of his perfect body. I wanted to trace my tongue along the dip between his pecs, down to the fine hair disappearing under the hem of his boxers. I'd never felt want like this. He was risking his position for me, and I wanted to risk something too.

I quickly tore my gaze from Fabiano and stepped into the changing room then closed the door before someone saw me. I needed to stop thinking like that about Fabiano. Touching him and having him touch me was okay, but if I allowed more, he'd stop respecting me. He'd lose interest. I *knew* it. Especially now that he knew what my mother was. The cool door under my palms grounded me. I didn't hear him approach but felt him close behind me, his heat pressing up against my back.

"You kept distracting me today," he murmured close to my ear. I shuddered at his proximity. Seeing him fight today had turned me on. There was no use denying it. The sport was brutal and hard, and Fabiano showed no mercy when he beat up his opponents, but my body responded to the sight of him. He'd looked invincible. Powerful.

The image of his hungry stare after he'd won sent a sweet tingling to the spot between my legs. "I can't stay here forever. People will start to wonder what we're doing."

I doubted no one had noticed me going into the changing room with Fabiano. I cringed at what they might think about me now.

"Let them wonder," Fabiano growled then licked my shoulder blade. "You taste perfect."

I shivered. "I'm sweaty."

He gripped my hips and whirled me around to face him, his head coming down and his lips claiming mine. I opened up, my tongue darting out to meet his. I ran my hand over his slick chest, my fingers trailing over the ridges. Perfection. He hissed when I slid over a cut.

"Sorry," I mumbled quickly but he quieted me with his tongue.

He backed me up until my legs collided with something hard. His arm wrapped around my lower back, and he lowered me until I lay on the narrow wooden bench. One knee between my legs, he bent over me, his mouth conquering mine, stealing my breath and making me dizzy with emotions and need. He didn't let up, and I could feel myself getting more and more aroused with every second. His tongue was so wonderfully skillful as it caressed mine. The scent of fresh sweat and Fabiano's own muskiness engulfed me.

He moved his knee up until it pressed against my crotch, and I moaned into his mouth at the sensation. I had to stop myself from rubbing myself shamelessly against his knee for some release.

"Stay like that," he ordered. Then he moved back, and only when he knelt on the floor between my legs did it dawn on me what he had in mind.

My eyes darted to the door. "Fabiano, please. What if someone comes in?"

"They won't."

"I'm sweaty. You *can't*." I shoved at his head, but he didn't let himself be deterred from what he was doing. He slid my skirt up then hooked a finger under my panties and shifted them to the side. Cool air hit my wet flesh, and my muscles tightened with need.

"Oh, Leona," he whispered darkly. "I thought you didn't like to see me fighting." He leaned his head against my inner thigh, his eyes darting from my most private area, wet and throbbing for him, to my face. I flushed with embarrassment but didn't say anything.

"But your pussy seems to enjoy it a lot."

Why did he have to use that word?

He blew against me and I quivered. I needed him to touch me. Shoving him away took a backseat in my mind as I watched him lower his hungry gaze between my legs again. And then he leaned forward, and I held my breath, every muscle in my body taut with tension. His tongue darted out, licking over my heated flesh, sending a torrent of sensations through my lower body. I squeezed my eyes shut and bit down on my lip to stop myself from making a sound. Outside music still blared, but I didn't want to risk anything. He took his time, exploring with his tongue. Good Lord.

I gasped and arched off the bench as he kept up his ministrations, mouth and tongue sure of every twitch and turn they did, driving me up toward a point I'd never imagined.

"You are perfect," he rumbled against me, and the sound of his voice was like a hot shower after hours in the cold.

I curled my fingers around the edge of the bench, clinging to it desperately as my legs began trembling. My breath came in short bursts. Fabiano closed his mouth over me and began sucking. I whimpered but he pressed on, tongue circling and flicking. I was falling. A different kind of falling than before. I let out a small cry, one hand darting out to grab his blond hair. He hummed his approval as I kept him in place. I needed this. He pulled a few inches back, and I huffed in protest. I was so close.

"Don't stop," I pleaded, not caring how desperate I sounded. I was so close to the edge with raw need.

A need so strong it *hurt*. I wanted to tumble over this cliff, and fall and fall. I needed that fall.

"But what if someone comes in," he asked in a low voice, his tongue sliding along my inner thigh. He was taunting me now.

"Fabiano, please. I don't care!"

He chuckled, holding my gaze as he lowered his head so very slowly. When his lips brushed my flesh, I almost cried from relief. He flicked his tongue over my clit, eyes possessing me, *owning* every inch of me, and I gasped as my body exploded with heat. I shook against the bench. If Fabiano's hands on my hips hadn't kept me in place, I would have tumbled onto the floor in a heap. Blackness seeped into my vision as the waves of pleasure raced through me.

My limbs felt heavy and sluggish. Gradually, the throbbing between my legs started to fade. Fabiano crouched over me, eyes full of possessiveness. I breathed heavily.

"That was perfect," I managed to get out.

He shook his head. "It's only the beginning."

There it was again. That promise sounding like a threat. Where was he taking me? Down a path I'd never chosen for myself, a path farther away from the mundane life I'd imagined for myself. He kissed my throat. "And happy New Year."

New Year. I'd almost forgotten. Would this finally be a good year?

Fabiano straightened, all flexed muscles and dark hunger as he towered over me. Even the loose fighting boxers couldn't hide his arousal. I pushed myself into a sitting position, knowing what he wanted, and wanting it too … but unsure if it was wise. We'd been in the changing room for too long already. But I stopped being wise a long time ago.

I peered up at him, my eyes locked with his. I reached out and pressed my palm against the bulge in his pants. His abs flexed, but he didn't make a sound. Still so full of control. I wanted to see him give it up, wanted him to fall like I had. Both in body and heart.

Rubbing him through the thin fabric, I felt him grow even bigger. I tugged at his waistband, wanting to see him in all his naked glory.

And for the first time I didn't care how it would make me look, wanting a man. I felt lust and acted upon it. I curled my fingers around his shaft, feeling it throb. It was hard and hot and yet smooth. Marvelous. Every inch of him.

I ran my fingers up and down slowly, but Fabiano gave a thrust of his hips. I peered up at him. "Leona, I'm in no state of mind for the soft approach."

Tightening my hold, I moved faster but eventually let him take control as he closed his hand over mine and thrust his hips in rhythm with his strokes. New blood dripped from the wound over his ribs, but he didn't seem to mind. I raised my gaze from our hands moving together to his face. Hunger and need. And that gentler emotion that scared me shitless, but it scared him even more. I knew that now.

When he tensed and his release took over, I watched his face in wonder, hoping for a revelation. He looked marvelous but not unhinged. Still in control, even now.

I think I love you.

His eyes peeled open, and his emotionless mask slid over his features as we stared at each other. He took my hand and led me toward the shower.

I followed even as I said, "Fabiano, we can't."

He ignored my protest and pulled my dress up over my head then removed my underwear. "You said you needed a shower."

I gave up on protesting and slipped under the warm stream with him. His hands slid over my slick skin and his lips found mine. Blood tinged the ground pink. He peered down at me as the water plastered his hair against his head.

"Do you still think I want to degrade you?"

I flushed, wanting to forget my words from that night. He had given me pleasure with his mouth, but it was different. "No," I said quietly.

"Good." And then his lips were back on mine, and I let him pull me out of reality as his warmth surrounded me. I placed my palm over his heart, feeling it beat. I wanted it to beat only for me. His fingers curled around my hand, and he pulled it away—away from his heart—and raised it to his lips for a kiss. I pressed my forehead against his shoulder.

This was enough.

SEVENTEEN

Leona

WHEN A KNOCK SOUNDED AT MY DOOR, I STIFLED A SIGH. I HAD TO leave for work in a few minutes and had no time for a talk to my father. Mom had moved in with us two days ago, so our already strained relationship took a nosedive toward worse. He only wanted money from me anyway. That was the only reason he even let me and Mom stay with him. I didn't have much money left. I'd given almost all of my savings to my mother, so she could pay part of her debt to the Camorra. And it still wasn't enough, which was why she was out on the street selling her body again.

I begrudgingly opened the door.

Dad was deathly pale, sweat coating his forehead.

"What's wrong?" I asked, even though I had a sinking feeling that I knew. It was always the same thing.

"I'm in trouble, Leona."

"You always are," I said, reaching for my backpack, ready to leave, but Dad gripped my arm. "Leona, please. They will kill me. He will."

I froze. "Why would they do that?"

"I owe too much. I can't pay them. I'm a dead man if you don't help me, Leo, please."

He used to call me Leo when I was a little girl, when he was occasionally a decent father.

He's not your business. That's what Fabiano had told me, and after these last few days of my father treating my mother like shit, I started to agree with him.

"How much do you owe them?"

"I don't know. Two thousand? I don't know! I lost track."

How could he lose track? I closed my eyes for a moment. The remaining money was supposed to get me into college, buy me a future, and again my father ruined it. I turned and took the money from its hiding place beneath the carpet and held it out to my father. He didn't take it.

"I can't bring them the money. They will kill me before I have a chance to hand it over. Leona, you must go for me."

I could go to Fabiano and give him the money, but he wouldn't take it. He would gladly kill my father. He had done enough for me already. "Where do I need to bring it?"

"It's called the Sugar Trap. That's where Falcone and his Enforcers hang around most days." He gave me the address then clutched my hand. "You have to hurry. Perhaps they already sent someone out for me."

I grabbed my backpack and headed for this Sugar Trap, wherever that was. I wasn't just handing over my hard-earned money for him, I was also going to be late for work. If Roger threw me out, I was screwed. I doubted I'd get a job on the Strip or anywhere else any time soon. We needed every cent I earned, with both my mother and father in Vegas.

When the red and yellow neon sign of the Sugar Trap caught my eye, I halted. The word was wedged between two open legs wearing high heels. The windows were tinted black so you couldn't look inside. I knew what kind of place this was, and it wasn't a place I ever wanted to set foot in.

There was a ginormous black man guarding the door. I approached him slowly. He didn't budge.

"I'm here to see Remo Falcone." Even as I said it, I realized how foolish I must have sounded. Remo Falcone was the Capo of the Camorra. He owned everything that mattered … if Fabiano was to be believed. Why on Earth would he waste his time with me?

The bouncer seemed to think the same because he snorted. "Mr. Falcone doesn't choose the girls who work here. Go away."

Choose the girls? "I'm not here to work," I said indignantly. "I'm here because I have money for him."

The man tilted his head to the side but still didn't let me pass. I tried to catch a glimpse at his watch to see how late I was for work. I pulled the money from my backpack and held it out to the bouncer. He reached for it, but I snatched it back. I didn't trust him to hand it over to Falcone. "Go away," he muttered.

"Let her through," came a cold drawl from behind me. I whirled around to look up at a tall man. Nino Falcone. He nodded for me to step into the gloomy light of the Sugar Trap. And I did, because *really* no one could refuse those cold eyes.

"Straight ahead," he said. I kept walking, even though having him behind me gave me the creeps.

The corridor opened up to a bar area of red velvet and black lacquer. There were poles and booths with velvet curtains and several doors that branched off the main room.

"Go ahead. First door on the right."

I peered at him over my shoulder. He walked two steps behind me, watching me with those cold, unreadable eyes. I showed him the money. "Perhaps you can give your brother the money. It's from my father. His name is Greg Hall."

"I know who he is," Nino Falcone said with absolutely no hint of emotion in his eyes. "Go ahead."

I shivered and moved toward the door he indicated. I pushed down the handle and stepped through into another long corridor with black walls and a red carpet. I kept walking to the end, where another door waited. The hairs on my neck rose at the proximity of Nino Falcone and at his quiet scrutiny.

"Let me," he drawled and stepped past me to open that door. He entered a long room without windows. There was a desk on the left side that looked untouched. To the left was a heavy bag and some couches. Remo sat on one of them, laptop on his lap. His eyes moved up when his brother entered. Then they slid over to me, and I knew it had been a huge mistake to come here. The man, Soto, who had attacked my father, stood off to the side as if he were reporting to his Capo.

Remo Falcone put aside his laptop and rose from the sofa. Where Fabiano was grace and control, this man was unhinged power and barely contained aggression. My fingers crumpled the money.

"She's here to pay her father's debts," Nino said. I wasn't sure he was talking about money.

"Is she now?" Remo asked curiously. He came around the sofa, closer to me, and I wished he didn't. A smile curled his lips, and I took a step back, but Nino's arm stopped my movement. He wasn't looking at me, only at his brother. Some silent understanding passed between them I wasn't in on. "I'll let you handle it, then. I'll be back later," Nino said and just left, closing the door in my face.

I stood there, feeling small and shaking but trying to look determined and strong. My eyes flitted over to where Remo propped his hip against the backrest of the sofa. Soto, behind him, had something eager and gleeful in his expression.

I held up the money uncertainly. "I have the money my father owes you."

Remo regarded me with unsettling intensity. "I doubt that."

I frowned. He couldn't possibly see how much money I held in my hands. It was a bundle of ten and twenty dollar notes. "It's one thousand dollars."

"One thousand?" Remo asked with a laugh. "How much do you think he owes us?"

I shivered. My eyes darted to Soto again then back to Remo.

I licked my lips nervously. "He said a couple of thousand."

Remo shook his head once and pushed away from the sofa. He came closer, and I fought the urge to run. There was no way I could have outrun him anyway. He scared me more than anything ever had, and *I* had been stupid enough to face him because my father couldn't get a grip on his addiction.

"Ten thousand, and that's without interest. In total he owes us close to fourteen thousand."

My stomach plummeted. "Four thousand in interest?" I gasped. "That's usury!"

"We're the mob, Leona," Remo Falcone said, amused. He knew my name? Had Fabiano talked to him about me? *Because of my mother.*

"Every day he doesn't pay us, another five hundred of interest gets added on top."

I couldn't believe it. My father must have known he owed much more than just a couple of thousands. Did he set me up? "But ... but I don't have that much, and there's no way I can earn enough money unless you stop adding interest."

Remo shook his head. "This isn't a negotiation, girl. Your father owes us money, and perhaps you forgot, but your mother does too. Your father was supposed to pay at midnight yesterday. He didn't." By now, Remo was only two steps away from me, and it set my body into flight mode.

"I have this." I held up my wrist with the bracelet Fabiano had given me for Christmas. Guilt filled me. How could I even consider giving his present away?

Something in Remo's eyes shifted, and he bridged the remaining distance between us. I bumped against the door, trying to evade him, but he gripped my arm tightly and regarded the bracelet. A fire simmered in his eyes when he looked up at me. "That would settle your father's debt. An expensive piece of jewelry for someone like you."

It would settle fourteen thousand dollars? I stared down at the bracelet. Remo released my wrist. His lips twisted cruelly. "Sadly, it's too late. Your father will pay his debt in blood."

"Please," I begged. "He won't ever owe you money again."

"Are you willing to swear on it?" Remo hissed.

I knew how much an oath meant to the Camorra. And I knew it would have been a lie. I averted my eyes from Remo's cruel ones. "Please. There has to be something I can do. Don't kill him."

Remo tilted his head. My begging did nothing. "It's not me who will kill him. It's Fabiano, but you must know that …" His voice was low and threatening.

"Isn't there something I can do?" I whispered desperately. Something flickered in his dark eyes. God, I wanted to swallow every syllable I'd just uttered. What did I say? My father sent me here to pay for his debts and I was risking my life for him.

For a long time, Remo didn't say anything.

I gave a jerky nod. "Okay. I'll just go."

Remo put a hand on the door. I sucked in a breath and backed away from him. I fumbled for my cell phone. Maybe Fabiano could help me. I didn't get far. Remo took it from my hand and glanced down at it.

"Just let me leave."

He shut off my cell with a thunderous expression. "It's too late for that, I fear." He nodded toward Soto, who came our way at once. "I think we need to set an example."

Soto gripped my arm. The excited gleam in his expression made terror soar through my veins. "The basement?" he asked with barely hidden eagerness.

Bile traveled up my throat. Remo gave a nod, his eyes slipping down to my bracelet again, recognition filling his eyes like he'd seen it before. "And, Soto, you'll wait until I give you an order before you begin. If you lay a finger on her before, I'll cut it off."

Soto pulled me down a flight of stairs and into a small room with only a mattress in one corner and a chair in the other.

"I can't wait to start, bitch. Fabiano will be fucking furious," Soto muttered then let go of me. I stumbled back against the wall. There was no escaping him.

I wasn't sure how much time passed as he undressed me with his eyes, but a low buzzing sound made me jump. Soto pulled out his mobile. Then he looked back at me with a leer. "Time to play."

EIGHTEEN

Fabiano

I CURSED WHEN GRIFFIN HANDED ME THE LIST OF PEOPLE WHO HADN'T paid their betting debts. Greg Hall. This time he owed more than he'd be able to pay back. He was third on the list. Leona would hopefully be gone by the time I paid him a visit.

Why did this fucker have to borrow money from us?

When it was finally his turn, I parked at the curb, pissed off. I got out, but the purr of my engine had caught Hall's attention.

He spotted me through the windows. He'd probably been watching the street all day. He knew the rules. He knew the consequences. This wasn't his first time, after all. But today he'd suffer more than a few broken bones. His life would end today.

He disappeared from view, probably trying to escape. As if that was going to happen. I jogged around the building and saw him rushing out of the back door of the apartment complex. Sighing, I ran after him. His legs were shorter, and he was too out of shape to evade me.

When I caught up with him, I grabbed him by the cuff of his stupid Hawaii shirt and slammed him to the ground. He cried out as he landed hard on his back, bloodshot eyes staring up at me with trepidation. The impact already made him cry out like a pussy, so I'd have to stuff his mouth with something or else he'd alert the entire neighborhood with his screaming. I punched him hard in the ribs, making him gasp for breath. That would silence him for a while. Then I dragged him after me, hearing his desperate attempts to speak past the lack of oxygen in his lungs. "Don't. Please," he managed when we reached the apartment door.

I ignored him. If I stopped whenever someone begged me, the Camorra would have no money. And a big part of me was looking forward to torturing him for his behavior toward Leona. He caused her nothing but trouble, and he would continue to do so.

I shoved him into the apartment that he hadn't bothered locking when he ran from me. He hit the ground, and I pulled my knife. Perhaps I'd finish my work on his back first.

His eyes zeroed in on the blade in terror. "I sent Leona to settle my debt! You don't have to do this."

I froze. "What did you just say?" I stalked toward him. If he'd agreed to let his daughter handle this, he was the worst scum on Earth. He nodded and disgust washed over me. I really wanted to plunge my knife into his cowardly eyes.

"I sent Leona—"

I crouched over him, lifting him by his collar. "Where did you send her?"

"To Falcone."

I thrust my fist into his face, breaking his nose and jaw. I would have beaten him to death if I thought there was time. If Leona was on her way to Remo, I couldn't waste a single second. "Where exactly?" Leona wouldn't walk into Remo's mansion after all.

"I told her to go to the Sugar Trap," he got out, blood dripping out of his mouth. I punched him again then jumped to my feet and gripped his collar. I dragged him toward my car.

"I told you I sent Leona! My debt will be settled!"

"Shut up!" I snarled.

I knew how much he owed us, and he knew it too. There was no way Leona had enough money.

The Sugar Trap was the worst place to send her, and I suspected he knew that. He sacrificed his own daughter to save his sorry ass. I opened the trunk and flung him inside, glaring at his terrified face in disgust as I closed it.

I raced down the Strip, only slowing when I came closer to the Sugar Trap, one of our whorehouses and the place where Remo dealt with women who gave the Camorra trouble. It wouldn't do any good if someone saw me hurrying. Remo would wonder why and put things together. Perhaps he had already.

I parked in my usual spot. Remo's Aston Martin was already parked in front and so was Soto's Buick. I hauled Leona's father out of the trunk then dragged him after me as I stalked past the guard without a greeting and crossed the public part of the whorehouse, to the back wing. He kept pleading and groveling. I found Remo in his office, as usual, not behind his desk but on the sofa, browsing through a car magazine. He didn't look up when I stepped in, but he knew it was me. He was waiting for me. I'd known him for years and knew the games he played. I'd been one of his best players for a long time. It took all of my self-control not to ask him about Leona right away. I needed to play this right or it would all be in vain.

"You're done early," he said, and when he met my gaze, there was something snake-like in his expression. I shoved Leona's father to the ground. He landed hard, his fucking beady eyes darting between Remo and me.

"The asshole told me he sent his daughter to handle his debt. I needed to check with you before I proceeded with him."

"Of course," Remo said with a cold smile. He didn't look at Hall. This was about me, about us. "It's the third time Hall is behind. His daughter offered to pay his debt."

I knew all that and didn't give a fuck. All I cared about was Leona not getting hurt.

"So you took her money?"

"I didn't ask her for money. She wouldn't be able to pay that much. But she was determined to save her father."

"Where is she?" I asked carefully. Every muscle in my body was tense because I knew if something happened to Leona, I'd fucking lose it.

"She's in the basement. Paying his debt the only way she can."

My blood ran cold. "Soto?" was all I managed.

Remo nodded but his eyes bored into my skull. "He went down with her a couple of minutes ago."

Two minutes. I didn't have much time. Leona didn't have much time. "I'm your enforcer. Let me handle her."

Remo came up to me, steps slow and measured. And for the first time, I tried to imagine what I'd have to do to beat him, to kill him. He was like my brother, and I hated that it had gotten this far. "You never deal with women. You asked me to let Soto handle that part of the business, and I granted you your wish, Fabiano."

He was right. He never understood, but because I was like his brother he accepted my reluctance. And Remo wasn't the accepting type.

"It's different with her," I said, letting my desire show but not my protectiveness. If Remo thought this was anything but fun for me, nothing would save Leona.

Her father was still crouched on the floor, and I made a silent vow to let him suffer before I granted him death.

"I don't think you handling her will have the desired effect," Remo said. "You have been seeing her for weeks. You fucking her in my dungeon won't really send a message."

"I haven't fucked her yet. She refused me."

"Refused you?" Remo asked, as if the word meant nothing to him. His eyes became calculating. "And you let her?"

Oh, Leona, I hope you are worth it. Remo was on the hunt.

I didn't say anything. I had a feeling it would make things worse. "Let me handle her," I said calmly. I put my hand on his shoulder, and that he let it happen gave me hope. Still like brothers. "You won't regret it."

"I know I won't," he said. "But perhaps you will." He paused. "Then handle her, Fabiano." I was about to turn around and storm into the cellar to get Leona, but his hand clamped down on my forearm. He turned it so the tattoo of the Camorra was facing up. "You are my enforcer, Fabiano. You have been at my side since the beginning. You never disappoint me. Don't start now."

"And I won't," I said fiercely. "I will take care of her."

Remo gave me a warning look. "Don't disappoint me, Fabiano. She is just one woman. Remember where your loyalties lie."

I barely listened. I hurried out of the room and down the stairs. I knew I had to make it there before Soto sank his claws in her. I took the stairs two at a time. I couldn't be late.

I knew where to go. Soto always chose the same room. I didn't bother knocking. Instead, I pushed open the door to our interrogation room. "I can't wait to have you suck my cock," Soto drawled. "Fucking choice be damned."

Leona was pressed up against the wall, looking terrified, while Soto was pulling down his pants, revealing his hairy ass. Terror filled Leona's beautiful face, and for a moment I considered putting a knife in Soto's back.

"Get out," I snarled. "I'm taking over."

Soto whirled around, showing me his pitiful cock. He gave me a stunned look. "I thought you didn't like to handle women," he said mockingly. "That's why Remo gave me the job."

"I changed my mind," I growled. "Now get out before I lose my patience."

Soto shot Leona another hungry look, but then he pulled up his pants and stalked past me, muttering curses.

The door slammed shut. I knew the camera was pointed at us, recording everything. Perhaps Remo was watching. This had nothing to do with Greg Hall and everything to do with me. Remo was testing me. Remo trusted me as much as a man like him could trust anyone, like he trusted his brothers, and now he felt the need to test me.

A small part of me felt fury toward Leona for being the reason for it.

Remo had never doubted me. *Never*. And I had sworn with my own blood to never give him reason to.

Leona pushed away from the wall, looking confused and hopeful and scared all at once. "Oh, Fabiano," she whispered, relieved. "I'm so glad you came. I was so scared."

I didn't go over to her.

I wasn't the savior she'd hoped for. She took another step in my direction then stopped, looking at me with fucking hopeful eyes. Slowly, the hope disappeared. "Fabiano?" she asked in the barest whisper.

I shut off my fucking useless feelings. I would be dead without Remo. Everything I was today was thanks to him. He saved me. I couldn't try to kill him, not even for Leona. And trying would be all it was. Remo was as strong as me, and he still had his brothers at his side.

I stalked toward Leona, and for the first time she backed off. When her back hit the wall, I was in front of her. I pressed my body against hers, caging her in, and sank my nose into her hair. The camera would make it look like I was cornering her. Her sweet flowery scent reached my nose.

"Fabiano?" she murmured. Hesitantly, she put her hands on my waist as if she wasn't sure if she should hug me. That would have been the end of everything. Fuck, but I wanted to wrap my arms around her.

Fuck me. Fuck us.

"I told you I'm not good," I said quietly.

She peered up into my eyes, and I knew what she would see, exactly what I needed her to see to be convincing. Leona started trembling against me, fear eating away at what little hope was left. I pulled her arms away from my waist, grabbed her wrists, and pinned them on top her head resting against the wall. I cornered her with my body, and she allowed it. She let out a choked whimper, a confused expression on her face. She should have fought by now. This brokenhearted surrender was something I couldn't handle. There was still that stupid fucking hope there. It was worse than begging and crying. Worse than anything had ever been ... because it meant she still believed there was more to me than the coldhearted killer.

Perhaps she still didn't understand what I was supposed to do to her.

I pressed my lips against her ear. "I can't spare you. We're being watched. If I don't do it, Soto will ... and I can't allow that."

Fear widened her eyes as she stared up at me. "Because you don't share, right?" she whispered miserably.

I wished it were only that. "Because Soto will *break* you."

"And you won't?"

We'd been talking for too long already. Every second that passed could seal both our fates.

"As a woman, you are granted a choice, unlike men. You can pay with your blood as a man would have to or with your body," I said sharply. I'd only spoken those damn words once before and never again after that. Remo had handed over the task to Soto because I couldn't fucking do it. He allowed me that one fucking weakness.

She raised her chin, and I knew she considered choosing the first option because she'd rather suffer through pain than become like her mother. Damn it. "Leona," I whispered, leaning into her again, surprised by the despair in my voice. Careful, Fabiano.

You are my enforcer.

"Number two. I can fake that one, but not the other."

Confusion filled her face.

"Choose the second option," I murmured again.

"Two," she said, resigned but still not understanding what I had offered.

She started crying softly. I watched the tears make their silent descent over her soft freckles. Her eyes held mine, and then just like that, she nodded. "Do what you have to do."

I'd wanted her from the first second I'd laid eyes on her, had wanted to be the one to rip her innocence from her, wanted to possess her in every way possible. But not like this, not in front of a fucking camera, not hard and fast and brutally as Remo expected. Was she worth the risk?

The Camorra was my family. My life.

In my darkest hour, Remo had been there to pick me up. He had showed me my worth. He could have killed me. He was a monster, but so was I.

Leona held my gaze. And I made my own decision. Fuck it. "I'll try not to hurt you. Fight me and cry. It has to look real," I whispered harshly.

Confusion filled her eyes.

I shook her wrists and tightened my hold. "Play your part or we are both dead."

I gave her a warning look then gripped her hips and threw her down on the mattress in the corner. She let out a terrified scream that bounced off the walls. I didn't give her time to recover. This needed to be convincing. I hoped the long wait in the beginning hadn't raised Remo's suspicions, because I knew he was watching. I climbed on top off her, pinning her down with my taller body. My mouth was back on her ear. "Trust me. Because from now on, I'll have to look the monster I am with everyone else. Now fight me with all you have."

I didn't wait for her reply because it didn't matter if she agreed or not. We were past that point. I grabbed her wrists in one hand and began pushing them up when Leona finally sprang into action.

She screamed, "No," and fought against my hold, her hips bucking, legs kicking, but it was no use. I shoved her wrists hard against the floor. She gasped in pain. Damn it. Playing rough was difficult without *actually hurting* someone. I loosened my hold, knowing it wouldn't be noticeable on camera. I squeezed her breasts through her dress then moved lower and pushed my hand below her skirt. I was glad she'd allowed me to touch and see her before so this wouldn't be her first experience.

"No, please don't! Please!" she cried, so convincing that something ugly and heavy settled in my stomach. This was why Soto had been responsible for that part of the job.

"Shut up, you whore!" I snarled.

Hurt settled in her eyes. I breathed heavily. I could not take my eyes off her face, off those cornflower blue eyes, off those damn freckles. She held my gaze and I hers. One second. Two seconds. I couldn't do this, not even pretending. I felt fucking sick to my stomach. Fuck. I'd cut men into tiny pieces, had done so many horrible things that had never bothered me, but this … this I could not do. Not for real. Not for show. Never.

I let go of her wrists. Her brows furrowed. I lowered my head until my forehead rested against hers, and she released a small breath then lifted her hand and touched my cheek.

I wasn't sure how much of it the camera recorded. I didn't care.

"Fabiano?"

I wasn't sure if I could save her, save us, after this. I pulled away and straightened before I helped her to her feet. She clutched my arm, still shaking.

"What's going to happen now?" she whispered.

Remo wanted blood. He wanted confirmation that I was his soldier, that I was capable of doing what had to be done. He wanted to see my monster. And he would.

Leona would hate me for it.

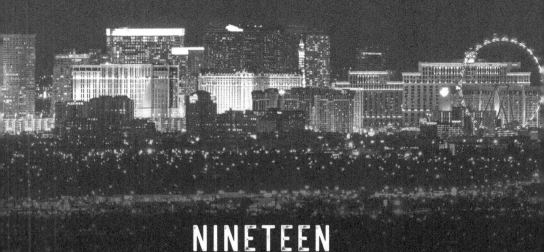

NINETEEN

Fabiano

WE HEADED UPSTAIRS. REMO WAS WAITING FOR US. NINO WAS THERE too, and at his feet cowered Leona's father, tape over his mouth but still very much alive. Leona stiffened, but my grip on her arm kept her at my side. I wasn't sure if she'd try to run toward him otherwise.

Remo regarded Leona from head to toe. He knew, had known before he laid eyes on her. Leona trembled against me.

That Nino was here told me two things: one, Remo thought he needed re-inforcement and that reinforcement wasn't going to be me and two, that reinforcement wasn't going to be me because he thought he needed reinforcement *against me.*

I released Leona but gave her a look that made it clear she needed to stay where she was. She understood.

I walked toward Remo. He didn't rise from where he was perched on the desk, but the look he gave me was one he only ever leveled at his opponents in the cage.

"So," he said tightly, "you didn't handle her."

"I didn't handle her because he is the one I should handle." I nodded toward her father. "Since when do we let out debtors get away with this shit? Since when do we let their daughters or wives pay for their crimes? Since when, Remo?" I was very close to him now, and finally he stood, bringing us to eyelevel.

"Since the moment I decided she was going to pay for her father. My word is the law."

"It is the law," I confirmed fiercely. "Because you are Capo. *My Capo,* and I've always followed your command, because you taught me the true meaning of honor and loyalty and pride." I took another step toward him so we were almost touching. "But there's nothing honorable about making an innocent woman pay for her father's debts, Remo."

His dark eyes pierced mine. I knew Nino was watching, probably with a hand on his gun. "We don't spare women."

"No, we don't spare women who are indebted to us, because they brought it upon themselves. They knew what they were getting themselves into when they asked for money. But this is different and you know it. I don't know why you feel the need to test my loyalty like that, but I ask you to reconsider. There's no reason for you to doubt me. Leona is only one woman. She means nothing to me. You are like my brother."

"Are you sure about that?" he asked in a low murmur. "Because when you look at her, she isn't just one woman."

My chest constricted. "I'm loyal to you, to the Camorra, to our cause."

"Someone will have to bleed for this," he said, and he settled back on the desk. Relief washed over me.

"And I will make *him* bleed for you."

"I know you will," he said quietly, challengingly.

I turned to her father. His eyes widened then darted over to Leona. She stood frozen. I wanted her to leave, but that wasn't what Remo wanted, and I couldn't ask for more than he'd already given. I nodded at Nino, and he understood. He moved to Leona, who took a step back. When his fingers closed around her upper arm to keep her from interfering, it took all my willpower not to snarl at him.

I prowled toward her father, who tried to scramble back but hit the couch. I yanked the tape off his mouth, and he cried out in pain.

"Fabiano, please," Leona begged.

It was either her father or her. Someone had to pay.

"When you sent your daughter to Remo to pay your debt, did you know what would happen to her? Did you know that she would bleed for you?"

His eyes darted to Leona again, looking for help.

I grabbed him by the shirt and hauled him up. "Did you know what would happen to Leona?"

"Yes!" he cried.

"And you didn't care?"

"I didn't want to die!"

"So you sent her so she could bleed and die for you?"

He gaped at me. *Oh, I would make him bleed.*

And I would enjoy every second of it. I didn't risk a look at Leona. Maybe someday she could forgive me. But I didn't think she'd ever look at me the same again. Not after what I had to do now. After what I *wanted* to do.

I extracted my knife. Her father tried to run, but I shoved him down and climbed on top of him. He struggled and I punched him. His head snapped back, but I needed to be careful not to knock him out. That just wouldn't do.

Remo's legs appeared beside me, and then he held down Hall. He gave me his twisted grin, and I felt my own lips curl. We would do this together. Together like in the beginning. I brought my knife down, and when the tip of the blade slid into Hall's stomach, parting flesh and muscle, everything else faded to black.

Remo and I did what we did best.

I wasn't sure if I'd been a monster before him, if I'd always had it in me and he only awakened that part, or if he turned me into one. It didn't matter.

When Hall's cries died and his heart stopped beating, I came back to myself. Remo and I knelt on the ground beside the body, in its blood. My hands were covered in it, and so was the knife still clutched in my hand.

Remo leaned forward, voice calm. "That's what you really are. What we both are. Do you think she can accept it?"

I didn't say anything. I was fucking scared to face Leona, to see the disgust and terror in her expression.

Remo nodded. "That's what I thought. She will leave. They all do. She's not worth the trouble. People like us are always alone." He touched my shoulder. "We are brothers."

"We are," I confirmed then finally dared to glance back at her. Leona and Nino were gone. I jerked to my feet, knife clattering to the ground.

"Where is she?"

"Nino dragged her out when she threw up because things got too rough."

I stared at the spot where she had been.

"Go clean up," Remo said. "I'll have Nino drop the body somewhere it will be found quickly."

I nodded but didn't move.

"And, Fabiano…" Remo waited until I met his gaze "…I let you refuse my order once. I let you spare her once. Remember your oath. The Camorra is our family."

I nodded again then went to change clothes before I went to search for Leona. I found her in the main room of the Sugar Trap, perched on a barstool at the bar, clutching a glass filled with a dark liquid in her hands. Nino leaned against the counter like a sentinel. She kept staring at her hands when I stopped beside her. Nino left without a word.

I reached for the glass, and she flinched away from me. There it was. Finally she reacted to my closeness the way she should have. And I fucking hated it. I took the glass and downed the burning liquid. Brandy.

"I thought you didn't drink," I said quietly.

She raised those cornflower blue eyes to me. Against her deathly pale skin, her freckles stood out even more. "Today is a good day to start, I think." She swallowed, lowering her gaze as if she couldn't bear looking at me. She was still in shock.

"No, it's not. Don't let it happen."

"Let what happen?" she echoed.

"Don't let my darkness drag you down."

Those fucking blue eyes filled with tears. I curled my hand around her wrist, ignoring her shiver, and tugged lightly. "Come on, Leona. We should leave."

For a long time, her eyes rested on my fingers. Then she finally slipped off the stool and followed.

I was a hypocrite because even as I'd warned her about my darkness, I knew I would never let her go.

Leona

My hands shook as I wedged them between my legs. Fabiano was silent beside me as he steered his Mercedes through traffic. He was clean now.

His fingers, his hands, his clothes.

The blood was gone.

My father's blood.

A new wave of sickness washed over me, but there was nothing left in my stomach.

Things had taken a turn for the worse that I hadn't expected.

You didn't choose your family. That was what people always said. And it didn't have to define who you became, but my mother and father had managed to steer me so far off the path I planned for myself, I wasn't sure I'd ever find my way back.

And now my father was dead. Killed by the man I loved.

God help me, I still loved him.

Still?

Still. After what I'd seen, after what he'd done.

And that was the worst. I could still feel something for him after I saw what he truly was. A monster.

My father was a horrible human being—had been a horrible human being.

He drove my mother to selling her body, even offered my body to Soto for his debts, and he pretty much admitted he'd let me die just so he could live. Perhaps he'd deserved death, but he didn't deserve what happened today. Nobody did.

I closed my eyes against the images of Fabiano with the knife, of the twisted look he shared with Remo. They had done this before. They *enjoyed* it.

Nino dragged me away after Fabiano began cutting my father. But the screams followed us until they were no more. I was relieved because it was over. Over for my father and over for my mother and me. No more betting debts or drunken fits. And that realization shattered me completely. I didn't miss my own father.

He set me up. I knew he was scared of the Camorra, but so was I.

Fabiano killed him.

My eyes shifted to the man beside me. His gaze was focused on the road ahead. In the past few weeks, we'd gotten to know each other—or I thought I'd gotten to know him, thought we'd built a connection. Now I wasn't sure that was real anymore.

Enforcer. The word held no meaning for me until now. I shuddered when I remembered the basement. How much horrors had those walls seen? And for how many of them was Fabiano responsible? How many people had he killed? Had he made bleed?

So much blood on his hands.

I pushed the thought aside. It led down a dark path I couldn't stomach right now. I had already dug myself into a deep hole I couldn't possibly ever get out of. Could I really love someone like him? And could someone like him *love* at all?

Love is a sickness, a weakness.

Leona is only one woman. She means nothing to me.

Those words had threatened to break me, but then Remo had said, "*Are you sure about that? Because when you look at her she isn't just one woman.*"

And those words still haunted me, after everything. Tears prickled my eyes. Fabiano was a murderer.

He did it for me, so he didn't have to hurt me. He protected me. And part of me was consoled by that fact. What did that say about me?

I closed my eyes again. I had to end this, had to leave. I couldn't stay, even though I loved him, or maybe I had to leave because I did. I had to break this twisted bond, had to do it as long as the memories of today were still fresh.

"Where are you taking me?" I asked as I realized we were heading to the better parts of Vegas.

"To my apartment."

I stared blankly. Did he really think I'd spend the night in the same bed with him after what he did today?

You want his closeness.

Still.

After everything.

Fear filled my veins. Not of him. I pushed through it, let it feed my next words. "Have you lost your mind? I'm not going home with you after what you did."

Fabiano jerked the car to the side and hit the brakes, making me gasp from the impact of the belt. I didn't get the chance to catch my breath. He wasn't strapped in so he leaned over me, eyes furious. "Don't you realize in what kind of trouble we are? I went against Remo's orders for you. I showed weakness. He will watch my every move now. He will watch us."

"You killed my father."

"I did, so I wouldn't have to hurt you, so Remo didn't feel the need to hurt you."

"Maybe I would have preferred if you let him hurt me."

Fabiano laughed darkly, blue eyes searching my face. "You can't still believe that after today. Remo has made grown men beg for mercy, for death even."

"So have you," I whispered. "You and him, you are the same. You both enjoyed this. I saw it in your eyes." I swallowed hard.

His eyes flickered with emotion and my heart broke seeing it. "You don't even realize what I'm risking for you. You made me go against everything I ever cared about."

Everything I ever cared about.

Cared. Past tense. As in not anymore?

Deep down, I knew the answer, and it terrified me because if he felt what I felt ... if he was capable of it, leaving him would destroy not only me.

"You should just have let Soto have his way with me."

His expression was blank. He was too good at this. Too good at all things dark and dangerous. "Perhaps I should have," he said simply. "It would have spared me a lot of trouble." He twisted a strand of my hair around his finger with a strange expression on his face. "After all, who says you are worth it?"

His words didn't hurt me because I'd seen the look in his eyes down in the basement—even if I hadn't dared believe it. Remo confirmed it wasn't my imagination.

Fabiano needed to push me way. And I knew I needed to let him so I could do what had to be done. "Don't pretend you acted out of the goodness of your heart. You saved me because you wanted to be the first one *to fuck* me."

The word left a bitter taste in my mouth, but it got a reaction from Fabiano. His lips curled into a cold smile. "You are right. I will be the first to fuck you." "Not if I have a say in the matter."

He let out a joyless laugh before he pulled the car back onto the street.

"You are a monster," I said harshly.

"I know."

Fifteen minutes later, we entered the underground parking garage. He was really taking me to his apartment. Fabiano opened the car door and held out his hand for me. I stared at it then up at his face. "Come on, Leona," he said quietly. "Don't make me carry you."

I took his hand and let him pull me to my feet. He didn't let go of me as he tugged me along toward the elevator that would take us up to his apartment.

Once we were inside the elevator, my emotions began to bubble over. Anger and terror and sadness and everything in between. "Why did you have to choose me?" I asked miserably. And *why, why, why* had my heart chosen him?

He didn't say anything, only gave me that impenetrable look. The elevator doors slid open, and he guided me into his apartment. He pulled me against his chest and kissed me fiercely, and for a second I kissed him back, kissed him with every twisted, horrid part of me that loved him.

My palms came up against his chest. "No," I said firmly and tore away from him. My pulse raced in my veins. Fabiano came around, never allowing me to pull away. Why couldn't he just let me be?

"You know," he said quietly. "I never meant for any of this to happen. You were just a poor, lonely girl. I didn't choose this, didn't choose you."

"Then stop this. Whatever it is between us, stop it. Now," I whispered, peering up at his cold, beautiful face.

He cupped my face. "Don't you think I would if I could?" His lips brushed mine. "But I can't. I won't. You are mine, and I will protect you no matter the price."

"Protect me?" I echoed.

Fabiano was a destroyer, not a protector. He was no knight in shining armor. "And who will protect me from you?"

"You don't need protection from me. Today should have proven that."

"Today proved that you have done horrendous crimes in your past and that you are still committing atrocious acts every day … and that you enjoy doing them."

"Leona," he said darkly. "I never lied to you. I am the Camorra's enforcer. I am pain and death. I never pretended to be anything else. Don't pretend you were ignorant to make yourself feel better."

I lowered my gaze, feeling guilty and furious because he was right.

Death. Blood. Pain.

That was what being with Fabiano meant.

And love.

I couldn't get one without the other.

That wasn't the life I'd imagined. And did he love me? Whatever he felt, whatever I had seen, whatever Remo had seen ... it wasn't love.

"Come on," Fabiano said, tugging me toward the stairs. "Let's talk in the morning. You've gone through a lot today."

What was there left to talk about in the morning? Yet I still followed.

I took a shower and Fabiano didn't join me. Perhaps he finally understood that his closeness was too much right now. I put on the T-shirt he'd laid out for me then walked into the bedroom.

Fabiano was already in bed, the covers pulled up to his waist, revealing his chest. Falling asleep against his chest had been the best thing about being with him these last few weeks. One last time, I promised myself. I slipped under the covers with him and rested my cheek against his chest, right over his heart. It beat a calm rhythm. If today's events didn't increase his heart rate, what could? His fingers stroked my upper arm, and I ran my fingertips over all the scars on his chest and stomach.

"This can't end well. It will get us killed, you know that."

Fabiano pulled me on top of his body. "Do you think I'd ever allow it? I will do anything to protect you."

"Even kill Remo?"

He grew tense. "Remo is like my brother. If he goes down, so will I."

I searched his eyes. He was serious. "You could leave Las Vegas. Start somewhere new."

Leona, stop this. End this.

He shook his head like I couldn't understand. "The Camorra is in my blood."

Blood. Screams.

I glanced at the tattoo on his forearm. The Camorra was the love of his life. Nothing could compete with that, least of all me. "Blood," I murmured.

Fabiano's eyes were like a stormy summer sky. "I will handle Remo. Don't worry about it. Now that your father is gone, things will settle down. You can continue with your life."

Gone.

Killed. Murdered. Tortured.

"Do you really believe that?" I asked. What life was I supposed to continue?

Fabiano

The look she gave me now was the one I'd expected in the beginning. It was a look I hated seeing now. I was risking my reputation, my life, and Remo's trust for her. All for her.

I kissed Leona hard. For a moment she froze, then she returned the kiss with the same force.

Deepening it, my hands moved down on her hips, and I rolled us over, stretching out over her. I supported my weight with my elbows as I kissed her harder. She returned the kiss with just as much need. I slid my hand under her shirt, my fingers trailing over her smooth thigh. I wanted her, never wanted anything as much in my life. She pulled away from my mouth, growing tense beneath me. "No, Fabiano," she got out from under me. "I can't do this now, not after everything that has happened."

I sucked in a deep breath. Who said there would be another chance for us? My cock was so hard it threatened to tear through my boxers. I had half a mind of ignoring her plea and just keep going. I could imagine how tight and warm she'd be, how her channel would squeeze down on my cock. Fuck. I wanted her. I wanted to have her before I faced Remo tomorrow, before I risked my life *again*. What if he changed his mind?

Her blue eyes met mine. I hated that the trusting innocence was gone from them, hated that I was the reason for it.

Fuck. What had I become?

I pressed my forehead against hers, breathing in deeply. "You'll be the end of me, Leona."

She didn't say anything. I rolled away, because staying between her legs gave me ideas I didn't need. I pulled her into my arms, and she didn't resist.

She held me just as tightly. "I won't," she murmured sleepily.

"Won't?"

"Be the end of you."

Her body went slack. I propped myself up on my elbow, trailing my fingertips over her throat, watching her sleep. I was glad she finally drifted off, glad her eyes weren't looking at me with that broken expression anymore.

She didn't understand what I'd risked for her today. She couldn't possibly understand.

I would do it again, would save her again, even if it meant risking Remo's wrath.

TWENTY

Leona

I WOKE TO SILENCE AND AN EMPTY BED. I ROLLED OVER, STARING AT THE rumpled sheets beside me. Burying my nose in the pillow, I inhaled Fabiano's familiar scent, letting it take me back to the time I was able to pretend I didn't know what he was.

Regret came over me. Last night when he'd wanted me, I should have let him. I should have allowed us that one night, that one moment to cherish. Too late now.

I allowed myself to lie in the feather soft bed for a few more minutes before I sat up, my legs dangling over the edge of the bed. Everything smelled fresh and clean, and the room was flooded with light. This was nothing like the places I'd grown up in. It almost seemed like a dream at times, Fabiano's attention, that someone like him could want me. I should have realized it wasn't meant to last. For girls like me, dreams always came with a price. The time for dreaming was over now.

I quickly gathered my clothes and got dressed, allowing myself a couple of seconds to admire the Las Vegas strip stretching out below the apartment. I felt uneasy about this luxury the first time I saw it. I'd seldom had more than a few bucks, and here I was standing in an apartment that had cost more than I'd make my whole life as a waitress. *"Beautiful things are always taken from you."* That was what my mother used to say. I hadn't wanted to believe her, even though this thing between Fabiano and me seemed too good to be true … especially in a city ruled by someone like Remo Falcone. And now her warning was true.

Once in the elevator, I closed my eyes, reliving everything that had happened since I set foot in Las Vegas. I wasn't that girl anymore. Fabiano had changed me, but I couldn't change him, and I wasn't sure I wanted to.

Fabiano. He was on his way to Remo again, on his way to do the man's bidding. I was grateful that he'd protected me—that he'd saved me—but the only reason why I needed saving was because of the one thing he gave his life to: the Camorra.

My father was responsible for his debts. My father had set me up. I knew all that. But my father, at least, had his addiction as an excuse. Fabiano, however, was in control of his own actions. He chose to be Remo's enforcer. He chose the Camorra every day. He chose darkness and violence. He chose this life. And now it was my turn to make a choice.

I could admit that I was scared of what I felt for him and had been from the start. Over the years, I watched my mother fall for one horrible guy after the other, dragging her deeper and deeper into her drug addiction. Everything had started with her first bad choice: my father, who had turned her into a whore.

Fabiano was a man people always warned me about, and yet I couldn't stay away from him. His family had shaped him just like mine had shaped me. We were two sides of the same coin. Perhaps that was why I knew I needed to leave as long as it was still a possibility. Part of me didn't want to go. There was nothing out there waiting for me. I was turning my back on something I'd longed for all my life: love.

I took a bus back home, even though Fabiano always urged me to take a taxi. I was out of cash, except for the few coins I'd found on the kitchen counter in Fabiano's apartment. Yesterday, I handed Remo everything I had. Now I had to start from zero. If things kept progressing the way they were, I'd never be able to pay tuition for college.

Maybe I wanted too much out of life.

I hesitated in front of the door to our apartment. He was dead. And in some way it was my fault.

I took a deep breath before I moved inside. The smell of fresh coffee wafted over to me and relief filled me. At least Mom was there. I quickly rushed into the kitchen to find my mother hunched over a cup of coffee. She looked up. There was a dark bruise on her cheek. I touched the spot. "What happened?"

"Your father and I got in an argument yesterday morning. He wanted money, but I told him I didn't have any."

I dropped my hand. And to think that I had risked my life for him. That because of him I'd been forced to see Fabiano's darkest side.

He paid for his crimes. Fabiano made him pay.

Her glassy eyes scanned me from head to top. "Where is your father?"

"Gone," I said hoarsely. "Dad is gone."

"Gone?"

"He killed him because of me," I admitted, and it felt good to voice the truth.

I put a hand down on my mother's frail shoulder. She didn't look sad. Relief filled her eyes. "He got himself killed. Bets. Always bets and gambling. I told him it would kill him."

"Yes, but in the end Fabiano killed him because of me. For me. To protect me."

Mom's bloodshot eyes were too knowing, and for once I wanted her in a drug haze. "That the one you love? The one with the cold blue eyes?"

"Yes," I whispered.

"I thought he treated you well."

"He did," I said.

"Men like him usually don't."

"I have to leave."

"Because of him?"

Because I loved him, despite what he was.

"Because if I stay I won't get the future I've always wanted," I tell her.

"Sometimes the future we thought we wanted isn't the future we need."

I shake my head. "He isn't a man I should love. That's why I need to leave."

Mom tilted her head. "Can't run from love."

It made no sense talking to her about this. Every life choice of hers had been a mistake. We both knew it. "You have to come with me, Mom. You can't stay here alone."

She shook her head. "I've got to pay off my debts to the Camorra. And I like it here. This apartment is better than the last one we had."

"It's Dad's apartment."

"Now it's mine," Mom said.

"Mom..." I gripped both of her shoulders, trying to make her see reason "... if you stay here, I can't protect you."

She smiled. "You have no business protecting me, Leona. I am your mother."

"Mom—"

She stood. "No, for once, let me be the mother. If you have to leave, then do it. But I can't run again."

"The Camorra will hurt you if you don't pay them. You should come with me, Mom. We can start over."

"Leona, it's too late for me to start over. And what can they do to hurt me that hasn't been done to me before? I've lived through it all, and I'm still here."

I stared at her. She was still here, but only because she numbed everything with drugs.

"Has he hurt you?"

It took a moment before I understood whom she meant. "Fabiano? He hasn't hurt me. But he hurts other people."

"If he's good to you, why leave?"

Fabiano had been the first person to take care of me, but he was also the man taking me down a path I shouldn't follow.

I reached for the cup of coffee. My hands shook as I brought the cup up to my mouth and took a long sip.

I had to leave. I closed my eyes against the sense of hopelessness that washed over me. I'd never really thought Las Vegas was my final destination, but I'd hoped I could use it as my starting point for something new and better.

Now I was even worse off than when I arrived in this damned city with my backpack and flip-flops. I didn't have any savings and not only that, now I lost my heart to a man whose own heart only beat for the Camorra. A man who was brutal and dangerous. A man who would eventually be my death because he couldn't possibly keep me safe and not betray his oath.

Still a small, stupid voice asked the same question my mother had: *Why leave?* That was probably the same voice my mother listened to every time she'd gone back to a pimp after he apologized for beating her to a bloody pulp. Perhaps Fabiano had been right on the night of our first encounter, that our DNA determined most of our decisions. Perhaps my mother's genes would always prevent me from living a normal life.

My eyes were drawn back to her wiry form hunched over the table again. She wasn't looking at me anymore. Instead, she was peeling off more of red her nail polish. Her hands were shaking. She needed a fix. She raised her eyes.

"You don't have any money for me before you leave?"

No. This wasn't my future. "I'm sorry, Mom."

She nodded. "It's okay. Just leave and be happy."

Be happy.

I didn't say anything. I grabbed a quick shower, feeling a bone-deep tiredness that didn't have anything to do with sleepless nights. I was leaving Las Vegas behind. I was leaving Fabiano behind and all that he stood for: blood and darkness and sin.

I leaned in the doorway to the kitchen. "I'm leaving," I told my mother.

She looked up. "And you won't come back?"

"I can't."

She nodded as if she understood, and perhaps she did. After all, we moved after each one of her breakups and never returned.

"I have to go now," I said. I went over to her and kissed her cheek. She smelled of smoke and faintly of alcohol. I didn't know if I'd ever see her again.

Thirty minutes later I arrived at Roger's Arena. I headed directly for Cheryl, who was as usual early. Her affair with Roger kept her busy until the early mornings most days. Sometimes I thought she lived at the bar. The moment she spotted me stark relief filled her face, and she rushed over to me, grabbed my arm, and dragged me toward a booth.

"Are you alright, chick?" she asked in a worried tone. I was startled by her concern. She pulled back. "Heard what happened to your father."

I stiffened, doubting she had heard what really happened.

"It was Fabiano, wasn't it?"

I looked away.

"I told you he was dangerous, chick. But don't blame yourself for what happened to your father. He had it coming for a long time. It's a miracle he lasted that long with all the gambling."

"Can you give me some money?"

She narrowed her eyes. "What happened to the money you earned? Did your no-good bastard of a father spend it on bets?" She crossed her arms over her chest as if that would make her insulting a dead man any better.

"Please, Cheryl." I didn't tell her I'd pay her back because I didn't think I could. I was never returning to Las Vegas, and if I sent her money, Fabiano would trace it back to me.

"You wanna run, right?"

I nodded. "I have to."

She pressed her lips together. "He won't be happy about it."

"It's my life. My choice."

Cheryl touched my cheek in an almost motherly gesture. "Chick, it stopped being your choice the moment he first laid eyes on you and decided he wanted to have a piece. He won't let you go unless he loses interest."

"I have to leave," I said again.

"What happened to your father finally made you see what kind of man he is?" She must have seen something on my face because her expression softened. "Did he hurt you too?"

I bit my lip with a small shake of my head. I couldn't trust her. What happened between Fabiano and me had to remain my secret. How could I explain to her that I'd fallen for someone like him?

"If I give you money and he finds out ..." She trailed off.

I hadn't even considered that. I pulled away and nodded. "You're right. I can't drag you into this. You warned me from the start. I didn't want to listen. Now I have to deal with the consequences."

She sighed then grabbed her purse and pulled out a few bills. "One hundred enough for you?"

I searched her face. Did she really want to do this?

She thrust the money at me. "Don't give me that puppy dog look, chick. Just take the money and run as fast as you can … and don't you dare come back."

I took it hesitantly then pulled Cheryl into a tight hug. After a moment of surprise, she squeezed me back. "Can you keep an eye on my mother? I know it's a lot to ask, but—"

"I will," she said firmly then pushed me away. "Now go."

And I did. I turned around and didn't look back.

TWENTY-ONE

Fabiano

I'd texted Leona twice, but she didn't reply. I wanted nothing more than to go to her at once, but I couldn't disappoint Remo again. This morning he acted as if everything was okay between us, but I was wary.

Still, I needed to see her, needed to see if that broken look from yesterday was gone. I couldn't think about anything else. I stood up from crouching over the men on the floor. "Today's your lucky day. I can't spare any more time for you," I said as I sheathed my knife. I went over to the washbasin and began cleaning my hands. It took a while before the water was clear.

The man lifted his bloody face from the ground. "I swear I'll pay tomorrow. I swear. I'll go to my brother …"

"I don't give a fuck where you get your money. Tomorrow we get our money or you'll spend more quality time with my knife."

He blanched.

I left him in his pitiful state and jogged to my car. I tried calling Leona again, but it went directly to her voicemail. What if Remo had changed his mind after all?

I called him as I headed toward Roger's Arena.

He answered after the second ring. "Done?"

"Yes, done. Is there anything else you need me to handle?"

There was a pause. "Come over later. Nino, Adamo, and Savio will be there. I'll order pizza and we can watch some old fights."

"Salami and peppers for me," I said then hung up. Remo didn't have Leona

I knew why. After she had fallen asleep in my arms last night, I thought she could forgive me for what I'd done, for what I had to do because her asshole father didn't leave me a choice.

I pulled up in front of Roger's Arena. Her shift began about one hour ago. I entered the bar. There were only few customers at the tables. They looked my way before whispering among themselves. Everyone knew about the bloody message Remo had left for our other debtors. Hall's corpse was a good warning. Most of them had paid their debts in the morning.

My eyes scanned the bar area, but instead of Leona's amber curls, I spotted horribly dyed black hair behind the counter. Cheryl, if I remembered correctly.

I stalked over to her. She straightened and put on a fake smile, but the fear in her eyes screamed at me. "Where is Leona?" I demanded.

"Leona?" she asked, puzzled, like she didn't know who I was talking about. One look from me, and she quickly said, "She didn't show up. I had to take over her shift. Roger is pissed."

"I don't give a fuck what Roger is," I snarled, making her recoil.

I stared at her for a few heartbeats. She squirmed under my gaze. "You sure you don't know where she could be?"

"She's a colleague, not a friend. I keep my nose out of other people's business. It's safer."

I whirled around and left. Where the hell was Leona?

I raced toward the apartment complex she lived in and hammered my fist against the door. The moment Leona's mother opened it a gap, I pushed inside. She stumbled back on her heels, colliding with the wall. She was only wearing a thong, revealing too much of her used up body, and a moment later I realized why. A fat guy emerged from another room, only in white briefs, sporting a fucking boner.

"Where is she?" I growled.

Leona's mother blinked. She was fucking drugged out.

Her john stared at me with an open mouth. It annoyed the fucking crap out of me. I gripped his throat and smashed him against the wall, making him sputter. Then I looked up at Leona's mother again. "I'll give you ten seconds to tell me where she is, or by God, I will make you watch me skin this asshole alive."

Terror shook his frame.

Leona's mother didn't seem to care. Her lipstick was smeared across her left cheek as if she'd wiped her mouth. I looked from her to her john, my lips curling with disgust. She probably wouldn't mind me cutting him to pieces. I shoved him away then advanced on her. I didn't like hurting women, and Leona would definitely never forgive me if I hurt her mother, but I needed to find her. That left me at an impasse. I tried to calm the fuck down and focus. Tried to read her as if we were facing off in the cage.

I softened my expression. "I protected your daughter. Your husband—"

"Ex-husband," she corrected.

"I got rid of him so he couldn't hurt you or Leona again."

I could tell that her resolve was slipping away, but it still wasn't enough to tell me what I wanted to know. I reached into my back pocket and pulled out two hundred dollars. I held it out to her. "Take it." She did, but she still hesitated. "I could give you some drugs every now and then ... for free."

Her eyes lit up. And I knew I won. Drugs won over her need to protect her daughter. "She left," she said in that raspy voice. "She packed her things and left about two hours ago. I don't know where. I didn't ask her."

"Are you sure you don't know?" I asked in a low voice.

"The stupid whore barely remembers her name or how to suck a cock," her john muttered, trying to side with me to save his ass. He was trying to get back up, but I shoved him to the ground and unsheathed my knife, cold fury burning in my stomach. "Did I ask for your opinion? Next time you interrupt us, I'll have to give you a taste of my knife, got it?"

Leona's mother met my gaze. "Leona went to the bus station. That's all I know. I swear." I searched her face. She was telling the truth. "So will you give me meth?"

"I will," I said, disgusted.

"What do you even want with her?" Leona's mother asked.

"She is *mine*," I told her.

"Don't hurt her. She loves you."

Shock shot through me. "You don't know what you're talking about."

She didn't say anything, and I stormed out of the apartment. I hurried into my car and hit the gas. Was she running from me? Did she really think I would let her?

She loves you.

If she did, she wouldn't run. I remembered Remo's words after we'd killed Hall. That people always left. Leona had left too.

I stopped the car at the bus station. One of the bus drivers honked because I was barring his way. When he spotted me as I got out, he quickly swerved the bus around my car and almost hit another bus.

I went to the ticket office.

"What can I do for you?" an older woman drawled in a bored voice.

I slid my mobile with a photo of Leona on the screen over to her. "Where did she go?"

The woman looked down at the screen then shook her head. "I can't tell you—"

"Where?" I repeated slowly.

She raised her eyes to mine. She didn't recognize me. I pushed back my shirt and showed her the tattoo on my forearm. If she lived in Vegas for more than a few weeks, she knew exactly what it meant.

"I ... I think she took the bus to San Francisco. It left ten minutes ago."

"Are you certain? I'd hate to waste my time." I took my phone back and stashed it in my pocket.

She nodded.

It took me ten more minutes to find the bus. I positioned myself in front of it and hit the breaks. The bus driver honked at me and tried to pass me on the left. I mirrored his move, so he had no choice but to come to a halt behind me.

I jumped out of the car at the same time as the driver opened the bus door. He was pulling his trousers that were way too big up over his paunch as he walked down the steps, shouting, "Have you lost your fucking mind? I'm calling the police!"

I ignored him and tried walking past him into the bus. His hand shot out, and he grabbed me by the arm. Then he swung his fist at me.

Wrong move, buddy. I brought my forearm up, dodging his punch, then rammed my elbow into his face, hearing and feeling the bones break. He sagged to his knees with a muffled cry. "Stay there. One more move, and you'll never see your family again."

He gave me a sideways glance, but after catching sight of my tattoo, he was too clever to act on his anger. This time he didn't stop me as I took the steps up into the bus. My eyes wandered the rows of seats until they came to rest on familiar amber curls in the second to last row.

I ignored the staring crowd and headed toward Leona, who watched me like I was a demon risen from hell. I stopped in front of her and held my hand out. "Come."

"I'm leaving Las Vegas," she said, but her words lacked conviction. Her blue eyes seemed to see into the deepest, darkest parts of my soul, and I knew she hated what she saw. Love. No, she couldn't love me.

"No, you are not. We have to talk. You are leaving the bus with me *now*."

"Hey, listen, dude, if the lady doesn't want to be with you, you have to grow a pair and accept it," said a guy who looked like he had no fucking care in the world. Some backpacker kid who looked like he came from a nice family and had had a sheltered childhood but was now out for some adventure. I could give him more than that.

Some of the bravado slipped from his face. He swallowed.

Leona practically jumped from her chair, gripping my arm, fingernails digging in. I averted my eyes from backpacker kid and turned to her.

"I'm coming with you. Just ... just let's go now," she whispered.

I took her backpack from her and gestured for her to walk ahead of me. She did without protest. Nobody else tried to stop me, especially backpacker kid.

Outside, a police car had pulled up beside the bus. The police officers were standing with the bus driver, beside my car, talking into their radio set. Probably checking my license.

Leona paused and gave me a questioning look. "You seem to be in trouble."

I put my hand on her lower back, ignoring the way she shied away from my touch. She stared stubbornly ahead, not giving me a chance to read her face. I could tell that the only reason why she was cooperating at all was that there were too many people around that I could potentially hurt.

The police officer lowered his radio set when he noticed me. He said something to his colleague. Then they gestured at the bus driver to follow them. He looked stunned as he pointed in my direction. The older police officer yanked down the man's arm and said something angrily then nodded back toward the bus.

Leona followed the scene with an incredulous expression. "Even the police?" she asked horrified.

I opened the car door for her. She hesitated.

"Las Vegas is ours."

And you are *mine*.

She sank down on the leather seat, and I closed the door. After I'd thrown her backpack in my trunk, I slipped behind the steering wheel and started the engine.

"Where are you taking me?" she asked.

"Home."

"Home?"

"To your mother. That's your home for now, right?"

She frowned. "I'm not going back there. I'm leaving Las Vegas."

"I told you you're not."

"Stop the car." She began shaking beside me. "Stop the car!" she screamed. If anyone except for Remo had taken that tone with me, they would have regretted it thoroughly.

I pulled into a parking lot and shut the engine off before turning to face her.

She was glaring at the windshield, and her fingers clutched her knees so hard her knuckles were turning white. "You can't make me stay," she got out.

"I can and I am," I told her. I knew I should have let her leave, should have given her the chance to move on, to find a better life, but I couldn't.

"Haven't you done enough already?" she asked in an angry whisper.

I raised my eyebrows. "I've never done anything to you."

"Do you really believe that?"

"I found your mother for you. I saved your life."

"You killed my father," she hissed.

"Don't tell me you miss him. Your mother definitely doesn't."

She paled as if I hit too close to home. "You dragged me into your darkness."

"I didn't *drag* you into anything. I didn't force you to go on that first date. I didn't force you to kiss me or to let me lick and finger you. You were a willing participant, and we both know you enjoyed it. My darkness turned you on."

Her eyes grew wide, but she didn't deny it. She couldn't. I leaned very close to her, relishing in that sweet scent of hers. Was she making me out to be the bad guy in this? Really? Did she not realize what I was putting on the line? Remo was going to be even more suspicious in the future. I was risking my status and what was I getting in return?

She pushed me away from her. "I will try to leave again and again. You can't always be there to stop me."

"Perhaps you should remember that your mother still owes us four thousand dollars."

She froze. "Are you threatening to kill her too?"

"No," I said. "Just reminding you that she needs someone who makes sure she pays us back." I was a fucking bastard for using her mother against her, but I'd do anything to stop Leona from leaving, even this.

"Just tell me what you want from me. You want me to sleep with you? Would that settle my mother's debt?" She said it with so much disgust that it set my veins aflame with fury.

"Do you really think fucking you once is worth that much? Leona, believe me, it's not. For you to pay off four grand, you'll have to let me have your pussy for a long time."

She slapped me hard, catching me by surprise. I grabbed her hand, my fingers tight around her thin wrist. I jerked her toward me, so our faces were inches apart. "This once. Only this once," I said in a low voice. "Never raise your hand against me again."

She glared at me with tear-filled eyes. "I hate you."

Those words weren't new to me, but coming from her …

"I can deal with hate. The sex is so much better when hate's involved."

"I'm never going to sleep with you, Fabiano. If that means I'm breaking some Camorra rule, then so be it. Torture me if you must, but I won't be yours. Not now, not ever."

I could tell that she was serious, but she knew nothing of torture. I leaned close to her ear. "We'll see about that."

She jerked open the door and fled the car.

"Don't forget your backpack," I called through the open window, popping the trunk. She went to the back and picked it up. "And, Leona," I said in warning. "Don't ever try to run from me again. I won't let you go, and I'll find you wherever you go."

She watched me, shoulders slumping, her expression desperate. "Why?" she murmured. "Why won't you let me leave? I'm not worth the bother."

Remo had said the same. And I knew they were right. She was nothing. I'd fucked so many women and could have many more. Leona was nothing to write home about.

"You're right. You aren't."

She flinched as if I'd gutted her. Those hurt blue eyes were what gutted me. She nodded then turned toward the apartment complex.

I almost called out to her, but what would I have said?

I'm sorry. The idea of you leaving me is the worst torture I can imagine. Be the woman Aria gave me that bracelet for.

Stay, even if I'm not worth it.

TWENTY-TWO

Leona

I PRACTICALLY RAN BACK HOME, MY HEART BEATING IN MY THROAT FROM anger and hurt. I couldn't believe what he said to me. Did he really mean it?

I was breathless when I arrived at the apartment. I unlocked the door and froze, on my way to my bedroom. Grunting and moans were coming from my father's bedroom. Was my mother already using it for work? He hadn't been dead for more than twenty-four hours, and she had moved on.

I hammered against the bedroom door until she finally opened it, dressed in a bathrobe with nothing beneath it.

"Leona?"

A hairy man, at least seventy, was sprawled on the bed, completely naked. I whirled around and stormed into the kitchen, holding on to the counter in a death grip.

Tears burned my eyes.

I could hear Mom's shuffling behind me. "Did you return because of that man? He seemed really intent on finding you. Looks like you really got under his skin," Mom said as she stopped beside me. I had a hard time ignoring her skinny nakedness.

The only way to get under Fabiano's skin was with a knife. It shouldn't have come as a surprise that my mother took Fabiano's possessiveness as a sign of him caring for me. She had a habit of making that mistake with her past boyfriends. "He didn't let me leave. I didn't want to return."

"Perhaps it's for the best."

I searched her face. "You told him I went to the bus station?"

She finally closed her bathrobe. "I think he really cares about you."

"What did he do? Did he threaten you?"

She looked embarrassed.

"He gave you what? Money? Drugs?"

"He promised to give me meth every now and then. For free, Leona. But I wouldn't have told him anything if I didn't think he meant well." Mom touched my hand. "It's not a bad thing to be with someone like him, especially if he is good to you. He holds power. He can protect you. What's so bad about being with him?"

"Mom, Fabiano killed Dad. Don't you remember?"

Mom's hand tightened on mine. "I do remember, but I also remember the first time I had to sell my body, back when we lived in San Antonio and your father owed one of the local MCs money. He asked me to help him, but behind my back he had already told their president I would spread my legs to pay off his debt. You were only a baby, and I was still recovering from giving birth to you. Five of them. I had to sleep with five of them, had to endure their filthy hands touching me everywhere. They took more than was agreed upon. And it was fucking painful, but you know what? Afterward, your father asked if I would fuck him too. I hated him. But he promised it was only this once. It wasn't. Next time he owed money, I had to do it again, and that time they gave me meth, and I took it because it made me forget. So yes, I remember that Fabiano killed your father … and I am thankful. While I was working the street, they told me what happened to him. All I could think was that I wished I could have been there to see it because he destroyed me. And I was never there for you because of it. I was a horrible mother."

I was speechless. I just stared at her with my mouth gaping.

"Your father only protected himself. That's all he cared about, saving his own ugly ass. So if you tell me that Fabiano kills someone to *protect you*, I'll tell you it could be worse. Would Fabiano ever make you pay off his debts with your body?"

"No," I said with conviction. "He would kill anyone who dared to touch me."

"Good."

"Hey, are you coming back? I paid you forty dollars!" my mother's john shouted.

Mom sighed. "I have to get back to *him*."

I watched her scurry back into the bedroom. Slowly, I loosened my death grip on the counter. I needed to figure out a way to get the money my mother owed the Camorra so she could stop selling her body. If I kept working in Roger's Arena, I would make enough money to pay for the apartment, food, and her drugs. She'd never have to bear anyone's touch again. I didn't want to think about what she said about Fabiano. Even before her words, back when I sat in the bus, I wondered if I should really leave him. If I should give up the chance of love. But Fabiano's harsh words today had taken that decision off my chest. This wasn't about love, not for him at least.

I pulled the rest of the money Cheryl had loaned me from my pocket. I still had fifty dollars left. Not much. But it could turn into more.

I grabbed my backpack again and headed out, glad for the silence in the bedroom. If I had to listen to my mother doing that old bastard, I'd lose it.

Cheryl's face fell when I walked into the bar. She dropped what she was doing and staggered toward me, ignoring the few customers waving at her to serve them. Mel took over quickly. Cheryl gripped my arm and pulled me behind the bar. "What are you doing here? Shouldn't you be gone by now?"

"Fabiano caught me," I said quietly. I didn't need people to overhear. I could tell from the looks people were giving me that they were already talking about me because of what happened to my father.

"Oh fuck." She sighed. "I told you."

"I know."

"You know, if he doesn't let you leave, maybe you need to beat him with his own weapons. Go along, let him have fun, give him what he wants until he doesn't want it anymore. Can't be that hard?"

I looked away.

"Or is he some kind of sadistic bastard in the bedroom too?"

I didn't say anything. I knew Fabiano wouldn't appreciate me talking about these kinds of things. For some reason, I didn't want to betray his trust, and I was uncomfortable talking about it with her. Because no matter what he'd said during our last encounter, he showed a gentler side when he was with me, a side he didn't want people to know about.

Sleeping with Fabiano didn't scare me for the reasons Cheryl suspected. He had been a far cry from sadist in the bedroom.

"I'll give you your money back as soon as Roger pays me, okay?" I told her.

She shrugged. "I don't care about the money. I wish it would have helped you."

I smiled. I'd never forget she was willing to help me. "Where is Griffin?"

Her eyebrows shot up. "Don't go down that road. It's a slippery one. You saw where it got your father."

She didn't have to tell me. I remembered what had happened to my father, had relived it in vivid color ... repeatedly. But after what Mom had told me today, I wasn't broken up over his death anymore. At least not because he was gone. I only wished I didn't have to see Fabiano do what he'd done. "I know what addiction does to people, and I have no intention of making betting a habit, believe me."

"Nobody ever does." She shrugged. "He's in the booth behind the cage."

"Thanks," I said then made my way to Griffin. He sat with his gaze glued to his iPad while he pushed fork after fork of fries into his mouth. I sat down on the bench across from him. He looked up then back down, muttering, "I don't need anything."

"I'm not here to serve you," I said quickly.

I pushed the fifty dollars over to him. "I want to bet against Boulder."

Griffin raised one gray eyebrow then nodded. Boulder had won every fight in the last couple of weeks. He was rumored to be Fabiano's next opponent if he won tonight. And everyone was certain he would win tonight.

"That's one to twenty," he said calmly.

So much money. "Can I bet money I don't have?"

"You can get a credit from us and use it for your bet," Griffin said then pointed at my wrist. "Or you could put that down for a bet. I'd give you five hundred."

"It's worth much more," I muttered.

He shrugged. "Then sell it somewhere else."

I fingered the delicate gold chain. "It's not for sale." Stupid. Stupid. Stupid. For some silly reason, I didn't have the heart to sell Fabiano's gift.

"Just give me two hundred as a credit." Indebting myself to the Camorra, what a day. If Boulder lost tonight, then Mom would be free ... and Fabiano wouldn't be able to hold her debt against me anymore.

Fabiano

I had to look a second time, unable to believe my eyes. Leona was handing over money to Griffin, our bookie. I'd only come to Roger's Arena to see if Leona already returned to work and to watch Boulder's fight. I stalked toward them. "What's going on here?"

Griffin nodded a greeting at me. "Earning money like I'm supposed to."

Leona gave me an indignant look.

"How much did she bet?"

"Fifty in cash and two hundred in advance against Boulder."

I shot her a look. Boulder was one of the best. He came directly after me and the Falcone brothers. He wouldn't lose his fight. "She's not betting," I ordered.

Griffin hesitated with his fingers against his iPad, finally looking up to me. A frown knitted his gray brows together.

"I am," Leona interrupted. "My money is as good as anyone's."

People around were starting to stare. I grabbed her by the arm and pulled her up from the leather booth, away from Griffin.

"Does that mean the bet is still on?" he shouted. That was why Remo liked him. He was always focused on the job at hand, never one to be distracted.

"Yes," Leona shouted in reply.

I dragged her toward the back and then downstairs into the storage room, seething. Only when the door shut behind us did I let go of her. "Have you lost your fucking mind?"

"I need money to pay my mother's debts off, remember?" she muttered. I staggered toward her, backing her into the wall. She was driving me insane. "And you think you can do that by making new debts? Boulder is going to win, and you'll lose not only the fifty you handed over but you'll be indebted with two hundred more. I don't think you have that, and soon it'll be twice as much."

She gave me a 'so what?' look. "I know what it means to be indebted to the Camorra." For the first time, she rolled the r's the same way I did. "I saw what it means to be indebted to *your Capo.*"

I pressed my palms against the wall beside her head, glaring down at her. "You have seen what it means to be indebted to Remo, but you have never *felt* what it means to be indebted to us. There's a world of a difference between those two scenarios."

She smiled joylessly. No. So wrong on her freckled face. These fake smiles were for others to have, not for her. "And who's going to make me feel what it means? Who's going to remind me of my debts? Who's Falcone going to send to do his dirty work? Who will he send to break my fingers or take me back to that basement?"

I didn't say anything.

"Who will be the one to make me bleed and beg, Fabiano? Who?"

She shook her head, looking crushed. "You are his enforcer. His bloody hand. You are the one I have to fear, right?"

She straightened her spine and reached for the knife in my chest holster. I let her do it. She held my gaze as she pulled it out. "Who's going to pierce my skin with this knife? Who's going to draw my blood with this blade?"

She pressed the tip of the knife against my chest. "Who?" The word was a mere whisper.

I leaned closer, even as the blade cut through my shirt and skin. Leona drew it back, but I moved even closer. "I hope you'll never find out," I murmured. "Because it sure as hell won't be me, Leona."

She exhaled, and I crashed my lips against hers, my tongue demanding entrance. And she opened up, kissing me back almost angrily. The knife fell to the ground with a clatter as I slipped my hand between us, into her panties, until I found her hot center already wet. I stroked my fingers over her clit, making her gasp into my mouth. I slid my finger into her tight heat. So fucking hot.

She tensed at the foreign intrusion but softened around me as I pressed the heel of my palm against her bundle of nerves. I finger-fucked her slowly, allowing her to grow used to the sensation. "I don't want to see you placing a bet ever again. You hear me? And no other messed up ways of earning money either. I won't always be able to protect you."

She huffed, her eyes glazed over with pleasure as I pumped into her slowly with my finger. "How am I supposed to pay back my mother's debt? Or perhaps you don't want me to so you can blackmail me with it?" Her voice was shaky with desire, the sexiest sound in the world.

I stroked my knuckles over her side up to her breast and brushed her nipple through her shirt, feeling her shiver against my touch. She was getting close. "This is a good start." I was *teasing* her.

She flinched, forcing me to pull my finger away. "No," she hissed like a wounded animal. "I told you no and that stands. You said it yourself: I'm not worth your time. I'm nothing, remember?"

I shook my head. "You aren't nothing." If she were, Remo wouldn't be breathing down my neck.

"What am I then, Fabiano?"

I leaned down and kissed her slowly, letting her scent and taste engulf my senses, before I drew back. Her cheeks were flushed. "You are mine."

I stepped away, turned around, and left her alone in the storage room.

Leona

"You are mine."

I watched him leave, stunned. For a moment, he looked at me like I was inexplicably precious.

Was this about more than him wanting to own me?

Don't be stupid.

He was a killer. A monster. He was Falcone's right hand man. He was his *enforcer.*

I shuddered at the idea of what he did to people on Falcone's orders. He wasn't the cute guy I'd taken him for the first time I'd seen him. How could I have ever taken him for anything other than a killer? Fabiano was many things, but cute and kind weren't among them. And yet I had fallen for him. What did that say about me?

This city was rotten, corrupt, and brutal. The Devil had his claws sunk deeply into Vegas soil, and he wasn't letting go. If I wanted to survive in this city, I had to play dirty like anyone else. I glanced down at my watch. Three hours until the final match, until Boulder would have to earn me my money back. Fabiano had said it himself: he couldn't always protect me, and I didn't want him to. I needed to take things into my own hands. Something on the ground caught my eye. Fabiano's knife. I picked it up.

I quickly rushed back up the stairs, searching the bar for any sign of Fabiano but he was gone. Relieved, I hurried toward Cheryl. "I need to leave for a while. I'll be back soon."

"Hey!" she called after me, but I was already on my way out.

I returned one hour later with a few of my mother's pills in my pocket. They were the ones she took when she couldn't get her hands on meth. They made her dizzy and her heart beat like drums in her chest. I hoped they'd do the same to Boulder.

My nerves were frayed as the second to last fight started. I hadn't seen Boulder yet. And if he didn't show up early for his fight, I wouldn't be able to hand him the bottle of water I prepared for him.

"What's the matter with you tonight?" Cheryl took the glass filled with beer from my hand. The foam head had dwindled. She tossed it into the sink then poured a new one and gave it to the man at the end of the bar.

Then the barrel-chested, bald man known as Boulder finally entered the bar and made his way toward the changing room. I took the bottle from the backpack beneath the bar and another untouched one for his opponent before I followed him. I glanced around before knocking on the door. People were occupied with the fight.

No sound came from inside, but I pushed the handle down and stepped in.

Boulder was sitting on the bench, staring down at the floor in concentration. He looked up, and I held the bottle out for him. He didn't take it, only nodded to the bench beside him. I was about to put it there when I noticed the white substance that had gathered at the bottom of the bottle. I gave it a quick shake then set it down beside him.

I waited a moment, but he didn't move to take it. His opponent came out of the toilet, and I handed him the other bottle.

I turned around and left. I always brought the fighters water, but I didn't hover to see them drink it. When I slipped out, I released a nervous breath then quickly went behind the bar before someone noticed something was off.

When Boulder emerged for his fight, he was holding the bottle in his hand. If he didn't drink it, I'd be digging myself a deeper hole. He climbed into the ring and raised the bottle then spilled some of the liquid over his head.

I held my breath, releasing it when finally he lifted the bottle to his lips and emptied it.

It took a while for the pills to take effect and the change was subtle. Hopefully subtle enough that no one would suspect anything. It merely looked as if he was lacking concentration, as if he was dazed, which could be explained by the hits his opponent landed against his head.

When Boulder went down and eventually surrendered, I could have died from relief. I waited for the uproar to settle down and most of the guests to leave before I approached Griffin. He handed me five thousand dollars, and the feel of the crisp bills soothed my nerves.

"This is your lucky day, I suppose," he said.

I nodded, suddenly terrified that he might be suspicious. I turned and left before someone else saw me with Griffin.

Grabbing my backpack, I stuffed the money inside and headed for the backdoor. What if this had been a huge mistake? If someone found out, I'd be dead.

Fabiano would be waiting for me in the parking lot, and I didn't want to face him now, not until I was sure I could convincingly lie about today. I stepped through the backdoor and breathed in the cold night air, trying to stifle my panic.

"Funny coincidence," said someone behind me.

I whirled around to find Soto a few steps behind me.

"You won quite a bit of money today."

I tightened my grip on my backpack. I still had Fabiano's knife buried inside there somewhere, but I remembered how little it had helped me against Fabiano. Soto wasn't Fabiano. I never saw him fight, but I suspected he had more practice handling knives than I did.

He moved closer. "Makes me wonder how you got so lucky. I'm sure Remo will wonder about it too … if I tell him."

I reached inside my backpack then drew the knife.

He laughed. "Ever since the basement, I couldn't stop imagining how it would be to bury my cock in your pussy. It's a pity that Fabiano got the honor of handling you."

"Don't come closer, or I'm going to—"

"Kill me?" He leered.

"Soto." Fabiano's voice sliced through the dim light of the back alley. I turned slowly. Fabiano was stalking toward us. Dressed in a black shirt and black slacks, his tall form blended in with the darkness.

Soto had his hand on the gun in the holster around his waist, his narrowed eyes on Fabiano. "I saw her bring Boulder water before the fight, and then he loses."

"She's a waitress, Soto. She serves everyone drinks. She served me water before my fights too," Fabiano said condescendingly as he positioned himself between Soto and me.

"She served you more than that from what I hear. She bet money against him and he lost. Remo won't believe it's a coincidence. Remo will love that. Apparently, you didn't do a good job in the basement, fucking some sense into her. This time I'll make sure Remo lets me handle it. And he will after your fuck up."

"You are probably right," Fabiano said slowly, eyes on me. I couldn't look away. His eyes were burning with emotion. "He will let you handle her." He held his gun in his hand, but Soto couldn't see it.

I didn't say anything.

He put a silencer on the barrel with practiced ease.

Heaven help me. I'd let him kill a man for me. Again. But this time I could have stopped him.

Fabiano held my gaze as if he waited for me to protest. I didn't.

Then he whirled around and pulled the trigger. Soto's head was shoved backwards by the force, and then he tumbled to the ground. I stared at his unmoving form. I didn't feel anything. No regret. No relief. No triumph. Nothing.

Fabiano dismantled the silencer from the gun and returned both to the holster around his chest. Then he walked up to me, took the knife from my shaking hands before touching a palm to my cheek. I looked up at him. "You killed him."

He killed one of Remo's men. Another Camorrista. For me.

"I promised I'd protect you, and I will honor my promise no matter the price."

The words hung between us.

"Leave. Go to my apartment and wait there for me. Take a taxi."

He held out his keys. I took them without a word of protest. He released me and I moved back slowly. "What are you going to do?"

"I'll handle this," he said, frowning at the dead body.

I swallowed then turned on my heel, hurrying toward the main road to catch a cab. I had to trust in Fabiano to handle this, to get us out of the mess I'd caused.

It felt strange entering his apartment without him. My body shook with adrenaline as I walked up the stairs to the bedroom. Fabiano had killed for me. And I had let him. I could have warned Soto. A word of warning was all it would have taken, but I had remained silent. And there was no guilt on my part.

Why wasn't there any guilt?

You're finally playing by their rules, Leona. That's why.

I took a long, hot shower to calm my frayed nerves. When I returned to the bedroom, dressed in one of Fabiano's crisp white shirts, almost one hour had passed. I'd hoped Fabiano would be here by now.

Worry twisted my stomach. What if something had gone wrong? What if someone had seen us and alerted Remo?

I felt dizzy with anxiety as I sank down on the bed. My eyes remained on the clock on the nightstand, watching one minute after the other pass, wondering why I needed Fabiano to return safely to me.

Betrayal.

I broke Omertà by killing a fellow Camorrista.

For Leona.

I considered my options as I stared down at Soto's body. I could, of course, make him disappear. Nobody would miss him, least of all his cowering wife. But Remo might be reluctant to believe that Soto deserted us. After all, the man had been loyal.

"Damn it," I muttered. *Loyalty.*

Loyalty to the Camorra and to Remo ... That was what I'd sworn, an oath that meant everything to me, but protecting Leona made keeping my oath impossible.

Remo didn't give a fuck about Soto or that I'd killed him, but he would care about me going around killing made men without his direct orders.

And then there was Boulder's miserable fight tonight. It was a big possibility that Remo was suspicious about that as well. God, Leona. Why did she have to bet money? Why did she have to meddle with things she had no clue about?

Because I backed her in a corner, and cornered dogs tried to bite. Fuck!

I could try to blame Boulder's failure on Soto. Tell Remo he had drugged the man and that I had killed him because of it, but Soto had no interest in changing the outcome of the fight. He hadn't placed a bet … No, Camorrista never did if they knew what was good for them. But Leona had, and Griffin would tell Remo if he asked. I grabbed Soto and dragged him toward my car. The parking lot was deserted, but if I wasted more time standing around looking for a solution to the mess I was in, that might change. I put Soto's body in my trunk and drove off, out of the city and into the desert. I had a shovel in my trunk, next to the spare tire.

When I found a promising spot, I parked the car, took the shovel from the trunk, and shoved it violently into the dry ground. It would take me hours to dig deep enough to hide the body. And all that hard work might be for nothing in the end.

I was covered in dirt and sweat when I finally unlocked my apartment door with my spare key. It was quiet inside. I closed the door and headed for the liquor cabinet. I didn't bother with a glass. Instead, I took a long swig of whiskey from the bottle. The burn of the alcohol cleared the fog of exhaustion.

Leona appeared at the top of the stairs, backlit by the soft glow from the bedroom. She was dressed in one of my shirts. She looked small in it. Vulnerable.

"Fabiano? Is that you?" she asked hesitantly.

I took another swig. I set the bottle down on the counter and moved toward the stairs, then took them one after the other. Leona's eyes took in my rumpled appearance.

"I was worried," she said as I stopped two steps below her, bringing us on eye level.

"It takes a while to bury a body in dry desert soil," I said, my voice raspy from the whiskey.

She nodded as if she knew what I was talking about. "I'm sorry."

"I'm sorry too," I ground out.

Her mouth parted. "You are?"

"For making you think you had no choice but to do something that foolish, for making you think you couldn't come to me to ask for help. Not for killing your father. I would do it again if it meant protecting you."

She averted her gaze, her chest heaving. "You look like you could use a shower."

I smiled wryly. "I could use a lot of things right now."

She tilted her head toward me, searched my eyes but didn't say anything. I walked past her into the bedroom and continued into the bathroom. I got out of my clothes. They were covered in dust and Soto's blood. I'd have to burn them tomorrow. Not that it would matter. I stepped into the shower. Leona stood in the doorway, watching me. I kept my eyes on her as hot water rained down on me. I liked the sight of her in my shirt. I would have preferred her naked.

Tonight everything had changed. I had made a choice, and I had chosen Leona. Over the Camorra. Over Remo.

What had happened in the basement was something Remo had been able to overlook, but today, me killing one of his men to protect a woman? No. That was something he'd never forgive nor comprehend. He wasn't the forgiving type. I wouldn't forgive me if I were him.

I shut the water off. Leona picked up a towel and handed it to me. Her eyes moved down my body then back up to my face. I wanted her. I wanted, I *needed* some small sign that I had chosen right. Fuck.

I dried myself off halfheartedly then thrust the towel on to the ground.

Leona didn't move as I advanced on her, gripped her hips and lowered my mouth to hers for a hard kiss. My fingers on her waist tightened when she kissed me back.

I began guiding her backwards, out of the bathroom and toward my bed. She didn't resist. Her legs hit the bedframe, and she fell backwards. My shirt rode up her thighs, revealing that she wasn't wearing panties. I breathed out harshly. My cock was already hard. I wanted to finally be inside her.

She must have seen it too, but there was only need in her eyes, not fear. I climbed on the bed and moved between her legs then pushed them apart and lowered my body on top of hers.

She sucked in a tense breath but didn't push me away or protest. I kissed her again, my tongue tasting her mouth. My cock was pressed up against her inner thigh. A small shift of my hips and I'd be buried in her tight heat.

Leona brought her hand up, the one with the bracelet, and raked her fingers through my wet hair, which dripped water down onto our faces.

I pulled back a couple of inches. "Why didn't you pawn it for your bet?"

She followed my gaze. "I couldn't do it. Because you gave it to me."

Fuck. The look in her eyes. "I thought you hated me. That's what you said."

"I was trying to. But …" She trailed off. "You saved me again. You are the only one who cares enough to risk anything at all for me. It's pathetic, but there's only you."

I couldn't say anything in response to her emotional words. Nothing that would have done them justice. "I want you," I rasped into her ear, then added in an even lower voice, "I *need* you."

Her eyes searched mine. She couldn't stop looking for something even after everything that had happened. She lifted her hips slightly, making the tip of my cock slide over her slick folds. I hissed in response to the silent invitation. It was too enticing to take her right now, no more waiting. But she was worth the wait.

I sat back on my haunches and unbuttoned her shirt then helped her pull it off, allowing my eyes to take in her flawless skin. I was tired and still riled up. My control was at its limit, but I forced myself to lower my mouth to her pussy. Surprise flashed across her face and then her lips parted in a soft moan as I dipped my tongue between her folds. After a few strokes along her heated flesh, I closed my lips around her clit. I was too impatient for the slow approach.

She rewarded me with a gasp and opened her legs even wider. My mouth on her bundle of nerves quickly had her panting and slick with arousal. I pushed a finger into her, fucking loving the way her walls clamped around me. I couldn't wait for them to do that to my cock. She bucked her hips, crying out, and I pushed a second finger into her. She shuddered as I guided her through her orgasm with slow strokes of my fingers and tongue. But my own need was too urgent now. My cock was close to exploding.

I straightened and reached for the drawer. I took a condom from it before I covered my cock with it. Leona watched me with a mix of trepidation and anticipation. I stretched out above her and guided my cock to her entrance. For a moment, I considered saying something, words she wanted to hear, loving words, gentle words, but I couldn't. I was filled with so much darkness and despair because I knew this was the only night we'd ever have. I felt it deep down.

I held her gaze as I pushed forward. My tip slid in, tightly gripped by her heat. She tensed, her breath stilling in her throat. Her eyes were soft and fucking emotional. I could not hold back. I didn't want to. I captured her mouth, my eyes boring into hers as I claimed her fully. Her resistance fell away under the pressure, and she gasped against my lips, her body taut under me.

"I betrayed for you, I killed for you," I said roughly, pulling out of her slowly until only my tip remained inside her. "I'll bleed and I'll die for you." I thrust back into her, trying to hold back.

Her eyes widened. From my words and pain. She clung to me. Those fuck-ing cornflower blue eyes never leaving my face.

I'll bleed and I'll die for you.

It wasn't a promise, not a sappy declaration of my feelings. It was a prediction.

I pushed deeper and harder with every thrust, and she held on to me, eyes boring into mine. And I claimed her with every thrust, trying to convince myself that this was worth it, that Leona was worth the trouble I was willing to take on for her. That she was worth dying for.

Because Remo would kill me.

She sucked in her breath a few times. I knew I needed to be more careful, to go slower, but I couldn't stop. It felt like our time was falling through our fingers, and I needed to make every moment count. She made me betray Remo, something I never considered before. She made me break my oath of putting the Camorra first.

Was she worth it?

As our sweat-covered bodies moved against each other, as her tightness squeezed down on me, as her eyes clung onto mine with trust and something stronger and more dangerous, I decided she was worth it. I wasn't sure how it had come to this. How could I have let it get so far? How could she still look at me with those fucking caring eyes after everything? She was messed up and so was I.

I held her tightly as I came inside her. She gasped again, her breathing la-bored, cheeks flushed. She blinked at me slowly as if she was dazed and only just waking from a dream. Her lips brushed mine softly, and I could tell from the look in her eyes that she was about to say words I couldn't say back. Words she shouldn't even consider saying, not after what I'd done, not after what she knew about me. Not when I was a dead man walking. No words would change that. Nothing could.

"Don't say anything," I whispered harshly, and she listened.

I rolled us over and pulled her close. She winced but then pressed up against me; her body against mine felt like it was supposed to be like that. But I knew it might be the only time I could hold her like that.

Leona

I woke to Fabiano's fingers tracing my spine. The touch was gentle, almost reverent.

I peered over my shoulder. He was propped up on his arm and followed the movement of his hand on my back. Hands that could kill without remorse, hands that were inexplicably gentle with me. His gaze found me, and I rolled over. Neither of us said anything. I kissed him.

I was sore from last night, but I wouldn't let that stop me, not only because he looked like he needed this more than air but also because I needed him. Last night, Fabiano, above me, in me, I felt like things had finally fallen into place. I never had a place to call home, but with him I felt anchored.

Things were complicated between us; they couldn't be anything else, given our pasts and lives, but I knew no matter what he was, nobody would ever make me feel more cared for than he did. We were twisted and broken and fucked up. Both of us. Why did I ever think I could be with someone straitlaced, someone with a normal past? That kind of man would never get me, not the same way Fabiano did. Reaching for his neck, I pulled him toward me. He didn't resist. Our lips glided over each other as he reached between us and found my opening to test my readiness. He shifted and his tip pressed against me. My fingers on his neck tightened as he claimed me with a slow push. My walls quivered in a mix of pain and pleasure. I exhaled sharply. He moved slowly, gently. Last night had been despair and possessiveness, and perhaps even fear and anger. This was different. It felt like … lovemaking. In a twisted way. Perhaps twisted was all I'd ever get.

His mouth found mine as his chest rubbed over my breasts. I moaned as he hit a spot deep within, lifted my butt, needing more. His fingers slipped between my legs, finding my bundle of nerves, and began their soft play. I gasped against his lips, and his tongue slipped in, meeting mine for a slow dance. My toes curled and my fingers scratched over the bed sheet as he sped up. Sparks of pleasure traveled from my core into every nerve ending.

I cried out, my hips bucking, and Fabiano pushed hard into me as he, too, lost control. We gasped, shaking against each other. Too many sensations, too many feelings. For a moment he didn't move, his hot mouth against my throat. Then he rolled over and pulled me with him so my cheek rested against his chest. It was almost as if he was trying to hide his face from me.

Our breathing was ragged.

"My sister gave it to me," he said. His words dragged me back to reality.

I followed his gaze toward the bracelet dangling around my wrist. I twisted my head to catch a glimpse at his expression, but he tightened his hold so I couldn't move.

"Your sister?"

"Aria, my oldest sister. Last time I saw her, she gave it to me."

That his sister had given it to him made it somehow even more precious. "When you were younger?"

"No," he said quietly. "Shortly before I met you. I was on a mission in New York." He fell silent. He didn't want to talk about the mission, and I wouldn't push.

"So she gave it to you so you'd remember her?"

He laughed, a raw sound. "She gave it to me so I would give it someone who would help me remember the brother she used to know."

"So you haven't always been like this." It was a stupid thing to say. Nobody was born a killer. They were turned into one by society and their upbringing. He finally allowed me to lift my face.

There was a strange smile on his face. "Like this?"

"You know," I said quietly, because what else was there to say. He knew what he was.

"I know," he murmured. "That's all I'll ever be. You know that, right?"

Part of me wanted to contradict him, but I couldn't. "I know," I said, and he smiled wryly.

"I gave the bracelet to you because I wanted it gone. It annoyed the crap out of me that my sister was trying to manipulate me somehow. But I think she got it right in the end."

I wondered what he meant by that, but his phone rang that moment. We both looked toward the nightstand and my heart skipped a beat when I saw who was calling.

Fabiano

I glanced down at the screen. Remo. I untangled myself from Leona and reached for my mobile.

Leona's eyes pleaded with me to ignore the call, but I needed to find out if Remo was on our trail. I picked up. "What's up?"

"I need you to kill Adamo for me," he muttered.

I sat up, shocked.

Leona threw me a worried look. I shook my head, trying to show her that we weren't in trouble. Yet.

"What do you mean?" I asked carefully. He couldn't possibly be serious. Adamo was a pain in the ass, but how could he be any other way. He was only thirteen and was only five when his father had been killed. Remo and his brothers had to go into hiding after that because their own family was fighting for the position of Capo and wanted them dead. They'd seen too much already.

"Cane told me he got word that Adamo did cocaine. Twice."

I grimaced. "You sure?"

"Apparently he's hanging with one of our errand boys. The fucker gave him the stuff." Remo paused. "Last night, he stole my Bugatti and drove it into a building."

Adamo had managed to steal another car?

"One day he's going to get himself killed. He doesn't seem to care about his life."

Remo was worried. Or as worried as Remo was capable of being. "What do you want me to do?"

"Give him a good scare. One that keeps him from doing shit like this. And kill all the other fuckers. Make him watch. Don't be lenient. Hurt him, Fabiano. If he gets addicted to the shit, he's fucking lost. A bullet to the head will be his end."

"Got it. I'll handle him."

Leona worried her lower lip. "That doesn't sound good."

"It's not, but it's got nothing to do with us," I said with a sigh. It was a good sign that Remo trusted me with Adamo. That meant perhaps I'd live to spend another night with Leona in my arms. "I have to deal with one of Remo's brothers."

Surprise filled her face, but she didn't ask for more details.

"Why don't you stay here and have breakfast? I should still have eggs in the fridge." I slid out of bed and dressed quickly. With a kiss and last glance at Leona's worried face, I headed out and went in search of Adamo.

I found the Bugatti on the side of the street, completely trashed. A tow truck from the company we worked with for the races was parked behind it, and Marcos, one of the other organizers of the races—and the driver of the tow truck—were walking around the car. I got out of my own car and strode toward them.

Marcos raised his palms. "I don't know how he managed to sneak into the qualification race. That boy is like fucking David Copperfield."

"Where is he?" I asked.

He shrugged. "He went off with two guys. That Rodriguez kid and the Pruitt kid, the one that sells snuff around here."

I asked around until I finally found one of our dealers who knew where Pruitt spent his days. It was an abandoned repair shop. I peered through the half-open gate.

Adamo and the two older boys were gathered around the hood of an old red Chevy. Adamo's long hair was matted to his head with blood, and yet he was laughing at something Pruitt said. The fucker shoved a piece of mirror with white powder on it over to Adamo, who looked fucking eager to get his nose down to business.

"Best nose candy, I'll tell ya," Pruitt said as he leaned down to sniff his own stuff.

I slid in. Adamo was the first to see me, and he opened his mouth for a warning. I gripped the back of Pruitt's head and shoved it down hard, smashing his face into the hood. "Enjoy your nose candy," I growled then ripped his head back. Blood was shooting out of his nose, and his face was covered in it and cocaine. His wide, dazed eyes settled on my face. I gave him a cold smile but released him when Rodriguez leaped toward me with an iron bar. Pruitt crumbled to my feet, and Rodriguez swept the bar at my head. I dropped to my knees. The bar crashed down on the hood. I pulled my knife and slashed it upwards, cutting him open. He dropped the iron bar then sank to his knees across from me, clutching his stomach. I rose to my feet then turned to Adamo. His shock was replaced by defiance when he met my eyes. He lifted his chin in challenge.

Oh, kiddo.

He took a step back from the hood and lifted his balled hands, one of them was clutching a knife, just like I'd taught him. "You think you are tough, don't you? That's what I thought when I was your age."

I approached and pointed toward the cocaine on the hood. "So that's how you want to end your life?"

"It doesn't matter. Remo sent you to kill me anyway!" he shouted. He glared, but there were tears in his eyes. "I crashed his favorite car. And I know Cane told him about the snuff."

"If you plan on using that knife any time soon, do it."

He ran toward me and slashed the knife sideways, as if he intended to cut my throat, but the attempt was halfhearted and his aim way too low. He wasn't into it. I grabbed his shoulder, thrust him down on the hood, then brought my elbow down on his wrist. He dropped the knife with a cry of pain. I released him and stepped back. He cradled his wrist, tears finally falling as he sank to the dirty floor. Still only a boy. Remo liked to forget. Since Remo had become Capo, Adamo had been alone too often. "Don't raise a knife against me again unless it's for training or you really mean to kill," I told him.

"Just do it," he muttered, but there was fear in his voice.

I crouched in front of him. "Do what?"

"Kill me."

"Remo doesn't want you dead, Adamo. And I think you know that. And you know I won't kill you. If all this shit is your way to get his attention, it's not working the way you want it to. You're only pissing him off."

"He's always pissed off since he's become Capo," Adamo said quietly. "Perhaps he needs to get laid more often."

I laughed because he was too young to pull it off. "You're the one who needs to get laid, but if you keep this shit up, you'll die a virgin."

He flushed and looked away.

"I'm sure Remo can ask a few pretty girls to take care of it for you."

"No," he said fiercely. "I don't like those girls."

I straightened and held out my hand for him to take. "Easy, tiger." He took my hand after a moment of hesitation, and I pulled him to his feet. He moaned in pain and cradled his wrist again. "I'll take you to Nino. He'll set it for you." Nino, being the fucking genius that he was, knew more about medicine than most doctors.

"Come on," I told Adamo. He swayed slightly—whether from the wound on his head from the car crash or because of the pain in his wrist, I couldn't say. I gripped his arm and steadied him. He only reached my shoulders, so it was no trouble keeping him upright. Pruitt was crawling away, off to another door. I pulled my gun out of my holster and put a bullet through his head.

Adamo winced beside me. "You didn't have to do that."

"You are right. I could have taken him to Remo." We both knew how that would have ended.

Adamo didn't say anymore as I led him toward my car and helped him into the passenger seat. "They were my friends," he muttered when I started the car.

"Friends wouldn't have given you cocaine."

"We are selling the stuff. Every junkie in Vegas is a customer of the Camorra."

"Yes. And because we know what it does to people, we don't take the shit."

Adamo rolled his eyes before he leaned his head against the window, smearing it with blood. "What's with you and that girl?"

I jerked. "What are you talking about?"

"The one with the freckles."

I narrowed my eyes in warning.

Adamo gave me a triumphant smile. "You like her."

"Careful," I warned.

He shrugged. "I won't tell Remo. At least she has her own free will. The girls Remo always brings home kiss the ground he walks on because they fear him. It's disgusting."

"Adamo, you are a kid. You need to grow up and learn when to keep your fucking mouth shut. Remo is your brother, but he is still … Remo."

Adamo did keep his mouth shut when we walked into the Falcone mansion. Remo, Savio, and Nino were sitting on the couches in the living room. Savio got up with a grin and punched his brother's shoulder. "You are screwed." Then he sauntered off. Sixteen and almost as intolerable as Adamo most days; Nino, on the other hand, he looked almost bored, but that didn't mean he wouldn't be able to recite every fucking word tomorrow.

Remo gave me a nod. Perhaps Remo hadn't lost his trust in me. Perhaps things would turn out okay after all. Remo turned to his brother. "Broken wrist?"

Adamo glared at the ground. I let go of him and took a step back. That was between Remo and him. Remo pushed off the couch and came toward Adamo. "You won't take drugs again. No cocaine, heroin, grass, crack, you name it. Next time, I won't send Fabiano. Next time, I will deal with you." If anyone ever killed one of his brothers, it would be Remo.

Adamo raised his head, the same fucking challenge back in his eyes.

I wanted to slap him.

"Like you dealt with our mother?"

Remo's face became still.

Nino slowly rose from the couch. "You shouldn't speak of things you don't understand."

"Because nobody explains them to me," Adamo hissed. "I'm sick of you treating me like a stupid child."

Nino positioned himself between Adamo and Remo, who still hadn't said anything. "Then stop acting like one." He gripped Adamo's arm and pulled him along. "Let me treat your wounds."

Remo hadn't moved yet. His eyes were like black hellfire.

Great. And I was left to deal with him like that.

"Set up a fight for me. Tonight. Someone who can hold his own against me."

The only people who could hold their own against him were Nino and me. Savio was on his way to getting there.

Remo's eyes settled on me, and for a moment I was certain he'd ask me to fight him. We hadn't ever fought in an official match. For good reason. There were no ties in the fighting cage. One of us would have to give up.

"Or better two. Alert Griffin. He should hurry with the bets."

I sighed, but it was no use arguing with Remo when he was in a mood like that. Perhaps this would distract him for a while. The longer it took for him to notice that Soto had disappeared, the better. I was about to set everything up when Remo's voice made me stop.

"Fabiano, have you seen Soto recently? I can't contact him and nobody seems to know where he is."

I forced my expression into one of mild curiosity. "Perhaps one of his clients gave him trouble today?"

"Perhaps," he said quietly, but his eyes said something else.

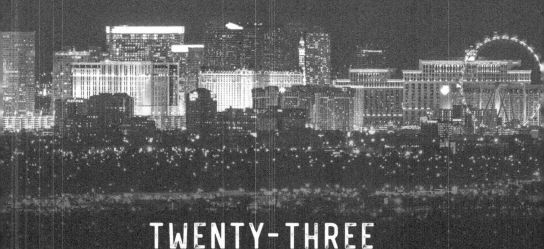

TWENTY-THREE

Leona

I HAD CONSIDERED CALLING IN SICK AT THE BAR AND STAYING AT FABIANO'S apartment, snuggled in the soft blankets that smelled of him, of us, but eventually the worrying in my head got too loud. I needed to distract myself.

And it worked. The bar was busy that day. People were overexcited about something. They drank and ate more than usual, and Griffin had a hard time taking their bets. I heard the name Falcone being mentioned a few times but wasn't sure which of them was going to go into the cage.

"Did you hear Remo Falcone is going to fight again tonight?" Cheryl said when I stepped up to her behind the bar.

Hearing his name turned my insides to ice. "And?"

"It's a big deal. He hasn't fought in almost a year. He's Capo, after all."

"Then why now?" I asked, suddenly worried.

"I hear his youngest brother wrecked his favorite car," she said. Good. Was that what Fabiano had to deal with?

Roger came up behind us with a crate of beer and set it down beside us with a resounding thud. "And I hear it's because one of his men disappeared, probably defected," he said. "And now stop gossiping. Falcone doesn't like it."

"Who was it?" Cheryl asked.

"A guy called Soto."

Coldness washed over me. "What do you mean he defected?"

Roger gave me a strange look. "He disappeared without a word. If the Russians or someone else got him, they'd have left a bloody message behind." He went past us toward Griffin and two fighters already dressed in shorts. I had seen them in the cage in the last few days. Both of them had won their fights.

"You look pale. What's wrong? You should be used to all this. It's daily business around here."

I nodded distractedly.

"When one speaks of the Devil," Cheryl whispered.

I followed her gaze toward the entrance. Falcone and Fabiano had entered the room. My eyes found Fabiano's. His were fierce and worried.

I clutched the edges of the counter.

I'd come to Las Vegas for a better life, for a future away from the misery that was my mother's existence. Away from the darkness that was her constant companion. And now I was caught up in something far darker than anything I ever knew existed.

Remo's eyes wandered from Fabiano to me, and something cold and frightened curled up in the pit of my stomach. If he found out that Fabiano had killed one of his men because of me, he'd not only end Fabiano's life but also mine. And it wouldn't be quick.

Remo finally averted his eyes from me, and I could breathe again. I quickly turned around and busied myself sorting the clean glasses Cheryl had brought in from the kitchen earlier. I kept my head down as I served beer to customers. I didn't want to risk catching Fabiano's eyes again.

Griffin climbed up on the platform of the cage, and I stopped what I was doing. He had never done that before. He raised his hands to quiet the crowd. "Death match," he announced simply and a hush went through the crowd, followed by thunderous applause.

"What does that mean?" I whispered.

Cheryl gave me a pointed look. "It's going to be ugly, chick."

Fabiano leaned against the side of a booth, where two of the Falcone brothers sat. He hadn't looked my way since he'd first come in with Remo. It was probably better that way. Deep down, I wished he'd give me a small signal of reassurance ... even if it was only show.

When Remo stalked toward the cage, a lump formed in my throat. This was going to get ugly ... just like Cheryl had said.

Remo's fight outmatched all the previous fights in its brutality. Remo was out to hurt. To break. To kill. This wasn't about winning.

This was madness and cruelty and bloodlust.

He faced two opponents, but the first was dead within two minutes. Falcone broke his neck with a hard kick. After that, he was more careful. The second opponent was the one I felt sorry for. His death wasn't quick. It was like watching a cat toy with a mouse.

Eventually, I had to turn my back on the scene. I pressed my palm against my mouth, breathing through my nose. When the crowd erupted with cheers, I dared to look back and wished I hadn't. Remo was completely covered in blood. The man at his feet was the source of it. I sucked in a deep breath, trying to fight my rising nausea.

"I think you should go outside and catch some air," Cheryl said. "If you throw up, it means only more work for both of us."

I gave a shake of my head. "I'm fine," I bit out. I forced a smile at a customer who was waving at me for more beer. I quickly loaded a tray and headed over to him. Perhaps work would keep me distracted from the cage. I never looked toward it or Remo. If I wanted to keep my composure, I had to pretend none of this had happened.

Roger was cursing as he cleaned the cage. Neither Cheryl nor Mel, and least of all I would agree to get in there.

Fabiano had disappeared with Remo and his brothers almost one hour ago, and I wondered if he would pick me up tonight. I suspected he might not risk us being seen together today. My suspicions were confirmed when I walked out to the parking lot and found it empty except for Roger's car.

I hesitated. Should I wait for him? What if Remo required his presence? Fabiano couldn't risk anything right now. Lifting my backpack on my shoulder, I decided to head home. I wrapped my arms around myself for warmth. I wasn't sure if my teeth were chattering because I was cold or because of what I had witnessed. I still had the money I won from my bet against Boulder in the backpack. I hadn't found time to give it to my mother yet. I wanted to get rid of the money as quickly as possible.

A new wave of panic washed over me. We needed to leave Las Vegas before Remo found out. And when had *I* become *we*? When I watched Fabiano commit the ultimate sin for me? He'd done it before, but this time I let him.

The familiar purr of an engine caught my attention. I stopped and turned to see Fabiano's Mercedes driving down the street toward me. Of course he would make sure I was safe.

I got in the moment he stopped beside me. He hit the gas and did a U-turn, taking us back to his apartment. After what had happened in the last twenty-four hours, it was difficult to form the right words … or any words, really. Fabiano didn't speak either. He was tense, his fingers clutching the wheel, eyes glaring out into the darkness.

"Does he know? Is that why he went berserk today?"

"That wasn't Remo going berserk, trust me. That was him trying not to go berserk."

So much blood and the sick excitement in Remo's eyes when he broke the neck of the first man, and then what came after … If that wasn't going berserk I didn't know what was. "Fabiano," I began, but he shook his head.

"At home. I need to think."

I gave him space and quiet, even if my own mind was whirring so loudly with thoughts I couldn't believe he didn't hear it.

He didn't say anything, but he took my hand as he led me toward his apartment. I squeezed to show him that I wasn't going to break, that I could handle things too. The moment the door closed, he cupped my cheeks and kissed me. He pulled back after a moment. "You should leave Las Vegas."

Fabiano

"What? You stopped me from leaving not too long ago," she said incredulously, stepping away from me.

I was equally surprised by my words. I didn't want Leona to leave. I didn't want to lose her, but if she stayed, I'd lose her too.

"I know, but things are different now. I can't protect you if Remo finds out about Soto."

"What about you? Don't tell me he'll forgive you."

I shook my head. "He won't." Forgiveness? No, that wasn't something Remo ever dished out. Leona squeezed my hand again as if I was the one in need of comforting. I couldn't remember the last time someone had tried to comfort me.

"Then come with me. We can leave Las Vegas together."

I glanced down at my tattoo, at the words that still filled me with pride when I read them. "I took an oath."

Leona shook her head in disbelief. "You took an oath for a man who will kill you."

"Yes, because I broke my oath by killing a fellow Camorrista. I can hardly blame Remo for that."

She shook her head again, only harder. "Fabiano, please. Can't we just go to New York … where your sister lives? She will take you in, won't she?"

Aria would take me in, but Luca … He would put a bullet in my head as he should. "Perhaps. She's stupid like that. Because she still thinks I can return to being the brother she knew, but I'm not him anymore, and I don't want to be." That boy had wanted to please his father so he'd deign him worthy enough to inherit his rank. I had learned to fight for it.

"She will learn to accept the person you are now."

"I doubt it."

"Why? I do." Her eyes had become soft and something in my chest tightened.

"Sometimes you actually remind me of Aria with your stubborn insistence on taking care of your mother, even if she doesn't deserve it."

"That's because I love her. I can't help it."

"Then maybe love isn't the right choice for you."

She regarded me with a strange expression, one I couldn't place. "Yes, very likely. My mother always loved the wrong people and things. I guess I got that from her."

She didn't say anything for a while, and I wasn't sure what to say.

I cleared my throat. "I won't leave Las Vegas, or the Camorra, or Remo and his brothers. I'll risk his wrath, but I'll keep my oath."

"Why does this mean so much to you? I don't get it." Her fingers clutched my shirt. "Explain it to me. Why would you risk so much for them?"

"My sisters and I we were a unit. We stuck together against our father and our mother. I thought it would always be like that. I was just a boy. Then, one after the other left until I was left in a huge house with my choleric father and his child bride. They thought I could handle myself, but back then I was still weak. And when my father decided he didn't need me anymore, I was lost. I didn't want to run to New York with my tail between my legs, like a fucking failure, and beg Luca to take me in. He would have done so only because of Aria."

I ran my hand down Leona's throat and shoulder, relishing in the softness of her skin. I could tell she was trying to follow my words, but for her, my world—the mafia—was foreign. If you didn't grow up like me or my sisters, you wouldn't understand exactly what it meant to be born into our world.

"I would have died without Remo. I was incapable of taking care of myself, of fighting, of pretty much anything, but Remo knew how to survive and he taught me. He took me in like I was another one of his brothers. Remo is a cruel fucker, but over all the years he fought to claim Las Vegas, and in the years that followed, he kept his brothers close. They were more of a burden than help in the beginning, especially Savio and Adamo who were too young. He could have controlled Las Vegas sooner, but he stayed in hiding to keep them safe. He protected them and me. I don't always know what's going on in his twisted mind, but he's loyal and a good brother."

I could tell that she didn't believe it, and from what she'd seen of Remo, her disbelief was understandable. "So you'll leave Las Vegas and take your mother with you, if you must, and move to the East Coast. Remo won't risk an attack on Luca's territory right now." I lifted her arm with the bracelet. "And if you don't know what to do, if you need help, then go to New York, to a club called the Sphere and show them your bracelet. Tell them Aria will recognize it. And tell Aria that you are the one."

"The one?" she asked with a frown.

"Aria will understand."

TWENTY-FOUR

Leona

I WASHED A FEW GLASSES THAT NOBODY HAD TAKEN CARE OF LAST NIGHT. This morning I'd finally given Mom the money I won. I hoped she'd use it to pay her debt. I warned her to not pay everything at once so it wouldn't raise eyebrows. She'd probably spend most of it on a supply of drugs anyway.

Cheryl was rolling cigarettes beside me. When things got busy later she would hardly find the time. Her fingertips had a slight yellow tinge. She'd been smoking a lot in the last few days. Considering my frayed nerves, I wished I had something to calm them.

She hadn't asked me about Fabiano in a while, and I knew better than to offer any kind of information to her. It was too complicated to involve more people.

The door swung open. "We're closed," she shouted without even looking up.

My eyes slid over to the entrance and my hands stilled. Nino Falcone and one of his younger brothers entered. Cheryl followed my gaze and set down her cigarettes. Her eyes darted to me.

They came over to us. They didn't hurry and seemed almost relaxed as if this were a friendly visit. But Nino's cold gray eyes settled on me, and I just knew that they were here for me. Iciness clawed at my chest. I quickly dried my hands, my right hand reaching for the mobile I'd put down on the counter beside me. I needed to tell Fabiano about this. Perhaps he could at least escape, but I knew he wouldn't.

Nino shook his head, an empty expression on his face, eyes hard. "I wouldn't touch that if I were you."

I snatched my hand back from my mobile. Cheryl took a step back from me, from them. Her eyes held worry and fear—whether for herself or for me, I couldn't say.

Nino propped his elbows up on the bar. He was wearing a black turtle-neck, and he looked like an Ivy League student, not a mobster. One look at his eyes and nobody would have taken him for anything but dangerous. And I had seen him fight, had seen the many disturbing tattoos on his body, always covered by clothing when he wasn't in the cage. He pointed at the Johnnie Walker Blue Label. "Give me a glass."

My hands were shaking when I filled the glass with scotch. He took a sip. "My brother and I are going to take you with us now. We have some matters to discuss." He scanned my face. "You won't fight us, I assume."

I swallowed. The younger brother came around. He was still a teenager, definitely a couple of years younger than me, but there was no sign of boyish innocence on his face. He didn't touch me as he stopped beside me. Cheryl's eyes filled with pity.

I gave her a small smile then nodded toward Nino in agreement. There was no other option. Fighting them would have been ridiculous. I heard Fabiano talk about their fighting skills. I saw Nino in the cage with my own eyes. They would have me on the ground in a heartbeat, and unlike Fabiano, they wouldn't take care not to hurt me. Quite the contrary. I grabbed my backpack and mobile.

"Savio," Nino said simply.

Savio held out his hands, and I gave him both without resistance. Then he jerked his head. I walked ahead of him, even if having him at my back raised the little hairs on my neck. Nino appeared at my side. Neither of us spoke as they led me outside toward their car, a black Mercedes SUV. Savio opened the backdoor, and I climbed in. They sat in the front, not bothering to tie me up. There was no running. Nino sat behind the steering wheel and we drove off.

My hands shook badly as I curled my fingers around my knees in an at-tempt to calm myself. This didn't mean we were in trouble. Perhaps something else was up. But I couldn't come up with an explanation that set my mind at ease. I caught Savio watching me through the rearview mirror on occasion, while his older brother was completely focused on the windshield.

The drive passed in utter silence. Eventually a high wall came into view, and we drove through the gates and up the driveway toward a mansion. It was a beautiful sprawling estate. White and regal.

The Falcone brothers got out. Then a moment later, Nino held open my door. I hopped out of the car, glad my legs managed to hold me up despite their shaking.

"Where's Fabiano?" I asked, trying to mask my fear and failing on a grand scale.

Nino nodded toward the entrance, ignoring my question … or perhaps answering it. I wasn't sure. Together, we walked inside the beautiful house. They led me into another wing and then into a large room with a pool table and boxing ring. In it, Remo was kicking and punching a heavy bag.

He wasn't wearing a shirt, and for some reason that sight more than anything else sent a wave terror through my body. His upper body was covered in scars, most of them not as faded as the one on his face, and like Fabiano, he was all muscle. A tattoo of a kneeling angel surrounded by broken wings covered his back. I'd never seen it up close. He jumped over the rope and landed gracefully on the other side, his eyes never leaving me as he approached me. My entire body seized.

"Where's Fabiano?" I asked again, hating how shaky my voice came out.

He tilted his head to the side. "He will be here soon, don't worry." His words weren't meant to be consoling. The menace in them prevented that.

Fabiano

I stared down at Remo's text: **Come over.**

Nothing more.

I paused, knowing immediately that something was up. I tried calling Leona, but I got her voicemail, and that was when a stab of worry went through me. I raced toward Roger's Arena.

Cheryl was having a smoke in front of the entrance, fingers trembling as she held the cigarette to her mouth. Fuck.

She shook her head at me. "She's not here. They took her." She took a drag. "I hope you're happy … now that you've ruined her life."

That was the first time she'd given me anything but fake friendliness. I had no time to waste on a reply. Instead, I slipped back inside my car and raced off.

Would Remo do the honors himself? Or would he ask Nino to put a bullet in my head?

That was assuming he'd allow me the privilege of dying a quick death at all, which I doubted. And what about Leona? I could handle his torture, but Leona … What if he hurt her in front of me and made me watch her die? My hands clawed at the steering wheel.

I pulled up in Remo's driveway and jumped out of the car, not bothering to close the door. A few of Remo's soldiers watched me like the dead man that I was. We all knew I wasn't getting out of here alive. I didn't have to ask where Leona was. I knew where Remo held these kinds of conversations. I didn't bother knocking and instead stepped right into the sparring hall.

Remo, Nino, and Savio were there. And Leona stood in the center. Her eyes darted to me and relief flashed in them. Her hope was misguided. This time I couldn't save her. We'd both die. I'd die trying to defend her, but it wouldn't help. Not against Remo, Nino, and Savio … and all the men gathered in other areas of the house.

Remo perched on the edge of the pool table. He looked controlled, which worried me. He wasn't a man that usually bothered controlling himself or his anger.

"Remo," I said quietly with a nod. I walked up to Leona. I needed to be close to her when things escalated.

Remo's eyes flashed with suppressed rage. I had to fight the urge to reach for my gun. Remo, Nino, and Savio appeared relaxed enough, but I wasn't stupid enough to think that they hadn't taken all necessary precautions to guarantee we didn't get out of here alive.

"What's the meaning of all this, Remo?" I asked carefully.

He gritted his teeth and pushed himself away from the table. "Still not admitting to it?"

My muscles tensed. "Admitting to what?"

I didn't know what exactly Remo had found out. Admitting to killing Soto for Leona would be suicide.

"When you started pursuing her, I thought it was a brief adventure, but you got yourself in over your head."

"I've been doing my job as always, Remo."

He stopped across from me. Too close. "I don't recall asking you to kill Soto."

There it was. The thing that sealed our fate.

I considered pretending I didn't know what he was talking about but that would have made things worse. I pushed Leona a step back so my body was shielding her completely.

Remo saw. "All this because of that girl," he snarled. "You betrayed me for the daughter of a cheap crack-whore and a gambling addict. After everything I've done for you, you stab me in the back."

I held Leona's hand in a crushing grip, shielding her with my body, even if it drove Remo into madness. My eyes did a quick scan of the room. Remo alone was a dangerous opponent, but I would have tried my luck. With his two brothers in the room with us, I stood no chance. Nino, too, was impossible to beat.

I would still fight them, but it was only postponing the inevitable. I allowed myself a glance down at Leona, who was watching me with trust in her eyes. She thought I could get us out. Slowly, fear replaced her trust. I squeezed her hand once. She rewarded me with a shaky smile, and I released her hand. I needed both of my hands if I wanted to stand the slightest chance at all.

I considered denying I had killed Soto, but while I could withstand torture, Leona wouldn't be able to keep our secret if Remo or Nino turned their special talents on her. "I never meant to betray you. And I never did. Soto was a rat. He wasn't a good soldier."

"It's not your place to decide who is a good soldier. I am Capo, and I decide who lives and dies," he said in his quietest voice.

Remo was never quiet like that. He wasn't just furious. He was fucking crushed because I betrayed him and that was so much worse to him.

"I shouldn't have. I have always been a good soldier and I will always be your loyal soldier if you let me."

"Are you asking for forgiveness? For mercy?" He laughed.

I smiled coldly. "No. I won't."

Leona looked at me like I'd lost my mind, but she didn't know Remo. I'd seen him laugh into the faces of the begging and dying for years and knew he didn't have a heart to melt.

"Do with me whatever you want. But as a favor for years of loyal service, I ask you to let Leona go."

Remo laughed again. The way his eyes wandered over Leona, he was probably already thinking about all the things he could do to her. Raw protectiveness crushed me.

"Let me fight for her life. I'll fight as many men as you want."

Remo walked toward me. I fought the urge to pull a weapon. He stopped right in front of me. Our eyes locked. Years of loyalty, of brotherhood, passed in that one moment, and deep regret settled in my bones.

"You will fight me to the death," Remo said.

I stared at him uncomprehendingly. Since my sisters had left, since my mother had died and my father had wanted me dead, he was the only family I had. He and his brothers. Fuck, we spent every day together for the last five years. Had bled together, laughed together, killed together. I swore loyalty to him. I would have put my life down for him.

I turned my gaze to Leona, who was watching me and Remo with her innocent doe eyes. For her … I would kill him. I would kill them all.

"If you win, she will be free," Remo said to Nino, who would become Capo if Remo died. "And you, Fabiano, will put your life down without another fight."

"I will."

He nodded. "Perhaps Nino will feel lenient enough to grant you life afterward." Nino's expression left me little hope for that. Not that it mattered. If I killed Remo, the Camorra would be in uproar. Nino would have his hands full with that. He would prevail, of course, but perhaps it would give me the chance to … to what? Run away with Leona? From Vegas, from the Camorra? Join the fucking Famiglia? Fuck. I wasn't sure I could do it. But it wasn't something I had to decide now, probably never.

"To the death," I told Remo, holding out my hand for him. He gripped it, and we shook hands. Then he stepped back, fixing his cold stare on Leona. "I hope you can live with yourself now that Fabiano's signed his death note for you."

Leona opened her mouth in what looked like protest, but I gripped her hand hard. She pressed her lips together.

"Tomorrow," Remo said then turned to Nino. "Set everything up. Call Griffin."

He fought two men only yesterday, but I knew the advantage that gave me was balanced out by the fury Remo felt.

His eyes found me again. "You will spend the night here, where I can keep an eye on you."

"You know I won't run," I told him.

"Once I *knew* you were loyal," he said.

He nodded at Nino and Savio, and they led Leona and me toward a panic room without windows and locked the door.

Leona gripped my shirt. "This is suicide. He wants to kill you."

"That he's giving me the chance to fight for your life is more than he would have given anyone else. That he fights me himself is the greatest proof of respect I can think of."

She didn't look like she understood. I didn't expected her to. "You will win, right? You are the best."

"I've never won against Remo."

Leona's eyes grew wide. "Never?"

I pulled her against me, my hands slipping under her shirt. I brushed my nose along her throat. "Never."

Her hands tightened on my shirt then she slid under the fabric, her fingers raking over my skin. Her need met my own as we tore and tugged at each other's clothes until we were finally naked. I tried to memorize every inch of her body, her smell, her softness, her moans.

Later, when we lay in each other's arms, I murmured, "I don't mind dying for you."

"Don't," she whispered. "Don't say that. You won't die."

I kissed the top of her head. "Love only gets you killed. That's what my father said. I suppose he got one thing right."

Leona stopped breathing. She raised her head. One look at her cornflower blue eyes and I knew she was worth it. "Did you just …?"

"Sleep," I said softly.

TWENTY-FIVE

Fabiano

"Y**OU ARE LUCKY MY BROTHER DOES THIS FOR YOU,**" N**INO SAID**. "I'd have cut your throat."

He said it in a clinical voice. For him this was about logic and pragmatism. For Remo, this was personal. For Remo, I was like a brother … and I had gone against him. Nino moved across the room to his brothers.

Every last seat was occupied. Even more spectators stood against the walls, eyes eager for the fight of a lifetime. Leona wrung her hands beside me, eyes sliding from me to Remo, who was surrounded by his three brothers. Even Adamo would be watching the fight for once. They knew it might be their last chance to say goodbye to him.

The excitement of the crowd slowly crept into my bones. The thrill of the fight took hold of me. Remo looked at me. Tonight we'd both die. We knew it. Every other outcome would be a miracle. Leona was reluctant to let me go when Griffin called my name. Before I loosened her grip, I kissed her in front of everyone, because it didn't matter anymore. I pulled back and climbed into the cage where Remo was already waiting for me.

Griffin was saying something to the crowd or to us … I wasn't sure.

Remo approached and only stopped when his chest almost touched mine. "I loved you like a brother. Tonight is where it all ends." He held out his hand.

I wasn't sure if Remo could love. Before Leona, I was sure I wasn't capable of it either. I gripped his forearm, my palm covering the tattoo on his forearm, and he mirrored the gesture. Then we let go and took a few steps back.

Griffin climbed out of the cage and locked the door before he shouted, "To

The bar erupted with applause, but it all faded to the background. This was about Remo and me. I charged forward and so did he. After that, our world narrowed to this fight, to this moment. Remo was fast and angry. He landed a few good hits before my fist collided with his abdomen for the first time. There was blood in my mouth and my right side ached fiercely, but I ignored both, focused on Remo, on his heaving chest, his narrowed eyes. He lunged and I tried to duck, but then he was upon me. We fell to the floor, his forearm pressed against my throat.

Remo tightened his hold until stars danced in front of my eyes. "And do you still think she's worth it?" he muttered into my ear.

I sought Leona's fear-stricken face in the crowd.

"Yes," I gritted out. Never had anything been more worth dying for.

Leona

Fabiano's face was turning increasingly red in Remo's chokehold. I couldn't breathe. The crowd around me cheered like madmen, as if this wasn't about life or death. For them it was pure entertainment, something to distract them from their miserable lives.

Fabiano's blue eyes fixed on me, fierce and determined.

I tried to give him strength with my expression, even though I'd never felt more helpless and desperate in my life. The man I loved was fighting for both of our lives. Love. When had it happened? I wasn't sure. It was creeping up on me. I didn't even tell him outright. Perhaps I'd never get the chance to tell him.

And even if he won, Nino might still end his life.

Suddenly, Fabiano arched his back and thrust his elbow into Remo's side, but Remo didn't budge. Fabiano bowed forward as much as Remo's hold allowed, and then he thrust his head back with full force, crashing against Remo's face. The crowd exploded with cheers and yowls.

And suddenly, Fabiano wound himself out of Remo's grip and staggered to his feet before aiming a kick at Remo, hitting him square in the ribs. Remo jerked but quickly rolled away and pushed to his own feet. Then they were facing off again. They were circling each other, both covered in blood from head to toe, littered with bruises and cuts. Two predators waiting for a flicker of weakness.

"Perhaps now you realize what you've done," Nino said from close behind me. I jumped and took a step away from him. I didn't take my eyes off the fight. What had I done? I allowed myself to get close to a man who should have been out of reach. I had proven that I was more like my mother than I wanted to admit. But I didn't regret it. And I wouldn't allow Nino Falcone to scare me. I was past that point.

Remo landed three hard punches against Fabiano's stomach before he got hit in the face, and then they were kicking and punching so fast I lost count. They thrust each other to ground, got up, hit and kicked some more.

Fabiano's face wasn't even recognizable anymore from all the blood covering it, but neither was Remo's. I shivered.

I lost track of time; their fighting grew more erratic and less cautious. There was no holding back. Even to someone who wasn't in on the rules, it would have been clear that these two men were fighting for their life.

Remo grabbed Fabiano and thrust him full force into the fence. Fabiano bounced off and fell to his knees. I gasped and took a step forward.

Remo gripped Fabiano's head, but somehow Fabiano managed to push off the ground and thrust his knee into Remo's groin. Both of them toppled to the mat, panting and spitting blood. For a split second Fabiano allowed himself another look at me. Why did it feel like saying goodbye?

I began walking toward the cage, needing to stop this madness. Nino stepped in my way, tall and cold. "You stay where you are unless you want to die."

"How can you watch your brother die?" I asked incredulously.

Nino's unrelenting eyes took in the fight in the cage where both men were beating each other with elbows and fists, half kneeling on the floor, too weak to get up from almost one hour of non-stop fighting.

"We all have to die. We can choose to die standing up or on our knees begging for mercy. Remo's laughing death in the face like any self-respecting man should."

Fabiano

With every breath I took, it felt like a knife was slicing into my lungs. I pressed my palm against my right side, feeling my ribs. They were broken. I spit blood on the ground.

Remo was watching me closely as I knelt across from him. He'd make sure to aim his next hits on my right side. His left arm was hanging limply after I had managed to dislocate it with my elbow. This time I wouldn't give him the time to set it in place.

I pressed my palm against the ground, trying to push myself back into a standing position. The floor was slippery with blood. The room shook with roars and clapping when both Remo and I had managed to get to our feet. We were both swaying. We wouldn't be able to last long. Every bone in my body felt like it was broken. Remo winced, not bothering to hide it. We were past the point of pretending we weren't in pain. This was coming to a close.

"Thinking about giving up?" I asked.

Remo pulled back his lips in a bloody smile. "Never. And you?"

He could have had me killed without getting his hands dirty. He could have put a bullet through my skull and would have been done with it. Instead, he chose to give me a fair chance. Remo was hated. He deserved that hate like few other men in this world, but for what he did today, I'd respect him till my last breath.

"Never."

I barreled toward Remo under the thunderous applause of the crowd. The money the Camorra would win with bets tonight would set new standards. My body exploded with pain as I collided with Remo. We both fell to the ground and began wrestling. We had no strength for kick boxing anymore. This would be settled on the ground, with one of us choking the other or breaking his neck.

Something exploded. Remo and I fell apart, disoriented. The door to the fight arena went down, and men stormed in. They shouted at each other in Italian and English. Not the Russians.

The Outfit or the Famiglia attacking Las Vegas on their own?

They flooded the room like wildfire, lighting it up with gunshots.

And Remo and I sat in the middle of the room, in an illuminated fighting cage, like goldfish in a bowl.

From the corner of my eye, I saw Nino pushing Leona to the side so she fell to the ground, out of the line of fire. He began firing at the intruders as he rushed toward us. Remo and I pressed to the floor, trying not to be hit by stray bullets. It wasn't an honorable death to die kneeling on the ground, unable to fight back.

I could see one tall masked intruder heading our way, already reloading his gun. This wasn't the end I'd imagined. Being shot in the head by some Outfit or Famiglia asshole.

Nino reached the cage when two men began firing at him. Before he dove under a table, he threw a gun over the top of the cage. It landed with a soft thud in the blood puddle between Remo and me.

Remo had only one good arm, though, so I dove forward and grabbed the gun with my right hand while I used my left one to punch Remo's dislocated shoulder, stopping a grappling match before it could even start. He growled as he fell back. I knelt immediately, gun pointed straight ahead.

Remo smiled crookedly and opened his arms in invitation. "Do it. Better you than them."

Sorry, Remo, not like that.

I took aim, trying to stop my bruised arms from shaking, and then I pulled the trigger. The bullet hit its target right between the eyes.

Remo whirled around to what was behind him and could only watch the attacker, who had been pointing a gun at his head, tumble to the ground. I stumbled toward Remo, ignoring my body's screams of pain. I didn't waste time nor warned Remo. Instead, I grabbed his dislocated arm and pushed it back in place with one practiced move. Remo groaned then stumbled to his own feet. I threw my arm over his shoulder and steered him toward the door of the cage, shooting at anyone who looked like they might be a threat. I hammered against the locked cage door, but people were busy saving their own asses. And Remo's men and brothers were having a shooting match with five attackers hiding behind the bar.

My eyes searched our surroundings. Where was Leona? Was she safe? She knew this place and would be hiding somewhere safe. She was clever. I tried to calm myself. It wasn't fucking working. I ripped at the door, but the thing was built to last. "Fuck!" I screamed.

Remo tried his luck as well, but that thing was too strong. It rattled but apart from that nothing.

Suddenly, Leona's head popped up before us. Her eyes wandered between Remo and me, but she didn't say anything. She'd probably given up understanding me and this world a long time ago. She fumbled with the key in the lock until finally the door swung open, releasing us. I let go of Remo and jumped out of the cage, gasping at the impact. I'd be bruised for weeks.

If Remo let me live that long ... I was still supposed to die for my betrayal. Remo landed beside me and picked up a gun from a fallen man on the ground. "I go ahead, you have my back," he ordered like in old times. I pressed a kiss to Leona's lips. He watched with an unmoving expression.

"Let's leave," she begged. "This isn't our fight."

I smiled apologetically. "This will always be my fight as long as Remo lets me." I pushed her under the side of the cage where she wouldn't be spotted easily. "Stay there. It's too dangerous."

She nodded like she understood why I had to do this as she pressed herself against the side of the cage.

Remo and I turned around, and then we did what we did best. It took another hour to break the attack. The last two men raised their guns to their heads to end their own lives before we could get our hands on them. I shot one of them in the hand before he could pull the trigger. Then I was on him. "You'll regret the day you decided to enter our territory."

He spat onto my naked feet. "Fuck off."

Remo chuckled then coughed and spit blood on the ground. "That's how your spit is going to look soon too," he murmured.

We let Nino and Savio bring the man down to the soundproof storage room. Adamo stood back against one of the booths, looking shaken. He held a gun in his hand and stared down at one of the attackers. Was this the day of his first kill?

I could feel Leona's eyes on me as I followed after Remo to force information out of the attacker. I knew she was appalled by what I was doing. But she knew what I could do, and yet she was still here.

It took forty minutes to get the information we needed. Remo and I both were bruised and tired and needed medical treatment. We couldn't waste time on elaborate torture methods. Luckily, Nino did most of the work. The man was lying on the ground, wheezing. Remo knelt beside him. "So let me get this straight," he said calmly. "The Outfit sent you to my territory. For what?"

The man shook his head. "I don't know. I'm following orders. Your territory is bigger than ours. We want a piece. This was a good time."

Remo nodded. "Playing dirty. I like it."

He stood and gave me a look. I shoved my knife up the sucker's throat.

"This means war. If the Outfit thinks they can play, we'll show them what we are capable of."

I wiped my knife on my bloody shorts. "I bet that would be interesting."

Remo raised his dark eyebrows. "Would be?"

I straightened, despite the pain in my ribs. "I'm supposed to die, remember?"

Remo and I stared at each other for a long time. Nino and Savio exchanged looks as well. I wondered what they wanted. Me dead? I couldn't say, and they weren't the ones to decide anyway.

Remo put his hand on my shoulder, eyes fierce and full of warning. "This once I will let you live. You proved your loyalty by putting a fucking bullet into the head of my enemy when you could have killed me instead. Don't go behind my back again, Fabiano. That time there won't be a death match. I'll just put a bullet through your skull."

"As you should," I told him then pressed my palm again my side again. "Leona must be safe. She must be mine. I want her at my side. I want to spend my life with her."

"If that's what you want."

I nodded. "She's seen me at my worst, and she's still here."

Remo waved a hand at me. He couldn't comprehend. "She is yours, no worries. Now go to her and get a nice long blowjob as a reward for your troubles."

I rolled my eyes and dragged myself up the staircase. I doubted I'd get it up today. Every part of my body was aching, but I was willing to give it a try.

The moment I stepped back into the bar, Leona hopped off the barstool she had been waiting on and rushed toward me, throwing her arms around my waist. I gasped from the stab of pain in my ribs, my shoulder—fuck, my entire body. She loosened her hold, worried eyes peering up at me. Her hair was all over the place, and there was a small cut over her cheekbone. I ran the back of my index finger over it.

"You're hurt."

She choked out a laugh. "I'm hurt? You are bleeding and bruised. I thought you would die in that cage, and when you disappeared with Remo down into the storage room, I feared you wouldn't come out again," she whispered.

"I'm fine," I told her, and she gave me a look. "I'm alive," I amended.

For my fucking body to get anywhere close to being fine again, that would take a while.

"But what about Remo? Won't he kill you?"

Wasn't she worried about her own life as well? Perhaps she'd forgotten, but my fight would have decided her fate too.

"We came to an understanding. He gave me another chance." Fuck, to think that I would see that day.

"He did?" Leona voiced the disbelief still anchored in my body.

I nudged her in the direction of the entrance. "Come. I want to go home."

She froze. "We're not going home. You need to go to the hospital. Remo must have broken every bone in your body."

"I broke just as many of his," I said immediately.

Leona shook her head, unbelieving. "I don't care about him. But you need treatment."

I leaned down, my mouth curling into a smile despite the fucking cut in my lower lip. "I know just the right treatment."

She angled her head away. "You can't be serious."

I brushed my hand over her side. "I am dead serious. Won't you honor the wish of a dying man?"

She shoved me, angry and half amused. I winced because my body fucking ached. "Sorry!" she blurted, fingers ghosting over my chest in silent apology.

"I almost lost you and my fucking life. Don't you think I deserve a reward?"

She shook her head again, but her resolve was melting. Her fingers lingered on my abs, the touch a mix of pain and promise. "I really don't think …"

"I won't go to the hospital," I interrupted her then buried my nose against her throat. "I want to feel you. Want to feel something else other than this fucking pain."

She opened the passenger door of my Mercedes for me. I raised my eyebrows. "You can't drive."

I handed her the keys without protest, enjoying her surprise. "Then you will."

I could tell she was terrified of wrecking my car. As if I gave a fucking damn about the thing. "Take us to our hill," I ordered when she pulled out of the parking lot.

Her brows pinched together again, but she did as I asked. After she parked, I pushed myself out of the car and carried myself toward the hood. I sank down and let my eyes take in my city. Leona stepped up beside me.

"And now?" she whispered.

I pulled her between my legs and kissed her softly, then harder but had to pull away when my vision began spinning. I tried to mask my dizziness, but Leona's eyes narrowed.

"Your body is a mess, Fabiano. Let's go to the hospital. There's no way you can do anything right now anyway."

I guided her hand to my dick, which was growing hard under her touch.

Her blue eyes met mine. "So every part of your body is hurting except for him," she said, squeezing my cock through the fabric. I chuckled and regretted it at once. "Seems so."

"Sure," she murmured doubtfully. "You should really go see a doctor."

"I will, later," I said quietly. "Now I want to remember why life is better than fucking death."

She leaned forward once more, kissing me sweetly and almost shyly, as if something in her mind was distracting her. When she pulled away, her uncertainty had been replaced by resolve. She slid down my shorts, grazing several wounds on the way, and got down on her knees before me. My cock jolted at the tantalizing sight. I hadn't expected her to do it after what she'd said about cock sucking being degrading and all, but I wasn't going to remind her. She wrapped her fingers around the base of my cock, opened her mouth, and slowly took me in inch by inch.

Holy Fuck.

I'd been with so many women, but every experience with Leona outshined my past. She gagged when my tip hit the back of her throat, and she quickly moved back. I had to resist the urge to grab her hair and hold her in place so I could fuck her sweet mouth. Instead, I forced my body to relax under her soft tongue, allowed her to explore and taste me. But eventually I needed more, so I took control. I began moving my hips, sliding my cock in and out of her warm mouth harder and faster every time.

Leona and I could have been dead by now. But we weren't. I jerked my hips upwards, and she let me. She struggled to take as much of me into her mouth as possible, and the sight fucking undid me. My balls tightened, and I called out a warning, but Leona didn't pull away. I released into her mouth.

It was the most painful orgasm I'd ever had, and yet as I watched Leona lick her lips with uncertainty, I decided it was also the fucking best. She ran a hand over her mouth, looking up at me. I could see the vulnerability in her eyes.

I pulled her up to me despite the agony that shot through my ribs, needing her to get it out of her head that anything I did was to degrade her. I needed her to understand what I felt for her, even if I had a hard time understanding it myself. "Leona, nothing I do will be to degrade you. And no one else will ever dare degrade you either." I softened my voice. "Are you okay?" I ran my thumb over her soft lips.

She ran a hand through my sweaty, blood-streaked hair. "Can we be together now? I mean for real?"

"We can and we will. I want you to move in with me. I want to bind you to me. I want to stop you from getting away ever again."

It wasn't romantic, it wasn't nice, but I wasn't either of those things.

"Then I'm okay."

I let out a small laugh, followed by a wince. She lightly traced my ribs but even that hurt.

"Why did you want me in the first place? I've been wondering about that from the start, but I knew you'd never tell me the truth anyway," she said.

"And now you think I will?"

She traced the cut below my cheekbone. "You are pretty rattled. I think now is my best chance."

"You are becoming more cunning."

She shrugged. "Survival of the fittest and all that. Or what did you call it?"

I slipped my hand under her shirt and bra and ran my forefinger over her nipple. It puckered immediately under the ministration. Leona licked her lips as her eyes glazed over. "Why?" she repeated her earlier question. I tugged at her nipple. She smiled. "Stop distracting me."

I slid my other hand up her thigh and into the leg of her shorts. My thumb brushed aside her thong and slid into her wet heat. She was still tight, but there was no resistance. Her walls squeezed around my finger as I slid it in and out slowly. She moaned and began bucking her hips.

"Why," she ground out again as she rocked her pussy against my hand. I exchanged my thumb for two fingers and moved faster. I stood and lifted her shirt then closed my lips around that perfect pink nipple. I tasted sweat on her skin. She'd been afraid for me, for us. I sucked her nipple harder. She gasped, slowly coming undone. I added a third finger, and she clawed at my shoulders, her expression a mix of ecstasy and discomfort. Pain shot through me when her fingers dug into bruised skin, but it felt fucking good. I thrust my fingers harder and faster into her, enjoying her tightness, her wetness, her whimpers. Fuck, those breathless sounds were music to my ears. Her walls clamped down on my fingers, and she threw her head back, letting out a long moan. I released her nipple and watched my fingers slide in and out of her. Her grip on my shoulders loosened. Slowly, her eyes peeled open and she watched me. I kept moving my fingers in and out of her, letting her ride out the last gentle waves of pleasure. "Because you didn't judge me. You didn't know me. You didn't go into our conversation hoping to get something out of it."

Leona smiled. "But I got something out of it. I got you."

I shook my head at her. I slid my fingers out of her. "You don't know what's good for you."

She released a small breath then lifted one shoulder. "Good's overrated."

I kissed her again, tasting myself on her.

"You almost died today ... for me," she whispered. "Nobody has ever done something like that for me. People can keep telling me to stay away from you if they want, but it won't make me love you any less."

My body grew taut at her admission. Love was a dangerous thing, something that had brought the hardest fighters to their knees. Weakness was something I couldn't afford, not if I wanted to stay on Remo's good side. But love wasn't a choice. It was like fucking torture. Something that happened to you and you were unable to stop it. It was the only form of torture I was unable to endure.

I brushed a sweaty curl out of her face, wondering how she could have put a hole in the impenetrable façade I'd built since my father had abandoned me. Leona, with her infuriating naivety, her shy smile ... I'd watched the people I cared about leave me one after the other. I swore to myself to never allow anyone else into my heart. And now Leona had changed everything.

"Your expression is a bit on the unsettling side. What's going on?"

I shook my head in exasperation. I hadn't been afraid of anyone or anything in a while, and here I was being a fucking pussy about this. "Fuck," I breathed. "I love you."

She took a small step back, astonishment reflecting on her beautiful face. "I didn't think you'd say it."

"You didn't think I loved you?"

She laughed then wedged herself between my legs again, bringing us closer and sending a stab of pain through my body from the movement, but I couldn't care less. If I didn't think it might shove one of my broken ribs into my lungs, I'd have fucked her right then. No, *made love to her*. God help me.

"After you agreed to a death match, I was fairly certain you did," she said with a small smile, "but I didn't think you'd admit it."

Sometimes I forgot how well she'd come to know me. That she still wanted to be with me filled my heart with a strange sense of comfort but also with a bone-deep fear I hadn't felt in a long time. The idea of a death match with Remo hadn't scared me, death and pain certainly didn't, but Leona's love and my love for her scared me shitless. It was something I'd just have to deal with because Leona wasn't going anywhere, and I wouldn't stop loving her.

TWENTY-SIX

Leona

FABIANO'S BRUISES AND CUTS HAD HEALED. ROGER'S ARENA HAD BEEN renovated, but I was no longer working for him. Fabiano didn't want me to. After all, now I was officially his girl. Even my mother stopped selling her body because she didn't have to do it anymore. She got her meth from Fabiano. The Camorra had more than enough of the toxic stuff. It wasn't what I'd wanted for her, and I still wished she'd stop taking the shit altogether, but it was her choice; I'd done what I could for her.

Suddenly people treated me differently. With respect. Not because of who I was but because of who I belonged to: The Enforcer of the Camorra.

It was nice in some regard, but I still preferred people respect me for my own accomplishments. One day perhaps.

I sat quietly beside Fabiano, watching Nino Falcone destroy his opponent in the fighting cage. Remo sat at the same table, but I ignored him. He was being civil toward me since the fight to the death, and I treated him with the respect he expected as Capo. I did it for Fabiano and because I wasn't suicidal. But I'd never like him. Too little humanity remained in him—if it had ever been there in the first place. His two brothers were at the table too. Savio, who whistled whenever his brother landed a hit, and Adamo, who seemed drawn into himself, not once glancing toward the cage.

Fabiano traced a hand up my thigh, startling me. My eyes met his then quickly did a scan of our surroundings. People were mesmerized by the fight and didn't pay attention to what was going on underneath our table.

Fabiano turned his attention back to the fight as well, but he kept stroking the inside of my thigh. Nino threw his opponent into the cage, and the room exploded with applause. Fabiano slipped his hand beneath my panties, finding me aroused, which was usually the case when he touched me. He leaned over, his breath hot against my ear. "I hope this isn't because of Nino," he said huskily.

I rolled my eyes.

"Tonight I'm going to fuck you in that cage."

He dipped a finger between my folds, and I had to stifle a groan. Remo's eyes slid over to me, and I quickly closed my legs, forcing Fabiano to pull his hand away. He smirked then commented on a move Nino did with his leg as if nothing had happened.

With an audible crack, Nino broke his opponent's arm. Adamo jerked back his chair and stood, eyes wild, then he turned and hurried off toward the exit. I wasn't sure why, but I pushed my own chair back and followed him. He was a Falcone, Remo's brother, but he was also only thirteen. And he obviously wasn't coping with what happened the last couple of weeks. I caught up with him in the parking lot, his hand on the door of a sleek red Ford Mustang.

"Your car?" I asked jokingly.

"Remo's," Adamo said, twisting car keys between his fingers.

"He lets you drive it?" I doubted anyone would let a thirteen-year-old drive a car around Vegas, but Remo didn't exactly play by the rules.

Adamo turned angry eyes toward me. "No, he'll probably kick my ass. I stole the key."

"Oh." He was still watching me, still twisting the key as if he needed the smallest reason to stay. I took a step closer. "I don't enjoy the cage fighting. Too brutal."

"Not as brutal as real life."

Mob life. His life … and now mine as well. "I dream about the attack." And about the hours before it, the fear of the death match.

He looked down at the key in his hand. "I shot someone."

"I know," I said quietly and took another step forward. I put my hand on his forearm lightly. His eyes met mine. Only thirteen and they looked jaded. "It was self-defense."

"It won't always be. I'm a Falcone. Soon, I'll be a Camorrista."

"True. But who says you'll have to hurt people. You could do street races. It's a big part of the business, right? So it would be good to have a Falcone showing off what he can do. I hear you are quite good already."

His lips twitched. "Yeah. But Remo thinks I'm too young."

"Once you're inducted, I'm sure he'll change his mind. If you can handle a gun, you can race a car, don't you think?"

He shook his head slowly. "Remo will attack the Outfit in retribution. He will need a fighter, not a race driver."

I'd figured as much from Fabiano's cryptic comments these last few days. Things would get rough pretty soon. "Why don't you come back inside? Stealing your brother's car won't get you any favors."

His eyes shifted between the car and the bar. Then he closed the door. We turned and headed back toward the entrance, where Fabiano was waiting with his arms crossed over his chest.

Adamo winced.

"Have you been spying on us?" I asked.

He pushed off the wall. "You both have a penchant for getting into trouble." I huffed.

Fabiano caught Adamo's gaze and put a hand on his shoulder. "Running won't help." He poked his index finger against Adamo's forehead. "Can't run from what's in there. Regret and guilt, they follow." Fabiano touched Adamo's forearm, and the boy gave a small nod as if he understood.

Fabiano tousled his hair. Adamo pulled back in protest. Then Fabiano feigned an attack and a grappling match ensued. After a moment, Fabiano pushed a smiling Adamo toward the door. "Inside."

Adamo entered the bar, and we followed. Remo's eyes zeroed in on us at once. His brother put the key down in front of him then slumped back in his chair.

Fabiano and I took our seats, and he took my hand under the table, linking our fingers.

Remo leaned over to me, and I tensed. Fabiano squeezed my hand in support, but his eyes were on the fight. "What did you do to stop him from driving off?"

It took effort to hold Remo's fierce dark eyes. "Tried to make him see light in the dark."

"Like you did for him," he said with a tilt of his head. It wasn't a question.

I glanced at Fabiano, but his eyes followed Nino's movements in the cage … at least it appeared that way. Before Remo turned away, a flicker of acknowledgement passed over his expression.

I didn't think he was serious, but Fabiano and I were the last guests in the bar. Cheryl cleaned the counter, eying us wearily. "We should leave too."

"I told you I'd have you against that cage tonight." He turned to Cheryl and raised his voice. "You can leave. I have the keys. I will lock up later."

Cheryl put down the cloth, picked up her purse, and walked past us. She'd been distant since I was officially at Fabiano's side.

He took my hand and pulled me to my feet then led me toward the cage in the center. My core tightened in anticipation as he leaped onto the platform and pulled me along. I climbed into the cage then heard the familiar click of the door closing. A pleasant shiver raced down my spine. Fabiano pressed up against my body from behind, his erection digging into my lower back. I arched my butt against him, needing his hands on me. After his teasing during the fight, it had been difficult to grasp a straight thought. He pulled my dress over my head and dropped it onto the ground then pulled down my panties.

Fabiano urged me forward with his body until I had no choice but to brace myself against the cage. He ran his hands over my shoulders and down my arms, then gripped my hands, lifting them above my head. I linked my fingers in the mesh of the cage as Fabiano pressed my body against the cold metal. My nipples hardened immediately. The feel of the unrelenting steel against my breasts and Fabiano's equally unrelenting muscles was oddly erotic. He stepped back and I huffed in protest, but when I looked over my shoulder, I saw him pull down his briefs. His cock was already hard for me. I shivered in anticipation. There was hunger in his eyes and the warmer emotion that he didn't try to hide anymore. His movements were lithe and dangerous as he stalked toward me. Fighter and killer and mine. I turned back to the cage and leaned my forehead against it. Not able to see him approach heightened my senses, made me even more aroused.

He slid a hand between my thighs and urged them apart. I complied eagerly then waited for his fingers to send me to Heaven. Instead, I felt his tip press against my opening. Surprise filled me, but then I arched my butt to show him I didn't mind him skipping foreplay. Being in a cage with him was all the foreplay I needed. But he didn't push into me. Instead, he ran his tip up from my opening to my clit and back again. I moaned, arching against him for more friction. My nipples rubbed against the metal deliciously.

And then he pushed into me with one hard thrust. I cried out, my fingers clinging painfully to the wire mesh. He slid in and out. His hand glided over my stomach and lower until his fingers brushed my clit. I cried out again, and he thrust even harder into me. His fingers established a slow rhythm while he fucked me fast. My fingers on the mesh tightened painfully as a wave of pleasure swept through me. I cried out his name, half delirious from the force of my orgasm. I had trouble staying upright. My fingers loosened their grip on the mesh fence, and Fabiano's hands covered mine, linking our fingers and holding me up.

His pelvis hit my butt again. I whimpered. The sensations were almost too much, but Fabiano knew no mercy. His pelvis slammed against my butt over and over again as he drove himself even deeper into me. Dots danced before my vision. "Oh God," I gasped. His next thrust catapulted me into sweet oblivion, a darkness of heightened senses and overwhelming pleasure. He turned me around and lowered me to the ground then lifted my feet to his shoulders, raising my butt. His tip rested against my sensitive flesh. His blue eyes looked unhinged. Out of control for once. He slid into me slowly then back out. The way he was holding my hips, I could see his erection sliding between my folds as I felt my walls yielding to him. Fabiano's muscles flexed as he took his time sliding in and out of me. I didn't think I was capable of another orgasm after my last, but seeing Fabiano's cock bury itself in me aroused me even more.

I began quivering. Fabiano smiled darkly and parted my folds with his thumbs, revealing my clit. If he touched me there, I'd fall apart. But he didn't. He only watched his cock slide in and out, his thumbs so very close to where I needed his touch the most.

I reached out, too desperate for my next release to wait for him to make a move, but he caught my wrist. He raised my palm to his mouth and pressed an open-mouthed kiss to my flesh, his tongue darting out and licking off sweat. I groaned at the sensation as it traveled all the way down to my clit. "Fabiano," I begged. "Stop torturing me."

A predator grin. "But it's what I do best."

Good God. There was no way I wasn't going to Hell for this. And I couldn't even pretend I cared. He slid into me again and then mercifully, he captured my clit between his fingers and twirled it between them. I came apart. My shoulder blades arched painfully against the floor, my nails searching for leverage. And then Fabiano followed after me with a curse and groan. I forced my eyes open, needing to see him. He had his head thrown back, eyes closed. The most amazing sight ever.

Slowly, he lowered his head and looked at me, his lips twisting wryly. "I truly corrupted you. You weren't even worried someone could walk in on us."

I turned my head to the side. The bar was deserted, but of course he had a point. We hadn't locked the doors, and it wouldn't be the first time Roger spent the night in his office.

I covered my eyes with my hand, trying to catch my breath. Fabiano took my wrist and pulled my shield away, then stood me up so I straddled his legs. I wrapped my arms around his neck, searching his eyes for confirmation that he was okay with me enjoying this so much. "

You were worth it, you know?" He nuzzled my neck and I smiled to myself.

"What exactly?" I whispered.

"The pain, the wait, Remo's wrath. Everything."

This was where it all started. Where my dreams of an ordinary life ended and something else, something equally good I realized now, had begun.

"I love you," I breathed.

"And I love you," he said. The words still sounded foreign from his lips.

I touched the tattoo on his forearm. "More than this."

"More than this." But because I knew he loved the Camorra, loved Remo as a brother—for whatever inexplicable reason—I would never ask him to choose.

He brushed my hair back from my sweaty forehead. "You should start looking into applying to college. University of Nevada is a good place to start."

I pulled back. "I don't have the money."

Fabiano smiled. "I might as well put all the blood money in my account to good use. The Camorra still needs a good lawyer. Why not you?"

I couldn't believe it. "You mean it?" I didn't dare hope I was hearing him right.

He nodded. "But I have to tell you that it has to be in Vegas. I can't let you go, being a possessive bastard and all."

I kissed him, excitement surging through me.

"My possessiveness never excited you that much before," he said wryly.

I shook my head, having a hard time forming words to express my gratitude. "I don't want to leave Las Vegas. Because Las Vegas is your home and you are mine."

He pulled me into a painful embrace and I sank into him. My protector.

THE END

TWISTED EMOTIONS

Book Two
The Camorra Chronicles

PROLOGUE

Kiara

THE FALCONES WERE GOING TO FEEL CHEATED. A SACRIFICIAL VIRGIN was to be given to the monsters in Las Vegas for a promise of peace. I was never given the chance to be a virgin. That choice had been taken from me. *Painfully ripped from me.*

Fear, acute and raw, clawed at my chest as my husband led me into our room for the night and closed the door to the grinning faces of his brothers. Nino released me, and I quickly created distance between us, moving toward the bed.

Six years had passed, but the memories still woke me at night. I was scared of being close to a man, to any man, especially this man—my husband.

Standing a few steps in front of the bed, my eyes swept over the white sheets—sheets my family expected to the see stained with my blood in the morning.

Blood that wouldn't be there.

I crept closer to the bed. There had been blood the first time, the second time, and even the third time. Lots of blood, pain, terror, and begging. There had been no presentation of the sheets back then. Our maid, who had never come to my aid, cleaned them.

I wouldn't beg tonight. It hadn't stopped my abuser many years ago.

It wouldn't stop my husband.

I knew the stories. I had seen him in the cage.

My only consolation was that I doubted he could break me more than I already had been all those years ago.

ONE

Before:

Nino

"**Y**OU DO REMEMBER WHAT I TOLD LUCA LAST TIME I SAW HIM? I doubt he'll have any kind of interest in working with us after that," Fabiano muttered, pacing the room. "He will kill me the moment I set foot in his territory, trust me. Fuck, I would kill me if I were him."

Remo shook his head. "He is angry, but he will see reason."

I nodded. "He wanted to protect his property, his wife, but he's still a businessman, and we have good arguments for cooperation. Drugs are still his main business, and our contact in his lab tells us they can't produce enough for the increasing demand. Luca needs to import drugs, but he can't because we hold the west and Dante holds the middle. His smugglers lose too much of the shit before it reaches the East Coast. If he works with us, we can guarantee safe transport through our territory and in return he promises us to stay out of our fight with Dante Cavallaro. We don't even want his help."

"We don't need it," Remo insisted, dark eyes hardening. We disagreed on that point; additional help facing an opponent like Dante Cavallaro would have been very appreciated, but like Luca, Remo let emotions get in the way of rational decisions.

Fabiano frowned. "Luca isn't like you, Nino. Not every single one of his decisions is based on logical reasons. He's furious because we insulted Aria, and his pride might stop him from making the logical decision. Trust me on that."

"If you tell your sister that you gave Leona that bracelet, she will convince him. She'll think you are her little brother again. She'll want to believe it. Take Leona with you. Make it out to be a family visit, for all I care, but convince Aria and Luca to talk to us. Tell him I'm going to meet with him personally," Remo said.

I gave Remo a slanted look. Last time he talked to Luca hadn't gone over too well. Years had passed, but if Luca held on to grudges, he'd remember that too. And Remo had a way of provoking people that didn't go over well with the other Capo.

"He won't believe that we're trustworthy," Fabiano said. "And you talking to Luca is the fucking worst thing that could happen. Remo, you are a fucking time bomb. You get a hard-on just imagining how it would feel to bathe in Luca's blood, damn it. Do you really think you could stop yourself from trying to kill him?"

Remo leaned back with a smile on his face that I'd learned to be wary of. "The Famiglia is all about bonds to ensure peace, aren't they? We give them what they want, what your sister wanted for you and everyone else."

He hadn't answered Fabiano's question.

Fabiano stopped his pacing and crossed his arms. "And what's that supposed to be?"

"Peace and love." Remo's mouth twisted as if he was going to start laughing. "We'll suggest a marriage between our families. It worked between the Outfit and the Famiglia for a while."

Remo hadn't mentioned anything to me. Usually he consulted with me before he made these kinds of decisions. For Remo, it was a surprisingly reasonable plan. Marriages had prevented many wars over the centuries of human history— of course, they'd started just as many as well.

Fabiano laughed but I could tell that he was displeased from the narrowing of his eyes. "For a few years and now they are back to killing each other."

"A few years is all we require," I told him. "Luca knows as well as we do that any kind of peace arrangement will always only be for a short period of time."

"You can't believe that Luca will agree to an arranged marriage."

"Why not?" Remo asked, grinning. "It worked for him and your sister. Look at them, sickly in love. I'm sure he can spare one of his cousins. Didn't you say his father had three sisters and two brothers? There have to be a few cousins in marrying age, or even a second cousin for all I care."

"One of those sisters was married to a traitor whom our father killed. I doubt she will give her daughters to us," I reminded Remo.

"One of her daughters is the fuck-thing of that bastard Growl. As if I'd accept her or her sister for our family," Remo spat. I inclined my head in agreement. It would send the wrong message if we allowed the Famiglia to give us the leftovers of our traitorous half-brother.

"Luca wouldn't choose either of them. But who the fuck is supposed to marry a woman from the Famiglia?" Fabiano asked, raising his blond eyebrows at my brother. "Don't tell me it's going to be you, Remo, because I won't make that fucking offer. We all know that you are the last person we can parade around as a husband. You lose your temper all the time. That will end in a fucking bloody wedding and you know it."

Remo grinned, his eyes shifting to me. That explained why he hadn't consulted with me. "I won't marry anyone. Nino will."

Lifting my eyebrows at him, I asked, "Will I?"

Fabiano sank down onto the sofa, grimacing. "No offense, but Nino isn't really the right person to play husband either."

I tilted my head. I'd never considered marriage. It seemed unnecessary. "If you're referring to my lack of emotions, I can assure you that I can fake them if required."

Remo shrugged. "It's not like it's a marriage for love. Nino doesn't have to feel anything to marry. He only needs to say yes and fuck his bride, perhaps father a kid or two, and keep his wife alive as long as we want peace with the Famiglia. You can do that, right?"

I narrowed my eyes, not liking his tone. "I can do that."

Fabiano shook his head. "That's a fucking bad idea and you know it."

"It's unconventional," I conceded, "but it's a practice that's been used in our circles for generations. Even before our families came to the US, they arranged marriages to establish bonds between different families. And the Famiglia has old-world values. They are the only family outside Italy that still follows the bloody sheets tradition. I'm certain that Luca's family will welcome the idea of another arranged marriage between families; Luca needs to keep the traditionalists in the Famiglia happy, especially now that he had to take in some of his relatives from Sicily. And there are still traditionalists in the Camorra who'll appreciate that kind of agreement."

Fabiano shook his head again. "I tell you again, Luca won't agree. He will kill me."

Remo smirked. "We will see. I hear he needs to protect his children."

Fabiano jerked. "Aria's got kids?"

Remo and I had known for a while. One of our contacts told us. Luca made sure to keep Aria and the kids out of the press and even killed a few photographers who didn't grasp the concept of privacy. Remo hadn't wanted

Fabiano to know because he worried Fabiano would get too emotional during his visit in New York. Apparently, he changed his mind.

" A daughter and a son," I said. "He needs to protect them, and if we offer him peace in the west, that should convince him."

Fabiano was silent. "How long have you known?"

"Is that important? It's not like Luca would have let you anywhere near his kids," Remo said.

Fabiano nodded but his mouth was tight. "You know Dante wasn't the main force behind the attack on us. It was my father." He looked at me then at Remo. "Dante might kill my father before we get our hands on him. I don't want that to happen. Let me go to Chicago and bring him to Las Vegas. We can still ask Luca for peace after that."

Remo gave me a pointed look, obviously needing me to be the voice of reason as usual.

"That seems unwise," I said. "You are too emotionally invested to lead an attack on Outfit ground, especially on your father. And we don't know for certain if your father acted without Dante's direct orders. Dante might not kill him."

"It was my father's plan. You heard what the Outfit fuckers said when we tore them apart. My father sent those fuckers because he wanted me dead," Fabiano growled. "And I want to kill him. I want to tear him apart limb by limb."

"And you will," Remo said firmly, touching Fabiano's shoulder. He paused. Again with that smile. "But it would be a good wedding gift. If we get our hands on Scuderi, we could have his death as a peace offering for Luca and his clan. After all, the Scuderi sisters don't hold much love for their father either."

"Of course they don't. He is a despicable asshole," Fabiano said.

"We can't waltz into Chicago and drag their Consigliere out. You realize that, right? Dante will have put every possible protection in place." I had to say it because it was becoming increasingly obvious that neither Remo nor Fabiano would make the wise choice when it came to bringing down the Outfit. "The only logical choice is to send me to New York for the meeting with Luca. I'm not emotionally invested. I will be able to deescalate the situation if required."

Remo shook his head. "I am Capo. I should be at the front. Only a fucking coward would send his brother out to risk his sorry ass in a situation like this."

"What about my fucking ass?" Fabiano muttered.

"Your ass is safe because of your sister. No matter what Luca says, he'll always think twice before putting a bullet in your head. With Nino, nothing's holding him back."

"He won't shoot me. His next delivery will have to pass our borders in the upcoming days ... if our informants in Mexico are to be believed. We intercept it, keep hold of his men and his drugs until the meeting, and I'll give the order to have them released as a peace offering, a sign of goodwill."

"Drugs and expendable soldiers won't stop Luca from killing you," Fabiano said.

"We will see," I said. "It's the only logical choice."

"Your fucking logic is pissing me off," Remo muttered.

"I'm the future husband, so it is the *logical* choice to send me. We're doing this on my terms, Remo. I won't have you two mess this up with your emotions."

"I think he's pissing me off on purpose," Remo said to Fabiano.

Fabiano nodded. "I think he is."

"It doesn't take much effort to piss you off, Remo."

Remo narrowed his eyes at me. "The logical choice would be to take some-one with you. You shouldn't go alone. Take Fabiano."

Fabiano rolled his eyes. "Yeah, take me. Because apparently I'm bulletproof because I'm a fucking Scuderi."

I regarded the blond man. "Maybe your presence would rip open too many wounds for Luca. We don't want to start on the wrong foot."

"I think that ship has sailed," Fabiano said.

"Do you want to come with me to New York?" I asked, my expression doubtful.

"I'd rather go to Chicago and kill my fucking father, but if an insane mar-riage between you and some poor Famiglia woman brings me closer to that goal, I'll go to New York and talk to Luca fucking Vitiello. But I don't think he'll be very happy to see me. He won't believe I've changed for one fucking second."

"You haven't really. Except for your behavior toward Leona. You are still a cruel bastard, so Vitiello shouldn't trust you," I said.

Fabiano looked between Remo and me. "Am I going or not? I'll have to fig-ure out a way to tell Leona about this without freaking her out."

Remo shook his head. "I should go as Capo."

"We'll save that reunion for the second meeting when Vitiello is convinced the benefits of a bond outweigh the joy of cutting off your head," I said.

"I take it that means I'm going." Fabiano got up. "I really hope this fucking ordeal allows me to kill my father, or you two will have a lot to make up to me."

I still wasn't convinced that Fabiano's presence would improve our situ-ation. He was Aria's brother, true, but even that wouldn't protect him forever. Taking Remo was out of the question. I'd have to make sure Luca and Fabiano would follow my reasoning and not let their unpredictable emotions run the show.

Kiara

I stood off to the side as usual, far enough away from the dance floor so no one would feel obligated to ask me to a dance. My eyes followed Giulia as she danced with her husband, Cassio. Her eyes caught mine briefly, and she smiled. She had already moved out when I had to move in with Aunt Egidia and Uncle Felix six years ago, but she and I had become close friends nevertheless, closer than anyone else, especially my older brothers. They were allowed to stay in Atlanta after our father was killed by my cousin Luca. I shivered at the memory.

Giulia was one of the few who looked at me with kindness and not a superior sneer. I resisted the urge to rub my arms; it seemed like I was always cold. Even the music failed to set me at ease. I couldn't wait to be back home and feel the keys of my piano under my fingertips.

My spine stiffened when Luca headed toward me. His wife, Aria, probably took pity on me and told him to ask me to a dance. I really wished he wouldn't.

"Would you like to dance?" he asked, holding out his hand. Since I'd turned eighteen last year, I was expected to attend social events. Even Aunt Egidia and Uncle Felix couldn't find excuses to keep me away anymore. I was still shunned by many, not openly, but I caught their looks when they thought I wasn't paying attention.

"It's an honor," I said quietly and took his hand. My body revolted at the physical contact, but I forced it into submission and followed Luca toward the dance floor. He was my cousin and I'd known him all my life, not that I knew him very well. We had too many cousins in our family to allow a closer bond.

I tried to brace myself for the next step, for his hand on my waist, tried to prepare so I wouldn't flinch, but the moment his palm touched my hip, my entire body seized. Luca regarded me but didn't pull back. He was probably used to that kind of reaction from people. His reputation and size would have sent even a normal woman running. I tried to soften my body in his hold as we danced, but it was a losing battle and eventually I gave up.

"Your father was a traitor, Kiara. I had to kill him."

I'd never held it against him. My father knew the consequences of betrayal, yet Luca seemed to think that was the reason I couldn't stand his touch. I wished it were that. God, how I wished it were only that, wished it was only Luca's touch that brought me close to panic. I swallowed the memories of the nights that had broken me.

"You had to," I agreed. "And I don't miss him. He wasn't a good father. I miss my mother, but you didn't kill her. That was my father."

In my head I began playing the melody I'd been working on over the last few weeks, hoping it would calm me. It didn't.

Luca nodded. "I talked to Aunt Egidia and Felix. They are concerned that you aren't married yet."

I was nineteen and hadn't been promised to anyone yet. "Who wants to marry the daughter of a traitor?" I muttered. Deep down I was relieved. Marriage would reveal a secret I needed to hold on to, a secret that would turn me into a pariah in our circles.

"You did nothing wrong. Your father's actions don't define you."

People were watching me. "Why don't you tell them," I spat, looking around at our audience. I cringed at my tone. "I'm sorry." Luca was Capo. I needed to show respect.

He regarded me, wearing a blank mask. "I don't want to promise you to a soldier. You are a Vitiello and should be married to one of my Captains or Underbosses."

"It's okay. I have time," I said quietly, my cheeks flushing in shame. I didn't really have time. I was getting older and being unmarried and a traitor's daughter would only make people talk more.

The dance was finally over, and I gave Luca a quick, forced smile before I made my way back to the side. After that, I did what I could do best—had learned to do best—I pretended I wasn't there. My aunt choosing modest dresses in subdued colors from last year's collection definitely helped with that. I couldn't wait for the Vitiello Christmas party to be over. Christmastime was connected to too many horrible memories.

Christmas Time seven years ago

I couldn't sleep. No matter how I twisted and turned, I always managed to lie on the bruises. Father had been in a horrible mood today. Mother said it had something to do with us being in New York. Tomorrow, we'd finally return to Atlanta, and then his mood would be better. Soon, everything would be better. Soon, Father would have solved all of his problems and we'd finally be happy. I knew it wasn't true. He would never be happy, never stop hitting us. Father enjoyed his unhappiness and he enjoyed making us suffer.

Something clanged downstairs. I got out of bed and stretched, trying to get rid of the soreness in my limbs from the beating I endured this morning. A sound in the corridor drew me toward the door, and I carefully opened it, peering out the crack. A tall man lunged at me. Something over my head gleamed in the light, and then a knife was wedged into the wooden doorframe. I opened my mouth to scream, but the man clamped his hand over my mouth. I struggled, terrified of the huge stranger.

"Not a sound. Nothing will happen to you, Kiara." I froze and took a closer look at the man. It was my cousin Luca, my father's Capo. "Where is your father?"

I pointed toward the door at the end of the corridor, my parents' bedroom. He released me and handed me over to Matteo, my other cousin. I wasn't sure what was going on. Why were they here in the middle of the night?

Matteo began to lead me away when my mother stepped out of the bedroom. Her terrified eyes landed on me a moment before she jerked and fell to the ground.

Luca threw himself to the ground as a bullet hit the wall behind him. Matteo shoved me away and darted forward, but another man gripped me in an unrelenting hold. My gaze froze on my mother, who stared at me with lifeless eyes.

Only Father had been in the bedroom with her, and he had killed her.

Dead. Just like that. One tiny bullet and she was gone.

I was dragged downstairs and out of the house, pushed into the backseat of a car. Then I was alone with the sound of my shallow breathing. I wrapped my arms around my chest, wincing as my fingers touched the bruises on my upper arms caused by my father's outburst this morning. I began rocking back and forth, humming a melody my piano teacher had taught me a few weeks ago. It was getting cold in the car, but I didn't mind. The cold felt good, soothing.

Someone opened the door, and I shied away in fear, pulling my legs up to my chest. Luca poked his head in. There was blood on his throat. Not much but I couldn't look away. Blood. My father's?

"How old are you?" he asked.

I didn't say anything.

"Twelve?"

I tensed, and he closed the door and sat in the front beside his brother, Matteo. They assured me I was safe. Safe? I had never felt safe. Mother always said the only safety in our world was death. She found it.

My cousins took me to an older woman called Marianna, whom I'd never met before. She was kind and loving, but I couldn't stay with her. As honor dictated, I had to stay with family, so I was sent to Baltimore to live with my Aunt Egidia and her husband, Felix, who was Underboss in the city like my father had been Underboss in Atlanta.

I had met her only during family festivities because she and my father hated each other. Luca took me to them a couple of days after my mother's funeral. I was silent beside him, and he didn't try to make conversation. He looked angry and tense.

"I'm sorry," I whispered when we came to a stop in front of a large villa in

Baltimore. Over the years, I'd learned to apologize even if I didn't know what I'd done wrong.

Luca frowned at me. "What for?"

"For what my father did." Honor and loyalty were the most important things in our world, and Father had broken his oath and betrayed Luca.

"That's not your fault, so it's nothing you should apologize for," he said, and for a little while I believed it to be true. Until I saw Aunt Egidia's disapproving face and heard Felix say to Luca that it would reflect badly on them if they took me in. Luca wouldn't hear it, so I stayed with them, and eventually they learned to tolerate me, and yet not a day passed when I wasn't acutely aware that I was seen as a traitor's daughter. I didn't blame them. From a young age, I'd learned that there was no greater crime than betrayal. Father had tainted our family name, had tainted my brothers and me, and we'd always carry the blemish. My brothers, at least, could try to make a name for themselves if they became brave Made Men, but I was a girl. All I could hope for was mercy.

Today

Being regarded as a traitor's daughter, facing the pitying or disgusted expressions wasn't the worst part about these gatherings. Not even close. He was. He caught my eyes from across the room, and his face held the knowledge of what he had done, the triumph over what he had taken. He stood beside my aunt—his wife— beside his children—my cousins—and was regarded with respect. His eyes on me made my skin crawl. He didn't approach me, but his leering was enough. His gaze was just like his touch; it was humiliation and pain, and I could not stand it. Cold sweat covered my skin, and my stomach churned. I turned around and hurried toward the women's restroom. I'd hide there for the rest of the night, until it was time to leave with my Aunt Egidia and Uncle Felix.

I splashed my face with water, ignoring the minimal makeup I wore. Luckily it was waterproof mascara and a hint of concealer to cover the shadows under my eyes, so I didn't do much damage. I needed the cold of the water to help me get a grip on my rising panic.

The door opened and Giulia slipped in. She was beautiful in her bold violet dress with her light brown hair. She carried herself with confidence and had for as long as I could remember. That was probably how she had managed to make her marriage with Cassio work despite their age difference.

She came toward me and touched my shoulder, her brows drawing together. "Are you okay? You left the party."

"I'm not feeling well. You know I'm not good around so many people."

Her eyes softened further, and I knew what was coming. "Luca would kill him if you told him what he's done."

"No," I croaked, my eyes darting to the door, afraid someone would come in and overhear us. I often regretted that I'd confided in Giulia shortly after it had happened, but I had been broken and confused, and she was always kind. "You swore not to tell anyone. You swore it, Giulia."

She nodded, but I could tell that she didn't like it. "I did, and I won't tell anyone. It's your decision, but I think Uncle Durant needs to pay for what he did."

I shuddered, hearing his name. Turning my back on her, I washed my hands again. "You know that I will be the one to pay, Giulia. This world isn't kind, least of all to a woman like me. I can't go through this. I will be worse off than I am now. Your parents already have trouble finding a husband for me. If the truth got out, I'd die a spinster. They would never forgive me."

Her lips formed a thin line. "My parents never treated you the way they should have. I'm sorry."

I shook my head. "It's okay. They took me in. They never hit me, never punished me harshly. It could have been worse."

"I could ask Cassio if one of his men would be a good match for you. There are many decent men in his ranks."

Decent. Cassio ruled over Philadelphia with an iron fist. What he considered decent probably didn't qualify as decent for other people, but I had no right to be choosy or judge others.

"No. That would offend your parents. You know how they are."

"Yeah, I know …" Her brows tightened.

"Don't worry about me. I'm in no hurry to marry," I said. Marriage would be my final ruin.

TWO

Nino

"I ASSUME YOU WILL HOLD BACK DURING OUR MEETING AND NOT offend Vitiello," I said as Fabiano and I boarded the plane.

"I'm not a genius like you, but I'm no imbecile either. Don't worry, I know when to shut up."

I nodded as I sank down into one of the comfortable leather seats. Fabiano usually had a good handle on his emotions, unlike my brother. "That Luca even agreed to meet us at all is a good sign."

Fabiano sat in the seat across from me. "It might be, yes, or Luca wants to put a bullet in our heads."

"No," I said. "He won't risk war with the Camorra. Remo would attack, and he wouldn't do it with subtle tactics like Dante Cavallaro. He'd go to New York and go on a killing spree they haven't seen in the Famiglia before."

Fabiano smirked. "Yeah, he'd do that. But I hear Luca has gone on a few impressive killing sprees in the last few years to get the Famiglia under control and shut up the Bratva. He and Remo are pretty similar when it comes down to it."

"To some extent, but Remo doesn't have a wife and children he needs to protect."

Fabiano raised an eyebrow. "Remo protects Savio and Adamo, and even you and me by some degree."

"That's different," I said.

Fabiano regarded me carefully. "You really think marrying is a good idea?"

"It's—"

"Don't say it's the logical choice," Fabiano muttered. "I want to know if you really think you can be with a woman like that. You are messed up, Nino. Not in the same way Remo is messed up, but still fucking messed up. Fuck, even I'm messed up, and it almost cost me Leona. And it's still fucking difficult sometimes to make this relationship work because I keep saying or doing things that unsettle her. And let's be real: I'm the fucking epitome of normalcy compared to you. Women aren't like us. They want their fucking knight in shining armor. They want roses and all that emotional shit. They want declarations of love. That's not something you're going to give your future wife. To be honest, I think most women would kill themselves within a few weeks of marrying you rather than live under a roof with all you Falcone fuckers."

"From what I know, arranged marriages aren't based on emotions. They are based on tradition and rationality. A woman who's given to me in marriage knows what's expected. She'll know it's business. She's a chess piece. And I can assure you, I will prevent her from ending her life for as long as her survival is required for peace."

Fabiano sighed, touching his temple. "Maybe you should keep your thoughts to yourself as well. Most of the shit coming out of your mouth won't set anyone at ease, least of all a woman."

My muscles tensed when I pulled our rental car up in front of the abandoned Yonkers power plant. After we landed in New York, Romero had sent me a text saying that was where Luca would meet with us. The building was decrepit, and the area was deserted. A good place to torture and kill, I had to give that to Luca.

"This is fucking great," Fabiano said, his lips curling. "I'm not in the mood to die today."

"Neither of us will die today," I said, pushing open the car door and getting out. My eyes searched the area. On the roof of the building, two snipers were lying in wait. The moment Fabiano stepped up beside me, a gate in the old factory building swung open and three men emerged. I recognized them as Luca, Matteo, and Romero.

"I assume you saw the snipers pointing their guns at our heads," Fabiano murmured. Despite his words, he appeared relaxed from the outside.

I inclined my head in confirmation.

The three men stopped about two car lengths away from us. Luca evaluated me for a moment before he narrowed his eyes at Fabiano. "Do you remember what I told you last time you were in New York?"

Matteo and Romero held their guns, the former particularly looking like he'd gladly put a bullet in Fabiano's head. I could tell that the feeling was mutual.

Fabiano nodded. "You told me I was a dead man if I returned to New York."

Luca nodded. "And here you are asking for death."

"We are here to offer truce, Luca." I interrupted what would have surely soon turned into a less than pleasant argument. "As Consigliere of the Camorra, I hold the power to negotiate a peace treaty between our two families."

Matteo snorted and exchanged a look with Romero.

Luca took a step forward. "You really think I'm going to work together with the Camorra after the message Remo sent me through Fabiano last time, after you threatened my wife years ago."

"Remo wanted to size you up. He didn't mean to insult you or harm your wife." That was only a half-truth, but there was no point in revealing it to Luca.

Luca sneered. "Every word out of your mouth is a lie. I know you caught one of my drug deliveries. You're probably having my soldiers dismembered as we speak. I have absolutely no reason to trust you."

"I don't trust anyone, Luca, and trust isn't required for truce."

Luca and I whirled around toward the voice. Remo sauntered in our direction, completely naked except for black briefs. "I'm not armed as you can see." My brother was even barefoot. I narrowed my eyes at him. This was insanity. I wasn't sure why I still bothered making plans if Remo always acted on his own accord.

"One day, I'm going to kill the crazy fucker," Fabiano muttered. "He just signed our fucking death warrant."

Remo gave me his twisted grin as he clapped my shoulder then Fabiano's before walking closer to Luca and the others. "I thought it would be good to talk face to face, Luca. From one man of honor to the other. From Capo to Capo."

Luca's face reflected hatred, but there was also respect present. "And I thought you were a coward who sent out his Enforcer and his brother to fight his battles."

"I'm many things, Luca. A coward isn't one of them," Remo said.

"You know what, why don't we put a bullet in your head and help Las Vegas to a new Capo. Someone less fucked-up," Matteo said, aiming his gun at Remo. Romero pointed his gun at me.

Fabiano pulled out his own gun, but Remo shook his head. I walked to his side. "Killing us wouldn't serve any purpose," I said calmly. "Savio will contact Cavallaro the moment we're dead and offer them cooperation, and even you can't fight both the Camorra and the Outfit."

"Your brother Savio is only sixteen. He won't be able to control the Camorra."

"I was only seventeen when I began my fight to win my territory back. You were only seventeen when you crushed a man's throat. Savio is a Falcone. He is a born killer, Luca. He can control the Camorra. The name Falcone holds power in Las Vegas and beyond," Remo said.

Luca narrowed his eyes, but I took it as a good sign that he hadn't killed us yet. "Do you want to risk cooperation between the Outfit and the Camorra? You can't have peace with Dante Cavallaro unless you send him your sister-in-law and your Captain." I nodded toward Romero.

Luca still didn't say anything. He was probably trying to decide if he should just end us. My finger rested loosely on my trigger, but with the snipers on the roof, even my skills wouldn't save us.

Remo moved even closer to Luca until they stood at arm's length. Luca was about an inch taller than Remo, but that didn't come as a surprise.

"What is there to talk about, Remo? And this time I know your brother Nino isn't aiming at my wife, so there's nothing stopping me from bathing in your fucking Falcone blood."

Remo grinned. "The Camorra doesn't have any interest in hurting your family, Luca. Not your wife *nor your children.*"

Luca lunged, his fingers clamping down around Remo's throat. My brother made no move to defend himself. He didn't take his eyes off the Famiglia Capo as he rasped, "We aren't the only ones who know about your children. The Outfit does and so does the Bratva. The Outfit attacked my territory when they thought I was vulnerable. Who do you think they will attack to hurt you, Luca? Scuderi tried to get rid of Fabiano, his own son, *his heir.* What will he do to the daughters who disappointed him so greatly, who ruined peace between the Outfit and the Famiglia?"

The Famiglia Capo looked like he wanted to crush Remo's throat, and I knew he could have done it. Remo was one of the most vicious fighters, brutal to the very core, but a fight with Luca would probably kill them both. Even Fabiano and I couldn't prevent that, not with Matteo and Romero and the snipers.

Remo's face turned red, but he kept talking. "Dante Cavallaro is our enemy, and I'm going to walk into Chicago and show him what it means to be at war with the Camorra, show him why we are despised even among our own. I will make him pay, and it won't be quick or fair. As for Scuderi, Fabiano is going to kill him very slowly, and if you want, we can send you the video footage so you can share it with the Scuderi sisters. You want Cavallaro's death as much as we do."

Luca released Remo. "Don't underestimate Cavallaro. He is a cold fish on the outside, but he is a cruel fucker like you and I. And Scuderi is a nasty piece of shit but a strategic genius. That's why he remained Consigliere under Dante's rule."

Fabiano made a low growl but otherwise remained silent.

Remo nodded, rubbing his throat. "I know what kind of man Cavallaro is. And I don't doubt that Scuderi is a mastermind of twisted plans, but I will attack where he and Cavallaro don't expect it. I will beat them at their own game. And I will enjoy every fucking minute of it."

Luca narrowed his eyes. "I'm not going to join you in your crusade. I have a feeling I won't like your plan. You are fucking insane."

"I'm not asking you to join me. I'm asking you to stay out of my fight. In the past, the Camorra and the Famiglia worked together. Peace in our territories can lead to peace between our families in Italy as well."

"My territory is my only concern."

Remo shrugged. "We can both profit from a union. I can offer you safe delivery routes for your drugs through my territory. You lose more than half of your deliveries because either my men or Outfit soldiers intercept them. Peace means you won't have to worry about it anymore. You can double your profits. And I will keep Dante busy with attacks so you can focus on the Bratva and not worry about your family so much."

"And all you want in turn is for me stay out of your war with the Outfit?" Luca sounded suspicious.

I spoke up. "Dante might approach you after we start our attacks. We want to make sure he doesn't manage to convince you to help him."

Luca smiled coldly. "I have no intention of working with the Outfit. I want Dante Cavallaro dead, trust me." He narrowed his eyes. "So how do you want to go about peace?"

"First, we will release your soldiers and your drugs," Remo said with a smile. He motioned at me, and I reached for my phone, causing all guns to swivel in my direction.

I sent a quick message to Savio so he'd arrange the release of the Famiglia men. I nodded. "Your men are being released as we speak, and your drugs will arrive safely in your territory."

"Why don't you just spill it?" Matteo muttered. "There's more to this. I'm running out of patience over here."

I tossed Remo a look. Matteo sounded just like him.

"We want to show you that the Camorra is willing to allow change," I said calmly. "Fabiano is allowed to be with an outsider. He gave her that bracelet your wife gifted him."

"I don't give a fuck about any of that," Luca growled. "I don't care if Fabiano's found a whore to fuck."

"Careful, Luca," Fabiano hissed, taking a step forward.

Luca raised his eyebrows.

"Why don't we get back to business," I suggested. "You need peace. We need peace. You want Cavallaro and Scuderi dead. We will kill them."

Remo opened his arms. "And to show you that we are very serious about truce with you and the Famiglia, I want us to arrange a marriage between one of yours and one of mine."

Matteo chuckled. "Oh, this is getting good."

"We're being serious," I said because Remo's expression worried me. I could tell that Matteo was starting to seriously piss him off. "Arranged marriages between Famiglias have ensured peace for centuries, and your Famiglia has always upheld the tradition. You and Aria are proof that it's the perfect solution."

Luca's mouth tightened when I mentioned Fabiano's sister. "It was supposed to bring peace with the Outfit and now there's war."

"Well," Remo said, gesturing at Matteo and Romero, "that was your Famiglia's doing. I can assure you we will uphold our part of the deal."

"If I gave one of our women to the Camorra, who would guarantee she was safe?" Luca asked.

"Our women are as safe as your women, trust me. They have nothing to fear in our territory," I said. Nothing that they wouldn't have to fear in every marriage in our circles, at least.

Luca's mouth curled in distaste as he regarded my brother. "I won't give a woman to you in marriage, Remo. I don't trust you one bit. You are too fucking crazy for my taste."

"I'm not the one who will marry. It's my brother Nino, and you will find that he's absolutely in control of himself. Look at him. Doesn't he look like every mother-in-law's dream?"

I gave my brother a warning look before I turned to Luca. "It's a good deal for the Famiglia and the Camorra. Don't let old grudges or feuds ruin your chances of optimizing the Famiglia's profits and securing your territory."

"This is ridiculous," Matteo said, but Luca was silent. He was a businessman. He knew what safe delivery routes through our territory could mean for him. Luca motioned for his brother and Romero to follow him. They walked out of earshot.

Remo smiled.

"I don't know what you're smiling about. This isn't Texas Hold 'em. Going all in isn't the way to go," Fabiano murmured. "This is a fucking train wreck."

"Luca will agree," I said firmly.

My brother and Fabiano looked at me curiously.

"Are you sure?" Remo asked.

"Luca isn't the man he used to be before he had his wife and children. He won't risk open war with the Outfit, but he wants Dante dead and he prefers us on his side. If you have something to lose like he does, you choose the safe option."

Romero walked toward us.

"He's the one who broke truce with the Outfit by popping your sister's cherry, right?" Remo whispered.

Fabiano grimaced. "He did, and I let them fucking shoot me so they could escape. I was a fucking idiot."

Romero regarded us with open distrust. "Luca will consider your offer. We have another drug delivery in three days. If it reaches our territory safely, we can discuss a truce in more detail."

"It will arrive safely, don't worry," Remo muttered.

Romero nodded. "Luca wants you to leave New York now. We will contact you in a few days if everything goes as planned."

"Everything will go as planned," Remo said, grinning widely. "Luca better start looking for a wife for my brother. We're looking forward to meeting her."

THREE

Kiara

D ESPITE THE WARMER TEMPERATURES THAT MARCH BROUGHT, I WAS glad for my thick wool sweater. I'd never grown used to the colder climate of Baltimore. The weather in Atlanta had been so much warmer. My fingers were stiff as I settled them on the piano keys and began to play. Melancholic low notes of music filled the room, a reflection of my current emotions. I had started fiddling with the composition a couple of days ago, but it was still far from good.

When my aunt stepped into the living room, perfectly styled—as always—in a beige cashmere dress, her dark hair piled on top of her head, I lifted my hands off the keys and the sound died off in a soft exhale.

Uncle Felix entered behind her. He was a tall man, heavy around the middle, with a mustache that twitched when he talked. They exchanged a look and something heavy settled in my stomach.

"We need to have a word with you," Felix said.

I got up from the bench and followed them toward the seating area. They sat on the couch, and I took the armchair across from them. It felt like I was facing a tribunal.

"It hasn't been easy on us, taking you in," Felix began, and I curled my fingers into the leather of the armchair. It wasn't the first time I heard it, but it still stung. "But we did what we could. We gave you what we could to raise you."

They had given me shelter and education, but affection or even protection from the harsh whispers of society … No. Never that. I was grateful anyway. I knew how important outward appearances were, and they had risked their reputation by taking in a traitor's daughter.

"But you are a grown woman now and it's time for you to have your own home, to be a wife and mother."

My insides tightened, but I kept my face blank. Over the years I'd learned to hide my emotions. "You found a husband for me?"

Who would have agreed to marry me? Perhaps they had settled on a soldier after all. It was for the best. If I married down, the wedding and marriage would be a low-key affair, no attention, little potential for scandal. A soldier might see me as a way to improve his position, because despite being a traitor's daughter, I was the Capo's cousin. Maybe that would make him overlook my defect.

Aunt Egidia smiled but her eyes showed guilt, perhaps even shame. Felix cleared his throat. "I know you aren't aware of the details of my business, but the Famiglia is at war."

As if anyone didn't know that. Even small children were brought up with the knowledge that we had to be vigilant because the Outfit might attack, or heaven forbid, the Camorra.

"I know, Uncle Felix," I said quietly.

"But Luca was approached with an offer of peace. You don't need to bother with the details, but it might be the final step to destroy the Outfit."

My breath stuck in my throat. What was he talking about? If the offer didn't come from the Outfit, who else was willing to agree on a truce?

"It's an honor, Kiara. After what your father did, we thought we would have to give you to a soldier or never find a husband at all."

"Who is it I am going to marry?" I forced the words out, but they sounded strangled.

"You will marry up," Aunt Egidia assured me with a tense smile, but her eyes … her eyes still held pity, and deep down I knew that whatever horrors my past held, they would soon be accompanied by new horrors.

"Who?" I rasped.

"Nino Falcone, second in command to his brother Remo Falcone, the Capo of the Camorra," Felix said, avoiding my eyes.

I heard nothing after that, rising without a word and walking out. I went upstairs, continued into my bedroom, and sank down on the chaise longue, staring blankly at my bed. It was neatly made. I didn't let the maids make it, hadn't let them make it in years. Every night I took my pillow and blanket and curled up on my chaise longue to sleep, and in the morning I returned everything and made my bed so no one found out that I didn't use the bed and hadn't in six years.

Six years. I was only thirteen.

As I stared at my bed, the horrors of the past took shape again like they did every night when I closed my eyes.

Six years ago:

It was dark in my room when footsteps woke me. I turned around and recognized my Uncle Durant under the gleam of moonlight. He had come to Baltimore with his wife, Aunt Criminella, to visit Aunt Egidia and Uncle Felix for a few days.

Confused by his presence, I sat up. His breathing was loud, and he was dressed in a bathrobe. "Shh," he said as he leaned over me, his body forcing me down.

Fear shot through me. I wasn't supposed to be alone with men in my bedroom. That was a rule I had learned from an early age. Stiff with terror, I watched as he removed his bathrobe; he was naked beneath. I had never seen a naked man. His hand grabbed my shoulder, and his other hand pressed down on my mouth. I was supposed to show respect to my elders, to men in particular, but I knew this wasn't right. I began struggling.

He tore at my clothes. He was too strong. He tugged and pinched. His hands hurt between my legs. I cried, but he didn't stop. He moved on top of me, between my legs.

"This is your punishment for being a dirty traitor."

I wanted to say I didn't betray anyone, but pain robbed me of my words. It felt like being torn apart, like breaking and falling and shattering. His breath was hot on my face, and I cried, whimpered, and begged. His hand only clamped down harder around my mouth, and he grunted as he shoved himself into me again and again. I cried harder because it hurt so much.

I hurt all over, my whole body and deep in my chest.

He kept grunting above me. I stopped struggling, breathed through my clogged nose. In and out. In and out. His sweat dripped down on my forehead. He shuddered and slumped down on top of me. His hand slipped off my mouth.

I didn't scream. I was quiet, motionless.

"Nobody will believe you if you tell them about this, Kiara. And even if they do, they will blame you and nobody will want you anymore. You are dirty now, Kiara, you hear me? Worthless."

He pulled out and I cried from the sharp pain. He slapped me. "Be quiet."

I pressed my lips together, watching him get up and put on his bathrobe. "Have you had your period yet?"

I shook my head because I couldn't speak.

"Good. Wouldn't want you to have a bastard, right?" He leaned over me again, and I flinched. "I will make sure the maids know you got your period, don't worry. I won't let anyone find out that you are a worthless little whore. I will protect you." He stroked my cheek before he pulled back, and I didn't move until he was outside. When his steps had faded, I pushed up and managed to stand despite the pain.

Something warm trickled down my legs. I stumbled forward, grabbed my discarded panties, and pressed them between my legs, crying out again. Shaking, I curled up on the chaise longue, staring into the darkness at the bed.

Before sunrise, the door opened again, and I pressed against the backrest, making myself small. One of the maids, Dorma, stepped into my room. She was one of the younger ones who looked at me like I was a bother. Her eyes moved over me. "Get up," she said sharply. "We need to clean you up before the others wake up."

I stood, wincing from the soreness between my legs. I looked down at myself. There was blood on my legs and something else that made my stomach pinch sharply. Dorma began gathering the sheets. They, too, were covered in blood. "You better keep this quiet," she muttered. "Your uncle is an important man and you are only a traitor. You are lucky they didn't kill you as well."

I waited quietly as she bunched up the sheets and set them down on the ground. Then she began tugging at my clothes, ignoring my flinching, until I stood naked. I felt dirty, worthless, and broken under her cruel eyes.

She added my nightgown to the bloody heap on the ground then helped me into a bathrobe. "We'll go to the bathroom now, and if anyone asks, you got your period, right?"

I nodded. I didn't ask why. I didn't fight it.

That night, Uncle Durant came into my room again, and again the night after, and again until he finally had to leave for Atlanta. Every morning Dorma cleaned the sheets and me. A few days after he'd left, she wore an expensive necklace. The price for her silence.

Today

A knock sounded, tearing me out of the painful memories. I took a deep breath and willed my voice to be strong. "Come in."

Aunt Egidia opened the door, but she didn't enter. Worry tightened her mouth. "Kiara, that was very rude," she said. She regarded me then averted her gaze, and again it was filled with a hint of guilt. "You should be honored to be given to someone of importance. With your background, it's a blessing. Your wedding will be a spectacle. It'll bring honor to your name."

"And yours," I said quietly.

She stiffened, and I instantly regretted my words. I had no right to criticize her or my uncle. "We braved a lot of unpleasantness because we took you in. You can hardly hold it against us that we are happy to have found such a honorable match for you."

"Has it been decided?" I asked quietly.

She frowned. "As good as. The Falcones insist on Luca's relative for the marriage, naturally, so Felix suggested you. Luca would like a word with you before he makes the offer, which isn't how it used to be done, but if he insists on your consent, we can hardly refuse him. We invited him and his wife over for dinner." Her eyes met mine, finally. "You will tell him you are delighted by the honor, Kiara, won't you? This is your chance to redeem your family and yourself. Maybe your brothers will even be allowed to become Captains if you marry someone like Nino Falcone."

My throat closed tightly, and my gaze found the bed again.

"Kiara, you will tell him you agree, won't you? Your uncle already told Luca you would. It will lead to rumors if you refuse."

I looked back at my aunt, who looked worried.

"I will agree," I whispered, because what else was there left to do?

That evening before dinner, Luca pulled me aside to talk to me without my aunt and uncle, which displeased them greatly, made plainly clear by the scowls on their faces.

"I'm not going to force you to marry if you refuse," he said. His presence made me nervous.

"I'll be twenty this fall. I need to marry."

"That's true," Luca conceded. His gray eyes regarded me as if he thought he could pull any truth out of me with just his watchful gaze, but I had learned to hold on to my secrets. "But you could marry someone else."

I could, but if I refused to marry Nino Falcone, I'd be even more of a pariah in our circles. Uncle Felix and Aunt Egidia would be disappointed, and they would have an even harder time finding someone else. And how would I justify my refusal? In our world, you married the man your parents chose for you, no matter how bad the choice. "Who would marry Nino Falcone in my stead?"

"Most of my cousins are promised or married. I'd have to choose one of the daughters of my Captains. A few of them will be turning of age this year and aren't engaged."

Another girl given to the monsters in Las Vegas. A girl more innocent than me. A girl who deserved a chance at happiness no matter how small it would be in our world.

Nobody had protected me all those years ago, but I could spare another girl this fate. "I will marry him. You don't have to choose anyone else." My voice didn't betray my terror. It was firm and determined, and I forced myself to meet Luca's gaze for the first time this evening.

Luca stared at me a moment longer, but I could tell he approved of my decision. Duty and honor were the pillars of our world. Each of us had to do what was expected. It would have made him and the Famiglia look bad if he couldn't have offered one of his cousins to the Camorra. These were the rules we lived by, and his own wife had been given to him for peace. This was how it was done, how it would always be done.

After dinner, it was Aria who approached me. She smiled kindly and touched my arm while the men drank their scotch in the smoking lounge and Aunt Egidia got espresso ready for us. "Nobody would blame you if you refused," Aria said.

"You married Luca. You did what was expected, what honor dictated, and I know the same is expected of me," I said with a smile.

She frowned. "Yes, but—"

"It's not like this has ever been my home. Even if I wasn't the one who broke his oath, I'm paying for my father's mistake. I want to move on from it. This is my chance to redeem myself. Las Vegas can be a new start for me."

Those were the words expected of me, but they fell heavily from my lips because I knew that my marriage to Nino could destroy everything. My reputation and any chance at peace. And beneath these worries, lay a deeper, darker fear—a fear born in the past that haunted my present and would determine my future.

Nino

"This was too risky and you know it, Remo. One day you will get yourself killed," I said as Remo and I settled at a table in the Sugar Trap. I knew he was starting to grow tired of my lectures, but as long as he acted impulsively, he'd have to listen to them.

Remo threw his feet up on the table, watching the stripper sway her hips, her tits bouncing up and down. The Sugar Trap was deserted, except for the women preparing for the evening.

"When that happens, you are there to rule over the Camorra."

I frowned. He was taking this too lightly. He was the born Capo. Nobody could scare people into submission as easily and fast as Remo. I didn't want to become Capo. That was Remo's birthright, not mine.

"Don't give me that look, Nino. I know you would have handled things differently."

"Anyone would have handled things differently."

"It worked. Luca got his drugs, and he agreed to give this union a chance. And I bet Aria played a part in the matter. She wants her brother back. She is a woman. They want peace and love. They like to meddle."

"You aren't an expert where women are concerned. When was the last time you talked more than two sentences to a woman?"

Remo swung his legs off the table and got up then pointed at the stripper. "I want to fuck. Get your ass into the changing room. I'll be there in two minutes. You better be naked." The woman nodded and hurried backstage. Remo raised one dark eyebrow. "See? Four sentences."

I sighed and rose to my feet. "That wasn't talking, that was commanding. A monologue, at best. For it to be an actual conversation, she has to say something in return."

Remo grinned. "Why would I want to hear what she has to say? I prefer her mouth filled with my cock." He pointed at another stripper who entered our club. "Why don't you take that one? In a few months, you'll be a married man. No more stripper pussies for you then." He laughed at his own joke, knowing Made Men could do whatever they wanted, and clapped my shoulder. "Come on, relax a bit before you have to meet with Luca tomorrow."

He had a point. I met the woman's gaze and motioned her toward me. I'd fucked her before. "C.J.," I said, and her eyes widened. They were always surprised that I remembered their names, but I never forgot a name or anything else.

"Yes, Mr. Falcone?" She licked her lips because she thought it was what turned me on. I found it more distracting than anything else. If I didn't already intend on fucking her, I wouldn't have called her over. There was no sense in trying to turn me on further. Remo had already headed backstage. I grabbed her wrist, led her to the restrooms, and fucked her up against the stall. She moaned, but I knew it was fake. She was wet around my cock, but she definitely hadn't come. Her body didn't exhibit the telltale signs of orgasm. As a whore, she was used to faking it to make her customers happy, but I fucking hated it. I gripped her harder, narrowing my eyes, and fucked her faster. "You know what happens to people who lie to me?"

Fear flashed across her face. I reached between us, flicked her clit, and eventually she had to surrender to me—as they always did—and she came. I followed a few moments later, pulled out of her, threw the condom into the toilet, and left her standing there.

Luca and I decided to meet in Nashville. It was neutral ground, which was the best option for a second meeting considering we'd both be alone. Luca sized me up as I walked over to him in the deserted parking lot of an abandoned cinema complex.

I held out my hand for him to shake. He took it and to my surprise he didn't try to squeeze my hand into dust like some people did when they wanted to intimidate. Maybe he knew it didn't have that effect on me.

"We meet again," he said with narrowed eyes. "Last time we didn't get to talk in private. You were the one who threatened my wife."

"I didn't threaten her," I objected. "I found a weakness in your safety measures, and Remo pointed it out to you to stop you from killing him."

Luca's gaze hardened. "You won't threaten my wife ever again."

Maybe the average person was afraid of him, but I regarded him coolly, my pulse as calm as always. "Scare tactics don't work with me. I don't have the disposition for them to have an effect on me. I have no intention of threatening your wife in the future. I think a truce between the Famiglia and the Camorra is the logical solution to our problem with the Outfit, and for truce to work, we will have to agree not to threaten or kill each other for the time being."

Luca regarded me for several seconds, a sneer on his face. "Are any of you Falcone brothers sane?"

"What is your definition of sanity?" I asked. "Society regards neither you nor I as sane. We are psychopaths because we enjoy killing. Or are you trying to tell me you feel guilty when you torture and kill?"

Luca shrugged. "Maybe we are psychopaths, but you and Remo make most psychopaths look sane."

I knew Remo and I were the result of the same catalyst. Animals adapted to their environment if they wanted to survive. It was an evolution process that sometimes happened on a small scale within a single being. Remo had turned toward his emotions, had let them loose, and as a result had barely any control over his rage.

My body had survived by getting rid of emotions altogether. I preferred my adaption to his. It made life more predictable.

Adamo hadn't been born when Remo and I became the men we were today, and Savio had been only three years old, too young to understand or remember. They didn't share Remo's and my dispositions. "I'm perfectly capable to act accordingly based on society's standards if I want."

"And you want to marry for truce?"

"It is the only reason why I would consider marrying," I said honestly. "Marriage really serves no other purpose. I don't need companionship. I have that in my brothers and Fabiano. And I don't need marriage to fulfill my sexual drive. There are enough women in Las Vegas for that."

Luca let out a dark laugh. "I believe you."

"I got the impression that you were in favor of a marriage between our families."

"I'm not in favor, but as you said, it is the logical choice. I have to think of the Famiglia and my own family. I don't want you crazy Falcone fuckers on my back. I prefer you making Cavallaro's life hell. I have my hands full with the Bratva. I don't want to deal with him. That you're going to kill Scuderi in the most brutal way anyone could come up with is an added bonus."

"Then it's settled. Given your family's background, your Captains and Underbosses are in favor of the union, I presume."

"They follow my judgment, but arranged marriages are very popular in the Famiglia, of course."

Arranged marriages were still popular even among the Camorrista. "Have you chosen a woman for me yet?"

Luca's mouth tightened. "It won't come as a surprise if I tell you that most of my Underbosses and Captains aren't eager to send one of their daughters to the Camorra. The name Falcone has a certain reputation."

"I'm perfectly capable of fulfilling my duties as a husband. I can provide protection, father children, and money isn't a problem either."

Luca grimaced. "I don't give a fuck about that. What I want to know is if I will have to attack Vegas to save one of my cousins from you and your brothers."

"You won't have reason to save anyone, and even if you tried, Las Vegas is too strong for you. But I assure you, my wife won't suffer violence." I paused. "And must I remind you that it's your family who upholds the tradition of bloody sheets and not ours? That forces any husband's hand on the wedding night."

"Some traditions can't be overruled."

"The question remains: Do you have someone in mind?"

Luca nodded. "One of my cousins is of marrying age. Her guardians sug-gested her for the union. She won't be sad to leave the Famiglia."

I narrowed my eyes. "Guardians? What is wrong with the girl?"

"Nothing. She's more than capable of becoming a wife, but her father, my Uncle, was a traitor, and many people won't let her forget it. She grew up with our Aunt Egidia."

"A traitor's daughter for us. Some people might consider that an insult."

"Will your brother Remo be one of them?"

It was always hard to say with Remo, but he didn't give a fuck about family history. "Remo judges people by their own actions, not by their parents' wrongdo-ings. And she is still your cousin."

He reached for his back pocket, and I lifted my hand to my holster.

Tension shot through Luca's body. "Phone." He pulled out his cell, and after a moment he turned it to me. On the screen was an image of a young woman with dark brown eyes and almost black hair but her naturally olive skin was rather pale, which suggested she didn't leave the house very often. "This is my cousin, Kiara Vitiello. Nineteen. An honorable woman." The last was said with a hint of warning.

"She will do," I said.

Luca put his phone back into his back pocket. He nodded once then sighed. "Then it's settled."

I returned late that night to our mansion. Remo was awake as usual. He never slept more than a few hours. He got up from the sofa the moment I stepped into our game room. Savio and Adamo were busy playing a video game, some kind of race. Adamo was in lead; just like in real life, he knew how to drive a car.

"And?" There was a hint of eagerness in Remo's voice. I wasn't sure if he hoped Luca had disagreed after today's meeting so we could attack the Famiglia or if he really wanted peace. Remo only ever thrived in chaos and violence.

"He suggested one of his cousins, Kiara Vitiello."

"If her last name is Vitiello, her father must be one of Luca's traitorous uncles."

"You are right. Her father was killed for betraying Luca."

"So he gives us the daughter of a traitor?" Remo asked in a low voice.

"We don't care about these kinds of things."

Remo threw one of his knives at one of the armchairs, and it wedged itself into the leather. There were more holes in it already. "But the Famiglia does. The arrogant asshole probably wants to send some fucking message with the marriage."

"Perhaps Nino is meant as a punishment for her," Savio mused as his car crashed into a wall, his brown eyes alight with what I assumed was amusement. Adamo didn't seem to care that he won the game. He put down his controller and regarded me with a face that was probably supposed to convey boredom.

"Sometimes I think Nino is my punishment as well," Remo said. "It makes sense that Luca would punish his cousin by giving her to Nino."

I had considered that option as well, but Luca wasn't the type to punish a woman like that, especially an innocent woman. "If it wasn't for me, you would be long dead."

Remo shrugged. "Maybe. We'll never know."

"So you're really going to marry?" Adamo asked. His hair had grown too long and fell into his eyes so he had to push it back constantly. Unlike me, he never put it in a ponytail or styled it back.

"I am."

"But you haven't even met the woman. What if you can't stand her?" Adamo asked.

Savio rolled his eyes. "Could you sound any more like a pussy? You really need to get fucked."

Adamo's face turned red. "Shut up."

"Come on, you are almost fourteen. When I was your age, I'd already fucked a few girls." Savio looked at Remo. "Lock him in a room with a few hookers so they can fuck him into shape."

Adamo shoved Savio's shoulder. "Shut up! I don't need your hookers."

"If you want to be a real Falcone, you can't be a fucking virgin. It's pathetic. Or perhaps you are a fag?"

Adamo jumped up and threw himself at Savio. They both tumbled to the ground and began punching. Adamo hadn't yet fought in the cage like Savio, so it wasn't wise of him to attack.

Remo shook his head, but he didn't intervene. I moved closer to get a better view in case things got too rough. Savio had gotten the upper hand and straddled Adamo, punching him hard once, twice, and then lifted his arm for another punch. I took a step forward to stop him, but Remo swung himself over the sofa, landed beside Savio and grabbed him by the collar before pulling him off Adamo and shoving him away. Savio landed on the sofa, breathing hard and making a move to get back up.

"You stay there," I ordered. His eyes held challenge before he nodded and slumped against the backrest.

Adamo was sprawled out on his back, face red and lips busted. He shook but made no move to stand. Remo bent over him and held out a hand. Adamo didn't take it, only glared. "Adamo," Remo said. "Don't try my fucking patience."

Adamo accepted Remo's hand and let him pull him to his feet. Adamo winced, then with a last glare at Savio, he stormed toward the French doors and fled outside.

"Fuck, perhaps he's really into guys," Savio said, scrunching up his face. Then his eyes widened. Sometimes when we were out on business, he managed to act like a man, but in moments like this it became obvious that he wouldn't be turning seventeen for another month. At his age, Remo and I had already been hardened by years on the street. I wasn't sure if we'd ever been teenagers. "Will you kill him, then?"

Remo got into Savio's face. "We are brothers. We will stand by each other. I don't care if Adamo is into fucking goats or ducks or men. He is our brother."

Savio nodded slowly. "He's annoying as fuck. If fucking a guy makes him more tolerable, I can live with that."

Remo snorted. Then he turned to me. "Talk to him. You are the only one who can deal with him."

I headed into the garden, following the stench of smoke, toward one of the lounge chairs beside the pool. Adamo was hunched over, smoking a regular ciga-rette. Since Remo's last warning, he hadn't touched anything harder. I was curious how long that would last. I ripped the butt out of his mouth and threw it into the pool. "No drugs."

"It's a cigarette, not pot or heroine," he mumbled.

I pulled another chair toward him and sat down across from him. "What's going on?"

He glared. "Nothing."

"Adamo, if you want to be treated like an adult, you have to act like one. Now tell me why you are acting the way you do."

His gaze lowered to his sneakers. "I don't want to screw a hooker or any of the strippers you take home."

"That became obvious when you attacked Savio. What did I tell you about fighting?"

"Only attack if you are sure you can beat your opponent."

"You can't beat Savio. Not yet."

"I won't ever be as good as all of you. I don't enjoy hurting people as much as you do."

I had figured as much. Adamo had never been a very violent child. "You are strong and a good fighter. You don't have to enjoy hurting or killing to be good at it."

He swallowed hard. "I don't want to kill again."

He had killed his first man during the attack on Roger's Fight Arena, and unlike Remo, Savio, and I, his first murder haunted him. "You will get used to it."

"Maybe I don't want to get used to it," he muttered. "I'm not like you."

"You have time," I said. There was no use discussing this now. He still had five months until he turned fourteen; he wouldn't be inducted until then. "What's your problem with the women your brothers and I take home?"

He stiffened and his head shot up. "I'm not gay."

I regarded him but his face remained in the shadows, making it even harder to read him. "Remo wouldn't punish you for it. We are brothers, Adamo. Nothing will change that."

Adamo gnawed on his lip then winced.

"I will have to stitch that up."

He nodded. "I'm not gay."

I tilted my head, but he continued without further prodding.

"I don't want a hooker because they don't even like you. They screw you because you are their boss or because they are scared. I don't want that. I want a girl who likes me and who wants to be with me."

"In our world it's difficult to find that."

"Because you aren't looking. Fabiano found Leona."

"He did, but he went through a lot of women before that."

Adamo shrugged. "I don't want to be forced to sleep with a hooker."

"Remo won't force you nor will I."

"Really?"

"Really." I couldn't understand Adamo's reasoning. He was a teenage boy. At some point his sexual drive would be too strong to wait for someone he cared about, even more someone who cared for him. "But, Adamo, we are Falcones. People always act differently around us. Finding someone to trust is difficult."

"Don't you want your future wife to like you?"

"Affection isn't necessary for a marriage. I have no expectations like that."

"But what if she wants affection?" His mouth twisted at the word, and he winced again.

I gave him a look and stood. "You know me."

Adamo shrugged. "I kind of feel sorry for her."

"Come on. Let me stitch up your lip now." Maybe I would have felt sorry for Kiara Vitiello as well if I were capable of it.

FOUR

Kiara

AUNT EGIDIA LOOKED INCREDIBLY PLEASED AS SHE ENTERED THE LIBRARY where I had been hiding all day from her and my uncle. "Luca had a meeting with Nino Falcone today."

I put down the book I was reading, trying to keep my face emotionless. "And?"

"Luca showed Nino a photo of you, and he agreed to marry you."

She watched me expectantly as if she thought I'd do a happy dance because Nino had approved of my looks. I swallowed hard. "That's good news." It was all I could manage, and it lacked enthusiasm.

My aunt pursed her lips. "Kiara, really, I don't think you grasp what this means."

Oh, I knew exactly what it meant, and that was the problem. "It takes some getting used to, the idea of marrying him, Aunt Egidia. Don't worry, by the time I'll have to marry him, I'll be able to convey my excitement properly."

It was a blatant lie. If I managed not to flinch at every touch, that would be a huge success.

"Well, you don't have much time. Remo Falcone insists things progress quickly. The wedding is set for four weeks from now."

I dug my fingers into the leather of the armchair, the color draining from my face. "Four weeks? But that's not enough time to plan everything."

Definitely not enough time to mentally prepare myself for marrying a Falcone— if I could even prepare for something like that.

"Don't worry. I already contacted a few bridal shops. Of course some of the most popular dresses are already sold out, but they assured me that they have enough beautiful pieces left."

"That's good," I said in a monotone voice.

Aunt Egidia nodded. "Aria and Giulia will join us. I already talked to both of them, and they are excited. Aria was so nice to make an appointment with the best bridal store in New York. New York seems the most sensible choice, given that we can't expect the wife of the Capo to travel all the way to Baltimore. Of course, the store managed to squeeze us in tomorrow. Who could refuse Aria Vitiello?"

"Tomorrow?" I asked horrified.

"Isn't it wonderful?"

"Wonderful," I managed to say.

Aunt Egidia frowned again. "Anyway, Felix and Luca are trying to figure out the best place to hold the wedding. It's not going to be New York. Luca doesn't want the Falcones in his city."

Didn't he? I almost laughed.

"I'm sure there are enough other options," I said quietly.

"Yes, yes. I'm sure," Egidia said, smiling. "I should call a few florists and make arrangements with them."

I didn't bother pointing out that it wouldn't make sense until we knew where the celebrations would take place. This was Aunt Egidia's show, even if I was the main attraction.

When she left, I closed my eyes. Four weeks.

Four weeks until my wedding night.

Four weeks until Nino would want to claim his prize.

Four weeks for me to figure out a way to hide that someone had taken that prize years ago. Sickness washed over me, and I pressed a hand to my stomach.

Ten minutes later, Giulia called. "Did my mother already talk to you?"

"A few minutes ago," I said.

Giulia sighed. "I don't like this, Kiara. Four weeks, really? It's like they can't throw you at Falcone quickly enough, as if they're worried they might start feeling guilty if they waited any longer."

"At least that leaves less time for me to fret." I'd worry anyway. My nights would be haunted by even worse nightmares than they had been before.

"Even Cassio is wary of the Falcones. He showed me a video of Nino Falcone in the cage. It's sick."

"A video?" I echoed. "Where can I watch it?"

There was silence on the other end. "Don't. Don't watch it."

My throat tightened. "Where?"

"It's a forum in the Darknet that the Camorra uses to show their cage fights and illegal street races."

"Give me the log in information."

"Kiara—"

"I'm nineteen, not nine. I want to see him, Giulia. *I need to.*" If I was faced with this monster the first time on our wedding night, I'd bolt. I needed to see what he was capable of, even if a cage fight wouldn't even begin to cover it.

"Give me a sec. I need to ask Cassio for the info again." I heard rustling followed by silence on the other end for a while until I heard muffled voices. After what felt like forever, Giulia spoke again. "Do you have somewhere to write it down? It's long and complicated. The Darknet uses several steps to keep people out."

I grabbed the pen and paper that I always kept close by when I read a book; I liked writing down my favorite quotes. "I'm ready."

After jotting everything down, I listened to another one of Giulia's warnings before we ended the call. Clutching the paper in my sweaty palm, I walked to my room to grab my laptop. My fingers shook as I logged into the forum. There was a list of fights from the last few years. I entered Nino's name in the search engine, and several fights popped up immediately. I clicked on the latest from only a few weeks ago.

The camera was trained on a massive cage. A broad man stood inside of it, but he was in his thirties and didn't have any hair. He was too old to be Nino Falcone. A hush went through the crowd and another man stepped into the cage, taller than the first, and I froze. For several moments, my breath stuck in my throat. If a mere video already summoned that kind of horror, what would real life Nino do?

Nino was tall and muscled, and every inch of his torso and arms was covered in tattoos. Flames and knives and screaming faces, and more images and words I couldn't make out. The flames traveled down his arms to his wrists. They also snaked into his fighting shorts, ending on his muscled thighs.

His expression was focused but completely emotionless.

My fear turned into pure terror when the fight began. Nino was a fighting machine. Every single one of his hits was *precision*, but what was worse was his analytic expression. He didn't look like he was fighting in a cage. When his opponent landed a hit, Nino's face hardly reflected any sign of pain. He kicked and punched hard and fast, without mercy, even as his opponent fell to his knees. Nino was on top of him in a heartbeat, ramming his knee into the man's back so he sprawled out on the bloody floor. Even that wasn't enough. Nino wrapped his forearm around the man's throat and cut off his air. His opponent thrust his elbow into Nino's side, but he didn't even wince, only tightened his hold further and eventually the man passed out. Nino released him then and stood. His gaze flitted over the crowd until it focused on the camera. It was as if he was looking straight at me, and the cold, hard look in his eyes awakened the horrors I couldn't shake off.

I couldn't believe this was the man I was supposed to marry.

I didn't sleep more than two hours. Every night, Uncle Durant's face haunted my dreams as he hovered over me and broke me, but this night it was a different face that had hovered above me, a beautifully cold face.

When our bodyguard drove us to Philadelphia to pick Giulia up, my aunt tried to involve me in a conversation about dresses, but I was too upset to engage in any kind of interaction. I was glad when Giulia joined us in the backseat. After one glance at me, she quickly distracted her mother by talking about her summer plans with the kids.

I sent her a grateful look before I trained my gaze on the window, watching as the landscape rushed past me.

Unlike many women, I didn't have a dream dress. I never looked at wedding dresses unless I was at a wedding.

Aria waited with her bodyguard inside the store because it was hailing. The moment we stepped inside, a vendor rushed over to us. "Who's the happy bride?"

Giulia, Aria, and Aunt Egidia looked at me, and the vendor touched my arm. "Exciting, isn't it? You're going to be a breathtaking bride. I can tell."

I gave her a small smile and followed her toward the display of dresses. "Why don't you browse the dresses and show me the ones you'd choose for me?" I asked, sinking down into one of the plush armchairs.

That garnered a look from the vendor, but at this point I didn't care anymore.

Aria and Giulia nodded immediately and set out to look for dresses, but Aunt Egidia's expression made it clear that she disapproved. However, after a moment she began looking for suitable dresses as well.

Of course, Aunt Egidia chose dresses that would have made most Disney princesses jealous. Too flashy, too eye-catching, just too much. Not me at all. Luckily, Aria and Giulia worked together and found dresses that were closer to my taste.

I chose a simple white mermaid, off-the-shoulder dress with lace trim around the neckline. A sheer veil was attached to the neckline as well and fell down my back and over my bare arms so I didn't feel quite so exposed.

"Beautiful," Aria said with a gentle smile. She was still trying to figure out my true feelings regarding the wedding, but I had learned to hide them well over the years. It was the only way to survive after what happened.

Giulia nodded, her eyes watering, and even Aunt Egidia seemed pleased with my choice—even if it wasn't as flashy as she'd originally planned. "You look very elegant and sophisticated. A true lady."

I took a deep breath, hoping Nino would treat me as a lady. The man I saw fighting in the cage didn't strike me as someone who would.

Nino

We pulled up in front of the massive stone and stucco Vitello villa in Baltimore, where the engagement party would take place. With only two days before the actual wedding, there was no logical reason to get officially engaged at all, but logical decisions weren't the Famiglia's forte. Savio, Adamo, and Fabiano remained in Las Vegas to make sure things went smoothly over there. They would only fly over for the actual wedding. It wasn't as if any of us cared for the festivities. It wouldn't be a huge affair like Aria and Luca's wedding had been many years ago. Our Underbosses and Captains would stay in their territory. Remo wouldn't risk anything after the Outfit attack.

"If they've invited that fucker Growl, I will paint their walls bright red with his fucking blood and that of any Famiglia fucker who gets in my way," Remo growled.

"He won't be invited, Remo. Luca won't risk it. He knows you and Growl will tear into each other."

"What about you? You'd fucking stand by and watch that fucker prancing around when he killed our father before we could?"

"Of course not. I'd slice him open ear to ear."

The moment we got out of the rental car, the door to the house opened, and Felix and Egidia Rizzo appeared in the doorway. Remo shot me a look, one corner of his mouth curling up. "Someone kept an eye on the window, it seems," he muttered as we walked up to my future wife's aunt and uncle. The engagement wouldn't be a grand feast, only held to appease the traditionalists in the Famiglia who required an official engagement before the wedding, but the Rizzos were dressed up in a tuxedo and a long evening dress anyway.

"I think we are underdressed," I said quietly. I had put on a black turtleneck and black dress pants with black wingtip shoes. Remo was dressed in a similar fashion, minus the turtleneck, which he'd swapped for a black dress shirt.

Remo shrugged.

"All in black," Mrs. Rizzo said with raised eyebrows after I kissed her hand. "What a curious choice for the occasion."

"It's the choice color for our profession. Blood is so very difficult to wash out," Remo drawled in his best Oxford English as he kissed her hand. That was pretty much the only thing he'd learned during our time in England. Of course, he only used it to unsettle people.

Mrs. Rizzo took a small step back from Remo, tugging her hand out of his grasp.

I shook hands with Mr. Rizzo, and he squeezed harder than was necessary. I tilted my head, eyes narrowing. If he tried this with Remo, the black shirt would prove its worth. "We are honored to give you Kiara in marriage," he said, releasing my hand. "Please call me Felix, and this is my wife Egidia."

I sent Remo a warning glance before he shook the man's hand.

"Come in," Felix said, stepping back. Remo and I followed him inside. It was a large old house with lots of dark wood and rugs in the entrance hall.

"The guests have already gathered in the living room and on the patio, but you and Kiara should enter together," Felix said then turned to Remo. "Perhaps you can join the guests. My wife will lead the way."

Egidia gave a tense smile and motioned for Remo to follow, but he made no move to do so. "I think for now my brother and I will stay together."

Felix blinked then nodded slowly. "Very well. Come on. I chose the library for your first meeting. It's the place Kiara spends most of her time."

I cocked an eyebrow. "She likes to read?"

Felix hesitated. "She does, but she is also very beautiful and demure. The perfect wife despite her intelligence."

Remo rolled his eyes behind the man's back. We stepped into a wide room that was filled with dark wooden bookcases. A book lay opened on the small table beside the reading chair. I walked toward it as Felix frowned. "She should be here."

"Perhaps she decided to run off," Remo offered helpfully.

"She wouldn't," Felix said quickly, but I caught the hint of worry on his face—and so had Remo.

I picked up the book. It was about the history of Las Vegas. It pleased me that she made an effort to learn about my hometown's history.

"There she is," Felix said loudly.

I put the book back down, and my eyes moved toward the doorway.

Kiara Vitiello was a fine-boned woman, shorter than I'd expected, almost breakable in appearance, but her hips curved nicely under her dress, and she had above-average-sized breasts. She wore a dress the color of light rose, almost white, but it made her look even more fragile. Clearly it was to emphasize her innocence, but I would have preferred bolder colors. Her dark eyes settled on my face—not my eyes, though—lower, perhaps on my nose, and her shoulders tensed ever so slightly. She hadn't moved from the doorway, appearing almost frozen. Her palm pressed up to the doorframe, and I knew it was to steady herself.

Remo looked at me, gauging my reaction, which was a futile effort on his part.

Her uncle motioned for her to come closer. "Come on, Kiara. Greet your future husband and brother-in-law."

A second passed before she pulled herself away from the doorway and walked toward us. Her movements were elegant and purposeful but underplayed with a hint of a tremor she couldn't suppress.

She stopped beside her uncle.

Even wearing heels, she only reached my chin. "It's a pleasure to meet you," she said in a soft voice. Her eyes darted from my face to Remo's then quickly back to her uncle.

"The pleasure is mine," I replied, and Remo's smile pulled wider. Kiara flinched slightly, almost imperceptible, but Remo had noticed, twitching his lip, and so had I.

Her uncle cleared his throat uncomfortably.

"I would like a few minutes alone with her to give her the ring and get to know each other," I said, never taking my eyes off her.

"Well," her uncle said, his eyes flitting between Remo and me and then to Kiara. "I'm not sure—"

Remo flashed him a twisted smile. "They will be married in two days. Then she will come to Las Vegas with us, but you are worried about her being alone for a couple of moments with my brother? She will be subject to his will for the rest of her life."

Kiara's shoulders rounded, caving in, and she swallowed hard.

Felix paled, his eyes hardening. "This is for peace. Don't forget that."

I spoke up before Remo could because he looked like he would have used his knife instead of words, and I wanted this annoying power play to end quickly. "You shouldn't forget it either. Kiara isn't your concern anymore. She is mine." I showed him the ring, and her eyes flitted toward it briefly. "Today, I will put this ring on her finger, and then my word is the law, not yours."

Resignation filled her face, and her shoulders slumped, but she caught herself quickly and straightened again.

"What do you say, Kiara?" her uncle asked. "Do you agree to talk to Nino?"

She met his gaze, her lips tense. "This is the first time you've asked me if I agree. As Mr. Falcone pointed out, I will be under my future husband's rule soon enough, so I don't see how it matters now."

Her uncle stared at her, a blank look on his face. Obviously he was not used to any objection from her. He gave a jerky nod and turned on his heel, rushing out of the room.

Before Remo moved to follow, he turned to Kiara. "Never call me Mr. Falcone again. That was my father, and I would have burned the fucker alive if I had been given the chance."

He stalked past Kiara, and she shied away from him so his arm wouldn't brush hers. Remo threw the door shut, and Kiara jumped. She wasn't naturally submissive, even if she acted that way.

I held out my hand, a silent order, and wondered if she'd comply. She stepped up to me and put her palm in mine, not meeting my eyes. I wrapped my fingers around her wrist, my thumb pressing against her veins. She shivered, goose bumps rising on her skin.

Dilated pupils, accelerated breathing, racing pulse, trembling, Kiara had the telltale signs of terror. I kept my thumb on her pulse point as I regarded her. She finally raised her gaze to mine, and her pulse sped up further. Her body's reactions could have been a sign for arousal as well, but I knew they weren't.

"So you didn't agree to marry me," I pointed out.

Her cheeks flushed, and her gaze returned to my chin. "I did agree when Luca asked me, but my uncle never asked when he made the offer."

"Why did you agree when Luca asked, then?"

Her brows drew together. "Because it wasn't really a choice; it was disguised as one. In this life women aren't given choices."

I regarded her for a few moments. She seemed angry. Her anger suited me better than the submissive terror she'd displayed before. I lifted her hand, and she tensed again as if she'd forgotten about my touch. Her pulse raced against my fingertips. I showed her the ring. "I won't tell you that you have a choice to accept this or not. We both know you will accept it like you will say yes in two days."

She blanched and gave a small nod. "Otherwise there won't be peace."

"Indeed."

Her fingers shook as I put the engagement ring on. The jeweler had recommended it after I told her money wasn't an issue. A simple gold band with a big diamond in the middle. I never understood the reason for engagement rings. She swallowed again, and I realized it was to contain some of her terror. "You realize this isn't a death sentence."

Dark brown eyes rose to meet mine. "Death isn't the worst that can happen."

"You will be my wife," I told her. Whatever she'd heard about my brothers and me, and what was going on in Vegas, she didn't have to fear that kind of thing.

The door opened and Kiara quickly pulled her hand from mine, swallowing again, but she didn't manage to erase the fear on her face. A woman with long brown hair, a lighter shade than Kiara's, poked her head in, eyes roving between Kiara and me. She narrowed her eyes then stepped into the room. "I'm not interrupting anything, am I?"

I recognized her from photos of the Famiglia Underbosses and Captains I'd studied. Giulia Moretti, wife to Cassio Moretti, Underboss of Philadelphia. "I think that was the purpose of your appearance, wasn't it?" I drawled.

She didn't look guilty as she moved to Kiara's side and gave me a haughty expression. "It's not proper for you to be alone with her yet. I don't know how you handle things in Las Vegas, but here we handle them like this."

I gave her a cold smile. "Don't worry, I'm very aware of your traditions, as peculiar as they may be with the presentation of the sheets."

If I'd thought, Kiara had been scared before, my mentioning of that tradition upped her fright.

I held out my hand but looked at Giulia. "Kiara and I are supposed to make an appearance together, Mrs. Moretti … unless that tradition has been changed recently?"

She glanced at Kiara, who gave her a firm smile. "He's right, Giulia. We don't want to disappoint the guests."

She slipped her hand back in mine and lifted her chin. My thumb found her wrist again, and she shivered. *Thud-thud. Thud.* An erratic rhythm. *Thud-thud. Thud.*

Giulia left, but she didn't close the door.

Without another word, I led Kiara into the living room, where the guests were waiting for our appearance. They began clapping when we entered. What a display of fake excitement. Remo stood beside Luca, his brother Matteo, and Romero. The women of the family were gathered on the other side of the room, probably because of my brother. Remo's expression didn't bode well. Maybe he was pissed that he didn't get the chance to spill our half-brother's blood, but I had told him Luca wouldn't dare invite him.

Luca and Kiara's uncle spoke a few words as was expected. After that, I released Kiara, so she could show off her ring to the women.

"And what do you think? Are you satisfied with your future bride?" Remo asked with a grin as I stopped beside him. Luca tossed us a hard look. Remo being his usual provocative self hadn't bothered to lower his voice.

"It's too early to assess my level of satisfaction yet," I said, considering her again. Her face was evenly shaped with the right proportions, pleasant to look at, and her dark eyes and hair contrasted in a pleasing way with her pale skin. Her body fulfilled all the requirements to attract male attention: narrow waist, slender legs, round ass, and bigger than average breasts. I would have no trouble claiming her on our wedding night.

"Done with your assessment?" Remo said as he followed me toward the spread of delicacies on the dining table. "You will definitely enjoy fucking her. I wish I could get a taste."

"But you won't," I said plainly.

Remo tilted his head. "In the past, the king had the right of the first night."

"Ius primae noctis."

"Maybe I should establish something like that in Vegas." Remo chuckled, his eyes scanning the crowd for suitable women. "Bring all your virgins so I can break them."

I shook my head. At least this time he had the sense to speak quietly. Luca needed peace as much as we did, but his patience certainly had its limits. "You aren't king, Remo. And you don't have a right to the first night with Kiara."

"Jealous isn't like you," Remo said with a hint of … was that curiosity?

"I'm not jealous, but there are a few things I don't want to share with you and Kiara is one of them."

Remo waved me off. "She is all yours. Don't worry." I wasn't worried. Remo was unpredictable, twisted, and brutal, but he was my brother and he would never lay hand on someone who was mine. "But I will have to give this … what did you call it?"

"Ius primae noctis," I provided.

"Yeah, that. Maybe I will have to give it another thought."

I regarded my brother, trying to figure out if he was being serious. It was often hard to tell with Remo, and my lack of understanding human emotions had little to do with it. "You realize that most men won't find the idea of you *fucking* their women very appealing. There is a limit to what people will take, even from you. Fear has its limits. At some point, humans revolt."

Remo rolled his eyes. "You realize you are human too, right?"

"I always got the impression that you and I had little humanity left."

Remo clapped my shoulder. "True." His smile turned dangerous. "Who needs emotions and morals when they can fuck and maim and kill as they please?"

I had never seen the appeal of having emotions.

Kiara glanced at me from across the room again but quickly looked away when I met her gaze. She was trying to hide her emotions, but I could sense her terror even from the distance. Emotions were always a weakness.

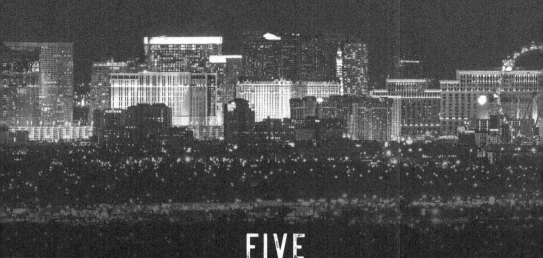

FIVE

Kiara

A**UNT EGIDIA HANDLED THE WEDDING PREPARATIONS WITH ARIA'S** help. The Falcones didn't seem to show much interest in the details of the celebration. For them it was business, nothing else. It was decided that the wedding was to take place in my parents' mansion in the Hamptons—the place where they had been killed. My mother by my father and my father by Luca. It was almost symbolic that this was the place where I would lose my life as well.

On the day of my wedding, I stepped into the foyer of the mansion, a place I hadn't set foot in for years. It had been mostly deserted since then. My brothers had inherited the place—not me since I was a woman—and they had preferred to stay in Atlanta, away from Luca and away from me. They were much older, so we never had much in common anyway. They were busy making names for themselves, despite our father's wrongdoings. My marriage to Nino was supposed to wash away the blemish of the past, but my secret could ruin us all.

Over the last few days, cleaners and interior designers had awoken the place from its desolate state. The main party would take place in a massive party tent in the garden. It was late April and planning the party outside without any shelter would have been too risky.

I walked up the stairs slowly, and my eyes found the spot where my mother had died. With a shudder, I quickly scurried into my old bedroom. It, too, had been prepared for the day. Fresh flowers had been set up in vases around the room, probably to cover the musty scent of neglect. My aunt was talking to the stylist, who'd do my hair and makeup, at the vanity. A floor-length mirror had been set up for the occasion. My dress was spread out on the four-post bed.

It was a beautiful dress: white, the color of innocence and purity.

I looked at my aunt and considered telling her what had happened to me six years ago. As always, I didn't because I'd be less in her eyes. Something broken, something dirty. Not worthy of that perfect white dress.

Giulia slipped into the room, already dressed in a beautiful burgundy dress, and hugged me. "I can't believe they chose this place for the celebrations," she muttered.

"It belongs to her closest living relatives, her brothers. It's what honor dictated."

Honor dictated so many things in our lives, it hardly left any room for choice.

Giulia rolled her eyes. "So it had nothing to do with the fact that nobody wanted to risk their mansion for the party because the risk of a bloodshed is too high? After all, that's why this isn't taking place in a hotel."

Aunt Egidia pursed her lips at her daughter. "Giulia, really, one would think your marriage to Cassio would have put a stop to your insolence."

"Cassio likes my insolence," she said, her cheeks flushing.

Aunt Egidia sighed then narrowed a nervous glance toward the stylist; she was always worried about leaving a bad impression in front of others. "I think we should start now. With your unruly hair, it'll probably be a while before your bridal hairdo is done."

My aunt proved to be right. The stylist took forever taming my curls into a braid that traveled down my back. A thin strand of gold leaves and pearls that she wound into it adorned the simple style.

"You are so very beautiful," Giulia said quietly.

Egidia clasped her hand in front of her stomach, regarding me with more affection than I'd ever seen before. "You are."

The stylist left the room with a small smile, which I returned even as my facial muscles felt ready to burst from tension.

Egidia smoothed out the veil lining my neckline again before she faced me, touching my shoulders. "As women, we have to fulfill our duty to our husbands …" she began, and I tensed because I knew where she was going with it. "You don't have to be—" She stopped herself. Don't have to be scared? Those were the words every mother spoke to her daughter on their wedding day. I knew because Giulia had told me Egidia said the same thing to her on her wedding day. I met Aunt Egidia's gaze and the guilt I'd seen in her eyes before was back. "Make him treat you like a lady."

Giulia stepped up to Egidia. "Mother, let me talk to Kiara, okay? I think she will feel more comfortable around me."

Aunt Egidia nodded, looking relieved. She patted my shoulder then walked out, leaving me alone with my stepsister.

Giulia sighed as she regarded me in the mirror. "I don't like this, Kiara. You shouldn't be marrying a Falcone. You are the last person who should."

"Why? Better than someone innocent."

Giulia gripped my hand hard. "Stop it. You aren't dirty or less or whatever you think you are because of what he did to you. And you don't deserve this."

"Who deserves this? I don't wish this fate on any other girl. I will survive."

Giulia perched on the vanity. "I don't know what to tell you."

"Don't say anything. There's nothing you can tell me that will set me at ease," I told her quickly. I knew what was going to happen tonight, and I had lived through it before. I swallowed. "I won't fight him. I will do what he wants. Then surely it will be endurable. I'm not thirteen anymore." My words were hushed, broken vowels strung together.

Giulia breathed deeply. "My God, Kiara. Tell Luca. He can still find a way out of this for you."

"Cancelling the wedding today? That would be a slap in Remo Falcone's face. He isn't a man who will turn the other cheek. He will seek revenge, no matter the price." I took a deep breath. "No. I will marry Nino. Did you get the pills I asked you for?"

She held out a small package to me. "One should do the trick, but I really don't think you should drug yourself to be calm."

"It's a light sedative. It won't knock me out." Although, I would have preferred that effect, but Nino would not appreciate it if I were unconscious when he claimed me. My stomach pinched sharply, and I pressed my palm against it.

"Kiara—"

"No. I'm doing this. Many choices have been taken from me throughout this life, but I choose to salvage my honor, choose to hold my head high no matter what happens. Let this be my choice."

Giulia nodded and got up. "Because the Falcones are feared, because they rule without mercy, doesn't mean Nino won't treat you with kindness. Some men don't bring violence home to their wives. Some men can distinguish between the ones they need to protect and those they need to break. I think Nino might be one of them."

I wondered if she really believed her words or if they were just to console me, but I didn't have the courage to ask her. I stuffed the pills into the small white purse that matched my dress. "Can you give it to me at the party? I can't carry it down the aisle."

Giulia took it and hugged me briefly. "Of course."

Nino

My brothers and I weren't religious, so we had refused to marry in church, much to the Famiglia's disapproval. I wasn't sure why they clung to their beliefs when they broke every rule established by their religion on a daily basis. Every man would end up in Hell, if what they believed was truth.

I waited at the altar that had been set up in front of the tent in the gardens. Remo stood beside me as my best man, his eyes undressing Kiara's bridesmaid Giulia in a way that made her husband Cassio scowl. I sent Remo a warning look but he ignored me. He probably would have preferred a bloody wedding, and from the look on Matteo's face as he sat in the first row, he would too. Adamo and Savio sat a few seats away from the Vitiellos. To my surprise, Luca had allowed Aria to sit beside Leona. They seemed to be getting along well, and even Fabiano exchanged the occasional word with his sister.

Remo rolled his eyes when he followed my gaze. He should have been happy that his insane plan was working. A truce between the Famiglia and Camorra seemed like a valid possibility.

A hush fell over the crowd when the music began to play and Kiara appeared at the end of the aisle. She had chosen an elegant dress with a veil that covered her shoulders. Felix led her toward me, but Kiara never raised her eyes to meet mine, instead keeping them fixed on my chest.

When Felix handed her over to me, her hand shook in mine. I pressed my thumb against her wrist, feeling her pulse raced under my fingertips. I regarded her face. Her expression was neutral, but in her eyes was a look I'd often seen in people's eyes before I started to torture them.

Given our reputation, her terror was understandable, but it was completely unfounded. She wasn't my enemy but my wife. I hadn't given her reason for that kind of reaction.

She never once glanced my way as the pastor gave his long-winded sermon and finally declared us husband and wife.

"You may kiss the bride," the pastor said.

I turned to Kiara and her pulse sped up even more. Her terrified eyes finally lifted to mine, and she swallowed hard. Holding her gaze, I cupped her cheek, ignoring her trembling, and pressed my lips to hers. They were soft and quivered against mine. When I pulled back, she swallowed again.

We made our way past the guests and stopped beside a table, which had been set up with champagne flutes.

After we'd accepted congratulations from our guests, the buffet was finally opened. Kiara was tense throughout dinner and hardly ate anything. She only relaxed when she got up and walked over to Aria and the other Scuderi sisters to talk.

"Excited about making your wife bleed tonight?" Remo asked the moment she was out of earshot as he leaned back in his chair. I was surprised he'd bothered to wait until she couldn't hear his words.

Leona's eyes widened, and she looked up at Fabiano. "He's referring to the tradition of the bloody sheets that the Famiglia still upholds. It requires the groom to present the sheets he and his bride spent the night on."

Leona pursed her lips. "You are joking, right?"

"And they call us barbaric," Remo said with a smirk. "But I have to tell you, I envy you your chance to spill some blood tonight. It's been too long. I really want to kill someone."

Fabiano rolled his eyes at Remo.

"When has there ever been a day without blood in our lives?" I asked.

Remo's eyes tightened with an emotion I could not read. "True," he said. "Remember, no taking her up against the wall or bent over the desk. Bloody sheets is what the dear Famiglia wants." He raised his glass and took a sip of wine, but neither of us would get drunk today.

"Don't worry. I will provide bloody sheets."

Remo smiled twistedly. "I know you will."

My eyes found my wife again. She was still talking to the Scuderi sisters but turned her gaze to me when she noticed my attention. She tensed and swallowed, the hand holding her glass shaking slightly.

Fearing me like she did, she'd probably bleed her second and third time as well. I knew how to please women with my hands, tongue, and cock, but even sexual skills had their limits when faced with terror.

When it was time for our first dance, I stood and Kiara came over to me, accepting my outstretched hand. I led her toward the center, and our guests gathered around us to watch. She allowed herself to look into my eyes for longer than she ever had. Fear and uncertainty flickered across her face. When she didn't find whatever it was she was looking for, she lowered her gaze back to my chest and swallowed hard. It must have been her way to suppress the fear.

I touched her lower back and pulled her against me. She made a small sound in the back of her throat, a strong sound of unease. I regarded her face. She was breathing faster and her cheeks had paled. This was only a mere dance. If this unsettled her, the consummation of our marriage would be particularly unpleasant. She wasn't the type to fight, too dutiful and raised to please. She would yield to me, but it wouldn't make things any easier for her.

Maybe words of consolation would have soothed her terror, but I wasn't a man who comforted others.

The song ended. As was expected, Luca, the Capo who had given her to me, stepped up to take over. Kiara didn't soften. She was as scared of dancing with him as she was of me. I forced myself to release her. She wasn't in danger. This was a dance. There was no reason to make it out to be more.

I turned to Aria. Luca narrowed his eyes at me. I ignored his unreasonable reaction and held out my hand to his wife. She took it and gave me a smile. She was a good actress. If it hadn't been for the slight tension in her fingers and the acceleration of her pulse, I might have believed her expression.

Pulling her against me, we began to dance. She was easy to steer, took my lead, and kept up a pleasant smile.

"You have Fabiano's eyes."

Her gaze flew up to mine, and her expression faltered. "He is my brother. Even if you made him believe something else."

"We didn't make him believe anything," I corrected. "We taught him that blood doesn't define your loyalties."

"You turned him into—"

"Into what? A killer? A torturer?"

She sighed.

"Every man in this room is a killer, and the boys are on their way to becoming one." And from what I knew of Luca, he definitely was one of the cruelest men in our circles, but Aria probably had limited knowledge when it came to her husband's business habits.

"This isn't wedding talk," she said. "I hope this wedding will allow us to find peace, and I hope your brother will allow Fabiano to be close to his blood family."

"It's up to Fabiano, but he is with the Camorra now. Don't forget that."

"I won't, trust me," she said sharply. Her eyes followed her husband and my wife as they danced. Kiara was stiff in Luca's hold.

"Kiara is very tense around men," I said.

Aria frowned. "Most women are tense on their wedding day."

"They are?"

She gave me a look, but I couldn't read it. "Men," she said under her breath. It had nothing to do with me being male, but I didn't elaborate. "For a bride, a wedding night holds quite a bit of terror."

"Fear of the unknown is common, but it is only the joining of two bodies. Nothing to be fearful of."

Aria blinked up at me. "Perhaps for you, but Kiara might disagree, like any other woman, especially considering who she has to join bodies with."

"I am more than capable of fulfilling my duties as a husband."

"I don't doubt that you can go through with it. The Camorra is notorious after all." She grimaced. "It's not my business."

But her voice made it clear that she wanted it to be her business. "It's not. You are right," I drawled. A truce didn't mean Remo or I would allow the Famiglia to meddle in our business.

When the last notes of the song faded, she rushed to say, "Her father hit her before he was killed. That might explain her problem with men. But I think there might be more ..."

"More?"

She stepped back. "Thank you for the dance." She turned and moved toward Luca, who was waiting for her at the edge of the dance floor. Kiara had already been handed off to Felix.

I moved toward Remo, who stood beside Fabiano close to the buffet. As my oldest brother, it would be his turn to dance with Kiara after her Uncle Felix. I grabbed his arm, and he raised his dark eyebrows.

"Try to scare her as little as possible."

"I can be pleasant and gentlemanly if I try," he said.

Fabiano laughed. "Sorry, Remo, but that's the best joke I heard in a while."

"What am I supposed to do to set your little wife at ease?" he asked, but his eyes followed a young woman who walked past us. I really hoped he wouldn't try anything with one of the Famiglia's women.

I was the wrong person to ask. "I don't know."

We glanced at Leona who flushed. "Perhaps smile?"

Remo's mouth pulled into a smile.

"I have seen hyenas with less unsettling smiles," Fabiano muttered, and Leona choked on her laughter and buried her face against his arm. The song ended, and Remo pulled free of my grip, heading for Kiara, who looked like a lamb facing off with a butcher.

Giulia surprised me when she asked for a dance. I was fairly sure that wasn't how things were usually handled, but I led her toward the dance floor and pulled her against me. Her husband watched us from his spot beside Luca at the buffet. They were both tall and muscled and shared a similar disposition for brutal leadership ... if rumors were to be believed.

"I don't know if you are even capable of such a thing, but I ask you to be kind to Kiara."

I glanced down at Giulia. "You ask me?" I said with raised eyebrows.

She frowned. "If you have a heart, please don't hurt her."

"I was told there's no way around hurting a woman in her first night."

Her eyes filled with tears but her expression looked angry. "You know what I mean!"

"Kiara is my wife, a grown woman, and from this day on she's part of the Camorra. She isn't your concern," I said in a warning tone.

Giulia tensed but didn't say anymore. The second the music was over I released her, and she returned to her husband while I went back to my brothers and Fabiano.

Kiara

Remo Falcone headed my way, and it took considerable effort not to run. His eyes were almost black like his hair. There was something in his face that spoke of unbridled violence, and that wasn't because of the scar trailing from his brow down his temple to his cheekbone. He held out his hand with a twisted pull of his mouth. It was reminiscent of how a lion regarded a gazelle.

His palm and fingers were littered with scars and burns.

"You are supposed to take my hand so we can dance," he said in what I assumed was annoyance.

Suppressing a shudder, I slipped my hand into his. I didn't look up into his face. It would have been my undoing. His fingers closed around my hand with less pressure than I had expected, and his other hand gently touched my back and pulled me against him. My body clenched, my breathing caught in my throat. I had to hold in a gasp. He led me along to the music, but my trembling didn't make it easy for him. He tightened his hold on me, bringing us closer, and I exhaled sharply at the feel of his hard body against mine.

My fingers on his bicep began slipping as I fought against the impending panic attack.

"Look at me," he ordered.

I couldn't.

"Look at me." A low murmur full of command, and I finally met his gaze. His expression wasn't angry, more assessing, as if he was sizing me up. "This is dancing. Don't make it into something more than that because you let your imagination run free."

I was momentarily startled. He sounded a lot like Nino; maybe he hid his intelligence behind his layers of violence.

"Now pretend you are a happy bride. This is a day of celebration," he said, and his own lips formed a scary smile.

I tried my best to relax in his hold, to make my face look pleasant, but I wasn't sure if I succeeded. I counted the seconds till the end of the song, but when it finally ended, Uncle Durant appeared at our side and terror from the past took hold of me. I dug my nails into Remo, clinging to him, undoubtedly leaving marks with my fingernails.

"I would like to dance with my niece now," Uncle Durant said to Remo, but his eyes were on me, full of knowledge and triumph as always.

He hadn't touched me since those nights. I clutched Remo tightly, looking up at him. His dark eyes regarded me, narrowing ever so slightly. *Please don't let me dance with him.* The words didn't leave my mouth. Durant reached for me, but Remo angled us so he was between my uncle and me.

Remo turned his gaze to my uncle, but he didn't let go of me. "I can't allow that unfortunately. My brother wants her back at his side."

"It's tradition in the Famiglia," Uncle Durant said. "Maybe you don't care about traditions over in Vegas, but here we do."

Remo's lips pulled wider, and I realized then that his smiles for me had been genuine; he was being nice. This smile had a sinister feel to it. "We honor our traditions as well. In Vegas, it's tradition that I cut out the tongues of people who annoy the fuck out of me. If you insist on your traditions, I will have to insist on mine. And your tongue will look good in my collection."

Uncle Durant's face turned red. His angry gaze settled on me briefly, and I pressed into Remo, but then my uncle moved away.

"You can release me now," Remo muttered.

I unfastened my hold and stepped back, ashamed. Remo held onto my hand, not allowing me to go. His thumb pressed against my wrist in a similar way like Nino had.

"What was that?" Remo asked in a low, dangerous voice.

"Nothing. I don't like him."

"That was not dislike, Kiara," he said, still in that terrifying voice. His fingers pressed harder into my wrist. I risked a peek at him. His eyes were narrowed at me, as if he could see into the deepest, darkest corners of my soul. "Dislike wouldn't have made you seek protection in my arms, trust me."

"I didn't—"

"Don't lie to me. I am your Capo now."

Nothing would make me reveal my secret, not even Remo's terrifying scowl. "I didn't ask for your protection," I whispered.

He stepped closer, and I cringed. "You begged me for protection. Unlike Nino, I have no trouble reading your emotions."

I wasn't sure what he meant.

"You didn't have to protect me. I'm not your responsibility."

"You are a Falcone now. My brother's wife. You fall under my rule. That makes you mine to protect."

He tightened his grip on my wrist, ignoring my flinching, and dragged me off the dance floor toward Nino, who raised his eyebrows at his brother. Remo practically shoved me into Nino's arm. Despite my tension, Nino wrapped an arm around my waist and left it there. "That was her last dance with anyone but us," Remo ordered. "I don't give a fuck about their traditions. She is under our rule now."

Nino narrowed his eyes. "What's the matter?"

"Nothing," Remo said. "But her family is starting to piss me off."

Nino glanced between his brother and me but didn't say anymore. After that, I didn't have to dance again.

SIX

Kiara

"**B**ED HER, BED HER!" THE CHANTING BEGAN BEFORE I'D MANAGED to mentally prepare myself. Perhaps I was stupid for thinking I could prepare for it.

My husband's brothers, Remo and Savio, shouted the loudest, but most of the other men were almost as loud. The youngest brother, Adamo, remained in his seat, lips pressed together in a firm line. He hadn't talked to me or danced with me or anyone else.

"Bed her, bed her!" the cries grew louder.

I sought Nino's gaze. He nodded at me, got up, and held out a hand. I took it because I could not refuse him with everyone watching us. Forcing down my fear, I stood and followed him past the rows of guests who had lined up to see us out. The men clapped Nino's shoulders; the women caught my gaze with pity and sympathy in their eyes. Giulia was pressed up against her husband, worry filling her expression. I quickly looked away.

"On to unchartered grounds!"

"We want to see the sheets!"

There were more comments like that, and they turned my stomach into solid rock.

Nino's face didn't betray his reaction to the shouts. His fingers pressed against my wrist tightly, and I was glad because they grounded me, kept me from faltering, from drifting off to the past.

Remo and Savio were close by as we went down the long corridor—a corridor that held many childhood memories, few of them good and tonight worse memories would be added to the list.

We arrived in front of the dark wooden door to the master bedroom, dozens of men behind us.

"No fucking your virgin bride up against the wall, remember?" Remo said with a laugh.

I jerked, my pulse doubling. Nino's fingers tightened against my wrist.

"Remo," he growled in a voice that sent fear into every fiber of my being.

"Have fun!" Savio shouted with a grin.

The Falcones were going to feel cheated. A sacrificial virgin was to be given to the monsters in Las Vegas for a promise of peace. I was never given the chance to be a virgin. That choice had been taken from me. *Painfully ripped from me.*

Fear, acute and raw, clawed at my chest as my husband led me into our room for the night and closed the door to the grinning faces of his brothers. Nino released me, and I quickly created distance between us, moving toward the bed.

Six years had passed, but the memories still woke me at night. I was scared of being close to a man, to any man, especially this man—my husband.

Standing a few steps in front of the bed, my eyes swept over the white sheets—sheets my family expected to the see stained with my blood in the morning.

Blood that wouldn't be there.

I crept closer to the bed. There had been blood the first time, the second time, and even the third time. Lots of blood, pain, terror, and begging. There had been no presentation of the sheets back then. Our maid, who had never come to my aid, cleaned them.

I wouldn't beg tonight. It hadn't stopped my abuser many years ago.

It wouldn't stop my husband.

I knew the stories. I had seen him in the cage.

My only consolation was that I doubted he could break me more than I already had been all those years ago.

I couldn't take my eyes off those perfect white sheets—as white as my dress. A sign of purity, but I wasn't pure.

"They are your traditions, not ours," Nino said calmly but loud enough to tear me from my thoughts.

I schooled my face into placidness. "Then why follow them?" I asked as I turned. My voice had betrayed me. Too hushed, laced with a terror that I hoped he mistook for virginal fear.

He wasn't as close as I'd expected. He wasn't even looking at me. Standing beside the desk, he read the note my aunt had written congratulating us on the nuptials. He put it back down then looked up at me. There was nothing on his face that gave me a sense of hope. No kindness, no pity. It was a blank canvas.

Beautifully cold with empty gray eyes, an immaculate short beard, and combed back hair.

As he shook his head, he destroyed what little hope I'd had. "The Famiglia wants blood, they get it."

He was right. It was what my family expected, what I was supposed to deliver, but they wouldn't get blood. And my husband would realize his prize was faulty. The Camorra would cancel the truce. My husband would rebuke the marriage, and I'd be left to live as a pariah.

It would be my ruin. My family would shun me. Nobody would ever want to marry me after that, and an unmarried woman in our world was doomed.

He began unbuttoning his shirt, calmly, precisely. Finally he shrugged it off, revealing scars and tattoos—so many, so disturbing—and steely muscles. I turned away, my pulse galloping in my veins. Terror, similar to that which I'd felt many years ago, clawed at my insides. I needed to rein it in, figure a way out of this mess. I needed to save myself, not from him claiming my body but from me losing my honor.

I reached into my purse, which dangled over my forearm, and freed a pill from the packet. My throat was tight, and I wasn't sure if I'd manage to swallow it without water, but walking into the bathroom seemed impossible in my current state. I wasn't sure I would make it without breaking down.

With shaking fingers, I brought the white pill to my lips. A hand curled around my wrist, stopping me. My eyes flew up to stare into Nino's narrowed eyes. I hadn't even heard him approach.

"What is that?" he asked forcefully.

I didn't say anything, too terrified for words. With his free hand, he reached into my purse and pulled out the packet. His eyes scanned the description. He threw it away before his gray eyes met mine, and he held out his hand. "Give me that pill."

"Please," I whispered.

Not a flicker of emotion on his beautiful, cold face. "Kiara, give me that pill."

I dropped it into his palm, and he threw it away as well. I could have cried. How was I supposed to rein in my terror, keep the memories at bay without something to calm myself?

His thumb brushed my wrist, and he murmured, "I won't have you drugged." He released me. I stepped back and turned around to face the bed, sucking in a deep breath. He was watching me.

I reached behind me for the buttons on the back of my dress. I would be the one to open them. That would give me a sense of control, unlike last time when my clothes had been ripped from me against my will, my body too weak to fight against it.

I swallowed the bile. My fingers shook too much to close around the tiny buttons.

"Let me," came the cool drawl from my husband who was close behind.

No! I wanted to scream, but I forced the sound down. "I want to do it my-self," I managed in an almost calm voice.

He didn't say anything, and I didn't dare look at his face. I fumbled with the buttons, and one after the other gave way. It took an excruciatingly long time. He waited silently. His calm breathing and my ragged breaths filled the room.

Then I remembered that the groom was supposed to cut the bride out of her gown with his knife. Nino must have forgotten—after all, that wasn't his tradition either. I didn't have the courage to remind him or to button my dress again so he could cut me out. I'd lose it completely.

I pulled my dress down and it pooled at my feet. Now only my strapless bra and panties remained. I discarded my bra but didn't have the courage to remove my panties yet.

Nino's cold gray eyes scanned the length of me. "Your hair ornaments need to be removed as well. They will be uncomfortable against your skull."

I choked back a desperate laugh but tried to loosen the fine gold string from my hair. My shaking fingers didn't allow it. Nino moved closer, and I re-coiled. His gray eyes locked on mine. "I *will* remove it."

Dropping my arms, I nodded.

His long fingers untangled the adornments from my curls quickly. Then he stepped back again.

"Thank you," I managed to say.

I forced myself toward the bed and lay down flat on my back, my fingers splayed out against the smooth fabric of the blankets.

Nino regarded me coolly. He stepped up to the bed. Tall and muscled and deadly cold, he didn't look like this affected him in any way. He reached for his belt and unbuckled it. Terror clogged my throat. I looked away, fighting weak tears. From the corner of my eye, I saw him remove his boxers, and then he climbed on the bed, naked and determined. I trembled. I couldn't stop myself.

His hand touched my waist then slid up slowly. The touch was light. I jerked away. "Don't touch me."

His eyes were hard and cold as he looked down at me. "You know I can't. I won't give your family any cause to take Las Vegas as weak." It wasn't said in a cruel way. He stated facts.

"I know," I whispered. "Just don't touch me. Just do what you must." If there was any leading up to what was to come, I wouldn't be able to contain my terror.

"If I don't prepare you, it will be very painful." He sounded like he didn't care either way. "It would be better if we got you to relax."

That wasn't going to happen. "Just do it," I said. Pain was okay. I could deal with it.

He regarded me for a couple of moments more. Then he pulled back his hand from my ribcage and sat up. His fingers hooked under the hem of my panties, and he slid them down. A low whimper wedged itself in my throat.

He moved one knee between my legs, parting them, his gray eyes on me. He was moving slowly, and I wished he wouldn't, wished he would stop looking at me. Panic began to claw its way out of my chest, and I tried to force it back. I squeezed my eyes shut, trying to block what was happening. When he knelt between my legs completely, I seized up with complete terror.

"If you don't relax, you will tear."

My eyes shot open, and a few tears slid out. He supported himself on one arm, hovering over me. Tall and strong. *No. No. No. No.*

"Try to relax." He was so clinical about it. His gaze followed the trail my tears left on my cheeks and throat. They didn't affect him. I tried to loosen up, but it was completely impossible. My muscles were frozen with fear. He gave a small shake of his head, almost disapproving. "This isn't working," he said. "I will have to use a lot of force to get past your tensed up muscles and all the way into you."

I could taste the bitterness of bile in my throat as memories from long ago slithered through my mind.

And something in me just … broke. Something dark and scared and deeply buried. There was no way for me to hold it in.

A bone-shattering sob ripped from my throat, and it hurt because of the memories that it brought up. I pressed my palms against my face hard then curled my hands to fists and pressed my knuckles against my closed eyes. Wanting the memories out of my head, I tried to claw them out like I'd clawed at my uncle many years ago, but just like in the past, there was no escaping.

I couldn't breathe. Could. Not. Breathe.

And I wanted to die. I needed the hurt gone. I didn't want to live through that horror again, and I didn't want new nightmares.

Strong hands curled around my wrists, pulling, and I resisted, struggling, but they were relentless and kept pulling until my hands came away from my face. My eyes snapped open, my vision blurry with tears. And through the fog, two intense gray eyes slowly came into focus, and then they were all I saw, all I could see, all that mattered.

So calm. Clinical. Cold.

Just what I needed. It was a cool flood against this terror-filled inferno. Blissfully emotionless. I stared into his eyes, stared for a long time, and he let me, until I brought the first breath of oxygen into my lungs.

I could breathe again, and the face of my husband came into focus, his narrowed eyes all too knowing.

Lowering my gaze to his chin, I tugged at his hold on my wrists. He released me, and I placed my hands into my lap. My naked lap. He, too, was completely naked, kneeling across from me. He must have pulled me into a sitting position some time during my panic attack.

This was it. He knew something was utterly wrong with me. I pulled my legs against my chest, swallowing.

I wished he'd kill me now. I'd often wished for death after my uncle had broken me.

"What happened to you?" His voice was emotionless.

I considered lying, but I had lied for too long. And I had a feeling he knew. "I was thirteen," I said, but then I couldn't say more. I began shaking again, and he put a hand on my shoulder. I didn't flinch this time. The touch was too clinical to elicit any terror.

"Someone raped you."

The word made me feel small and dirty and worthless. I gave a nod.

"Your father?"

I shook my head. He was already dead by then, and he would have never done that. He knew I would have been ruined. He hit me and screamed at me, but he never touched me like that. Maybe he would have later on if Luca hadn't killed him.

"Someone from your extended family, then. Girls like you are protected. It must have been someone you were related to."

I nodded.

"Who was it?" he asked firmly. "Your uncle who raised you?"

I licked my lips. "My other uncle."

"For how long?"

I lifted four fingers.

"Four years?"

I shook my head.

"Four times?"

Only four nights, yet every day since.

Ever since.

"I dream about it every night," I choked out. That admittance felt good. I was doomed anyway. I had sealed my fate. Nothing mattered anymore.

I didn't dare look up to see his disgust, his anger at having been given some-one tainted. "You know," I said quietly. "A kind man would spare me the humilia-tion of having to face my family, living in shame, and just kill me."

"A kind man might," he said in a low voice.

I raised my eyes, resigned.

A terrifying smile played across Nino's face. It didn't reach his eyes. "*But I will find the man who did this to you and make him feel the same terror you did that night and pain unlike anything he thought possible. And eventually, when he has been begging for it for a long time and when he's given up hope, I'll grant him death.*"

My breath caught in my throat. I stared. I could do nothing else. He was calm about it, but in the depth of his eyes there was something dark and dan-gerous. Not directed at me. And I didn't dare hope that this could really be the truth.

"And what will you do to me? I'm not what was promised. I'm not a virgin."

He looked at me almost as if I'd said something stupid. "I don't care if you are a virgin. It's a small piece of flesh that's completely useless. But I'm aware of the importance it holds in the minds of so many people, even yours."

"Then why are you furious if it's not because someone stole what you wanted for yourself?"

"Because someone stole what you weren't willing to give," he murmured.

I looked away because stupid tears gathered in my eyes. I didn't understand his reaction or him for that matter. I'd heard the rumors about Vegas, about how they dealt with women who didn't pay their debts or displeased Remo Falcone in some other way.

I gestured at the sheets. "It's tradition. My family expects to see blood." I swallowed. "If you take me with force, will I bleed?"

He nodded, his expression impassive. "It's been years for you and you only had sex a few times, so if I use enough force, you will most definitely bleed. Your vaginal muscles are very tense from fear, and you will tear when I force myself into you all the way."

My stomach constricted. He sounded like a doctor explaining the physical effects of his actions. My lips fought to form the words that rationality wanted to say. "Then do it so my family and the Famiglia get the blood they expect."

He leaned forward, his beautiful, cold face so close I could see the dark specks in his gray eyes. "They will get blood, don't worry."

I nodded and moved to lay back, but he stood from the bed and put on his briefs. Confusion filled me. "I thought you would …?"

He got into his pants and buckled his belt. He didn't say anything until he was dressed in his black wedding suit again and had strapped on his knives. "I will find the man who raped you and slaughter him like a pig on these sheets. Do you think that will be enough blood for your family?"

I choked, sliding off the bed, clutching the blankets against my nakedness. "That means war. Luca will kill us all."

Nino didn't say anything, but he moved closer. I tensed but didn't back off. He raised his hand, and I flinched. I hadn't been hit in years, not since my father—and later Uncle Durant—but my body still expected it.

"I won't hit you." I opened my eyes and stared at his white shirt. He put a single finger under my chin and lifted my gaze. His cold face peered down at me, almost curiously as if I was something he needed to understand. "Do you want your uncle to live?"

"No," I admitted.

And that sealed all our fates.

Nino

I dropped my hand and walked over to the desk to pick up my mobile then raised it to my ear.

Remo picked up after the second ring. "Shouldn't you be busy?"

"I need you to come over."

"I assume it's not because you want me to help you fuck your wife."

"No, that's not it."

Silence. "Two minutes. This better be good. I chose a waitress to fuck."

He hung up, and as promised he knocked two minutes later. I opened the door, and his dark eyes went to something past me. I stepped back and he entered. Kiara backed away, the sheets still clutched to her naked body, her face tearstained.

Remo turned to me with raised eyebrows. "That was quick. You realize you can't give her back once you've opened her, right?"

"I'm going to kill someone. And I wanted to give you fair warning."

His twisted grin slipped right off his face. Remo tilted his head. "So you aren't asking for my permission."

"No, not this time. I will kill that man and nothing will stop me."

Remo looked at Kiara, and she flushed, trying to make herself even smaller. Her shoulders rounded in, her arms wrapping the sheets tighter around her body.

"Someone got her before you could? You want to cancel everything?"

"Someone raped her when she was a *child*." I paused, regarding my wife, who now stared at the ground, shaking. "And she will come to Las Vegas with me."

She raised her widened eyes.

"Her rapist is among the guests. He's the husband of Luca's Aunt Criminella, Underboss of Pittsburgh," I said. Remo needed to know the extent of our problems.

"I know."

I raised my eyebrows. "You knew?"

He shrugged then cracked his neck, stretching out his hands. "Then I better sharpen my knives and load my guns."

"We could prevent war if we gave Luca a warning."

"Ask him for permission to deal out revenge on someone who attacked your property?" he snarled. "He gave us less than was promised and you think we owe him anything?"

"Not ask but warn him," I said. I turned to Kiara, who had pressed herself against the wall at Remo's outburst. "Get dressed."

Her gaze flickered between Remo and the bathroom door he stood beside.

Remo understood her expression before I did. He walked over to me, away from the bathroom door. Kiara grabbed her bag and quickly rushed into the bathroom.

I raised my eyebrows at him.

"She was scared to walk past me," Remo said with a shrug.

"She's fearful."

"Aren't they all?" He pulled out his phone. "I'm going to call Fabiano. Savio better stay with Adamo before the kid gets himself killed."

"Come on," I said and led him out into the corridor. It was deserted.

Fabiano arrived a few minutes later, his eyes narrowed. "Don't tell me you killed the girl."

I raised one eyebrow. "I'm not prone to emotional outbursts like Remo."

"Perhaps you faked your emotions too well," Fabiano muttered.

"I didn't. Kiara is alive and well, considering her circumstances."

Fabiano threw a glance at Remo. "Nino wants to spill the blood of her uncle. Fucked her when she was a kid," my brother said.

Fabiano grimaced in what I assumed was disgust. "Killing off Luca's family won't go over well."

"Luca would kill him if he weren't family. I saw the look he gave the old fucker. And the guy isn't even Luca's blood. He's married to Luca's aunt."

"It's one of his men. He will insist on dishing out punishment himself."

"No," I said. "He punished Aria's cousin for leering at her on Outfit territory. He will understand that I need to kill his uncle myself."

Fabiano considered my words. "Maybe. But it's not a good start to this union." He regarded me. "But I see that you will do it no matter what I say, so I will go looking for Luca and attempt damage control. Maybe he hasn't left for his own mansion yet." Fabiano paused. "Where will you take the asshole?"

"I will tend to him on my wedding sheets," I said, and my mouth pulled into a smile.

Fabiano sighed then turned on his heel and went in search of the Famiglia Capo.

"Ready to pick up your date for the night?" Remo said with a laugh.

I tried to figure out what he meant with it.

"I assume you are going to fuck him with your knife." I stared down at the blade in my holster.

I nodded slowly. "I'm going to take my time breaking him, body and mind."

"I hope you let me in on the fun."

I inclined my head. It would be unreasonable to prevent Remo from participating. I knew every spot on a body that brought agony, but Remo knew how to break them with mind games. Both were more effective if applied in combination.

"Let's go," I said, and Remo let me lead the way because this was my crusade.

Keeping to the shadows, we found Durant in the gardens with his wife, laughing loudly and clutching a wine glass in his hand. "I hope he's not drunk," Remo muttered. "Don't want him to miss the night of his life."

"We will get him sober," I said quietly as I regarded him. He was a tall man, wide shoulders but had a paunch that told me it had been a while since he'd really fought. Not that it mattered.

Remo sneered. "Fucking a kid. That gives even me the creeps. I hope he isn't one of those that passes out quickly."

"We will make sure he stays awake." I wanted him to enjoy every second of his last hours.

Fabiano stood over to the side, beside the buffet, with Luca. It wasn't difficult to read the Capo's emotions. He was furious.

"Come on," I said to Remo. "Let's grab Durant."

He didn't need any further encouragement. I gripped my bowie knife, fingers curling around the smooth wood handle, as Remo and I moved along the fringes of the party. Most people still around were shit-faced. The moment Durant spotted me and my brother, his eyes widened. He dropped the glass and turned, fleeing the party and leaving his wife standing there with a dumbfounded expression.

Remo sighed. "Why do they always think they can escape?"

I began jogging and spotted Durant stumbling down the slope leading to the water. Maybe he hoped he could reach one of the boats and escape. When I reached a good spot, I stopped and flung my knife. The Damascus blade gleamed magnificently in the moonlight before it impaled itself in Durant's calf. His ear-piercing scream was a good start to the night. No cries of pleasure tonight. Only agony.

Durant fell to his knees, clutching at his calf.

"Nice," Remo acknowledged as he came to a stop beside me. We walked down the hill slowly as Durant pushed to his feet and tried to hobble toward the nearest boat, but he couldn't put any pressure on his injured leg. He should have pulled the knife out; it either would have helped him move faster or it would have made him bleed out quickly. Both would have been better outcomes than what awaited him under Remo's and my hands.

We reached him and Remo walked around to face him. "Why are you leaving? The fun is about to start."

Durant took a step back. I kicked away his legs so he fell to his knees. I reached for the knife and twisted it. He screamed, his eyes flying up to meet mine. "Whatever she said, the little whore lied."

"How do you know this is about Kiara?" Remo asked quietly. "Perhaps I can't stand your face. Nino and I have killed for less."

Durant's gaze flitted between my brother and me, his breathing picking up. Terror started to fill his veins like poison. I knew the telltale signs. This was only the beginning.

I leaned down, my mouth curling. "You will admit to it soon enough, and before the sun rises, you will beg Kiara for forgiveness, trust me."

Twisting the knife again, I left it in his leg. I gave Remo a sign, and we hoisted Durant to his feet, gripping his arms.

As we dragged him back toward the house, Luca and Fabiano stepped in our way. Luca regarded his uncle without any emotion. "This is my territory, and Durant is part of the Famiglia."

I met his gaze. "That's true, but I will be the one to tear him apart. Or are you telling me you would have acted differently if someone had dishonored Aria before her wedding night?"

Luca smirked. "I would have killed everyone who would have stopped me from dishing out punishment." Then his expression hardened. "I need to see Kiara before I can allow you to begin..." his eyes darted to the knife in Durant's calf "... or to continue."

"Luca," Durant began, but Remo jerked his arm, causing the words to die in a scream.

"We will continue, Luca, but of course you can have a quick word with my wife *if she agrees.*"

Luca's mouth tightened, but he gave a sharp nod. He followed us as we dragged Durant toward the mansion. A few people caught sight of the scene and stared openly. Matteo jogged over to us, but Romero stayed back with the Scuderi sisters.

"I knew this day would end in a fucking bloody wedding," Matteo muttered after Luca had filled him in on the details. "Of course, I'd hoped it would give me the chance to stick my knife into one of you fuckers."

"Ditto," Remo said with a dangerous grin.

We didn't stop and as we passed the patio, Giulia caught sight of us. She ripped away from her husband Cassio and stormed toward us as we stepped into the foyer.

"You should leave," Luca told her firmly.

She stepped in our way and glared at Durant. "Tonight you will finally get what you deserve for what you did to Kiara." She met my gaze. "Make him pay."

"Oh, I will."

Cassio arrived and pulled his wife back. He looked at Luca, resting his hand on his gun. "Do you need help?"

"No," Luca said. "This is a Camorra matter."

I inclined my head, surprised by his answer. When we entered the master bedroom, Kiara stood in front of the window, dressed in pants and a thick sweater. She paled when she spotted her uncle and backed away, bumping against the wall.

Remo and I dropped her uncle on the floor.

"What did you tell them, you traitorous whore?" he snarled.

I yanked the knife out of his calf with a sharp twist as I bent over him and rammed my fist into his throat to silence him. He sputtered and fell forward.

Kiara watched the scene with wide eyes.

Luca took a few steps toward Kiara, but she flinched, still crippled by her terror. I barred his way. "Unfortunately, I can't allow you to go any closer to my wife."

Luca frowned but nodded. "She is yours." Then he spoke to Kiara. "I can only allow Nino to punish Durant if I know he deserves it."

Kiara wrapped her arms around her chest, swallowing hard as she glanced at her uncle then looked away. For a while she didn't say anything but she began shaking. "I was thirteen," she whispered then released a broken sob. Her dark eyes met Luca's, and whatever he saw on her face convinced him because his expression turned to stone as he leveled his gaze on Durant. "You are subject to the Camorra's judgment, *Uncle*." His lips pulled into a smile not unlike the ones Remo was notorious for. "I'd tell you to hope for mercy, but we know you won't receive any from Nino and Remo."

Mercy? No.

Durant coughed, still trying to get his voice back after my throat punch. "Luca, I'm your family."

Luca sneered. "You are a child fucker. You aren't family." Luca looked from Kiara to Durant then to me. "Don't get blood on the ceiling and the walls. It's a pain in the ass to paint them."

"Luca! You can't do that!" Durant begged. He fell forward and clutched Luca's feet. "I beg you."

Luca narrowed his eyes. "Let me go." When Durant didn't, Luca grabbed him by the collar and threw him away from himself. Durant clambered to his feet with a wince, and I stepped in his way.

Matteo came in and held out rope for Remo, who took it with a twisted smile. Then the Famiglia Consigliere left.

Luca walked out as well, but before he closed the door, he said, "Don't disturb the neighbors with his screams and don't feed him his dick. I want to present it with the sheets in the morning to get a message to my men."

"There are enough other parts of his body we can feed him, don't worry," Remo said. "His balls might work well."

Luca closed the door.

Durant glanced at Kiara, who sat frozen on the sofa beside the bed. "Please, Kiara."

I smashed my fist into his mouth. He fell backwards, screaming hoarsely. "You won't address her. You won't look at her, unless she gives you permission."

Durant cupped his bleeding mouth, moaning and crying.

"If this makes you cry already, the night won't be easy for you," Remo said, pulling his knife out. Then he laughed.

"Do you want my help?" Fabiano asked. He had already rolled up his sleeves and was always a useful asset when it came to torture, but tonight Remo and I would handle this.

"No. Ask the Famiglia doctor for transfusions. I don't want him to die too soon," I told him. Fabiano rushed off at once.

Durant scrambled backwards as I advanced. I grabbed him and shoved him toward the bed. He tried to climb off, but I pushed him down and thrust my fist into his balls. He screamed and I leaned over him, staring down at his pain-filled and terror-widened eyes as I wedged a sock into his mouth. "Your screams won't be heard just like Kiara's weren't when you forced your cock into her." I showed him my knife and murmured, "I will force my blade into every fucking inch of your body. I hope you enjoy it as much as I will."

I motioned at Remo, and he came forward with rope. We tied Durant down spread eagle.

Pushing off the bed, I began unbuttoning my shirt and shrugged it off. Remo took his shirt off as well. There was no sense ruining our white shirts.

"Do you want her to stay?"

I chanced a glance at Kiara, who hadn't moved from the sofa, her eyes huge as they regarded her uncle.

"You can leave," I told her.

"Go to my room," Remo said. "You can sleep there. I will be too riled up after this to sleep."

She blinked once then gave a small nod but still didn't move. Maybe she needed to watch. I turned to her uncle. "First, I'm going to break each of your fingers," I explained to him. "Fingers that touched without permission."

I nodded at Remo. I grabbed Durant's left hand and Remo grabbed his right. "This will be painful. But don't worry, you'll get used to the pain. When that happens, I'll make sure to go a bit harder on you."

SEVEN

Kiara

I FLINCHED EVERY TIME MY UNCLE'S STIFLED CRIES RANG OUT AS Remo and Nino broke each of his fingers. My eyes weren't on my uncle, though, but instead on my husband's face. His expression was keen and attentive as he watched my uncle like he was conducting an interesting experiment.

Next, they began cutting his clothes off his body, slicing his skin over and over in the process. I jerked to my feet. I couldn't watch this, couldn't see him naked, couldn't listen to his muffled cries anymore.

Nino looked over to me and stopped his brother from removing my uncle's underpants. Nino walked toward me. "Do you want to hear what he has to say before you go?"

I wasn't sure but I gave a very small nod.

Nino went back and pulled the sock out of my uncle's mouth. "I'm sorry," Durant croaked. "Please forgive me." His eyes begged me.

Nino looked at me, cold gray eyes emotionless despite what he had been doing to my uncle. "Do you forgive him?"

Could I forgive him? Can you forgive having your childhood destroyed? Having your innocence ripped from you? Losing that childlike trust in your family in the worst way possible? "No," I said.

Nino stuffed the sock back into Durant's mouth.

I had to go when Nino brought the knife down onto my uncle's chest. I closed the door and took a shuddering breath then stiffened when I noticed Fabiano heading my way, carrying transfusion bags. I moved to the side so he could enter, but he returned a moment later with empty arms. "I'm going to take you to Remo's room. Nino will join you later."

I didn't say anything, just watched the tall blond man. We walked in silence, and when I stepped into Remo's room, he left me alone. I walked over to the bed and crept under the blankets, staring into the darkness. The bed was too heavy with the memories of the past, even if it wasn't the same bed where it had happened.

Slipping out of the bed, I curled up in one of the armchairs, not bothering with a blanket. Much later, the door creaked open. As the light spilled in from the corridor, I could see Nino dressed in his wedding suit. Then he closed the door, bathing us in darkness. He stopped halfway to the bed. "You can sleep in the bed. Remo won't require it tonight. It's ours."

I swallowed. "I haven't slept in a bed in years."

"Why?" There was no judgment in his voice, only mild curiosity.

"Because that's where it happened," I choked.

"He begged for death in the end if it's any consolation."

I sucked in my breath. Was it? It shouldn't have been, but part of me felt consoled. "Thank you," I whispered.

"The power he still holds over you … that's something you have to break."

I stood and slowly walked toward the bed. In the dim light I could only make out Nino's tall form, but I had a feeling he was watching me.

I lay down and covered myself with the blanket.

Nino's shadow shifted and I could hear clothes rustling. He was getting out of his wedding suit. The remnants of fear made my breathing change. Perhaps it would always be like that. Would he try again? I was his wife after all.

"You should try to sleep," he said in that calm drawl as he slipped under the covers. He didn't come close enough so we would touch.

"I can't."

"The nightmares won't stop because he's dead," he said, and I knew he was right, but it was unsettling that he *knew*. They'd called him a genius, as twisted and dangerous as he was intelligent. And I realized he was all that and more. *Monstrous.*

Every cut he'd inflicted on Uncle Durant in my presence spoke of clinical precision, of years of practice, and I knew what came after I'd left had been worse.

He begged for death in the end.

"But he won't ever hurt you again, and nobody else will either," he said as if him speaking the words made it law.

Because of the bloody message he sent today. "What about you?" Silence. "Will you hurt me?"

He shifted and the bed moved under his weight. I sucked in a breath before I could stop myself. Even in the dark, I could see him turn to face me. "I won't hurt you either. Physically at least."

"But you will abuse me mentally?" I asked.

"No. Not intentionally." He paused. "But I don't feel."

"Feel what?"

Pity? Mercy?

"*Feel.*"

I tried to understand what he meant. "You don't feel emotions?"

"Haven't since I was a child." He paused. "Not like people usually do. It's difficult to explain."

A sociopath. That was what people like him were called.

"I recognize them and I can simulate them in a satisfying manner if I want, but I don't feel them."

I wasn't sure what to say. Perhaps his admittance should have scared me. "So what does that mean for us?"

"That means that I will never act on anger or fear or sadness, but ..."

"But never on love or affection either," I finished. I wondered why he had slaughtered my uncle if it wasn't for anger. Was it habit? Because that was how things were handled in Vegas? Even in New York any Made Man would have killed the man who'd dishonored his bride.

"Indeed."

I didn't need love as long as I knew I was safe from him. Besides, I had gone without real affection for years now. I could live through more. "What about desire?"

"That isn't an emotion. It is animalistic drive. And basically humans are animals."

Not so safe after all. "So you act on desire." Fear was back in my voice, and my body clammed up with it.

In the dark I could see the slight movement of his face. "I do. And to be upfront, I desire your body."

There it was. My pulse sped up, and I could feel a new wave of panic begin to rise.

"But I won't act on it."

"You won't?"

"At some point it might be required that we produce offspring, but until then I can seek out other women to handle my needs ... if that's what you prefer?"

So clinical and emotionless. "Yes," I said, relieved that he'd suggested something like that. I could have cried from relief.

He didn't say anything. For him this was settled. I closed my eyes. It felt like a weight had been lifted off my chest, and I could breathe freely again.

I fought him, tried to push him off, but he was too strong. Gasping, I woke and panicked because something was holding me down. I struggled harder, terror clawing at my chest. Only one of my arms was free. I flailed.

A firm hand caught my wrist, and I let out a choked sound.

The lights came on, and I blinked against the brightness.

"Calm down, Kiara. You are tangled in the covers."

It took me a moment to realize who was speaking, who was holding my wrist. Nino's face came into focus above me, and I cringed into the pillow. I tugged at the wrist he was holding and he released me.

"Let me help you." He reached for me and I stiffened, watching his hand. He grabbed the covers and yanked. They came loose and I was free. I sucked in a deep breath.

His hair was disheveled and with it not being combed back or in a short ponytail he looked more human, almost approachable. Of course, that changed the moment my eyes dipped below his throat, where his tattoos began. Almost every inch of his torso was covered in them. They barely touched his neck so they weren't visible if he wore a shirt. The tattoos snaked over his shoulder on his back and down to his arms, reaching his wrists like sleeves. They didn't hide the steely outline of muscles or the raised scars.

I swallowed and sat up. My skin was slick with perspiration, but I shivered. "I'm not used to that much space. The chaise longue I slept on didn't allow for me to move enough to get entangled like that."

Nino was still propped up on one arm. His gaze trailed over my face, and it made me acutely aware of our proximity and the rude way I woke him. He must have realized what kind of lousy deal he'd gotten by now. I was nothing like the promised prize. He couldn't claim me, and I stole his sleep. "I'm a mess," I whispered. "At least, you don't have to worry about other men making a move on me."

"I'm not worried about that," he said in a low voice.

I tilted my head. "Have you discovered that you got a faulty prize?"

"Faulty?" he inquired.

I motioned at myself. "Broken. I'm not what was promised. You should give me back."

Nino pushed himself into a sitting position and brought us closer. I forced myself to remain still, but my body tensed. His eyes flickered over me, perhaps noticing my reaction, but he didn't pull back. "I was promised a Vitiello woman in marriage. A woman with beauty and grace. You fulfill my requirements."

I stared. "You think I'm beautiful?"

"*To think* it would suggest it's born of my imagination, but your beauty is fact. And the reason why I'm not worried about men making a move on you is because you are a Falcone now, my wife, and in Las Vegas nobody goes against us."

I swallowed harder.

"The dark holds power over you because he came at night for you?"

I nodded, followed by another hard swallow.

"Your nights are safe. You are safe now, Kiara. Even in the dark there's nothing you have to fear, no one, because I am there and they will have to go through me. And no one ever has won against me. I am the most dangerous thing in the dark, but you don't have to fear me."

I lowered my eyes, not understanding. "Why?"

"Why what?"

"Why don't I have to fear you? You are a Falcone."

"I am. And my brothers and I protect each other because we are family, and we protect Fabiano because we made him family, and now we will protect you because you are my wife and that makes you family as well. That's what family is supposed to be, don't you think?"

I looked up at him with a shaky smile. "Was that how your family raised you? How your father raised you? Because my father beat me and killed my mother in an attempt to save his own life. My Aunt Egidia and Uncle Felix treated me like a burden and pariah because my father was a traitor, and my uncle Durant, he … he …" I still couldn't say it.

"My father and mother were never family. They were blood, nothing more. My brothers and I are blood, but we also decided to be more, to be a unit. We are blood and chosen family. And we protect family." His expression was more animated than I'd ever seen it, and I wondered if he realized it … if he really was as emotionless as he claimed to be. "If you choose to be a Falcone, if you choose to be our family, if you choose to be mine not just on paper and because it is your duty, then we will protect you."

"What do I have to do to be family? To be yours?"

"Be loyal. Be trustworthy. Forget your blood family and New York. Cut the bonds that tie you to them and become a Falcone. It's us against the rest. It will always be like that."

"I can do that." Nothing in New York was holding me back. The only person I cared about and who cared about me was Giulia, and we had barely seen each other because she lived in Philadelphia and I lived in Baltimore with her parents. She also had Cassio's children to take care of.

He gave a nod and reclined in bed. "Try to sleep now."

I lay back down on my side, and Nino extinguished the lights. As always, my body seized with fear in the dark. I focused on Nino's calm breathing. He was too far away for me to feel the warmth of his body, but I heard him. He wasn't asleep. I don't know why I knew it, I just did. I closed my eyes and counted his breaths until sleep dragged me down.

Nino

Kiara's breathing remained tense for a long time after her nightmare. I knew she was trying to make me believe she had fallen asleep, and I allowed her to think she was succeeding. It was curious how often people forgot about the little details when it came to their body language. Breathing in sleep had a different quality than when awake, especially if your waking moments were filled with fear.

Other people's fear was something I was used to; people feared me because of my name and my Camorra tattoo. Even if they didn't know me, they feared me because they saw me in the cage or because they realized I didn't feel. It deeply unsettled most people once they realized that my blank expression wasn't forced. It came naturally.

Kiara shifted slightly. She was asleep now, but neither my mind nor my body craved sleep. Usually, I had no trouble finding sleep after torturing some-one. It didn't raise my pulse up or make my blood boil, and yet this time there was an underlying restlessness in my limbs as I lay beside Kiara.

I wasn't sure why I had reacted so strongly. Maybe it was that as my wife I felt obligated to protect her.

I slipped out of bed eventually and left the room. It was quiet in the house and gardens at this hour. People had left the party while Remo and I had been busy with Durant. I assumed Luca had strongly advised them to take their leave. The dark had never harbored horrors for me like it did for Kiara. I enjoyed its peaceful quietness. I went downstairs and followed a slight breeze toward the French windows. As expected, Remo was awake as well. He stood on the crest of the knoll and stared out toward the ocean. He hadn't bothered getting dressed in pants or a shirt after we were done with Durant. He stood only in his briefs.

His body tensed briefly at my approach, but then his muscles slackened.

I stopped beside him, but he didn't turn to look at me. The scent of copper flooded my nose, and my eyes trailed down his body. Even in the dim moonlight it was obvious that he hadn't even bothered cleaning up yet.

"Why are you still covered in his blood?" I asked curiously.

"When has there ever been a day without blood in our lives?" He threw my earlier words back at me. I frowned. Remo was in a strange mood.

"Do you know what day today is?"

"April 25," I said, but I knew that wasn't where he was going with his words.

He turned his head, and his expression would have sent most people running. "It's her fucking birthday."

"I know."

"Right this moment she's fucking taking a breath, a breath she shouldn't be taking. She should burn in hell."

My chest became tight as it occasionally did when Remo felt compelled to mention our mother. "We can still kill her," I said.

Remo balled his hands to fists. "Yeah. We could." His eyes assessed me. "Fourteen fucking years and she's still breathing."

"We could ask Fabiano to do it. He would understand."

"No," Remo growled. "That day is between us. And if anyone kills our mother, it's going to be us. Together." He held out his hand, his Camorra tattoo on display.

I nodded and gripped his forearm as he gripped mine. "I would go through fucking fire for you."

"You already did, Remo," I said.

He released my arm and took a deep breath. "The smell of blood always reminds me of that day. Isn't that kind of ironic considering how much blood we've spilled over the years? You'd think it would manage to drown out that one fucking day."

"Some things stay with you," I said.

Remo nodded. "You being here I assume you didn't fuck your wife."

"Her past stayed with her too. Killing her uncle didn't change that."

"Would killing our mother change things for us?" he asked quietly.

I considered that, but for once I didn't know the answer. "I don't know."

EIGHT

Nino

A S ALWAYS, I WOKE AROUND SIX IN THE MORNING, ON MY BACK, STARING at the ceiling. I had slept about two hours, which wasn't much worse than my average night. I turned my head toward the sound of soft breathing. Kiara was curled into herself, her face hidden under her wavy dark brown hair. After her nightmare, she had slept soundly, and once I'd returned to the bedroom from my conversation with Remo, I had quickly found sleep as well. I had no trouble sleeping beside her, even if it had been years since I'd shared a bed with anyone; back then it had been with my brothers because we only had two beds.

I sat up, wanting to prepare everything for the presentation of the sheets—and Durant.

Kiara jerked awake, eyes wide and terrified as they settled on me. Her body coiled tighter before she swallowed visibly and then finally relaxed. "Sorry."

"For what?" I asked. She said sorry a lot for her body's natural reactions. I wasn't sure why she thought her fear would offend me. After what she had been through, and considering who I was, it was natural for her to react the way she did. Killing her uncle and not laying claim on her body wouldn't change that.

She didn't say anything, and I couldn't read her expression. I swung my legs out of bed and stood.

Kiara gasped behind me. I glanced over my shoulder at her. I was naked because I preferred to sleep without clothes. "I'm going to take a shower. Does my nakedness bother you?"

She moved her head in a twitchy mix of nodding and shaking, looking down at the blankets.

"Is that a yes or a no?"

"You are my husband."

"I am. But that doesn't answer my question." I turned, fully facing her, to try and coerce a stronger reaction.

She swallowed, her cheeks turning red. "It doesn't bother me."

I narrowed my eyes. "Being trustworthy means no lies, Kiara."

Her eyes snapped up to my face, and she pursed her lips in … frustration? "Okay. I lied. It bothers me very much. You scare me when you are naked. Happy?"

"I can't see how that would make me happy."

She shook her head. Then her eyes darted to my groin area, and she tensed again and looked away.

"My nakedness doesn't pose a risk to you. It doesn't make me more dangerous nor would clothes offer you any kind of protection. It's a matter of physical strength, not layers of clothing."

My words didn't have the intended effect. She slumped her shoulders, making herself smaller. Fear. I wasn't sure how to handle her. My lack of emotions had never been much of a problem when dealing with my brothers or Fabiano; they weren't offended easily, and even harder to scare. With others, my lack of emotions had been a useful asset.

"Kiara," I softened my voice, something I had never done. Her hazel eyes flickered up to my face. "I'm stronger than you. That is fact. If I wanted to hurt you, nothing would stop me. That is also fact. But as I told you, I have no intention of hurting you. My being naked doesn't change that in any way. Nor would you being naked around me change it. I'm more than capable of controlling my urges just as any other man would."

"My uncle," she murmured.

"Your uncle didn't want to control his urges, and he paid for it with his life." For me the topic was settled, so I turned and headed for the shower.

When we were both dressed, I checked the time. It was only seven-thirty. Still early. "Why don't we head for breakfast before the presentation of the sheets?"

Kiara's eyes widened. "What sheets?"

"The sheets your uncle bled out on," I told her.

"Everyone will realize what happened to me," she whispered, her face scrunching up.

"Are you ashamed?" I asked, because I still had trouble reading her face and eyes. It would take me a while to link her facial expressions to the appropriate emotions.

She gasped out a laugh and swallowed hard. "Of course I am."

"You have nothing to be ashamed of. You did nothing wrong. Don't turn yourself into the aggressor when you were the victim."

She shook her head at me, eyes wide. "You don't understand. It doesn't matter that he did this to me. They will blame me. Somehow the victims always end up being treated like accomplices. You are a man. You don't understand."

Her voice and words made me realize that the emotion her face displayed was anger. "It's not a matter of being a man. It is fact that you did nothing wrong. He forced you."

"Don't you understand? I'm a woman. I'm guilty by default. It's always like that. They will say I asked for it. A smile means I'm flirting. A nice word means I'm asking for it. Revealing clothes mean I'm inviting touch. *That is fact*, Nino."

I regarded her, surprised by her vehemence. The women my brothers and I dealt with weren't prone to wordy comebacks, but Kiara was eloquent and intelligent, and she could hold her own if she got past her fear of me and men in general.

"If you feel ashamed, if you allow them to make you feel that way, you cement their ignorance. Fight it."

"I fought once in my life, and it only made him hurt me worse!" she screamed. She swallowed again. I assumed it was her attempt to control her emotions, to stop her tears, but they had gathered in her eyes anyway. Maybe I should have prolonged her uncle's torture over a few days, but we were supposed to return to Vegas today.

Her eyes flickered over my face, and she stiffened. "I'm sorry."

I tilted my head. "What for?"

"For screaming at you. I shouldn't do that, shouldn't provoke you."

"Provoke me?"

She frowned up at me. My words seemed to make as little sense to her just as her words made little sense to me. She wrapped her arms around her chest in a protective gesture.

Was she scared of my reaction?

"Voicing your opinion doesn't provoke me, Kiara. And as I said, I don't act on anger. You don't have to be submissive. I won't feel attacked if you stand up to me. I'm aware of my status and power and don't need your submission or flattery."

The frown deepened, but she dropped her arms. Her breasts settled nicely against her top as she did so, but I moved my gaze to her face. Another thought crossed my mind, something I hadn't considered before. "When he came for you, there must have been blood on the sheets."

She blanched. "It was. Every time."

"Why didn't the maids who cleaned your sheets alert your guardians? Your uncle Felix would have acted if Durant dishonored you under his roof. It's what honor dictates."

She was visibly fighting with herself, and I allowed her a few moments to form an answer. "He paid one of the maids to clean me and the sheets after … after he was done with me."

Without conscious decision, I touched her shoulder, knowing many people found comfort in physical closeness. Her body was pleasing to look at and felt good to the touch. She didn't flinch away. She swallowed again and gave me a small smile.

"What's her name?"

"The maid's?"

I nodded.

Kiara hesitated, her eyes searching my face, but whatever she wanted to see, it wasn't there.

"Why do you want to know?"

"What is her name?" I repeated the question but made my voice more dominant.

As expected, she yielded to dominance. She'd been brought up to comply. "Dorma. She works for Uncle Felix and Aunt Egidia." Her eyes widened. "What are you going to do to her?"

"I'm not going to do anything," I said truthfully, and she relaxed. Remo would.

I held out my hand. "Come on. Let's grab something to eat." After a moment of hesitation, she slipped her hand into mine. My brothers, Kiara and I, and Fabiano and Leona were the only ones who stayed overnight in the mansion, but people were supposed to arrive for brunch and the presentation of the sheets in a couple of hours.

Kiara followed me quietly through the house.

"This belonged to your parents before they were killed."

"Yes, now it belongs to my brothers."

"Luca killed your father."

"He did," she said simply.

"You don't miss him?"

She met my gaze briefly. "Do you miss your father?"

I inclined my head. "No." We stepped into the kitchen. A few maids from the Rizzo and Vitiello households were busy preparing everything for the brunch.

My brothers were already at the kitchen table, having breakfast. Fabiano and Leona were still upstairs, probably busy fucking.

The maids turned around when we entered, and as they spotted me, they quickly ducked their heads. One of them, a woman in her thirties with short brown hair, moved her gaze over to Kiara, whose pulse sped up under my thumb. That must be Dorma.

I tugged her toward the table and sank down on the chair beside Remo. He was in sweatpants, nothing else. Probably Savio's clothes since Remo hadn't returned to the bedroom to grab his own. Kiara sat down next to me with a hesitant smile. "Good morning."

"Morning," Adamo said. "How did you sleep?" His eyes darted to me, and he flushed. Remo leaned over the table and tapped his forehead with a smirk. "She didn't. What do you think?"

Kiara gave me an uncertain look as if she wasn't sure how to react. She would have to learn not to look for my approval. I released her wrist and grabbed an apple and bit into it.

"It would have been a better morning if you'd let me be part of the fun," Savio said to me.

Adamo glanced at Kiara again. "Las Vegas is really kind of cool. There's a lot you can do."

"I'm sure I'll like it there," Kiara said softly.

Remo cocked one eyebrow at me as I leaned over to him and whispered in his ear, "After her uncle raped her, one of the maids of the household helped him keep it a secret. She cleaned Kiara of the blood."

Remo drew back, his mouth pulling into a smile. "Where do I find her?"

My eyes went to the woman with the short hair. Remo followed my gaze then he looked back at me, an excited gleam in his eyes. "I will take care of her after the presentation of the sheets. I don't want to miss that."

"Should I tell our pilot that we'll leave later?"

Remo considered that. "I won't take too long."

Dorma walked over with a massive pan. "I made some eggs and bacon as you asked," she said to Remo.

He smirked. "Yes. I need to replenish my reserves." She put some eggs and bacon down on his place.

She looked at me. "Do you want some? I'm sure you'll need some after your wedding night." Her eyes moved to Kiara, who sank deeper into her chair.

"That's true," I said in a low voice. My gaze rested on the expensive necklace around her neck. "An exquisite piece of jewelry you got there. Do the Rizzos pay you that well?"

She blinked and touched the necklace, her eyes going to Kiara once more. "It … it was a gift," she said indignantly.

I smiled coldly. "Are you sure? Or did someone else pay the price for it, *Dorma?*"

She blanched and took a step back. Remo watched her like a cat would a mouse. She turned and put the pan down on the stove then stepped closer to the other maids. Now and then she sent a glare at Kiara, who continued to flinch every time.

"She's seriously starting to piss me off," Remo murmured. He got up and stretched. All the maids looked at him. This was his show. His sweatpants hung low on his hips, and they stared at his scarred chest. Remo, like me, was ripped from years of fighting. You could tell our muscles weren't just from lifting weights. We had bled for them. He picked up his knife holster and put it on over his naked chest. Kiara's eyes widened. Then she quickly looked away. The maids were caught up somewhere between open-mouthed shock, fear, and fascination.

Savio rolled his eyes and muttered. "Show-off."

Remo strode over to the maids and stopped right behind Dorma.

"That looks delicious," he said darkly as he glanced over her shoulder at whatever she and another maid were preparing. Of course he wasn't referring to food. Dorma edged closer to the countertop, but Remo leaned in closer. "I can't wait to get a taste. I'm *starving.*"

Adamo shook his head and scowled down at his plate.

Dorma shook her head. "It's for later. You can't have it now."

Remo brought his mouth close to her ear. "I can wait. Don't worry. It will be worth it."

She shuddered visibly, but Remo retreated, snatching another piece of bacon from the pan before he returned to the table.

Kiara remained in the kitchen with Leona, Adamo, and Fabiano as Savio, Remo, and I led Luca and Matteo upstairs to the master bedroom.

I opened the door so Luca could step in. He and his brother took in the bed and its surroundings.

"Didn't I tell you not to get blood on the walls?" Luca said in annoyance, but there was a flicker of something else in his eyes. "The only way this room can be cleaned is by hosing it down."

"Better yet, burn it," Matteo suggested. He shook his head and exchanged a look with his brother.

Remo offered him a shrug and one corner of his mouth tipped upwards. "Things got a little out of hand in the end."

"I don't doubt it," Luca said dryly, sizing up the other Capo.

Savio walked around the bed, regarding Durant. "Man, next time call me when you're having fun. Why did I have to babysit Adamo while you went all-out?"

Luca shook his head. "Fuck, you Falcones are all bat-shit crazy."

I gestured at the scene. "I assume the room will suffice to send the message you intended?"

Matteo snorted. "*Suffice*, my ass. It is kind of ironical that you were the ones to deliver a message against rape."

I regarded the other man calmly then looked at Luca. "You disapprove of our ways."

"I do," Matteo said, showing teeth.

"How do you punish women in your territory?"

"If possible, we don't."

"What do you do with female drug dealers who steal money or betray you and sell out to the Bratva? How do you deal with whores who don't pay for hitting your streets or women who borrow money and don't pay it back?"

Remo stepped up to Matteo. "You deal with them as you deal with men, I assume. Or have you found a way to torture them in a female-friendly way? Have you found a way to make death less final for them?"

Matteo's hand twitched closer to his knife, and I rested my hand on my gun, but Remo could hold his own, and he had seen the movement of Vitiello. He grinned. "We give them a choice. And what do you think do they all choose?"

Matteo sneered. "Then you should reconsider your methods."

Remo chuckled. "Don't worry about my methods. I am Las Vegas. I own every club and whore and drug dealer. And soon I will have banished every fucking Bratva fucker from my whole territory, and after that, I will deal with the fucking Mexicans and then I will be the West."

It wouldn't be as easy as that. Las Vegas and Reno were under our complete control, but we still had to share many of the other cities in the West with the Russians and the Cartel. To banish them from every city would take considerable effort and forces. Forces that we were currently utilizing for our revenge on the Outfit.

"We have guests who need to see this," Luca said firmly. "But I think we will exclude the women from the spectacle. I don't think most of them have the ability to stomach *this*."

"Perhaps you should stop coddling them like fragile porcelain dolls," Remo muttered.

Luca smiled coldly. "I do as I please in my territory and you can do as you please in yours."

We headed back downstairs. In the living room, Luca's Underbosses and Captains had gathered, as well as their wives and a few low-ranking Famiglia soldiers. They regarded us with open curiosity. Fabiano, Leona, Kiara, and Adamo came over to us.

"There's a slight change of plans," Luca said. "We'll hold the presentation of the sheets in the master bedroom."

A murmur went through the guests.

"I'd strongly advise people sensitive to large amounts of blood to stay here," Luca said. Some people laughed hesitantly but fell silent when they realized he wasn't making a joke.

Every man in the room followed. Of course, they would never admit to having a problem with blood, but a few women followed along as well. Among them were Kiara's aunt Egidia and Giulia, despite her husband's obvious aversion to the idea. Durant's wife Criminella wasn't there. She had returned home after Luca had told her what her husband had done. She knew what the penalty for that kind of thing was. Everyone knew.

As expected, the sight of Durant caused the desired shock effect. Egidia rushed away toward the bathroom and didn't return, and Giulia staggered into her husband, burying her face in his chest. He regarded the scene with the same mild surprise as Luca and Matteo had before.

"Tell your soldiers, tell everyone that this is what happens to child fuckers in my territory," Luca said. When the guests had filed out and returned downstairs for brunch, only Felix remained with Luca, Matteo, Remo, and myself.

"I didn't know," he said quietly, pointedly not looking at Durant.

"I find it difficult to imagine that you wouldn't have noticed a change in Kiara's behavior after the rape. She's still horrified of male closeness. I reckon that couldn't have been much better when she was thirteen," I said sharply.

Luca cocked an eyebrow. "That's true, Felix. You know that I would have expected to be informed of such a crime so I could dish out the suitable punishment."

Felix paled. "I didn't know. Kiara isn't my daughter, and she has always been peculiar. If she ever acted in an odd fashion, I put it down to what happened to her father."

I narrowed my eyes at him. Even someone with mediocre perception would have noticed something was off if they paid attention. But Kiara, being a traitor's daughter, probably lived most of her life in the shadows. She was a Falcone now. She'd learn to hold her head high.

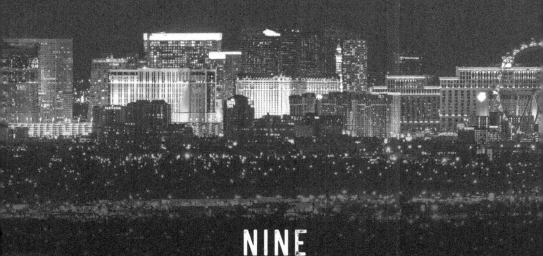

NINE

Kiara

A FTER SAYING GOODBYE TO GIULIA, I WAS SHAKEN. IT FELT LIKE MORE than just a temporary goodbye. We'd always lived in separate cities, but this was different. I was part of the Camorra now. If the truce didn't hold, and from what I'd heard it wouldn't last for very long, I'd never see her again.

But that wasn't the only thing that turned my stomach into a pit of snakes. So far Nino had been kinder than expected. What if this was part of the plan? What if his pleasant mask slipped the moment we were in Las Vegas? That was their territory. That was where they could do as they pleased. It wasn't like I could return to Baltimore if things didn't work out—much less now that everyone knew what Durant had done to me.

The pitiful stares had been almost too much to bear, but the occasional assessing looks were even worse. It was as if people wondered if I had been the one who'd brought this down upon myself.

Leona and I walked ahead with the men behind us. She gave me a hesitant glance. We hadn't talked much so far, but she seemed nice, and I couldn't see any judgment in her eyes, even now that she knew about my past.

We stepped into the private jet, and I paused, unsure of where to sit. Leona smiled. "Why don't you sit with me so we can get to know each other? I think the men have some things to discuss."

Relieved about her offer, I followed her toward the back, and we sat across from each other. Nino, his brothers, and Fabiano settled on seats close to each other on the other end of the plane.

Nino didn't seem to mind that I hadn't chosen to sit beside him. This mar-

"So you're married to Fabiano?" I asked Leona.

She flushed and it made her freckles stand out even more. Her eyes darted to the blond man. "Oh … no … we aren't married. We haven't been together for very long."

"And your family allows you to be with him before marriage?"

Leona let out a laugh. "I'm not Italian. I'm an outsider."

My eyes widened in surprise. "Oh. I wasn't sure because of your name. They allow that in Vegas?"

Leona pursed her lips. "I'm not sure it's something that's allowed, but Remo allowed it for Fabiano."

I knew at once that Leona was as wary of the Camorra Capo as I was. Everyone except his brothers was probably wary of him.

"So you grew up in a normal family?" I hadn't had contact with outsiders often, so I found their company exciting.

Leona grimaced. "Well, I wouldn't call my family normal by average standards. My parents are addicts. I mean were … my mother still is." She took a deep breath.

"What about your father?"

"Fabiano killed him."

I froze, my eyes moving to her boyfriend. As if he could feel my gaze, his blue eyes settled on me before they moved over to Leona and warmed. Trying to suppress my first reaction, I asked, "Why are you with him if he killed your father?"

Leona turned to face me. A hint of guilt flickered across her face before it disappeared, and she gave a small shrug. "My father wasn't a good man."

"And Fabiano is a good man?"

"God no," Leona said with a laugh. "These men over there … they aren't good." She nodded toward the Falcones and Fabiano.

I nodded. "But is he good to you?"

Leona smiled. "He is." Her blue eyes searched my face. "I don't know what happened between Nino and you last night, but he killed the man who hurt you, so I think he wants to be good to you."

I regarded Nino. He leaned back in the seat, looking relaxed, his lips pulling into an almost smile. I wondered if it was something he had to force or if his facial muscles did it on their own when his body registered a certain level of satisfaction. He met my gaze. I wasn't sure if he wanted to be good to me or if he even knew what he wanted with me at all. I averted my eyes because his scrutiny made me feel self-conscious, even if I was the one who had begun staring.

"He doesn't feel emotions, right?"

Leona shrugged. "He doesn't show emotion. I don't know what's going on in his head. To be honest, I don't want to know. He and Remo…" she shook her head then caught herself "…sorry. Nino is your husband now."

"No," I said, waving her off. "I understand. I feel the same way."

I wasn't sure what to make of my husband yet. He wasn't what I'd expected. I had expected cruelness, and I knew it was in his nature considering what he and Remo had done to Durant. Even if my uncle had deserved to die, from Giulia's shaken state, I could only guess how bad it had been. Would his cruel side eventually emerge when he was around me?

The thought of lowering my guard and then being hit with cruelty I no longer expected was something I'd once endured, and I didn't want to go through again.

The mansion was a sprawling white estate with several wings, each of which belonged to one of the Falcone brothers. Still, I would have preferred to have more distance between Remo and me. Savio didn't scare me as much, and Adamo was still a kid, even if he was already taller than me. Remo, Savio, and Adamo headed to their respective parts of the house when we arrived, leaving me alone with Nino. I was still unsure how to act around him. I was still scared of him, but not as much as before.

"Come on, I'll show you around the house," he said, gripping my wrist again. I didn't even flinch this time because I'd expected it. He did it frequently, and I wondered why. Was holding hands too personal? Was it about dominance when he held my wrist like that?

From the foyer we moved into a massive high-ceilinged open space with French windows taking up an entire wall. I supposed this had been the living room once. Now it looked like a massive game room with a pool table, pinball machine, and bar with shelves full of liquor. A boxing bag hung from the ceiling and two huge sofas sat in front of a television screen that took up most of the wall. But the strangest thing was the boxing ring on the right side of the room.

"Before our father died, this was the living room and the dining room. We tore down the walls. This is where my brothers and I spend most evenings unless we are out." Nino's brows pulled together as he regarded me. Maybe he realized now this wasn't an all-boys house anymore. I was the intruder who ruined it all.

"I won't bother you during your family time," I said, sparing him the trouble of trying to let me down easily. I'd spent most of my life on the fringes. It wouldn't break me.

"You are family now."

I doubted Remo and Savio agreed with him. Adamo seemed nice enough, but he was probably only trying to be polite, and I wasn't really sure if I wanted to spend excessive time with the Falcone brothers.

"I'll show you the kitchen, but we almost never use it. We only keep a few things for breakfast. We order takeout for dinner every day."

"Don't you have maids or something like that?" I asked, following him to the back of the house toward the kitchen. It was all stainless steel and large enough to prepare dinner for many people.

"No. We have two cleaning people who come over twice a week to take care of the worst of it, but we don't really like people around."

"Oh." I never attempted to cook because our maids had always done it, but I wouldn't mind giving it a try. Without any maids breathing down my neck, now it was an option.

We continued our tour into Nino's part of the house. It consisted of a smaller, sparse living room with nothing but a couch and a TV. On the ground floor was a guest bathroom and another room, which was stuffed with old furniture. On the first floor were three more bedrooms and a master bedroom—the room Nino's and I would now share.

I stepped into the large bedroom with a massive four-poster bed on the left, which faced the door way. High windows framed both sides of it. Dark red drapes partially covered the windows.

Nino tightened his fingers around my wrist. "I told you there's no reason for fear."

I gave him a confused look, but he didn't elaborate. To our right, I noticed two doors. One of them was ajar, exposing a black marble floor. The door next to it was closed. Nino followed my gaze. "That's the walk-in closet. There's enough room for your clothes. I don't need much space."

He released me, and I moved into the adjoining bath and found a floor-level shower, a Jacuzzi tub, and double sinks set in a black marble countertop. A window behind the tub looked out onto the vast gardens.

Nino waited in the bedroom for me, next to the bed. Taking a deep breath, I walked closer. He looked relaxed, calm, in control. "We will share a bed."

"Of course," I said quickly.

"Have you changed your mind about me seeking satisfaction elsewhere?" he asked neutrally, but I wondered what his thoughts were about it.

My stomach tightened. His eyes traced my face with a hint of curiosity. For some reason it took me a second longer to give him an answer. "No," I finally said.

He nodded. "I won't bring women here with me, so you don't have to be worried."

"Thanks." I wasn't sure what else to say.

"Let's go back downstairs. I haven't shown you the library or the gardens yet."

My excitement spiked. "You have a library?"

Nino's mouth twitched. "I do, yes. It's in the main wing, though, but my brothers don't really read."

I followed Nino back downstairs, but then I paused in the living area. There was still so much room, and I hadn't seen a piano anywhere. I hadn't even considered not having a piano at my disposal. Music had always been a part of my life. I couldn't imagine living without it. "Do you have a piano somewhere in the house?"

Nino shook his head. "No. Do you play?"

"Yes. Well, I would if I had a piano."

"Where would you put a piano?"

I looked around the room. It was minimally furnished. I didn't think Nino spent a lot of time here. The Falcone brothers seemed to prefer spending time in the main wing during the day, if the amount of empty glasses and plates in the gaming room had been any indication. I motioned toward a spot close to the French windows. It would allow me to watch the sky while playing the piano. "This would be a good place, I think."

Nino nodded but didn't say anything.

"To the library?" I prompted, and he motioned me to follow him. As I walked beside Nino, I risked the occasional peek up at him. His expression was relaxed, at ease, but I supposed that was his default expression given his lack of emotions. The long-sleeved shirt hid his tattoos, and I realized his clothes always covered them. I wondered why he kept them hidden under layers of fabric. Weren't most people proud of their body art? And it wasn't like he had to cover his tattoos because of a straight-laced job. Even without the disturbing tattoos on display, Nino managed to carry a vibe of otherness, a subtle violent energy. It wasn't as blatant as Remo's, but it was there. Everyone who looked at Nino knew he was a man you shouldn't cross. Not because of the muscles or his movements that screamed strength but because of a certain air of self-assurance, a confidence that said he knew he was deadly.

Nino's gray eyes met mine, and I flushed. How long had I been staring? I quickly ducked my head and felt a rush of relief when he opened the door to a library. It made the one I'd had access to in Baltimore look like a measly broom closet. Situated in the back of the main wing, it was two stories high, and the shelves reached all the way to the top. A ladder on small wheels leaned against every row and reached the books at the very top. My heart skipped a beat as I tried to guess the number of books.

"Wow," I breathed.

"I should give you fair warning: our selection of fiction titles is limited. Most of them are old classics or horrid bodice-rippers my mother used to read when she still lived here. I don't read fiction and have switched over to buying books in ebook format since it simplifies storage and accessibility."

I only half-listened as I walked through the nearest aisle, my eyes gliding over the spines. There were books about history and science, medicine and warfare. Classics like *1984* and *Animal Farm*, *Jane Eyre* and every play written by Shakespeare. Then I spotted the entire Harry Potter series, the spines cracked as if the books had been read too often. I touched the first book. I'd read it in the darkest time of my life and finding refuge in the world of those books had been the only light for me. I stopped, drawing in a deep breath. Books and music had always been my salvation. The scent of old leather and dusty paper was pure comfort. I could spend a lifetime in this room and die happy.

When I finally turned away from the books, I caught Nino watching me with a small frown. I flushed. I must have looked like a lunatic, inhaling the library scent and smiling to myself.

I cleared my throat. "Are there any parts off limits for me?"

Nino raised his dark eyebrows. "Like the Dark Arts area?"

I froze, speechless, frozen, and utterly shocked. I swallowed. "Did you … did you just make a Harry Potter reference?" He must have noticed me touching the books.

"I did," he said dryly, and I had to stifle laughter.

"Don't tell me you read the books."

"I didn't read them for my own enjoyment. I read them to Adamo when we were on the run. He was obsessed with them, and Remo didn't have the necessary patience to read bedtime stories. Besides, he had a habit of letting the Death Eaters and Voldemort win, and that upset Adamo when he was little."

I laughed then fell silent, confused and overwhelmed by everything that I'd found out about Nino in these past few days. He was a man of many layers, and I didn't think I'd ever manage to fully grasp the top layer. I walked over to him. "It must have been hard to protect your little brother when you were fighting for your territory."

Nino shrugged. "It was difficult, but Remo and I killed anyone who posed the slightest risk to Savio or Adamo. We couldn't bother asking too many questions. The motto we lived by was kill first. Once we had established a stronghold on the territory, we made sure to torture people for information before we killed them."

I looked up at him, trying to imagine what it must have been like back then. During the day Nino and Remo slaughtered their enemies and at night they came together in whatever dingy place they were hiding in at the time and read bedtime stories to Adamo and Savio.

"You confuse me," I admitted quietly.

Nino nodded thoughtfully. "That's a compliment I can return."

"Thanks," I said then cleared my throat.

"I'll show you the gardens now. You can roam the premises as you please but stay out of Remo's and Savio's wing, especially Remo's. He won't take it kindly if he finds you in his domain." I nodded. I had absolutely no intention of going anywhere near Remo if I could avoid it. "Adamo probably won't mind you being in his space, but he's a pig and a teenager, so you will see and smell things not intended for females."

I laughed again, and Nino regarded me curiously. My cheeks heated under his scrutiny. He reached out and brushed a fingertip over my burning skin, almost as if he was trying to make sense of my reaction. I didn't pull back, growing more and more confused by the second.

"You wanted to show me the gardens?" I croaked, clearing my throat again.

He dropped his hand and turned. I followed a step behind him, trying to understand my husband, but he was an enigma.

There was something I noticed on our way through the gaming room heading toward the garden. "I don't see guards anywhere."

"We don't need them. Even Adamo is capable of defending himself," Nino said as he led me toward a square swimming pool. "I swim laps in this pool every morning. My brothers occasionally use it for the same purpose, but they prefer more hands-on workouts."

"I'm not capable of defending myself," I pointed out after a moment.

He frowned, his eyes trailing over my body. "That's true. You are an easy target. As I said, we don't want people in the mansion. Remo and I will have to figure it out. It'll be for the best if one of my brothers or Fabiano is always around when I'm not here. They can accompany you wherever you go."

"So they are my babysitters?"

"As you pointed out, you can't protect yourself, and while people in Vegas fear us, there are outside forces that might risk an attack and could target you," he said and motioned me to follow him around the house toward another pool area. This space was definitely created for recreational purposes and not working out. It was a meandering pool landscape with small waterfalls and fountains. A ginormous inflatable sofa floated gently on the water. "You better not touch it. That's Savio's, and he uses it for female company."

I grimaced. "Thanks for the warning." Nino nodded.

"Have you told your brothers yet that they are supposed to play babysitter?" As hard as I tried, I couldn't imagine Remo guarding me. I would probably manage to set him off with something I'd say and he'd end up killing me.

"They will protect you because you are a Falcone."

Kiara Falcone. It was still difficult to believe that I was really someone's wife. The wife of Nino Falcone of all people. My eyes traced his cold, perfectly sculpted face, wondering again why he hadn't claimed me on our wedding night, why he was being nice. Though, nice wasn't the right term for Nino's behavior. I wasn't sure what to call it. It seemed as if he wasn't sure what to do with me. Marriage must not have ever been part of his life plan.

I couldn't believe that my panic had warmed his heart. After all, he wasn't capable of emotions, but I wasn't brave enough to question his motives lest he begin to question them as well.

"But it's crucial that you become capable of defending yourself. I don't understand why the Famiglia keeps their women unable to defend themselves. It's an unnecessary risk."

I frowned. "You want me to learn how to fight?"

Nino shook his head, his mouth twitching as if I'd said something amusing. "I don't think that makes much sense at the moment, given your fear of physical contact. Maybe later. But you will have to learn how to shoot a gun. That's the first step and will give you a sense of security."

"You will allow me to run around with a gun?" I asked, shocked.

His brows drew together. "Of course."

"Okay." I wasn't sure what else to say. I thought he'd be wary about having me armed, but maybe he was so sure of his own fighting abilities that he didn't worry about it.

"I think it's best to make something clear from the start," Nino began, and I stiffened, worried what he was about to say. "If something my brothers and I do bothers you or if you want something, you have to say it outright. No subtle hints or secretive expressions. Neither my brothers nor I are good at female subtlety, and we lack the patience to figure it out. So speak your mind if you want to make it easy on all of us."

"I can do that," I said, but it would be a new experience for me. My family had raised me to be careful with words and not speak my mind. Voicing my opinions to men like my husband and his brothers seemed like an even bigger challenge. He was right. If I wanted to stand a chance surviving with the Falcone men, I'd have to get over my fears. But there were so many of them, some of them so deeply burnt into my very being, I wasn't sure I had any chance of fighting them.

TEN

Nino

K IARA KEPT THROWING POORLY VEILED GLANCES MY WAY AS WE WALKED into our gaming room. Remo was already there doing some recreational kicks against the punching bag. He paused when we stepped in, his gaze narrowing on Kiara briefly before starting to kick again. "I'm starving. Let's order pizza."

Upon seeing Remo, Kiara had stiffened beside me and her breathing turned erratic. I wasn't sure if it was because he was only in his fight shorts or because he was beating the shit out of an inanimate object, but her fear of him was obvious. I snatched the delivery menu to one of our favorite pizza places from the bar. It was stuck to something that had spilled. I turned to her. "You will have to get used to Remo's presence."

She jumped, tearing her eyes away from my brother. "I don't know if I can. I heard what he does, what he likes doing," she whispered.

I regarded my brother, who watched us from across the room as he landed another kick against the punching bag. Remo did a lot of things, which were unsettling to someone like Kiara, and he enjoyed them all. "He isn't a danger to you."

She raised her eyes to mine, shivering, goose bumps rising along her smooth skin. "Are you sure?"

"Yes." There was no hesitation in the word. I knew with absolute certainty that Remo wouldn't lay a hand on Kiara because she was mine.

She nodded slowly, her eyes filled with unease. She was reluctant to believe me. She didn't know Remo like I did. Very few people in this world were safe around my brother, there was no denying it, but the same could be said for me.

"Why don't you take a look at the menu and see what kind of pizza you want?" I held it out to her.

She took it from me, eyeing it warily. The stained paper looked like it had seen better days.

I made my way over to my brother, who stopped kicking and raised his eyebrows at me. "That look means I won't like what you have to say."

"You scare her."

Remo gave me an amused smirk. There were very few people who weren't terrified of my brother.

"I'd appreciate it if you try not to scare her quite so much."

Remo chuckled, ramming his knee into the bag a few more times before he said, "I didn't do anything."

"I know," I said. "We don't do well with sensitive women, but Kiara lives under our roof now. She is part of our family, and we should make sure she feels as comfortable as possible given her past and our disposition."

He tilted his head. "You want us to treat her well?" I followed his gaze toward Kiara, who was assessing the bar area, which was piled with dirty glasses, beer bottles, and plates. The cleaning people were coming in the morning.

"Yes. I want her to be treated like family. I want her protected. I want her safe from any threat. She is a Falcone now. She is mine."

Remo nodded, not taking his eyes off my wife. She placed the menu down on the bar then glanced up and noticed our gazes. She blinked, stiffening, and then swallowed, quickly picked up the menu again, and fumbled nervously with it. *Fear.*

"She is safe, Nino." Remo turned to face me, gripping my forearm. "You are my brother and she is yours. I will make sure everyone in this city, and beyond, realizes she's under our protection."

Remo didn't have many redeeming qualities, much like me, but one of them was his loyalty. If he decided someone fell under his protection, he would stop at nothing to make sure that person was safe.

He let go of my forearm. "And? Have you finally fucked her?"

I rolled my eyes at him. "No. And I won't until she wants me to. She is too scared because of the rape."

Remo's eyes moved back to Kiara. She was still staring intently at the menu. She must have memorized every pizza they offered by now.

"Kiara isn't capable of protecting herself. We need to make sure she is safe wherever she is," I said.

"I don't want our soldiers in the mansion. This is our home."

"I agree. That's why you or Savio, or even Adamo, should guard her when I'm not around to do it."

Remo smirked. "Are you sure Kiara wants me to guard her? She might die from fear if I'm alone with her."

"She will get used to you."

"I doubt it," Remo said with a grin.

"It won't be easy, but eventually she'll come around if you don't lose your shit around her."

"I'll do my best."

We both knew what that meant. I returned to Kiara's side. She was biting her lip, and her body was tense. "So did you find a pizza you want?"

"I'm not very hungry," she said softly. "Is it okay if I only order a salad with mozzarella and olives?"

"You can eat whatever you like. And if you're still hungry, you can have a piece of one of our pizzas," I told her.

She smiled. "Okay. Thanks."

Remo stalked toward us and stopped beside me and Kiara.

"Ready to order?" he asked.

"I will place the order. Will Fabiano be coming over?"

"Yes. Leona spends the evenings with her crack-whore of a mother."

Kiara's eyes widened. I wasn't sure if it was the insult or because another man was joining us tonight.

I picked up my phone and gave our favorite Italian restaurant a ring. Their pizzas were the best in town. We all got our usual orders, so the addition of a salad caused a bit of a stunned silence on the other end.

"Why don't you sit down? You can turn on the TV if you want. The food will be here in thirty minutes," I told Kiara, who stood frozen beside Remo and me.

She nodded and moved to the sofa where she sank down in the middle.

"I hope she loses that submissive behavior soon. It's fucking annoying," Remo muttered.

"This is new for her. She wasn't as tense when I was alone with her."

Five minutes later, Fabiano sauntered in. He had a spare key and never bothered ringing the bell. "I need a scotch," was the first thing out of his mouth. "Leona's mother is a fucking nightmare. That woman smokes and shoots up more crystal than most people and manages to survive."

"That's because you offer her a free supply. Her tolerance to the substance grows," I explained.

Fabiano glared. "I know. But if I don't give it to her, the stupid whore will hit the streets again, and it fucking kills Leona to see her mother sucking ugly dicks."

Kiara sucked in a soft breath on the sofa, and we all turned to her. She flushed. Fabiano reached over the bar counter and grabbed a bottle of scotch from the shelf then poured himself a generous glass. "Anyone else?"

"I'll have one," Savio said as he walked in, clapping Fabiano's shoulder. "I hear you're being pussy-whipped."

Fabiano shoved him. "I can still wipe the floor with your ugly face, Savio, don't forget that."

Savio smiled cockily. "Not much longer. I'm a fucking natural when it comes to fighting."

I opened the fridge under the bar and took two bottles of beer out, one for Remo and one for me, then glanced over at Kiara, who was focused on the TV. The local news was reporting about a fire that had burned down one of our soldier's restaurants.

"Turn that off," Savio shouted. "The fucking news grates on my nerves. They always get it wrong."

Kiara jumped and quickly turned the TV off. "Mind your tone," I said to Savio, who raised his eyebrows at me. I turned to Kiara. "What would you like to drink?"

Her eyes darted from me to my brothers and then Fabiano. "Something non-alcoholic, please."

"Alcohol adds to the fun," Savio said with a grin.

Kiara flinched. Adamo skidded down the stairs in that moment. "Get Kiara one of your Cokes from the kitchen," I ordered.

He groaned but turned on his heel and went off. The pizza arrived shortly after. Fabiano and I carried it over to where Kiara sat and spread the boxes out on the wide table. I sat down beside her, and Remo took up her other side; it was his usual spot. Kiara's shoulder stiffened, but she didn't react any other way. I handed her the salad. "That's yours."

"I really don't get why girls always eat salad. It annoys the fuck out of me," Savio said as he grabbed a piece of his pizza.

Adamo threw himself down on the sofa between Fabiano and Savio, causing them to scowl at him. He handed a bottle of Coke to Kiara. She who took it, mumbling a thanks, and poured herself a glass.

"What's on?" Adamo asked between bites.

"We tested a race in Kansas. It was a huge success," Remo said eagerly, turning on the TV and opening the recording of the illegal street race.

"Cool," Adamo said, eyes keen when the camera zoomed in on the line of cars.

Kiara ate quietly among us. If I closed my eyes, I wouldn't have even known she was there at all, except when I got the whiff of her flowery perfume. It was obvious that she was uncomfortable surrounded by so many men, and the alcohol seemed to bother her additionally. She'd have to get used to it. This was how it always was in our home.

"Maybe we can convince Vitiello to extend the races into his territory," Savio suggested.

"I don't think Luca wants to cooperate with us any longer than he has to. We all know that this truce won't last forever. Then all bets are off."

Kiara shifted. I inclined my head toward her, but she was focused on the salad.

Fabiano cocked an eyebrow at me as if I knew what was going on in her head.

"It would do Luca good to remember that he's lucky having us on his side," Remo said, reaching for a piece of my pizza; we usually all shared pizzas. He leaned over Kiara's legs to reach the box, brushing up against her leg. She gasped, jerked back, and dropped her salad. Pressed up against the backrest, chest heaving, she regarded Remo as if he was going to jump her. His eyes narrowed, and I knew this wasn't going to go over well. "What the fuck is wrong with you, woman?" he growled. "I was going to grab a fucking piece of pizza, not grope you. I have no intention of fucking you, not now, not ever. For one, there's no fun in breaking someone broken, and secondly you are Nino's, so he's the only one who's going to get your pussy. Nobody else is going to touch you like that, got it?"

Tears welled in Kiara's eyes.

"Oh fuck," Savio muttered.

"Remo," I said in a warning voice.

He scowled, grabbed the piece he'd wanted in the first place, and leaned back. "Shut up, Nino. I'm fucking sick of her flinching. It's fucking annoying, especially because I didn't even give her reason to flinch. This is my home, and I'm not going to walk on eggshells because she can't get a grip on herself."

Kiara swallowed audibly and picked up the few pieces of lettuce she had dropped on her jeans with shaking fingers. Then she rose slowly. "Do you have a mop so I can clean this?" she asked quietly.

"Leave it. The cleaning people are coming tomorrow."

"I don't want them to find cheese and salad on the floor," she said.

"Trust me, they've seen much worse on these floors," Fabiano said.

She gave a jerky nod. "I'll go clean up and then go to bed." She pressed herself past my legs. To my confusion, she didn't move toward the guest bathroom, instead she walked toward the French windows and slipped outside into the gardens.

"Why's she going outside?"

Fabiano shook his head. "For fuck's sake, she's going outside because she's going to cry in peace."

I regarded him, and he narrowed his eyes. "You are a fucking genius, but you're still a stupid asshole when it comes to women."

"You should probably go after her," Adamo suggested.

I frowned. "If she wants to cry in peace, she probably doesn't want my company."

"Women," Remo muttered, shoving another piece of pizza into his mouth.

"Listen to the kid," Fabiano said. "Go to her and console her or whatever it is you are capable of doing."

"I've never consoled a woman."

Fabiano sighed. "Then improvise, simulate emotions or whatever. I don't give a fuck."

"Since you are the one who has a girlfriend and who has experience dealing with female emotions, it seems logical that you should go outside and console her."

Fabiano snorted. "I knew this marriage was a fucking bad idea." He leaned back. "I'm not the one she wants to see, trust me. She'll probably scream bloody murder if I go after her in the dark. You are her husband so act like one."

I stood.

"Good luck," Savio said, stifling his laughter.

It didn't take me long to find Kiara. She was perched on a sun chair. The bluish glow of the pool highlighted her face, and I could see tears running down her cheeks. She quickly ran the back of her hand over her skin, but it was too late. I sat down beside her, ignoring her body tensing. "I'm sorry for ruining your dinner."

"You didn't ruin anything. We've had far worse incidents, and most of them involved broken bones, so this is nothing."

I reached for her and brushed another tear away. She became very still and stopped breathing. I grabbed her shoulders and brought our faces closer. She sucked in a breath, but I needed to get through to her. "If something bothers you, say it. If you don't want Remo to trample all over you, you will have to stand up to him. I can protect you, but it won't bring you the respect of my brothers. If you want to be a part of this family, you need to gain their respect. Being submissive and shying away like that doesn't cut it, okay?"

She averted her eyes.

"No," I ordered.

Her gaze flew back to meet mine. I tightened my hold on her shoulders, and she winced.

"I'm not sure if I can do it. My fear is too strong."

"Your fear is useless. It cripples you. Don't let it."

She narrowed her eyes. "It's not that easy."

"It's not as hard as you make it out to be either. It's your choice to face your fears or to let them rule over you."

"Let me go," she said with a shaky exhale.

I nodded and released my hold on her shoulders. "That's a start."

Standing up, I held my hand out to her. "Now come. We'll return. You can have pizza."

She hesitated but then she took my hand and straightened. Her pulse was still racing under my thumb, but she looked less shaky. "I can't eat your pizza."

"We always share our pizzas. Nobody will mind."

"I'm vegetarian. Your pizzas all have some kind of meat on them," she said.

I hadn't noticed that she hadn't eaten meat at the wedding. "Next time we'll order a vegetarian pizza for you."

She became tense as we stepped back into the gaming room, and her skin reddened in embarrassment. I led her back to the sofas and sat down beside Remo so Kiara didn't have to. Remo pretended he didn't notice and kept watching the race on the screen. Kiara squeezed my hand briefly before she released me and took a gulp from her Coke.

Fabiano gave me a look that probably conveyed recognition, though I wasn't sure why. Nobody mentioned Kiara's exit or her puffy eyes, and eventually she became more relaxed and watched the race with us.

Her eyes started drooping but she didn't get up; she probably wasn't sure if she was allowed to leave. I decided to make it easy for her. "Let's go to bed," I suggested and stood.

That was obviously the wrong thing to say because the tension in her body returned full force. I sent Fabiano a questioning look. After all, he was the woman whisperer. He only shrugged.

"Good night," Kiara said before she followed me silently into our wing. I tried to figure out the reason for her tension. I thought I was doing her a favor when I suggested we go to bed. I wasn't even tired.

When we arrived in our bedroom and her gaze lingered on the bed, she swallowed thickly and it dawned on me. "Are you worried because you think I want sex?"

She bit her lip. "I'm a horrible wife."

"I'm not a good husband either. It is what it is." I pointed at the bed. "As I said before, you don't have to fear me. I won't touch you unless you desire it. We discussed this. I assumed you understood that our bedroom doesn't pose a threat to you."

"I guess it's difficult to believe," she said.

"I keep my word."

I wasn't sure if it finally sank in or if it needed more time. When I joined her in bed later, she had her back turned to me and was half hidden beneath the covers. I couldn't see if she had tensed but her breathing definitely changed. I waited for her to fall asleep before I got up. This was going to be one of those nights where I wouldn't get any sleep. With a last glance at my sleeping wife, I walked out into the corridor. I was never going to be a good husband; my disposition would always prevent that.

Kiara

When I woke, it took me several moments to realize where I was. Once I did, my pulse quickened. I sat up, looking around. Nino was gone, and I didn't hear any sounds coming from the bathroom either. I got out of bed and headed into the bathroom. As I'd noticed yesterday, there wasn't a lock on the door. It was a bit unsettling since Nino could walk in at any point. For that very reason, I hurried through my shower and quickly got dressed in a maxi dress with a high neckline. Even if I preferred to keep most of my body covered, it was too warm outside to wear something long sleeved. My eyes were drawn to the window behind the Jacuzzi tub and the blue sky outside. From the looks of it, it was going to be another hot day in Las Vegas. The sprinklers in the gardens were spewing water. I supposed there was no other way to keep the grass this beautifully green.

After that, I busied myself by putting away my clothes into the drawers that Nino must have cleared for me in the walk-in closet. When I was done, I hesitated, not sure how to proceed. I was hungry and I couldn't very well stay in the bedroom all day, but the mansion didn't feel like home yet. I wasn't sure if it ever would, so walking around on my own felt like I was intruding.

Eventually, my hunger drove me outside. It was quiet in this part of the house, which wasn't surprising considering its size. Nino was probably in the main wing with his brothers. I wasn't really sad that he didn't wake me when he left the bedroom this morning. I was used to being alone most of the time and preferred solitude over the company of people.

I moved downstairs into the smaller living area in Nino's wing and froze on the last step. There, beside the French windows, stood a beautiful Steinway D piano. I couldn't do anything but stare. I took the last step down then approached the instrument almost fearfully. How did Nino manage to get it over here so quickly? But this was Las Vegas and he was a Falcone, so he probably had his ways. The more important question was why did he buy this for me?

Of course I told him I loved to play, but it wasn't as if he needed to put in an effort to win me over. We were already married, and I was bound to him forever. If anyone was required to please someone, then it was me as the wife. And so far, I'd failed miserably.

I sank down on the black leather bench, letting my fingers glide reverently over the smooth black and white keys, and then I began to play, but to my surprise it wasn't the song I'd been working on these past few months. It was something new entirely, a melody I hadn't even known was in me, but as my fingers moved over the keys, it took shape. Slowly, the knot around my chest loosened, and I realized the notes were my emotions shaped into music.

The sound was haunted and frightful, the notes chasing each other, quick and erratic then slowing almost abruptly. Tumult and fear, resignation and defiance, and beneath it all an underlying pain I could not shake.

I couldn't stop playing, even as I began the melody anew, reformed it, but the emotion remained, and it filled the room and me. For a moment, I felt at home, felt almost at peace.

"I see you discovered your piano," Nino drawled, and my fingers dug into the keys, making the beautiful instrument cry out almost angrily.

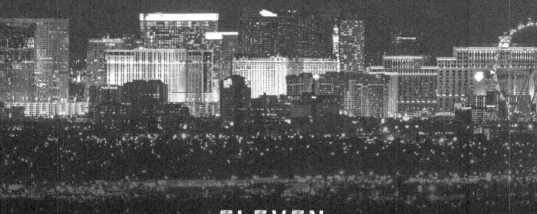

ELEVEN

Kiara

MY EYES DARTED TO MY LEFT, WHERE NINO STOOD, WATCHING ME WITH mild curiosity. He was dressed in black pants and a tight black T-shirt that exposed his tattooed arms. His hair was pulled back in a very short ponytail.

I flushed and quickly stood. "I'm sorry. I should have asked before I started to play. I don't even know if I'm allowed to."

Nino frowned and moved closer and didn't stop despite my growing tension. He leaned against the piano, close but still more than an arm's length away. His eyes scanned me from head to toe, and I forced myself to stand still, allowing him his appraisal. It was his privilege. Finally, his eyes met mine. "Why wouldn't you be allowed to play the piano?" he asked. "I got it for you and it's meant to be played."

"Thank you," I said quietly. "You didn't have to do this. It's too expensive."

Nino's mouth twisted in dark amusement. "I didn't, but I wanted to, and money isn't an issue, Kiara. We have more than we could ever spend."

I glanced back down at the keys and brushed them with my fingertips.

"Play that song again," Nino said.

"I only started working on it today. It's not ready yet." I didn't mention that I'd never been happy with a song I'd created and avoided playing in front of others if possible. Music was emotional for me. Laying myself bare to other people like that had never seemed wise.

"Play it," Nino ordered.

My eyes flew up to his face. His expression was commanding but not cruel. I sank back down on the bench, taking a deep breath, and rested my fingers against the first notes.

I closed my eyes because with Nino's intense gaze on me, I couldn't focus. Then I began to play, and the melody came to life, flowed around me, *evolved* as I added a few more notes.

The last note had long died off when I dared to open my eyes. Nino regarded me, and heat rose into my cheeks. "It's not good, I told you, but—"

Nino leaned in, and I held my breath. "Don't put yourself down. You are a Falcone now."

I blinked and gave a nod. I'd been put down all my life by others and by myself. Giulia had said the same thing to me before, but none of her words had ever had an effect. Upon looking into Nino's beautifully cold face and seeing the dominance in his eyes, it seemed impossible not to take his words to heart.

When it became clear that Nino expected an answer, I said, "Okay."

He gave a small shake of his head, but I wasn't sure what it meant. He straightened. "I have to leave to meet with the owner of our fight club, Roger's Arena, now. You can spend the day as you please. You are free to walk around the premises and the mansion, but as I said, don't go into Remo's wing." Remo probably had a poor woman locked into a dungeon there. I shivered.

"I will be alone?" I asked.

Nino shook his head. "Savio will stay with you."

Relief flooded me when I realized the Camorra Capo wasn't on babysitting duty, even if the younger Falcone made me nervous as well. After the embarrassing incident yesterday, I really wasn't looking forward to meeting either Falcone brother.

"If you want to leave the house, tell Savio and he will drive you wherever you want to go. Tomorrow, I will have time to show you around Vegas." He waited for a response, so I nodded.

He returned a curt nod before he left.

I stared at his back, dumbfounded.

For a moment, I wavered between sitting back down at the piano and going to find something to eat, but then my rumbling stomach won that struggle. I headed down the connecting corridor into the main part of the house. It was still quiet, but when I moved closer to the kitchen, I could hear a male voice. When I stopped in front of the door, I recognized Savio's voice. "I'm stuck here babysitting. I'll come over when Adamo takes over when he gets out of school."

I was about to turn around and return to Nino's wing despite my hunger, when the door swung open. I tried to stumble back but still managed to get hit in the shoulder, landing on my butt. I gasped from the sharp twinge then flushed with embarrassment when I found Savio staring down at me with narrowed eyes.

From my position on the floor, he looked even taller, which didn't help with my anxiety.

"Did you eavesdrop? Never heard about privacy?" he muttered. He stuffed his phone into his pocket then bent over me, and I flinched. He froze, his eyes widening a moment before he controlled his expression. He was almost as good as Nino. "Jeez, I wasn't going to grope you, *woman*." He held out his hand. "Stop the cowering and take my hand."

I did, and he pulled me to my feet then released me. I quickly straightened my dress, flustered. "I'm sorry. I didn't mean to eavesdrop, and I'm sorry that you have to play babysitter when you have obviously better things to do."

Savio shrugged. "Nino asked me to do it, and you are defenseless."

Defenseless. He sounded almost disgusted as he said it. I wasn't sure how to react, so I said, "I was going to make breakfast. Do you want something too?"

Savio snorted. "Good luck. There's no food in the fridge, only beer. Nino is pretty much the only one who remembers to buy food, and he's been busy these last few days."

"Oh," I said.

Savio sighed, running a hand through his dark hair. It was shorter than Nino's and a bit darker. "Let's grab something to eat. We can do a quick detour so I can check in with one of our soldiers who's having trouble with vandals."

My eyes widened. Like Nino, Savio told me about business. It was mostly frowned upon to involve women in any kind of business, to even mention it around them, in the Famiglia.

"We don't have to go out," he said, assessing my expression. "But then you'll have to go without food."

"That's not why I was shocked. I'm not used to hearing about business."

Savio shrugged. "It's what my brothers and I are doing all day, so it's a constant topic around here. Except for Adamo, whose main activity is sulking."

I laughed. Savio looked at me like he was trying to figure me out.

"You can go outside and wait in the driveway. I'll grab a few more guns and then we can head out."

A few more guns? He already had a holster strapped around his chest, which held a gun and a knife, but it wasn't my place to comment, so I headed outside. It was warm and sunny. Several cars were parked in the driveway; one of them was a Ferrari in a metallic copper tone, which glowed in the sunlight. My eyes were drawn toward what must have been a marble fountain once. Now the broken down remains of a statue lay in a heap in its middle.

Savio jogged outside. He tossed on a black leather jacket, probably to hide his guns, and nodded toward the metallic Ferrari. Of course. I followed him toward the car and got in. I jumped when the engine roared to life like a beast risen from Tartarus. Savio steered the car down the long driveway and through the gate. "Why is the fountain broken?"

"It was our father's pride and joy. He had it made in Italy and shipped here. When my brothers and I returned, after we came into power, Remo smashed it with a sledgehammer."

I could picture it in my mind, Remo wielding that sledgehammer like a madman. "You didn't try to stop him?"

"There's no stopping Remo when he's murderous," Savio said as he steered us down a wide road with casinos and smaller hotels on either side. "We hated our father. We were busy burning the painting of him and our mother."

His voice held a tension, and I decided to change the topic. "You aren't trying to blend in, are you?" I asked, motioning to his car.

Savio rolled his eyes. "With a name like Falcone and with this tattoo…" he moved his arm so I got a peek at his forearm tattooed with an eye and blade "… there's no way in hell I could blend in around here. And why would I want to? My brothers and I have brought honor back to the Camorra. I'm proud of who I am, of what I am, why would I want to hide it?"

I nodded. It was a foreign concept for me. Most of my life I'd tried to blend in, tried to hide.

"It's a bit strange that you are my babysitter even though I'm two years older than you, don't you think?"

Savio's expression hardened. "Age doesn't matter. I have been a Camorrista for close to four years. I have fought in the cage. I have killed and tortured. I am capable of defending you and myself, and I have no qualms doing it."

"Four years?" I asked incredulously. "But that means you were only thirteen back then."

He nodded. "I wanted to become a Camorrista, and my brothers needed me."

"What about Adamo? Has he been inducted yet?"

Savio's mouth thinned. "No. Remo thinks it's better to wait until he is fourteen so he has some time to pull his head out of his ass."

Savio pulled the car up at the curb in front of a café then got out without another word. I quickly got out as well and immediately realized that the Savio in the mansion or in the car wasn't the Savio that the outside world got to see. His expression had hardened, not as cruel as Remo's and not as cold as Nino's but enough to send a shiver down my back. He no longer appeared like a teenager. He looked a man.

He surprised me when he stepped closer. I gave him a curious look. "I'm supposed to protect you. I'm not going to be the one who gets his ass handed to him by Nino because something happened to you."

I doubted Nino would care. Maybe he'd be displeased because his possession had been damaged or maybe even worried that it would endanger the truce with the Famiglia. "I thought Las Vegas was safe."

"It is," Savio said, his eyes scanning the sidewalk and street. The few passersby looked like tourists, even though we weren't near the Strip. "But since the Outfit attacked, we are more careful."

It made sense. Being attacked in your own territory must have been a hard blow. Savio motioned for me to follow him toward the café, and I tried to stay close to him. He didn't make me quite as nervous as Remo, which was a relief. He held the door open for me, and I stepped in. The barista behind the counter gave me a smile, but it dropped the second Savio entered.

He strode toward the counter. After we'd ordered coffee to go and a few donuts, we moved over to wait for our order. The barista's hands shook so much she kept spilling the milk. Her eyes kept flitting toward Savio and occasionally me. I couldn't help but feel bad.

"Is everyone around here this scared of you and your brothers?" I asked when we were on our way back to the car. I took a sip from my coffee, watching Savio.

"Not everyone, no. Her brother owes us money. He got a visit from Fabiano recently. That's why she's like that."

The moment I buckled up, Savio pulled the car away from the curb. He awkwardly steered the car with his cup wedged between his legs because there was no cup holder.

I took a sip then lifted the box with the donuts. "Is eating in your car off limits?"

"No. Hand me one with lemon glaze. The cleaning people can get rid of the crumbs."

I handed him one of the donuts and took a plain one out for myself. I took a bite, and we settled into silence. I glanced at him again.

"What?" he muttered.

"You changed when we were outside."

Savio narrowed his gaze at me. "We Falcones need to display a certain image outside. Even Adamo knows it. You should remember it too."

"Me?" I asked, surprised.

"You are a Falcone now, aren't you?"

I nodded. "Yeah. You're right." A Falcone. It would take a long time to come to terms with the fact that I was a part of the most notorious family in the US.

Savio parked. "I have to handle some business, but you have to come along."

I quickly emptied my coffee then followed Savio. We were in front of an Italian restaurant called Capri. "As I said, this restaurant belongs to one of our soldiers. His son is a friend and also a soldier."

This time, when we stepped inside the gloomy restaurant, the reactions were quite different. No fear or hands shaking. The restaurant hadn't opened yet. Two guys around Savio's age and two older men sat around a table and were arguing about something. They all looked our way the moment we entered. They nodded at Savio, but then their eyes were glued to me. Uncomfortable under their scrutiny, I had to fight the urge to lower my gaze, remembering Savio's words.

He walked toward the men, and I followed a couple of steps behind, not sure if I was supposed to stay at his side when he'd soon have to discuss business. The younger guys got up. Both hugged Savio and clapped his shoulder. Then the tall, bulky one let out a low whistle. "Nice catch, Savio. New girl for the week?"

Savio glanced toward me, and I could feel my cheeks heat. When he turned back to the men, his smile had thinned. "She's Nino's wife."

An awkward silence followed, and the bulky guy flushed, which seemed to amuse Savio if the twitch of his mouth was any indication. One of the older men shot to his feet and hit the teenage boy over the back of the head. "Apologize now, Diego!"

"I didn't mean any disrespect," Diego mumbled.

"Good thing Nino isn't here," Savio said with a shrug. "He's a possessive bastard."

Was Nino? Or was that part of the outward appearance the Falcones wanted to present. I wasn't sure. I didn't know Nino.

"Why don't you join us? I'm sure our cook can prepare a quick meal for you?" the older man said. He and Diego shared the same sharp facial features, father and son I assumed.

Savio tilted his head in agreement and sank down on one of the chairs then pushed back the one beside him for me to sit. I sat down, glad that the men were now purposely trying to avoid looking at me, though that, too, felt weird.

"Go into the kitchen and tell them we have guests, Diego," the father said.

When Diego returned, he didn't look quite so shaken anymore and eventually got over his initial shock. "So you are the Vice's cousin?"

Now their full attention was back on me.

"I am, but Luca has many cousins."

"How is he?" Diego asked.

His father gave him a look, and Savio rolled his eyes.

"He's a strong Capo. Merciless and well respected."

"Nobody's stronger than our Capo," Diego said, and all the men nodded. Savio's eyes lit up with pride.

I nodded because it was expected of me. I wasn't sure who was stronger, Remo or Luca. Remo had the advantage of having three brothers at his side, even if Adamo wasn't inducted yet.

"I'm here to discuss the attack on your other restaurant, Daniele. Do you have any clues as to who did it?"

"I don't know. A few years back I would have said the Bratva, but since you chased them out of the city, that seems unlikely."

"Maybe they're thinking about returning," Diego suggested.

"Let them try," Savio said fiercely. "We will slaughter them all."

The door to the kitchen opened again. An plump woman and a girl around thirteen or fourteen with long dark hair and startling olive eyes came through it, each carrying a tray with pastries, bread, and cheese. The girl was a bit of a tomboy, and her eyes narrowed when she spotted me. She set down the tray in the center of the table.

"Who's this?" she asked curiously, nodding in my direction.

The woman made a shush noise.

"I'm Kiara, Nino's wife," I said, and she relaxed. Her eyes darted to Savio, and I knew why she'd been wary of me. "So, Savio," she said. "When are you going to fight me as you promised?"

"I never promised anything," Savio said with a smirk.

"Gemma, stop bothering him. Savio doesn't have time to play around with annoying little girls," Diego muttered.

She reached over the table and punched his shoulder. He tried to grab her, but she dashed away before he could, poking her tongue out at him. Then with a last smile at Savio, she slipped through the kitchen door. I was relieved to see that not everyone in Vegas was terrified of the Falcones.

When we returned to the mansion in the early afternoon, I was more relaxed than I'd been in weeks.

"Thank you for spending the day with me," I said as we entered the living area.

Savio gave me a strange look. "It's not like it was my choice, but you are far less bothersome than most women."

My eyebrows shot up. "Umm, thanks?"

He nodded toward Adamo, who was slouched on the sofa, headphones in his ears, playing a video game. "It's his turn now."

With that he walked off, leaving me standing there. I felt like the bothersome little sister who was handed from one older brother to the next, which was idiotic since they were both younger than me.

Adamo lifted one of his earphones. "Wanna join me?"

I glanced at the screen. He was playing a race game. I'd never played a video game because my uncle and aunt didn't own any consoles, and I didn't think that it was anything I'd enjoy. I nodded anyway and sat down across from Adamo. So far, I had barely spoken to the youngest Falcone. He was the most approachable of the lot, almost normal, except for the fact that a gun rested beside him on the sofa.

He put down the earphones. His curly brown hair was a hopeless mess. I didn't think he bothered brushing it after getting up this morning. "I hope Savio wasn't an asshole. If he was, don't worry. It's his go-to mode."

"He was nice," I said.

Adamo gave me a doubtful look, his brown eyes so much kinder than those of his brothers. "Have you ever played this game?"

"I have never played any kind of game."

His eyes grew wide. "Shit. Really?"

I smiled. "I suppose it's something I shouldn't miss."

"Better sit beside me so I can explain the controller to you."

I got up and Adamo put the gun on the table in front of him so I had room to sit down. For a moment, I hesitated. Adamo grimaced. "You don't have to be scared of me."

I plopped down closer than I would have with any of his brothers. Adamo was a kid, even if he was taller than me.

He held out the controller. I grabbed it with an honest smile. "I fear you'll have to start with the basics. I'm completely clueless."

"It's easy," he promised with a grin of his own. He pointed at the buttons and patiently explained them.

It didn't come as a big surprise that I was absolutely horrible. I constantly crashed my car against the wall.

When Nino came home later that afternoon, Adamo's face was red from laughing at my lack of video game skills.

Nino's cool gaze flitted between his brother and me. "Having fun?"

I nodded, but soon my smile diminished. Nino still made me nervous with his cold aloofness. I had no way of guessing what was going on in his head. He surprised me when he came toward us and sat down beside me. He regarded me for a moment longer before saying, "If you want, I can take over."

I held the controller out to him, and he took it, his fingertips brushing my skin. I shivered slightly at the contact. Nino leaned back, controller in hand, but he narrowed his eyes at me for the briefest moment. It wasn't out of anger, I knew that now. He was trying to make sense of me.

Adamo didn't look too pleased about having to play with Nino. It didn't take long for them to be in a serious battle, including snarky comments from Nino and fervent cursing from Adamo.

A small smile tugged at my lips. My siblings and I had never been close. It was good to see that despite everything, the Falcone brothers had managed to stay a family. I only wished I'd figure out a way to feel like part of it.

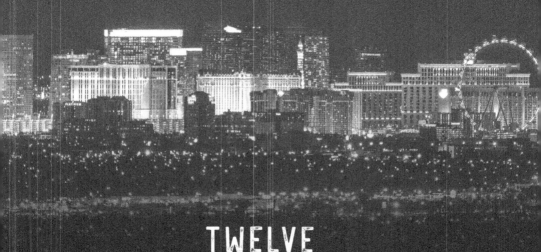

TWELVE

Nino

J UST LIKE I HAD EVERY DAY, I GOT UP AT SIX IN THE MORNING AND grabbed my swim trunks. Kiara stirred behind me, so I moved into the bathroom to change. I was wearing briefs at night for her benefit, and it seemed to have decreased her anxiety around me. She was still wary in bed with me. I wasn't sure why she thought the bed was a particularly dangerous place. If I wanted to fuck her, I could just as well do it in the living room or any other room in the house.

Upon returning to the bedroom, Kiara was propped up against the headboard, the covers gathered around her waist, her dark hair sticking out all over the place. Her slender shoulders and arms were on display, and her thin nightgown did little to hide the outline of her nipples. My body definitely wanted to lay claim on her, but it would have given me little satisfaction having her terror-stricken, crying body under mine.

"Good morning," she said in a slightly deeper voice, which added to her sexual appeal. I could feel a traitorous stirring in my cock but suppressed it quickly.

"I'm heading out for my morning swim. Once I'm done, we can leave. I want to show you the city as promised, and early in the morning it's less crowded."

She nodded. "I'll get ready." My eyes lingered on the swell of her breasts. Then I turned and left. The cold water would do me good.

She was quiet beside me as I drove us down the Strip. It was where every Las Vegas tour should start, but my favorite places were on the fringes, especially the canyons and creeks. Kiara's eyes were drawn to the spectacular hotels lining the street on both sides, but she didn't look that impressed. "You don't enjoy the tour?" I asked.

She shook her head quickly. "It's fascinating, but I'm not the city type. I prefer landscapes and tranquility."

"Then we'll change our plans." I turned the car and headed out of the city boundaries and toward the Red Rock Canyon.

Kiara's eyes grew wide when the glowing red rock formations rose up around us.

"This is a place I like to visit when I'm in the mood for rock climbing."

"You climb?" she asked.

"Climb and hike. It's a good workout with the added bonus of being in nature." I steered us along the scenic loop drive but eventually stopped at a high point lookout. Kiara and I got out and sat down on one of the benches there. She was silent as she regarded the multi-colored mountains around us. Her expression was as peaceful as it had been when she'd played the piano. No fear or tension or worry.

"Beautiful," she whispered.

"It is," I agreed, looking directly at her.

She turned to me and smiled. "Thanks for taking me here. I prefer it to the city."

"I come as often as I can, which isn't very often. Now that we're about to attack the Outfit, there will be even less time. There's always a fight to win, an enemy to hunt down, or a city to win over or defend."

She pursed her lips. "Isn't it tiring to fight all the time? You fought for years to win your territory back, right?"

"We did. After our half-brother killed our father, Las Vegas was in shambles. Without a strong Capo, every Underboss in the West decided to do as he pleased. They didn't follow Vegas' lead because there was a new Capo in the city every few months."

"How long have you been in power?"

"Almost five years, but Remo is in power. I'm his Consigliere."

Kiara shook her head, playing with the thin fabric of her dress absentmindedly. "You rule together. You do everything together."

"Remo is still Capo, and that's good. He's meant to rule."

She worried her bottom lip again. I reached for the hand resting on her thigh and pressed my thumb against her wrist. Her pulse wasn't fast enough for fear.

Her brows formed a V as she peered at my finger against her wrist then up at my face. "Wouldn't it make more sense to have someone run the Camorra who doesn't let emotions overrule logic?"

"No. Our soldiers look up to Remo. His fierce brutality, his uncontrolled anger and passionate loyalty … that's something they seek in a leader. Not logic. Humans don't want logic. They want feelings."

"I suppose."

Kiara

I jerked awake from a nightmare and realized I was alone in bed. My fingers searched my nightstand for my phone until finally the screen lit up under my touch. It was two in the morning. Confused, I sat up. Nino always went to bed with me so where was he? Since our tour through the Red Rock Canyon two days ago, I had only seen him at dinner every evening, where we ordered either pizza or pasta. Aside from eating together, I spent my days alone in the library while my babysitters, Savio or Adamo, stayed somewhere in the house.

Now wide awake, I decided to go into the kitchen to grab something to drink and perhaps an apple. I doubted the kitchen had ever been used before. All these evenings ordering takeout had seriously reduced my fruit and vegetable intake, and I was hungry despite the late hour. I put on a bathrobe and slipped out of our bedroom then continued downstairs. The door to the connecting corridor was closed, which was strange, but I opened it quietly, careful not to wake anyone. I headed through the connecting corridor and into the kitchen, where I grabbed a glass of water and an apple. Then I started to make my way back to our bedroom.

A strange noise made me pause briefly. I couldn't place it. Through the dark, I slowly crept in the direction of the sound. A dim light from the gaming room filtered into the hallway. Maybe Adamo was playing a game. He seemed to be doing nothing else when he was home.

I stepped out of the dark corridor and froze, my body seizing up with shock. It took my brain a second to comprehend what was going on. Remo had a woman bent over the pool table, holding her down by the neck, as he slammed into her from behind. She moaned loudly despite her cheek being pressed against the table. At the other end of the room, a woman was on her knees in front of Savio, his hand fisting her blond hair, guiding her movements.

The glass slipped from my hand and shattered at my feet as panic filled my body. Savio and Remo's eyes zeroed in on me. I tried to whirl around and run, but my feet slipped on the spilled water, and I landed on my butt. Pain sliced through my thigh, a sharp burn that stopped my breath but not my body.

Scrambling to my feet, I stormed off, my bare feet slipping as I fought for balance. My breaths came in short gasps, my vision turning black at the corners. I could hardly breathe from fear as I rushed into the master bedroom and locked the door. Then I stumbled into the bathroom. For a moment I was sure I'd throw up, but after I'd splashed water in my face, my nausea ceased. I couldn't shake the feeling of being dirty. I knew it was just in my mind, which summoned the memories that haunted my nights.

A sharp twinge in my inner thigh caught my attention momentarily, and I stared down. Blood trickled down my leg. Red rivulets slithered down my skin.

I started shaking, more horrible memories resurfacing and clawing out of my chest.

Slowly, I lifted my nightgown to find a piece of glass in my upper thigh. I clutched the sink. Blood covered my legs like it had so many years ago. I kept picturing Remo and Savio with these women.

Shaking, unable to stand, I sank to the ground.

The sound of the bedroom door being busted open registered in my foggy mind, and then two strong male legs came into focus. Nino came in, dressed only in briefs.

"Kiara?"

Nino

Savio barged into the guestroom without knocking, pulling up his pants in the process. I stopped and the whore on her knees before me threw a look over her shoulder.

"What's the matter?" I asked.

"Your girl walked in on us fucking the whores. She freaked."

"Fuck. Didn't I tell you to take your fucking into a room?"

"We were in a room. And why should we hide in our own home?" Savio muttered.

I pulled out of the whore's ass, grabbed my briefs, and put them on before I followed Savio back into the living area.

Remo stopped fucking his whore when he spotted me. "You stay like this. I'm not done with you," he growled as he released the woman's neck, pulling out of her and coming toward me, not bothering to cover himself.

Shards and water as well as blood covered the ground. There wasn't much blood, though, to have been anything serious. "What happened here?"

"She panicked, fell, and cut herself," Remo said. "You need to get a handle on her."

I left him standing there and headed for the master bedroom but found the door locked. "Kiara?"

No answer. I wasn't sure how badly she'd injured herself. A glass shard could cause serious injuries depending on where it cut. The amount of blood on the ground hadn't given me cause for worry, but if she'd removed the glass without checking its position, she could bleed out within minutes.

When she didn't reply after another louder knock, I kicked the door in and stepped inside. The bedroom was empty, so I continued into the bathroom. Blood stains covered the cream-colored marble, and Kiara was sitting on the ground, staring down at herself.

I moved closer. "Kiara?"

I'd seen a similar look on her face on our wedding night. Her past held her in its unrelenting grip once more. Blood covered the inside of her leg, but her nightgown hid the source from my view. I knew she wouldn't handle my touch well, but I couldn't be bothered to take that into consideration when she had a wound that needed to be treated.

I bent over her and picked her up. She tensed and made a small sound in the back of her throat but didn't react otherwise. I hoisted her up on the marble surface of the sink.

"Kiara, look at me," I ordered firmly, and she raised her eyes to meet mine. She wasn't as far gone as on our wedding night, but I wasn't sure what had caused her episode. The sight of my brothers banging their whores, the blood on her legs, or a combination of the two.

"I need to take a look at your wound."

She blinked at me then gave a small nod, but I wasn't sure if she'd really registered what I said. Her dark curls stuck to her sweaty forehead. I reached into the drawer and took out a first-aid kit then grabbed a washcloth, soaked it with cold water, and wiped Kiara's face with it. She shuddered, but her gaze became more focused. I dropped the washcloth and reached for the hem of her nightgown. She seized up and her breathing changed. *Fear.*

I searched her face. She was watching me with wide eyes, her chest rising and falling fast. She didn't stop me, however. I pushed the fabric up until it bunched around her pelvis. I could see the top of a glass shard, but with her legs closed together, I couldn't get a good look. I put my hands on her knees and pressed. She resisted. I could have parted them, but that seemed an unwise choice given her past.

"Kiara," I said firmly, "I need to take a look at this."

Her leg muscles softened under my palms, and I could finally push her legs apart, revealing white lace panties and a shard protruding from the sensitive skin on her upper inner thigh. "Lean back a bit." She did and I propped her injured leg to the side, opening her up.

She sucked in her breath.

"Relax. I'll take care of your wound, that's all, Kiara."

"I know," she whispered.

I disinfected my hands. The shard wasn't in very deep from the look of it, but I'd have to feel it to make sure. "This might hurt a bit," I warned before I felt the area around the shard with my fingertips. She flinched violently, whimpering. I glanced up and saw tears welling in her eyes.

She was very sensitive to pain. I mostly dealt with my brothers or Fabiano when treating wounds, so I hadn't taken her reaction into consideration. We didn't have any numbing spray, and Tylenol wouldn't help with the immediate pain.

"Kiara, I need to remove the shard. It will be painful. I'll do it quickly." I didn't tell her yet that I would still have to stitch up the wound. More bad news after the initial injury.

She swallowed then gave a small nod. I grabbed the edge of the shard with my fingers and curled my free hand around Kiara's hip to steady her, pressing between her legs so she wouldn't be able to jerk them closed. Her breathing hitched, but I didn't give her time to worry. I wrenched the shard out in one sharp movement.

She cried out, jerking violently in my hold. She dipped forward and rested her forehead against my chest, panting, still trembling. I brushed my thumb over her side. "This was the worst," I said. She didn't react. "Kiara, you need to lean back so I can take a look at your wound now."

Slowly, she straightened. Her face was pale and tears trailed down her cheeks. I dropped the shard in the sink and crouched down before Kiara to get a better look at the cut. It had started bleeding again because the shard was removed. As expected, it wasn't very deep. I cleaned it carefully, ignoring Kiara's flinching. I wasn't sure if it was from pain or from fear because my fingers had to work close to where she felt most vulnerable. When I reached for the needle to stitch her up, she exhaled sharply.

I looked up at her. "Have you ever been stitched up?"

She shook her head.

It was going to be very uncomfortable for her. There really was no preventing it. The wound needed stitches, and I couldn't take her to a hospital or call one of the Camorra's doctors. The former because we didn't involve outsiders and the latter because I didn't trust these men to do a better job than I could. I considered her wound again. Five stitches would do and I'd be quick.

Kiara whimpered but otherwise didn't make a sound when I worked the needle into her flesh. Her thigh muscles quaked under the needle, and I pressed my palm over them so the motion wouldn't ruin my stitch work.

"Done," I said eventually and straightened out before washing my hands. Then I took a new washcloth and wiped the excess blood off Kiara's legs.

Kiara was still very quiet. I nudged her chin up so she had to meet my gaze. "What happened?"

Her eyes flitted away.

"You walked in on my brothers having sex." Especially Remo. Kiara didn't need to see him in action.

She exhaled.

"It brought back memories?"

"Yeah," she murmured.

"I will have a talk with them to keep their activities to their parts of the house from now on," I told her. Remo wouldn't like that one fucking bit, nor would Savio, but Remo was the one I needed to convince.

"Where were you?" she asked in a soft voice.

I evaluated her expression, but her eyes were downcast and it was obvious she was trying to keep her face impassive. "We agreed that I seek pleasure elsewhere, Kiara. Or did you change your mind?" She didn't appear like she'd be ready to submit to me in bed yet.

"No," she said quietly, but I noticed the hesitation.

"But?"

"No but," she said more firmly.

"Okay." It was obvious something was still bothering her, but she wasn't willing to share. I handed her two Tylenol, which she popped into her mouth. "Why don't you go back to bed?"

I lifted her down from the counter and led her into the bedroom. She was still a bit unsteady on her legs. She climbed under the covers and lay down. "Won't you join me?"

I paused. I'd intended to return to the whore I'd fucked before Savio had interrupted me, but something in Kiara's eyes made me slip under the covers with her. The whore would eventually realize I wasn't going to return. Maybe Savio or Remo had use for her. I couldn't grasp Kiara's reasons for wanting me to stay. She lay on her back but with her head tilted toward me. I shut off the lights.

"Can you tell me something about yourself I don't know yet?" came her soft voice out of the dark.

"What *do* you know about me?"

There was silence for a moment. "I know your father was Capo before

Remo took over. I know you and your brothers lived in England for a while but returned to the States to get your territory back after your father was killed by his Enforcer, Growl. I know you are a genius."

Those were the basics. It was difficult to decide what kind of information to divulge at this point. "I speak five languages fluently. Russian, Italian, English, Spanish, and French."

"Let me guess," she said. "Russian and Spanish so you can better deal with the Bratva and the Cartel."

"That's true. It makes little sense to torture someone for information if you don't understand what they're saying. That negates the purpose."

Kiara let out a small noise, but I couldn't tell if it was a stifled laugh or a huff.

"Why French?"

"Because of the Corsican Union in Canada. They haven't been involved in our business so far, but it's good to be prepared. Their territory is close to Dante's. He might seek their support."

"Is there anything you do that doesn't serve a purpose or is illogical? Something you do because you enjoy it?"

"There are plenty of things. Sex, for one." I didn't have to see Kiara to know she'd stiffened again. "Though one might argue it serves the purpose of relaxing me. Maybe hiking and climbing."

"I'd like to go hiking one day," she said.

"There are a few smaller canyons around Vegas that are good for hikes, and the Red Rock canyon offers a few trails that are more advanced. I could take you to one some time. Or you could go rock climbing with me."

"I'm not very fit, so take it easy on me," she said then yawned.

"Sleep now," I told her.

"Okay," she whispered, her voice already heavy with sleep. "And, Nino, thank you for everything so far."

I frowned into the dark. I didn't know what she had to thank me for.

The next morning Kiara was still in a deep sleep when I got up and headed down to the pool to swim my laps. Afterward, I went into our gaming room where I found Remo stretched out on the couch, a cup of coffee in his hand. He was on the phone, looking annoyed. Nobody had cleaned up the shards and blood yet, and if I didn't do it, nobody would until the cleaning people arrived tomorrow.

"Don't worry. That delivery will go through. We always keep our word. You just make sure you keep yours," Remo muttered before hanging up.

"Famiglia?"

"Matteo fucking Vitiello. That motherfucker sets my nerves on edge."

"Because you have a similar temperament," I said.

Remo narrowed his eyes. "So, how's your wife doing? Has she gotten over her shock of seeing how fucking is done right."

"I had to stitch her up because she got cut by some glass. I think it would be wise to keep your sexual activities in your own wing. Now that Kiara lives under the same roof, the risk is too high that she walks in on you again."

"This is my home. We don't have any maids because we didn't want to feel like we were being watched in our home, and now you want me to hide in my own wing when I want to fuck a whore?"

I sank down across from him. "Don't turn this into a bigger deal than it is. You have more than enough places to go about your fucking, Remo. When Adamo was younger, we were more careful as well, and you could deal with it."

"Your wife is a grown woman. Shouldn't she be able to handle it?"

"You know why she doesn't. She's too scarred from her past, and even if she weren't, I don't want her to see you or Savio fucking around. She doesn't need to see your dick."

Remo chuckled. "She doesn't see yours either. Maybe that's the problem. Maybe you can fuck the messed-up past out of her."

Remo was trying to piss me off, and despite my lack of emotions, I was growing tired of this discussion. "I never ask you for favors, Remo, but this I ask of you."

Remo's expression turned serious. "Why do you give a fuck about her?"

"As I told you before, she is now part of the family. Just like we protected Adamo and Savio, we should protect Kiara now. She is innocent and at our mercy, and we should treat her as she deserves, as my wife and as a Falcone."

Remo shook his head and set down his coffee cup with an audible clang, spilling some of the liquid on the table. "Fuck. Did you come up with that speech just now? But if you ask me to do it, I will. Savio will be a pain in the ass because of it, I'm sure."

The sound of movement made us both fall silent. I knew from the soft footfall that it could only be Kiara. Adamo trampled through the house to annoy us, and Savio's steps were more confident. Her steps were slow and hesitant, as if she worried about what she would find in the living area this morning.

"The coast is clear," Remo shouted. "No fucking about happening here ever again."

I shot him a look, but he gave me a twisted smile.

Kiara emerged from the connecting corridor. Her eyes landed on the shards and her spilled blood on the ground. A pink color filled her cheeks. She glanced toward Remo then quickly to me. "Where do you have a mop so I can clean this up?"

I got up. "Let me do it." I moved into the small cleaning closet that none of my brothers had ever set foot in. They didn't mind if the house was dirty until the cleaning personnel showed up again, but I preferred things neat and clean. Living under the same roof with those pigs, it was a losing battle to keep everything clean.

Kiara followed close behind. "I should do it. After all, I caused the mess."

"Following that logic, Remo and Savio should clean up," I said.

"That's not going to happen," Remo shouted.

"Is he angry?" Kiara asked quietly.

"Remo is always angry. You have to be more specific than that."

"Because I disturbed him and his … woman."

"You didn't disturb him. Trust me. Remo is used to a lot of shit. You freaking out on him won't stop him from fucking a whore."

Kiara tensed. "Do you call all women whores?"

"No, but that's what they were. They work in the Sugar Trap for us."

Her nose wrinkled. "So you always use whores?"

"No. But if things are busy, it's the easiest way to get sex. Finding a regular woman requires we go out and charm them. That's considerably more work."

Kiara sighed. "You and your brothers are messed up."

Remo got up from the sofa. "Is there any food in the fridge? I'm starving."

"I bought eggs and bacon yesterday." I took the mop, a dustpan, and a small broom out of the closet as Remo disappeared from view. Kiara took the broom and dustpan from me and walked somewhat stiffly back to the remains of the broken glass on the floor. I filled a bucket with water before I followed her.

"How's your wound?" I asked.

"It stings, but your stitches seemed to hold," she said, her expression softening. "You're really good at playing doctor."

"I have years of practice stitching up my brothers and myself, though Remo has provided me the most practice."

"You all have a lot of scars," she said, her eyes tracing my upper body. I had trouble reading her expression. She didn't seem unsettled by my half-dressed state.

"Everyone has scars. Some are skin deep, others reach beyond that."

"Soul deep," she whispered.

"Are you referring to yourself?"

She watched me mop up the blood and brushed the shards into the dustpan then smiled strangely up at me. "I don't think my scars will ever fade."

"They don't need to fade." I grabbed her hand and touched it to the scar above my bellybutton. Her fingertips fluttered over my skin, her eyes wide with shock. "A knife went in there. Dirty blade. The wound wouldn't heal for a long time. For a moment, I was sure it wouldn't heal at all. How does it feel?"

She frowned. "The skin is a bit harder, but your tattoos cover up everything."

"The skin is harder there because of the thick scar tissue. It's less sensitive to pain and cold and heat. It's stronger."

Her brown eyes held my gaze. "I don't understand."

I moved my face closer. "The scars he left, your body can heal them if you let it, and the result will be stronger than what was there before."

THIRTEEN

Kiara

GOT UP WHEN NINO DISAPPEARED IN THE BATHROOM TO CHANGE INTO his swim trunks. Every morning since I'd moved in three weeks ago, he followed the same ritual. I had occasionally watched him from the window in the beginning until I'd found the courage to follow him outside one day a week ago. Now he always waited for me.

He raised his eyebrows when he saw me putting on my bathrobe and grabbing a book. "Ready?"

"Ready."

I followed him downstairs, my eyes darting to his body. He looked good in his swim trunks. In the last few days, I'd often caught myself staring at him. His body fascinated me, I could admit that, and touching his scar hadn't summoned past demons as I'd feared. His scars and tattoos made me want to find out the story behind each of them. Nino's story.

Stretching out on one of the sun chairs, I watched as Nino made his way toward the edge of the pool and jumped in elegantly. He always followed the same routine. Two rounds of the butterfly stroke, two rounds of the backstroke, and two rounds of the crawl. Then he repeated everything from the start. He never faltered in his movements throughout the thirty minutes that he swam, and I didn't read a single word. I couldn't take my eyes off him, off the muscles in his arms and back as they flexed. It was mesmerizing and beautiful, graceful.

May mornings in Las Vegas were surprisingly warm, and I relished the feel of the sun on my skin as my eyes rested on my husband.

My husband. It didn't feel real yet. He had kept his word, had never made a move to touch me, and sometimes I caught myself wondering how it would be if he did touch me ... if we were closer. I knew it wasn't a possibility I should bother entertaining.

When he swam toward the ladder, I quickly lifted my book and returned my gaze to the page, but above the edge of the book, I watched Nino getting out and a small shiver trailed up my spine.

After a moment of Nino soaking in the sun—a sight that always halted my breath in my throat and sent spears of heat through my body—he headed my way, dripping water. I handed him the towel he'd put down on the sun chair beside mine and tried not to act like I had been secretly watching him the entire time.

"Thanks," he said and began drying himself. "You can use the pool as well, you know."

"I haven't swam in many years, and I was never very good," I admitted, having a hard time focusing on his face. For some reason, Nino's presence was even more overwhelming when he stood right in front of me, soaking wet.

"I can teach you if you want," Nino drawled.

"Maybe in a few weeks or so," I said quickly because I wasn't sure if I was ready to be in only swimwear around Nino, even if he had already seen me naked on our wedding night. That day seemed like a lifetime ago.

"I have to take out your stitches today. If I hadn't been busy these last few days gathering information on Outfit buildings, I would have done it before. Why don't we do it right away and have breakfast afterward?"

I smiled. "That sounds good." Then added quickly, "Not the part about the stitches but the breakfast part."

He held out his hand. My stomach flopped strangely when his warm fingers closed over my skin and he tugged me to my feet. His brows pulled together when his finger brushed my wrist, but then he released me.

"What kind of information did you gather?" I asked as we walked back to the house.

"Remo is planning an attack on Chicago. We assume Fabiano's father was the driving force behind the attack on our territory. He has powerful supporters in the Outfit, one of them is Fiore Cavallaro, and as long as the old man lives, Dante probably won't get rid of Scuderi."

"But Scuderi is Fabiano's father. Why would he try to kill his own son?"

"He tried to kill him before when Fabiano was a kid. Remo found him shortly after, and Fabiano's been part of our family ever since. Scuderi holds a grudge against his children. I'm sure you know the story of why war broke out between the Outfit and the Famiglia."

"Of course. Fabiano's sister Liliana killed her husband with the help of a Famiglia soldier and ran off."

"Scuderi wants to salvage his honor, if Fabiano is to be believed."

I frowned. "But what does that have to do with you gathering information?"

"As I said, we intend to run an attack in summer. It's our goal to extract Scuderi so Fabiano can kill him and we can send his remains back to Cavallaro as a present."

That sounded like an insane plan. Kidnapping the Outfit's Consigliere was an impossible task. Men like that were always surrounded by soldiers and guards. We arrived in our bathroom, and I stood awkwardly beside the sink as Nino took out the instruments he needed to pull out my stitches. "Where do I sit?"

"I'll lift you onto the counter. That way I don't have to bend too low."

Nino stepped up close and his clean, manly scent flooded my nose. My cheeks heated, and I jumped when his strong hands touched my waist as he lifted me up onto the wash table as if I weighed nothing. I opened my bathrobe and waited nervously.

Nino touched my knees, and I became very still. His touch was light, purposeful—not at all sexual but a mix of fear and excitement shot through me anyway. The latter caught me by surprise, but Nino didn't give me much time to consider this because he nudged my legs apart. My body's natural reaction to clamp shut lasted only a moment. Then I allowed him to part my thighs so he could take a look at my wound.

My cheeks turned hot when he crouched before me and pushed my nightgown up, giving him a clear view of my panties. It was a vulnerable position, but despite the nerves coursing through me, my fear was only a distant voice in the back of my mind, where I'd buried my most hurtful memories.

Nino's fingers were gentle and clinical as he felt my wound. "Does it still hurt?"

I shook my head, startled by the light tingling his touch caused. I hoped Nino didn't realize how my body reacted to him.

He was very careful when he pulled out the stitches, so it only stung the slightest bit. When Nino had pulled the last stitch, his eyes took in the small scar, and he brushed his thumb over it. My breath got stuck in my throat from the sensation that traveled all the way to my center. I'd never experienced anything like it.

Nino straightened. "All done. The small scar will fade."

"It's not like anyone but you will ever see it," I said, and his expression became strangely intent.

"That's true."

He gripped my waist again and set me down. This time his hands lingered on my waist a moment longer, and I swallowed, my stomach fluttering again. But Nino dropped his hands. He motioned toward the shower. "I'm going to shower now. After that, we can make breakfast."

I left but listened to the sound of the running water, confused by my reaction to Nino's body and his close proximity to me. He was still intimidating because of his strength, coldness, and reputation, but part of me had come to trust him a little. Nino had never done anything that had unsettled me.

When he emerged with only a towel wrapped around his waist, the overwhelming feeling of his mere presence resurfaced. "While you take a shower, I'll head into the kitchen and see what I can do."

I nodded silently and quickly disappeared into the bathroom, closing the door behind me.

When I walked into the kitchen thirty minutes later, Nino was chopping onions and occasionally checking his iPad, which was propped up on the counter.

"You can cook?" I asked in surprise.

"I wouldn't say I can cook. But it's not very difficult as long as you follow instructions."

I stopped beside him. A recipe for a cheese omelet was open on his iPad and hash browns were cooking in a pan on the stove. It smelled delicious and the onions were chopped with the precision of a chef. "Can I help you with anything?"

"Why don't you make another pot of coffee. My brothers will probably be coming down soon like hungry wolves. The smell of bacon will draw them out of their hibernation."

As if on cue, the door swung open and Savio stumbled in, yawning, wearing only sweatpants. He didn't greet us. Instead he sank down in a chair, rubbing the back of his head. He glanced between Nino and me. "You two cook together now? Nino's been the only cook around here."

"I'm not a good cook," I said.

The door opened again, and Remo entered, dressed in only briefs, revealing those steely muscles and unsettling scars. He had an erratic air about him, which set alarms off in my body. "I need to have a talk with you two," he said to Nino and Savio, grinning in a way that didn't bode well.

My interactions with the scary Capo had been limited to dinners and the occasional breakfast.

"About what?" Nino asked as he flipped the omelet.

"Nothing I'm supposed to discuss in front of Kiara if I remember your lecture," he bit out, dark eyes settling on me.

"I can go," I said.

Nino shook his head. "It can wait until after breakfast."

Remo's expression made it clear that he disagreed, but as usual, he held back when I was around. I quickly ate my omelet before I excused myself to tinker with a new song.

Nino

Remo was unusually excited, even by his standards. He leaned back in his chair, lips pulling wide in a very dangerous way.

Savio raised an eyebrow, but I shook my head. I didn't know what was going on.

"Kiara is gone. You can talk now," I said.

Remo glanced down at his phone. "Wait a sec."

Sometimes my brother drove me up the wall with his antics. Steps sounded in the corridor. A man. Adamo was in school, but given Remo's relaxed stance, it could only be Fabiano.

The blond man shoved open the door and strode in, looking less than pleased about being here. "I have a full schedule of kicking debtors' asses, Remo." He nodded at us before he took the chair beside Savio. "What's going on?" His eyes moved over to me.

I shook my head. "Remo hasn't revealed anything yet."

"I changed my mind about our plans," Remo said.

"Regarding the Outfit attack?" I asked. I'd spend days trying to gather useful information about Scuderi's weekly habits, upcoming social events he might have to attend. Now Remo decided to change our plans.

Fabiano propped himself up on his forearms, frowning.

Remo nodded with a wide grin. "Dante is a man of logic, like you Nino. He will expect us to target him, or Scuderi, or one of the other men in his family. But I won't do it because history has proven that there's no better way to demoralize your enemy than to target the people they are supposed to protect." He paused, excitement flashing across his face. "Their women."

I narrowed my eyes. "Dante will have put every possible protection in place to make sure we don't get anywhere near his wife or their children."

He made a dismissive gesture and took out his phone then showed it to us.

On the screen was a young woman with blond hair and blue eyes, standing beside Dante Cavallaro. She had the same aloof expression on her face.

"Do you know her?"

"That's Serafina," Fabiano said slowly. "She's Cavallaro's niece."

"You met her?"

"I used to play with her and her twin brother when we were little," he said, his expression turning wary. "What's your plan?"

Remo looked down on the screen with a twisted grin. "Her wedding to the Underboss of Indianapolis is scheduled for August first. I've always wanted to crash a wedding."

Fabiano shook his head. "You want to waltz into Chicago and attack a wedding celebration? All the Captains and Underbosses will be there. Maybe we get in, but we won't get out. Trust me on that, Remo."

Remo chuckled. "No, we will attack the day before. The future bride will spend the night before her wedding in a hotel in Indianapolis with the women of her family. The men of the family will be at stag night. There will be only the usual guards."

"Are you sure there won't be additional safety measures in place?" I asked.

Remo raised his eyebrows at Fabiano, who shrugged.

"They won't expect an attack like that. It's never been done before. To disturb a wedding is regarded as somewhat sacrilegious by most members of the Outfit."

Remo snorted. "Sacrilegious," he said. "Dante attacked my territory. I will show them my version of sacrilegious. Don't worry."

"I told you before, it was my father's doing," Fabiano muttered. "We should try to get our hands on him and not a woman."

Remo's grin turned dangerous. "You will get him. I'm sure Dante will see reason and exchange him for his niece … *eventually*. I will show him just how sacrilegious we are in Las Vegas."

Fabiano grimaced. It was obvious that he didn't like the idea, but he knew better than to argue with Remo when my brother was this excited about an idea.

"This is genius or insanity," Savio said with a laugh. "Given that it's your plan, Remo, it's probably insanity."

"I think I have a better plan," I began. "It'll send a more symbolic message. The bride will probably be taken to church from the hotel in a limousine. There will be even less people around. She will have her mother in the car with her, a bodyguard, and the driver, and perhaps one or two cars as a convoy. We can attack then. It would be absolutely dishonorable to do so, but we have always had our own interpretation of honor."

Remo laughed darkly. "Nino, you are a fucking genius. The girl will already be in her wedding dress. We will steal a bride from under their noses, right before her wedding night. No better symbol than that."

Fabiano shot me a look, but if he thought I had the power to stop Remo at this point, he hadn't seen the way Remo looked at Cavallaro's niece. Remo got up, obviously unable to sit still any longer.

"I'd prefer if we could keep that plan from my wife. It might trigger some images from her past that I don't want to resurface."

Remo waved me off, pacing the room like a caged tiger. His eyes focused on the image on his phone screen.

"If we attack Dante's family, he will take war to a new level," Fabiano said.

"I hope he does," Remo murmured.

Two hours later, I found Kiara at the piano, her eyes closed, head tilted to the side as she played a melody she had been working on since she moved here. She never talked about her music, but I had a good ear. "I made time for gun training today," I said.

She jerked upright, her dazed eyes zeroing in on me. Slowly, she stood. She wore one of her modest dresses that reached her knees, but even those clothes did nothing to hide the enticing swell of her breasts, her narrow waist, or soft curve of her hips.

"Where?" she asked curiously as she padded toward me on bare feet. To my surprise, her toes were painted red. It was a color I'd favor in her clothes as well.

"I set up a target in the garden." I gestured at my gun holster. "And you have a selection of these guns or we could go down into the basement to our weapon room."

She laughed then bit her lip. "I think one of your guns will do."

I led her outside to the west side of the gardens, and we stopped close to the target. "Have you ever held a gun?"

"No," she admitted.

I shook my head. Growing up in the mafia, girls should learn how to handle guns from a young age. They were smaller and less muscular than men. Why add the disadvantage of being inept at using a gun? I handed Kiara my semi-automatic. It was easy to handle. She took it carefully, but her grip was all wrong. I moved around her and positioned myself behind her back. Her sweet perfume wafted into my nose. I'd never thought I'd like it, but Kiara obviously used a brand my senses favored. She glanced over her shoulder with a hint of shyness. I was glad that her facial expressions were slowly becoming less of a mystery to me. It made my life and her life indefinitely easier.

"Lift your arms and aim at the target."

She did, but we had work to do. "I will adjust your hold and stance," I explained. I touched her hips, and she stiffened, but I angled her the way I wanted her then moved on to her arms and pushed them down a couple of inches. I faced her again and corrected her fingers on the gun. "I'm not sure if it's a good idea for you to stand in front of the barrel. What if I shoot you by accident?"

"You'd have to release the safety first. That would give me time to get out of the way."

She drew her lower lip between her teeth again. It was awfully distracting. "I'm so clueless."

"That's why I'm here, to teach you all you need to know." A delicate blush spread on her cheeks, but I couldn't link an emotion to it.

I guided her hand for her first few shots to let her get accustomed to the recoil. She jumped every time the shot sounded, but eventually she seemed to enjoy herself and even laughed when she managed to hit the target without my help. It was satisfying to see her gain confidence.

FOURTEEN

Kiara

FABIANO DROPPED LEONA OFF AT THE MANSION ON HIS WAY TO WORK. It was only the second time she was over in the four weeks since I'd moved to Las Vegas. Occasionally, we exchanged texts, though. I waited in the doorway as she kissed Fabiano in his Mercedes before she got out, and he drove off with a short wave at me.

Leona was dressed in jean shorts and a tank top. It was already uncomfortably warm outside. "Beautiful dress," she said with a smile as she hugged me. It was one of my many maxi dresses. I wasn't sure why I still hesitated to walk around in shorts. None of the Falcone men had made a move toward me, not even Nino.

"Thanks. I love your shorts."

She glanced behind me. "Who's on guard duty?"

I huffed. "Adamo. It's the weekend, after all."

"Mafia men are protective."

"I hope one day I'll be able to protect myself. I've had another gun lesson with Nino. I'm improving."

"Fabiano has been trying to improve my self-defense skills for months now, but it's such a slow process. And most of the time we end up making out ..." She trailed off, her skin turning red. "Sorry. TMI."

I smiled. "Don't worry. I don't mind." I led her onto the patio. A large umbrella shaded the lounge furniture so we didn't suffer a heat stroke in the midday sun. "I thought we could order sushi?"

"Oh yes." She lifted her bag. "I brought a bikini. It's going to be really hot. I thought we could take a swim in the pool later."

Thirty minutes later, we were settled on the lounge chairs, plates of sushi spread out on the table in front of us. "When did you know that you wanted to be with Fabiano?" I asked, picking up a piece of avocado maki.

Leona considered the question, chewing thoughtfully. "You mean in a physical sense or in a relationship?"

"Both, I guess."

"It was a gradual process. I was attracted to him from the start but also worried about getting close to him. Eventually, my heart and body won over my rationality." She laughed.

"Sometimes I wonder how it would feel to be with Nino," I blurted.

Leona put down the piece of sushi she was about to push into her mouth and blinked. "You haven't been with Nino yet?"

I flushed. Should I have kept it a secret? Maybe Nino didn't want others to know that he wasn't the monster—no, didn't *act* like the monster he was. But I needed to talk to someone about it, and Giulia was no longer an option because I was now part of the Camorra and she was part of the Famiglia. Truce or not, the families were enemies. Our phone calls had been a difficult task, telling her about my daily life without revealing any important information to her, and I could tell it was the same for her.

"No, I freaked out on him on our wedding night, and he hasn't tried anything since then."

Leona blinked at me. "Wow. Really?"

"Really. I told him to seek out other women if he needed to satisfy his needs."

Leona shook her head with wide eyes. "And it doesn't bother you? The mere thought that Fabiano could touch another woman makes me sick."

"It didn't in the beginning."

"But now it does?"

I tried not to think about it, but when I did, it bothered me a lot. "Yes, it does. I actually enjoy spending time with Nino. He is calm and incredibly intelligent. He makes me feel like I'm safe around him. Is that weird?"

Leona frowned. "Well. I feel safe around Fabiano and most people are terrified of him, so I'm not the right person to ask."

I dipped a piece of sushi into the soy sauce and put it in my mouth, chewing slowly to gather my thoughts. "I don't know if I should even consider changing our relationship."

"Talk to him. Tell him you would like to be with him. He probably won't say no."

He wouldn't. "What if I can't go through with it? What if the memories stop me again? Or what if Nino wants all or nothing. I'm not sure how far I can go just yet."

"You won't find out if you don't talk to him. If he hasn't pushed you yet, do you think he would do it after you ask him for more?"

I wasn't sure. But if I got close to Nino, I needed him to stop seeking out other women, and I wasn't sure if he'd agree to that as long as I wasn't giving him what he needed. Why should he do this on my terms?

I was nervous all day because of my conversation with Leona, and even music hardly managed to set me at ease this time. My fingers kept stumbling over the notes, so I had to keep starting from scratch.

When Nino came home late in the afternoon, looking as beautifully cold as ever—dressed all in black, tall and muscled—and leaned against the piano to listen to me play, I finally gathered my courage. "I'd like to go out for dinner."

His brows drew together. "Of course."

"Just the two of us," I blurted.

He regarded me calmly, his eyes searching my face. I wondered how much of my feelings he could guess and how much of them would always remain a secret to him. Sometimes it came as a relief that he had trouble reading emotions. "Tonight?"

My fingers stopped on the keys. "That would be lovely. But can you get a table that quickly?"

He chuckled, and I let out a small laugh, remembering who I was talking to. "Never mind."

"What would you like to eat? Asian? European?"

"Asian. I haven't eaten much of it yet except for sushi."

"Then I'll book a table at the best Szechuan restaurant in town."

"What do I have to wear? Is there a dress code?"

Nino's eyes trailed over me. "Something red."

I blinked. That wasn't the answer I had expected. "Why red?" I couldn't imagine guests were required to wear a certain color, but this was Las Vegas and anything was possible.

"Because I think it will go well with your dark hair and honey skin. I want you to stand out, not blend in."

I stared down at my arm. Nobody had ever described my skin as honey colored. A pleasing warmth settled in my chest. "I don't have anything in red. Most of my clothes are meant to make me blend in," I said.

Nino nodded. "I got that." He glanced down at his watch. "If we head out now, we can buy you something and still have enough time to return home and get ready, if I book the table at eight." He didn't wait for my reply. Instead, he picked up his phone, dialed a number, and two minutes later we had a table. Another customer would hear some kind of excuse why they wouldn't be dining at Chengdu tonight.

"Come now," Nino said, holding out his hand. I had to admit that I enjoyed his small touches. My hand in his didn't feel as if it was caging me in or anything close to it. It made me feel safe.

I put my palm in his and followed him to his Bugatti Veyron. "Where are we going?" I asked as we pulled down the driveway.

"It's a boutique where Fabiano occasionally buys dresses for Leona. From what he tells me, they have extravagant pieces. I've never been there. They don't sell men's clothing."

I laughed nervously. "How much attention am I supposed to draw to us?"

"As much attention as you deserve, Kiara. You are too beautiful to lurk in the shadows. And as my wife, you will have to get used to the spotlight."

My insides warmed at his compliment. He'd told me that he found me beautiful before, but it still felt wonderful to hear him say it again.

The store offered an overwhelming selection of dresses in all colors, and from the moment we entered, the saleswoman hovered around us like a mother hen. She kept throwing Nino nervous glances, obviously eager to please him, but, of course, his face gave nothing away.

"We're looking for dresses in red," he said, his palm still pressed lightly against my back.

"Oh, we have a few beautiful pieces in that color. Let me show you. Your wife will look absolutely stunning in them."

Nino looked at me with a glint in his eyes. "That she will."

I shivered, and again it wasn't in fear. I wasn't sure what was going on, but my body reacted to Nino in a way that was unsettling and exhilarating at once. We followed the woman back toward a secluded part of the boutique where the changing rooms were. "I'll be back in a moment. Would you like something to drink?"

"No, thank you," I said with a smile.

Nino nodded his agreement. Then the woman dashed off. He lowered his hand from my back. The saleswoman returned with three dresses thrown over her arm. I slipped into the changing room, and she handed me the first dress. It was like a second skin and went to my knees, accentuating every curve with a high collar and no sleeves. People would be staring if I wore this, especially men.

Nerves fluttered in my stomach as I stepped out. Nino leaned against the wall, arms crossed, looking every bit like a runway model. He straightened the moment he saw me, his gray eyes sliding over my body.

"It's too sexy, don't you think?" I whispered.

Nino moved closer. "It's perfect." He tilted his head. "Don't you want people to see how beautiful you are?"

I shifted. "I'm not used to it."

"You will grow used to it. Don't worry."

I tried on a long dress with a high slit and another one with a low neckline and even lower back, and they, too, would definitely not help me go unnoticed, but the way Nino regarded me in them gave me a strange shiver of delight. In the end, we bought all three dresses and even a red jumpsuit. When we were back in the car, I couldn't help but laugh. "You are really into red."

Nino didn't look away from the street, but the corners of his mouth tipped up in the ghost of a smile. "I don't favor one color over the other, in general, but red is your color, and I like its symbolic value as well."

"Red like blood," I said.

"Yes. It's always good to unsettle people."

I didn't say that he didn't need me at his side wearing a blood red dress to unsettle people. Nino was unsettling on his own, and he knew it.

Two hours later, I was dressed in the knee-length skin tight dress and matching blood red heels. I wore my hair down because it made me feel less exposed, and I preferred to have my neck covered.

Nino was waiting for me downstairs, leaning against my piano, dressed in all black, as usual. The fitted dress shirt and tight pants fit him like a glove. He wore his hair down for once, but it was slicked back. His eyes followed me as I descended the stairs. I took his outstretched hand, and his thumb found my wrist as he leaned close.

For a heartbeat, I was sure he'd kiss me, and my lips parted in a mix of anticipation and nerves, but he leaned toward my ear and whispered, "Tonight people will start talking about another Falcone. The lady in red."

I shivered, my eyelashes fluttering at the feel of his warm breath on my ear and his scent filling my nose. Then he pulled back but didn't release my wrist.

"Ready?" he asked in a low voice, and for some reason he made it sound as if he wasn't referring to going to dinner.

I gave a mute nod, trying to gather my wits about me. Nino led me into the main part of the mansion. Remo was sitting on the sofa, his laptop in front of him. His eyes moved up when we entered, and they locked on me. I didn't move.

Nino's grip on my wrist tightened, and his thumb brushed my skin lightly. "We'll be going for dinner now."

Remo nodded, his lips pulling wide. "Blood red. Good choice." They exchanged a look. "You look good enough to devour," he said to me, and my heart rate quadrupled.

"Thanks," I barely got out.

Nino pulled me outside toward his car. "Remo is no danger for you, Kiara. Trust me on that. His words are meant to unsettle. It's how he is. But you are mine and that makes you off-limits. Remo would never lay a hand on you. Never."

"You trust him?" I asked as I settled into the passenger seat.

"I trust him absolutely. With my life. With yours."

"Okay," I said, trying to share his confidence that Remo would protect me. He had protected me from Durant on my wedding day, but with Remo there really was no telling what he'd do.

Every table in the restaurant was occupied when we arrived, but the manager greeted us personally. He shook Nino's hand and bowed his head slightly before turning to me. I held my hand out with a smile. He hesitated briefly, but after Nino inclined his head, he took it and kissed the back of my hand. "Your wife is stunning, Mr. Falcone."

"She is," Nino drawled.

People at the surrounding tables were throwing veiled glances at us, and as the manager led us to our table with a stunning view over the Strip, they began whispering.

My cheeks felt hot when I sank down into the chair the manager held out for me. Nino seemed completely unfazed by the force of attention. He regarded me over the menu. "You look flustered."

I laughed. "I am. Everyone's talking about us."

Nino shrugged. "Let them talk. I'd be more worried if they didn't."

"Do you never wish to blend in, to walk the streets unnoticed?"

Nino lowered the menu, a hard look on his face. "My brothers and I were in hiding for a while when our family was hunting us down. We fought to get back what was ours. We killed and we bled for our birthright. We tore Las Vegas from the bleeding hands of unworthy men. We fought for the spotlight. We are done hiding."

The waiter brought us our wine at that moment. A blood red Shiraz. Nino raised his glass with a strange smile. It was so very difficult to read him. "To a place in the spotlight. No hiding ever again, Kiara."

I clanged my glass against his and took a deep gulp. "No hiding ever again."

The waiter arrived with the appetizers a second later. Everything was delicious, spicy, and extravagant. Nino was easy to talk to. I could have listened to him answering my questions about Las Vegas history all night.

He knew everything. Eventually, more personal questions crossed my mind. "Why did your father send you to boarding school in England? Most Made Men keep their sons close because they want to teach them everything they need to know to become Made Men themselves."

The mentioning of Benedetto Falcone brought an immediate change to Nino's body language. When before he had been relaxed, his shoulders now tensed considerably and his expression turned colder. "Our father didn't want Remo and me under his roof, and he knew he didn't have to prepare us for becoming Camorrista anymore."

"But you were twelve and fourteen at the time, and your brothers were even younger."

Nino smiled, and I took another deeper gulp of wine because his expression gave me the chills. "Our father knew Remo and I would have killed him if we stayed. Remo killed his first man three years before at eleven, and shortly before our father sent us away, I had killed my first man together with Remo. Our father knew he had no way of controlling us, so he sent us away. He knew we wouldn't leave without our brothers, so he sent Adamo and Savio away as well."

"That's horrible," I whispered.

Nino took a swig of his own wine. "It made us stronger, brought us closer. Regret over the past is wasted time."

I could feel the effects of the wine by now. Red wine was definitely stronger than the occasional glass of champagne or white wine I'd had in the past.

Nino tilted his head. "I think you've had enough wine."

I smiled. "You think?" For some reason, I took another gulp of the red liquid, and Nino shook his head, his mouth twitching.

"You will regret this tomorrow morning."

"I thought regret is wasted time," I said.

His mouth twitched again. "It is, but right now you still have the chance to prevent yourself from regretting anything."

"I think it's too late for that," I said. I felt hot and fuzzy. I'd probably have the headache of my lifetime in the morning.

Nino waved over the waiter and paid for our dinner. I got up and immediately realized that I was a bit tipsier than I thought, but I straightened my spine, not wanting to appear drunk in public. Nino wrapped an arm around my waist, and I was too grateful for its steadying effect to tense up at the contact. He led me out of the restaurant.

"Thank you for the lovely evening," I whispered before I plopped down in the car seat with less grace than intended.

"It was surprisingly pleasant," Nino agreed, and I burst out laughing. I couldn't help it. The wine had loosened my control.

Nino raised his eyebrows and closed the door. I leaned against the window, closing my eyes.

I woke with my head against something hot and hard. My body stiffened when I realized I was in someone's arms, being carried.

"Shh, Kiara. You are safe."

I peered up at Nino's calm face and forced my body to relax in his hold. "Where are we?" I asked groggily. My brain felt foggy.

"At home."

It took me an embarrassingly long time to figure out what he meant. Then I recognized our bedroom. He set me down in the center of the room. "Why don't you get ready for bed?"

I nodded and immediately regretted the motion. Nino gripped my hip to steady me. "Can you do this?"

"Yes," I said quickly because I didn't want Nino to undress me.

I wasn't sure how long it took me to get out of my dress and go through my evening routine, but it felt like forever before I finally lay down in bed.

Nino joined me shortly after. "Tell me if you're going to be sick." He touched my forehead with his palm, and I leaned in to the touch, but then he dropped his arm. He stretched out on his back beside me, and I scooted closer, reaching for his arm. My fingertips curiously traced the tattoo of a shadowy figure amidst surging flames. When my eyes managed to focus, I realized a name was written in the flames. It was small and you had to take a closer look to distinguish it from the fire. Remo.

"You have Remo's name tattooed on your arm."

Nino regarded me without a flicker of emotion. "I have Savio's and Adamo's name tattooed on my other arm."

"Why is he burning?"

"Because he burned for me," Nino said quietly.

I searched his face but could tell he wasn't going to tell me more. My fingertips followed the flames down to his wrist. I frowned when I felt something rigid under my fingertips. I turned his arm slightly so I could see his forearm. Under his Camorra tattoo, which was surrounded my flames as well, a long thin scar ran along his vein. I looked up at him, and he stared right back. I didn't dare ask because for once his eyes didn't appear emotionless at all.

I stroked the scar lightly. "Does it bother you if I touch you like this?" I asked in the barest of whispers.

"Your touch doesn't bother me, Kiara."

I wished he could touch me like that without my body wrenching me back into the past, without my fears taking control. "I wish … I wish I could be touched without fear."

"Eventually you will. You will kill the part of your uncle I couldn't kill for you."

He sounded absolutely sure as if it wasn't a matter of if but when. And because this was Nino Falcone, and maybe because I was drunk, I believed him.

FIFTEEN

Kiara

NINO STIRRED BESIDE ME, AND MY EYES PEELED OPEN. JUST LIKE I HAD the last few mornings since our dinner, I was snuggled up to him at night and wedged myself under his arm, my head in the crook of his neck, my knees pressed up against his side. His warmth and comforting scent wrapped around me and managed to banish the nightmares.

"Sorry," I murmured like I did every morning because I was fairly sure that the position couldn't be comfortable for Nino, but he never pushed me away. I sat up, freeing his arm.

"Your subconscious seeks protection at night, and I can provide it," he said with a shrug as he stood. The tight briefs did nothing to hide the outline of him.

I forced my eyes away from it, my heart thudding faster. He grabbed his swim trunks and went into the bathroom to change, but he didn't close the door. It was only for my benefit that he didn't undress in the bedroom. I had considered telling him that I could deal with his nakedness, but every time I was on the verge of saying those words, my courage left me.

Getting up as well, I grabbed my satin dressing gown. It wasn't because it was cold but because I felt uncomfortable walking around the house in only my nightgown.

Nino returned and opened the door for me. Grabbing my book from the nightstand, I followed him in silence down the stairs and out through the French doors. It was already warm outside. I settled on the lounge chair close to the pool and opened my book, but my eyes weren't drawn to the letters on the page. Instead, I watched as Nino stepped up to the edge of the pool and dove in, his muscles flexing as he did.

He swam his laps in the pool, and I observed him over my book from my spot on the chair. Eventually, I had to remove my robe because the sun relentlessly beat down on me despite the early hour.

Sometimes I felt ridiculous for even bringing a book with me. I hardly ever read a word. My gaze was drawn to the man in the water. The book was like my safety shield because I was too cowardly to admit that I enjoyed seeing Nino— and definitely too terrified of him finding out that I did.

After thirty minutes, he swam over to the ladder and climbed out. Water dripped off him and down his sculpted body. My eyes trailed from his muscled shoulders, down to his eight-pack and his narrow hips to his muscled thighs. His tight swim trunks hardly hid his body, and I could see the outline of him beneath the wet fabric again. The horrid tattoos, with their flames, agonizing faces, and words of pain and blood that ran from his forearms up over his shoulders down to his pecs and around to his shoulder blades didn't scare me any more like they had done in the beginning. Nino was a piece of art.

His movements were unhurried and exact as he rubbed himself dry. I couldn't take my eyes off him. His cool, gray eyes met mine, and I sucked in a sharp breath and quickly looked back down on my book. When his shadow fell over me, I had no choice but to stop pretending I was reading. I hadn't paid attention to my book in a while.

"You pretend to read but you watch me every morning," he said. There was no judgment in his voice.

I wasn't sure what to say. Embarrassment crawled up my neck. "I—I didn't..." I began to protest but upon raising my head, his expression silenced me. He knew I'd been watching him. Of course he'd noticed. This was a man who had been raised to watch his surroundings. Denying it would have been ridiculous.

"You can watch. You are my wife," he said. He tilted his head down, his eyes searching my face, and it felt like he could read my every thought. A few distracting droplets of water trailed down his beautiful face. What millions of male models probably had to practice for years, that cool, otherworldly expression, came naturally to him. "But I wonder why you do it. I thought my body scared you."

It still did. Nino oozed strength. But fear had become a very small part of what I felt when I watched him. There was also that flicker of curiosity in the pit of my stomach and the burst of warmth deep inside of me when he moved in a way that accentuated his muscles.

I put down my book on the small side table, not sure how to say what I wanted to say and not sure I should even consider saying it. Some doors should stay closed. But what was holding me back—and would perhaps always hold me back *if I let it*—was something forced upon me in the past, something I wanted to be freed of.

"Sometimes I wonder how it would be to be more like husband and wife," I admitted despite the heat in my cheeks, despite the spike of fear and worry about Nino's reaction. Falcone or not, he had never given me reason to be truly fearful of him.

"You mean in a physical sense?" Nino asked in a low voice. There was the hint of something in his tone that I couldn't place, but as usual, his face didn't reveal anything.

I nodded, releasing a tense breath. I hadn't thought I'd dare admit it, but Nino was always in control. I didn't have to fear an emotional outburst from him. Sometimes I felt like I didn't have to fear him at all.

He put down the towel, allowing me to view the length of him. I followed the invitation and slowly trailed my gaze over every inch of him. He didn't move, but his stare was an insistent presence on my skin. "We could explore the physical options of our relationship, if you like. To be honest, I want you."

He'd told me so before, but it still scared me. I glanced down at my hands, fumbling with the hem of my nightgown. Only one man had ever wanted me, and he'd taken what he wanted without asking. Nino wasn't like that. He could have had me on our wedding night and every night since. There was certainly nobody who could have stopped him, least of all me.

"What are you thinking?" he asked.

I sighed. "I'm scared."

"Did I give you reason to be scared?"

I looked back up at his attentive face. "No, but I'm scared because you want me, and because I want you, but I don't know if I can do it."

"We can set limits, and we can go step by step." He paused, his expression becoming contemplative. "If my physical strength unsettles you, we could try to have me restrained. I don't mind."

My mouth opened in shock. "You mean have you tied up?" Images of Nino with silk ties bound to the headboard entered my mind and almost had me laughing out loud. It seemed impossible that a man like him would suggest something like that.

Nino nodded. "That way you'd be free to explore without having to fear me."

"But then I would have to lead."

"Isn't that what you'd prefer, given your past experiences? I have no trouble being dominant, but I doubt you'd react well to it."

I wasn't sure what to do. It seemed like the perfect solution, but it still terrified me, only now for a different reason.

"Have you ever reached climax?" he asked quietly, still staring at me with his quiet scrutiny.

My eyes widened, and I gave a jerky shake of my head. My stomach plunged into an abyss as I remembered how it had felt to have *him* in me. "All I felt was pain … and shame."

He lightly grazed my shoulder, the touch warm and gentle. How could he always be so warm when his face was so beautifully cold? "I didn't mean when you were raped. I mean later. Did you ever touch yourself and feel good?"

I bit my lip, trying to shake off the memories and focus on the present. "Not really. I tried to touch myself a few times, but it felt wrong."

Nino surprised me when he perched on the edge of the lounge chair, his bare back brushing my naked calves. I didn't pull away, and I had a feeling it was an attempt for him to see if I could stand his closeness. "It would be good if you explored your body and figured out what you like and conditioned your brain to realize that sexual touch can be very pleasurable."

My face became impossibly hot, even when Nino looked as if we were talking about what we'd have for dinner tonight.

"I'm not sure my body is capable of finding anything *pleasurable*," I whispered.

Nino angled his body to the side and slowly reached for my ankle. I tensed briefly, more out of confusion than anything else. He paused, his eyes narrowing, and when I relaxed, his fingers brushed my ankle before he cupped my heel. He began to apply light pressure with his fingers as he stroked the underside of my calf and looked into my eyes. His fingers never reached higher than my calf, but the touch seemed to send tingles up my knee, my thigh, and straight to my core.

My eyes wandered over to Nino as he stroked me, over his strong arms, his muscled chest, and his ripped stomach. After a while, my breathing picked up, and the tingling increased until I could feel wetness gather between my legs. Startled, I rocked my hips lightly.

Nino let go of my calf, his mouth curling at the corner. "I think your body will adjust well to pleasure."

My cheeks heated even more, but more than embarrassment, I felt relief. Nino swallowed once before he murmured, "Now that your body is already aroused, it would make sense for you to explore yourself."

"You want me to touch myself?"

"Yes," he rasped. "Not here. Somewhere private, where you feel relaxed. I would recommend you focus on your clit at first. Try to rub it lightly with two fingers, and if you feel close to release, you can try to dip a bit lower and give your labia some attention. That's a spot many women are very sensitive, some even favor it over their clit. I don't think you will feel comfortable with a finger inside you yet, but it would add to the overall pleasure."

My center had become warmer and even wetter, hearing his deep voice.

"It would also help if you imagine something that arouses you."

"You," I burst out, feeling suddenly emboldened.

Nino heaved a deep breath and something in his eyes shifted. "If that helps, yes. Imagine me." His voice had dropped lower than ever before, and a slight stiffness had taken hold of his upper body. Confused, I was about to ask if I had offended him somehow when I registered the way his swim trunks tented.

I sucked in a breath. A flicker of fear coursed through me, but I was far more curious than afraid.

"I told you I desire you," he murmured. "And if you want to explore physical options, you'll have to get over your fear of my erection."

"I'm not scared," I said then amended my words because of his no lying rule. "Mostly."

He rose to his feet, and again, my eyes were drawn to his groin area. "Why don't you go into our bedroom and do what I suggested and find some relief?"

"What about you?"

"I'm going to seek relief as well," he said matter-of-factly.

Would you prefer if I sated my sexual drive somewhere else? I'd said yes on our wedding night.

"Where?" I asked.

He didn't say anything, only watched me with cold intensity.

I stood as well because it made me feel stronger, even if Nino still towered a head over me. "I don't want you to seek out other women anymore."

There. I said it. And relief washed over me. It had bothered me for a while, ever since I realized I wanted this marriage to be more than about necessity. I wasn't sure how they handled things here in Las Vegas, if maybe he never meant to be faithful, if he expected to keep sleeping around simply because he could, but it wasn't something I could ever accept if we really moved our relationship to a physical level.

Nino regarded me. "So you want me to seek you out to satisfy my sexual needs?" His voice held a strange note, and he took a step toward me.

There was the hint of curiosity in his eyes. This was him conducting an experiment, I realized. I'd learned to read him much better. I stood my ground and didn't back away. He moved even closer until I could almost feel the heat radiating off his body. He wasn't touching me.

"Eventually, yes," I said quietly. "Obviously I'm not able to do it yet." To be honest, I wasn't sure I'd ever be able to do it, but I wanted to.

"So until you feel ready, you suggest I get myself off with my own hands?"

I frowned. Was he mocking me? Or being serious? It was so hard to tell because he's said it dryly, without the hint of emotion. Suddenly, I felt foolish for having brought up the matter. This was Las Vegas, he was a Falcone, and despite his consideration toward me so far, he was still a man used to having women, money, and power at his disposal. Why should he give up one for me? I meant nothing to him. I was a pawn in this game for power.

I looked away, unable to bear his cold beauty. Turning around, I was about to leave when he stepped in my way. My eyes flew back up to him.

"Answer me, Kiara. Is that what you suggest?"

Sighing, I nodded. "I know how things are. I know your clubs are filled with willing women, but yes, I want you to be faithful to me. I can't explore physical closeness with you as long as you see other women."

"You realize that you can't explore your sexuality with anyone but me."

"Is that so?" I wasn't sure why I said that.

And for once, Nino let his expression become the one most people knew, one of dominance and suppressed violence. "It is. I won't ever push you past your boundaries, but just because I haven't claimed your body with my cock yet doesn't mean I haven't laid claim on you. You are mine. Mine alone. And for as long as I live, no one will touch you but me."

It was the least restrained I'd ever seen him, and it reminded me of the man he really was. I felt overwhelmed and on the verge of taking flight.

Nino let out a harsh breath and took a step back from me then sank down on the chair.

I blinked. Was he making himself small on purpose? He was watching me closely.

"Better?" he asked quietly, in control again.

"Yes."

"I didn't want to scare you."

"Didn't we agree on no lies?" I asked teasingly.

Nino's mouth twitched. "We did. And you are right to some extent. I knew you'd yield to my view of things if I exerted dominance, and given your history, I could foresee how it would make you feel. But it wasn't a conscious decision to scare you."

"Okay."

His brows pulled together. "When I first suggested satisfying my sexual drive elsewhere, you were relieved."

Back to the topic at hand. Nino never let himself be distracted.

"I was, but I don't want that anymore. I want us to have a real marriage."

"Isn't this a real marriage? It's official, after all."

I shook my head. "That's not what I mean. I want a normal marriage. For me that means being faithful and being intimate only with your partner. It means taking care of each other, showing affection, trying to love each other." The last slipped out because it was something I wanted deep down inside.

Nino pushed to his feet again and moved closer. "I can be faithful and I can show you affection …"

"But you can't love, I know."

Nino startled me by cupping my cheeks, his eyes warmer, his expression softer than ever before. "I can simulate emotions very well, Kiara. If it helps you feel more comfortable, I can fake affection and even love."

I peered up at him. Without his words, I would have believed the tenderness on his face to be real. I swallowed hard. "Don't pretend to care for me. Don't lie."

His expression became one of cold beauty again, and my heart clenched tightly. "I want to take care of you, and even if I can't feel emotions, seeing them on your face, particularly happiness and joy, give me a certain level of satisfaction. I can't give you more than that."

"Okay," I whispered, because there was nothing else to say. It had to be enough. I'd expected so much less out of this union, and so much worse. I couldn't hold it against Nino that he couldn't feel.

"Would you like to go inside now?"

"I don't think I'm in the mood for exploring anymore," I said quietly.

He tilted his head. "I understand."

"Maybe later?" I asked quietly.

"Of course," he said. "How about I get dressed and we practice your shooting skills some more."

For him it was always easy to move on because no topic ever moved him so much his brain couldn't proceed, but I didn't want to make a bigger deal out of this than it was so I nodded.

He returned thirty minutes later in black pants and a black shirt, his go-to clothes. I had seen him in similar clothes so often before, and yet the sight got to me today. He looked tall and strong and graceful, and the tattoos on his arms created just the right contrast to his perfectly beautiful face.

Two guns hung from the holster strapped to his chest, but I knew he hid more weapons on his body. I had become a better shot over the course of our last few lessons, but today my concentration was frayed.

A few hours later, I sat in our living room and played the song I'd started work-ing on almost six weeks ago. It was a song that helped me deal with my mar-riage with Nino, helped me understand my feelings toward the man. The breeze streamed in through the windows, and I breathed deeply. I missed the scent of ocean in the air, but Las Vegas' warmth felt good. I didn't feel constantly cold anymore.

"What song is that?"

My fingers jerked against the keys and the piano released a low whine in response.

"Sorry, I didn't mean to startle you," Adamo said as he stepped into the room through the open French doors.

I relaxed and smiled. "It's okay. I startle too easily."

He shoved his hands into his pockets and nodded toward the piano. "You can keep playing. I like to listen."

Had he listened to me play before? I settled my fingers lightly on the keys and began where I'd left off when he'd startled me. He moved closer and propped up his elbows on the wing. A bruise bloomed on his left cheekbone, and his lip was busted. I didn't think I'd ever seen him without a busted lip.

"What happened to your face?"

"My brothers practice fighting with me."

"When will you be inducted?"

He looked down at his bloody knuckles. "In two months. August. On my fourteenth birthday."

"But you don't want to?"

Adamo shrugged. "I'm a Falcone. The Camorra is my destiny." His brows drew together. "But I don't want to do most of the things expected of me."

"Kill people."

"That," he agreed, a dark look passing over his face. "I already did. Kill someone. Shot him. I'm a good shot."

I nodded and stopped playing again.

"I don't enjoy killing, and I don't want to torture people or hurt women," he whispered.

"Then don't," I said and realized how stupid I was. Adamo couldn't choose his path, not as others could.

He pressed out a laugh. "I have to."

"What would you rather do?"

His eyes lit up. "Race cars."

"You can drive a car?"

"Remo let me drive his car when I was eleven, and I managed to sneak into a few races since then. I crashed two of his cars. He was majorly pissed, and now he keeps a closer eye on me so I can't do it anymore."

"Is that why you are sulking around the gardens and listening to me play?" I asked with a smile.

"I'm supposed to watch you."

I burst out laughing then quieted at the indignant look on his face. I still found it funny that the youngest Falcone was supposed to be my bodyguard. "Sorry."

"I'm a good shot and a decent fighter, and it's not like someone is going to attack our mansion. It's the safest place in Vegas."

"Because people are terrified of Remo."

"And Nino," Adamo added then curled his lips in disgust. "Since he fought his first official cage fight, Savio's even cockier than before. He thinks he's as scary as them, but he's not. Not even close."

"Agreed. Nobody does scary as well as Remo and Nino," I said. Luca had been terrifying, but maybe because I'd known him from a young age, I could deal with his brand of scary better than that of the Falcones.

"Yeah," Adamo murmured and then became serious, his brown eyes hesitant. "Is Nino nice to you?"

I pursed my lips. Nice wasn't really a term I'd use for Nino. "He is …"

"Present," Nino drawled, making me jump and Adamo as well.

I turned toward his voice. He was leaning in the doorway, tall and cold, muscled arms crossed over his chest. For once he wore a shirt with the sleeves rolled up, revealing his tattoos.

"You should be doing homework or work on your knife skills," Nino said, pushing off the wall and striding toward us.

Adamo jutted his chin out, but he didn't protest. "Bye, Kiara," he muttered before he walked out of the French doors.

Nino propped his hip up against the piano as he always did, and my eyes took in the way his pants accentuated his muscled legs, the way his shirt clung to his torso. "And am I being *nice* to you?"

I nodded, but I couldn't stop looking at him and remembering his suggestion from this morning.

"Would you like to go to our bedroom and explore?" he asked calmly.

Despite the heat in my cheeks, I nodded. Nino straightened and held out his hand for me to take, and I did as always. His fingers curled lightly around me but in a way that suggested I could pull away any time. With a deep breath, I got up from the bench, startling slightly as his thumb pressed against my wrist. Why did he always do that?

My eyes trailed over his muscular, inked forearm as I followed him upstairs. The moment we stepped into our bedroom and my eyes landed on our bed, my pulse began racing in my veins.

Nino peered down at me. "Fear or arousal ... or both?"

"What?" I asked confused.

He pressed his thumb against my wrist. "Your pulse picked up."

"That's why you always touch me there?"

"It's a good indicator of your mood and helps me figure out your emotions combined with your expression and breathing."

I laughed then quieted when he led me closer to the bed. Nino raised one eyebrow.

"Both," I admitted.

He sank down on the bed, tugging me along so I'd stand before him. "It would be good if we could manage to reduce one and increase the other."

"Which one would you like to increase?" I said in the same scientific tone as he had used.

His mouth twitched. "Well," he began in a low voice. "Fear would be easier to increase than arousal with you being you and me being me, but I prefer difficult tasks. Which do you prefer?" He raised my hand to his lips very slowly, his eyes never leaving my face, and pressed an open-mouthed kiss to my pulse-point then trailed his tongue over it.

A small shiver passed down my spine. How was it possible I could feel that all the way between my legs?

He regarded me intently. "Fear?"

I shook my head, my tongue heavy.

"Both?"

I considered that and gave a hesitant shake of my head.

Nino's eyes became even more intent. "Are you sure?"

I wasn't because he evoked sensations in my body I'd never felt, but the tingling between my legs had increased, and I felt hot and wet down there. "No."

Nino nodded. "Let's try to change that. Okay?"

Good Lord, he sounded so sure of himself, as if he just knew he would make it good for me.

Nino

Kiara's pulse rate spiked again. "Okay."

Releasing her hand, I reached for the top drawer of my nightstand and pulled out the handcuffs I'd stored there.

Kiara released a choked laugh. A quick scan of her face told me she was nervous.

"I don't usually have cuffs in my drawer," I said before she could draw conclusions that would unsettle her. I'd never seen the appeal to restrain myself like that and preferred to dominate in bed, so I never allowed a woman to do it, and the other way around would have made as little sense because I didn't need cuffs to restrain anyone. "I put them there after we talked this morning."

Kiara bit her lip, but she didn't react in any other way.

"I can cuff one of my hands to the headboard. What do you say? That would give you a sense of safety, don't you think?"

"I think so," she said hesitantly.

"Would you like me to undress?"

She shook her head quickly. "No."

I regarded her closely. "Kiara. We don't have to do this."

"I want to. I'm just a bit overwhelmed by the situation that's all."

I nodded and moved back on the bed until my back rested against the headboard and then cuffed my left hand to it.

Kiara hadn't moved from her spot.

"What would you like to do first?"

She flushed, tugging a strand of hair behind her ear. "I don't know. What would you suggest?"

She was sending out mixed signals. On one hand she was scared of losing control, but on the other hand she needed me to take control. "How about we start with kissing?"

Her eyes darted to my lips, the blush on her cheeks darkening as she nodded. She climbed on the bed. I tried to sit as relaxed as possible, my legs crossed at the ankles and my unrestrained arm lying in my lap while I watched her. Her eyes on my face, she moved closer until she was kneeling beside me, her knees pressing up against my hip.

I didn't move.

She exhaled softly. "I've never kissed before."

"It's not difficult, Kiara, trust me."

She gave me a look I couldn't place. "Easy for you to say. How many women have you kissed?"

I couldn't see how that was of any relevance. "One hundred and twelve. I don't kiss every woman I fuck."

She choked. "You've slept with more than one hundred women?"

"Yes. I was a late bloomer in comparison to Remo and Savio. Had my first woman at almost fifteen."

"Then I had my first time before you," she said bitterly, swallowing hard and staring down at the bed.

I lifted my hand and nudged her chin up to see her expression. "You haven't had your first time yet. What you had doesn't count. What we are going to do has absolutely nothing to do with what you experienced."

Her eyes watered, and I dropped my hand, unsure if my words had upset her, but she scooted closer and hesitantly brought one hand up to my shoulder. "How can you say things that make me feel better when you don't even understand what I feel?"

"I'm stating facts. That's all."

She laughed. "*Facts.*" Then her eyes lowered to my mouth, and she licked her lips. I doubted she noticed, but the sight had an immediate effect on my cock.

"Are you going to kiss me?" I asked her.

She nodded but didn't move.

"Kiara, if you want to be in control, you actually have to take control." She was a woman I'd have pegged as the submissive type in bed, and under normal circumstances I'd have naturally taken the lead, but as long as she was caught in the memories of her rape that would have ended badly.

She finally leaned forward and pressed her lips to mine, eyes closing. I would have preferred for her to keep them open so I had a chance of reading her, yet as it was I had no choice but to trust she'd pull back if something unsettled her.

Her lips were very soft and the pressure was light, almost nonexistent like our kiss on our wedding day. Resisting the urge to pull her closer and show her how good kissing could feel, I let her be in control. After a moment, she pulled back with a frown, her skin reddening. "This feels odd because you aren't moving."

"I wanted to let you be in control."

"It's okay if you take the initiative and lead because you know what to do and I don't, and it's making me nervous."

I regarded her, not exactly sure what she needed me to do. "We had me restrained so you'd feel in control."

"Yes, and that's okay, but I want you to kiss me as you normally would."

"Normally, I lead."

She bit her lip again. Nerves. I reached for her wrist and pressed my thumb against it. She huffed out laughter. "You can lead … I mean, you can lead without being all dominant and rough."

"I won't be rough with you, Kiara. And if you ever feel like I'm being too dominant, you tell me and I will adapt my behavior, all right?"

She smiled slightly, but her pulse spiked up anyway. She was very difficult to read. "Can we try again?"

"Of course. I'm going to touch your back."

Again a spike in her pulse rate. I released her wrist and put my hand on her lower back and began rubbing it lightly with my thumb. Her cheeks were flushed, and she was soft under my touch. She leaned slightly forward until her lips almost touched mine.

Deciding to see if me taking lead would work, I caught her lips with mine, applying more pressure than she had and nudged her lips with my tongue. She parted them without hesitation and I dove in. Her taste and the soft warmth of her mouth went straight to my cock. She submitted to the kiss without hesitation, following my lead.

She yielded so easily to my demands, so readily, I knew she would continue to do so if we moved further, and it made me want to do just that, but I reined myself in.

I widened my strokes on her back, brushing over her spine. She made a small sound in the back of her throat, tightening her hold on my shoulder. Her other hand pressed up against my chest, grazing my nipple, and I kissed her a bit harder.

Moving my free hand up her back, I wanted to cup her head, but the moment I touched her neck and my fingers slid into her dark waves, she jerked back. "No," she whispered quickly.

I pulled my hand away, seeing the remnants of panic on her face. It wasn't a touch I'd considered problematic, so her reaction surprised me.

"Your hair?"

She gave a quick nod. "And my neck." She swallowed. "My uncle … he held me there … He held me down when he forced me to …" She looked at me with despair. I had no trouble reading it on her face, and I didn't have to touch her wrist to know her pulse was racing because she remembered how her bastard of an uncle had forced her to suck his cock when she was only a child. And once again, I wished I had prolonged his torture. He had suffered thoroughly under mine and Remo's hands, and yet it didn't seem enough.

"I understand," I said.

She shivered helplessly, and then she just fell forward, catching me by surprise as she pressed her face into the crook of my neck and began shaking. I touched her back and her shaking got worse. Then something wet hit my skin. She was crying.

"Kiara?"

She clung to my shoulders and I wrapped my free arm around her. She pressed even harder into me. I let her cry herself out. Maybe it would help her. Pulling back, she kissed me softly, her eyes probing as if she was searching for something. I returned the kiss, tasting her tears.

"I'm sorry," she said after a moment.

"For what?"

"For becoming emotional." She sighed and closed her eyes briefly. Then she opened them again and nodded toward the cuff. "Where's the key?"

"Drawer."

She leaned over me and gave me a look at her round, firm butt. My body definitely reacted strongly to her assets. She unlocked the handcuff. "I think I'm going to take a bath." I didn't stop her as she retreated into the bathroom.

Instead, I walked out and headed for our gaming room. Remo was there, sprawled out on the sofa, watching the latest cage fights in Roger's Arena.

He glanced toward me as I sank down on the armchair, reached for the bottle of bourbon on the table, and poured a glass.

Remo nodded toward my wrist, which had red marks from the metal cuffs. "What happened there? Already getting kinky with your wife?"

"Kiara's scared of my physical strength, so I cuffed myself to the bed."

Remo leaned back, eyebrows raised. "As if that would stop you."

"It wouldn't, but she feels safer, and that's what this is about. She needs to feel comfortable around me."

Remo narrowed his eyes. "So you still haven't fucked her?"

I took a sip of the bourbon. "We didn't progress beyond kissing, so no."

Remo was quiet for a moment, and that was usually never a good sign. "You have the patience of a saint. Do you want me to call some entertainment over?"

"I agreed to not seek out other women anymore."

Remo laughed. "Right." And then sobered. "You are being serious?"

"I am."

"Are you trying to become a straight-laced citizen?"

"I have no ambitions in that regard, no."

Remo shook his head. "First Fabiano, now you. Why's everyone becoming pussy-whipped?"

"Since I'm not getting any pussy, your term is misleading."

"Oh, fuck you, Nino. Don't be a fucking smartass. Do you really think you can make a marriage work? Even if you don't fuck other women, you won't be a caring husband and you know it."

I shrugged. "I know, but for now I'm going to give this a try and see where it takes me."

"So this is some kind of scientific experiment for you?"

"Maybe." It was something new, something I had no experience with and couldn't say how I'd deal with it long-term, but I was curious and Kiara wanted this marriage to be real.

SIXTEEN

Kiara

I COULDN'T SLEEP AFTER THE KISS. MY MIND REPLAYED IT. NINO'S MOUTH had been so warm and gentle. It was nothing like I'd imagined, nothing like I'd feared. He managed to surprise me every day and had done so since our wedding night.

The door creaked open and someone stepped in. Opening my eyes, I peered through the gap in the blankets. I had them pulled up to my ears because it made me feel safer that way. I left on the light in the bathroom because the dark still held power over me. I could see Nino's tall form in the warm glow.

My cheeks heated when his eyes settled on me. I'd fled into the bathroom after our kiss, not because of it, though. I had been embarrassed about breaking down and crying in Nino's arms. I needed time to get a grip on myself. For a man as controlled and emotionless as Nino, being married to me must be a particular difficult task for him. In the beginning, I was sure my marriage to Nino was punishment for my father's actions, but now I was fairly sure he was the one that could have made a better deal.

"It's late," he murmured.

"I can't sleep."

He nodded before he moved into the bathroom and closed the door. Barely any light spilled into the bedroom through the narrow gap beneath the door, but I focused my eyes on it and listened to the sound of running water.

After a few minutes, Nino came back out, dressed in briefs. I knew he preferred to sleep naked and now only wore clothes at night to set me at ease. Even in his own bed, he had to hold back on my account. He turned off the light in the bathroom and approached me in the dark.

My pulse quickened when the mattress dipped under his weight—but for much different reasons than it had in the past. What would it be like if I just leaned over and kissed him? No warnings, no handcuffs. Only my lips touching his, my body pressed against him. How would it feel to be free and act on my desires? How would it be not to be shackled by the past?

"Are you alright?" Nino drawled.

How could he know? He hadn't touched my wrist, so my pulse couldn't have given me away. "Why do you ask?"

"Because your breathing changed. That's usually a sign that you're unsettled by something. Is it because of our kiss?"

I hesitated, wondering what to say, but opted for the truth. "Yes."

"You changed your mind about the physical aspects of our marriage?"

I wished I knew what he was thinking. He said he wanted me, but maybe my kiss and the teary outburst afterward made him change his mind.

"No, I enjoyed our kiss," I admitted.

"Good."

That wasn't quite the answer I'd hoped for. Had he enjoyed it as well? Did he want to kiss me again?

"Would you like to kiss again?"

It was sometimes scary how easily he could read me, even in the dark, even without understanding my emotions. The inner workings of Nino's brain were completely inexplicable to me. "What do you want?"

He was quiet. "In terms of kissing or in general?"

"In general," I whispered, my stomach tightening with nerves.

"Give me your wrist," he said, and I complied. His thumb pressed against my pulse point, and I had to stifle laughter. It quickly died down when he started to speak in that low, deep voice.

"I want *you* in every regard. I want to kiss you, of course. I want to show you pleasure, Kiara." My pulse galloped with every word. "I want to give you an orgasm with my mouth and my fingers. I want to taste you everywhere, and I want to … sleep with you."

I could tell he had wanted to use a different term, but he chose to soften his words for my benefit. My chest warmed at his consideration. Despite who he was, Nino would always represent safety for me.

"I know every spot on your body that will increase your arousal. If you let me, I'll make you come again and again."

I swallowed audibly. My core seemed to liquefy, throbbing with a need I hardly understood.

He tapped my wrist. "Fear?"

I laughed nervously because right now fear was only a small flicker in the corners of my consciousness. "No," I admitted in the softest whisper.

Nino waited patiently for me to say more. As my eyes grew used to the dark, I could make out the outline of his strong shoulders. He was facing me, breathing calmly, relaxed. Those words … didn't they affect him?

"Arousal?"

I gave a nod, not sure if he could see it.

"Good," came his low voice.

I shivered. "And you?"

"Are you asking if I'm aroused?"

I nodded.

"I am," he said.

My pulse really started racing. "Kiara?"

"Both," I said quickly, because I was equally scared and aroused by his admittance.

"What can I do to banish your fear?"

"Nothing," I said, because deep down I knew it was a battle I had to fight on my own. "But I want to try something."

"Okay," he said slowly.

"Can we kiss without you being restrained?"

"Of course. Now?"

"Yeah," I said quietly and scooted a bit closer to him until his warm breath fanned over my face and the sheer volume of heat radiating from his body told me how big he was, how much taller and stronger.

I caught the hint of alcohol on his breath, something smoky and spicy. "You smell like … bourbon?"

"I had a glass," he said. "But you don't have to be concerned. It's not enough to lower my inhibitions. Not even close."

"I'm not concerned about that." I leaned closer until his face hovered right in front of me, and then I bridged the remaining distance between us and pressed my lips to his. He waited a couple of seconds before he increased the pressure, and his tongue slipped between my lips, exploring my mouth. His fingertips moved up from my wrist, stroking the soft skin of my forearm, the crook of my elbow, then a little higher before trailing back down. Finally, his thumb pressed against my wrist again.

He did it because he needed it to read me better, to make sure he noticed when I felt overwhelmed or scared. That realization did a strange thing to my heart.

We kissed for a long time, and I started to feel hot between my legs. Nino's kisses were incredible, overwhelming; he led easily without making me feel like I was under his control. His breathing deepened ever so slightly as his mouth slid over mine, and the friction sent a new surge of heat through my core. I squirmed, pressing my thighs together. If Nino noticed, he didn't react, but his grip on my wrist tightened the slightest bit.

I put my free hand up against his naked chest and felt his muscles flex beneath my fingertips. His skin was covered with scars, and I began tracing them curiously until I accidentally grazed over his nipple. He groaned into my mouth, jerking slightly, and the motion caused something hard to dig into my thigh.

I froze against him. Fear and my own arousal battled within my body. He had told me he was aroused, but feeling it made things more real.

He stopped kissing me and took a deep breath. "Tell me how you feel."

"I'm okay."

"That's not a feeling."

"I'm feeling okay," I said again with more force. "Only startled."

"Maybe we should stop, then."

I didn't want to stop, but maybe Nino was right. Even if my body screamed for more, I wasn't sure if I could actually handle it. I felt … overwhelmed again. "You're right."

He released my wrist and rolled over onto his back, farther away from me. A gaping hole opened in my stomach. I swallowed hard once then a second time. I knew I told Nino I didn't need him to fake affection, but maybe I was wrong.

Nino's head shifted toward me. "You are upset again."

I wasn't sure how he'd noticed this time. Maybe my breathing had changed again.

"I … I changed my mind about the simulated affection." I was treading across a dangerous path. Living a lie wasn't something I wanted to do, but with Nino it was all I could have. Maybe simulated affection was better than nothing.

"Okay," he said quietly. He angled his body toward me. "Would you like to fall asleep in my arms?"

My throat tightened. I didn't say anything and moved closer to him. He wrapped an arm around my shoulder and pulled me against him. His touch was light, never like a cage, always considerate. Stupid tears gathered in my eyes as I rested my cheek against his strong chest. His heart beat a calm rhythm. Did it ever speed up? Did it ever clench when he looked at me like mine sometimes did when I looked at him or like it had when I realized he always touched my wrist to make sure I was all right.

When I woke the next morning, Nino was gone. It was already past nine, so I missed watching him do laps in the pool. I went through my morning routine, put on shorts and a simple top, and headed downstairs. I walked through the main part of the house and into the kitchen. After making myself a quick breakfast of porridge, I decided to eat it outside so I could enjoy the beautiful weather. As I headed outside, the sound of a video game drew me into the gaming room. Adamo was in there again, focusing on a car race on the ginormous screen on the wall.

"Hey, Kiara," he said without looking away from the game. "Fabiano brought over Leona this morning. She's sunbathing in the garden."

"Why didn't anyone tell me?"

He gave me a strange look.

I smiled at him. "Never mind. Enjoy your game." I hurried out of the French doors and down the small path to the swimming pool and lounge chairs. Just as Adamo had said, Leona was stretched out on one of them, reading a book. Something about the history of the Supreme Court. She glanced up as I approached, smiling, and put the book down on the table beside her.

"That doesn't look like light reading," I said, taking a seat on the chair across from her, my bowl of porridge wedged between my thighs.

"It's not, but I want to prepare for college. I'm starting in a few months, and I don't want to be completely clueless. What about you? Have you considered going to college?"

I frowned. I was raised to become a wife and mother. "To be honest, I've always only wanted to be a mother," I said quietly. "I want a family to take care of. Boisterous kids that fill the house with life and laughter." Maybe it was something I longed for because I never had a family like that. Unconditional love was something only children could offer in our world.

"That's okay," Leona said with a smile. Then her brows dipped in thought.

"What?"

"I'm trying to imagine Nino as a father and Remo as an uncle…" she shook her head "…but I just can't. They aren't really the family type. I mean they are close as brothers, but otherwise … no."

I knew what she meant. Nino and his brothers were more than close. They were a unit. *It's us against the world.* He'd probably want to keep living with them even if we had kids. Boisterous, loud-mouthed kids around Remo? That was definitely something that made me wary. I shrugged.

"It's not like we'll have kids any time soon." I pointed at my porridge. "Would you like some as well? I made more than I can eat."

"I already had breakfast with Fabiano."

I nodded and ate a spoonful. For some reason I wasn't hungry anymore.

"How are things between you and Nino going?"

My cheeks heated as I tried to form a reply. "Better than I thought they would. He is being very considerate."

Leona's eyes widened. "Really?"

I giggled at her expression. "Really. I mean, it's obviously not easy for him to understand my emotions, but he does his best and that's all I can ask for."

"I admire your strength. To be honest, Nino scares me shitless, almost as much as Remo."

I smiled because I understood her so well. "I know. And Remo still does. I don't think that will ever change. There's something so … unhinged about him."

"Unhinged is a bit of an understatement," Leona said. "The way he rules over Vegas …" She sighed.

"I'm not married to him. That's a blessing, I suppose."

"I really hope he never finds a poor woman he wants to marry."

I couldn't imagine Remo settling down for a woman. Perhaps it would just be for the thrill of the conquest or that satisfaction of breaking her. I shuddered and pushed any thought of him aside. "Your Fabiano isn't any less scary than Nino. You haven't even grown up around men like him, yet you are with him. He is the *Enforcer*."

Leona sat up, her expression thoughtful. "I know what he does is, what they all do is wrong, but I love him. I can't help it. No one has ever been good to me, but he is. Maybe I'm selfish."

I put down my bowl of porridge and reached for her hand, squeezing it. "You don't have to justify your love. It's something pure and beautiful, and I'm sure everything happens for a reason. Sometimes we just don't understand why."

Her blue eyes searched mine. "What do you feel for Nino?"

I wasn't sure. Gratefulness. Affection. And sometimes something warmer and deeper that scared me. "Falling in love with Nino would be foolish. He can't return my feelings no matter what they are."

"Love tends to turn us into fools," Leona said quietly, but she dropped the subject and reclined on the lounge chair.

I decided to stretch out as well, even if I wasn't wearing a bathing suit like Leona. Thinking about my situation, I had no intention of becoming that kind of fool. Falling in love with someone without emotions would be a horrible mistake.

In the early evening, I was back at the piano, tinkering with my song, when Nino walked in. My fingers stumbled over the next few notes. He was dressed in only fight boxers, his skin covered in a fine sheen of sweat that made his tattoos stand out even more. My eyes trailed down his ripped stomach then followed over to his muscled arms and his strong hands wrapped in white tape. They were red in places. I quickly tore my eyes away, too late of course, because Nino regarded me with a knowing expression. Thankfully, he didn't say anything.

"Remo's ordering pizza for us now. I'm taking a quick shower then we can head over."

"Sure," I said slowly. "I'm not sure Remo likes to have me around all the time when you have dinner." In the past few weeks, they had been increasingly busy planning their attack on the Outfit, so I often had dinner with Leona in our wing or even ate with Adamo, who wasn't involved in the Camorra's dealings yet. Nino had also taken me out to dinner twice. Thankfully, spending evenings with all of the Falcone brothers had been a rare event.

Nino tilted his head. "You are my wife. You are family. He can deal."

My eyes lowered to his chest again, wondering how it would feel to explore every inch of his skin with my fingertips. I'd only briefly touched his chest.

Something in Nino's expression shifted, and he prowled over to me. There really was no other way to describe his movements. He lowered himself to his haunches beside me so we were almost at eye level as I sat on the piano bench. My breath caught in my throat when his mouth curled into a smile and his eyes reflected warmth.

My God, he was so good at faking affection. Too good. This was going to be my downfall, I knew it, but I could not tell him to stop. The scent of him washed over me, manly sweat and something that was only Nino.

My breathing quickened and so did my pulse. Nino reached for my hand, which lay limply on my thigh, and pressed his thumb to my wrist. Then he brought it up to his face and pressed a kiss to my palm, his gray eyes on my face the entire time. And I stared at his face in turn. That beautiful face, always perfectly cold but now filled with consciously created warmth. Even though I knew this was a lie, a lie that could break me in the end, I leaned forward and kissed him because with him giving me that tender look, I needed to be closer.

He returned the kiss and touched my cheek with his calloused hand. Not wanting him to read what this did to me, I closed my eyes. If I wanted this to work, I needed to either make peace with the truth that Nino was faking emotions for me or I would have to try to pretend they weren't faked. I knew the latter would be easier because Nino was so scarily good at simulating.

Pushing any thought out of my mind, I allowed myself to drown in Nino's kiss, in his closeness and scent, and my body sprang to life. When Nino pulled away eventually, my cheeks were flushed, and I was panting. His thumb was stroking my pulse point lightly, and the small touch traveled through every part of my body. He wasn't only good at simulating emotions, he was good at this as well. Genius and monster.

"We can do some more exploring after dinner if you like?" His voice was deep and raspy.

I gave a small nod, not trusting my voice to come out as more than a squeak. Nino kissed my palm again before he stood, giving me a view of the bulge in his fight shorts, before he turned and headed upstairs to shower. My eyes followed his muscled, inked back, his narrow hips, and his firm butt.

I pressed shaking fingers to the piano keys. Where had I left of? I couldn't remember. Instead, I turned my current emotional state into music. It was fast and erratic, but eventually the melody mellowed out, and my heartbeat calmed. I found my way back to the song I'd been working on before Nino had arrived. With every passing minute, I relaxed further.

"You have been working on it for a while now," he commented. I jumped. As usual, he moved so quietly that I didn't hear him approach. Now he leaned against the wall, hands in his pockets. He was wearing a tight white T-shirt that accentuated his muscles and showed the dark outlines of his tattoos beneath.

"You recognize the melody?" I asked, surprised.

"I have good hearing and a good memory."

"Is there anything you're not good at?" I stood and moved over to him. His own eyes lingered on my bare legs, then moved higher, pausing briefly on my chest before they stopped on my face. Warmth flooded my body. It wasn't the first time I noticed him looking at me like that.

"A couple of things," he said quietly, holding out his hand. I slipped mine into his grasp without a second thought. "Come on. Remo will be intolerable if the pizza gets cold."

"Isn't he always?"

Nino's mouth twitched. "He'll be even more intolerable."

"We don't want that. One of these days, he'll make a widower out of you."

Nino's hand tightened around mine. "You are the safest woman in the city. Trust me."

As we headed into the main part of the mansion, I risked the occasional glance at his face. He didn't exactly look emotionless, more relaxed.

He glanced at me. "Everything okay?"

I nodded quickly, glad that we'd arrived in the gaming room where Savio and Remo were already waiting on us. As usual, dinner wouldn't take place in the dining room at a proper table but on the sofa with pizza cartons strewn haphazardly around the living room table.

A fight was playing on the big TV screen. Remo sat on one sofa and Savio on the other. Neither wore shirts. It was hot outside, but I really wished they had chosen to wear more than sweatpants. Unlike Nino, they didn't have any tattoos on their torsos, only the marking of the Camorra on their forearms and Remo's angel on his back.

They hadn't begun eating yet.

"Where's the kid? He's driving me up the wall," Remo muttered then shouted, "Adamo, get your fucking ass down here. Pizza's getting cold."

I had eaten more pizza in my marriage to Nino than in my entire life before him. Nino led me toward Remo's sofa, but thankfully he sank down beside his brother. The sofas were huge, so we didn't even have to sit very close, and yet sitting beside Remo would have been too much. Nino released my hand and grabbed a beer from the selection on the table.

I regarded the five extra-large pizzas. It was pretty clear which one was mine. Spinach, feta, tomatoes—the only one without any kind of meat.

Steps thundered down the stairs, and a moment later Adamo appeared in the living room. Without a greeting, he grabbed a piece of pizza, dropped down beside Savio, and began eating.

Remo shook his head but reached for a piece as well. They all shared pizzas, of course none of them touched mine. I gingerly picked up a slice then looked around for napkins that the delivery service usually packed but found none. "Do you have napkins?" I asked but got empty looks back.

"We have some in the bar, I believe," Nino said. He was about to get up, but I beat him to it. I turned to head for the bar.

"She's got a nice ass if she doesn't hide it under her clothes," Savio commented.

I stiffened but kept moving.

"Careful," Nino murmured in a voice that made the little hairs in my neck rise.

"She isn't one of our whores, Savio. She is Nino's, and you better remember it the next time you open your fucking mouth," Remo muttered.

"Fuck. Don't get your panties in a bunch," Savio said.

Relaxing, I found a handful of napkins next to a few dirty whisky glasses, picked them up, and headed back, hoping my cheeks weren't red. Nino's intent gaze traced my face as I sank down beside him. I put the napkins on the table then placed one on my lap before I grabbed my piece of pizza.

"Savio is sorry, you know? He's just a stupid idiot," Adamo said, catching my gaze across the table with a grin. I smiled back.

"Oh, shut up," Savio said.

I met his gaze. His dark eyes held wariness but also curiosity. He still regarded me as an intruder. I understood it. And other than Remo, he showed it openly. It was one of the few things that reminded me that he was two years younger than me.

Taking another bite of pizza, I was glad when the attention shifted back to the cage fight on the television screen, which I was trying to ignore. I knew Leona had worked there for a while, and I wondered how she could stand the violence.

"Where's Fabiano?" Adamo asked with a full mouth.

"With Leona," Nino said simply.

Savio rolled his eyes. "Pussy-whipped."

After my third piece, I was stuffed. More than half my pizza was left. The men had wolfed down every last morsel of their food, of course. "You can eat my pizza if you are still hungry," I suggested.

Four heads turned my way.

"There's nothing dead on it," Savio said.

"We can change that in a heartbeat," Nino said dryly.

"I'm sure there are a couple of limbs you don't need," Remo added, exchanging a smirk with Nino.

Savio snorted. "If anything's going on that pizza, it's Adamo's dick. He's not using it anyway."

Adamo flushed, glancing at me before scowling at his brother. They probably would have started fighting if I wasn't there.

"It's delicious. You don't need to add limbs or other body parts, believe me," I said before it got out of hand.

Nino shrugged and grabbed a piece then took a huge bite and gave a satisfied nod. "It's edible."

I huffed. Leaning back against the headrest, I curled my legs under me. Nino put his arm on the rest behind me. I scooted a bit closer to him until I was tucked against his side. His gray eyes paused on my face for a moment before he lowered his arm and put his hand on my hip.

"Why don't you eat meat?" Remo asked, reclining against the backrest, on his second piece of my vegetarian pizza. He looked fairly relaxed.

"I like animals," I said. I didn't want to argue with them about animal cruelty in meat factories because I doubted they would understand; they tortured humans on a daily basis, after all.

"I like them too. Better than most humans," Remo said with a shrug. "Doesn't mean I don't eat them."

"I prefer them in sausage form," Savio said with a grin, but he, too, ate a piece of my pizza and stretched out on the sofa, putting his bare feet on Adamo's legs, who in turn wrinkled his nose.

"Great, now I have to smell your feet all evening."

I couldn't help laughing. Nino gave me a look, but I couldn't read his expression. Remo, too, had his eyes on me, and for once he didn't look pissed or furious, but he, too, made it difficult for me to gauge his emotions.

"How about we watch this fight now?" Remo said after a moment and turned up the volume.

I risked a look at the screen, where a massive man with arms as thick as my thighs was beating up his opponent before throwing him into the cage. I shivered at the rattling of the cage and the drunken cheers of the crowd.

Nino reached for my wrist, never taking his eyes off the screen, and I stifled a smile, which died when the giant grabbed his opponent and smashed him down on his knee. The man's back gave a sickening crunch, and he fell to the ground motionless.

I flinched violently against Nino, and his arm tightened around me. "Is he … is he …?" I swallowed, my pulse racing. Nino brows drew together.

"Dead," Remo said with a shrug.

My stomach turned violently.

"That was a spectacular move," Savio commented, stuffing his face with another slice of pizza. How could he eat while a man died?

Nino tapped my wrist, drawing my attention to his face. "We can switch to one of the street races."

I caught the look Remo sent Nino. He disagreed, and he was right.

"No. If I want to be part of this family, I better get used to watching this."

Savio leaned back, a challenge in his eyes. "Then you should come to Roger's Arena in two weeks. That's when Nino's got his next fight."

"What?" I leveled my widened eyes at Nino.

"I haven't fought in a while. It's time."

"That's why we are watching this," Remo added. "The huge fucker is his opponent."

I stared at Nino in disbelief. "You can't be serious. He broke someone's back."

"I will break his neck. That's easier and has the same effect," Nino drawled.

I reached for the beer bottle he still held in the hand that wasn't busy checking my pulse and took a deep gulp. Then I began coughing from the horrible taste.

Nino gently pried the bottle from my hand, emptied it with one long sip, and set it back on the table.

"Women," Savio muttered under his breath.

I put my head down on Nino's shoulder and focused on his chest as the next fight played out on the screen. When I felt Nino's hand on my ankle, I peered up at him, but his full attention was on the fight. All I could focus on were the small strokes of his fingers against my skin. The brothers began discussing strategies for Nino's next fight as they watched the giant's previous fights. Nino's hand shifted again, sliding up to my outer thigh. I stilled, my breathing hitching in my throat. His warm, rough palm felt surprisingly good despite its proximity to more problematic areas, areas that held painful memories.

He didn't move his hand, only rested it there, and I wasn't even sure if he'd realized it or not because he was in an argument with Remo about whether it was best to kill fast or let the fight play out for a while to entertain the audience. Eventually, he must have noticed my stillness and lowered his gaze to me. He moved his thumb lightly over my skin, his eyes remaining on my face. Goose bumps flashed across my skin. He leaned down to my ear, whispering. "Fear?"

I considered it for a moment then shook my head. Nervous, definitely yes, but not scared.

He nodded, obviously pleased.

"If this is turning into a fucking session, warn us, all right?" Savio muttered.

Nino narrowed his eyes, expression hardening. "Savio, watch it."

"What? Now I can't say fucking because *she* is here?" He sat back up, scowling at me. "No strippers, no whores, and now you don't want me to say fucking?" He looked at Remo. "Tell him he needs to stop acting like a fucking pussy and show Kiara who's boss."

"I think she knows who's boss," Remo said with a twisted smile. "And you stop bitching. Take a whore into your room if you are eager for pussy."

Savio leaned back with a challenging glint aimed at Nino. "What no 'watch it' when Remo says pussy?"

Nino rolled his eyes and relaxed again. "With you there is still hope. Remo is a lost cause."

Savio chuckled. "Yeah, that's a given."

"I don't care if you say fuck," I said. "This is your house and you can talk however you like."

"It is *our* house," Nino said firmly. "And he can say fuck and whatever else he wants as long as he doesn't insult you. You are mine, and I won't have him insult you."

"Geez, I didn't insult her. I asked if you were about to fuck. That's a valid question, don't you think?"

Adamo gave me a look, which made me laugh again.

"We aren't about to fuck, satisfied?" Nino asked.

Savio grinned. "More satisfied than you, obviously."

Luckily, the conversation returned to fight strategies after that, but Savio's words kept replaying in my mind. Would I ever be able to satisfy Nino? I wasn't even sure I would ever be able to touch him *there*.

When Nino stepped out of the bathroom in only his briefs, I realized how stupid my concerns were. My eyes never seemed to get enough of watching him, but my fingers now itched to touch as well.

"What do you want?" he asked as he walked toward the bed.

"Touch you," I admitted.

He stopped right in front of the bed, allowing me to see him in all his muscled glory. I swallowed, getting overwhelmed again.

"Do you want me to keep my briefs on?"

I nodded quickly because if he got naked, I'd lose my courage.

"Of course." He nodded toward the nightstand. "Cuffs?"

"Yes."

He grabbed the handcuffs from the nightstand, cuffed his left hand to the bedpost, and stretched out on the bed.

I knelt beside him. Nino looked completely at ease as he lay sprawled out on the bed. His eyes trailed over me, taking in every inch.

"You can touch me wherever you want."

"Where do you want me to touch you?" I knew the answer to that question, of course.

"This is about you, Kiara. Touch me where you want."

Gathering my courage, I ran my hands over his chest then down his abs until my fingertips grazed his waistband. Then I quickly backed up. I kept my eyes on my hands as I explored his muscled chest, but his eyes were on me the entire time. I ran my fingernails lightly over his chest, scraping across his nipples, and he exhaled deeply.

I stifled a smile and repeated the motion then moved lower. Avoiding his briefs, I moved on to his legs, massaging his strong thighs, before I returned to his torso once more. A while after my ministrations, he grew hard under his briefs. My hands paused on his abs.

"You are in control," he assured me. His voice was deeper than ever before.

My uncle had guided my hand last time, forced it down onto his erection, forced me to rub him. I'd hated the feel of him. Swallowing the growing lump in my throat, I pushed any thought of the past aside.

I ran my hands back up to his chest then down again, over his hips and down his thighs, and then on the way up, I brushed over him with my thumbs, barely touching him. He grew harder immediately, and I repeated the motion then moved back up to his chest. Nino's eyes were keen as he watched me, his breathing deeper and his body taut like a bowstring. His hand came up to stroke my upper arm, a whisper of a touch that sent tingles into every nerve ending. "I can touch you like that as well if you want."

"But won't you need both your hands?"

He tilted his head. "It would add to your enjoyment, but if you feel threatened we should keep me restrained."

"No, let's try it without the cuffs." I leaned over and opened them for him. He lifted up, bringing our faces close. I pressed my mouth against his, and he took the lead as he always did. My eyes fluttered shut as warmth settled in my core from the skillful way his lips and tongue worked me. I moaned softly into his mouth, and he pulled back. I peered up at him questioningly.

"I think we can move on now," I said.

His mouth twitched in an almost smile and a hint of warmth reflected in his eyes. Simulated affection but so good.

"What should I do?" I asked uncertainly.

"You could lie on your back, and I'll start massaging your legs and arms and see how you like it."

I scooted lower and lay back. Nino knelt beside my legs, giving me a perfect view up his strong body. The overwhelming sense of losing control, or worse fear, never set in. He reached for my left foot and began massaging my sole with just the right amount of pressure. Then he moved on to my ankle. His touch switched between featherlight and more pressure as he worked his fingers up my calf.

My core throbbed, and I could feel myself growing wetter under his touch. His gaze followed the trail of his hands. "Can I remove your shorts?"

"Sure," I said quietly.

He unbuttoned them slowly and pulled them down my legs, his fingers grazing my skin. My heart felt ready to burst out of my ribcage. Nino raised my foot up onto his thighs and stroked my knee then applied gentle pressure on the skin just above it. I released a soft breath. Watching my face, he grabbed my ankle again and raised it as he bent forward. He pressed a kiss to the inside of my ankle before his tongue tasted the same spot, hot and wet and inexplicably perfect.

I shivered and could feel myself grow even more aroused. How could this feel so good? He shifted my leg again and pressed a light kiss to my calf. Finally his eyes lowered from my face and darted lower. It took me a moment to realize what he was looking at. The way he held my leg, he could see up to my panties that clung to my throbbing, drenched center.

He released a long breath and his expression became more strained. Embarrassment and insecurity filled me, accompanied by a hint of wariness because of my exposed state.

Nino met my gaze, and his eyes sent another pleasant shudder down to my core. He looked immensely pleased.

"Your body responds perfectly to stimulation," he murmured. "This is very good. It will make our explorations very pleasurable for you."

"So confident," I said with a small, nervous laugh.

Nino smirked and kissed my calf again before he sucked the skin into his mouth and nibbled lightly while his other hand trailed up my arm. I shuddered again. This felt impossibly good.

He released my skin. "I would like to give your chest some attention."

I paused. My nipples were already painfully straining against my clothes, but I wasn't sure if I was ready to get out of my shirt and bra yet. Nino had seen me like that before, but for some reason I still had trouble baring myself to him.

"You can keep your shirt on, and I'll just push it up a bit. The skin over your ribs and on your belly is very sensitive. If I give it some attention, you might come close to climax without any friction between your legs, which I know you aren't ready for yet."

It was so very scary how easily he could read me.

"Okay," I said breathlessly.

His strong hands reached for the hem of my shirt and slowly pushed it up. I shivered when his thumbs lightly grazed my skin as he did it. His eyes locked with mine as he lowered himself to his side, his head level with my ribcage. My stomach twisted with nerves but I wanted this. Nino put his palm against my belly, and my muscles constricted under his touch.

"You tell me when you want me to stop."

I nodded. He began moving his thumb, brushing my skin and raising goose bumps all over my body. His eyes trailed from my stomach, down to my black lace panties, then over the length of my legs before they focused on my eyes. "You have a beautiful body," he said appreciatively.

I flushed. "Thank you."

He moved his hand over my belly and dipped his fingertips under the waistband of my panties. When I tensed, he pulled back. He didn't go near my panties after that and instead stroked my belly. I held my breath when he lowered his head and pressed a kiss to the skin. How could he be this good at gentleness?

Nino was a patient man. Whenever I flinched, he stopped, only to try something else. Soft kisses and touches. His lips took a long time on the sensitive skin over my ribs, kissing and nibbling. My nipples strained against the fabric of my bra, and Nino regarded them as he kissed the spot where the fabric was bunched. His gray eyes rose to meet mine.

"Would you like to have me restrained again?"

For a moment, I was so caught up in the sensations he had summoned that I wasn't sure what he was talking about, but I nodded anyway. He got off the bed and came back with the handcuffs. Then he cuffed one of his hands to the headboard as he leaned his back against it. I pulled my shirt over my head before my brain could get in the way.

"If you lean over, I can kiss your breasts if you like."

So calm, controlled, and clinical but with an underlying tension in his silky voice that betrayed his arousal.

I flushed and reached behind myself to unhook my bra. My hands shook too much.

Nino regarded me calmly. "I can use my free hand to unclasp it. It's my left, so I may take a bit longer."

I moved closer and he reached up and unclasped my bra after a couple of seconds. Then he dropped his hand again and rested it on his ripped stomach. I lowered my bra. He had seen me naked on our wedding night, but I was still uncomfortable with his calm scrutiny. I had no way of knowing if he approved of what he saw.

"Scoot up," he said.

I did and knelt beside him. He reached up slowly and touched my shoulder, his palm warm against my skin. He applied the lightest pressure until I leaned down, bringing my breast toward his face. He parted his lips and closed them around my nipple in a delicious cocoon of heat and wetness. I gasped from the sensation and had to support myself against his chest, bringing my breast closer to his face. His eyes seemed to see right through me and knew exactly what I desired as his tongue began to circle my nipple.

It was incredible, overwhelming, and so good.

He settled back and began to leisurely suck at my nipple, tugging, swirling, nibbling until I was sopping wet. I had never been aroused like this, but Nino's mouth and his intense gaze caused unexpected sensations. I pressed my legs together, feeling like I was going to implode if I didn't find some relief soon.

Nino eyes were drawn to the movement, but he kept up his ministrations. I couldn't look away from his face, from the desire in his eyes and the way he lavished my breast.

He released my nipple with a wet sound and exhaled. My cheeks burned. He lifted his hand off his stomach and moved it to my leg then rested it lightly on my knee. I stilled, but my core sprang to life, needy and desperate. I didn't know it could be like this.

He lay still too, gray eyes tracing my face. "You can lead my hand if you want."

"What?" I whispered, my brain barely functioning.

"If you would like to have me touch you and give you pleasure, you can lead my hand."

"But I wouldn't even know what to do. You are the one who does."

"I do, and my touch will be very pleasurable, but you are still tense."

My brows drew together at his confidence. "You are a bit full of yourself."

He tilted his head with the hint of amusement. "I'm only good at estimating my own talents, and I'm good at giving pleasure."

"And inflicting pain," I added.

"That too, but that's not something you have to worry about." His thumb stroked my knee lightly. "Why don't you let me suck your nipple again. You seemed to enjoy that."

I nodded and leaned forward. He latched onto my nipple, and I instantly moaned. "Now your other breast," he murmured when I could barely hold myself up above him. I shifted and he circled his tongue over my nipple then sucked it into his mouth while his hand came up to knead my other breast. My center began to pulsate, lightly at first, and then a shudder passed over me, spreading out from between my legs.

Nino sucked my nipple a bit harder. I gasped and felt more wetness pool between my legs as my center throbbed. I froze above Nino, and he released my nipple.

"What happened?" I asked, stunned.

"I think you might have had an orgasm. It wasn't a strong one, but my sucking of your nipple was enough to stimulate your pussy without friction."

Heat rose into my cheeks. "Oh, wow."

Nino's eyes were intent as they trailed over my chest then lower. "If I touch your pussy, it will intensify tenfold, trust me."

I regarded him and my gaze darted down to the hard outline of him beneath his briefs. Not giving myself a moment to worry, I reached for him and cupped him through the material. He let out a sharp exhale and twitched against my palm. I scooted down, despite my racing pulse.

Nino was handcuffed to the headboard. It was safe for me.

I was done allowing the past to hold me down. I was done being a prisoner of Durant's. He was dead. Nino had tortured and killed him for me. Now it was my turn to kill the man's memory.

Fingers shaking, I hooked them under Nino's waistband and pulled his briefs down. His stomach rippled with tension, but he made no sound. I didn't dare look up at his face for fear of losing my courage.

I had seen Nino naked before, but I'd never risked more than fleeting glances. This time I allowed myself to watch his erection as I brought my palms down on his thighs. There was no reason for me to be afraid of Nino's nakedness. And I wasn't disgusted by his body, not even his erection, like I had been of Durant's. Nino was beautiful all over, even with the scars and the tattoos—or maybe because of them. They were part of him, and I couldn't imagine how he would look without them.

My eyes lingered on his erection. He was long and thick and circumcised. A brief moment of panic burst through me at the idea of having him inside of me, remembering the pain from long ago, but I pushed it aside. I curled my fingers around the base, and Nino released a low breath, but he kept very still. I was in control of this. Nobody forced me to do this. I wanted it. *My choice.*

I began moving my hand slowly, up and down, focusing on the present, on my breathing, on Nino's low exhales, on the silkiness of him in my palm. He was tense under my touch, and when I finally dared to look up, his eyes burned into me with desire.

I shuddered, my movements faltering for a moment, but then I tightened my grip and sped up. This time I kept my eyes on his face, needing to see him, needing to see what I did to him. Nino never looked away as I rubbed him harder and faster, his breathing turning into pants. My own breathing turned labored as I watched him, watched his beautiful face. His free hand gripped the edge of the mattress as his expression twisted and his thigh muscles contorted under my hand. "If you keep it up, I'm going to come," he rasped.

I didn't stop. I needed to continue. My lips parted when Nino's eyes closed. His hips thrust upwards, and he came with a shudder. Nothing was more beautiful than Nino's perfectly cold face alight with passion. My gaze flitted down to my hand as he came over my fingers.

Stilling, my breathing lodged in my chest. He twitched twice, and then Nino, too, stilled. It became very quiet around us except for the pounding of my heart in my ears.

Nino

Kiara stared down at her hand wrapped around my softening cock with my cum all over it. She was tense and her expression was impossible for me to read. I sat up, unlocked the handcuff, and gently pried her hand off me. Then I stood and tugged her along. She followed me without a word into the bathroom, where I turned the water on in the sink on and held her hand under it, washing my cum off. I could only assume it had triggered memories from the past.

Her brows drew together, and finally she raised her eyes to mine. "Why did you do that?"

I regarded her, trying to read her expression, but it was only puzzled not upset. I dried her hand then curled my fingers around her wrist. Her pulse was fast but not as fast as it was when she was scared. "I assumed you were upset because I came over your hand."

"I wasn't," she said quietly.

I tilted my head. "Then why did you tense? You looked upset."

"I was stunned and relieved," she said slowly. "Because I was worried I couldn't do it. That it would remind me too much of what he did, but it didn't. I wasn't disgusted."

"That's good," I murmured. I hadn't expected her to touch me today, but she must have felt safe with me being restrained. She smiled up at me, and I returned the smile. Her expression softened further. She pressed up against me, and my hands automatically wrapped around her hips. "Let me touch your pussy, Kiara. I want to make you feel good. I want to make you come hard."

A blush spread on her cheeks. There was still uncertainty on her face.

"My fingers won't bring pain, only pleasure. Trust me."

"I do," she said quietly.

I led her back into the bedroom, and Kiara lay down on the bed, watching me with a small, tense smile. I knelt beside her. "I will massage your legs and work my way up. For now, you'll keep your panties on, okay?"

She nodded.

As I put my palms on her thighs, her skin tightened under the touch. "You just say 'stop' when you want me to stop," I told her firmly, meeting her gaze.

"Okay," she said.

I began kneading her outer thigh, and after a moment she relaxed, but I didn't move on. Eventually, I widened my movements, my fingertips stroking the soft inner side of her thighs where the small scar was. Kiara's breathing deepened. I brushed my palm higher, finally reaching her panty-covered mound. She sucked in a breath, and I glanced up at her and found her watching me.

"Do you want me to stop?"

She gave a quick shake of her head, and I smiled. "Good."

I ran my palm over her panties again, and she rocked her hips lightly. This time as I brushed my hand over her, I slid my middle finger over the little dip, brushing her folds and clit. She arched up with a surprised little moan, and I repeated the motion. Her panties stuck to her wet flesh, giving me a perfect view of her slit. Slowing my hand as I ran it over her, I made sure the pad of my finger rested against her nub. I kept my palm pressed against her pussy. Her heat and wetness was tantalizing against my skin. Her heady scent teased my nose and made me want to bury my face in her lap and lick up her arousal.

I moved my fingertip lightly over her clit, and Kiara moaned then flushed, biting her lip. I repeated the motion. "Don't quiet yourself. Let me hear you. That way I know you enjoy what I'm doing." Though, her soaked panties were a fucking good indicator as well.

Lightly rocking the heel of my palm against her, my finger brushed her clit. Eventually, she moved her hips against me, her hands fisting the sheets.

Her eyes lowered to my groin area. I knew she'd find me hard.

"Come for me, Kiara," I ordered.

She moaned again, almost helplessly, her body beginning to shake under my touch. I sped up my finger. "Nino," she gasped. "I … I … oh God." Her eyes widened and then her hips bucked, and she cried out as she shuddered violently. I slowed my strokes, enjoying the way her panties clung to her with arousal.

My cock ached for another release, for her pussy, her taste and warmth. She was so fucking wet. It would have been so very pleasurable if I'd fucked her now, but her fear still prevented it.

Lifting my finger, I kept up the pressure of my palm against her center, knowing it would prolong her orgasm.

She watched me with parted lips, her curls a wild mess around her head. "Thank you," she whispered.

"For giving you an orgasm?" I asked with a hint of amusement.

I climbed back up to her and stretched out beside her. She moved closer, and I wrapped my arm around her. "For never going beyond what I can take," she said quietly. "For showing me that being touched there doesn't have to be painful."

She put her head down on my chest, and my body relaxed at the feel of her warmth.

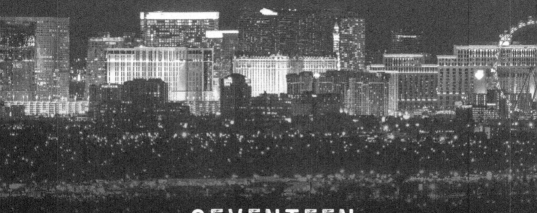

SEVENTEEN

Kiara

I WAS A NERVOUS WRECK. THIS WAS THE FIRST TIME I'D BE RETURNING TO
Baltimore since marrying Nino, after the bloody sheets scandal. Giulia's
description of the aftermath of that day was probably softened for my sake.

I'd be the center of attention. People would whisper behind my back. They
would judge me for actions that weren't even my own.

Nino stepped up to me. "We should head out now. The plane ride takes
almost five hours, and we need to be at your uncle's house around seven p.m."

I nodded and my stomach tightened even more.

"Where's your dress?" he asked.

I pointed toward the dark blue modest dress hanging on the door. It was
one of the dresses Aunt Egidia had bought for me a couple of years back. It was
the safe choice.

Nino shook his head once. He walked into our walk-in closet and emerged
a few minutes later with the long red silk dress I bought a few weeks ago.

My eyes widened. "If I wear that, people will be staring even more."

Nino tilted his head. "You are a Falcone, my wife, and you won't try to hide.
You will hold your head high and show them that they are beneath you. Show
them how beautiful you are. Let them stare."

I blinked and nodded mutely. He made it sound so easy.

Remo, Nino, and I took the private jet to Baltimore. Savio, Adamo, and
Fabiano stayed in Vegas since this was more of a family matter, it being my uncle's seventieth birthday. Remo, as the Capo of the Camorra, was invited as a
guest of honor, though I assumed that my aunt and uncle weren't too enthused
about having him under their roof.

We would be staying in a hotel this time because Giulia and Cassio, as well as my other step-siblings, were already spending the night at my aunt and uncle's house. And of course because pretty much every member of the Famiglia had grown even more wary of Nino and Remo since they killed Durant on my wedding night.

Sometimes I wondered if something was wrong with me because I didn't feel guilty for what happened to him. I didn't see his corpse, but from the reactions of everyone who had, I knew it was bad.

I regarded Nino and Remo over the top of my book. They were discussing an upcoming meeting with Luca.

We arrived later than expected at our hotel, so I had to hurry getting ready. When I was dressed in the red dress with a slit going all the way up to my upper thigh, combined with the low-cut neckline, I couldn't tear my eyes from the mirror. My dark hair fell in waves down my back and shoulders, and I put on lipstick in the same blood red color as my dress. Lady in red.

Nino came up behind me with a pleased look. "You will be the center of attention, Kiara, as you should be. You are a sight to behold. Blood red is your color."

I huffed out a laugh. "People will think of the bloody sheets, no doubt."

Nino put his hands on my hips, and without thinking about it, I leaned back against him, relishing in the feel of his strong body pressed up against my back. "Let them remember the sheets. It's what will happen to anyone who dares to touch you."

I shivered at the expression on his face. So cold and cruel. So beautiful. Nino in his black tux and blood red bowtie was a breathtaking sight on his own, but together we looked perfect, like we were meant to be together. It was a ridiculous thought, a romantic notion I would never utter aloud because Nino wouldn't understand.

"Come now, we don't want to be late," he murmured, but his eyes traveled over my neckline once more, and the desire in his expression tightened my core.

Remo was already waiting in the lobby of the hotel when Nino and I arrived. Remo, too, was dressed in a tuxedo, but he wore a black bowtie. I'd never seen him this dressed up, not even at my wedding.

His eyes took their time assessing me. Then he smirked. "I bet a few people will be hit with unpleasant memories when they see your dress."

I wrung my hands as the rented limousine dropped us off in front of my old home. Nino wrapped his arm around my waist, his hand resting possessively on my hip.

I took a deep breath.

"Hold your head high," Nino reminded me quietly.

Remo looked at us curiously. "Don't let any of those fuckers put you down because your father was a traitor. Don't let them put you down for any other shit either. You are a Falcone now. If one of them doesn't show respect, tell me or Nino and we'll handle them."

"Thanks," I said with a small smile.

Remo gave a quick nod. I wasn't quite as terrified of him as I had been before, and he tried not to scare me too much. Maybe we'd come to an understanding eventually.

The door to the mansion swung open. Aunt Egidia and Uncle Felix came into view. Their eyes widened when they settled on me.

Nino squeezed my hip, and I raised my head, forcing a smile.

Kiara Falcone. Someone new. Not the girl who hid in the corners.

When we arrived in front of them, there was a moment of awkward silence, then I said quickly, "Happy birthday, Uncle Felix." I kissed his cheek and his expression softened.

"Thank you, Kiara. You look incredible."

"You do," Aunt Egidia agreed. "What a strong color."

I gave her a quick hug as well then stepped back so Nino and Remo could greet her and my uncle. Nino handed the expensive limited-edition scotch to my uncle, who visibly relaxed. It became apparent very quickly that neither Egidia nor Felix enjoyed being around Nino and Remo.

We followed them inside. The house had been decorated with fresh flowers, and the living room was filled with guests and so was the garden. A buffet had been set up in the adjoining dining room, and waiters walked around with trays loaded with champagne and appetizers. The moment Nino and I entered the room, all eyes turned to us, and most people didn't manage to hide their surprise seeing me dressed like this.

Giulia motioned for me to join her and Cassio. I glanced at Nino, who released my waist. "Remo and I will go talk to Luca. Why don't you head over to your stepsister?"

I nodded and quickly made my way over to her. She wrapped me in a tight embrace then pulled back and scanned my outfit, a proud expression on her face. "Finally, you're showing off your curves. You look absolutely stunning."

I smiled then nodded at Cassio. He made no move to touch me. He had always been careful not to do so unless absolutely necessary. Giulia and I had never discussed this, but I was fairly sure she had talked to him about what happened to me years ago. He was her husband, so it was only natural to share intimate details.

"How are things in Las Vegas?" he asked, but from the tension in his expression, I could tell that Giulia must have given him a hard time because she'd been worrying about me.

I gripped my stepsister's hand and squeezed. "I'm doing well. You don't have to worry anymore."

Her eyes darted over to Nino, who was listening to something Luca had to say. "You can tell me if something's wrong, Kiara. We can help you."

I laughed. "Giulia, I don't need your help. I'm now a Falcone. I'm well protected."

She regarded me with surprise then exchanged a look with her husband. "Wow. What did they do to you?"

I glanced toward Nino, and as if he could feel my eyes on him, he turned, meeting my gaze. My lips pulled into a smile. "He taught me my worth."

Giulia touched my bare shoulder, her lips parting. "You like him?"

I couldn't look away from Nino. "I like him," I said quietly, and my body warmed at my admittance. Deep down, I realized that perhaps I did more than just like him.

Giulia grabbed my hand and led me outside into a secluded part of the garden. "Kiara, how is this possible?"

"What? I thought you'd be happy that I feel home in Las Vegas, that my marriage to Nino isn't hell as I'd originally feared."

"I am happy for you, it's just so hard to believe that the Falcones treat you right."

I shrugged. "It is like you said: some men don't bring violence home with them. Nino is one of them. He knows how strong he is, how powerful. He doesn't have to humiliate me to feel powerful."

The first real smile spread over Giulia's face, and she hugged me again. "I'm so happy for you."

People kept staring when we returned to the party, but they kept their distance. In the past it had been because they didn't want to be associated with a traitor; now it seemed as if they were scared. Eventually, I found myself back at Nino's side, his hand a reassuring presence on my hip.

"You're doing good," he murmured. His praise filled me with pride.

I felt relieved when we returned to our hotel later that night. Even after less than two months, Las Vegas already felt more like a home than Baltimore ever had, and I longed to be back where people didn't judge me for my past.

A couple of days later, I woke with Nino when he got up for his swim. I decided to stay in bed for once and grab a couple of hours of additional sleep. Nino surprised me when he sat down and leaned in close, mouth near my ear. "Tonight, I want to explore every inch of your body with my mouth," he said, and heat rose to my cheeks. "It'll be more intense than anything we've done so far. I'm very good at it."

All I could do in response was nod, stunned into silence, but my body exploded with heat. Nino got up, his swim trunks tenting, and turned to leave.

I closed my eyes, trying to imagine his mouth between my legs, wondering how it would feel. Restless and hot, I clamped my thighs together. My fingers found their way between my legs, and I stroked myself the way Nino had told me to, imagining his deep, low voice, his hands, his mouth ... and I came with a small shudder, but it wasn't enough. Not even close.

Slipping out of bed, I opted for a long shower to clear my mind.

That evening I prepared dinner for the first time. I wasn't sure if the men would appreciate it, considering it was meatless, but the three-cheese lasagna sounded delicious and as it cooked in the oven, its enticing scent gave me hope that I actually managed to create something edible.

I went in search of the men but found only one, Remo, who was kicking the punching bag as if it had personally insulted him. It was his favorite pastime.

He tossed a look my way but didn't immediately stop his assault.

"Where's Nino?"

"Shower." Kick. "He worked out with Adamo today." Kick. Punch. Punch. Kick.

"I cooked for us."

Remo paused, his dark eyes narrowing. "For you and Nino?"

"For all of us," I said quietly, shifting nervously under his harsh glare.

He moved closer despite my rising tension. Grabbing a towel thrown over the sofa, he stopped in front of me. "No running or flinching today?"

I pursed my lips. "I never ran from you."

"You did when I fucked the whore on the pool table."

Steps sounded a moment later, and Nino appeared at my side, lightly touching my back. "That is an unsettling sight."

"Your wife cooked for us," Remo said.

Nino glanced down at me. He smelled of his spicy shower gel. A few wet strands hung down his forehead and temples.

"Adamo took me grocery shopping today. I thought it would be nice to have a home-cooked meal for once."

My eyes darted to his mouth, trying to imagine how it would feel, but I came up short. My imagination wasn't very good.

"I assume no animal was harmed," Remo muttered.

Nino sent his brother a warning look.

"It is vegetarian, yes, but your cholesterol levels will get their fill. Don't worry. It's layered with mozzarella, pecorino, and taleggio cheese."

"About three pounds of cheese," Adamo added as he sauntered down the steps, his wet hair tousled.

"Do you need my help?" Nino asked.

"You could carry it over here. The pan is heavy."

Nino followed me into the kitchen, his warm palm pressed up against my back.

"It needs five more minutes," I told him after another peek inside the oven, avoiding looking at his face because that led to me looking at his mouth and that led to more distracting thoughts. Nino regarded me quietly. He cupped my face and brushed his thumb over my cheekbone.

"You are nervous."

I licked my lips, my eyes drawn up to his mouth then a bit higher. He moved closer and kissed me, slow and hot and with a promise of more. His tongue was almost playful as it circled mine, teasing but still dominant. Flustered, I pulled back. It was the first time Nino had initiated a kiss, the first time we'd been intimate outside of our bedroom.

"That's what I'll do tonight," he murmured then added in an even lower voice, "Between your legs."

I shivered. Nino was less careful around me; it was exciting and terrifying, and I didn't want it any other way.

He pulled back, gray eyes evaluating my face. He reached for my wrist, brushing his thumb across the sensitive skin before he kissed it. "Remember, there's nothing for you to fear when you are in bed with me."

I nodded. My dry throat made swallowing difficult. "I think the lasagna is done."

Nino took out the large pan and carried it into the gaming room. I carried plates, napkins, and cutlery. Savio, Adamo, and Remo had already taken their usual seat. For a moment, I considered asking them to have dinner in the dining room but then decided against it.

"That smells good," Adamo said as he leaned over the lasagna the moment Nino set it down on a wooden trivet.

"Are you sure she didn't poison the food?" Savio asked with a grin, but he was already loading up his plate with lasagna.

Nino put his hand on my knee as he sat down beside me. "Kiara and I have plans for tonight, so I don't think she will poison me just yet. Am I right?"

Heat blasted my cheeks.

"TMI, Nino," Adamo muttered.

"TLI if you ask me," Savio said with a grin. "It was more fun when you still shared your fuck adventures with us, Nino. Now I only get to hear Remo's twisted shit."

I was sure my head would explode with embarrassment any minute.

"If you don't want to hear my twisted shit, I'll share it with only Nino and Fabiano in the future."

"I don't think anyone wants to hear it," I said.

Remo leaned back, regarding me with a sinister smile on his face. "Not everyone's cut out for shitty vanilla sex, so sue me. And if I remember right, Nino and Fabiano enjoyed the rougher side of things too before your women castrated you."

I chanced a look at Nino, but his face didn't give anything away. The lasagna was delicious, and the men dug in as if it were their last meal. As usual, they taunted each other and argued. It always gave me a strange sense of belonging when they acted like family around me.

After dinner, Nino and I retreated to our wing. When Nino closed the door to our bedroom, I peered up at him curiously. "What did Remo mean with the rougher side of things?"

Nino shook his head. "It doesn't mean what you think it means."

"You don't know what I think," I said quietly. "Maybe you are a genius, but you aren't a mind reader."

Nino wrapped his fingers around my wrist and tugged me closer. Then he leaned down. "I don't have to be a mind reader to recognize the look on your face, Kiara."

I sighed. "So you never …?" My voice shook.

"Never," he said firmly and relief filled me. His thumb stroked my wrist. "How about we explore some more now?"

I gave a mute nod, excitement coursing through my body. Nino led me toward the bed. "If you want me to go down on you, it would be wise not to have me restrained … unless you feel comfortable sitting on my face."

My eyes flew open in shock. "No," I finally managed. "Definitely not."

Nino's lips twitched at the corners. "That's what I thought."

My cheeks were hot as I rolled my eyes. Stepping closer, I stood on my tiptoes and curled my hand around Nino's neck. He lowered his head at once, claiming my mouth and wrapping an arm around my back. I lost myself in his kiss until he began to lower us to the bed. I felt the soft mattress beneath me as Nino hovered over me.

He pulled away, his eyes tracing my face. "Fear?" he asked quietly, holding his body above me.

It was ridiculous to be scared because it was Nino, but how Durant had felt hovering over me always returned to my mind, even if I didn't want the memories to hold me back.

Nino lowered himself to the bed beside me, and I quickly returned kissing him. He complied without hesitation and as usual took lead. I surrendered to his expert tongue, feeling my center heat. His hand stroked my side then slipped below my shirt, touching skin and creating goose bumps. His fingers reached higher then brushed over my lace bra. My nipples puckered under the touch, and I moaned into Nino's mouth. His hand cupped my breasts and kneaded lightly at first then his touch grew firmer. Gathering my courage, I reached for Nino, needing to feel him. My hands slid over his muscled chest, down to his ripped stomach until I reached the hem of his shirt. I tugged at it.

Nino pulled away from my mouth, sat up, and yanked his shirt over his head. My eyes took in his torso, the muscles, the scars, the tattoos, and as usual, my body filled with thousands of butterflies. Before he had even lain back down, my hands were already roaming over his chest. He propped himself up to allow me to explore. His eyes were on my face, but my eyes remained on my fingers as they stroked his pecs then grazed his nipples.

He exhaled, and I repeated the motion, loving that I could break through Nino's cold demeanor with such a small touch. It felt empowering. Exhilarating.

"How about we get rid of your shirt as well?" Nino murmured, hands reaching for the hem of my shirt. I raised myself up so he could pull it over my head.

His eyes traveled over my body, lingering on my breasts, and then his lips returned to mine as his fingers tugged at my nipple through the lace. He helped me out of my bra. Fingers and lips caressed my breasts, shoulders and stomach, as he left a burning need in their wake. Despite my body's need, I froze when Nino reached for my panties. So far he'd touched me through the fabric. It gave me the illusion of safety.

I lifted my hips, and Nino took me up on my invitation, but his eyes remained on my face as he laid me bare to his eyes. His palm stroked my thigh then slowly up it, moving over the small patch of dark hair between my legs. I held my breath when his thumb touched my slick nub for the first time without a barrier. Arching up, I moaned.

His finger nimbly stroked my folds, but he never dipped between them. I wasn't sure how good he was at reading me … if he understood that having his fingers so close to my entrance scratched the surface of painful memories. Nino moved to the end of bed and eased my ankles apart. I knew what he was about to do and tried to make my body relax.

He stretched out between my thighs, his tattooed biceps flexing as he parted me wide. My center clenched, followed by my thighs, when he lowered his gaze to my center.

"Fear?" he asked quietly, intently. I wasn't afraid of that. *He* had never done that to me.

"Nerves," I admitted.

"Of what?" His breath ghosted over my wet heat, and I trembled with anticipation, nerves, and need.

It was hard to explain. "I don't know."

He leaned forward. "This is going to be good for you, Kiara. Try to focus on my tongue and my lips. Don't think about anything else."

His breath fanned over my clit, and then his tongue slid over me lightly, dipping between my folds before it fluttered over my nub. I whimpered from the sensation.

"Good?" Nino asked against me, his voice deep and calm.

I nodded, my fingers digging into the bedsheets. Nino's tongue did a small flutter again, and my muscles finally loosened. He eased my thighs farther apart with his shoulders and dragged his tongue down to my opening. I tensed briefly, and he moved back up quickly. Again, his tongue fluttered over my clit then over my folds before he dipped lower and repeated the same motion over my entrance. Intense pleasure coursed through me, and this time my body didn't tense. Nino's tongue flicked lightly over my opening then he twirled it around and increased the pressure, easing the tip into me. I released a surprised gasp.

He let out a low hum, which sounded like approval, and my eyes darted down to watch him. His gaze rested on my folds as he circled my opening with his tongue. He seemed to enjoy it, and that realization banished the last of my nerves. He flicked his tongue over my clit again, with light nudges and twirls, and then I could feel something building; tension tightened deep in my core, mounting with every lick and flick, until I shattered. I cried out, shuddering through my release.

Nino groaned against me, moving lower, and lapped at my entrance with slow strokes. My eyes widened as my walls clenched again under his ministrations.

"Ride it out," he ordered in a low voice.

He began to use firm licks to heighten my pleasure again. It was incredible, *impossible*. This felt better than anything ever had.

"Nino," I whimpered as he worked me with gentle care. "This feels so good."

"Good," he rasped against my folds, and I trembled at the sound. "I want you to come again for me, Kiara. Can you do this for me?"

"Yes," I gasped out, and he flicked his tongue along my clit before he focused his attention on my entrance. He pressed his mouth firmly against me and his tongue entered me again. His tongue felt so good inside of me as he moved it slowly. His thumb found my clit, and he rubbed the same soft circles.

I bucked my hips restlessly, overwhelmed with the wondrous sensations. It was building even quicker this time, my flesh oversensitive but still eager for more. My hand flew down to Nino's head, gripping his hair, and then I came even harder.

Nino's fingers stroked my folds. "I'd like to put my finger in you."

I met his gaze. His expression was calm, self-assured. I swallowed.

He dipped one finger between my lips. "Say something. Tell me to stop if you don't want this."

"I … I'm worried it'll hurt like last time."

"It won't," Nino said firmly with certainty. The tip of his finger moved a bit lower. I tensed, remembering the pain from long ago, the feeling of breaking, of helplessness.

Nino regarded me, his finger lightly tracing my opening, but he didn't push in. He reached up with his other hand and stroked my lower belly. "Try to loosen up, Kiara. You are very wet, and my finger will be very pleasurable against your sensitive walls if you allow it."

I tried to relax, but my body clamped down with fear from the past. Nino kept stroking my opening and folds. "Let me help you," he murmured.

He startled me when his hand fluttered up from my stomach to the ticklish spot over my ribs. I gasped out in laughter and twitched. Then Nino slipped his finger into me. He immediately stopped the tickling.

"Oh," I breathed out and stilled. It didn't hurt at all. Slowly, his eyes found my face. He began moving his finger, and I moaned at the sensation.

"Why did you tickle me?" I asked thickly as Nino kept thrusting inside me with his finger. He rubbed my clit lightly.

"I distracted your body. Your brain had assumed my finger against your opening was a threat because you expected pain, so I went and posed another threat your synapses had to focus on. Usually it works best with actual pain, but tickling is effective too because the body reacts in a similar way."

I shook my head. "You are good at this."

His lips twitched, and his gray eyes questioned me. "I've studied the workings of the body for a long time, especially its reactions to pleasure and pain."

I didn't doubt it. I moaned as he did something with his finger inside of me, a light rotation.

He repeated the motion and rubbed his thumb lightly over my clit. "Do you like this?"

How could he even ask? "Yes," I managed to get out. His lips took the place of his thumb over my clit as his finger slid in and out slowly.

"Come again for me," he said in that silky, dominant tone, and I fell apart under the combined sensation of his finger and his mouth.

My entire body burst with waves of pleasure. I trembled for a long time, trying to catch my breath. Nino pulled his finger out and then shocked me by lifting it to his lips and putting it into his mouth.

"I enjoy your taste, Kiara," he said in a more textured voice as he knelt between my legs. My eyes were drawn to his pants. He was hard, aroused because he'd had his mouth on me.

I sat up, reached for his briefs. "I want to give back."

Nino slipped out them then knelt on the bed again. I was in front of him and reached for him. He groaned. I moved slowly then leaned forward, and he met me halfway. His lips claimed mine and tasted like me. We kissed as I pumped my hands up and down, his eyes boring into me with more than cold scrutiny. Our kiss turned desperate, uncoordinated. Nino tensed in my grip. I watched the small twitches of his muscles, the sharp pull of his mouth, listened to his quick pants, and it felt right.

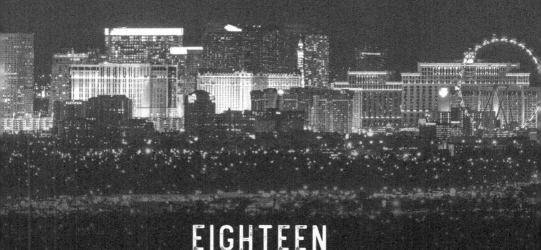

EIGHTEEN

Kiara

L EONA GAVE ME A LOOK. "ARE YOU NERVOUS TOO?"

I laughed. "Nervous doesn't even begin to cover it. I don't think I'll be any good at fighting." I paused. "But why are you nervous? I thought you've practiced with Fabiano before."

"A few times, yes, but we've always been alone. Now there will be people watching."

I nodded. I wished Nino had chosen to practice alone with me, but I knew he had a lot on his plate because of his upcoming fight against that giant man.

When we stepped out into the training hall, my eyes had trouble taking it all in. The chandelier dangling from the ceiling, the red and gold wallpaper, the broken roulette tables, the beautiful dirty, seashell-shaped windows … It was so typically Falcone to choose something as flashy as an abandoned casino building for their fighting gym.

The men had already gathered around the boxing ring. They were only in fight shorts, and my heart thundered faster at the sight of all that muscle and scars. Even Adamo was muscular for an almost fourteen-year-old.

"Thank God, not the cage," Leona muttered, and I gave her a questioning look. She smiled. "Fabiano always insists we work out in the cage, and it honestly gives me the creeps."

My eyes wandered over to the cage, and I had to agree. I was already nervous as it was.

Nino touched my hip when I arrived beside him. "Leona will go first because she already has some practice."

Fabiano parted the ropes for Leona, who climbed in with a nervous look toward the Falcone brothers. "Are you all going to watch?"

"No," Nino said. "I'm going to attack you."

Leona's eyes widened. "What? I thought Fabiano would train with me?"

Fabiano shook his head. "Not this time. Being faced with an opponent that makes you nervous is closer to reality."

Nino swung himself over the rope and faced Leona, his arms hanging down at his side in a relaxed way. "Watch closely, Kiara," he said.

I nodded.

Nino lunged at Leona, and I noticed Fabiano's body rocking forward slightly. Leona let out a surprised cry when Nino's hand clamped down her wrist. He jerked her toward him, and then she was already on her back. He knelt between her legs.

"Leona," Fabiano hissed. "Remember what I taught you."

Leona began struggling, but Nino pressed her wrists into the ground above her head, lowering himself, parting her legs further with his muscular thighs.

Remo made a buzzer noise. "There's no way for you to escape now. You acted too late. Now he's got you exactly where he wants you."

I shivered.

"He would have to open his pants. That might give her an opening to attack him with her free hand," I said.

Everyone looked at me, and I swallowed but stood my ground.

Nino grabbed both of Leona's wrists in one of his despite her wriggling and showed me his free hand. "Free to open my pants."

Nino straightened and pulled Leona to her feet.

"Why did you act so late?" Fabiano asked with a frown.

"I was startled, and to be honest … Nino scares me," she said indignantly.

"Then let's hope your assailant announces his attack ahead of time and doesn't scare you," Remo muttered.

Obviously losing interest, Savio and Adamo moved into the cage and began sparing with each other, but Savio definitely had the upper hand and didn't take it easy on his younger brother, judging by the force of his kicks and punches. No wonder Adamo was always beat-up.

"Again," Fabiano said.

Nino grabbed Leona's arm, but this time she acted instantaneously. She brought her hand up to claw at his face, but he blocked it with his elbow, at the same time dodging her kick aimed at his groin with his hip. Then he threw her down. They ended in the same position as before, and Leona huffed.

"Better," Nino said with a nod, pushing off her and pulling her to her feet.

"I still ended up on the ground."

"Your attacker won't be Nino," Fabiano said. "He probably won't be half as fast or strong or skilled."

They did two more drills until Leona's face was bright red and covered in sweat. Nino looked like he'd just finished a nice, slow morning walk.

I stifled a smile and when he met my eyes and the corners of his mouth twitched. My body filled with warmth as it so often did in Nino's presence.

"Your turn," he said and parted the ropes for me.

Gulping, I climbed inside the ring, and Leona quickly scrambled out, whispering, "Good luck."

Fabiano immediately wrapped his arm around her waist possessively. Remo shook his head and jumped up on the edge of the ring then swung himself inside.

I stared at Nino, my pulse hammering in my veins. "You will train with me, right?" My voice trembled.

Nino regarded my face then shook his head. "I want you to face your fears. They might immobilize you during a real fight."

I started shaking as I looked at Remo, who stood with his arms crossed over his chest, watching me with dark amusement.

I shook my head. "No. I can't." I backed into the rope. "Please, Nino."

Nino exchanged a look with his brother, who rolled his eyes.

"I can take over," Fabiano suggested.

My head swiveled toward him. He terrified me too, but not nearly as much as Remo.

"Then do it," Remo growled, but he walked toward me, his dark eyes hard. "As long as you don't face your fears, you will be weak. He will keep power over you as long as you let him. If you ever stop being a coward, come to me and I will show you how to fight an opponent set on hurting you."

He jumped over the rope and walked toward Adamo and Savio to join them in the cage.

Nino touched my waist, his eyebrows pulled together. "Don't mind him."

"Do you agree with him?" I asked quietly.

Nino nodded. "Remo would be the best option if you wanted to simulate an attack."

"I can be as scary as Remo if you want me to be," Fabiano said with a shrug.

"No," I said quickly. "Thanks."

Fabiano was scary enough with his assessing blue eyes.

"You saw what Leona did," Nino began. "Of course her past doesn't harbor the same demons, so you will have to fight two enemies: Fabiano and your memories. I can tell you how to do the first, but the latter is your fight." He motioned for me to get closer to Fabiano. "You are smaller and weaker, so you will have to make every hit count. Aim where it hurts the most. His balls." Nino pointed at Fabiano's groin area, who cocked an eyebrow. "Solar plexus." He pointed at the area below the ribs. "Under his chin. Eyes. Nose." He gestured toward Fabiano's face.

"Here, let me show you," Nino said and positioned himself in front of Fabiano, whose lips widened into a smile.

Nino brought his knee up sideways toward Fabiano's groin without making contact. Then he curled his hand into a fist and pretended to punch Fabiano's stomach twice. Then he pushed the heel of his hand up toward Fabiano's nose. "You can also scratch or bite, but don't waste too much time. You will tire eventually."

Nino stepped back and gave Fabiano a nod.

Fabiano came at me at once, and I seized. Everything happened so fast, and suddenly I was on my back and he was between my legs. Panic choked me. I let out a terrified sob, clenching my eyes shut, and began to shake.

"Fuck," someone said. Then another cold and compelling voice spoke above me. This voice had brought me back before.

"Kiara, open your eyes." And I did, looking up into cool, gray eyes. Nino. "Don't allow the past to control you. You are safe. Nothing will happen to you. I am here."

I swallowed and gave a small nod. Fabiano had sat back on his haunches, regarding me with a deep frown. I closed my legs, embarrassed. "Sorry."

"You don't have to be sorry," he said with a shrug, but his eyes were a bit softer than before.

Nino helped me to my feet. "Again?" His eyes held mine, and I gave a small nod. He turned to Fabiano. "This time straddle her legs only."

Fabiano nodded. "Ready?"

"Yes," I said, and he reached for my arm, and again, I found myself on my back with Fabiano straddling my thighs. Panic clawed its way out of my chest, and I tried to fight it, but I couldn't. My vision turned black. Fabiano shoved off me, and I sucked in a deep breath. Nino knelt beside me, touching my shoulder.

"I don't think it's working," Fabiano said. "She is too scared."

Nino nodded but he kept his eyes on me and his warm palm on my shoulder. "You can leave. I will take it from here."

Fabiano gave me a tight smile. Then he climbed out of the ring.

"I'm sorry," I said, embarrassed that I'd broken down like this even though this had been fake, even though Fabiano hadn't meant to hurt me.

"I underestimated your fear of men. With me, you've been relaxed."

"That's because I trust you," I whispered.

His brows pulled together, and he didn't say anything. "That's why I wanted you to fight Remo or Fabiano. You are wary of them. It would make the fight more real."

"I know, but it's too much right now. Can't you train with me?"

"Of course, but I will go hard on you, Kiara. It makes no sense to stay within your comfort zone. You won't improve if you feel safe."

My stomach clenched with nerves as Nino pulled me to my feet. Nino had a point, and I wanted to show him that I wasn't weak, and more than that, I wanted to show myself that I could beat my past once and for all. I'd allowed it control my life for too long.

"Step closer." As I did, he grabbed my wrists, and I tensed in preparation for his attack, but he put my palms up on his shoulders. "Use this to gain momentum and now jerk your knee up as hard as you can."

I hesitated.

"Do it," he ordered, and I did. Nino blocked my knee with his thigh so I wouldn't connect with his groin. I jumped from the impact, a dull pain spreading through my knee and upper thigh. "Sorry."

"Don't apologize. You are supposed to hurt me. Again, and harder this time."

I jerked my knee up again and rammed his thigh. He gave a curt nod. "Better. Still too hesitant. Now make a fist."

I lowered my hands and curled them into fists.

"Hit my stomach."

I punched him, but even I could tell that I was holding back. Nino grabbed my hand and curled my fist even tighter. Then he touched it to the spot where he wanted me to aim. "Here. And hard."

I punched him again, and his mouth tightened. I wasn't sure if it was because I'd actually managed to hurt him or if he was still not satisfied with my performance. Probably the latter. "Now open your hand and bring the heel of your hand up to my nose."

I did as he instructed, and he changed the angle of my hand slightly. "Like this. If you use enough force, you can break your opponent's nose."

"You perhaps."

He shook his head. "You can. Trust me. If I use that move with full force, I can kill my opponent by shoving his bones up into his brain, not just break his nose."

My face scrunched up in disgust.

"Now let's move on to actual defense. I will attack you, throw you on the ground, and force myself between your legs, and you will try to stop me with everything you have. Don't hold back, Kiara. You can't hurt me."

"Okay," I said. I wiped my hands of my pants because they were sweaty from nerves.

Nino regarded me calmly, but then something in his expression shifted, becoming calculating and predatory, and I knew he was about to pounce. Despite that knowledge, I yelped when he grabbed me by the hips. After a second of freezing, I brought my knee up, but he dodged it with his thigh and pressed me to the ground with his body. Then he was over me, kneeling between my legs, his pelvis pressed to mine. My wrists were pinned above my head and no amount of struggling made him budge. My breathing turned ragged as panic swirled in the pit of my stomach, not as bad as before, but it was definitely there.

"Fight it," Nino ordered sharply.

I knew what he meant, but it was so very hard to fight my own mind. I focused on his cool, gray eyes. They had now freed me from my panic twice, and they did again. Slowly, my terror waned and my breathing slowed.

Nino shook his head as he released my wrist, but he stayed on top of me. "It's good that you find comfort in my eyes, Kiara, but it won't help you if you ever get attacked."

I closed my eyes. "Maybe we just have to accept that I will never be able to defend myself and that the next time someone like my uncle comes around, he can take whatever he wants from me."

Nino's lips brushed my ear, making my eyes shoot open in surprise. "You will learn to defend yourself, and I swear nobody will ever hurt you again. Nobody will ever get close."

He pulled back and his expression set my heart aflame with silly emotions. For a moment neither of us moved, and I touched my palms to his muscled chest. My breathing quickened for another reason. For the first time in my life, I was comfortable with a man being on top of me, with him between my legs. Nino finally broke the moment, pushing himself off me, and held a hand out for me. I took it and let him pull me to my feet, but my body still tingled from his closeness.

"Again," he said and the tension in his voice overpowered the fluttering in my belly.

Nino

After working out and we came home, Kiara kept throwing glances my way, but the moment I returned them, she looked away. I couldn't read her mood. She seemed nervous. I went into the shower after she was done but kept the door open as usual. Kiara never came in. My nakedness still made her nervous and it wasn't only from fear.

Remo had been right. She needed to learn to fight someone who scared her, and that person wasn't me. Kiara had come to trust me, and I hadn't expected it. Of course, I had treated her in a way that made me hope for her to be able to relax in my presence. Her cowering fear wasn't something I could tolerate in a wife. I needed someone who could stand up to me, and Kiara was getting there. We still had a ways to go, but unlike my brother, I was patient.

Leaning back against the shower stall, I turned the water to cold so my cock didn't get any ideas. I had a feeling Kiara wouldn't be ready for more exploring today. The fight with Fabiano had unsettled her. And if I was being honest, it had been difficult for me to stand back and watch him touch her, hold her, kneel between her legs. It was something I had never experienced before. I couldn't place an emotion on what I was feeling.

When I entered the bedroom after my shower, Kiara was propped up against the headboard, wearing a thin, silk nightgown that did little to hide her nipples. Her lean legs were crossed at the ankles, a place where Kiara was beautifully sensitive. Her eyes darted up from the book she was holding and did a quick scan over my naked chest, lingering on my briefs, before she returned her gaze to the book, but she wasn't able to focus on what she was reading.

Drying my hair, I walked over to where she pretended to read. "What is wrong? Did I do something to make you nervous? Is it because of the training today? I have to make sure you learn to defend yourself. Going easy on you won't have the desired effect."

I thought we had settled into some sort of understanding. I wouldn't budge on the subject of self-defense. Kiara was well protected. As a Falcone, her last name carried fear through the streets in Las Vegas. Everyone knew she was mine. Everyone knew Falcone protected what was ours and our revenge was cruel and merciless. She was as safe as a woman in our world could be, however, I couldn't see why we shouldn't guarantee the highest level of safety by making Kiara a difficult target. Her gun skills had improved, but she needed to learn to defend herself without the aid of weapons.

She blushed and set down her book then finally looked up at me. Her eyes trailed over my torso and down to my briefs then quickly back up to my face. I narrowed my eyes, trying to gauge her mood. She was nervous. I dropped the towel I'd used to rub my hair dry and sank down on the bed beside her.

"If you don't tell me what bothers you, I can't change my behavior."

"You did nothing," she said quietly. Again, her eyes did a quick scan of my upper body, dipping lower, then jerked back up to my face. This wasn't her being upset over today's events, I realized. I was fairly sure she was aroused, but as usual, I allowed her to make the first move.

"I—I want to sleep with you."

My body reacted at once, blood shooting straight into my cock, but I didn't act on the impulse. I turned toward Kiara, angled my body closer, my arm supporting myself beside her leg, and she scooted forward, dropping her book on the ground. Her lips pressed against mine, and her tongue slipped in. I fought the urge to press her down into the mattress, to cover her with my body and grind myself against her pliable body. I wanted to sink myself into her fucking tight channel, wanted to feel her around my cock and lose myself. There was no denying it.

"Would you like me restrained?" I asked between kisses.

Her brown eyes held mine, and she gave a small shake of her head. "I trust you. I'm not scared of your strength anymore."

I ran my knuckles down her arm. Trust, it was a fragile thing. I knew. I'd only ever trusted my brothers, but I was starting to trust her too. "I will make this good for you, Kiara."

She exhaled and a hint of anxiety tightened her lips. "It won't be like last time, right?" Her voice shook and her eyes looked at me as if she knew I'd keep the past at bay. And fuck, I wanted to do this for her, wanted to show her that what she had gone through wasn't something she would ever relive again.

I traced her breasts through her top. "It will be nothing like that." I kissed her chin down to her throat and collarbone, breathing in her sweet scent, relishing the feel of her silk-soft skin against my lips. "There won't be pain or fear. You will be in control."

Her fingers found the back of my head, and she pushed me down. I complied, brushing her strap off her shoulder and laying her breast bare. I closed my mouth around her erect nipple, and sucked it into my mouth, enjoying the way it puckered under my ministrations.

She gasped, goose bumps rippling over her skin. My hand cupped her other breast, massaging gently before my thumb found her nipple and swiped over it, eliciting a moan from her. I swiped again as I circled her other nipple with my tongue. She began shifting restlessly beside me as she knelt on the bed.

"Nino," she whispered. "Please."

"Please what?" I asked in a raspy voice. I was painfully hard in my briefs, but I tried to shove my need to the back burner.

"I need to come."

"Do you want my mouth?"

She gave a jerky nod.

"Then lie down."

She scooted back and lay down. I climbed on the bed then hooked my fingers in her panties, and when she didn't tense, I pulled them down. She lifted her butt to make it easier for me. Slowly, I eased a knee between her legs, watching her face. There was a second of resistance before she opened up for me. Putting my second knee between her legs, I brushed her thighs lightly and eased her legs farther apart. The sight of her glistening folds sent a ripple of desire through my body, straight into my cock.

Patience was a virtue, but at this moment, being patient felt like an insurmountable task. Taking a deep breath, I stretched out between her thighs as she watched me with need, lips parted, eyes wide and trusting.

She was already very aroused from my ministrations to her nipples, aroused enough for sex, but I wanted her to be relaxed from several orgasms before I entered her. I kissed her thigh, working my way higher to where she wanted my mouth. I breathed over her folds, causing her legs to tremble with need. I kissed her pubic bone then her folds before I took a long lick, tasting her, not caring that it made my cock even harder. Her taste was like a fucking catalyst of my own lust.

Kiara breathed deeply, almost relieved. I established a rhythm of light flutters over her clit and slow circles over her opening until she was writhing and panting. When she was making small, desperate rocking motions with her hips, I pressed my tongue up against her clit firmly, and she fell apart with a cry. Her hand came down on my head, holding me in place, as I focused on her entrance, dipping my tongue in, burying my face all the way in her perfect lap.

I stroked her thigh then moved my hand closer to her pussy and brushed my fingers over her wet flesh. Tracing my index finger along her slit, I waited a few moments, but she didn't tense, and so I slipped one finger into her. My cock jerked, knowing that soon I'd be buried in her wet heat. I began fucking her with my finger slowly as I circled her clit. And that sight lit me on fire. I imagined this came close to feeling emotions, this burning, all-consuming need. Better than the feel of her arousal was the breathless moan falling from Kiara's mouth, the softness of her thighs telling me she enjoyed this without any reservations because she trusted me to be good to her.

I raised my eyes to watch her.

My finger was engulfed by her wetness, and she was fisting the bedsheets, making desperate little moans in her throat. I pulled back a couple of inches.

"How is it, Kiara?" My voice was tight and deep—*on edge*—but Kiara didn't seem bothered by it. A strange warmth settled in my chest, one I couldn't place.

"Good," she whispered then gasped as I curled my finger inside of her, pressing my pad lightly against her G-spot.

"Good?"

"So good, Nino. So good." She sounded as if this was a fucking miracle, as if it was a revelation I had offered her, and something strangely possessive filled my chest.

Kiara was mine.

"Good," I murmured against her wet flesh before I closed my mouth over her clit again and brushed her G-spot. She came again, arching up, clawing at the sheets, gasping and moaning, and I softened my ministrations, allowing her to ride this out. I knew I needed to test her readiness with another finger, but warning her about it posed the risk that she'd tense again. However, she needed to feel in control. "I want to put a second finger in you."

A moment of hesitation. "Okay."

"Try to relax or I will tickle you again," I warned as I slid my finger in and out slowly.

She laughed, and I eased my second finger into her. She tightened in surprise and I didn't move, letting her realize that no pain would follow. She was too wet for that. "Good?"

"Okay," she said.

"Then let's try to make it good." I moved up her body, keeping my fingers inside of her and closed my mouth over her nipple. I teased it for a while before I began moving my fingers in a slow rhythm.

Kiara's walls hugged them tightly, and I couldn't wait to feel them around my cock. After a few seconds, Kiara met my thrusts with her pelvis as I sucked her nipple harder. I released her nub to ask how it was, but Kiara was faster.

"Good, Nino. Please don't stop."

I returned my mouth to her waiting nipple, lightly nibbling, and soon Kiara arched under me, crying out her release. I eased my fingers out of her, which were coated in her juices, and that sight almost undid me.

Her eyes fluttered open, her gaze unfocused, lips pulled into a small, satisfied smile.

"Your body is ready," I rasped, teetering on the edge of control. I'd rarely allowed myself to lose control, and tonight would definitely not be the day.

"I'm ready," she said softly, eyes searching my face. I smiled at her, knowing she needed it to be set at ease.

I pushed myself up and off Kiara. "I think it's best for you to be on top."

"I'm not sure I can do this. Can you be on top?"

I nodded but given her nerves as soon as she realized my physical power, being on top seemed a bad choice. In the boxing ring today, she had handled it well, but it was different than submitting to someone in a bed. I got out of my briefs. I was already painfully hard, but I knew I needed to go slow for Kiara. Never in my life did I have to hold back for someone. I took whatever pleasure women could offer me, and they could offer plenty, but Kiara was my wife and I wanted to treat her right, treat her like a wife was supposed to be treated.

Kiara wasn't a whore or debtor. She was my wife. A Falcone. My responsibility.

She watched me with nerves and trust. I wasn't sure why the realization that she trusted me pleased me as much as it did; only my brothers trusted me, and now Kiara—even though her past had taught her that the people she trusted ended up hurting her.

I climbed back on the bed, and Kiara smiled, but her lips trembled as she did so. I wanted to be in her.

"We don't have to do this," I told her, even if the words flowed painfully from my lips.

"No," she said immediately, touching my chest. Her fingers were shaking. I brought her palm to my mouth and kissed it. She relaxed slightly, reacting well to tenderness, as usual. I enjoyed being gentle with Kiara because the way she responded gave me a great deal of satisfaction. It was a new experience that I hadn't thought possible.

I moved over her slowly, and she opened her legs for me so I could kneel between them. Supporting myself on my arms, I looked down at my wife. I could already see that she was getting overwhelmed by my presence. Her breathing had quickened, and her lashes were fluttering nervously. I wished there was a way for her to realize that this had nothing to do with the rape of her past. Her being on top of me still seemed like the best solution to the problem.

I hovered over her, not moving. "You will feel even more out of control if I enter you. My weight will press you into the mattress, and you will have to yield to the pressure I apply. There really is no helping it," I rasped, trying to ignore the way my cock jerked as I grazed the inside of her thigh. A slight shift of my hips and one thrust was all it would take to sate the burning desire in my veins.

"Why do you want this position?" I asked quietly.

"Because I want you to take lead … and I want to be close to you when we have sex with each other."

"Even when you sit on top of me, I can hold you in my arms. I can easily lead even when you ride me."

Her cheeks flushed at the word ride.

I pushed myself off her and sat back against the headrest. "Move on top," I ordered, deciding to take the decision off her hands.

Kiara got to her knees, biting her lower lip in uncertainty. I softened my expression and brushed her unruly curls away from her face. She leaned into the touch at once. I stroked her cheek with my thumb then ran my fingers down her throat and over her arm. She let out a small breath.

"Ready?" I asked in a forced calm voice.

Kiara nodded and moved closer to me. I grabbed her waist and helped her settle on my lower abdomen. I exhaled when her arousal pressed up against my abs. Her body was so fucking ready. Wrapping my arm around her back, I pulled her toward me, my lips claiming hers in an unrestrained kiss.

Kiara returned the kiss eagerly and rubbed her wet pussy over my pelvis, unconsciously slipping down. I stifled a growl. I just wanted to bury myself in her, but I held back for her, let her feel comfortable on top of me.

When she finally leaned back and looked at me for help, I said, "Lift up a bit and scoot back." She did until she straddled my thighs. I curled my hand around my shaft. She swallowed thickly. "It will be good. I will take care of you, Kiara."

She nodded with a small smile as she gripped my shoulders and positioned herself above my cock. Slowly, her palms slid down until they pressed against my chest and her sopping wet entrance brushed my tip. I restrained a groan, not wanting to startle or scare her.

My balls tightened, my muscles clenching. Fuck. I couldn't remember the last time I'd wanted someone as much as I wanted Kiara right this moment.

"It might sting a little, but you are very aroused, Kiara." I knew I'd find no resistance if I plunged into her. Her body was ready for claiming, but her expression displayed apprehension. I was better at reading her emotions now.

"Help?" she whispered, her dark brown eyes trusting, and my heart picked up its pace for some inexplicable reason.

I pressed my heels into the mattress for leverage and grasped her hips to hold her in place. "I'm going to shift my hips now and enter you," I warned. "I will go very slow so your body can adapt. Tell me if you need me to stop."

Pushing up slightly, my tip slipped in and I suppressed a groan as her walls fisted me tightly. Her lips fell open, brows pulling together. She leaned forward, bringing our faces even closer so her sweet breath ghosted over my face. Her wide eyes held mine.

"Pain?" I asked, my voice harder, rougher than I wanted it to be. With how wet she was, I couldn't imagine she felt pain, but she was also very tight, a delicious combination for my cock and one that made me want to plunge hard and deep into her.

"No," she said. "Stretched."

I waited, even if my body screamed for me to buck my hips and impale her on my length. Her eyes held so many emotions, I had no way of grasping a single one. How must it feel to have that kind of chaos inside your body?

She moved her pelvis, and I took that as permission to lift my hips. I slid deeper into her, her tight heat encasing me perfectly, and she closed her eyes.

"Kiara," I forced out. "I need to see your eyes." I had trouble reading her facial expression without seeing the look in her eyes.

Her lids fluttered open. "Sorry."

I stroked her sides, and she licked her lips. "You can go deeper."

And I did. This time I didn't stop. As I raised my hips, I helped her down until her pussy pressed against my pelvis. I lowered myself to the mattress and took her with me. She became still on top of me as I filled her completely. Fuck. This felt as close to perfection as I could imagine.

She breathed out, and her fingers flexed against my skin. I swallowed. Never before had someone felt as good around my cock. My body screamed to move, to seek the pleasure her tightness could offer. She clung to me, completely motionless.

"Okay?" I asked in a low voice.

Kiara exhaled again. "It feels … good." Tears filled her eyes, and I became as still as she was.

"Why the tears?"

She leaned forward to kiss me and shifted my cock inside of her. I moaned against her mouth, and she gave a small shudder. Her lips brushed mine, and I took her up on the invitation, tasting her mouth. Kissing had always seemed a necessary evil many women required during intercourse, but with Kiara it spiked my own arousal.

Slowly, she pulled back, eyes dark and teary. "I feel like I'm finally free of him."

I stroked her back gently, trying to understand. I had killed him as brutally as I was capable of, and yet this act of tenderness finally destroyed the demons of her past, the memories of his actions. I tightened my hold on her, bringing our bodies flush together, my back pressed against the headboard. For once I didn't know what to say, and it was an unsettling experience.

I began moving, rotating my hips slowly, gently, and she gasped. She looked into my eyes and brushed her lips over mine. Trust. Tenderness. And so many more emotions I didn't understand. I'd never truly resented my incapability to feel, but in this moment I did.

"It feels so good, Nino."

I angled my hips the same way, and Kiara's lids fluttered, but she didn't close her eyes. It was as if she needed to see me, so I returned her gaze. Her lips parted for a soft moan. It was a perfect sound, more perfect than any melody Kiara had ever created on her piano and she had created some of the most beautiful melodies I'd ever heard.

Brushing my thumb over her clit, it moved easily over her heated flesh coated with her juices. My other hand cupped her breast, my thumb flicking over the hardened nub. She cried out and clenched around me.

My eyes rolled back as I fought for control. I wanted to go harder, faster. Fuck. I forced the urge down and focused on my wife as she rocked her hips almost helplessly, trying to find more pleasure but uncertain of her moves. I let her discover the motion she loved as I kept slowly thrusting upward. Every time her eyes widened or her lips parted, my fucking heart clenched. I wasn't sure what was wrong with me. It wasn't a physical response I'd ever encountered during sex.

I flicked my thumb over her clit faster and sped up my thrusts. Kiara's walls clamped tightly around my cock, her nails digging into my skin. She rocked faster, barely meeting my thrusts. It was uncoordinated and unpracticed and yet the best thing I'd ever watched. *The fucking best thing I'd ever felt.*

Her eyes grew wide, body tightening as she came with a loud moan. And finally I let loose, slamming harder into her and hoping she could take it but too far gone to ask, until my release hit me like a tidal wave. My head fell back against the headboard as I spent myself inside her. The fucking tightness in my chest remained.

She fell forward and clung to me, her face buried in my neck, her lips leaving kiss after kiss against my sweaty skin. I ran my hands over her back and arms but stayed away from her neck. That was still a spot she was nervous about. She softened under my touch, breathing deeply.

"I love you," she whispered, and we both stiffened at the same time.

Her breathing hitched against my throat.

Love?

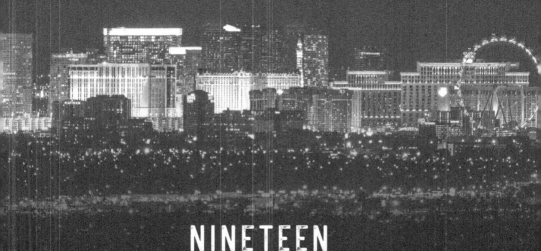

NINETEEN

Kiara

I LOVE YOU.

Nino grew tense beneath me, and I stiffened in turn. I closed my eyes. I couldn't believe I uttered those words. I hadn't considered saying them because I knew Nino couldn't say them back. Love. For him it was something unfathomable, illogical, impossible. He simulated affection for me. Every act of tenderness, every smile and soft expression was a conscious effort.

I swallowed. The words had slipped out without my intention because I'd been so relieved and happy and grateful. I had never told someone I loved them, not even my mother, and no one had ever said it to me.

Nino had been nothing but patient and gentle with me, and it wasn't something I'd expected. Not in my wildest dreams, not from a man like him, and not from a Falcone. I felt safe with him. But saying the words I'd barely dared to admit to myself had been a mistake. I knew it deep down.

Gathering my courage, I pulled back and sat up. Nino was still inside of me, but he was starting to go soft. I was afraid of looking into his face and seeing him stare blankly at me. It was impossible for him to understand why I had said these three words.

When I raised my eyes, Nino looked like he was trying to comprehend what had just happened. His brows drew together, his gray eyes piercing me to the very core as if he was trying to see into my heart and soul, laying me bare when I had already bared myself to him by admitting to my foolishness.

Embarrassment washed over me, and a deep longing that seemed to tear at the seams of my heart filled my chest. I began to pull away, but Nino wouldn't let me. His arms tightened around me. "No," he said firmly. "Don't run."

Had it been that obvious on my face that I wanted to run away, even if there was no way for me to run from my emotions?

He cupped my cheek and kissed me, his expression softening. "You are overwhelmed and relieved because we had sex. It's okay. Don't be embarrassed."

Deep down, I knew this act of kindness as well was a conscious effort. He made his facial muscles go soft because he knew I wanted it, because he knew I needed it.

"I meant what I said," I whispered because I was done running. Nino was right. All my life I'd run from memories, from my family, from men. I was done running, and even if Nino couldn't understand my feelings, that didn't change the fact that I had them.

Nino regarded me, his eyes almost … expressive for once. "Kiara," he began in a low voice.

"I know," I said quickly, my throat tightening. "I know you can't return the emotion. I know you don't feel anything for me, and it's okay. You are trying to be a good man, even though it's not in your nature. You are treating me right, you are simulating affection for me, and that's all right. It's more than I expected when we married and it's enough."

His gaze became searching, and again, I got the feeling that he was trying to peer straight into my heart. Maybe he succeeded because he asked quietly, "Are you sure?"

No, it had been a big fat lie. The idea that Nino could never feel for me what I felt for him filled me with despair, but he had been upfront about his disposition from the very start. I couldn't hold it against him. I wouldn't.

"Does it matter? You can't change who you are. You can't make yourself feel, so even if it bothered me, that wouldn't change a thing. I prefer not to fret over things I can't change."

"That is a logical choice, but you aren't the logical type, Kiara."

I kissed him fiercely, my lips lingering against his as I looked into his gray eyes. As soon as I did, they softened again. Simulated affection. He was so horrifyingly good at it.

"I can try to simulate love," he murmured, and my heart jerked violently. "It's not difficult. Humans have a certain way they act around each other when they are in love."

I was torn between wanting to agree … because if Nino was as good at simulated love as he was at everything else, he could make me believe his emotions were real. I could allow myself to believe a lie. I knew it. But what happened in the moments when I realized the truth, when he forgot to show emotion? These moments would tear me apart if I allowed myself to believe his love could actually be real.

"Kiara," he said quietly, softly, and even that timbre in his voice was fake, and yet my heart surged with warmth upon hearing it.

I shook my head, my lips brushing against his because we were still so close. "Don't simulate love. Everything else, I can deal with, but not love. If you ever tell me you love me, it has to be because you really do love me."

Nino's arms tightened around me and a flicker of wariness filled his expression. He knew it was never going to happen. Nino loving me was an impossibility.

Could you love someone who didn't have emotions? Someone who analyzed love as if it were a mathematical problem?

It wasn't a question that needed answering.

I knew the answer.

I loved Nino, even if he could never love me back.

I had fallen asleep in Nino's arms. And as usual, when I woke the next morning, I was curled into him just like every morning, but today felt different. Light streamed in through the gap in the curtains, and I sighed, my fingers tracing along Nino's stomach.

"How do you feel?"

His voice startled me, even though I'd known he was awake. He always woke before me. I didn't lift my head and pressed my cheek tightly against his chest. "Good."

Nino's hand stroked my arm. "No lies."

"I'm not lying," I said and finally looked up into his calm face. It wasn't exactly cold. "Yesterday, I finally freed myself of him and you helped me do it. That's all that matters."

Nino's fingers moved to my spine then slowly trailed higher, brushing my neck, and I stilled, waiting for the flicker of panic; there was a moment of unease, more because I waited for the panic and memories to surface than because of Nino's touch. He eased his fingers into my curls, cupping the back of my head, and I smiled.

"See. I told the truth."

His eyes narrowed slightly, but I wasn't sure why. He looked almost confused, which was strange for Nino. I propped myself up on his chest and kissed him, and he readily returned the kiss and soon pulled me on top of him, his erection digging into my thigh. He pulled me down until his tip brushed against my opening, but he didn't slip in. Instead, he kissed me and his hands massaged my ass cheeks. I allowed myself to drown in the taste of his lips, allowed the strokes of his rough fingertips to steal the last of my tiredness.

He pulled back slightly, his expression tense with desire. "I want you."

I kissed him harder, answering him with my body and not with words. His fingers moved between my legs, slipping between my folds, and he exhaled.

"So wet," he murmured.

I bit my lip when two of his fingers pushed into me. The sensations spread from my core into every nerve ending, and I arched up, allowing him to push deeper into me. How could I have ever thought this wouldn't be good? Nino managed to make everything good for me.

He watched me with toe-curling intensity as I rocked my hips against his fingers. My pleasure was mounting, and I could feel myself getting closer. Nino pulled his fingers out before I could find my release, and I huffed in protest, squirming on top of him for some friction against his pelvis.

"You'll get it," he growled, and I shivered hearing his voice.

He gripped my hips and pulled me down until finally his tip slipped into me, and I moaned at the sensation. He pushed his hips up, sliding all the way in, and I shuddered through my release, desperately clinging to him as my walls clenched around his length.

I buried my face against his throat as he rocked his hips, driving himself into me again and again. No pain, no fear, no memories.

Only Nino's warmth and the pleasure only he could bring me. Clinging to his shoulders, I looked into his eyes, and in my mind three words repeated themselves over and over again.

I love you. I love you. I love you.

Neither of us broke eye contact as Nino slammed into me over and over again, and when his thumb flicked over my clit, I threw my head back as pleasure coursed through me. Nino growled against my throat, his tongue swiping over my pulse point. Then he bit down lightly as he released into me.

Listening to his pounding heart, I relaxed. Love: a game for fools. I wasn't sure where I'd read the phrase, but I knew it was true.

That night Nino had his first fight since we got married. I was more nervous than he was, which wasn't really all that difficult. But still, I was *really* nervous.

I put on the elegant red cocktail dress that I had bought with Nino. It wasn't as luxurious as the other dresses, but it accentuated my curves in a way I had never allowed before. I had always been worried that displaying my body would make people blame me for what happened, that it would make them see that I wasn't the epitome of purity I was supposed to be, but I wanted to be rid of that thinking as well.

Nino had already left an hour ago so he could prepare for his fight, and I was supposed to ride with Savio. In the last few weeks, he had avoided me, probably because he resented me for the whore-ban in the communal space in the house.

When I walked toward the main part of the house, I found Savio lounging on the sofa, texting someone on his phone. He had a strange smile on his face as he stared at his screen, but he quickly shoved his phone into his pocket when he noticed me and straightened. His dark eyes scanned me from head to toe, and despite him being two years younger than me at only seventeen, he managed to make me nervous with his attention.

"You look hot in red," he said, surprising me.

"Thanks?" I said hesitantly, not sure how to handle his compliment.

He nodded and came toward me. Savio was almost as tall as Nino and held himself with complete confidence.

I tensed when he stopped beside me.

"You don't have to get all tense because I'm close," he said. "You are family. I'm here to protect you."

I raised my eyebrows. "So far you haven't seemed too happy having me around."

He shrugged. "It's annoying that I can't fuck girls where I want now that you're here. I have to go to my part of the house. I really liked to fuck on the pool table."

I grimaced. "Okay. I'm glad you and Remo both fancy the table."

He smiled, and it transformed his face, making him more approachable. He was more controlled than Remo in some regards but nowhere near as calm as Nino, and he was way cockier than both of them.

"Come on. I don't want to be late for the fight. Nino's going to rip that ass-hole a new one."

Savio led me toward his Ferrari. He drove like a madman, and I clutched the seat as if that would save me if he crashed the car. Apparently, Adamo wasn't the only one who enjoyed racing. I definitely wasn't a speed junky.

When Savio and I entered Roger's Arena, a shiver passed through my spine. The place was crowded with people. Every table and booth was occupied, and many people stood against the wall. The scent of blood, beer, and sweat hung in the air, and the neon tubes attached to the mesh wire on the bare concrete walls emitted an eerie glow.

My eyes scanned the words they formed. Honor. Pain. Blood. Victory. Strength. The bar was cast in the same red glow, and the women behind it worked in overdrive to serve the customers quickly. Looking down at myself, I realized how well the blood red of my dress fit the occasion.

Savio nodded toward a red leather booth close to the cage, where Fabiano and Leona were sitting. "Come on. Let's go over to them."

In passing, we greeted his friends and their fathers and a few people I didn't know but who obviously knew who I was.

Arriving at the booth, Leona gave me an encouraging smile. "It'll be okay. Nino is undefeated in the cage."

Fabiano nodded. "He's brain and muscle … that's too much for most opponents."

I gave them both a grateful smile as I slipped into the booth across from them. "I know, but I'm really not looking forward to seeing Nino getting hurt."

Savio snorted. "Don't worry. My brother is invincible."

Nobody was, not even Nino, even if his emotionless mask made everyone believe it. Nino was human. He could fail. He could get hurt.

Leona regarded me curiously, and I wondered if my feelings for Nino were obvious to people around me. I hoped I could hide them, because how foolish would I appear if people realized I'd come to love someone incapable of emotion?

"I'll be back in a few minutes. I need to talk to Diego," he said. His friend was giving him signs. Savio walked off without another word, and a waitress with long black hair and pink lipstick appeared at our booth. She gave Leona a tense smile, ignoring Fabiano, and finally turned to me with a wary expression. "What would you like to drink, Mrs. Falcone?"

That name still made me pause. "Do you have wine?"

The waitress pursed her lips. "This is a fight bar. We have liquor or beer."

"Careful, Cheryl," Fabiano said in a low voice that sent a shiver through my body. His blue eyes held a clear warning as he regarded the waitress. "You better remember who she is."

Leona touched his arm, which was propped up on the table, but Fabiano didn't take his eyes off the woman. Enforcer. It was easy to forget what that meant.

I felt bad for her and quickly said, "Then a beer." I needed something alcoholic to calm my nerves and hard liquor was out of the question. I didn't have the necessary tolerance for it.

"And one for me," Remo said as he appeared close behind Cheryl. She tensed and stepped aside to let him pass.

"I'll bring it over in a moment," she said then rushed off.

To my surprise, Remo slipped into my booth. As usual, my body tightened with unease at his closeness. He gave me a challenging look but didn't come close enough so we'd touch. "Still?" he asked with a twisted smile.

He didn't have to elaborate. I knew what he meant, and I didn't think I'd stop being wary of him anytime soon. He hadn't given me reason to do so, but something about Remo just screamed danger, and I wasn't the only one who felt that way.

Leona rolled her eyes when Remo turned to Fabiano.

"I saw that," he said under his breath.

I stifled a laugh. Sometimes, very rarely, I managed to get past my fear of Remo. In those moments, I almost understood why Nino thought so highly of his brother.

Two men in fight shorts entered the cage. My brows furrowed. "I thought Nino's fight was next?"

"The biggest fight is always last," Fabiano explained. "There are two fights before Nino's. Whoever wins might end up fighting me or perhaps Savio next."

"Why do you do this? Why do you keep fighting? It's not like people don't fear you enough."

"If you get comfortable, you get weak. That happens to many people in positions of power. It's good to prove to people and to yourself that you are still someone to fear," Remo said, his dark eyes passionate and fierce.

The referee gave the signal. At once, the two men barreled toward each other and collided with grunts. I winced as I watched their kicks and punches. Cheryl returned with our beers, and I took a deep gulp despite my aversion to the taste. One of the men flew against the cage and blood spurted out of his mouth.

I covered my own with my hand. "Oh God."

Remo cocked an eyebrow. "This is nothing."

"Maybe for you," I muttered.

"You'll get used to the sight." He nodded toward Leona. "She did."

"I still don't enjoy it," Leona said. "Especially if Fabiano's in the cage. It's horrible seeing him getting hurt." She shuddered.

"I'm not getting hurt," Fabiano said firmly. "I always win."

Savio returned and sank down beside Remo. "Because you've never fought against me."

"I've fought against you, and I kicked your ass," Fabiano muttered.

"That was more than a year ago."

The crowd burst into applause, and my eyes darted toward the cage where one man lay unmoving on the floor while the other stood above him with raised hands.

My heart beat in my throat when the referee finally announced Nino's fight. His opponent, a man the size of a giant, was already waiting in the cage when Nino stepped out of the changing room.

The crowd regarded Nino with respect and fear as he walked through the aisle they'd made for him. His eyes were directed straight ahead at the cage with an expression of cold determination, yet something was different about him. For once the emotionless mask seemed almost forced, as if he had to make it appear that way. Or maybe my own nerves had me imagining things.

Nino climbed into the cage under the roaring applause of the crowd. In his fight shorts and with his gruesome tattoos, he was an intimidating sight. The moment Nino had entered the room, Remo, Savio, and Fabiano had changed their behavior. There expressions showed no hint of doubt or worry, only pride and the grim knowledge that Nino would win.

I knew Nino was a good fighter, but his opponent was several inches taller and much wider than Nino. My husband didn't seem impressed by the man in front of him, and the moment the ref got out of the cage and closed the door, he switched into predator mode. His entire body became taut, his eyes cautious as they regarded their opponent.

The man was the first to attack. I tensed when he barreled toward Nino, who jumped to the side and landed a hard kick in the man's side. Remo cheered loudly, and Savio and Fabiano applauded, but I could not move.

Nino seemed off. I couldn't quite pinpoint what it was. His opponent got him good in the first few minutes of the fight. Nino was thrown against the cage and landed on the floor hard. I jerked violently, clamping my hand over my mouth to stop a scream as tears formed in my eyes. Remo tensed, leaning forward as if he was on the verge of jumping up.

I sucked in a deep breath, trying not to cry. Remo looked, scanning my expression and eyes. "Don't lose it. This is public."

I blinked. "What if he loses?" I whispered. "What if he dies?"

Remo narrowed his eyes in anger, but there was something else there. Worry. "Nino won't lose, and he definitely won't fucking die. Understood?"

I gave a nod, and to my relief, Nino was already back on his feet. For a moment, he didn't move, only regarded the man who was taunting him. Then his eyes moved toward me for a second, and my body exploded with emotions.

He turned back to his opponent and as if a switch was turned, Nino dropped the analytic calm. I had never seen that look on his face. He lunged at the other man and attacked viciously. He looked unhinged, hungry for blood and death, and he kicked and punched his opponent over and over again, not stopping even as the man dropped to the ground.

It was a deeply unsettling sight.

"What's gotten into him?" Savio muttered.

Remo didn't take his eyes off the cage, but his mouth thinned. "I don't know."

Nino thrust his fist down on the unconscious man one more time. Then he staggered to his feet, covered in blood, gray eyes alight with fury. Even scarier was how quickly the emotion was replaced his usual calm. What had just happened?

Nino left the cage before the judge declared him the winner and stalked toward the changing rooms under the applause of the crowd.

I jumped to my feet. "Let me out," I said.

Remo stood as well and gripped my arm. I tensed but didn't pull away because people were watching, and I knew how to keep up appearances. "I don't think this is a good time for you to go to Nino. I will handle him."

"Nino won't hurt me," I said quietly.

Remo tilted his head. "Are you sure about that?" His voice held a challenge.

I gave a resolute nod. "Absolutely. Let me go to him."

Remo smiled coldly and motioned for Savio to make room. They both stepped out of the booth so I could leave before sitting back down.

Remo held my gaze. "I've never seen Nino like this, but if you think you can handle him, be my guest."

Straightening my spine, I moved through the crowd, who backed away from me as if I was contagious. Some people gave me pitying looks; others regarded me as if I was someone to be scared of. *Kiara Falcone.* I heard their hushed whispers.

I was glad when I reached the changing room and stepped inside.

Nino wasn't in front of the lockers, but I heard the shower running and walked around the corner until I caught sight of him in the last stall. He was braced against the tiles, head hanging low as water poured down his body. His head turned and the look in his gray eyes sent a stab of worry through me.

"Are you all right?" I asked breathlessly.

Nino straightened in all his naked glory, covered in cuts and bruises. Magnificent. "Come closer," he said in a strange voice.

I moved toward him but stopped in front of the shower. Nino stared down at me as if I was a problem he wanted to solve. His expression was intense, on the verge of angry, which didn't make sense considering this was Nino. He didn't feel anger. He didn't feel anything.

He curled his fingers around my wrist and pulled me toward him, his eyes not once breaking their staring. "Nino," I protested. "My clothes."

But he didn't hear me. His lips claimed my mouth, stopping me from saying any more. He pressed into me, his tall frame caging me in. His hand brushed my thigh, pushing up my dress, shoving aside my panties. He slipped a finger into me, his mouth still soft yet dominant, and I arched back against the tiled wall. He followed, not allowing me to escape his overwhelming presence as his free hand cupped my breast through my wet dress. I wasn't sure what had gotten into him. His touch and kisses were overwhelming, but my body reacted with a tidal wave of arousal as he slid his finger in and out of me.

He nipped at my lower lip then licked water off it and claimed my mouth again, possessive, unrelenting, desperate ... but how was it possible?

His thumb swiped over my clit as he moved his finger faster. "Nino," I gasped out. "What—"

Again he interrupted me with an almost harsh kiss. I blinked up, confused and turned on, and a bit unsettled but not enough to stop. He added another finger, and I grasped his shoulders to steady me. He hooked one of my legs over his hip, opening me up so he could slam his fingers deeper into me. I rocked against his hand, clinging to him as his mouth ravaged mine, all the while his eyes never looking away from mine as if he was trying to devour me. As if he needed me. He flicked his thumb over my clit again, and I cried against his lips when my orgasm rocked through me. Stars burst in my vision, an almost blinding pleasure. My fingers dug deeper into Nino's skin.

I stared at him, openmouthed, panting. He slowed his thrusts then eased his fingers out.

He released me but moved even closer until he filled all of my vision and breathed harshly as he stared down at me. He was hard, digging into my stomach, but he made no move to take things further, and it confused me, like his expression confused me.

"Nino?" I reached for his chest, trailing my fingers over it then moving lower. He didn't take his eyes off me, but when I curled my fingers around his shaft, his hand came down on them, and he leaned forward, his mouth brushing my ear.

"If I fuck you now, it's going to be against this wall. It's going to be hard and fast, and nothing like last time. Nothing like you want. Nothing like you need."

I shivered at the underlying threat in his voice. I gazed up into his eyes, and again they shifted between anger and absolute calm. I didn't understand any of it. Had the fight unchained him that much? Remo and Savio had been stunned by his behavior, so it wasn't something that happened with every fight.

"You won't hurt me."

He took a deep breath, chest heaving, and closed his eyes. My dress clung to my body and my feet swam in my heels, but I stayed where I was, close to Nino, as he battled whatever demons the fight had summoned. His breathing slowed and his hand around mine loosened until he finally released me completely.

I kept my fingers around his erection and lightly brushed my thumb over the silky tip. Nino's eyes jerked open, but this time he didn't stop me. I moved my hand slowly up and down, not hard and fast, trying to give him comfort and not let this be his outlet for the violence brooding in his body. He braced himself, placing his hands on both sides of my head, and regarded me through half-closed eyes.

He rocked his hips in rhythm with my pumps, and eventually some of the tension slipped away. His breathing deepened as I rubbed him, and when I used my second hand to cup his balls, he let out a low breath and pumped even faster. I wanted to comfort him, wanted to show him that I was there for him.

Nino lowered his head, and I tilted mine back to meet his mouth for a kiss. It was gentle, unhurried, and deliciously slow. No anger or violence, only beautiful sensuality. My own body responded to the kiss and the feel of Nino coming undone under my touch. His moves became less controlled and his kiss more passionate, and then his body tightened, and he groaned against my mouth. He jerked in my hand, his eyes closing. I kept stroking, and for a long time he stayed still, his forehead lightly pressed up against mine, his chest heaving.

I released him and the water washed away every trace of our juices. Nino opened his eyes again, and his expression was back to the familiar calm. I was torn between missing the more unhinged version of him, the one he'd never shown before, and being relieved that Nino hadn't lost it completely.

He straightened, robbing me of his heat. He turned the water off, his eyes trailing the length of me. "You can't walk out of the changing room in wet clothes," he said matter-of-factly.

I searched his face for a hint of something, but he returned my gaze steadily, eerily. He stepped out of the shower and grabbed two towels. "It's probably for the best if you undress and dry yourself. I will get dressed and see if I can organize clothes for you."

Nodding mutely, I took the towel, wrapping it around my curls to stop them from dripping all over the place. I peeled my soaking dress off my body. Despite his words, Nino didn't leave or move to get dressed. Instead, he watched me remove my dress then my underwear. "Nino, are you all right? You've been off since the fight."

"I'm fine," he murmured then finally dried himself off and got dressed. "I'll be back in a few minutes."

"What if someone comes in?" I asked, a hint of worry creeping into my voice.

Nino shook his head. "Nobody will dare to come in. Trust me. I won't be gone long."

He disappeared, and I wrapped another towel around myself, staring down at the red heap at my feet. What had gotten into Nino?

As promised, he returned a few minutes later with jeans and a plain black T-shirt. "Roger's waitresses keep spare clothes in case they spill something."

I took the clothes and put them on. They were a bit too big on me, but at least they smelled clean and were dry. I cringed, thinking about what people would say if I came out in different clothes than before.

"Something is bothering you," Nino said, coming a bit closer, his brows drawn together.

"I'm worried what people will think of me."

He gripped my waist and pulled me toward him. "They will think that you gave your husband a prize for winning."

My cheeks grew hot. "Yeah, that."

"And?" he asked quietly, the strange look still in his eyes. He nibbled my throat, then my ear. "You are my wife."

My lashes fluttered, and I released a strangled breath. I was already getting aroused again. He picked my dress up from the ground, wrung it out, and put it into his bag before taking my hand. I took my slippery heels in my free hand and followed Nino out of the changing room, barefoot.

Most people had left the bar by now, but everyone who was still there stared at us. It took all of my self-control not to duck my head under the force of their scrutiny. Nino's presence helped. He appeared completely unfazed, of course. When we arrived at the booth with his brothers and Fabiano and Leona, they all regarded us strangely. My face heated, knowing what they were thinking.

Remo's evaluating gaze was especially hard to bear. His eyes narrowed as they moved between his brother and me. "I take it you fucked his strange behavior right out of him?"

My mouth fell open. "I—I didn't—"

Nino squeezed my hand. "Let's go home. I'm done with this day."

Remo nodded then exchanged another look with Fabiano and Savio. They were as puzzled by Nino's strange behavior as I was.

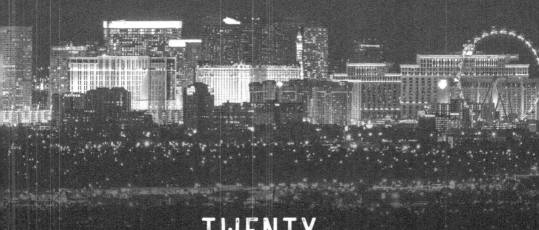

TWENTY

Kiara

NINO DIDN'T SAY ANYTHING ON OUR DRIVE HOME. I KEPT GLANCING AT him but his eyes were closed. There was a cut over his cheekbone, and the skin around it was swelling. At least it wasn't bleeding.

Remo watched us occasionally through the rearview mirror as he drove his car, but he didn't say anything.

When we walked into the mansion, Nino headed straight toward our wing. Remo gripped my wrist before I could follow.

I flinched, but he didn't release me. "Will you stop this shit?" he growled. I forced myself to meet his angry gaze. "Keep an eye on my brother. I don't know what's gotten into him. Usually he would analyze the fight like a fucking computer program right after. That he's like this is a fucking bad sign."

"Has he ever been like this?" I asked.

Something in Remo's eyes shifted as if he was remembering something. He loosened his grip. "Just keep a fucking eye on him."

I turned and continued toward our wing of the mansion then upstairs into the bedroom. Nino was perched on the edge of the bed, arms propped up on his legs as he stared down at the ground. He was completely naked.

I approached him, but he didn't move. Slowly, I raked my finger through his still damp hair, and finally he raised his eyes to meet mine. "I want you," he said quietly.

Leaning forward, I kissed him, my fingernails scratching his scalp, making him shudder and release a low breath. He tugged at my jeans and pushed them down my legs. I wasn't wearing panties. He leaned forward and kissed my hipbones, biting down lightly and making me jump. Then he soothed the spot with his tongue. Slowly, he trailed his tongue down from my hipbones to my upper thigh and then between my legs.

I gasped when he slipped his tongue between my folds. I was already aroused, but the feel of his mouth against my heated flesh increased it even further. Nino hooked a palm under my knee and lifted my leg, propping it up on the bed and opening me for him.

Watched him through half-closed eyes, his lips moved over my folds and his tongue slid along my crease, tasting me. His eyes met mine, and I couldn't look away despite the embarrassment heating my cheeks. Never taking his gaze off me, he ran the tip of his tongue up and down before he circled my clit.

"Nino," I gasped, parting my legs wider, needing to feel more of his mouth on me. He buried his face in my lap, his mouth closing over my folds as his tongue worked me. His hands cupped my ass, and he massaged my cheeks, pushing me even harder against his face. I couldn't hold back anymore, starting to shake and rocking my hips almost desperately as I held on to Nino's shoulders. My moans spurred him on, and he licked and nibbled greedily until I was sure I'd come again, but then he pulled away, his face glistening with my arousal.

His eyes were alight with desire. I quickly pulled my shirt over my head then bit my lip. "How?" I asked quietly.

He curled a hand over my hip and tugged me toward the bed. I climbed on top of the mattress. "Lie down on your side," Nino instructed in a low voice.

Surprised, I stretched out, my back facing Nino. He lay down behind me and pressed up against my body, his erection digging into my butt. I tensed. His mouth grazed my ear. "Trust me. I'm not going to do anal, Kiara."

I felt foolish but nodded. Nino slid one arm under me then lifted my upper leg with his other and moved it slightly back so my foot rested on his strong calf. Then he pressed his pelvis against my butt, and I felt his tip nudge my opening. He changed the angle slightly and slowly slid in. I arched back against him.

He didn't go as deep in this position, but I loved the feel of his chest against my back, his hot mouth against my shoulder and neck, his arms around me from behind. His movements were slow, but his tip seemed to rub my clit from the inside, and when he trailed his hand down between my legs, I released a low moan.

"This position okay for you?" he rasped against my ear as his next stroke hit me even deeper.

"Yes," I gasped.

Nino's closeness, his warm embrace, his soft kisses along my shoulder blade … they made this perfect. Nino cupped my breast, fingers tweaking my nipple as his other hand worked nimbly between my legs. He slammed into me over and over again, slow, precise strokes that curled my toes and made my eyes roll back with pleasure.

It was beautiful and breathtaking, and I let myself fall completely. I trusted Nino without reservation to guide me over the edge, to take care of me, and he did.

I tightened as my release hit me, and I cried out Nino's name. He rasped mine into my ear, the word almost desperate as he spilled inside me moments after my orgasm. He didn't pull back, holding me closely against his body, still buried deep inside of me.

He eased out of me, and I turned in his embrace. I lightly traced the skin around the cut in his cheekbone then the blooming bruises over his ribs. He tensed under my touch.

"Sorry," I breathed. "Are you in a lot of pain? Clearly, I have nothing better to do than to rub myself against you when you're bruised."

He tangled his hand in my curls, regarding me with an unreadable expression. "I was the one who initiated sex, Kiara. I wanted you. I..." He trailed off, brows pulling together "...I've survived many fights. I'll be healed in a few days."

I didn't say anything, only snuggled against Nino's chest, careful not to apply pressure to his ribs. I kissed his shoulder blade, and uttered in my head the words I'd never say aloud again. *I love you.*

A low noise I couldn't place tore me from sleep. Even with Nino beside me, I was a light sleeper, quick to wake from the slightest noise. I stared into the dark and there it was again: a throaty sound full of dark despair. What was that?

A wave of fear shot through me when a familiar tone caught my attention. Nino? Was that Nino?

The sound stirred memories within me, but I pushed them aside and rolled over. In the dark, I couldn't make out more than the outline of Nino's back, but the bed was shaking from the force of his body tremors.

"Nino?" I whispered, but my voice was so hesitant and quiet I could barely hear it.

My first instinct was that it had to be a seizure, something physical because it seemed impossible that emotions forced these sounds out of *Nino.* These throaty inhales—not moans, not gasps, but something in between—were full of emotion. I didn't understand. Slowly, I sat up, unsure if I should wake him, completely at loss what to do. Nino was always in control. He *was* control.

Reached over to my bedside, I turned on the light, needing to see him and at the same time terrified of it. Nino was lying on his side, shaking, one hand curled around the edge of the bed, clutching it tightly; his brows formed one hard line and his forehead was covered in sweat.

My fingers shook as I reached for him. My God, what was going on with him?

The second my fingertips brushed his shoulder, his eyes flew open and the look in them made me recoil. Nino lunged for the knife on his bedside table, clutching it in his hand as he staggered out of bed. His gaze pinged around the room then settled on me, the way I was pressed up against the headboard in confusion and fear. His legs gave out. Pressing the knife to his chest, he bent forward, braced against the ground with one arm, heaving deep breaths.

"Nino?" I whispered, crawling to the edge of the bed.

Nino said he wasn't capable of emotions, that he couldn't feel, but in his eyes and on his face was pure unbridled emotion. And he couldn't handle it, didn't know how. Maybe this was the first time in a long time that he was submitted to something like that.

His back was heaving, arms shaking, and somehow in the diffused glow of the bedside lamp, his tattoos seemed to come alive, the inked flames leaping up, the contorted faces mocking yet agonizing at the same time.

My throat clogged with emotion, helpless and terrified and worried that this was it, that something had snapped Nino's sanity—whatever was left of it. My love for him didn't make me blind to the truth: Nino and Remo both were messed up in a way that couldn't be resolved with a few pills and countless sessions with a shrink. Something awful had twisted them into what they were today, twisted Nino's emotions into a tight knot. Something had managed to untie it. Seeing him like this made me think that maybe there had been a good reason why his mind and body had tied that knot in the first place.

I slid out of bed and approached Nino hesitantly, but he jerked his head to the side. "Remo," he croaked. Then it got louder, more desperate. "Get Remo!"

Stumbling toward the door, I ripped it open and ran down the corridor. My heart beat in my throat and my bare feet smacked loudly against the cold granite. What was going on with Nino?

Fear, raw and unhinged, rushed through me. What if I lost Nino to whatever this was?

I crossed over into the east wing, Remo's domain. I'd never been there before and I knew I wasn't welcome, but Nino needed his brother, so no matter how scared I was of Remo, I would get him.

It took me a moment to get my bearings in the unfamiliar part of the house. I wasn't sure where Remo's bedroom was and with only minimal moonlight streaming in through the window at the end of the corridor, it was difficult to make out more than the hazy outlines of doors. Panicking, I ripped open the first door, and even in the dark I could make out the shape of a bed. An old smell hung in the air, something dusty and abandoned. Nobody had lived there in a while.

There were so many rooms in this house, I'd never find him in time. I felt the wall for a light switch, but my body shook and I couldn't get my bearings. The dark was beginning to close in on me, but I moved on to the next door, my finger curling around the handle. Then there was a warm breath against my ear and a low murmur. "What the fuck are you doing here?"

I screamed and lashed out instinctively, my hand colliding with a stubble-covered chin a moment before I realized whom I'd just hit. A strong hand clamped down on my wrist. I stilled, suddenly glad for the dark because it hid Remo's expression from me.

"Let me go," I whispered, voice shaking.

He released me, and I stepped back. "I'm sorry for hitting you," I got out. "You scared me."

He remained silent for another moment, towering over me with that unsettling vibe of violence. "Answer my question," he ordered.

"It's Nino. I don't know what's happening with him. He's upset."

"Upset," Remo said doubtfully.

"Remo, please, can you turn on the light." I swallowed. "It's making me nervous being in the dark with you."

He shifted and his arm brushed mine, then light flooded the corridor. When my eyes grew accustomed to the blinding light, Remo came into focus, tall and naked except for briefs. His eyes slid down my body, dressed only in my thin nightgown, before they returned to my face. His chin was slightly red from when I'd hit him.

"I'm losing my patience here, Kiara."

"Nino needs your help!" I said annoyed, because there was no way I could explain Nino's situation to him. And finally something went through to him, and he turned around and began running. I had absolutely no chance to catch up with him with his long legs.

Panting, I arrived in our bedroom a couple of minutes later.

Remo was kneeling beside his brother, who was on the ground, his hand on Nino's shoulder. They both looked like fallen angels with their curved backs, their scars and tattoos, the muscles formed from years of fighting. Remo's fallen angel on his back with the broken wings had never made more sense than it did now.

"What's happening?" I croaked, and Remo looked up from where he knelt beside his brother. For a moment he looked as helpless, as terrified as I felt, and that sight undid me because this was Remo, this was a man always commanding, always hard and powerful and cruel and not afraid of anything. It came almost as a relief when he narrowed his eyes at me, his mouth pulling into a twisted smile, as if this was my fault, as if without realizing it, I had broken Nino even though I held nowhere close to the power over him to do so.

"Get out," Remo growled, but I didn't want to leave. "Get out!" he snarled, and I knew he'd make me if I didn't, so I rushed out and ran along the corridor, down the stairs, and into our living room, which wasn't really called that because most living room activities took place in the shared area of the mansion when all the brothers were together. This was my sanctuary and sometimes Nino's when he tried to simulate affection for me.

I sank down on the piano bench. My fingers instantly found the keys, needing to feel their cool smoothness. The first notes of the song I'd written for Nino rang out. Desperate, drawn-out, low notes in the beginning then hesitant, higher notes, lighter notes until the melody seemed almost excited in their staccato, followed by overwhelming, high-pitched notes until finally the melody became a gentle flow, a song of acceptance, but this ending seemed wrong now, and my fingers moved on, the notes reaching higher and higher, filling me up until my emotions created this melody.

I breathed harshly as Nino's despair became music, as my fear let the melody burst through me with hard, short notes. Emotion was everywhere and I could not stop and felt like this was the only way I could get through this.

Heavy steps sounded and my fingers slid off the keys as Remo stalked into the room and toward me, still only in his briefs and a look of murder on his face. I stiffened but didn't follow my impulse to run. Instead, I lowered my shaking hands to my lap and returned Remo's gaze. He stopped halfway into the room as if he was torn between anger and despair, but then he bridged the remaining distance between us, dwarfing me with his height and sheer, brutal presence.

He leaned down, and I drew back but didn't look away. "What the fuck did you do?" he rasped.

"I didn't do anything," I said. What could I have possibly done to unhinge Nino like that? I was only a woman. I didn't have any power over him.

"Bullshit."

"Remo, leave her alone." It was Nino's voice, strangled, raw, and yet cool and controlled. I sagged with relief. Remo stepped back from me and turned to his brother, opening my view to Nino as well.

Like Remo, Nino was only in briefs, and yet there were layers over layers of barriers I could never bridge. His expression was the blank canvas I'd grown used to, but there was something haunted, *something hunted* in his gray eyes as he stared at Remo; a look passed between the brothers that spoke of horrors I could not grasp, a look that made me realize that one brother could never be without the other.

Whatever had shaped them into ice and fire, it had also forged them together in a way that couldn't be broken. Maybe Nino had become the cold flood against Remo's raging inferno. Perhaps Remo was the outlet for emotions Nino had locked behind impenetrable walls. I couldn't and would never be able to understand these two men.

Nino tore his eyes away from his brother and looked at me. My chest tightened with relief and warmth, and I wanted to go to him and hug him, wanted to soothe him with words, give him comfort with my touch, but Nino wasn't like that. He didn't need comfort, or tenderness, *or love...*

"Play that song again," he said quietly.

I touched my fingertips to the keys and began the song, a song that wasn't just a string of notes but a gaping hole in my heart. Nino approached me slowly, and as he did, Remo backed away a few steps but kept watching us.

Nino lowered himself beside me on the bench, but I didn't stop playing. I closed my eyes and let the music flow, wishing he could understand that this song encompassed everything I felt for him, everything I'd ever felt for him. Then new notes rang out, and my eyes jerked open, my fingers faltering as Nino began to play the song as well. *What?*

He added his own notes, and I realized it was on purpose. I joined in and played my melody, the two melodies seeming to flow around each other. It was more beautiful than anything I'd ever heard. Nino's eyes were on my face as he played the song from memory without faltering, but I had to return my gaze to the keys because I couldn't understand the look in his eyes.

Remo met my gaze briefly over the piano, and his expression was just as unreadable. Then he turned around and left. I didn't understand any of this, but hearing Nino's melody merge with mine, creating something inexplicably beautiful ... it felt like a gift.

Nino and I played until the sun rose over the mansion and filled the room with light. Our melody had evolved, a string of beautiful notes, and my heart seemed to burst with emotions when our fingers finally lifted off the keys. Nino looked exhausted, and my own body yearned for sleep too, but at the same time, I felt like screaming my feelings from the rooftops.

I stood and took Nino's hand. His cool gaze flitted up to me. "Let's go to bed," I whispered.

Something shifted in his eyes as if for once there was something that scared him, as if he didn't trust himself while asleep.

"We don't have to sleep, but you need to rest for a bit," I told him, and finally he got up from the piano bench and followed me upstairs.

Nino lay down, and I stretched out beside him, close but not touching. I wanted to press up against him, give him closeness. In the past he'd held me to comfort me, not because he required that kind of attention.

My gaze flickered across his face. His eyes were distant, and there was tightness to his mouth that suggested he was still fighting something within him.

I couldn't hold back anymore and reached out for him, laying one hand hesitantly on his arm. It was ridiculous for me to be worried about touching him. We'd been closer than that, but I didn't want to push something onto Nino if he didn't want it just because it would have helped me.

His eyes zeroed in on me, and he lifted his arm so I could move closer, and I snuggled up to him, my hand coming to rest on his hard abs. I wished I knew if this was something he wanted, something he needed, or if he did it for me as part of his simulated affection.

I didn't dare ask him what had caused this episode, or what he had seen in his mind to bring him to his knees like that, but the question burned on my tongue. Maybe one day he would tell me.

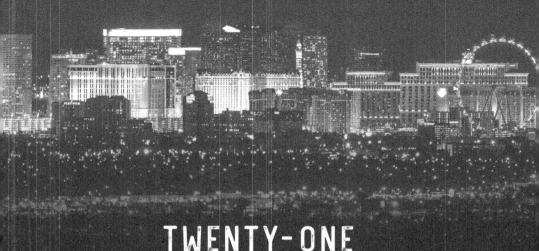

TWENTY-ONE

Kiara

WE STAYED IN BED UNTIL MIDDAY, AND FOR ONCE, I WOKE BEFORE Nino. I was wedged against his side as usual, and he looked peaceful sleeping, no sign of last night's episode visible on his face. His cheek bone was swollen with a bluish tint as expected, but it didn't make Nino less attractive. For some reason this small blemish on his perfect face made him even more beautiful.

He stirred and opened his eyes. I smiled at him. "How do you feel?"

He remained silent for a few heartbeats. "Different."

"Different?" I echoed, confused, but he didn't elaborate. He untangled himself from the blankets and sat up with a slight wince, his palm pressing up against his ribs.

"Do you need something for the pain?"

"No," he said. "It'll fade. And pain is a good motivator. Next time I'll have to be better so my opponent doesn't land hits like this."

I climbed out of bed as well and hovered beside him. "Will you go swimming?"

Nino nodded. "It'll help with the tiredness."

I grabbed my book and put on my bathrobe while Nino put on his swim trunks. He didn't bother going into the bathroom anymore. We were past that point. We headed outside in silence, and I took my usual place in the lounge chair while Nino dove into the water. His movements weren't as rhythmic or as smooth as usual. He drove himself harder than ever before, swimming fast and almost angrily. I wasn't sure how one could swim angrily, but it sure looked like it.

I put my book down and stood to get a better view. Nino's breaths were short, less controlled, as he swam one round after the other. This was a much longer swimming session than his daily thirty minutes. Worry gnawed at me as I watched him overexert him as if he was trying to swim away from something.

Finally, he stopped and held himself against the wall of the pool, his chest heaving, panting. He pushed himself out of the water, inked arms flexing, and staggered to his feet. I handed him his towel, and he pressed it against his face. When he lowered it to dry the rest of his body, the calm returned to his expression, but it looked wrong. Off. I couldn't even pinpoint why.

"Let's go inside. I'll make us something to eat."

Nino didn't bother changing out of his swim trunks, and he followed me into the kitchen. I began to gather everything needed to make pancakes. The sounds of the clanking pots had Remo joining us. He was dressed and looked surprisingly well rested despite my intrusion last night.

His eyes darted from me to Nino, who was reading the news on his phone without looking up. Remo moved to my side, as usual ignoring my personal space as his hip bumped against mine. He watched me whip together the batter.

"How's he doing?" he murmured, his dark eyes filled with worry.

I paused because that sight still got to me. "I don't know. He's still acting weird."

Remo moved to the kitchen table and sank down in a chair across from Nino. "So are you up for work today?"

Nino put down his phone and looked up. "What do you have in mind?"

"We caught two Outfit bastards. I thought we could get some information out of them. When we're done, we can send them back to Cavallaro in a few nicely wrapped packages. What do you think? Will a nice round of torture lift your spirits?" Remo smiled twistedly.

Was he being serious? Did he really want to involve Nino in something this brutal when he wasn't quite himself? "I don't think that's a good idea."

Both Nino and Remo glanced my way. Nino furrowed his brows in an almost confused expression while Remo had murder on his face. I was growing used to it.

"You better remember your place," Remo said harshly.

Nino met my gaze. "Your worry is unnecessary, Kiara."

I doubted it, but I kept my mouth shut and prepared the pancakes, dividing them between three plates, and carried them over to the table.

Remo seemed surprised.

"I assumed you'd want to eat with us. Even if you threaten me, I won't let you go hungry."

His dark eyes assessed my face, and I returned his gaze. Didn't he always insist I needed to learn to be a Falcone? Not cowering to him was a good step toward that goal. I couldn't be sure, but I thought I saw a flicker of respect in his eyes.

"I like you better now that you aren't scared of your own fucking shadow anymore."

I shrugged. "And I like you better when you're not being scary and bossy."

"Then you don't like me very often," Remo said, digging into his pancakes. I sat down beside Nino, and he surprised me by putting his hand down on my thigh and squeezing. When I chanced a glance at him, he was focused on eating.

"When do we need to leave?" Nino asked his brother.

"The assholes are in the basement of the Sugar Trap. Savio and Fabiano are already there. I wanted to wait for you before we started."

Nino nodded and finished his pancakes. "I'll get dressed and then we can leave." He turned to me and hesitated. "Is Adamo here?"

"He should be here, but the asshole snuck out this morning and took my Bugatti. If he gets back, I'll kick his fucking ass. Until then, your girl will be alone here."

Nino shook his head. "No. She can't defend herself yet."

I frowned. "The mansion is safe, and I'm good with a gun. Well … decent, but that should be enough."

"Decent is not good enough against most of our enemies. Cavallaro will soon realize we have his soldiers. I won't leave you unguarded."

"She can come with us," Remo said with a shrug.

I knew the Sugar Trap was a strip club and whorehouse. But if the Camorra's enemies were taken there, that probably wasn't all it was used for.

Nino regarded me. "That is a difficult place for Kiara."

"I can deal," I said firmly.

The second we stepped into the Sugar Trap, everyone's eyes swiveled toward us. A few scantily clad women were gathered around the bar, talking to a tall, black guy sorting bottles. He nodded at Remo and Nino but regarded me curiously. The women, however, only mumbled a few words of greeting before they returned to what they had been doing. Poles were spread around the room on small stages, and there were several doors branching off the main bar. I assumed they were for private sessions.

Remo's hard eyes only brushed over the women as if their mere presence annoyed him. Nino turned to me. "You can wait in our office while Remo and I are in the basement."

I shook my head. "No, I'll stay here and talk to the women."

Remo snorted. "They are whores. Talking isn't what they're good at."

I bit back a comeback and turned to Nino, trying to hide my worry. It must have showed because he brought my hand up to his lips and kissed my wrist. Several women gaped at us from their spot at the bar, and even Remo looked caught off guard. Public displays of affection weren't usually Nino's style.

Nino leaned forward, whispering in my ear. "I've survived every horror you can imagine, Kiara. Don't waste your worry on me. Torturing Outfit bastards won't do anything to me. I don't feel their fear. I don't care about their begging." He pulled back, and I released a breath. Without another word, Nino and Remo walked through the backdoor.

The moment they were gone, the five women dared to stare at me again, and the guy behind the bar watched me too. I walked toward them. "Hi," I said, trying to hide my embarrassment. "I'm Kiara Falcone."

The guy laughed. "Everyone knows who you are, Mrs. Falcone. I'm Jerry. What can I do for you?" His white teeth contrasted with his dark face, and I liked him at once.

The women whispered among themselves but didn't say anything directly to me. A few months ago this would have driven me away, but I'd learned to brave unsettling situations.

"What do you have?" I asked Jerry.

"Everything you want. Wine, beer, shots, cocktails. And even if we don't have it, I'd get it for you, Mrs. Falcone."

I couldn't help but laugh. "No need for that, please. Just give me a Coke. It's too early for wine."

"If you ask me, every hour of the day is wine o'clock," the woman closest to me said as she raised a glass with red wine. She was very tall and had long blond hair, and was heavily made up like the other women. I supposed it was required in their field of work. I'd never before dealt with a sex worker. As my eyes took in the five women, I wondered how many of them had started working here of their own free will and how many had been dragged into this by a Romancer or to pay of their own debts. The other women, too, had wineglasses in front of them. I supposed alcohol made it easier to live a life like that.

"Give me a glass of white wine," I said. I couldn't help but wonder with how many of these women Nino had slept, but I decided not to ask.

Jerry chuckled. "Don't let their alcoholism rub off on you." Despite his words, he poured me a generous glass and slid it toward me.

"Free alcohol is one of the few perks of working here," another woman muttered.

I took a sip from my wine and regarded them, looking for signs of abuse. A few of them had small bruises on their arms or legs but nothing major.

"I'm C.J.," said a younger woman with long brown hair and a kind smile.

"She's a Falcone," the woman beside her hissed.

I took another sip. "I am," I confirmed. "I'm also a person and a woman. You don't have to fear me."

The tall woman shook her head. "You are not one of us, that's for sure."

"I'm not, you are right, but I understand more than you think. I'm not your enemy."

C.J. walked around and leaned against the bar counter beside me. "We heard what happened in New York, what the Falcones did to your uncle."

Jerry shoved her shoulder lightly. "Why don't you shut up?"

I swallowed, but then I forced a smile and nodded. "Nino and Remo killed him."

"Slaughtered him," the tall woman butted in.

"Got what he deserved, if you ask me," C.J. muttered.

"Many men deserve the same," the tall woman said.

I put down my glass and blurted, "Are you sex slaves?"

C.J. shrugged. "Not the kidnapped-in-the-middle-of-the-night kind, no. Most of us started this because we didn't have a choice. We needed the money, we felt obligated, and most of us stay because once you're in this, it's hard to work a normal job again. Once the debts to the Camorra are paid off, we earn good money."

The tall woman narrowed her eyes at me. "There are very few women in this business who do this because they enjoy it. Maybe johns want to believe most of us are nymphomaniacs who became hoes to get more dick. Fucking assholes. As if any of us enjoy sucking the dick of an old, hairy, unwashed bastard."

"Here comes the prick responsible for fresh meat," C.J. whispered, and the look in her eyes made it clear; he was the reason why she worked at the Sugar Trap.

I turned around and a tall, brown-haired man, maybe a couple of years older than me, entered the club. He was very handsome, and I understood why he had become the Camorra's Romancer. It was his job to make women fall for him until they were in so deep that they would do anything for him; even sell their bodies. He didn't give off the scary vibe so many Made Men did. He knew how to hide it, which was probably crucial if you wanted to lure women into your trap. His eyes wandered over the women without a hint of guilt. Then they settled on me and his face was puzzled. I hadn't met him yet, or at least, I hadn't noticed him. Something in his behavior shifted ever so slightly, as if he wasn't sure where to put me, but then he strode toward me and recognition flashed across his face.

He ignored the women beside me, shook hands with Jerry, then turned to me. "I'm Stefano," he said in a silky voice. "It's a pleasure meeting you." His charming smile hit me full force.

Remo prowled through the backdoor, covered in blood, and tapped the counter. "Four scotches, Jerry." Then his dark eyes moved on to Stefano. He shook his head and narrowed his eyes before walking around to meet us. I couldn't take my eyes off his blood-spattered arms and throat. His shirt was black, but I was sure it was drenched in blood too.

He grabbed Stefano's shoulder. "That is a conquest you wouldn't survive, Stefano. I'd hate to lose my best Romancer, but I'd have to put you down, and you'd fucking thank me for it because Nino would fucking tear you into bite-sized pieces and feed them to you."

Stefano watched Remo's bloody hand on his white shirt, curling his lip. "I know who she is, Capo. I was only introducing myself."

"We know how it goes. You charm them and then they fall head over heels and lose their few remaining brain cells." Remo flashed a cruel smile at the gathered women.

I rolled my eyes. "First, I'm not going to fall for him. I'm Nino's. And second, I have more than a few brain cells." I didn't mention that no matter what Stefano did, he couldn't win my heart because my heart belonged to Nino.

Stefano's eyes widened, and he looked at Remo as if he expected his Capo would strike me dead for the audacity.

"Indeed." Remo smirked and released Stefano, leaving a bloody handprint on the man's shirt. Jerry handed Remo a tray with four glasses of scotch. "We're almost done," he said to me, then to Stefano, "Hands off." The women backed away as he passed them with the tray.

Stefano let out an Italian curse under his breath as he regarded his ruined shirt.

"I suppose you won't charm your way into girls' hearts with blood on your shirt."

He shrugged. "If I told the right story, they'd believe I saved a man's life and that's why I have that handprint on my shirt. Women believe all kinds of shit if an attractive man makes them feel special and tells them how gorgeous they are, even if they're average at most."

I took a deep swig of my wine, not sure what to say to *that*.

But C.J. found my words. "You're an asshole."

Stefano grinned at her. "That's not what you said when I fucked your brains out and you declared your love for me."

She paled then whirled around and disappeared through the door behind the bar.

"That was very rude," I said. "I don't know why you think you can treat women like you do."

"Because they allow me to treat them like that," he said quietly, his brown eyes hard. "Everyone gets what they deserve."

I shook my head at him and hopped off the barstool to find C.J. A corridor led to a staff-only door that was left ajar, and I stepped in, finding C.J. leaning against a sink, crying.

"Hey," I said hesitantly, suddenly unsure if it was a good idea that I was here. I was the wife of the man who owned the Sugar Trap and even more places like that. C.J. and the other women belonged to the Camorra, and basically Nino as well. He wasn't Capo, but none of Remo's decisions were made without consulting Nino first.

I handed her a tissue. "I'm sorry for what he said."

"Why? It's the truth. I fell for him because he said exactly what I wanted to hear, what no man had ever said to me. He seemed too good to be true, but I didn't want to see the signs pointing toward the truth."

"Sometimes it's easier to believe a lie," I said quietly, because I believed Nino's simulated affection too, much too eagerly.

She met my gaze. "I slept with Nino."

My body seized with shock. I had guessed that some of these women had slept with him, but hearing her say it still hurt.

"But it's been a while. I haven't seen him with any of us in weeks."

Some of the weight lifted off my chest—probably since I'd told him I wanted him to stop being with other women. So he had kept word. "He's slept with many women before me," I said with a small shrug.

"Yeah, they all do," she said bitterly.

"Did … did he force you?"

She tilted her head. "I'm a whore."

"That doesn't mean you don't have the right to say no."

She smiled. "That's not how it works. But he never forced me. I never said no. Why would I? There are far worse men out there than Nino Falcone. He's good looking and not cruel during sex. That's a good thing."

I nodded quickly, glad when she stopped talking about having sex with Nino. "Why don't you leave? Or are you still paying off your debt?"

"Not anymore, no. It's been paid off for a year now, but I don't have anything to return to. I've grown used to this life. If you've been around here for a while, it's not like you can work a normal job. We've all seen too much. We could work as waitresses in one of the Camorra's clubs or bars, but there aren't many other options once you're in this."

"So you are a prisoner of the Camorra."

C.J. touched my arm. "Aren't we all? Don't tell me your life has ever been yours?"

No. It wasn't. Born in blood. That was what every child, girl or boy, was in our world. I was no longer bound to the Famiglia. Now I was bound to the Camorra. But free? That wasn't something I would ever be. It wasn't something I'd ever considered an option. A bird born in captivity will never know the feeling of unbridled freedom the open sky can offer. How can you long for something you have never experienced?

"It's okay. Don't blame yourself. Some things just can't be changed."

"I know," I said, but it didn't change the fact that I wanted to change them.

Nino was clean when he emerged from the backdoor and so was Remo. I was back at the bar with C.J. sitting beside me, drinking our second glass of wine. "I should leave," she said quickly. "The first customers will arrive soon."

I nodded. I had every intention of making it my goal to visit the whore-houses of the Camorra and get to know the women there. If I knew them, I'd feel even more obligated to help them—even if I knew it was a losing battle. Remo would never listen to me, and even Nino wouldn't let me meddle in their business.

I searched his face as he stepped up next to me, looking for signs that what he'd been doing had bothered him, but he looked calm, which should have terrified me, but I was only relieved. Nino's eyes followed C.J. as she walked off. Then he frowned at me.

"What did she say?"

"Nothing important," I said with a smile.

Nino didn't look convinced, but he didn't press the matter, only curled his hand around my wrist and led me out of the club.

The moment we were back home, we gathered in the living area, and Remo ordered pizza.

"How can you be hungry after what you've been doing?" I asked curiously as I sank down on the sofa.

Nino gave me a blank look. "The body still requires a certain calorie intake to keep up its functions."

Remo rolled his eyes. "One of these days, I'm going to lose my shit on you when you sound like a fucking text book."

Nino cocked his brows at his brother. "You've said it countless time. It loses its power if you never act on it."

Remo pulled out his knife and flung it at Nino. I jumped as the knife impaled itself in the armrest beside Nino's leg. "You, Savio, and Adamo are fucking nuisances."

I smiled. "Thanks," I said. When Remo gave me a blank stare, I added, "For not including me."

"She's getting too daring," Remo muttered, but he didn't look angry.

Nino looked relaxed, back to his usual calm self. Maybe he'd overcome whatever had haunted him last night. "Where's Adamo? Is he still gone?"

Remo's face darkened. "Adamo!" he roared. "Get your ass down here." There was silence. Remo picked up the phone, ordered pizza, then called again. "Adamo, I swear, if you're upstairs and don't get down here right this second, I'll come and get you, and you will fucking regret it."

Steps sounded from upstairs and then Adamo appeared on the stairs. He hesitated in the middle of them, looking nervous as he regarded his older brothers.

"What did you do?" Nino asked.

Adamo glanced at Remo, who was snarling. "Don't tell me you crashed my Bugatti."

Adamo shook his head. "There's only one dent in the back because someone bumped into me."

Remo staggered toward his brother and gripped him by the collar. "What the fuck is wrong with you? I told you to stop racing. You'll get yourself killed."

"So what? In a few weeks, I'll be initiated. I'd do everyone a favor if I got killed before becoming like you."

I held my breath. Nino, too, tensed beside me.

Remo pulled Adamo even closer, glaring down at him. "You are a fucking child. You don't know what you're talking about. Maybe I protected you for too long. Maybe I should have initiated you sooner like Savio."

"When did you ever protect me?"

Remo released him with a hard smile. "I ordered pizza. Or are you *too good* to eat with us?"

Adamo hovered on the staircase then slowly skulked down and moved toward us. He flung himself down on the sofa across from us. He gave me a smile then nodded toward Nino.

"Where's Savio?" he mumbled.

"Out with Diego," Remo said.

"Maybe you should go out more often too," Adamo muttered.

Remo sat down beside Nino. "Someone has to make sure the west stays in our hands. I fought too hard for this to lose it because of laziness."

I realized Remo and Nino hardly ever went out. With Nino, I'd thought it was because I was his wife now, but Remo, too, was mostly at home unless he was out doing business with his brothers or Fabiano. They lived in their own small world, a world I'd been allowed into. I was getting used to being a Falcone.

Nino and I returned to our bedroom after dinner and watching a few videos of past races with his brothers. We got ready for bed. I was sitting against the headboard when he joined me, looking almost wary. Was he worried about tonight?

"Did C.J. tell you I slept with her?" he asked quietly as he stretched out beside me.

"Yeah ... she did. But it's the past. I'm not holding your past against you. You didn't hold mine against me."

Nino frowned. "There was nothing I could have held against you because you didn't do anything wrong."

"I know," I said.

"Do you?"

I sighed. On a logical level, I did, but sometimes I still felt like I was to blame, which was stupid, but it was something deeply ingrained in me and difficult to shake. "Do you ever feel guilty for what you do? For what you did today?"

Nino considered that. "Not really. As I said, I don't really feel pity. And those Outfit bastards would have done the same if they got their hands on one of ours."

I yawned. He lifted his arm, and I snuggled up to him, propping myself up on his chest, and kissed him softly. We seldom kissed, mostly just during sex.

Nino gently touched the back of my head as his other hand brushed my arm. "What's that for?"

"I just wanted to kiss you," I admitted. "Or does it bother you if I do? Outside of sex, I mean."

Nino tilted his head, his thumb lightly rubbing my neck. "Why would that bother me, Kiara? I enjoy kissing you. Did I ever give you reason to believe otherwise?"

"No, but you never kiss me during the day. We only ever kiss when we're about to have sex."

"When would you want me to kiss you?"

I sighed. "I don't want you to kiss me because I want it. I want you to kiss me because you want to do it, because you feel like it." I realized how foolish I sounded. Nino would never feel like kissing me. Every act of tenderness was for my benefit.

Nino searched my face and pulled me toward him then kissed me, the brush of his lips soft, his gray eyes almost unsure.

I blinked at him. "Why did you do that?"

"I don't know," he said quietly.

I lowered my head to his bare chest, my cheek pressed up to his warm skin, confused by his actions and words.

TWENTY-TWO

Kiara

T HAT NIGHT, FAMILIAR SOUNDS OF DISTRESS WOKE ME. I SAT UP AND fumbled for the light switch, blinking against the sudden brightness.

Nino jerked upright beside me, his hand reaching for the bedside table and grabbing his knife.

His wild eyes locked on me, chest heaving, his fingers clutching the handle.

"I'm getting Remo," I murmured and slowly slid out of bed, worried about startling Nino. His free hand curled around my wrist, stopping me.

I gasped in surprise, my gaze searching his face. The wild despair was gone from his expression, replaced by a mix of confusion and the familiar blankness he had always displayed in the past. "Stay," he said quietly.

Hesitating, I climbed back into bed, and Nino pulled me toward him. I settled on his chest. He put the knife back down on his nightstand, but the tension remained in his body. Tracing the tattoos on his torso, I tried to count his scars to distract myself, but it was difficult to determine where many of them ended and others began.

"All these tattoos … why did you get them?"

Nino's fingers trailed up my spine and continued to my neck, then higher up, tangling in my hair. His lips brushed my forehead, and I peered up at him. Was this simulated affection? Simulated tenderness?

"Pain and pleasure," he said in a low voice. "I can feel those like anybody else, maybe even stronger."

"But if you feel pain even stronger than others, why would you submit yourself to having a needle pierce your skin over and over again for many hours? Why do you go into the cage? Why do you seek out pain?"

His mouth twisted. "To remind myself that I'm alive."

My brows drew together.

"To remember who I am, what I am."

"I don't understand," I admitted. "What happened to you and Remo to make you the way you are?"

Nino tilted his head down to me and regarded me. I returned his gaze, even if I didn't know what he was looking for. "Like you said, it's not only my story but also Remo's."

"I won't talk to him about it," I promised at once. I would never think about talking to Remo about something that obviously affected both him and Nino like that. It would be suicidal.

"Our mother was insane," Nino began in a distant voice. "Maybe she always was or maybe our father made her that way. I only remember her like that. She had better days when our father stuffed her full of pills, but on this particular day, she was heavily pregnant with Adamo. She couldn't take the pills. Maybe she had wanted to kill herself for a while."

Something tight coiled in my stomach, and I almost asked him to stop because I knew that day was when Nino's childhood ended. Nino's mother wasn't the first wife of a Capo who ended her life. Being married to someone raised to be cruel could destroy anyone.

"Our father had sent us all to our cabin out in the Rockies because he wanted us gone from Vegas. We were a burden. One night, our mother pulled me out of bed and led me into her bedroom. Savio was already there, but he wasn't moving. She'd given him her sleeping pills. I didn't know what was going on, but she gripped my arms and slit both my wrists with a knife. She wanted to kill us too. Maybe to punish our father."

I sucked in my breath, fingers seizing on Nino's stomach, but he was stock-still. Those scars on his wrists, they were remnants of that day.

"I was confused and scared." His brows drew together as if he was trying to remember how being scared felt. "She left after that and came back with Remo a few minutes later. I think she took him last because she knew he'd be her biggest challenge. The house was filling with smoke by then. She'd set fire to the kitchen and living room. Remo rushed over to me, and she locked the door and shoved the key under the gap below the door. Then she moved to cut Remo's wrists, but he fought her, unlike me. She managed to cut him over and over. That's where he got the cut on his face. When she realized she couldn't hold him down, she set the curtains on fire and then slit her own wrists. The room filled with smoke, and I sat in my own blood. Savio wasn't move on the bed."

Nino's voice was mechanical, detached, cold. His eyes were as smooth and impenetrable as mercury, but each of his words burned into me, wedged itself like a knife into my heart. The horrors he described, they were incomprehensible. I had lived my own share of horrors, true, but somehow hearing him describe what he'd gone through as a young boy broke me. "How did you get out?"

"Remo threw a lamp through the window and got burned ripping the curtains off the ceiling. Part of his clothes began burning too, but he didn't stop. My father's men were trying to get inside the house and trying to extinguish the flames. Remo grabbed me and helped me out of the window. I jumped and broke my leg from the impact. Remo jumped out with Savio in his arms. He broke his elbow and shoulder because he tried to protect Savio. Our mother was saved by my father's men later."

I swallowed hard, unable to speak, and Nino fell silent as well.

"It seemed to take forever as I watched my own blood run down my arms. I felt the deep burn and it was almost soothing." He lifted his arms, wrists up, showing me the long thin scars covered by dark ink. I leaned forward and kissed both of his wrists, my heart aching for Nino—and for Remo.

I tried to picture Nino as a child, kneeling in his blood, watching his mother cut Remo, smelling the smoke. I could picture how scared he must have been, how utterly broken and shocked that his own mother had tried to kill them in a barbaric way. It explained so much, explained why he had shut off his emotions and why Remo had turned toward them. Different ways to cope with the same horror.

"Where is she now? Did your father kill her after what she did to you?"

Nino shook his head. "After the doctors cut Adamo out of her, he sent her off to psychiatric hospital for a while, but eventually he moved her back home."

"He forced you to live under a roof with the woman who tried to kill you?"

Nino's eyes were focused on his fingers, which ran up and down my side. "For the first few years. What doesn't kill you makes you stronger." The smile on his face felt like a bucket of ice. "But things were difficult. Remo became harder to control, and my lack of emotions eventually unsettled my father too much, so he sent us off to boarding school in England, up in the countryside north of Norwich."

"But what about Savio and Adamo? Weren't they too young?"

Nino nodded. "Adamo was four and Savio seven when we were shipped off. At the time, Remo had already been inducted and killed a few, but he wouldn't let us be separated, so we went together to England. Of course, that's what our father had intended. He wanted Remo and me gone. He was scared of us."

I couldn't imagine Remo in a posh boarding school. Nino could look like a sophisticated gentleman when he covered his tattoos and tried to form his expression into one of pleasantries, but Remo was far from restrained and posh.

"That didn't work out long," Nino said quietly. "Eventually, we ran off and returned to the States to kill our father."

"But you didn't. Luca's Enforcer, Growl, did."

"That's something Remo will never forgive our half-brother for. He robbed us of the chance to destroy our father, piece by piece."

I tended to forget that the Falcones and Growl were related. "I'm sorry," I whispered eventually, my insides churning and hoping that Nino couldn't see how much his story had affected me.

Nino made a low sound in his throat, a sound I'd only heard twice before, when he'd been on the verge of snapping, but his face was still unsettlingly void of emotion. His hand on my side dipped lower, over my hip and between my legs.

I jumped, surprised that he was looking for that kind of closeness in a situation like this. His fingers found my clit. He hovered over me and kissed me, harder than ever before, and his fingers strummed a fast rhythm between my legs. Despite the jumbled mess that was my emotions, my body responded to his kisses and touch.

Suddenly, he pushed himself up and moved on top of me, his strong arms on either side of my head. I stilled as he held himself over me, his eyes not emotionless at all. Instead, his expression twisted with something akin to despair. He'd never been on top of me during sex.

"Tell me this is okay for you, Kiara," he managed to say in a raw and dark voice. "I'm not sure I can be as gentle as you need me to be. If you can't do this, tell me and I'll leave, but ..." He shook his head.

"It's okay," I whispered, because I wanted to console him in any way I could. If this was what he needed, I could give it to him. I wasn't scared of Nino or his body.

Nino

Kiara looked up at me with trust that I had no trouble reading in her eyes. Her hands curled around my shoulders, holding on to me, and I grabbed my cock and guided it toward her pussy. She was wet and soft, even though she had been anxious about this position because it made her feel like she had no control, because my physical strength intimidated her. I lowered myself to my elbows. The closeness would calm her, not unsettle her, and I felt her body become even softer under me.

She tugged me down for a kiss, and I allowed her this small sliver of control, even if I was longing for something harder, darker. Even if I wanted to exert dominance and not gentleness.

But I needed to be inside her. Now. I slid in without pause, until her pussy touched my pelvis. I shuddered, needing more, needing it fast, needing to get rid of the sudden pressure on my chest that had never been there before.

I forced myself to wait a couple of heartbeats, allowed her body to adapt, forced down the raging flood of need in my body. I had never felt like this, like I needed to consume Kiara completely. Like she was the only thing that could satisfy a hunger unlike anything I'd ever felt.

My chest was tight, my stomach hollow, and I wasn't sure what was going on. Why suddenly every look from Kiara made my insides explode with fire, almost painfully but good too.

I pulled out and thrust back into Kiara, and her nails dug into my back, leaving scratches. It felt like relief, an outlet for the pressure. My lips found hers as I slammed into her, and she returned my gaze with a burning need of her own. Again, that same ache for something I didn't understand. I had always been in control, but I couldn't control this. I reached between us and rubbed Kiara's clit then latched onto her nipple, sucking and nibbling as I drove her into the bed with long, hard thrusts.

Even her smell opened the hole in my chest wider. Everything about her made my body react, made me long for something impossible, for something foreign and inexplicable.

Kiara started to shudder under me, but I kept thrusting even as her walls tightened from the force of her orgasm. I got on my knees for more leverage and kept thrusting, hoping it would fill that hole in my stomach, would satiate the deep hunger of my soul, but even as I came with a violent jerk and my cock softened, the longing remained wedged in my chest.

I sank down on top of Kiara and breathed harshly against her throat. Her fingers played with my hair, and she kissed my ear, then my temple, and for some reason those two meaningless gestures fulfilled some of my longing.

I twisted my face to look at her. Her skin was flushed, and she was breathing fast. She looked stunned, overwhelmed as she met my gaze.

"Did I hurt you?" I rasped.

Her brows pulled tight. "No. When you said you couldn't be gentle, I'd expected worse."

So had I. It had felt like I was on the verge of losing control, but somehow Kiara had held me fast through it all.

"Nino?" she asked quietly. "That look on your face, what does it mean?"

If only I knew.

She kissed me. "I know our pasts hold horrors, but we can get beyond that, don't you think?"

I stroked her cheek. I had gotten past the horrors. I'd seen and done so many horrible things, how could an event from long ago still hold any power over me?

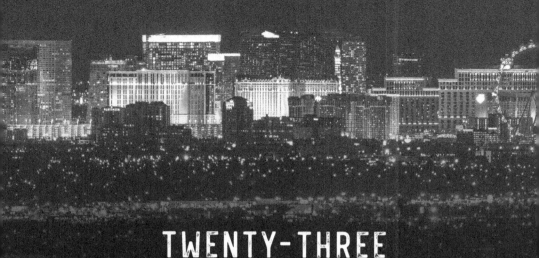

TWENTY-THREE

Kiara

THE NEXT MORNING I FOUND REMO PUMMELING THE LIFE OUT OF THE punching bag, but all I could think of were Nino's words, and I knew I'd never see Remo the same way again. Christ, he still terrified me, but I almost understood him—part of him anyway. Remo was cruel and brutal, merciless and quick to snap, but it wasn't all there was to him.

"Why are you staring?" he panted as he sent the bag flying with another hard kick.

I wasn't even sure why I had come here. It was where Nino and his brothers hung out to play pool, watch fights and discuss business, or pummel a punching bag during the day. In the evening when we all had dinner together, my presence was tolerated, but I usually stayed away the rest of the time, giving them their space.

My eyes were drawn to Remo's back. I had never been close enough to him to notice that the tattooed fallen angel covered up burn scars. I hadn't realized the rough patches on his palms were burns and healed wounds from fending off his mother.

Remo turned to me fully, narrowing his eyes, and for a moment I wanted to go over and hug him, hug the young boy who saved Nino and Savio and even the unborn Adamo, who fought an insane mother and burned so they could all live, but Remo was a man now and not one you wanted to console. My eyes lingered on the scar crossing his eyebrow, and compassion for him filled me. Maybe Remo was beyond redemption in many people's eyes, but he had saved his brothers, had saved Nino.

I wondered how he remembered that day, but I wasn't brave enough to ask him. Remo stalked toward me, and I looked up into his face when he stopped right in front of me. "Why are you giving me that fucked-up look?" he growled, but for once there wasn't only anger in his eyes ... there was apprehension.

I shook my head. "I wanted to thank you for saving Nino."

Remo stiffened and something hard and dangerous curled in the depth of his eyes.

"Two nights ago," I added, because self-preservation kicked in, but Remo knew that wasn't what I'd been referring to.

Yet he stepped back and gave a tense shrug. "Someone had to snap him out of it."

I took a step back as well.

"Oh, and Kiara, not a word about any of this to Savio and Adamo. They don't need to know."

About Nino's breakdown. About the past. They didn't remember, didn't know, and keeping that truth from them was probably another way Remo protected them.

My eyes were closed as I listened to the music, my fingers gliding over the keys. Nothing brought me more serenity than creating melodies. It was an outlet for the chaos of emotions inside of me.

"You're really good at it," Remo said.

I jumped, my eyes flying open and settling on Remo. He stood in the door-way for a moment then walked toward me. As usual, my body tensed in his presence.

"Still?" he asked with a wry smile. He leaned against the piano, looking down on me with these impossibly dark, dangerous eyes. "Still terrified of me."

I laughed. "Remo, is there a woman in Las Vegas or anywhere else who isn't scared of you?"

His smile pulled wider. "There's no man either."

I sighed. My gaze flickered to the scar on his face, remembering the story Nino had told me, wondering how a man capable of unspeakable acts could have risked his life to save his brothers. Remo Falcone was a complete mystery to me.

Remo's eyes narrowed, and he moved closer, leaning over me, one hand braced on the keys, causing the piano to release a high-pitched whine. "Why are you looking at me like that?" he growled. "What did Nino tell you?"

I swallowed. "Don't come so close," I said firmly.

Remo's lips tightened dangerously, but he straightened his body, giving me more space. "I told you before and I will tell you again: You are Nino's. You are safe."

"I know," I said. "But I can't help my body's reaction to you. Maybe it'll fade."

He shrugged. "He told you about our mother, didn't he?"

There was a tone to his voice that made the little hairs on my neck rise. "He did."

Remo gave a sharp nod. Then he warned in a low voice, "Some things need to stay buried. She is one of them. And Nino's emotions probably too. I don't know what you want from him, but for his sake and yours, don't push him."

Early the next day, Nino and I set out for our first hike together. I wasn't overly fit, but having Nino to myself, surrounded by beautiful red stone formations, was too enticing. He took us back to the Red Canyon National park. He was quiet during the ride, focused on the street, but his eyes seemed to see beyond the road ahead.

He surprised me when he took my hand, resting both on my bare thigh. His warmth seeped into me, but that wasn't why my chest felt warmer.

We parked our car and set off for the circular trail. Nino was dressed in a tight, white T-shirt and gym shorts, his hair falling into his eyes. He also carried a massive backpack with provisions. I had opted for shorts and a top. It was only seven o'clock, but the day would be hot.

Nino lightly touched my back. "Ready for your first hike?"

I smiled. "With you at my side, I can do anything."

His expression softened. He nudged me closer and kissed me before he straightened and pointed at the trail. I was still taken aback by his show of affection. Not trying to analyze it, I fell into a stride beside Nino. He pointed out particularly beautiful stone formations. They glowed in different shades of red and orange.

Despite nature's beauty, my gaze kept returning to Nino. He had been different since I'd told him I loved him. Did he feel pressured to simulate emotions more often? Was that why he had been acting off? But I couldn't imagine that Nino yielded under pressure. Nino was strong, hardened. He was a Falcone.

Nino slowed his pace when he noticed I was having trouble keeping up. Eventually he chose a spot overlooking a valley of smaller stone formations, so we could take a break. We sat down on the ground, hip to hip, and Nino handed me a sandwich.

"And? Do you enjoy it?" he asked.

I tilted my head at him. "The hike or the sandwich?"

"Both would be optimum."

I shook my head. "*Optimum...*" I put my chin down on his shoulder "...I bet in school the other kids hated how clever and proper you were."

Nino's eyebrows shot up. "I was not proper. And the kids hated me for many reasons."

"But I doubt they ever teased you."

"When Remo and I first started boarding school in England, the kids didn't know who we were. We were supposed the blend in. I was two years ahead, same year as Remo. Many of the boys in my classes were taller. They tried taunting me at first."

"That didn't go over well."

"A few of them had unfortunate incidents leading to hospital stays," Nino said. "Most of them were Remo's doing, but I got a few of them as well."

"And you weren't thrown out of school?"

"The teachers knew who we were," Nino said with a dark smile.

I searched his face, trying to imagine how he had been as a child. Nino met my gaze, and something softer, warmer filled his eyes. He leaned forward, touched my hip, and claimed my mouth for a kiss. I kissed him back, and eventually we stretched out on the warm stone, Nino leaning over me, kissing me, stroking my waist and ribcage. He rolled us over until I was lying on top of him. His hands roamed over my back, but the sound of a twig breaking tore us apart and Nino sat up with me still on top of him. His eyes scanned our surroundings. Then he relaxed again. His lips left a soft trail along my cheek down to my throat. His gentleness, his loving gestures, they made my heart throb with love and despair.

He simulated love for me. Sometimes, I managed to forget. But whenever I remembered, the pain was acute and heartbreaking. I shoved that thought aside. Nino cupped my cheek again, angled my head until our mouths connected. The kiss was all consuming, and I let it pull me down, let Nino's hands banish any logical thought. When he settled between my legs and claimed me, nothing else mattered but having Nino above me, inside of me, his mouth on mine, his gray eyes alight with desire and more ... I didn't care if it was simulated or not.

Afterward, we got dressed and continued our hike. His expression was calm and serene as it scanned the landscape around us, as long as he wasn't trying to simulate emotions. Was that how we would all be, calm and serene if we hadn't been burdened with the ability to feel at birth?

Calm and serene. I wished I could be like that, but my thoughts and emotions were a whirlwind in my body, confusing and terrifying and completely foolish.

A few days later, Nino had gone to train for a fight with Fabiano, and I was left alone with Remo. It was the first time he was the one to guard me. Nino had mentioned that Remo would be leaving soon for a mission in Outfit territory, which was why he was busy with last minute preparations at home.

I found him in his favorite spot on the sofa, checking something on his tablet. He didn't look up when I entered, and I watched him silently.

He raised his head, his expression hardening. "What now?" His voice was low, on the verge of angry.

"Why do you enjoy hurting women?" I whispered.

Remo narrowed his eyes. "I enjoy hurting *people*. I don't differentiate if it's a man or a woman."

"And yet you punish women differently than men," I said.

"Do I?" he murmured, dark eyes burning into me. He put down his tablet and stood. "They get a choice. They can submit to torture or ..."

"Submit to another form of torture," I said, growing angry. "You give them a choice between two forms of torture."

He stalked toward me, but for once I didn't back away. Almost three months in his presence gave me the necessary courage, that combined with the knowledge that Nino trusted Remo. "But one of them is far less painful than the other. It's a choice. More than men get."

I shuddered. "I can assure you that it was very painful for me."

Remo regarded me a moment. He was close enough I could see the myriad of scars marring his upper body. He seldom wore shirts in the house. In the beginning, I thought it was to unsettle me even more—like Remo wasn't unsettling enough on his own. "You were a child. Nobody touches children in my territory nor underage girls."

"Don't they bring more money?" I muttered.

"Of course. Most fuckers would pay a fortune to pop a girl's cherry, but we don't allow that kind of thing in our territory."

"Why not? You allow sex slavery, don't you? You have Romancers who seduce women, make them believe they are being loved and then turn them into whores."

Remo sneered. Sometimes I wondered how a single person could harbor so much violence and hatred. "These women start working as whores because they want to please a man they should kill instead. If a woman allows a man to treat her like that, it's as much her fault as it is his. They agree to sell their bodies because they think they are in love. That's stupid, and they pay for their stupidity."

"They want to help someone they love," I said indignantly. "Your Romancers make them believe they are indebted to the Camorra, and then the women take over the debt and have to work it off as whores. That's horrible."

Remo took another step closer to me, but I still didn't back off. "If women act as the weaker sex, they will be treated that way. Why don't these idiotic women tell my Romancers to go fuck themselves?"

"You will never understand because you've never loved someone."

Remo smiled wryly. "Loving someone who doesn't love you back is the biggest kind of stupidity I can imagine."

I flinched, because this hit too close to home, and because I knew he was right. Realization filled Remo's face and my insides twisted. Now he knew I loved Nino. I turned to leave, but he grasped my wrist.

"Let me go."

For once, he didn't. Instead, he drew me back so I had to face him. I glared up at his cruel, dark eyes. He shook his head, and I waited for him to taunt me. "He can't feel."

"I know," I muttered, tugging at his hold, but his fingers tightened around my wrist. Finally, my anger and despair bubbled over. "Do you think I don't know that? But I can't change how I feel! Don't you think I would change it if I could? But love doesn't work that way. You will never understand."

"You are right," he said in a low voice. "I can't and I won't. Why would I want to be a fucking fool?"

"I hope one day you will find someone you want so much it burns you up inside, and then we'll talk when she doesn't return your feelings."

Remo backed me against the wall, his expression hard and cruel. "That will never happen. And I've burned before, Kiara. I can brave flames and torture. I'm not weak like you."

"I'm not weak." I wrenched my wrist out of his grip and shoved him hard. He took a deliberate step back, staring down at my hands still pressed against his chest. I dropped them quickly, shock filling me.

Remo raised his gaze, and I tensed, worried about his anger, but he was smirking. "Finally, you didn't let your fucking fear win."

I blinked at him, but he stepped back and turned around, heading toward the door, but before he reached it, he stopped and looked at me over his shoulder, his eyes hard. "Oh and, Kiara, you will never speak to me like that again. I am your Capo. Understood?"

I gave stunned nod and watched as he left.

Nino

Fabiano aimed a kick at my head. I dodged it a bit too late, and he lightly grazed my chin.

Surprise crossed over his face, which I used to land two hard punches against his lower back. He gasped but quickly recovered and got in a hit of his own.

He tilted his head. "What's up with you?"

"What do you mean?" I asked carefully, grabbing the towel I'd thrown over the rope. I wiped my face and chest.

"You have been … less focused today. And it was the same during your fight."

I leaned against the post in the corner. My current state wasn't something I wanted to discuss until I had a better handle on things and had a chance to thoroughly analyze my predicament. "You don't like the idea with Cavallaro's niece."

Fabiano narrowed his eyes, obviously dissatisfied with the topic change. "Do you really think Remo's plan is good?"

Remo's plan was emotional, fueled by revenge and hate. It was dangerous but it could prove to be effective. I regarded Fabiano. "You know the girl. You feel pity for her?"

He grimaced. "You know me, Nino. I will follow Remo through hellfire, but unlike you, I still have a couple of emotions."

"Before Leona, you convinced everyone that wasn't the case."

"Before Leona, I had convinced myself that I wasn't capable of emotions," he said, then narrowed his eyes as if catching himself.

"Remo's plan will create upheaval in the Outfit. Cavallaro's sister will be devastated that her daughter got caught by us, and Dante will feel responsible for his niece. His wife will be worried as well because of their own daughter. This might be one of the times Dante forgoes logic and acts. If that happens, we can beat him."

"Probably. Because no matter what, we can always count on you to be the voice of logic, Nino."

I gave a tense nod. Indifference and logical analyzing had guided me through my life, had saved mine and Remo's life on many occasions when his temper had gotten the better of him. But when I was around Kiara, logic was difficult to hold on to. Since the night she told me she loved me, something had shifted. It had started as a small crack but had continuously widened, and I had no way of stopping it. "Are you sure you will be able to do what must be done once you're in Chicago? You won't get distracted by thoughts of your father?"

Hate flashed across Fabiano's face. "I've waited a long time. I can wait a few more weeks or months. You don't have to worry. I will stand by Remo no matter how insane his plan is. I doubt it's only motivated by strategic motivations."

"Remo's plans never are. He wants to play with Dante, wants to tear the Outfit apart from the inside. Remo is the best at mind games."

"Yeah. Remo knows how to fuck with people's brain," Fabiano said with a dark laugh.

He did, and Cavallaro and Scuderi would soon realize their mistake of fucking with the Camorra.

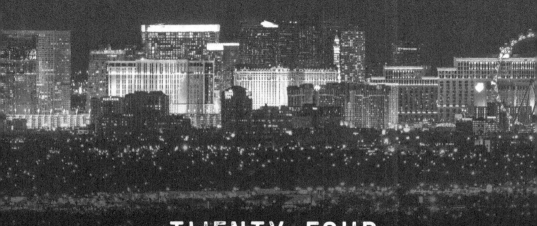

TWENTY-FOUR

Kiara

NOTHING BROUGHT ME AS MUCH COMFORT AS PLAYING NINO'S SONG, which was ironic considering it filled me with a crushing longing and wistfulness at the same time.

When my fingers got to the part where I came to the realization of my feelings, the melody turned low and dark, as if the piano was reluctant to play the notes, like I had been reluctant to admit my feelings to myself.

Nino stepped in and regarded me silently for a while. I didn't glance up from the piano keys, playing the song to the end, shivering as the low notes faded away.

"What does it mean?" Nino murmured. "Since you started the song, it has evolved more and more."

I raised my eyes to his. "It's the story of my feelings for you," I admitted. "How I came to accept that I love you and that you can never love me back." As usual, my throat tightened at my admittance.

Nino's expression softened ever so slightly and warmth filled his gray eyes, and today I could not take it. This simulated emotion, no matter how good he was at it, would never be enough. I knew it, deep down. "Stop it," I whispered harshly.

His eyes narrowed, and he moved closer, his motions graceful as always. And I resented even that. He could be so beautiful and intelligent and powerful, but he could never be the one thing I longed for: emotional.

I glared up into his beautifully cold face. "You are too good at this. Too good at simulating affection, at pretending that you care for me. So good, sometimes, I almost believe you could really love me, Nino." Tears welled in my eyes.

Weak. A fucking fool. What else had Remo called me? He had been right in every regard.

Nino braced himself on the piano, staring down at me. "Maybe I don't have to simulate," he said in that smooth voice. "Maybe I love you."

This was the last straw. I could not take anymore. I jumped up from the bench, wishing he could understand how it tore me apart knowing that I loved someone who could never grasp what it meant to look at another and feel like you would shatter if that person was taken from you.

I gripped the front of his shirt, turning toward my anger. "Don't lie to me. I told you not to say those words to me if you didn't mean them. So just don't."

I released his shirt, stunned by the look in his eyes. It seemed as if they were burning with emotion. How good was he at faking this?

Swallowing thickly, I whirled around, needing to get away before I allowed myself to become trapped in this horrid simulation again. A clear, low note rang out when I was halfway up the stairs, and I froze, listening to the melody unfolding. It was a beautiful melody, every note complimenting the other. It was well composed but lacked emotion. It was a melody a computer might have created because it was just a bunch of notes strung together to please the average ear. You could listen to it over casual dinner with strangers because it never got your pulse rate up, never tore at your heartstrings or filled your body with sweet longing. Never made you want to cry from the sheer force of emotion it carried.

Then something shifted. At first it was subtle, a slight hiccup in the perfect composition. Darker notes begged for attention and were followed by short, high notes until they battled each other and what appeared to be a perfect composition. Slowly, I turned, terrified of what I would see.

Nino sat at the piano, eyes closed, head tilted to the side, as his fingers flew over the keys. He was a sight to behold with his gruesome tattoos, countless scars, and that perfectly sculpted, emotionless face. I was sure no matter how long I'd live, I would never see anything more breathtaking than Nino forcing wondrous notes out of my piano.

The perfect composition battled with the unhinged notes, and then suddenly, inexplicably, they were no longer fighting for dominance. They wound around each other and it was more perfect together than any calculated symphony could ever be because it carried longing and hope, fear and resignation, love and hate. It carried it all, and I couldn't protect myself from it.

The tears I'd been holding back slipped out, and I wrapped my arms around my chest as if that could stop my heart from jumping out of my ribcage. When the last note died off, I stood there shaking.

Nino opened his eyes and looked at me. And I knew then that if what I saw in Nino's eyes, what I saw on his face, was simulated, then I could live with it because it filled my heart with so much warmth it burned me from the inside out.

"What is this?" he asked in a raw voice.

I took a step toward him. "What is what?"

"Tell me," he said as he rose. "What is this if not emotion?"

I stared, not able to comprehend what he was saying, not daring to hope. "The song ... that's what you feel?"

Nino walked toward me slowly and regarded me as if I had shattered everything he believed. He stopped right in front of me, standing two steps below me so we were on eyelevel, and I could barely breathe. "Before you, there was calm. There was order and logic."

I remembered the beginning of his song, that perfect composition. "And now?" I let out a hoarse exhale.

"Now," he growled and his expression twisted, "now there's chaos."

I swallowed. What was I supposed to do with that kind of revelation? He startled me by cupping my cheeks, bringing our faces close, breathing harshly against my mouth, his eyes almost desperate.

"And you want the calm back," I whispered.

His brows drew together as he regarded me. He dipped his head and kissed me, soft and slow, nothing like what I'd expected from the look in his eyes. "Yes and no. Perhaps. I don't know," he said quietly. "It takes some getting used to."

And it lodged itself in my heart again, that stupid hope that perhaps one day Nino could ... Nino would love me.

Nino

Remo watched me warily as he put a few more guns into the trunk of his car. He'd be leaving for Chicago in a few hours with Fabiano. We were meeting in the Sugar Trap in thirty minutes for a few last-minute preparations. "I still think I should come with you," I said firmly. "You and Fabiano are a volatile combination in Chicago."

"Fabiano knows more about the Outfit than any of us, and you need to make sure nothing happens here. You can keep things in order if Fabiano and I don't return."

"Your chances of returning would increase if I came with you."

"These last couple of weeks, you have been erratic, Nino. I think it's best if you stay here."

I frowned. I had a better handle on myself, and the nightmares had stopped. But I wasn't the same as I had been before. There was no denying it.

Remo touched my shoulder. "What is going on? Do I need to worry?"

"I'm not how I used to be," I began, not sure how I could describe to him what I could hardly understand myself. "I feel things. It's still a struggle, still not how normal people feel, I'm sure of it, but it is there."

Remo had become very still. "It is because of Kiara?"

I nodded. "Because of her. She fought the demons of her past and made me realize that I, too, was shackled by memories, controlled by something I thought I had put past me."

Remo looked away, fury contorting his expression. "Our mother should be dead. Father should have killed her after cutting Adamo out of her. I should have killed her when I took over, but she is still there. Still fucking alive."

I touched Remo's shoulder. "She's as good as dead. A shadow of a person. She is the past."

Remo gave a jerky nod and met my gaze, something dark and dangerous in his eyes. I knew that look and had seen it many times before. "Are you still at my side now that you have gone all soft because of Kiara?"

I gripped his forearm over the Camorra tattoo, and he mirrored the gesture. "We are brothers. Not just by birth, but by choice, and I will stand by your side until I take my last breath. Nothing will change that. Kiara knows it, and she accepts it. I have your back." I paused. "And I'm not going soft, don't worry. These new sensations … I worried they would weaken me, that I couldn't be what you needed anymore, but they don't and they won't. I still don't feel a flicker of pity or guilt when I kill and torture for our cause, and that won't change."

Remo nodded and released me. For him, it was settled. He knew I was still there for him. "Now that I know you can take care of Vegas while I'm gone, I'll have to focus on kidnapping the lucky bride."

I shook my head. Remo was obsessed. I should have been the voice of reason in this and made sure our plan actually worked. Emotions wouldn't change the fact that I was the voice of logic between the two of us. That I would always be better at controlling my emotions, but Remo would follow his plan no matter what I said.

Kiara had freed me from the shackles of my past, and I wished the same for Remo. But Remo was Remo, and he would never allow a woman to see any side of him that didn't evoke terror and fear.

When I returned home early in the evening, Kiara was outside in the garden and practicing how to shoot a gun. She had improved greatly since she'd first held a gun in her hand. Adamo was beside her, adjusting her arms every now and then. He'd be inducted in three weeks, on his fourteenth birthday, and now he'd pulled back even further from Remo, Savio, and myself. The only person he still spoke to on a daily basis was Kiara. She shot again, hitting bull's-eye. Adamo smiled. Then he spotted me and stiffened. After saying something to Kiara, he walked off.

Kiara headed my way, the gun still in her hand. She was beaming, looking fucking proud, and my heart did that strange flip again. It always startled me.

"Did you see that?" she asked as she stopped in front of me.

"You're a good shot."

Her brows drew together. "Everything all right? You have a strange look on your face again."

I took her hand and led her inside the mansion. She followed without hesitation but chanced the occasional confused look at me. When we arrived in our bedroom, I took the gun from her and set it down on the nightstand. Then I pulled her against me and kissed her. Her hands came up to my chest, stroking and tugging, as her mouth moved against mine. She tasted like peppermint and chocolate, and I couldn't get enough of it.

Lifting her up, I laid her down on the bed then climbed on top of her, pressing my hard cock against her center. She moaned into my mouth and wrenched my shirt out of my pants. I sat up and quickly discarded my shirt before lowering myself back onto Kiara's soft body.

Her hands roamed over my back up to my neck, pulling me closer, and I kissed her harder and rocked my hips against her pelvis. She gasped. "Nino. I need you."

I pushed her shirt over her head then sucked her breast into my mouth through her lace bra as my hand traveled down to her shorts. I opened them and slipped my hand into her panties, over her soft hair and between her folds, finding her hot and wet and ready.

Fuck. I ripped her shorts down her legs then made quick work of her panties as well and pushed down my own pants and briefs before I moved back between her legs and thrust into her in one deep, hard move. We groaned and Kiara's nails raked over my back. I growled as my balls twitched. I guided one of her legs up then began fucking her in slow, hard thrusts. Her eyes remained on mine as I elicited from her lips one moan after another. There was trust and love in her eyes. I could see it now. I wasn't sure why I ever had trouble reading those emotions in her gaze. My own chest tightened, and my dead heart swelled with fucking emotion.

Fuck, it was painful, but it was the best pain I'd ever felt. I wrapped my arms around Kiara, bringing our bodies even closer, needing her fucking closer because only she filled the hole in my chest. Only she could look down into the black abyss that was my soul and find something lovable in it.

My throat became tight, but I forced the words out that I'd wanted to say for days now. "I love you." My thrusts faltered when I heard those three words aloud, heard them spill from my lips.

Kiara tensed under me, her eyes widening, and I fucking pulled myself together and thrust into her again. "You do?" she whispered.

"I do, with my fucking dead heart. With every fucking fiber of my being."

She gasped as I angled my thrusts higher, and her eyes still showed incomprehension, like she couldn't believe it. I reached between us, touching her clit, and claimed her lips. She arched up, shuddering, and I let loose as well. I kept my eyes open, kept watching Kiara's gorgeous face contort with pleasure. I'd always enjoyed sex. It was the closest I could come to feel, but sex with emotion was something else entirely. It was fucking perfection.

I remained on top of Kiara even as I began to go soft and kissed her once more.

"You love me," she whispered. "For real?"

"I love you. For real. No simulated affection or love ever again, because with you, I don't need to simulate. You dragged that dead part of me out of the past and revived it. I didn't die fifteen years ago, but I didn't live either … until you."

She held even tighter on to me. "I love you, Nino. A part of me died six years ago, but you helped me live again."

We had both been scarred by our past, but together we fought our demons and came out as the champions. Never had a victory felt better.

To be continued in
TWISTED BONDS,
Book 4 in the Camorra Chronicles

TWISTED
PRIDE

Book Three
The Camorra Chronicles

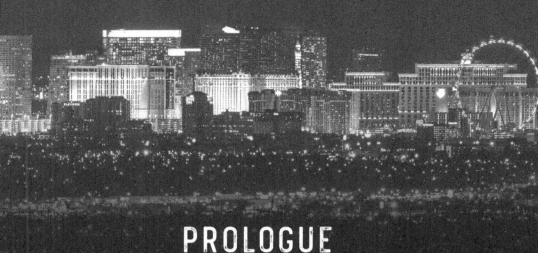

PROLOGUE

Serafina

ALL MY LIFE I HAD BEEN TAUGHT TO BE HONORABLE, TO DO WHAT WAS expected of me. Today I went against it all.

Dark and tall, Remo appeared in the doorway, come to claim his prize. His eyes roamed over my naked body, and mine did the same.

He was cruel and twisted. *Beyond redemption.*

Brutal attractiveness, forbidden pleasure, promised pain. I should have been disgusted by him, but I wasn't. Not by his body and not always by his nature.

I shut off the water in the shower, scared of what he wanted, completely terrified of what I wanted. This was his game of chess; he was the king and I was the trapped queen that the Outfit needed to protect. He moved me into position for his last move: the kill. Check.

He began unbuttoning his shirt then shrugged it off. He moved closer, stopping right before me. "You always watch me like something you want to touch but aren't allowed to. Who's holding you back, *Angel?*"

ONE

Serafina

"I CAN'T BELIEVE YOU'RE GETTING MARRIED IN THREE DAYS," SAMUEL said, his feet propped up beside mine on the coffee table. If Mom saw she would strangle us.

"Me either," I said quietly. At nineteen, I was already older than many other girls in our world when they entered the holy bond of matrimony, and I had been promised to Danilo for a long time. My fiancé was only twenty-one himself, so an earlier marriage wasn't very desirable. I certainly didn't mind. It had given me the time to finish school and stay home with Samuel for another year. He and I had never been separated for long, except for a few days when he had business to conduct for the Outfit.

Because of his father's sickness, Danilo was still busy taking over Indianapolis. A later wedding would have been even better for him, but I was a woman and supposed to marry before my twentieth birthday. I eyed the engagement ring on my finger. A prominent diamond in the center, we had to widen the band over the years as my fingers grew. In three days Danilo would put a second ring on me.

Mom came in with my sister, Sofia, who upon spotting us ran in our direction and wedged herself on the sofa between me and Samuel.

Samuel rolled his blue eyes but wrapped an arm around our little sister as she pressed up against him with big puppy dog eyes, tousling her brown mane. She had taken after Dad and hadn't inherited the blond hair of our mother like Samuel and I. "It's unfair that you're leaving right after Fina's wedding. I thought you would have more time for me."

I nudged her. "Hey." I wasn't really angry at her. I understood where she was coming from. Being eight years younger than us, she had always felt like a fifth wheel, since Samuel and I were twins.

Sofia gave me an embarrassed smile. "I'll miss you too."

"I'll miss you too, ladybug."

Mom cleared her throat, standing tall, her hands linked in front of her stomach. She was dressed in a fitted, elegant green dress. Her blue eyes lowered to our feet resting on the table. She tried to look stern, but the trembling of her mouth made it clear she was fighting a smile.

Samuel and I dropped our feet off the table at the same time.

"I thought I should warn you that Danilo just called. He's coming over because he just arrived in town and is supposed to meet your father and uncle."

Now I understood why Sofia, too, was dressed in a pretty summer dress. I didn't even know my father was expecting him. I was leaving for Indianapolis tomorrow.

I jerked to my feet. "When?"

"Ten minutes."

"Mom!" My eyes widened in horror. "How am I supposed to get ready with that much time?"

"You look fine," Samuel drawled, smirking, his short blond hair purposefully in a disarray. He could pull off the disheveled look, but I definitely couldn't.

I narrowed my eyes. "Oh shut up." I ran out of the room, almost bumping into Dad. He stepped back, looking down at me with a questioning smile.

"I need to get ready!"

I didn't have time to explain. He could ask Mom. I took the steps two at a time. The moment I stumbled into my bathroom and saw my reflection, I cringed. My God. My skin was flushed, and my hair curled wildly around my shoulders. My simple jeans and T-shirt didn't scream poised future wife either. Damn it.

I quickly washed my face then grabbed a flat iron. My hair was naturally curly, but I always straightened it when people other than my family were around. This time I had five minutes to do it. I stormed back into my bedroom, tore through my wardrobe. Choosing the right dress for such an occasion would have taken at least one hour. Now I had one minute, if I still wanted time to put on makeup. I grabbed a pink dress I ordered online a while ago but never wore and slipped it on. I was immediately reminded why I hadn't worn it before: it ended several inches above my knees, revealing more of my long legs than I usually displayed, especially when men were around. Danilo would be my husband in three days. It was only fair that he saw a bit more of what he was getting.

A nervous thrill took hold of my body, but I pushed it aside and quickly slipped on matching heels then hurried to my vanity. I didn't have enough time to put much effort into my makeup. My skin was quite flawless, so I decided against foundation and only put some blush and mascara on before rushing out of my room and down the corridor toward the stairs.

I slowed my steps considerably when I heard Danilo, Samuel, and Dad in the foyer below. It wouldn't be wise to appear as if I had rushed to get ready for any man, not even my fiancé.

They were shaking hands and exchanging pleasantries.

I had met Danilo a few times before. I'd been promised to him since I was fourteen and he sixteen, but this time felt more intimate. In only three days I would become his wife and share a bed with him. Danilo was very attractive and had much success with women, a ladies' man, but to me he had always been a perfect gentleman. He wore a white dress shirt and black pants, his dark hair immaculate.

I took the first step, placing my foot on the creaky stair on purpose, one long leg extended, my head held high.

All eyes turned to me. Danilo's gaze zeroed in on my exposed legs, then he quickly snapped his brown eyes up to meet my eyes, smiling. Dad and Samuel both looked briefly at my legs, but their reaction was less than thrilled. Dad was patient and loving with Mom and us kids, even Samuel, which made it easy to forget that he was Underboss of Minneapolis—and a feared one at that. I was quickly reminded just how scary he could be as he put his hand on Danilo's shoulder, wearing a hard expression on his face.

"I'd like to give you something in my office, Danilo," he said in a cold voice.

Danilo wasn't impressed by my father's mood change. He was going to be the youngest Underboss in the history of the Outfit, and he was practically already ruling over Indianapolis because his father was so sick. He gave a curt nod. "Of course," he said calmly, appearing so much older than his years. Hardened, grown-up. More man than I felt woman. Danilo gave me another smile then followed my father.

I descended the remaining steps, and Samuel barred my way. "Go change."

"Excuse me?"

He pointed at my legs. "You're showing too much leg."

I pointed at my arms and throat. "I'm also showing my neck and arms." I lifted one leg. "And I have nice legs."

Samuel stared down at my leg then up at my face with a frown. "Yeah, well, Danilo doesn't need to know that."

I snorted then quickly looked around, worried Danilo was close enough to overhear. "He will see more than my legs on our wedding night." Involuntary heat blasted my cheeks.

Samuel's expression darkened.

"Get out of my way," I said, trying to pass him.

Samuel mirrored my move. "Go change, Fina. Now," he ordered in a voice he probably reserved for business with other Made Men.

I couldn't believe his nerve. Did he think I would obey him only because he was a Made Man? That hadn't worked these last five years. I quickly reached for his stomach and pinched him hard, which wasn't easy considering Samuel was all muscle.

He jerked in surprise. I used his momentary distraction to slip past him then made a show of swaying my hips as I headed into the living area. Samuel caught up with me. "You have an impossible temper."

I smiled. "I have your temper."

"I'm a man. Women are supposed to be docile."

I rolled my eyes.

Samuel crossed his arms and leaned against the wall beside the window. "You always act like a well-behaved lady when others are around, but Danilo will get a nasty surprise once he realizes he didn't get a lady but a fury."

A flicker of worry flooded me. Samuel was right. Everyone outside my family knew me as the Ice Princess. Our family was notorious for being poised and controlled. The only people who really knew me were my parents, Sofia, and Samuel. Could I ever be myself around Danilo? Or would that put him off? Danilo was always controlled, which was probably why Uncle Dante and Dad had chosen him for my husband—and because he was the heir to one of the most important cities of the Outfit.

A knock sounded and I turned around to see Danilo step in.

His brown eyes met mine, and he gave me a small smile. Then his gaze moved on to Samuel leaning against the wall behind me. Danilo's expression tightened the slightest bit. I risked a look over my shoulder and found my brother glaring at my fiancé as if he wanted to crush him to dust. I tried to catch Samuel's gaze, but he was content killing Danilo with his eyes. I couldn't believe him.

"Samuel," I said in a forced, polite voice. "Why don't you give Danilo and me a moment?"

Samuel tore his gaze away from my fiancé and smiled. "I'm already giving you a moment."

"Alone."

Samuel shook his head once, his smile darkening, eyes returning to Danilo. "It's my responsibility to protect your honor."

Heat rose to my cheeks. If Danilo hadn't been in the room, I would have lunged at my brother and wrung his neck.

Danilo stepped up to me and kissed my hand, but his eyes were on my brother. Releasing my hand, he said, "I can assure you Serafina's honor is perfectly safe in my company. I will wait until our wedding night to claim my rights … when she is no longer your responsibility." Danilo's voice had dipped in a threatening way. He had never hinted to sex before, and I knew it was to provoke my brother. Power plays between two alphas.

Samuel rocked forward, away from the wall, his hand going to his knife. I turned and stepped up to my twin, placing my hand against his chest. "Samuel," I said in a warning tone, digging my nails into his skin through the fabric of his shirt. "Danilo is my fiancé. Give us a moment."

Samuel lowered his gaze to my face, and for once his expression didn't soften. "No," he said firmly. "And you won't defy my command."

I often forgot what Samuel was. He was my twin, my best friend, my confidant first, but for five years he'd been a Made Man, a killer, and he wouldn't back down in front of another man, especially not someone he would have to meet as a fellow Underboss. If I pushed further, he would look weak, and he was supposed to take over as Underboss from Dad in a few years. Even though I hated doing it and had never done it before, I cast my eyes down as if I was submitting to him.

Danilo might be my fiancé, but Samuel would always be my blood, and I didn't want him to look weak in front of anyone. "You are right," I said obediently. "I'm sorry."

Samuel touched my shoulder and squeezed lightly. "Danilo," he said in a low voice. "My sister will leave now. I want a word alone with you."

My blood boiling, I gave Danilo an apologetic smile before I left. Once outside, my smile fell and I stormed through the foyer, needing to vent. Where was Dad? I turned the corner and collided with someone. "Careful," came a drawl I knew well, and two hands steadied me.

I looked up. "Uncle Dante," I said with a smile then flushed because I'd barreled into him like a five-year-old throwing a tantrum. I smoothed my dress, trying to look poised. After all, my uncle was *pure control*. He had to be as Boss of the Outfit.

Dante tilted his head with a small smile. "Is something the matter? You look upset."

My cheeks heated further. "Samuel embarrassed me in front of Danilo. He's alone with him now. Having a word. Can you please check on them before Samuel ruins everything?"

Dante chuckled but he nodded. "Your brother wants to protect you. Where are they?"

"Living room," I said.

He squeezed my shoulder before walking away. Anger was still simmering under my skin. I would make Samuel pay for it. I made my way upstairs and into his room. A few knives and weapons belonging in a museum decorated the walls, but apart from that it was practically furnished. In a week or two Samuel would move into his own apartment in Chicago and work directly under Dante for a couple of years before returning to Minneapolis and eventually taking over for Dad.

I sank down on his bed, waiting. With every second that passed, I became more nervous. I got up and paced the room. When I heard his steps, I stopped and hid behind the door, carefully slipping out of my heels. The door opened and Samuel stepped in. I jumped, trying to land on his back and wrap my arms around his neck like I'd often done in the past.

Samuel caught me, hoisted me over his shoulder despite my struggling, and threw me down on the bed. Then he actually held me down, tousling my hair and tickling me.

"Stop!" I screeched between laughter. "Sam, stop!"

He did stop but gave me a smug grin. "You can't win against me."

"I liked it better when you were a scrawny boy and not this killing machine," I muttered.

Something dark passed over Samuel's eyes, and I touched his chest and lightly shoved him, a distraction from whatever horrors he was remembering. "How badly did you embarrass me in front of Danilo?"

"I went over the details of your wedding night with him."

I stared at Samuel in horror. "You *didn't.*"

"I did."

I sat up. "What did you say?"

"I told him he better treat you like a lady on your wedding night. No dominant shit or anything."

My cheeks blazed with heat, and I hit his shoulder hard.

He frowned, rubbing the spot. "What?"

"What!? You *embarrassed* me in front of Danilo. How could you talk about something like that with him? My wedding night isn't your business." My entire face was burning from embarrassment and anger. I couldn't believe him. He had always been protective of me, of course, but this took things too far.

Samuel grimaced. "Trust me, it wasn't easy for me. I don't like to think that my little sister is going to have sex."

I hit him again. "You are only three minutes older. And you have been having sex for years now. Do you even know how many women you've slept with?"

He shrugged. "I'm a man."

"Oh shut up," I muttered. "How am I ever going to face Danilo after what you did?"

"If it was up to me, you'd become a nun," Samuel said, and I lost it.

He had a way to drive me up the wall. I lunged at him again but like before it was futile. The last time I stood a chance fighting Samuel was more than five years ago. Samuel wrapped his arms around me from behind and held me in place.

"I think I'll carry you downstairs like this. Danilo is still talking to Dante. I'm sure he'll love to see his future wife this disheveled. Maybe he'll decide against marrying you if he sees you're not quite the obedient lady you want him to believe you are."

"You wouldn't dare!" I kicked my legs but Samuel carried me, lodged against his chest like I was a puppet.

Dad came in, his eyes moving from me pressed against Samuel to my twin gripping me tightly. He shook his head once. "I thought you'd stop the brawling once you got older."

Samuel released me and I stumbled to my feet. He smoothed his clothes, righting his gun and knife holsters. "She started it."

I gave him a look. Smoothing my hair and clothes, I cleared my throat. "He embarrassed me in front of Danilo, Dad."

"I told Danilo I'd rip his balls off if he didn't treat her right on their wedding night."

I scowled at my twin. He hadn't mentioned that detail to me.

Dad gave me a wistful smile, touching my cheek. "My little dove." Then he moved to Samuel and clapped his shoulder. "You did good."

I gave the two of them an incredulous look. Stifling my annoyance—and worse, my gratefulness for their protectiveness—I walked out of Samuel's bedroom into my own. I sat down on the bed, suddenly overcome with sadness. I was leaving my family, my home, for a city I didn't know, a husband I barely knew.

At the sound of an unfamiliar knock, I stood and walked toward my door, opening it.

Surprise washed over me when I saw Danilo's tall form. I opened my door wider but didn't ask him in. That would have been too forward. Instead, I stepped out into the corridor. "I can't ask you in."

Danilo gave me an understanding smile. "Of course not. In case you're worried, your uncle knows that I'm up here."

"Oh," I said, overwhelmed by his presence and the memory of what Samuel had done.

"I wanted to say goodbye. I'm leaving in a few minutes," he continued.

"I'm sorry," I said with as much dignity as my burning face allowed.

Danilo smiled with a small frown. "What for?"

"For what my brother did. He shouldn't have talked to you about … about our wedding night."

Danilo chuckled and moved closer to me, his spicy scent wrapping around me. He took my hand and kissed it. My stomach fluttered. "He wants to protect you. That's honorable. I don't blame him. A woman like you should be treated like a lady, and I will treat you that way on our wedding night and on every night that follows."

He leaned forward and lightly kissed my cheek. His eyes made it clear that he wanted to do more than that. He stepped back, letting go of my hand. I swallowed.

"I'm looking forward to being married to you, Serafina."

"Me too," I said quietly.

With a last look at me, he turned around and left. My heart pounding in my chest, I returned to my room and plopped down on my bed. I wasn't in love with Danilo, but I could imagine falling for him. That was a good start and better than many other girls in my world got.

A few minutes later, someone knocked again. This time I recognized the unabashed pounding of a fist against wood. "Come in," I said.

I didn't have to look up to know who it was. I recognized Samuel's steps with my eyes closed. He sank down beside me. "Thank you for obeying me when Danilo was around," Samuel said quietly. He took my hand.

"You need to appear strong. I didn't want to make you look weak." I looked up at him, tears gathering in my eyes.

His expression tightened. "You hated it."

"Of course I did."

Samuel looked away, glaring. "I hate the thought that you will have to obey Danilo or anyone for that matter."

"I could do worse than Danilo. He's a gentleman when he's around me."

Samuel laughed darkly. "He is as good as the Underboss of Indianapolis, Fina, and despite his age, he has his men under control. I've seen him in action. He is a Made Man like me and Dad. He expects obedience."

I regarded him curiously. "You never expected obedience from me."

"I wished for it," he muttered jokingly then turned serious again. "You are my sister, not my wife. That's different."

"Will you expect obedience from your wife?"

Samuel frowned. "I don't know. Maybe."

"How do you treat the women you are with?" I'd never met any of them. Made Men took outsiders into their beds before marriage, and those women weren't allowed into our homes.

Quickly and unexpectedly, Samuel's face seemed to close off. "It doesn't matter." He stood. "And it doesn't matter how Danilo is used to treating his whores. You are a mafia princess, my sister, and I swear by my honor that I will hunt him down if he doesn't treat you like a lady."

I smiled up at my twin. "My protector."

Samuel smiled back. "Always."

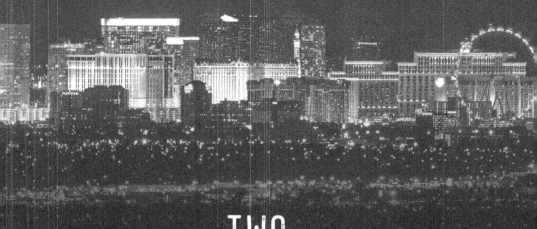

TWO

Remo

"**A**RE YOU READY? WE'VE GOT A WEDDING TO CRASH," I SAID, grinning. Excitement sizzled under my skin, a low fire that burned brighter with every second I got closer to my goal.

Fabiano sighed, checking his gun and shoving it back into his holster. "As ready I as I'll ever be for this insanity."

"Genius and insanity are often interchangeable. Both have fueled the greatest events in human history."

"I think you annoy me the most when you sound like Nino with your own brand of crazy," Fabiano said. "I can't believe I'm only a few miles from my father and can't rip him to shreds."

"You will get him. My plan will bring him to you eventually."

"I don't like the eventually part. I have a feeling this plan is about more than killing my father and punishing the Outfit."

I leaned back against the car seat. "And what would that be?"

Fabiano met my gaze. "About you getting your hands on Dante's niece for whatever insane reason."

My mouth pulled into a dark smile. "You know exactly why I want her."

Fabiano leaned back in his own seat, expression tightening. "I don't think even you know exactly why you want her. But I do know the girl will pay for something she wasn't responsible for."

"She's part of our world. Born and bred to be a mother to more Outfit bastards. Born and bred to obey like a mindless sheep. She was brought up to follow her shepherd without hesitation. He led her toward a pack of wolves. It's his mistake, but she will be torn apart."

Fabiano shook his head. "Fuck, Remo. You are a crazy fucker."

I wrapped my fingers tightly around his forearm, over his Camorra tattoo—the blade and the eye. "You are one of us. We bleed and we die together. We maim and kill together. Don't forget your oath."

"I won't," he said simply.

I released him. My eyes moved to the front of the hotel where Serafina's parents, Ines and Pietro Mione, had just walked out the door with a young dark-haired girl between them. Dressed in evening wear for the wedding of the year, Ines looked remarkably like her brother. Tall and blond and proud. So fucking proud and controlled.

"It won't be long now," I said, glancing down the street where the car with my two soldiers was waiting.

Fabiano put the keys in the ignition as we watched the Miones drive off. "Her twin will stay with her," he said. "And then there's the bodyguard."

My eyes sought out the middle-aged guy behind the wheel of a Bentley limousine parked in the driveway of the hotel. A fucking flower arrangement on the hood. White flowers. I wanted to squash them under my boots.

"They're making it too easy figuring out the car of the bride," I said with a laugh.

"Because they don't expect an attack. It's never been done before. Funerals and weddings are sacred."

"There have been bloody weddings before. They should know better."

"But those weddings became bloody because the guests got into fights with each other. I don't think anyone has ever attacked a wedding, especially the bride, on purpose. Honor forbids it."

I chuckled. "We are the Camorra. We have our own set of rules, our own idea of honor."

"I think they will realize that today," he said tightly.

My eyes scanned the front of the hotel. Somewhere behind its windows, Serafina was getting ready for her wedding. She'd be groomed to perfection, an apparition in white. I couldn't wait to get my hands on her, stain the perfectly white fabric blood-red.

Serafina

"You don't have to be scared, sweetheart," Mom said quietly so Sofia wouldn't hear her. My little sister was busy tugging at the pins keeping her hair in place on top of her head, grimacing.

"I'm not," I said quickly, which was a lie. It wasn't that I was overly scared of sleeping with Danilo, but I was nervous and worried about embarrassing myself. I didn't like to be bad at things, and I would be bad given I had no experience.

She gave me a knowing look. "It's okay to be nervous. But he's a decent man. Dante always talks in glowing terms about Danilo." Mom tried to sound casual but failed miserably. She stroked my hair like she used to do when I was little.

We both knew that there was a difference between being a decent man and a loyal soldier to the Outfit. Uncle Dante was probably basing his judgment of Danilo on the latter. Not that it mattered. Danilo had always been a gentleman, and he would be my husband in a few hours. It was my duty to submit to him, and I would do it.

My hairdresser took Mom's place and began pinning up my blond hair, arranging pearls and strings of white gold in it. Mom noticed Sofia fighting with her hairdo and quickly moved over to her. "Stop it, Sofia. You've already untangled a few strands."

Sofia dropped her hands with a resigned look. Then her blue eyes found mine. I smiled at her. Avoiding Mom's tugging hands, she came to my side and peered up at me. "I can't wait to be a bride."

"First, you will finish school," I teased her. She was only eleven and hadn't been promised to anyone yet. For her weddings were about looking pretty and the chivalrous knight she would marry. I envied her the ignorance.

"Done," the hairdresser announced and stepped back.

"Thank you," I said. She nodded and quickly slipped out, giving us a moment.

The dress was absolutely stunning. I couldn't stop admiring myself in the mirror, turning left and right. The pearls and silver embroidered threadwork caught the light beautifully, and the skirt was a dream consisting of several layers of the finest tulle. Mom shook her head, tears blurring her eyes.

"Don't cry, Mom," I warned her. "You'll ruin your makeup. And if you start crying, I will cry too and then my makeup will be ruined as well."

Mom nodded, blinking. "You are right, Fina." She dabbed her eyes with the corner of a tissue. Mom wasn't the emotional type. She was like her brother, my Uncle Dante. Sofia beamed up at me.

A knock sounded and Dad poked in his head. He froze and slowly stepped inside. He took me in without saying a word. I could see the emotion swimming in his eyes, but he would never show it openly. He came toward me and touched two fingers to my cheeks. "Dove, you're the most beautiful bride I've ever seen."

Mom raised her eyebrows in mock shock. Dad laughed and took her hand, kissing her knuckles. "You were, of course, a breathtaking bride, Ines."

"What about me?" Sofia asked. "Maybe I will be even more beautiful?"

Dad lifted a finger. "I will keep you as my little daughter forever. No marriage for you."

Sofia pouted and Dad shook his head. "We need to go to church now." He kissed my cheek then took Sofia's hand. The three of them walked out. Mom turned once more and gave me a proud smile.

Samuel appeared in the doorway, dressed in a black suit and blue tie. "You look dapper," I told him and felt a wave of wistfulness. He would be hundreds of miles from me once I moved into Danilo's villa in Indianapolis.

"And you look beautiful," he said quietly, his eyes taking me in head to toe.

He pushed off the doorframe and moved toward me, his hands in his pockets. "It'll be strange without you."

"I'll tell Sofia she needs to keep you on your toes."

"It won't be the same."

"You will marry in a few years. And soon you'll be even busier with mob business. You won't even notice I'm gone."

Samuel sighed then glanced down at his Rolex that Dad had given him for his initiation five years ago. "We need to go too. The ceremony is supposed to start in forty-five minutes. It'll take at least thirty minutes to reach the church."

The church was outside city limits. I wanted the celebration to take place in a renovated barn in the countryside, surrounded by forest, not in the city.

I nodded then checked my reflection once more before I took his outstretched hand. With linked arms we walked out of the suite and down into the hotel lobby. People kept glancing my way, and I had to admit I enjoyed their attention. The dress had cost a small fortune. It was only fair, since as many people as possible would see me in it. This wedding was the biggest social event in the Outfit in years.

Samuel opened the door of the black Bentley for me, and I slipped onto the backseat, trying to gather the skirt of my dress around me. Samuel closed the door and got in the front beside the driver, my bodyguard.

We pulled away and my stomach burst with butterflies. In less than one hour I'd be Danilo's wife. It still seemed impossible. Soon, the tall buildings gave way to the occasional field and trees.

Samuel shifted in the front seat, pulling his gun.

"What's wrong?" I asked.

We sped up. Samuel glanced over his shoulder but not at me. I turned as well and saw a car close behind us with two men. Samuel took his phone out and lifted it to his ear. Before he could say anything, another car came from the side and collided with our trunk. We spun around. I cried out, gripping the seat as the belt bit into my skin.

"Down!" Samuel shouted. I unbuckled and threw myself forward, my arms over my head. We collided with something else then came to a stop. What was going on?

Samuel shoved open the door and began firing. My bodyguard followed him. The windows burst, and I screamed as shards of glass rained down on my skin. A man cried out, and my head flew up. "Samuel?" I screamed.

"Run, Fina!"

I pushed through the gap between the front seats and found Samuel leaning against the side of the car, blood spilling out over the hand he pressed to his side. I struggled out of the door and sank to the ground beside him, touching him. "Sam?"

He gave me a strained smile. "I'll be fine. Run, Fina. They want you. Run."

"Who wants me?" I blinked at him, uncomprehending. He fired at our attackers again. "Run!"

I bolted to my feet. If they wanted me, they'd follow me if I ran and leave Samuel alone. "Call reinforcement."

I kicked off my heels and gripped my dress and began running as fast as I could. White petals from the destroyed flower arrangement stuck to my toes. Nobody shot at me. That meant they wanted me alive, and I knew that couldn't be a good thing. I turned to the right, where a forest spread out in front of me. It was my only chance to lose them. My breath came in short gasps. I was fit and a good runner, but the heavy fabric of my dress slowed me down. Twigs tugged at the dress, tearing it, making me stumble.

Heavier steps sounded behind me. I didn't dare look over my shoulder to see who was chasing me. The steps closed in on me. Oh God. This dress was making me too slow.

Had Samuel called reinforcement yet?

And then a worse thought banished my last. What if Samuel didn't make it? I turned to the right, deciding to run back to the car. Another set of steps joined the first. Two pursuers.

Fear pounded in my veins, but I didn't slow. A shadow appeared in the corner of my eye, and suddenly a tall shape came from my side. I screamed out a second before an arm slung around my waist. The force of it made me lose my balance, and I fell to the ground. A heavy body crushed mine. The air rushed out of my lungs and my vision turned black from the impact of landing hard on the forest floor.

I started kicking, thrashing, clawing and screamed at the top of my lungs. But a few layers of tulle covered my face and made movement difficult. If Dad and Dante had arrived with reinforcement, they needed to hear me to be able to find me.

A hand clamped down on my mouth, and I bit down.

"Fuck!"

The hand pulled back and the voice was distantly familiar, but I couldn't place it in my panic. The tulle still obstructed my view. I made out two shapes above me. Tall. One dark, one blond.

"We need to hurry," someone snarled. I shivered at the stark brutality of the voice.

A heavy weight settled on my hips, and two strong hands gripped my wrists, shoving them down on the ground. I tried bucking away, but a hand came toward my face. I tried to bite again, but I didn't reach it. My range of motion was limited with my arms above my head. The tulle was removed from my face, and finally I could see my assailants. The man sitting on my hips had black hair and black eyes and a scar on his face. The look he gave me sent a wave of terror through my body.

I'd seen him before but wasn't sure where. My eyes darted to the other man holding my hands down, and I froze. I knew the blond man and those blue eyes. Fabiano Scuderi, the boy I'd played with when I was younger. The boy who had run off and joined the Camorra.

Finally, it clicked. My gaze darted back to the black-haired man. Remo Falcone, Capo of the Camorra. I jerked violently, a new wave of panic giving me strength. I arched up but Remo didn't budge.

"Calm down," Fabiano said. One of his hands bled from where I'd bitten him. Calm down? Calm down? The Camorra was trying to kidnap me!

Opening my mouth, I tried to scream again. This time Remo covered my mouth before I got the chance to hurt him. "Give her the tranquilizer," he ordered.

I shook my head frantically but something pricked the inside of my elbow and pierced my skin. My muscles became heavy, but I didn't black out completely. I was released and Remo Falcone slid his hands under me, straightening up with me in his arms. My limbs hung limply down at my sides, but my eyes remained open and on my captor. His dark eyes settled on me briefly before he started running. Trees and sky rushed by as I peered up.

"Fina!" I heard Samuel in the distance.

"Sam," I wheezed, barely a sound.

Then Dad. "Fina? Fina, where are you?"

More male voices rang out, coming to save me.

"Faster!" Fabiano shouted. "To the right!" Twigs snapped under foot. Remo breathed heavier, but his grip on me remained firm. We burst out of the forest and onto a street.

Suddenly, tires screeched and hope filled me, but it crashed when I was put inside a vehicle in the backseat, and Remo slipped in beside me.

"Drive!"

I stared up at the gray ceiling of the car, my breathing ragged.

"My, what a beautiful bride you are," Remo said. I raised my eyes and met his, wishing I hadn't because the twisted smile on his face burned through me like a thunderstorm of terror. Then I passed out.

Remo

Serafina passed out beside me. I regarded her closely. Now that she wasn't thrashing or screaming, I could admire her like a bride deserved. Dots of blood splattered her dress like rubies and marred the creamy skin of her neckline. Pure perfection.

"We seem to have shaken them off," Fabiano muttered.

My eyes were drawn to the back window, but nobody was following us for the moment. We had injured, not killed Serafina's two companions, so part of the forces would waste time tending to their injuries.

"She is a nice piece of ass," Simeone commented from behind the steering wheel.

I leaned forward. "And you will never look at her again unless you want me to rip your eyeballs out and shove them up your ass. One more fucking disrespectful word from you and your tongue will keep your eyeballs company, understood?"

Simeone gave a jerky nod.

Fabiano caught my gaze with a curious expression. I leaned back and returned my gaze to the woman curled up beside me on the seat. Her hair was pinned tightly to her head as if even that part of her needed to be tamed and under control, but one wayward strand had freed itself and curled wildly over her temple. I wrapped it around my finger. I couldn't wait to find out how tame Serafina really was.

I carried a limp Serafina into the motel room and set her down on one of the two beds. Reaching for a twig that had tangled itself in her hair, I removed it before undoing her updo, letting her hair spill out on the pillow. I straightened.

Fabiano sighed. "Cavallaro will seek retribution."

"He won't attack us as long as we have her. She's vulnerable and he knows he can't get her out of Vegas alive."

Fabiano nodded, his eyes moving to Serafina who lay limply on the bed, her face tilted to the side, her long elegant neck on display. My gaze lowered to the fine lace above the soft swell of her breast. A high-collared dress. Modest and elegant, nothing vulgar or overly sexy about Dante's niece, and yet she would have brought many men to their knees. She looked like a fucking angel with her blond hair and pale skin, and the white dress only emphasized that impression. The epitome of innocence and purity. I had to bite back a laugh.

"What are you thinking?" Fabiano asked warily as he followed my gaze toward the bride.

"That they couldn't have emphasized her innocence more if they'd tried." I moved closer, my gaze trailing over her narrow hips. "I prefer the blood stains on her dress."

"It was her wedding. Of course they would emphasize her purity. You know how it is. Girls in our circles are kept protected until they enter marriage. They must lose their innocence on their wedding night. Cavallaro and her fiancé will probably do anything to make sure she returns to them untouched. Danilo is Underboss. Her father is Underboss. Dante fucking Cavallaro is her uncle. No matter what you ask of them, they will deliver. If you ask them to hand over my father now, they will do it and we will be rid of her."

I shook my head. "I won't ask for anything yet. I won't make it that easy for them. They attacked Las Vegas. They tried killing my brothers, tried killing you and me. They brought war into my city, and I will bring war into their midst. I will destroy them from the inside. I will break them."

Fabiano frowned. "How?"

I regarded him. The hint of wariness in his voice was barely noticeable, but I knew him well. "By breaking someone they are supposed to protect. If there's one thing I know, then it's that even men like us rarely forgive themselves for letting people they are supposed to protect get hurt. Her family will go crazy with worry over her. Every day they're going to wonder what's happening to her. They're going to imagine how she's suffering. Her mother will blame her husband and brother. And they will blame themselves. Their guilt will spread like cancer among them. And I will fuel their worry. I will tear them apart."

Fabiano lowered his gaze to Serafina, who started stirring slightly. The rip in her wedding dress shifted, exposing her long bare leg. She was wearing a white lace garter. Fabiano reached for the skirt of her dress and covered her leg. I tilted my head at him.

"She's an innocent," he said neutrally.

"She won't return to them innocent," I said darkly.

Fabiano met my gaze. "Hurting her won't break the Outfit. They will come closer together to bring you down."

"We will see," I murmured. "Let's call Nino and see which route to choose next." Fabiano and I moved toward the desk and put the phone on loudspeaker.

We had just finished our call when Serafina moaned. We turned to her. She woke with a start, disoriented. She blinked slowly at the wall then up at the ceiling. Her movements were slow, sluggish. Her breathing picked up, and she looked down at her body, her hands feeling her ribs then lower, coming to rest on her abdomen—as if she thought we'd fucked her while she was passed out. I supposed it made sense. She would have been sore.

"If you keep touching yourself like that, I won't be responsible for my actions."

Her gaze darted to us, her body stiffening.

"We didn't touch you while you were unconscious," Fabiano told her.

Her eyes darted between him and me. It was obvious she wasn't sure if she could believe him.

"You would know if Fabiano or I had fucked you, trust me, Serafina."

She pressed her lips together, fear and disgust swirling in her blue eyes. She began squirming and wiggling as if she was trying to get off the bed but couldn't control her body. Eventually she closed her eyes, her chest heaving, her fingers trembling against the blanket.

"She's still drugged," Fabiano said.

"I'll get her a coke. Maybe the caffeine will sober her up. I don't like her this weak and unresponsive. It's no challenge."

Serafina

I watched Remo leave the room and forced myself into a sitting position. "Fabiano," I whispered.

He came closer and knelt before me. "Fina," he said simply. Only my brother called me by that name, but Fabiano had always played with us when we were little and knew me by the nickname.

My mother hadn't raised me to beg, but I was desperate. I touched his hand. "Please help me. You were part of the Outfit. You can't allow this."

He pulled his hand away, his eyes hard. "I *am* part of the Camorra."

He stood and looked down at me without a hint of emotion.

"What will happen to me? What does your Capo want with me?" I asked hoarsely.

For a second his eyes softened, and that was the most terrifying answer he could have given me. "The Outfit attacked us on our own territory. Remo is out for retribution."

Icy terror clawed at my insides. "But I have nothing to do with your business."

"You don't, but Dante is your uncle and your father and fiancé are high-ranking Outfit members."

I looked down at my hands. My knuckles were chalk white from clutching the fabric of my dress. Then I noticed the red stains and quickly released the tulle. "So he's going to make them pay by hurting me?" My voice broke. I cleared my throat, trying hard and failing to hold on to my composure.

"Remo didn't divulge his plan to me," he said, but I didn't believe him for one second. "He might use you to bribe your uncle into handing over parts of his territory … or his Consigliere."

Uncle Dante would never give up part of his territory, not even for family, no matter how much my mother begged him to, nor would he hand over one of his men, *his Consigliere*. He couldn't, not for one girl. I was lost.

My vision swam again and I slumped back down onto the mattress.

Through the fogginess I heard Remo's voice. "Change of plans. Let her sleep the drugs out of her system while we drive. We've spent too much time at this place. Nino called again. He suggests we head out now. He sent our helicopter to pick us up in Kansas. He heard from Grigory that Cavallaro has called upon every soldier to search for his niece and we are still on the fringes of his territory."

Dante was trying to save me. Dad and Danilo would be searching for me as well. And Samuel, my Samuel, would look for me. If we were still on Outfit territory not all hope was lost.

THREE

Serafina

I WOKE IN A CAR, CURLED INTO MYSELF, HALF TANGLED IN MY DRESS. Fabiano was in the backseat beside me but didn't look at me. Instead, he was checking the rear window. Another man sat in the front behind the wheel and beside him was Remo.

I wasn't sure if they'd given me another tranquilizer or if my body had trouble fighting the effects of the first injection. I hadn't eaten all day and hardly had anything to drink. A low moan slipped past my lips.

Fabiano and Remo both looked down at me. Remo's dark eyes sent a shiver of fear down my spine, but Fabiano's gaze didn't offer any consolation either. I closed my eyes again, hating how vulnerable I felt.

I wasn't sure how long we'd been driving, but the next time I woke we were in a helicopter. I struggled into a sitting position. The strip with hotels and casinos spread out below, and my stomach constricted as the helicopter started its descent over Las Vegas. I didn't say a word to either Fabiano or Remo, and they didn't talk to me either. The tension was still palpable in the helicopter, but they had escaped from the Outfit and now I was in Las Vegas. In Camorra territory. At their mercy.

The moment we landed, Fabiano helped me out of the helicopter while Remo talked to someone on the phone. I needed to wash my face and clear my head so I could think straight again. I had been in my wedding dress for almost twenty-four hours. I felt sticky and sluggish and exhausted. And underneath it all a terror I had trouble containing throbbed inside of me.

I was pushed into another car, and eventually we pulled up in front of a shabby strip club called the Sugar Trap.

Fabiano gripped my arm again as Remo went ahead without a single glance at me.

"Fabi," I tried, but he tightened his hold. "I need to go to the bathroom and wash my face. I don't feel good."

He led me inside the deserted strip club toward the ladies' room and followed me inside to wait at the washbasins. Remo had ignored me mostly, but I had a feeling that would change soon.

I went to the toilet, hating that I knew Fabiano could hear me. There was nothing I could have used as a weapon, and even if there were, how would that help me surrounded by Camorrista? I dropped my skirt when I was done, breathing deeply, trying to hide my emotions.

"Serafina," came Fabiano's warning voice. "Don't make me get you out of there. You won't like it."

Straightening my shoulders, I came back out, feeling shaky from dehydration.

I bent over the washbasin and washed my face then drank a few gulps of water.

"You can have a coke from the bar," Fabiano said. Before I could say anything, he gripped me by the arm and dragged me out. My bare feet ached. I must have cut them on the forest ground. My eyes flitted around the room. It wasn't deserted anymore. As if drawn out by the commotion, several scantily clad women had gathered at the bar.

They avoided looking at me, and I realized I couldn't hope for their help. Not a single person in Las Vegas would probably risk helping me.

"Coke," Fabiano barked at a dark-skinned man behind the bar, who grabbed a bottle, opened it, and handed it to Fabiano. The man purposely wasn't looking at me.

Good Lord. Where had they taken me? What kind of hellhole was Las Vegas?

"Drink," Fabiano said, holding the bottle out for me. I took it and had a few long sips. The cold, sweet liquid seemed to revive my brain and body.

"Come." Fabiano led me through a door and along a bare-walled corridor toward another door. When he opened it and stepped inside with me, my stomach revolted.

Inside were two unknown men, both of them Falcones, I assumed. All of them were tall, with hard expressions and this air of unbridled cruelty that they were famous for. One of them had gray eyes and looked older than the other guy. I tried to remember their names, but then my eyes met Remo's and my mind turned blank.

The Camorra Capo had shed his shirt. There was a fresh wound on his left side that had been stitched up, but there was still blood around it. My pulse stuttered in my veins at the sight of his muscles and scars.

"Your twin almost got me there," Remo said with a dark laugh. "But not enough to stop me from capturing his beloved sister." He said beloved like it was something filthy, something worthless.

Fabiano released me and joined the other men, leaving me standing in the middle of the room like a piece of meat that needed inspecting. Dread settled in my bones because maybe that was exactly what I was to them. Meat.

Remo pointed at the gray-eyed man. "That's my brother Nino." Then he gestured at the younger man beside him. "And my brother Savio."

Remo stalked closer, every muscle in his upper body taut, as if he was a predator about to pounce. I stood my ground. I wouldn't give him an inch. I wouldn't give him anything. Not my fear and not a single tear. He couldn't force those from me. I didn't kid myself thinking that I could stop him from taking anything else.

"Serafina Cavallaro." My name was a caress on his lips as he slowly walked around me. He stopped close behind me so I couldn't see him.

I suppressed a shiver. "Not Cavallaro. That's my uncle's name, not mine."

Remo's breath fanned over my neck. "In every regard that matters, you are a Cavallaro."

I dug my nails into my palms. Nino's gray eyes followed the movement without a flicker of emotion on his face. Fabiano perched on the desk, looking at the man behind me but not me. Savio regarded me with a mix of curiosity and calculation.

I didn't say anything, only stared stubbornly ahead. Remo circled me and stopped in front of me. He was a tall man, and I wished for my heels. I wasn't exactly small, but barefoot only the top of my head reached his chin. I lifted my head slightly, trying to appear taller.

Remo's mouth twitched. "I hear you were supposed to marry your fiancé, Danilo Mancini, yesterday," he said with a twisted grin. "So I robbed you of your wedding night."

I remembered Mom's consoling words. That Danilo would be good to me. That I didn't have to be scared of him claiming his rights after our wedding. And Samuel's words that he'd hunt down Danilo if he didn't treat me like a lady.

As I stared up into the face of Remo Falcone, my worry of having sex with Danilo seemed ridiculous. The Camorra wouldn't be good to me. The name of their Capo was spoken in hushed, terrified whispers even among women in the Outfit. And a terror unlike anything I'd ever encountered gripped me, but I forced it down. Pride was the only weapon I had, and I would hold on to it until the very end.

"I wonder if you let your fiancé have a taste before your wedding," Remo murmured, his voice a low vibrato full of threat, his dark eyes raking over me.

Indignation filled me. How dare he suggest something like that? "Of course not," I said coldly. "The first kiss of a honorable Outfit woman happens on her wedding day."

His grin widened, wolf-like, and I realized my mistake. He'd led me into a trap. My own pride a weapon he used against me.

Remo

She held her head high in spite her mistake. Her long blond hair trailed down her back. Cool blue eyes assessed me like I wasn't worth her attention. *Perfect.*

Highborn and about to take a deep fall.

"So proud and cold," I said, trailing a finger down her cheek and throat. "Just like good ol' Uncle Dante." She turned her face away with a disgusted expression.

I laughed. "Oh yes, that stupid Outfit pride. I can't wait to rid you of it."

"I'll take that pride to the grave with me," she said haughtily.

I leaned even closer, my body lightly pressing up against hers. "Killing you is the last thing on my mind, believe me." I let my eyes travel the length of her body. "There are far more entertaining things I can think of."

Terror flashed over her face, only briefly, then it was gone. But I saw it. So death didn't bother the girl, or so she thought, but the idea of being touched by me put a chink into that prideful exterior.

"So you have never kissed a man before," I mused, leaning in so close that our lips were almost touching.

She stood her ground, but a slight tremor went through her body. She pressed her lips together, refusing an answer.

"This will be fun."

"My family and fiancé will tear down Las Vegas if you hurt me."

"Oh, I hope they do, so I can bathe in their blood," I said. "But I doubt you'll be worth their trouble once I'm done with you. Or will your fiancé settle for the leftovers of another man?"

She finally took a step back.

My smile pulled wider. Her eyes darted to something behind me. To someone. I followed her gaze to Fabiano. His eyes met mine, his expression hard and unrelenting, but I knew him inside out. He'd known Serafina as a child, had played with her. There was a hint of strain in his eyes, but he wouldn't come to her aid, neither would Nino or Savio.

I turned back around to her. "Nobody will save you, so you better stop hoping for it."

She narrowed her eyes at me. "I decide what to hope for. You might rule over Las Vegas and over these men, but you don't rule over me, Remo Falcone."

Never before had someone spat out my name like that, and it sent a fucking thrill through me.

"Oh, Serafina," I said darkly. "That's where you're wrong, and I will prove it to you."

"And I will prove you wrong." Her blue eyes held mine, back in control, back to being her prideful self. But she had given me an opening earlier, had shown me a crack in her mask, and she couldn't undo it. I knew how to get under her skin.

"As much as I enjoy chitchatting with you, I need to remember the purpose of why you are here. And that's to pay back your uncle Dante."

A flash of fear in those proud eyes. I let my gaze travel the length of her, over her torn and bloody wedding dress.

"We need to send your uncle a message, a nice video of you," I murmured. I nodded toward Fabiano. "Take her into the basement. I'll join you in a few minutes." I wanted to see how he'd react.

Fabiano's jaw tensed but he gave a terse nod. He grabbed Serafina's wrist, and she tensed but didn't fight him, not like she would have undoubtedly fought me. He began to tug her along. She didn't beg him like I thought she would. Instead, she gave me another disgusted look. She thought she could defy me, thought she could hold on to her pride and anger. I would show her why I had become Capo of the Camorra.

"What are you going to do to her?" Savio asked, trying to sound unfazed, but he wasn't like Nino and me. He had some humanity left in him.

"What I said. Let her speak a message to her Uncle Dante ... and record some additional material."

"So you're going to fuck her for the camera?" Savio asked.

I glanced at Nino, who watched me with narrowed eyes as if he, too, wasn't sure about my motives. I smiled. "Don't spoil my surprise. We'll all watch the video together once it's done."

I gave them a nod and headed downstairs. The moment I entered the corridor in the basement, Fabiano stepped out of the last door and closed it. His eyes settled on me. He met me halfway and gripped my arm. I raised my eyebrows.

"Serafina's virginity can be used as leverage against Dante and Danilo."

I narrowed my eyes at him. "Thank you for your input, Fabiano. I am Capo. I've thought my plan through. Don't worry."

"Have you?" Fabiano muttered, and I brought us nose to nose.

"Careful. You've betrayed me for a woman once before. Do not make it a habit."

Fabiano shook his head. "Fuck. I won't betray you. I went to Indianapolis with you and kidnapped Serafina. I didn't hunt down my father like I wanted to. I put her in your fucking cell for you. I am loyal, Remo."

"Good," I said, stepping back. "Serafina is my captive, and I decide what happens to her, understood?"

"Understood," Fabiano said, gritting his teeth. "Can I go to Leona now?"

"Go. I'll have Simeone watch her cell tonight."

"He's a fucking pervert, Remo."

"He also knows I'll cut his dick off if he goes against my orders. Now go have fun with your girl while I take care of mine."

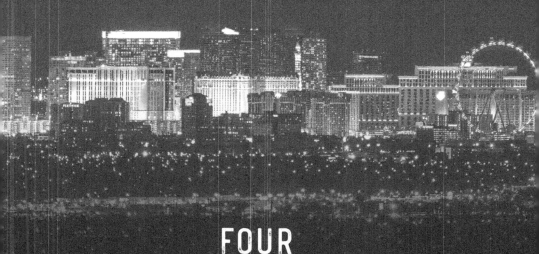

FOUR

Serafina

FABIANO DRAGGED ME DOWN A FLIGHT OF STAIRS INTO A BASEMENT.
"Fabi," I said imploringly, tugging at his hold.

"Fabiano," he growled, not even looking at me as he pulled me through another narrow bare corridor. He seemed furious.

Before I could utter another word, he opened a heavy door and stepped inside a room with me. My eyes darted around. A cell.

My stomach lurched when I saw the toilet and shower in one corner, but even worse when I took in the stained mattress on the floor across from them. Red and yellow stains. Terror gripped me hard, and suddenly I realized what was supposed to happen here.

My eyes flew up to a camera in the corner to my right then back to Fabiano. He was Enforcer of the Camorra, and while my parents had tried to shelter me, Samuel had been more forthcoming with information. I knew what Enforcers did, especially in Las Vegas.

Fabiano scanned my face and released me with a sigh. I stumbled back and almost lost my balance when my feet caught in my dress. "Will you …?" I pressed out.

Fabiano shook his head. "Remo will handle you himself."

I froze. "Fabiano," I tried again. "You can't allow that to happen. Don't let him hurt me. Please." The word tasted bitter in my mouth. Begging wasn't something I had been taught, but this wasn't a situation I had ever prepared for.

"Remo won't …" Fabiano trailed off and grimaced.

Pushing past my fear, I moved closer to Fabiano and gripped his arms. "If you are unwilling to help me, then at least tell me what I can do to stop Remo from hurting me. What does he want from me?"

Fabiano stepped back, so I had to release him. "Remo hates weakness. And in his eyes women are weak."

"So I'm at the mercy of a man who hates women."

"He hates weakness. But you are strong, Serafina." He turned and left, closing the heavy door and locking me in.

I whirled around, my eyes scanning the surroundings for something I could use against Remo, but there was nothing, and he wasn't a man who could be beaten in a fight. Strong? Was I strong? It didn't feel that way right now. Fear pounded in my chest, in every fiber of my body.

My eyes darted to the mattress once more. Yesterday Danilo was supposed to claim me on satin sheets in the holy bond of matrimony. Today Remo would break me on a dirty mattress like a common whore.

I braced myself against the rough stone wall, fighting my rising panic. All my life I had been raised to be proud and noble, honorable and well-behaved, and it didn't protect me.

The creak of the door made me tense, but I didn't turn to see who had entered. I knew who it was, could feel his cruel eyes on me.

I peered up at the camera once more. Everything that happened would be recorded and sent to my uncle, fiancé, and father. And worse … Samuel. I swallowed. They would see me at my worst. I wouldn't let it come to that. I'd hold my head high no matter what happened.

"Are you ignoring me?" Remo asked from close behind me, and a small shiver shot down my spine.

"Does that ever work?" I said, wishing my voice came out stronger, but it was already a fight forcing those four words out of my tight throat.

"No," Remo said. "I'm difficult to ignore."

Impossible to ignore.

"Turn around," Remo ordered.

I didn't move, focusing on the gray stone in front of me. It wasn't only an act of defiance. My legs refused to move. Fear kept me frozen, but Remo didn't need to know that.

His hot breath ghosted over my neck, and I closed my eyes, wedging my lower lip between my teeth to stifle a sound. "Open disobedience?" he asked in a low voice. His palms pressed down on my shoulder blades, and I almost crumpled under their weight, even though he didn't put much pressure behind the touch.

"On second thought," he said gently. "This position works well too."

The soft clink of a blade being unsheathed made me jump. Remo braced himself to both sides of me, a long dagger in one hand. His chest pressed up against my back. "I'll give you a choice, Serafina. You can either get out of your dress by yourself or I'll cut you out of it. What is it?"

I swallowed. I had expected another choice, one Vegas was famous for. A rush of relief filled me, but it was short-lived. I shifted my hand and covered the blade with my palm then curled my fingers around the cold steel.

"If you give me your knife, I'll cut myself out of my dress," I bit out.

Remo chuckled. A dark, joyless sound. "You want my knife?"

I nodded, and to my utter shock, Remo released the handle, and I held his dagger by the blade, the sharp edge cutting into my flesh. Remo stepped back, his warmth leaving my body. I stared at the deadly weapon in my hand. Slowly, drawing in a deep breath, I straightened and reached for the handle. I knew Remo hadn't given me a fair chance. He was playing with me, trying to break my spirit by showing me that even a knife didn't change the fact that I was at his mercy.

What he didn't know was that Samuel and I had spent all our lives fighting with each other, like siblings always do, but when he'd become a Made Man, he started working with me on my fighting skills because he knew how our world treated women. He had tried to make me strong, and I was. I knew how to handle a knife, how to defeat an opponent. But I had never won against Samuel, and he was always careful not to hurt me. Remo was stronger than Samuel, and he would hurt me, would enjoy it. I could not beat Remo in a fight, not even when I had a knife and he didn't.

Fabiano's words flashed through my mind. *Remo hates weakness.* Even if I couldn't beat Remo, I could show him I wasn't weak.

"Maybe I should take my knife back since you don't know what to do with it," Remo said, almost disappointed. He stepped closer.

In a fluid motion, I turned around and jabbed at Remo while my other hand pulled up my dress. Remo blocked my attack by hitting my wrist. My years of training with Samuel prevented me from dropping the knife despite the sharp pain in my wrist.

A smile crossed Remo's face, and I released my dress and rammed my fist into his abdomen while I slashed the knife at him once more. The blade grazed his arm and blood trickled down, but Remo didn't even wince. His smile got wider as he took a step back, completely unfazed.

I lunged at him but got caught in my long skirt. I barreled into Remo and tried to land another deadlier cut. We fell and Remo landed on his back with me on top of him. I straddled him and stabbed at his stomach, but he gripped my wrist with a twisted grin on his face. I tried to force the knife down, but Remo didn't budge. And then, suddenly, he showed me what it was like when he actually tried fighting back.

He bucked his hips, and before I could react, I landed on my back and Remo was on top of me. I struggled but he shoved my skirt up and knelt between my legs, moving closer until his pelvis thrust against me and I couldn't use my legs to push him away. His fingers curled around my wrists and he pressed them into the mattress above my head, the knife still in my grasp and utterly useless. He had me pinned under his strong body, completely at his mercy, both of my hands fastened to the ground.

His dark eyes held excitement and a flicker of admiration. For a moment, I felt proud, but then my situation dawned on me. I was on my back, on a dirty mattress, under Remo. He had me where he wanted me from the start.

Fear overpowered my determination, and my body stiffened, my eyes darting to the disgusting mattress under me. I sucked in a deep breath, trying to keep my panic at bay. Remo regarded me intently. "Let go of the knife," he murmured, and I did. I didn't even hesitate.

Be strong.

I swallowed hard, reminding myself of the camera. I'd take my pride to the grave with me. "Just get it over with, Remo," I said in disgust. "Rape me. I'm done playing your sick game. I'm not a chess piece."

Remo's dark eyes wandered over my face, my hair, my arms stretched out above my head. He leaned down, his cruel face coming closer. He stopped when our noses were almost brushing. His eyes weren't black; they were the darkest brown I'd ever seen. He held my gaze, and I held his. I wouldn't look away, no matter what he did. I wanted him to see me as I was. Not a weakness, not a pawn, but a human being.

"Not like this, Serafina," he said. His voice was low and dark, mesmerizing, but it was his gaze that held me captive. "Not like a whore on a stained mattress." He smiled, and it was worse than any glare or threat.

He brought his mouth down until his lips touched mine lightly, just barely, and yet a current shot through me. "I haven't started playing, and you aren't a mere chess piece. You are the queen." He took the knife and straightened, releasing me in the process. He stood slowly, drawing up to his full height and staring down at me.

"And what are you in this game of chess?" I whispered harshly, still lying on the mattress.

"I'm the king."

"You aren't unbeatable."

His eyes trailed over me until they returned to my face. "We'll see." He sheathed his knife. "Now get out of that dress. You won't need it anymore."

I sat up. "I won't undress in front of you."

Remo chuckled. "Oh this will be fun." He waited, and I returned his gaze steadily. "The knife it is, then," he said with a shrug.

"No," I said firmly, struggling to my feet. I glared at him and reached behind myself, pulling down the zipper with an audible hiss. Never taking my eyes off him, I pulled at the fabric until it finally fell to the ground, a fluffy halo around my feet.

"White and golden like an angel," Remo mused darkly as he took in every inch of me.

Even force of will couldn't stop my cheeks from blazing with heat, being exposed like this in front of a man for the first time. Left in nothing but my white garter, white lace panties and a corset, goose bumps rippled across my skin at Remo's scrutiny.

He bridged the distance between us, and I held my breath. He stopped close to me, dark eyes tracing my face, and he raised his hand, causing me to stiffen. The corner of his mouth twitched. Then his thumb brushed over my cheekbone. I drew back, away from the touch, which made him smile again.

"Virgin bashfulness, how endearing," Remo said darkly, mocking me. "Don't worry, *Angel*, I won't tell anyone that I'm the first man who saw you like this."

I glared at him, fighting tears of embarrassment and fury as he bent down, reaching for the dress. "Step back." I quickly stepped out of the dress, and Remo straightened with the stained fabric wedged under his arm.

He regarded me. "You are a sight to behold. I bet Danilo would have had a boner from merely looking at you. I can only imagine what he feels now, knowing you are in my hands, knowing that he will never get what was promised."

I shook my head. "Whatever you take, it'll always be less than what he would have gotten, because I would have given myself to him willingly, body and soul, and there's nothing you can do about it. You will have to settle for the consolation prize, Remo Falcone."

Remo moved back slowly, a strange expression on his face. "You should take a shower, Serafina. I will have one of the whores bring you fresh clothes." He turned and disappeared with a soft click of the door.

The air left my lungs in a whoosh. I wrapped my arms around myself, trembling, trying to keep it together. It had taken considerable effort standing up to Remo, and now everything fell off me in waves of emotion. I stiffened when I remembered the camera, but then I decided it didn't matter. Remo knew I was terrified of him. My brave front wasn't fooling him.

Remo

Serafina was everything I'd hoped for and so much more. A queen in my game of chess, indeed. Noble and proud like a queen and arrogant and spoiled like one too. She made me want to break her. Break those white wings. An angel in appearance but one with clipped wings, happy to be grounded, happy to never roam the sky. Content to become the beautiful tamed bird in Danilo's gilded cage.

I emptied my scotch and hit the bar. Jerry refilled my glass. The whores had gathered at the other end of the bar as far away from me as possible. As usual.

"She's so beautiful," the whore who had brought Serafina clothes said to the others.

She was. Serafina was a masterpiece, almost too beautiful. Her golden hair and unblemished skin against the dirty mattress had felt like sacrilege, even to me, and I had committed almost every sin conceivable.

I drank another scotch, considering returning to the basement, to Serafina. *Whatever you take, it'll always be less than what he would have gotten. You will have to settle for the consolation prize.*

Her words were an insistent pounding in the back of my head. And fuck, I knew she was right. Taking from Serafina what I wanted wouldn't feel like a victory. There was no challenge in doing so. She was weaker and at my mercy. I could have her in every way by the morning and be done with it, but it would feel like a fucking defeat. It wasn't what I wanted. Far from it. I had never settled for a consolation prize. I didn't want less than what she would have given to Danilo. I wanted more. I wanted everything from her.

I slammed the glass down on the counter and turned to the nearest whore. "In my office. Now."

She nodded and rushed off. I followed her, already painfully hard. Fucking hard since I'd seen Serafina in her underwear. Fucking desperate to bury myself in her pussy and rip her innocence from her. I always got what I wanted. I didn't wait for anything. But if I wanted the ultimate triumph, I would have to try my hand at patience, and it would be the biggest challenge of my life.

The whore perched on my desk but got up when I entered. I unzipped my pants and shoved down my briefs. She knew her cue. We'd fucked before. I often chose her. She got down on her knees as I tangled my hand in her red hair and started fucking her mouth. She took all of me as I thrust into her, hitting the back of her throat, making her gag, but for once it did nothing to sate the burning hunger in my veins. I scowled down at her face, trying to imagine it was Serafina, but the whore regarded me with that fucking submissiveness, that disgusting reverence. No pride, no honor. They all got a choice and chose the easy way, never the hard painful one. They would never understand that nothing could be gained without pain. Weak. Disgusting.

I tightened my hold on her hair, causing her to wince, as I came down her throat. Stepping back, my dripping cock slid out of her mouth. She peered up at me, licking her lips like I had given her a fucking gift. My fingers itched to reach for my knife and slash her throat, relieve her of her pitiful existence.

She lowered her gaze.

"Get up," I snarled, losing my patience. She scrambled to her feet. "Desk."

She turned around and bent over the desk, sticking her ass out, then reached behind herself and pushed her skirt up, revealing her naked ass. She parted her legs and braced herself against the desk. No pride. No honor.

I stepped up behind her, pumping my cock, but I was already getting hard again. I reached for a condom, ripped it open with my teeth, and rolled it down my dick. Spitting down in my hand, I lubed my sheathed dick then pressed up against her asshole and began pushing into her. The whore's knuckles turned white from her grip on the desk. When I was buried up to my balls in her ass, I leaned forward until my chest was flush with her back, and for the first time she tensed. I never got this close to her. I brought my mouth close to her ear as my fingers clamped down on her hips.

"Tell me, Eden," I whispered harshly. She held her breath hearing me say her name. I never had before. They thought I didn't know their names, but I knew every fucker I owned, soldier and whore. "Have you ever considered telling me to go fuck myself?"

"Of course not, Ma …"

"What did you want to call me? Master?" I slammed into her once, making her gasp. "Tell me, Eden, am I your fucking master?"

She hesitated. She didn't even know how to answer that fucking question, and it made me furious. "I'm not your fucking master," I growled.

"Yes," she agreed quickly.

I turned her face so she had to stare into my eyes. "Do you have a sliver of honor in that used up body of yours?" I asked gently.

She blinked.

My mouth pulled into a snarl. "No. Not one fucking ounce." I gripped her neck and started thrusting into her. She winced and it made me raving mad. Still slamming into her, I muttered in her ear, "Do you ever wonder where Dinara is?"

She tensed under me, but I didn't let up. "Have you thought of her at all?"

She let out a sob. She had no right to cry, no fucking right, because she wasn't crying for her daughter but only for herself. A fucking disgrace of a mother. "Do you ever wonder if I do to your little girl what I do to you now?"

She didn't say anything. I straightened and kept fucking her until I finally came. I stepped back, thrust the condom down on the ground, and cleaned my-self with a towel that I kept handy before I pulled up my briefs and pants.

She turned, mascara smudged under her eyes, and I tossed the towel at her. "Clean yourself. And dispose of the fucking condom. It's dripping my cum all over the floor." She picked up the towel from the floor and wiped the floor first then cleaned herself. Dirty whore.

"Get out of my sight before I kill you," I said.

She rushed past me, opened the door, and almost bumped into Savio, who stepped back with a disgusted expression. He cocked an eyebrow as he stepped in. "You're still fucking that bitch? Why don't you just kill her like she deserves?"

"She doesn't deserve death. It would be too kind to kill her." And I gave Grigory my word that the bitch would suffer.

Savio nodded. "Maybe. But I thought you'd be up virgin pussy, not this used up piece of trash."

"I'm not in the mood for virgin pussy."

Savio looked curious. "I imagine it'll be really tight and kind of hot knowing you're the first to be in there."

"Never been with a fucking virgin, so I can't fucking tell you. Is there a rea-son why you're here disturbing my post-fuck-fury?

"What's the difference between that and your pre-fuck-fury? Or your gen-eral mood for that matter?"

"You're a fucking smart ass like Nino."

Savio sauntered in and leaned his hip against the desk. "I thought I'd tell you Simeone went into the basement with a tray of food for your girl and didn't come back up yet."

I shoved past Savio, so fucking furious I had trouble not killing every single person in the fucking bar. I raced down the stairs when I heard Simeone's cack-ling and spotted him in the doorway to Serafina's cell, not inside of it. I slowed, knowing there was no rush. He wasn't that stupid. Stupid enough, but not so stupid to try touching something that was mine.

"Get out, you disgusting pervert," I heard Serafina's voice.

"Shut up, whore. You aren't in Chicago. Here you are nothing. I can't wait to bury my cock in your cunt once Remo is done breaking you in."

"I won't shower in front of you. Get out!"

"Then I will call Remo and tell him to punish you."

Oh … so he would call me? Interesting. I stalked closer, not making a sound. Simeone's back twitched like he was busy jerking off, which was probably the case.

My mouth pulled into a snarl, but I held back my anger.

More silence followed and I approached without making a sound. Simeone's profile appeared in my view, leaning in the doorway with his hand clutching his ugly dick as he rubbed it furiously. I stopped a few steps from him, and there was Serafina in the shower, her back turned to him.

Simeone was practically salivating on the ground and jerking off, watching Serafina shower. She was a sight to behold, no argument. Her skin was pale like marble. Her ass two white orbs I wanted to sink my teeth into. There wasn't a blemish on her body, not a single imperfection, so unlike my own. She had been protected all her life, kept safe from the dangers of this world, and here she was at my mercy.

"Turn around. I want to see your tits and cunt," Simeone ordered, his hand moving faster on his cock.

Simeone was so wrapped up in watching her and wanking off, he didn't notice me. "If you don't turn around, I'll call Remo."

"I won't turn around, you pig!" she hissed. "Then get Remo. I don't care!"

"You little whore! I will turn you around myself."

Simeone made a move as if to push off the doorway, when Serafina turned around, one arm wrapped protectively over her breasts, the other hand shielding her pussy. The water pouring down her face almost hid her tears. She gave Simeone the most disgusted look I'd ever seen, her head held high ... and then she spotted me.

"See, that wasn't so difficult, was it?" Simeone rasped.

My lip curled. I pulled the knife from my holster, slid my fingers through the knuckle holder, relishing in the feel of the cold metal against my skin. She watched unmoving as I stepped up to Simeone. Her perfect proud lips wouldn't utter a warning.

I wrapped my arm around his throat in a crushing grip and pressed my knife against his lower abdomen. He cried out in surprise and let go of his cock. "You were going to call me?" I asked.

His terror-widened eyes blinked up at me as his face turned red from the pressure of my grip. I loosened my hold so he could speak.

"Remo, I made sure she wasn't messing around. It's not how it looks."

"Hmm. Did you know that no man has ever seen what you just saw?"

He shook his head frantically. I lifted my gaze to Serafina, who was watching with a frozen expression.

"You see, now you have seen something that I had no intention of sharing," I explained in a pleasant voice. I slid the knife into his abdomen, only a couple of inches. He cried out, flailing in my grip. I held him fast, my eyes never leaving Serafina. Blood trickled down over my hand. His filthy blood.

Serafina dropped her arms to her side. I didn't think she noticed. She stared at me in open horror. For once her prideful mask had slipped and revealed her true nature: a softhearted, breakable woman. And I took in the sight of her firm breasts and the golden curls at the apex of her thighs, perfectly trimmed into a triangle. For her wedding night. What a pity that poor Danilo would never get to see it. She was mine for the taking.

"Remo," Simeone spluttered. "I won't tell anyone what I saw. Please, I beg you."

"I believe you," I said mildly. "But you will *remember*." I drove the knife deeper into his flesh, moving slow, letting him savor every inch of the blade. "Did you imagine how it would be to sink your filthy cock into her pussy?"

He gurgled.

The knife was buried to the hilt in his abdomen. "Did you imagine to bury yourself to the hilt inside her?" His eyes were bulging, his breathing labored.

I twisted the knife and he screamed again. Then I pulled it back out as slowly as it had gone in. His legs gave way, and I let him drop to the ground. He clutched his wound, crying like a coward. It would be another ten or fifteen minutes before he died. He'd wish it were less. "Remember what I told you about your eyeballs and tongue? Your cock will join them."

I brought the knife down on his cock, and Serafina whirled around with a gasp.

Serafina

My hands were splayed out against the white tiles of the shower. I couldn't breathe. Terror clogged my throat. Nothing in my upbringing had prepared me for this. Nothing could have. I was falling apart fast. Faster than I'd ever thought possible.

Pride and honor were the pillars of our world, the pillars of my upbringing. I needed to cling to them. He could take everything from me, but not that. Never that.

Simeone was screaming and I pressed my palms against my ears, trying to shut him out—to no avail.

Ice Princess no more.

My eyes were blurry from tears and water. But the image of Remo sinking his knife into a man with that twisted smile on his face was etched into my mind. How was I supposed to stay prideful? How was I supposed to hold my head high and not let him see my fear? Nothing had ever scared me more than Remo Falcone.

Monsters aren't real, my mother had told me a long time ago when I was afraid to sleep in the dark and kept crawling into Samuel's bed. I hadn't believed her back then, and that was before meeting Remo.

The screaming stopped.

I shuddered and lowered my hands slowly. Something red caught my eyes. I looked down at the shower floor where red water was pooling around my feet. I blinked. And then it clicked. Floor-level shower. Remo bringing down the knife on the man's … My feet looked even paler against the red. My vision shifted and something broke apart in me. I was standing in someone's blood.

I heard myself screaming and tried to get out of the blood but the ground was slippery. I twisted around, holding onto the shower walls. And then I saw the rest of the cell. The entire floor was covered in blood, and amidst it all stood Remo, tall and dark, knife still gleaming in his hand. His chest and arms were smeared with blood. Red. Red. Red. Everywhere.

I was still screaming and screaming until I couldn't scream anymore because there was no air left in my lungs. And I could not breathe.

Remo sheathed his knife and stalked toward me.

I flailed, trying to get away from him, from the blood, from the sight of the dead man behind Remo.

My feet slipped on the floor, and I was falling. My knees sank into the blood, my hands followed.

Remo pulled me up, my body pressed against his, and the smell of blood filled my nose. I clutched at his shoulders for balance. And then I pulled one hand back and it came away red. And one glance down. Red. My skin. Red. Everything red.

My eyes found Remo's blood covered body. Red. Red. Red.

I started struggling against his hold. I fought with all I had. "Please," I gasped out. Remo lifted me in his arms, and I had no fight left in me. He carried me barefoot through the cell, stepping over the dead man. When had he got rid of his shoes?

A hysteric laugh bubbled up my throat, but it turned into a sob. This was too much.

Remo walked into another cell and set me down on the floor of the shower. I sank down, curling up on my side, unable to remain in a sitting position. My chest was heaving, but I wasn't breathing. Through my foggy vision, I watched Remo getting out of his bloody clothes and coming toward me. Naked. I didn't register more than that.

I closed my eyes.

He moved his arms under my knees and back and lifted me once more.

Then cold water splashed down on me, and I sucked in a deep breath, my eyes shooting open. Remo shifted with me in his arms, leaning forward, his forehead pressed against the tiles as he looked down at me. His body shielded me from the cold water raining down on us, and his dark eyes held mine.

"It takes a while before the water gets warm down here," he said calmly.

So calm. My eyes searched his face. Eerily calm. No sign that he had just killed a man in a barbaric way. I shuddered, my teeth chattering. Even when the water turned warm, my teeth kept clanking together, and they didn't stop even when Remo stepped back out of the shower with me still in his arms.

Remo walked out of the cell and carried me through the corridor. Panic tore at my chest.

"Fuck," someone said. A man.

"Get me a fucking blanket, Savio," Remo growled.

He tightened his hold as he carried me upstairs. I closed my eyes, too shaken to put up a fight. Something soft and warm covered me, and then I was put down on warm leather.

"You can't drive through the city naked. And there's still blood on your body."

"You can drive," Remo said, and then his body eased in beside me.

"Where the fuck are we taking her?"

"Home."

"Nino won't like that one fucking bit. You know how protective he is of Kiara."

"I don't give a fuck. Now shut up and drive."

I focused on breathing, focused on remembering what made me happy. Samuel. Mom. Dad. Sofia.

I wasn't sure how much time had passed. The minutes seemed to blur together, when Remo picked me up again and eventually put me down on something soft. My eyes peeled open, heavy-lidded and burning from crying.

The first thing I registered was the bed I was lying on. Soft satin sheets, blood-red. A majestic canopy bed made from black wood, the posts twisting as if two branches had wound around another to form each. Heavy blood-red drapes hung from the canopy, blocking the bright sunlight streaming into the bedroom. I put my trembling hand flat against the smooth sheet, white against red, like in the shower. I shuddered and started hyperventilating again.

Remo appeared beside the bed and sank down, causing the mattress to dip under his weight. He was naked except for a knife holster, which was strapped to his chest. Muscles and scars and barely restrained strength.

I averted my eyes, my teeth beginning to chatter again. Remo reached over me. "Don't," I said weakly. Then firmer, "Don't touch me."

Remo's dark eyes held mine with intent. He bent low until his face filled my vision. "After what you saw me do today, you still defy me? Don't you think submitting to me will make things less painful for you?" His voice was soft, low, almost curious.

"Yes," I whispered, and something shifted in his eyes … was that disappointment? "But I'd rather take pain than submit to your will, Remo."

He smiled darkly and reached over me again. Before I could react, he pulled a blanket over my body, covering my nakedness. My eyes widened.

"How can you know what you prefer if you've never experienced either? Neither pain…" he brushed his lips lightly across my mouth, not a kiss but a threat "…nor pleasure."

A shiver traveled down my spine. My throat was dry, my limbs heavy.

"I want to show you both, *Angel*." He paused, his dark eyes burning into me. "But I fear you'd rather kill yourself than give yourself to me." He pulled his knife out and put it down beside me. "You should end your life, take the easy way out, because nobody will come to save you, and I won't stop until I've broken you, body and soul."

I believed him. How could I not with the intense determination and coldness in his dark eyes? I reached for the knife then pushed into a sitting position and pressed the blade against Remo's throat. He didn't flinch, only regarded me with unsettling eyes.

"I won't ever kill myself. I won't do that to my family. But you will never break me. I won't let you."

Remo tilted his head, again with a hint of curiosity. "If you want to kill me, do it now because you won't get another chance, *Angel*." My hand holding the knife shook. Remo didn't take his eyes off me as he shifted closer to me, climbing up on one knee then the other until he leaned over me. I pressed harder and blood welled to the surface. My eyes focused on the red coating the blade against Remo's skin.

Remo moved over me and drove the knife harder into his flesh. I yielded, fixated on the blood trickling down his throat, on its smell, its bright color.

Remo lowered himself on top of me, the knife between our throats, his body covering mine with only the blanket between us. He regarded me, dark eyes peeling away layer over layer of protective walls that I tried to put up.

Hysteria swirled in my chest, the memories of the basement clawing at the fringes of my mind. Remo curled his hand around mine and the handle then slowly pried my hands off it and took the knife from me. He dropped it to the bed beside us.

I could feel every inch of his strong, muscled body against mine, but my eyes couldn't focus on anything but the blood on his skin, dripping from the cut I had inflicted. He pressed two fingers to my throat, feeling my erratic pulse. "Still in the grasp of panic, hmm?"

I swallowed. He pulled away and stood. Then he bent over me. "You are safe in your weakest moments, *Angel*. I don't enjoy breaking the weak. I will break you when you are strong."

He grabbed the knife and turned around, presenting his back to me. My eyes traced the tattoo of the kneeling fallen angel. Was that how Remo saw himself? A fallen angel with broken wings? A dark angel risen from Hell?

And what was I?

Before he left the room, he glanced over his shoulder at me. "Don't try to run, *Angel*. There are more men like Simeone waiting to get their hands on you. I'd hate having to send them after you and hurt you."

As if anyone could hurt me worse than Remo would.

I forced a smile. "We both know you're lying. You won't let anyone hurt me."

Remo cocked one dark eyebrow. "I won't?"

"You won't because you want to be the one to break me, to make me scream."

Remo's mouth pulled into a smile that raised the little hairs on my skin.

A smile that would haunt me forever.

"Oh, I will make you scream, *Angel*. That I swear."

Suppressing a shudder, I dug my nails into my palms and forced more words from my tight throat. "Don't waste your time. Kill me now."

"We all have to let part of ourselves die to rise up stronger. Now sleep tight. I'll return later for a proper video message for your family."

"Why did you even save me from Simeone? Why not let him start the torture you have in mind for me? Why bring me here to your mansion?"

Remo regarded me as if he, too, was wondering the same thing, and his silence told me that my guess had been right; this was indeed the Falcone mansion. It surprised me that he would risk bringing me into his family's home.

"Like you said, I will be the one to make you scream and no one else." He closed the door.

I shut my eyes and pulled the covers tighter around myself.

A power play. A twisted game of chess.

I wasn't going to be a pawn or a queen, and Remo wouldn't be the king.

FIVE

Remo

I GRABBED SWEATPANTS TO PUT ON BEFORE I HEADED DOWNSTAIRS INTO our gaming room, where Savio, Nino, and Adamo were sitting. Since Kiara had joined our family, my days of walking through the house naked when I pleased were fucking over. My brothers regarded me as if I was a bomb about to detonate.

I flashed them a smile.

Adamo shook his head but didn't say anything. He didn't try to hide his aversion toward me or his reluctance about becoming a Camorrista.

Nino rose slowly. "You shouldn't have brought her here."

I grabbed the pizza menu. "Savio, order pizza for us and an extra one for Serafina."

Nino came around the sofa. My eyes flickered over the tension in his limbs. "Remo, take her somewhere else."

"No," I said. "She will stay here, under this roof, where I can keep a fucking eye on her."

My brother stopped in front of me, a deep frown pulling his brows together. That was the equivalent of an angry outburst from him. "This situation might cause another one of Kiara's episodes."

"Kiara is your wife, not mine. Make sure she doesn't see anything that she isn't supposed to see. Where is she anyway?"

"In our wing. The moment Savio told me you were bringing Serafina, I told her to stay there."

"See? No problem." I moved past him toward the bar and grabbed a beer. Nino followed as Savio ordered pizza in the background.

"It is a huge problem. Your captive is upstairs, free to roam the place as she sees fit. She could walk around the house and cross Kiara."

"I doubt Serafina will do that right now. She's too shaken and probably taking a beauty sleep as we speak. She can't escape from the premises, and one of you will have to guard her to make sure she doesn't do something stupid."

Nino assessed me. "I really hope you know what you're doing. This is supposed to bring the Outfit down. Don't forget that, Remo."

My mouth pulled wide. "It will crush them. They will bleed out slowly, painfully, without ever feeling my blade. This will destroy them."

Nino gave a nod because even if emotions were still hard to grasp for him, he knew the effect mind games had in a war.

"You disgust me," Adamo muttered.

"Four days," I reminded him.

He stood, jutting his chin out. "What if I say no?"

Savio shoved him. "You'd be a fucking disgrace, a traitor. What would you do? Where would you go?"

Adamo shoved him back. "I don't give a fuck. Anything is better than becoming like you."

I stalked toward him. He lifted his chin. "You say this because from the day of your birth you've been protected. You've never been subjected to true cruelty. You are a Falcone, Adamo, and one day you will be proud to be one."

"I wish I wasn't a Falcone. I wish you weren't my brother."

"Adamo," Nino warned, looking at my face.

"Fuck you!" Adamo shouted and ran off upstairs.

"He'll come around, eventually," Nino drawled.

"How much time until the pizza arrives?" I asked Savio.

He exchanged a look with Nino before replying, "Twenty minutes."

"Time for a phone call," I said, nodding at Nino, who hesitated briefly but then took out his mobile and scrolled through it.

Nino handed me the phone with the number I didn't recognize. "That's Dante's number if he hasn't changed it from our last call years ago."

"Good. Get some of Kiara's clothes. A white nightgown if she has one."

Nino frowned deeply but walked past me and disappeared into his wing.

"How are you going to keep her in check? Make sure she doesn't try to run or kill herself?"

"She's been sheltered all her life. She's far from home, far from the men who've protected her. Freedom scares her more than captivity."

Savio laughed. "You sound awfully sure of it."

I grinned. Nino returned, looking as close to pissed as he ever did. He held the clothes out to me. Among them a silvery satin nightgown. Perfect. "Kiara suspects something's the matter."

I took the clothes, not bothering to comment, and walked past him toward my wing where I barged into Serafina's room without knocking. My eyes wandered from the empty bed toward the wall behind it, where Serafina tried opening the window, which she couldn't do without the necessary keys.

She whirled around, the blood-red sheets wrapped around her body, her blond hair a wild mane slithering down her shoulders. Her skin glowed so innocently white against the red of the covers. I wanted to run my tongue over it to see if it would taste as pure as she looked.

Not cowering in the bed as I'd expected but trying to escape. This little birdy seemed desperate to escape my cage, only to flutter right into Danilo's. Her eyes and face held remnants of her earlier panic, but she tilted her chin upward and narrowed her eyes at me. Determined to play with the big boys.

I strolled into the room. Her shoulders pulled back, an act of defiance, but her hand flew up to press the sheet against her body, her fingers splayed out against the red, visibly shaking. My eyes never leaving her, I set the clothes down on the bed, catching the hint of her sweet scent. I'd caught it earlier, as if she'd been massaged with vanilla oil in preparation for her wedding night. My nostrils flared. "Trying to escape my cage, little bird?"

She tossed me a haughty look. "You're awfully fond of creatures with wings."

"I enjoy breaking them."

Her lip curled, and still she managed to be perfectly beautiful. I could guess the images that ran through her mind, of me torturing tiny animals. That was for cowards, for men not capable of facing a worthy opponent. "I'm not that kind of psychopath."

"What kind are you, then?"

I smiled. "You won't be able to open the window. Don't waste your energy trying to escape."

"Did you have the locks installed specifically for me, or do you make a habit of locking women in your bedroom so you can rape and torture them for your personal entertainment?"

I stalked toward her, backed her against the windowsill then braced myself against the glass, glaring down at her. "No," I said. "My father had them installed for my mother."

Disgust flashed across Serafina's face. "You Falcones are all monsters."

I leaned down, breathing in her scent. "My father was a monster. I'm worse."

Her pulse thudded in her veins. I could see her fear throbbing against the unblemished skin of her throat. I stepped back then nodded toward the clothes. "For you. Tomorrow morning you will wear the silver nightgown."

Serafina walked toward the bed sideways to keep an eye on me then scowled at the heap on her bed.

I raised the phone to my ear and pressed the call button. After the second ring, Dante's cold voice sounded. "Cavallaro."

"Dante, good to hear your voice."

Serafina's head jerked toward me, and she sank down on the bed, her prideful mask cracking as her fingers curled into a fist, gripping the sheet.

Silence rang on the other end, and I smiled. I wished I could see Cavallaro's expression as he was being faced with the consequences of his actions, and the realization that his niece would pay for his sins.

"Remo."

I heard male voices in the background and a hysteric female one. Serafina's mother. "I would like a word with you, Capo to Capo. From one man who had his territory breached to another. Two men of honor."

"I'm a man of honor, Remo. I don't know what you are, but honorable isn't it."

"Let's agree to disagree on that."

"Is Serafina alive?" he asked quietly.

I trailed my eyes over the glaring woman, clutching the red blankets around her naked body.

I heard a furious voice in the background. "I will break every fucking bone in your body!"

"Is that her twin?"

Pain flashed across her face, and she swallowed.

"Is she alive?" Dante repeated, his voice shaking with anger.

"What do you think?"

"She is, because alive she is worth more than dead."

"Indeed. I don't have to tell you that I will kill her in the most painful way I can think of if a single Outfit soldier breaches my territory to save her, and I can be very creative when it comes to inflicting pain."

Even from a distance I could see her blood pounding furiously in her veins as she stared down at her fist.

"I want to speak to her."

"Not yet."

"Remo, you crossed a line, and you will pay for it."

"Oh, I'm sure you think so."

"What do you want?"

"It's not time for that kind of conversation yet, Dante. I don't think you are quite ready for it. Tomorrow morning we will have another date. Set up a camera. I want you, her brother, father, and fiancé in a room in front of that camera. Nino will give you instructions how to set everything up. I will set up a camera myself so we can see and hear each other."

Serafina's eyes met mine.

"Remo—" Dante's voice held a warning, but I lowered the phone from my ear and ended the call.

Serafina stared at me, wide eyed. I moved closer, and she stiffened but otherwise didn't show her fear, despite the exhaustion on her face. "Tomorrow we will start playing, *Angel*."

I left, wanting her to ponder my words. Nino waited in the corridor as I closed the door. I raised my eyebrows in passing. "Pizza's arrived?"

Nino followed close behind me then grabbed my shoulder. "What kind of video do you have in mind for tomorrow?"

I regarded him, trying to gauge his mood, but even now it was still difficult. "I'll give her a choice."

Nino shook his head once, almost disapproving. "This woman is innocent. She's not a debtor. Not a whore who steals money. She hasn't done anything."

"Kiara changed you."

"Not in this regard. We've never preyed on the innocent, Remo. We've never laid a hand on someone who didn't deserve it, and this woman, this girl … she did nothing to deserve that choice."

I held his gaze. "You know me better than anyone else," I murmured. "And yet here we stand."

Nino tilted his head, gray eyes narrowing. "You're playing a dangerous game. You don't know your opponent well enough to be sure of her choice."

"She will choose what they all do, Nino. She's a woman. She's been coddled all her life. She will take the easy way. I want to hear her say it in front of that fucking camera, want Dante hear his niece offer her fucking body to me, want them all to hear it, and she will."

Downstairs, I grabbed one of the pizza boxes before I returned to the guest bedroom in my wing. This time, Serafina sat on the bed and didn't look up when I entered. She held the silver nightgown in her hands. "What if I refuse to wear it?"

"You can wear your nightgown for the show or be naked. Your blood will look just as enticing against your white skin as it would against the nightgown."

A small shiver rippled through her body, and she let the piece of clothing flutter to the ground at her bare feet.

I walked closer. "Here. You haven't eaten in more than a day." I set the pizza box down on the nightstand.

She eyed it suspiciously. I waited for her to shove it away, to try punishing me by starving herself, like my mother had always tried with our father. It hadn't worked with him, and it wouldn't work with me.

"I hope it's poisoned," she muttered then reached for a slice and took a big bite. She chewed then raised her eyes to mine. She swallowed almost defiantly. "Are you going to watch me eat?"

Maybe breaking her wings wouldn't be as easy as I'd thought.

Early the next morning Fabiano came over. I was doing kicks against the punching bag in our game room, needing to release my pent up energy.

He leaned against the doorframe, assessing me for a couple of heartbeats.

"Say what you've got to say," I growled and landed a hard kick.

"Jerry called me into the Sugar Trap a couple of hours ago so I could deal with the mess you created. I found Simeone with his cock stuffed into his mouth. I'm not sure I want to know what happened."

I narrowed my eyes. "If you didn't want to know, you wouldn't be here."

He pushed away from the doorframe and moved toward me. "Did he touch her?"

I stopped my kicks. "He didn't. He thought he could watch Serafina showering."

Fabiano evaluated my face. "Where is she?"

"In bed."

His eyebrows rose. "In your bed?"

I didn't say anything, but I met his eyes straight on.

He sighed. "So, you …" He searched for the right word then gave up. "I thought you wanted to use her virginity as leverage against Cavallaro and her fiancé?"

I tried to gauge Fabiano's feelings, but he was too good at masking them. If he put that kind of effort into hiding his feelings, he would only disapprove of me taking Serafina with force.

I stalked toward him. "Do you harbor feelings for her?"

He grimaced. "Really? I have Leona. I'm not interested in Fina."

"But you don't like the idea of me hurting her?"

"You are Capo. You do with her whatever you want, but no, I don't like the idea of you punishing her for something the Outfit did."

I respected Fabiano for his honesty. Most men were too cowardly to tell me the truth to my face. "Then you should leave now because I have a call set up with Dante and her family in two hours, and Serafina will play the leading role."

He looked away, a muscle in his cheek twitching. "I should return to Leona."

"You do that. Go to your girl. And I will go to mine."

"She isn't yours, Remo. She didn't choose you. That's a big difference," Fabiano said before he turned and left. I returned to the punching bag and kicked it harder than before.

Serafina

Even the next morning, the pizza lay heavily in my stomach, but at least now my stomach was churning for another reason than terror. I considered eating another piece for breakfast. I needed all the energy I could get if I wanted to figure out a way to beat Remo at his own game because no matter how sheltered I was, I knew Remo wouldn't have set up a video call with my family if he didn't know he had something to show them that would hurt them.

I barely slept through the night. Remo hadn't locked my door after he left, but I didn't try venturing outside, fearing it was a trap. I was still too shaken to plan my flight in a way that would guarantee its success.

I slid the satin nightgown over my head, even if I didn't want to give Remo even that small victory, but I'd have to pick my battles if I wanted to survive.

Steps in front of the door made me stiffen, and I got up from the bed, preferring to stand when facing Remo, but it wasn't the scary Capo who entered. Savio Falcone stood in the doorway, his brown eyes taking in the length of me. I wrapped my arms around my chest before I could think better of it.

"Come," he ordered with a nod toward the open door.

I walked toward him, and he made a move to grab my arm. "Don't you dare touch me," I hissed.

His eyebrows shot up, and he smiled arrogantly. "Then move your pretty ass. And take my advice, don't ever talk to Remo like that or you'll find yourself wishing you had never been born."

I sent him a scathing look as I followed him through the house, taking in my surroundings. It was a spacious, twisted place that quickly left me confused. I could feel Savio's eyes on me occasionally, more curious than sexual, but still his presence made me nervous. He was tall and muscled and too confident.

Eventually he led me down a steep staircase into a basement.

"Of course you Falcones have your own underground torture chamber," I muttered, but even I could hear the undercurrent of panic in my voice.

A desolate, abandoned smell hung in the air. Thankfully no excrements or blood.

Savio didn't say anything, but he motioned for me to enter a room on the right. Remo was already inside. "Here she is. I'm meeting Diego. Tell me how it went," Savio said with a laugh.

"You'll get to see the recording," Remo said, his dark eyes locked on mine. "Stand over there," he ordered, pointing at a spot in the center of the room. I followed his command, my brain whirring. The room was empty. No mattress, no chair, nothing except for a table with a camera that was pointed at me.

Remo walked around me, scanning my outfit. The silvery satin nightgown clung to my body, and as my nipples puckered in the cold basement, Remo's eyes were drawn to them. I shivered.

Nino came in as well, and my terror increased as I watched him re-adjust the camera and put a big screen on the table in the corner. He turned the screen so it was facing our way. "Remo," he said, and his brother went over to him. Nino frowned, but Remo touched his shoulder then looked at me. My nails found their way into the soft flesh of my palm.

The screen flashed to life, and on it I saw my family and Danilo, and my legs almost buckled.

Samuel jerked, his eyes so full of despair it tore at me, and Dad had dark circles under his eyes. Dante and Danilo were better at controlling their emotions, but they, too, didn't look their usual composed selves.

"I'm so glad you could make it," Remo said in a British accent, all posh and sophisticated. Wrong. A man like him shrouded in an air of violence and cruelty was anything but an English gentleman.

Remo smiled cruelly at them then turned to me, and his dark eyes flashed with excitement. "Serafina, in Las Vegas women get a choice …" His voice had returned to its normal, low, threatening vibrato.

"Don't you dare!" Samuel shouted, lunging toward the camera as if it was Remo. Dante gripped his arm to stop him, but even my uncle appeared at the edge of control.

Remo ignored them, except for a twitch of his lip. He pulled out the knife he'd used to slaughter Simeone and showed it to me. "They can pay for their sins with pain or pleasure."

I shuddered. "You have no right to judge other people's sins," I whispered harshly. Remo slowly walked behind me, too close, his breath hot against my neck. My eyes landed on the screen and met Samuel's desperate gaze. He looked on the verge of breaking. I needed to be strong for them, for him and Dad, and even Dante and Danilo. For the Outfit.

"What do you choose, Serafina? Will you surrender to torture or pay with your body?"

I held Samuel's gaze. I'd take my pride to the grave with me. Women were built to give birth. These men could brave pain and so could I.

Remo stepped back into my view. "If you don't choose, I will make the choice for you." His eyes and face said he knew my choice, was sure of it, because I was a woman, weak and insignificant.

I smiled arrogantly. "I will choose the bite of cold steel over the touch of your unworthy hands any day, Remo Falcone."

His eyes flashed with surprise, respect … and terrifying excitement. "I will enjoy your screams."

"Remo, this is enough," Dante ordered.

Remo only stared at me, murmuring, "We have only just begun." Without a warning he gripped me, whirled me around, and jerked me against his body—his chest, *every inch of him* pressing against my back and ass. His hand cupped my chin, tilting my head up so I was forced to look at him. He wanted to see my eyes, my expression, my fear and terror when he made me scream.

I returned his gaze with all the hatred and disgust I could summon. I hoped I'd be strong enough to deprive him of my screams, prayed for it. "Where would you like to feel my blade?"

He held the gleaming steel right before my eyes, letting me see the sharp edge of it. I had seen that both Remo's and Nino's Camorra tattoos covered scars on their forearms. Maybe it meant something, maybe not. I had nothing to lose at this point.

"Or did you change your mind about your choice? Will you pay with your body after all?"

I didn't trust my voice because terror clogged my throat, and Remo could see it. I gripped his wrist and guided the knife to my arm until the cool blade touched the soft skin of my forearm, close to my veins.

Something flickered in Remo's eyes and triumph filled me, because for some reason this spot got to him. I kept my hand on his as the blade rested against my sensitive skin.

Remo pressed and I tensed at the slight burn, but he wasn't really cutting yet—as if he couldn't bring himself to do it. I couldn't believe it was because he had reservations about hurting me; this was the cruelest man in the west after all. And it definitely wasn't because he couldn't bear to destroy my unblemished skin. I was sure he'd love to be the first to leave a mark. There was something else holding him back, something dark and powerful. I pushed against his hand, pushed it down on my arm, and the blade cut my skin, but Remo resisted.

I searched his dark eyes, wondering what went on in their depths, terrified of ever finding out. Remo's eyes hardened, turned harsh, brutal, and finally he pressed the blade down and it cut through my skin. Sharp pain burned through me, and I shook under the force of it, my hand still on top of his as he drew the knife across my skin, but not stopping him. For some reason his eyes reflected my pain as if he could feel it more profoundly than I did.

Remo released my chin, his arm snaking around my waist to keep me upright, but I kept my head tilted up, my eyes burning into his. I bit down on my lower lip as a scream clawed up my throat. Copper filled my mouth. Then it spilled over my lip, down my chin.

Remo stopped the blade, something in his eyes keeping me frozen.

"Enough!" Dad roared. "Stop it. Stop it now!"

Remo's brows drew together as our gazes remained locked. He released my waist and stepped back. My legs buckled, and I fell to the ground, my knees colliding with the hard floor. I barely registered the pain. I sat back on my haunches as I cradled my arm in my lap. The cut wasn't as deep as I thought, but blood soaked my silver satin gown, and the blood from my lip quickly joined it. I looked up to see Remo turning off the camera then the screen. Samuel's desperate face disappeared from view.

Nino stood against the wall, his eyes on my wrist and an unsettling expression on his face. Remo had his back turned to me, facing his brother, but his shoulders were heaving.

I forced my body to stand, despite the shaking of my legs, and let my bleeding arm hang in front of me on display.

Nino tore his gaze away and stared at Remo. I wasn't sure what passed between them, not sure I ever wanted to find out.

Remo slowly turned his head, his cruel eyes meeting mine, dark pools of rage leaving me breathless. For once he didn't smirk or smile, didn't look superior or furious. He looked almost confused in his own terrifying, otherworldly way.

And I swore to myself that no matter the price, no matter what it would cost me, one day I would be the one to bring Remo Falcone to his knees, the one to break the cruelest man I knew.

SIX

Remo

NINO'S EXPRESSION WAS STRAINED, BUT HE WASN'T ABOUT TO LOSE HIS shit again. He was staring into my eyes, no longer at Serafina. He swallowed then the cold mask took hold of his face and he straightened. My eyes fell to the scars on his wrist covered by our tattoo, then to similar scars on my skin, not as straight, not as focused. I almost touched the fucking scar over my eyebrow like I'd done in the weeks after...

"You will have to stitch her up yourself. You played this game and lost. You underestimated your opponent," he drawled then left, leaving me standing there, fucking furious and fucking ecstatic.

I turned around slowly. Serafina was swaying but trying to stand tall. Her chin was covered in blood from the wound in her lip, from biting down on it to stop a scream. She didn't give me a single one. My gaze dipped lower. Her nightgown was stained with the blood still trickling from the cut in her arm, which she cradled against her chest.

She was supposed to choose differently like all the other women always did. Instead, she'd caught me off guard, had taken the painful road, had forced my fucking hand. She hadn't given me the triumph of offering her body to me on a silver platter in front of Dante fucking Cavallaro and her fiancé. Nino was right. I'd underestimated my opponent because I compared her to the women I'd dealt with so far, but Serafina was nothing like them. Proud and noble. I wouldn't underestimate her again.

And I would get that fucking scream. I would get more than that.

My eyes were drawn to her arm. Why had she chosen that spot? When I looked back up, Serafina met my gaze with one of triumph. She knew she had won.

I stalked toward her, anger simmering under my skin. She tensed, swayed again but didn't fall. I took her arm and inspected the wound. It wasn't deep. I hadn't put enough pressure behind the blade to cut deep. I hadn't wanted to cut her at all, which was a new experience. Seeing the blood on her perfect skin didn't give me the deep satisfaction it usually did.

"How did it feel to hurt me? Does it excite you?" she asked fiercely.

I leaned close, cupping her chin. She held her breath as I trailed my tongue over her lower lip, tasting her blood. I smiled darkly. "Not nearly as much as this."

She jerked back and stumbled, but I caught her, because this wasn't the fall she would take.

"We need to treat your wound."

She didn't protest and followed me silently back upstairs to the first floor, and my grip on her arm held her steady. I led her into my bedroom then my bathroom, where I kept the only medical kit in my wing. Nino was the one who usually handled this kind of shit. She leaned against the sink. "You should sit down," I told her.

"I prefer to stand."

I let go of her and she clutched the edge of the sink to steady herself. I bent down to retrieve the medical kit, but my eyes were drawn to the high slit in her nightgown revealing a long, slender leg. She shifted so her front faced me. I smirked up at her, but her skin was pale and a fine sheen covered her face. I grabbed the medical kit and straightened, regarding her more closely to judge whether she was going to pass out or not. She narrowed her eyes at me and straightened her shoulders with obvious effort.

The corner of my mouth twitched. I took out tissue adhesive. The wound wasn't deep enough to require stitches. I couldn't remember the last time a cut from me didn't lead to stitches—or a funeral.

I took out disinfectant spray, and she stiffened but didn't make a sound when the stinging spray hit her wound, but she did bite down on her lower lip again.

"If you keep doing that, the result will be twice as painful."

She sent me a scathing look but released her bottom lip.

I began to put the adhesive on her wound, feeling a strange aversion to seeing the cut I had inflicted. I couldn't quite define the feeling; it was foreign to me.

"So is this how it's going to be? You cutting me open and stitching me back together?" she seethed.

"I'm not stitching you up. I'm gluing you together."

She didn't say anything, but I could feel her eyes on me. She tapped my forearm with my Camorra tattoo, brushing the crisscrossing scars there. "I wonder who inflicted those cuts," she mused.

I froze and my head shot up. She held my gaze with the same look of triumph I had seen in the basement.

"I wonder who stitched you up afterward? Did you and Nino cut each other in some twisted brotherly ceremony and stitch each other up when you were done? You have the same cuts. Maybe I should ask him."

I pushed her against the sink with my body, my hands clamping down on the marble counter as I shook with rage ... and other emotions I would never allow.

Serafina looked at me, despite the fear taking over her perfect features.

"Never mention those scars again. And you won't talk to Nino about this, not a single word, understood?" I growled.

She pressed her lips together, not saying a word. A droplet of blood squeezed past her lips and trickled down on her chin.

Exhaling, I stepped back, grabbed a washcloth and soaked it with warm water. I grabbed her chin but she reached for my wrist.

"Hold still," I ordered, and she dropped her hand and let me clean her chin. Then I took a closer look at her lip. Her teeth had only nicked the upper layer of skin. "You are lucky. This will heal on its own." I was so close to her, her scent hit me again.

Her voice snapped me out of it. "How long will you keep me here?"

"Who says I'm ever letting you go?" I asked in a low voice before I drew back and led her out of my room.

After returning Serafina to the guest room, which I locked this time, I was about to start doing my daily training, kicking the punching bag, when Kiara stormed into the game room. Nino was close behind her and tried stopping her, but she tore away from his grip and stalked toward me, looking furious.

I turned to her, raising my eyebrows. She didn't stop until she was right in front of me and shoved me hard, her eyes brimming with tears. I caught her wrists because she looked like she would slap me next, and that was something we both didn't want to happen.

A second later, a steely grip closed around my forearm. "Release her now," Nino ordered.

I met his gaze, not liking his tone one bit. His grip tightened further. A warning. A threat. We had never really fought against each other, for good reason, and I would lay my fucking life down before I would allow it to happen. But Kiara could be the reason why Nino might risk it.

Savio rose slowly and even Adamo put down his controller.

I let go of her wrists, and Nino unfastened his hold on my arm. He tilted his head in acknowledgment, a silent thank-you.

"What are you doing to that girl?" Kiara asked forcefully.

I narrowed my eyes. "I can't see how that's any of your business."

"It is my business if you are forcing yourself on a woman," she hissed, but her voice shook.

"I'm Capo. I rule over this city. I decide what happens to the people in my territory."

I turned to face the punching bag, but Kiara squeezed in front of it. Fury burned through me, but I shoved it down my throat despite the fucking bitter taste. She was Nino's. She was a fucking Falcone. I grabbed her by the waist and set her to the side like a fucking doll before I faced the punching bag once more. She had frozen under my touch as usual. Unfortunately, that lasted only one fucking second.

She stepped in front of me again.

"Kiara," Nino said in warning, but she glared at him.

"No! Nobody protected me. I won't stand by when the same happens to someone else."

"Get out of my way," I said in a low voice, feeling my own anger rising.

"Or what?" she whispered harshly.

"I said get out of my way, Kiara."

She took a step toward me, bringing us almost chest to chest. "And I said no. It's a mountain I'm willing to die on. I don't care about your vendetta with the Outfit or what happened in your past. An innocent woman won't suffer for it."

I couldn't believe she mentioned our fucking past. Nino should have never told her about it!

Nino moved closer, watching me, not Kiara. Fucking dread flickered in his eyes—something I still had to get used to because my brother had always been emotionless until he met Kiara.

I tried stepping past his wife, but she grabbed my wrist. My gaze darted to her thin fingers then back up to her face. Nino shifted slightly, muscles tensing. I gave him a wry smile. Was he thinking about attacking me? His expression stayed cautious. I met his gaze and twisted my free hand so he saw my tattoo and the crisscrossing scars beneath it. He should know that no matter how infuriating his wife was, I'd never hurt her. His brows drew together, and he relaxed with a small nod.

Kiara tightened her hold. "You protected me from my uncle when he wanted to humiliate me by dancing with me on my wedding. You helped Nino kill him—"

I interrupted her, growing tired of her emotionality. "You can calm down. I want Serafina to come to my bed willingly and not by force. So you can fucking release me now."

She regarded me closely. "She won't. Why should she? You kidnapped her."

"And you were forced into an unwanted marriage to my brother. What's the difference?"

She removed her fingers from my wrist. Nino wrapped his arm around her shoulder. "It's not the same," she whispered.

"The only difference is that in your case your family decided who got you, while Serafina's family had no say in the matter. Neither of you had a real choice."

She shook her head and peered up at Nino with so much fucking love I knew I could never hurt a single hair on her body. She returned her gaze to mine. "Let me talk to her," she said, not asking but *ordering*.

"Is that a fucking order, Kiara?" I asked in a threatening voice. Maybe she needed reminding that I was her Capo.

Nino squeezed her shoulder, but she held my gaze then stepped forward out of his grip and closer to me. "No," she said softly, looking at me with those big brown eyes as if that would warm my heart. "I am asking you for permission as your sister-in-law and as a Falcone."

"Fuck," I snarled and glared at Nino. "Couldn't you have chosen an airheaded wife? She's as good at manipulation as you are."

Nino's mouth twitched and he looked proud. Fucking proud.

"I'm not sure why I put up with all of you," I muttered.

"Does that mean I'm allowed to talk to her?" Kiara asked hopefully.

"Yes. But I should warn you … Serafina isn't as docile as you are. If I were you, I'd watch my back. She might end up attacking you to save herself."

"I'll take my chances," she said then turned on her heel and headed straight for my wing. Nino followed her because he was obviously concerned for her safety.

I released a harsh breath and kicked the punching bag with so much force the hook ripped out of the ceiling and the bag crashed to the ground.

Savio chuckled as he came up to me. "At first, I really loathed the idea of having Kiara under our roof, but I enjoy her presence more every day."

"Why don't you call someone to fix this fucking bag instead of grating on my nerves."

Savio grinned. "Will do, Capo. I know someone you can release your pent-up energy on. I was supposed to train with Adamo. Why don't you take over? The kid needs a good ass kicking."

"Why don't I just hang you from a hook and use you as a punching bag instead?"

Savio laughed and sauntered off.

Staring at the mess on the floor for another moment, I turned around to Adamo, who had his arms crossed over his chest and was glaring. "Come on, kiddo. Train with me."

Adamo and I had never trained together unless you counted the mock fights I'd entertained him with when he was a small kid and didn't hate my guts yet.

For a moment, he looked like he was going to refuse, but then he pushed up to his feet. He trudged after me in that annoying way he'd adopted recently, just to drive me up the walls. I grabbed my keys then tossed them toward Adamo. "Catch."

He did, frowning.

"You're going to drive us there."

"Really?" he asked and for once wasn't glaring at me.

"Really. Now move. I don't have all day."

Adamo hurried past me, not trudging, and I followed after him, shaking my head and smiling. Nothing got that kid as excited as driving cars or rather racing them.

When I arrived in the driveway, he was already behind the wheel of my new neon green Lamborghini Aventador, grinning like the cat that got the fucking cream. The moment my ass hit the passenger seat, he revved the engine and we shot down the driveway.

"There's a gate at the end. You remember that, right?" I muttered, buckling up.

Adamo hit the button and the gates slid open, and we raced through them with about an inch between the side mirrors and the unrelenting steel.

I shook my head but Adamo didn't slow down. We weaved through traffic, and honks followed us everywhere. A police car shot out of a side alley and started chasing us with sirens howling and lights flashing.

"Oh man," Adamo whined, hitting the breaks and pulling over.

The officer got out, hand on his gun, and strolled toward us while his colleague stayed back, his gun at his side. That was the problem with a new car.

Adamo let the window down, and the officer looked at him. "Get out of the car."

I leaned forward, my forearm with my tattoo propped up against the dashboard and smiled darkly at the man. "Unfortunately, Officer, we have somewhere we need to be."

The police officer registered my tattoo then my face and took a step back. "This is a misunderstanding. Safe travels."

I nodded and sank back against the seat. "Drive."

Adamo looked at me with a hint of admiration in his eyes. Then he pulled away from the curb in a slower pace but still too fast. His mood soured the moment we got out of the car in front of the abandoned casino that served as our gym.

I waited for Adamo in the cage, but he took his sweet ass time getting ready. When he finally shuffled toward me, I really wished he were someone else because I wanted to viciously destroy my opponent. Adamo climbed in and closed the door before he faced me.

He had grown these last few months. He was still much scrawnier than Nino and me, and even Savio, but he was filling out nicely despite his reluctance to fight. His arms hung limply at his side as he watched me with apprehension.

"Come on, kiddo. Show me what you got."

"Don't call me kiddo," he grumbled.

I smiled challengingly. "Make me. So far nothing I've seen has hinted at you being more than a sulking kid."

He curled his hands to fists, eyes narrowing.

Better.

"At least I don't enjoy hurting girls."

So that was what had his panties in a bunch. "You don't enjoy doing anything else with them either," I taunted, trying to finally get him to act on his anger. I couldn't give any less fucks if Adamo was a virgin or not. I didn't understand it one bit, but he could fuck whomever, whenever, however he wanted.

"I like girls."

"Not their pussies, obviously."

He flushed bright red. We still had a lot of work to do.

"Have you kissed a girl at least?" I took a step closer to him.

He looked away and my smile widened. "Who was it? A girl from school? Or a whore after all?"

His eyes flashed with anger, and he charged at me. His kick was surprisingly well placed, but I blocked it with both of my forearms then punched Adamo's side hard—not nearly as hard as I wanted, though. He gasped but still sent several punches my way.

We found a good rhythm, and I could see Adamo getting into it, as if this was one of his annoying video games. I had to admit I enjoyed the sparring. It wasn't more than that, though, because if I had really fought Adamo, the kid would have been on the ground. Eventually, we leaned against the cage, sipping water and dripping sweat.

"I didn't think you'd hold back. I thought you wanted to kick my ass because I'm a fucking disappointment in your eyes."

I lowered the bottle. "What makes you think I held back?"

He snorted. "You are the strongest fighter I know. I wouldn't stand a chance against you."

"Not yet. Maybe one day. And you aren't a disappointment."

He shook his head. "I'll never be like you and Nino or even Savio."

"I don't want you to be like any of us. I only want you to be a Falcone and be proud of it."

Adamo stared at me with a frown then looked down at his bottle. "Can we do another round?"

"Sure," I said, even if I was eager to return to Serafina.

"Don't hold back as much this time," Adamo said.

My lips pulled wide, and I set the bottle down. I should have fought with Adamo before.

Serafina

I lay on the bed, staring up at the ceiling, worrying about my family, especially Samuel. He was so protective of me, what if he did something stupid like attack and get himself killed? I wanted to be saved but if something happened to Sam, I wouldn't survive. I'd rather suffer pain and endure Remo's presence than see my brother get hurt.

A heavy weight settled in my stomach when I remembered the look in his eyes when Remo had put the knife against my skin. That look had hurt so much more than the shallow cut. But the cut had given me an important piece of information about Remo. He had a weakness, and it had something to do with those scars and his brothers.

Steps sounded in front of my door and someone knocked. I sat up, surprised. Nobody had bothered to knock.

The lock sounded and the door swung open as I stood, and a young woman with dark hair and dark eyes, wearing a red summer dress, stepped in. She was shorter than me, and must be the source of the clothes Remo had brought me to wear; it explained why the maxi dress I was wearing ended mid-calf.

I had never met her, but I knew who she was. Not a single person in our world didn't know her.

"Kiara Vitiello," I said. The poor Famiglia woman who was thrown to the Falcone wolves to be devoured. Everyone had heard of that union. It had been the gossip of the year among Outfit women. I had only felt pity for the girl, but she didn't appear as if she needed or wanted it.

"Kiara Falcone now, but yes, that's me." She looked over her shoulder with a small frown, and I followed her gaze, finding Nino Falcone standing behind her.

"You don't have to stay. Serafina and I are going to talk. She poses no danger to me."

He was worried I'd attack his wife? Maybe using her as a human safety shield would have gotten me out of the mansion, but I wasn't that brave. If I failed, I knew what that would mean because the look in Nino's eyes sent an icy shiver down my spine.

"I will stay," he said firmly, looking straight at me as he walked in, closed the door, and leaned against the wall. "And if you make a move toward my wife, the consequences will be very unpleasant."

Kiara's cheeks turned red. She gave me an apologetic smile before stepping close to him, touching his chest. I didn't hear what she was saying, but Nino's expression remained stoic. He shook his head once, and she sighed.

She came toward me. I eyed her warily. Not only had she been a Vitiello, but she was now a Falcone. Neither were names that set me at ease.

"I'm sorry. He's very protective," she said with a small smile.

I gave Nino the once-over. "That's obvious."

His expression remained a cold mask. Remo would have given me his twisted smile or that scary signature look, and I had to admit I preferred it to Nino's unreadable face, because I had no doubt that he was just as brutal and messed up as his brother but even harder to read.

Kiara extended her hand. "Call me Kiara."

I hesitated then took it. "Serafina."

Her eyes fell to my arm. "I'm sorry."

"That's not your apology to hand out," I told her as I returned to the bed and sank down.

"I fear it's the only one you're going to get," she said with a hint of disapproval. At least she seemed appalled by her crazy brother-in-law hurting me.

"I don't want Remo's apology. I want him lying at my feet in his own blood."

I sent Nino a smile, gauging his reaction, but his expression didn't change. He might as well have been carved from ice. If he couldn't be taunted into carelessness, my chances of getting past him were nil. If I ever tried an escape attempt, I would have to make sure he wasn't close by.

Kiara's eyes widened a tad as she perched on the edge of my bed, smoothing out her dress. "I think you will have to join the end of the queue. The world is full of people who want the same."

Oh, I liked her. Stifling a smile, I asked, "Are you one of them?"

She pursed her lips. "No, I'm not."

"He's the one hurting you then," I said with a nod toward her emotionless husband, only now something dangerous flickered in his eyes. He definitely wasn't indifferent to his wife.

Kiara glanced at Nino, and the smile tugging at her lips surprised me. "Nino would never hurt me. He is my husband."

She sounded honest and more … she sounded in love. I'd heard the rumors of what had happened to her and what the Falcones had done to her uncle. Maybe she was just grateful.

"Why are you here?" I asked eventually.

"I thought you'd like female company."

"I'd like to return to my family, to my home. I'd like Remo to stop his twisted games. That's what I'd like," I whispered harshly, feeling bad for snapping at her but not being able to help myself.

She nodded. "I know."

"I doubt you've come to offer your help. You are loyal to the Falcones."

Again, her eyes moved to Nino. "I am. They are my family."

I looked away, thinking of my own family, of Samuel, and my heart clenched tightly. She startled me when she leaned closer, and Nino, too, tensed and straightened. Despite my apparent apprehension, she brought her mouth close to my ear and whispered, "These men are cruel and brutal, but it's not all there is to them. I think you can get under Remo's skin. I wish it for both of you." She pulled away and straightened. "I'll see what I can do so you are allowed to spend your days outside of this room. We could sit in the garden. There's no reason why your captivity should be more unpleasant than absolutely necessary."

I stared at Kiara. She surprised me, but if she really thought anyone could get under Remo Falcone's skin, then life in Vegas had twisted her brain.

SEVEN

Serafina

T HERE WASN'T A CLOCK ANYWHERE IN THE ROOM, BUT IT MUST HAVE been early afternoon by now. Except for the cold pizza and the tap water, I hadn't had anything to eat or drink. Maybe this was another part of Remo's game.

Glancing out of the window, I tried to find the end of the premises, but from my vantage point the gardens surrounding the Falcone mansion appeared endless.

What was Samuel doing now? I closed my eyes. He would blame himself for what happened. I knew him. He had always seen himself as my protector. I wished I could hear his voice, could tell him that it wasn't his fault. And Mom and Dad …

I hoped they had at least found a way to keep the truth from Sofia. She was too young, too innocent to be burdened with the cruelness of our world.

The sound of knocking followed by the lock being turned made me face the door. I winced at the dull pain in my forearm. A teenage boy in fight shorts and a T-shirt stepped into my room. He had slightly longer curly brown hair and was lean but muscled.

"Hey," he said hesitantly, brown eyes kind. "Remo sent me to get you."

I didn't move from my spot at the window. "What are you, his servant?"

The boy smiled an unguarded, honest smile. A smile few could afford in our circles. "I'm his youngest brother, but that's as good as the same in Remo's eyes."

His kindness confused me. It didn't seem fake. My eyes flitted down to his forearm, free of the markings of the Camorra, the knife and the eye. "You haven't been inducted yet."

The smile dropped. "I will be in two days."

"But you don't want to," I said curiously.

Caution replaced the open friendliness. "We shouldn't keep Remo waiting."

He opened the door wider and gestured for me to walk through. I wondered what he would do if I refused to follow him. He was taller than me and definitely stronger, but I got the impression he would have a hard time laying a hand on me. If he'd been my only opponent, I might have taken my chances, but Remo was downstairs.

Finally, I moved toward him and followed him through the long winding hallway.

"I'm Adamo, by the way," he said.

I glanced up at him. "Serafina."

"I know."

"I suppose you Falcone brothers were all in on the kidnapping," I muttered.

His brows drew together, but he remained silent. There was a hint of … embarrassment and disapproval on his face.

After a few minutes, we arrived in the lower part of the mansion, in some sort of entertainment hub with a bar, sofas, TV, and a boxing ring. A punching bag lay amidst rubble, and Remo was glaring down at it as if it had personally insulted him. He, too, was in fight trunks and nothing else.

The memory of how he'd held me under the shower, of how I'd been pressed up to him completely naked resurfaced. I hadn't registered much at the time, and even in the immediate aftermath, but now my gaze trailed over the display of hard muscles, the many scars that spoke of his violent past and present. Every inch of Remo screamed danger. His height, his muscles, his scars, but worse: his eyes.

They found me and as always it was a struggle to meet them. Around Remo you felt like the omega in a pack of wolves. Your eyes wanted to avoid his out of a deeply buried *primal* impulse because Remo *was* the alpha. There was no mistaking it.

Adamo left my side and went over to the sofa, where he plopped down and picked up a controller. A gun lay on the coffee table in front of him.

Remo stalked closer. "Adamo," he clipped, indicating the gun. Damn it.

Adamo grasped it and shoved it under his leg.

"I wouldn't even know how to use it," I lied.

Remo smiled darkly. "You are a good liar." His skin glistened with a fine sheen of sweat as if he hadn't bothered showering after a workout.

"Why did you call me down? Do you have another torture session planned for me?"

Remo glanced down at my wound, his expression hardening—all sharp cheekbones and tight jaw. "There's food in the kitchen for you and something to drink, unless you prefer hard liquor, then this is where you'll get it." He nodded toward the bar to my left where an array of bottles, most of them less than half full, awaited consumption. Scotch, bourbon, whiskey, gin …

I definitely wouldn't get intoxicated while I was being held captive by the Camorra. "I'm free to walk around the house?" I asked.

Remo smirked. "I don't think we've reached that level of trust yet."

"We won't reach any level of trust, Remo."

Steps echoed out in the hall behind me, and I turned halfway but not enough to lose sight of Remo. I preferred keeping him in my line of vision. As if he knew exactly what I was doing, one corner of his mouth twitched upward.

Savio walked in with that arrogant swagger. "Got someone to fix the punching bag."

Remo tore his gaze from me. "And it took you four hours?"

"Took care of some other business while I was at it," Savio said with a shrug.

Remo shook his head with obvious disapproval. "One day I'm going to seriously lose my shit on you."

Savio didn't look concerned, and I doubted it was because he was as emotionless as Nino. Savio knew he had nothing to fear from his older brother. The realization surprised me, and I filed it away for later use.

"Now that you're here, keep an eye on our guest while she's eating in the kitchen. I'll take a shower then take over her watch."

My mouth curled. "I'm not your guest. I'm a captive."

"Semantics," Remo said.

Maybe in his twisted mind.

"I could have watched her too," Adamo grumbled from his spot on the sofa.

Savio and Remo exchanged a look. Either they worried their younger brother would help me or they worried he wouldn't be able to stop me from escaping. Interesting.

Remo narrowed his eyes at me then strode past me, his arm brushing mine, causing me to draw back.

"Come," Savio ordered. My eyes lingered on Adamo, who was scowling at Remo's retreating back. Maybe the Falcones had a weak link in their midst.

Tearing my gaze away, I followed Savio to the back of the ground floor and through a door, which opened to a huge kitchen.

He pointed toward a pot on the stove. I approached it and lifted the lid, finding a creamy orange-colored soup. "What is it?"

"How would I know?" Savio drawled, sinking down on a chair at the kitchen table. "Probably something without meat. Kiara is vegetarian."

I frowned, trying to decipher the emotion in his voice. I thought I detected a hint of protectiveness when he said her name. Turning on the stove, I took a whiff. "Pumpkin soup," I said.

Savio shrugged. "I'm having a bowl as well."

I stared at the arrogant bastard. Did he think I'd fix him lunch? "Why don't you haul your lazy ass off the chair and get your own bowl?"

He *did* haul his ass off the chair and advanced on me. He braced himself against the stove on either side of my waist, cornering me. "I'm not Remo," he said quietly, "but I'm a Falcone, and I love bloodshed. You better watch your tongue."

I didn't say anything. Savio was scary in his own way. The soup started bubbling behind my back, and Savio finally withdrew, turning around. I opened a drawer to look for a ladle when a plan took form. Remo was upstairs, showering. I hadn't seen Nino anywhere, only Adamo was in the living room, and potentially a workman, who, knowing Vegas, wouldn't come to my help. It was the best opportunity I've had so far.

I gripped the heavy pot by its handles and swung back to gain momentum, but before I could release my hold, Savio whirled around. I catapulted the pot with the boiling soup at him. In an impressive show of reflexes, he lunged to the side, avoiding the pot and most of its contents. Splatters of yellow soup covered him from head to toe. I took my chance and tried to rush past him. His hand shot out, clamping down on my wrist, and he shoved me away with an infuriating air of arrogance. Spinning myself around, my hipbones collided with the edge of the table. I fell forward, my elbows hitting the hardwood, my butt jutting out in an undignified way.

"I like your ass from that vantage point," Savio commented.

"As long as you like it from a distance," Remo warned.

I whirled around.

Standing in the open door, Remo took in the mess on the floor and on his brother. "What the fuck happened here?"

Savio grimaced at his shirt then scowled at me. "That bitch tried to boil me alive."

I straightened, trying to hide my fear of what my punishment would be for the attack, but then Remo laughed, a low rumble that raised goose bumps on my skin.

"I'm glad you find it funny," Savio muttered. "I'm done. Next time you're busy, do me a favor and ask Nino to watch her." He stalked out without another glance.

"Clean that up," Remo ordered with a nod toward the floor, the amusement gone from his voice.

I remained where I was.

Remo walked around the lake of orange on the floor and stopped right in front of me, forcing me to tilt my head back. He cupped my chin. "Let me give you a piece of advice, Angel. Choose your battles wisely," he murmured threateningly. "And now you will clean the floor. I don't give a fuck if your highborn hands aren't supposed to get dirty."

I lowered my eyes from the harshness of his gaze but tried to mask it as me drawing back from his touch. "Where's a mop?"

Remo turned and headed for the door. "I'll be back in exactly two minutes and you won't move a fucking inch, understood?"

I pressed my lips together, a small act of defiance—if it could even be considered that—because Remo knew I'd obey. Very few people would have dared to defy Remo in that moment. I hoped one day to be among them.

Remo

I headed for the utility cupboard. Savio leaned against the bar, nursing a drink and his bruised ego. "Next time you should pay more attention."

He glared. "I think from the two of us, you have more reason to worry. She's yours, not mine. Wait till she tries to boil your dick."

"I can control Serafina. Don't worry." I took a mop and a bucket out of the closet before I returned into the kitchen. Serafina stood at exactly the same spot, frowning down at the floor.

She kept surprising me. The photos I'd seen of her on the internet and the accompanying articles had suggested she was an ice princess. Cold, prideful, fragile. As easy to crush as fresh snow, but Serafina was like eternal ice. Breaking her with force was difficult, not impossible, because I knew how to break, but that would have been the wrong approach. Even eternal ice yielded to heat.

I handed her the bucket and the mop, which she both took without protest. She avoided my eyes as she set out to fill the bucket with water and put it down on the ground. It became apparent pretty quickly that Serafina had never wielded a mop in her life. She used too much water, flooding the floor.

Leaning against the counter, I watched her in silence. She should have taken a rag, gotten down on her knees, and cleaned the floor properly, but I knew her pride would stop her from kneeling in my presence. Proud and strong and painstakingly beautiful, even sweaty and covered with soup.

The floor was still smeared with soup when she finally gave up. "The mop's not working properly."

"It's not the mop's fault. Trust me."

"I wasn't raised to clean floors," she snapped, wayward strands of hair clinging to her cheeks and forehead.

"No, you were raised to warm a man's bed and spread your legs for him."

Her eyes widened, anger twisting her perfect features. "I was raised to take care of a family, to be a good mother and wife."

"You can't cook, can't clean, and probably have never changed a diaper in your life. Being a good mother doesn't seem to be in your future."

She shoved the mop away so it clattered to the floor and moved closer then jerked to a halt halfway. "What do you know about being a good mother? Or a decent human being?"

My chest constricted briefly, but I pushed through it. "I know how to change a diaper for one, and I provided my brothers with protection when they needed it. That's more than you can say for yourself."

She frowned. "When did you change a diaper?"

"When Adamo was an infant, I was already ten," I said. It was more than I had wanted to reveal in the first place. My past wasn't Serafina's business. "Now come. I doubt you can do better than this. The cleaning staff is coming in the morning anyway."

"You let me clean this even though you have people for it?"

"Your pride will be your downfall," I said.

"And your fury will be yours."

"Then we'll fall together. Isn't that the beginning of every tragic love story?" My mouth twisted at the word. What a waste of energy. Our mother had loved our father. She'd hated him too, but her love had stopped her from doing what was necessary. She'd let our father beat and rape her, had let him beat us because it meant he wouldn't lay a hand on her. She never stood up to him. She cowered and worse … turned his anger toward us to protect herself. Her one act of fucking defiance was to punish our father by killing his sons. She tried to pay him back by killing her own flesh and blood because she was too fucking weak to retaliate in any other way. In a house full of weapons, she couldn't find the courage to ram a blade into our father's back like she should have done the first time he laid a hand on her. She chose the easy way.

"We won't have a love story. Not a tragic one, not a sad one, and definitely not a happy one. You can have my hatred," Serafina said fiercely.

"I'll take it," I murmured. "Hatred is so much stronger than love."

Nino joined me on the terrace in the evening. "Savio told me what happened."

"She's strong-willed."

"She's trouble," he corrected. "Keeping her under this roof poses a considerable risk."

I gave him a wry smile. "Don't tell me you are scared of a girl."

Nino's expression didn't change. "Fortunately, fear isn't among the emotions I've unlocked."

"Then keep it that way," I said. Fear was as useless as love—and even more crippling.

"I'm concerned about Adamo. His initiation is in two days. Keeping Serafina as a captive in the mansion might increase his reluctance to take the oath."

I turned to him. "You think he'll refuse the tattoo?"

Nino sighed. "I don't know. He's slipping away. I can't get him to talk to me anymore. Kiara is the only one he spends time with."

"Adamo is rebelling, but he's still a Falcone. Should I push him more?"

Nino shook his head. "I think that would make him pull away further. We have to hope that he comes around eventually."

"The initiation is in front of our underbosses and captains. If he refuses ..." I trailed off.

Nino nodded because he understood. Adamo refusing the tattoo would be shameful, a betrayal. There was only one punishment for refusing the tattoo: death.

"I suppose it wouldn't be the first time we'd have to kill a considerable number of Camorrista," I said.

"These men are loyal. It would be unfortunate to dispose of them, and we'd be faced with too many opponents at once."

"It won't come to that."

Nino nodded again and stood quietly beside me. "Have you given Serafina something for the pain?"

"Pain?" I echoed.

"Her wound might sting."

"It's a shallow cut. It can't possibly cause her more than slight discomfort."

Nino shook his head. "That's what I thought when I treated Kiara's wound, but she was surprisingly sensitive to pain. And Serafina won't be any different. Maybe worse. It's probably the first cut she's suffered, probably the first act of violence at all, Remo. She'll feel pain more profoundly than you and I do."

I considered his words and realized he was probably right. From what I'd gathered, Serafina had probably never even been hit by her parents. The first act of violence ... I didn't dwell on those thoughts. "Do we have anything for pain?"

"I have Tylenol in my room. I can bring it to her after dinner. Kiara is cooking her cheese lasagna again."

"No, I will give it to her when I bring her a slice of the lasagna."

"Okay," Nino murmured, regarding me carefully.

"What?" I snarled, his silent judgment grating on my nerves.

"Originally the plan was to keep Serafina in the Sugar Trap."

"Originally I didn't know what kind of woman she was. And she is safer here. I don't want anyone to get their hands on her. It would ruin my plans."

"I'll get the Tylenol," Nino said, turning around and leaving me standing there.

I went inside and made my way into the kitchen, which smelled of herbs and something spicier. Kiara glanced up from the chopping board. She was slicing tomatoes and throwing them in a bowl with lettuce.

"No one's eating salad around here," I told her as I strode toward her. The tensing of her body was barely noticeable anymore.

"I'm eating it, and Nino will too, and maybe Serafina prefers to stay healthy as well," Kiara said. I stopped beside her and glanced into the oven where a big pan was bubbling over with cheese.

"Serafina has more pressing problems."

Kiara's eyes shot up, and I gripped her hand before she could chop her fingers off. "Nino needs to show you how to hold a knife properly," I demanded then released her.

She put down the knife. "When will you send her back?"

I stared down at her.

She pushed a strand behind her ear, looking away. Kiara was still quick to submit. "You *will* send her back, right?"

Nino came in with the Tylenol, glancing between his wife and me. He frowned but didn't comment.

"When's the lasagna done?" I asked.

"It should be ready now." She gripped the handle, and I stepped back so she could open the oven. She nodded. "Perfect."

Nino took oven mitts and gently pushed his wife to the side. "Let me."

He set the bubbling pan onto the stove, and Kiara smiled at him, touching his arm. "Thank you."

His expression softened, and I still couldn't wrap my mind around it. My brother loved—or whatever he was capable of—Kiara. Taking the Tylenol from his pocket, he handed it to me. "Give me a piece of lasagna for Serafina."

Kiara pursed her lips but did as she was told. "Why can't she have dinner with us?"

"She's a captive," Savio muttered as he came in. He was still pissed because of the soup incident.

"She can be a captive and eat dinner with us, don't you think?" She looked up to Nino for help. He touched her waist and a look passed between them I couldn't read.

Sick of their silent exchanges, I left with the lasagna and the Tylenol. When I stepped into the bedroom, Serafina was sitting on the windowsill, her arms wrapped around her legs. I wondered what kind of clothes she'd worn in Minneapolis. I couldn't imagine she'd opted for floor-length dresses like Kiara. Serafina didn't turn my way when I stepped in, not even when I crossed the room and set the plate down on her nightstand.

"Tell Kiara I'm sorry I wasted her soup."

"Are you sorry?" I asked as I stopped in front of her. Her blue eyes were still firmly focused on the window.

"I'm sorry for wasting it, not for throwing it at your brother. I'm sorry I missed, though. You can tell him that."

I stifled a smile and regarded her closely, her elegantly curved mouth, her immaculate skin. My eyes lowered to her forearm. She held her arm at an awkward angle so it wasn't pressed up against her leg. I held out the Tylenol. "For the pain."

Her gaze fell to my palm. Then she looked up. I could tell she considered refusing, but again she surprised me by taking the pills, her fingertips brushing the scars on my palm. Her blond brows furrowed.

"Those are burn marks, aren't they?"

I withdrew my hand and curled it into a fist at my side. "Eat. I have plans for you tomorrow." I turned on my heel before I walked out and locked her door.

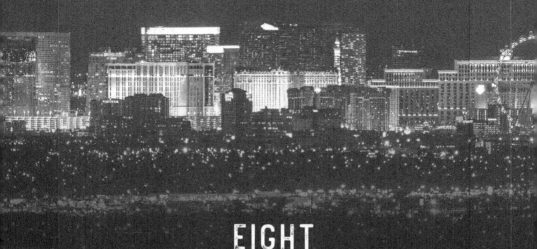

EIGHT

Serafina

THE NEXT MORNING I TOOK A QUICK SHOWER, HOLDING MY ARM OUT OF the stall so it wouldn't get wet. The painkillers had helped with the sting. I hadn't expected that kind of consideration from Remo, and I suspected he had ulterior motives for the gesture, but it had given me another piece of the puzzle. The scars on his palms held a special meaning. I had a feeling they were connected to the scars his tattoo covered.

The sound of the lock startled me, and I quickly put another one of Kiara's long summer dresses on before I stepped out of the bathroom, my hair still damp and barefoot.

Remo stood with his arms crossed in front of the window, tall and dark and brooding like the love interest in romance movies. He turned and scanned my body. It was unsettling how physical his gaze felt on my skin.

"I'm taking you outside for a walk in the gardens."

I raised my eyebrows. "Why?"

"Would you prefer to spend your captivity holed up in here?"

"No, but I'm wary of your motives."

Remo smiled darkly. "I want to keep you sound of mind and body. It would be a shame if these four walls broke you before I can."

I glared at him, glad he couldn't hear my thundering pulse.

"Now come," he ordered with a nod toward the door, his eyes lingering on my body.

I followed after him and almost bumped into him when he paused in the hallway, glancing down at my feet. "Won't you put on shoes?"

"I would if I had any that fit me. Kiara is a six and I'm a seven and a half."

Remo regarded me a moment before touching my lower back, and I lurched forward in surprise. He indicated I walk ahead, the corners of his mouth tipping up, those dark eyes assessing me.

My body tingled from his touch, and my heart throbbed in my chest. Remo's closeness terrified me, and he could tell. I made sure to keep my distance, but Remo trailed after me, his gaze burning my neck, his tall frame a shadow over my back.

I managed to relax when we stepped outside into the bright sunshine. Remo led me through the sprawling gardens that had different pools, shooting targets set up, and perfectly manicured greenery. The warm grass felt wondrous under my bare feet, but I didn't let it distract me from my main objective: scouting my surroundings.

Remo was oddly quiet, which was unsettling because it meant something was going on behind those dark cruel eyes.

"You can try to run, but you can't escape," Remo said firmly when I scanned the property boundary. The high walls around the premises were topped with barbed wire, and when we walked close enough I could hear the hum of electricity.

"Are you looking for a weakness in our safety measures?" he asked with a hint of dark amusement. "You won't find any."

"Everything, *everyone*, has a weakness. It's only a matter of finding it," I said quietly, stopping.

Remo stepped in front of me, his dark eyes triumphant as they slowly traced the length of me. "And you are Dante's weakness, Serafina."

"I'm only his niece. Dante has condemned so many men to death in his life, do you really think he cares about the life of one girl?"

Remo cupped the back of my head, holding me in place as he brought our faces closer. I let him, softened in his hold, knowing it wasn't the reaction he wanted. His dark eyes searched mine, and I had to fight not to look away.

"I wonder if you really believe it or if you hope I believe it," he said in a low voice.

"It's the truth."

His lips widened in a harsh smile. "The truth is that you are a woman, something precious, something they must protect. It's engrained in them, burned into them irrevocably from the day of their birth. Their honor dictates they keep you safe, and every second you are in my hands, they are failing you, failing themselves. With every second that passes the shame of their failure eats away at their honor. As Made Men we live on honor and pride. They are the pillars of our world, of our fucking self, and I'm going to tear them down pillar by pillar until every fucking member of the Outfit is crushed beneath the weight of their fucking guilt."

My breath had lodged itself in my throat, and I could do nothing but stare at the man in front of me. Maybe he'd underestimated me, but I—and I feared even the Outfit—had underestimated Remo Falcone as well. His actions spoke of barely restrained violence and led you to believe that he lacked any sliver of control, that he could be driven into rash acts. But Remo was dangerously intelligent. A ruthless man with the power and wit to get his revenge.

"Maybe they will feel guilty, but they won't waver. They won't risk any part of the Outfit for me. Not for the soundness of my body, not for my life, and least of all for my innocence, Remo. So take either or all. You won't weaken Dante or the Outfit."

Remo's thumb stroked the side of my throat. I wasn't sure if he did it on purpose or without noticing, and it wasn't the touch but the look in his eyes that made me shiver.

"They will protect your innocence at any cost because it's the only pure thing in their fucking lives. They think your innocence could wash away their sins, but they breathe sin. We all do. One hundred virgins can't wash the sin from our veins. Definitely not from mine."

""Not even an angel?" I murmured, tilting my head up, peering at him through my lashes. My pulse throbbed in my veins, aware of the risk I was taking. But I was forced into Remo's game, willing or not, and I could either be a pawn or a player.

Something in Remo's dark eyes shifted, something hungry and lethal unfurling. He leaned closer, his breath hot against my lips. "You are playing a dangerous game, *Angel*."

I smiled. "So are you."

His lips pressed against mine. I hadn't expected it. Almost kisses, like threats ghosting over my skin, had been his tactic … until now. This wasn't a ghost touch. It was substantial, and yet it felt like the promise of a kiss, a threat of what lay ahead. Stunned by Remo's action, I held his gaze. Finally, I ripped away and raised my palm to slap him, but he caught my wrist. He jerked me closer once more.

"That's the kiss Danilo would have given you in church, and maybe even later on your wedding night. Polite. Controlled. Reverent." His voice dipped low. "That's not a kiss."

Anger surged through me. "You—"

Remo's mouth crashed down on mine, fingers bruising my hip as his other hand cradled my wrist between our bodies. His lips conquered mine, his tongue tasting the seam of my mouth, sucking at my tender lower lip, demanding entrance. Heat flushed through me, and my lips parted slightly. Barely. A flicker of submission and Remo plunged his tongue into my mouth, tasting me, consuming me. His taste was intoxicating, his body's heat overpowering. His thumb pressed into my wrist, his palm sliding from my hip to my lower back. Small sparks of electricity followed in his touch's wake.

My head swimming, I was unable to pull back, unable to move at all. Finally, Remo let me free. I sucked in a desperate breath, lightheaded, confused, my body tingling from head to toe.

Remo exhaled. "That, *Angel*, was a kiss. It's the only kind of kiss you'll ever get from me, and it's the kiss you'll use to measure every kiss that follows."

I stumbled away from Remo, shaking. "What have you done?" I stammered. I pressed shaking fingers to my lips, horror striking down on me like lightning. That was supposed to be Danilo's privilege. My first kiss.

Remo had taken it.

No.

I had given it away.

Remo shook his head, glowering. "I cut you with my blade and you didn't shed a single tear, but a kiss makes you cry?"

I turned away, trying to get a grip on my emotions. All my life I had been raised to be the perfect wife, to gift myself to my husband. And just like that I'd allowed Remo to plunder part of my gift. For a moment, I felt like bawling. Then I felt Remo's warmth against my back, not touching but lingering between us.

"Are you scared of Danilo's wrath if he finds out his angel hides a few black feathers beneath the glowing white of her plumage?"

I glanced over my shoulder at his striking face. "You don't know anything about Danilo or me."

"I know your weakness, and I know his."

I faced him once more. "You, too, have a weakness, and one day your enemies are going to use it against you with the same cruelty you bestow upon them."

"Maybe," he growled. "Maybe they'll rise after I've burned down their pride, but not everyone is built to rise from the ashes."

I scoffed. "You sound like a martyr. What do you know about burning?"

Remo didn't say anything, only looked at me with cruel intention, the same expression I'd seen when he'd cut me.

My eyes darted down to the wound on my arm, and Remo's gaze followed. Brick after brick, I was tearing down a wall Remo had no intention of lowering.

Remo grabbed my arm and led me back toward the mansion. I didn't say anything, didn't even look his way. I knew when to retreat, knew when to give in, because this battle had only just begun.

The second I was alone in my room, I headed into the bathroom and splashed cold water on my face to clear my head. Looking up, I cringed at the state of my lips. Red and swollen.

I could still feel Remo's touch, could still taste him. How could I have let that happen? I should have pushed him away, but I didn't. Remo had stopped. Not only had I allowed him to steal my first kiss, I'd enjoyed it in a twisted, all-consuming way.

I walked back into the bedroom and dropped down on the bed, staring up at the dark canopy. Something about Remo overwhelmed me. He had a way of drawing me in. I lifted my arm to stare at my wound. It still felt tender but seemed to be healing. I was glad for its presence; it had not only allowed me a glimpse behind Remo's cruel mask, it also served as a reminder of what he was: a monster. One kiss didn't change that. I couldn't let his manipulation get to me. Remo was Capo. He knew how to make people act how he wanted them to act.

I covered my face with my palms, taking deep, calming breaths. I wished I could talk to Samuel, see his face, be in his arms. Without him, I felt lost. He'd figure something out. My stomach constricted thinking of my brother. If Samuel knew I had allowed Remo to kiss me, hadn't raised even a finger against him to fight him off, what would my brother think of me then? And what about Danilo? He was my fiancé. That kiss had been promised to him.

Samuel remained at the forefront of my mind. He was the person I really cared about. And my family. God, my family. I wished they'd never find out about the kiss, but I had a feeling Remo would tell them all about it.

Remo

A fucking kiss when I wanted so much more. But kissing Serafina had been like the first hit off a crack pipe. It got you addicted from the very first taste. I wanted to kiss her again, wanted to steal every piece of her innocence.

The sound of steps made me look up. Nino was headed my way and sank down on the sofa across from me. He assessed me in that analyzing way he always had.

"What happened?"

"Got a taste of Serafina."

Nino nodded, his eyes narrowing in thought. "You kissed her?"

"Yes, but it won't be the last taste I get of her."

"How did she react?"

"She didn't fight it if that's what you're asking," I said quietly.

He frowned. "I didn't come to talk to you about Serafina. It's obviously a topic you won't allow me to reason with you."

"What do you want to talk to me about, then?"

"I think we should have a conversation with Adamo. Tomorrow is his day, so I want to make sure he's on the same page as we are."

I nodded. "It's probably for the best. Where is he?"

Since he wasn't playing his games, he could only be upstairs sulking or wanking off. Probably the latter considering he didn't get any action. "I got something to sweeten the deal for him," I said.

Nino raised his eyebrows. "Don't tell me you got him a car?"

I grinned. "He's turning fourteen so why not? I'm tired of him crashing my cars. Maybe he'll treat his own possessions with more care."

"The legal driving age is fifteen in Nevada."

"And drugs and homicides are against the law. What's your point?"

"He'll get himself killed in one of our races," Nino drawled. "Are you going to discuss the drug issue with him?"

"I will. Why don't you get him? We'll take him on a test drive and have a word with him."

"Who's going to watch over Kiara and Serafina? Savio went off to meet with Diego again."

"I'll call Fabiano while you find our little brother."

Nino got up and disappeared, and I speed dialed Fabiano. "Remo, what do you need? I'm busy with that asshole Mason."

"Make it quick. I need you here to watch Serafina and Kiara while Nino and I have a talk with Adamo."

"About tomorrow, I assume," Fabiano said. I could hear a man crying in the background.

"Yeah. Be here as quick as possible."

"Fifteen minutes." Fabiano hung up.

Upstairs I could hear a commotion. Adamo was stomping and Nino was speaking to him in a calm drawl.

I stood and moved into the entrance hall, grabbing the keys to Adamo's first car. Nino appeared on the stairs, a disapproving look on his face. Adamo followed close behind him with a scowl on his own baby face. Nino stopped beside me, and I could see that he wasn't impressed by Adamo's antics, which was why he'd gone upstairs and I hadn't. Losing my shit on him today wouldn't help matters.

Adamo came to a halt on the last step with his arms crossed over his chest. "What do you want? I'm busy."

"Calm," Nino murmured to me. After training together, I'd thought Adamo and I had come to a sort of truce. Apparently he'd changed his mind again.

I grabbed the front of his shirt and jerked him closer. I cut him some slack because he was a kid, but my patience had its limits. "Why don't you wipe that sulk off your face, kiddo, or I'll give you a reason for it."

He jutted his chin out. "Do it. Then I'll have another reason to refuse the tattoo tomorrow."

"Adamo," Nino warned.

My fingers tightened and I stared into his eyes long and hard. "Do you think you can survive on your own?"

"I have friends," he muttered.

"Friends who keep you around because you give them weed and crack for free. They don't give a fuck about you. If you can't provide them with free drugs, they'll drop you," I growled.

Adamo blanched. "Who told you?"

"Do you think I didn't notice that someone's been stealing our shit for months now? Fabiano has been keeping a fucking eye on you."

"The punishment for stealing from the Camorra is death," he said challengingly.

"It is," I said. "But not for you."

The entrance door was unlocked, and Fabiano entered, shirtsleeves rolled up, forearms tinged pink. Blood was difficult to wash off.

Adamo's eyes widened. "What did you do?"

Fabiano nodded at Nino and me in greeting.

"Fabiano talked to one of your friends, that useless piece of shit Mason."

"You killed him?" Adamo asked horrified. Fabiano raised one eyebrow at me.

I shook my head. It wasn't time to divulge information yet. Adamo could do the talking.

"Don't hurt Harper," Adamo whispered.

I frowned at the tone of his voice. "That girl in your junkie group?"

Fabiano grimaced. "She was with Mason when I went after him, sucking his cock."

"You're lying!" Adamo jerked out of my grip and lunged at Fabiano, trying to land an uppercut. Fabiano blocked him and shoved him to the ground, but Adamo pushed up to his feet and went for it again. I didn't intervene. Adamo needed to realize that his actions had consequences, and it gave me the time to stomach the fucking truth that my brother had fallen for a useless bitch who probably whispered sweet nothings in his ear in exchange for drugs.

Fabiano grasped Adamo's arm and thrust him face-first into the wall. "Stop this shit," he warned, "or I'm going to defend myself for real."

He released Adamo, who turned at once, head flushed and eyes full of dread. "What did you do to Harper?"

Fabiano glanced at me. Nino shook his head at me, obviously worried I was going to lose my shit.

"Don't tell me the little slut gave you head in return for drugs, Adamo. You should know better." We had so many fucking whores who could suck cocks, why did he have to find a girl who used him?

Adamo glared. "Harper and I are in love. You wouldn't understand."

"She sucked another man's dick. How does that mean 'I love you?'" I snarled.

"She wouldn't! You're trying to ruin things for me."

Fabiano sighed. "I'm not lying. Mason had his cock shoved up to his balls inside her mouth."

"Shut up," Adamo said fiercely.

"I told you it's difficult to find what you're looking for," Nino told our brother. "People will always try to gain something from being with you."

Adamo shook his head, a stubborn gleam in his eyes. "What did you do to her?"

I nodded at Fabiano.

"Nothing. I sent her away before I beat some sense into your friend."

"He's alive."

"Broke a few of his bones, but alive, yes," Fabiano said.

I should have had him killed. If I had known the exact details, I would have given the kill order.

Adamo looked relieved. "You kept them alive so I'll take the tattoo tomorrow, right?"

"That wasn't the plan," I said. "I thought you'd want to be a Falcone."

Adamo looked away. "You never spare anyone without good reason."

"Get a drug test, Nino," I ordered.

Nino disappeared into his wing.

"I'm clean," Adamo blurted but his voice shook.

I turned my back to him, my fingers curling to fists. Why did Adamo have to make this so fucking hard? I wasn't sure how to deal with his shit, especially the drugs. He needed to realize that he was treading a dangerous path.

"I told the truth," Fabiano said to Adamo.

"Maybe Mason forced her. You don't know anything," Adamo muttered.

Nino returned and motioned for Adamo to follow him into the guest bathroom so he could pee on the test strip. When they emerged and I saw Nino's expression, I lost it. I grabbed Adamo by the collar and threw him to the ground.

"What did I tell you about taking drugs? Do you want to end up like all the lost losers roaming our streets? What the fuck is wrong with you?"

Adamo shrugged. "My friends and I only take it now and then to relax."

I breathed harshly. Adamo lay completely still beneath me. I took a deep breath, stifling the fury burning through me, then got to my feet. "You won't ever take anything again or I will kill every single of your so-called friends. Rich parents or not. And now you will take your new car for a test drive to Harper's home and tell her you won't give her free drugs anymore. If she wants drugs, she can come to me and pay the regular price. Understood?"

Adamo blinked up at me. "Understood," he said slowly, sitting up. "My new car?"

I thrust the keys to the ground beside him. "Bought you that Ford Mustang Limgene in red and black that you've had as your screen saver for months now."

Adamo took the keys. "For my birthday?"

"For your birthday and your initiation. Now talk to Harper and take Nino with you," I said then walked into the living room, straight toward the punching bag. I began kicking and punching, but my rage didn't lessen.

Fabiano joined me after a moment. "I suppose I don't need to watch the girls anymore?"

I didn't say anything. I didn't want to think about Serafina now because if I started thinking about her, I might end up ruining my own fucking plan.

Fabiano stepped in my line of vision. "That girl led him on."

"I know," I growled and sent the bag flying. The hook groaned but stayed anchored in the ceiling. "How about a sparring match?"

"You don't look like you want to spar. You look like you want to destroy someone," Fabiano commented, but he began unbuttoning his shirt. I tugged at my own T-shirt and dragged it over my head then shoved down my pants and swung myself into the boxing ring, wearing only my briefs.

Fabiano did the same and stood across from me. I motioned him forward, and he went into attack mode at once.

We hit and kicked hard and fast. Fabiano's punches spoke of suppressed anger, and my own were fueled with fury. I shoved him into the ropes, but he caught himself. "Is this because of Serafina?" I taunted.

"No," he shot back. "I always enjoy kicking your ass, Remo."

He lunged at me again.

"What's going on here?" Kiara asked from the entranceway.

We ignored her.

"If nobody bothers to give me an answer, I'll head upstairs and talk to Serafina."

"You won't," I ordered, and Fabiano landed a hard punch in my side.

Snarling, I did a sidekick and got his shoulder. "Kiara!" I held up my palm toward Fabiano to pause the match.

She froze. "I thought she could have dinner with us. I have mac and cheese in the oven."

"You won't go anywhere near her without someone to watch your back, understood?"

She nodded eventually. Then her eyes moved on to Fabiano. "Why don't you call Leona. I made enough food so you can join us."

"That's a good idea," I said then jumped out of the ring. It was obvious that I wouldn't get rid of my anger today.

"Will you bring Serafina down, then?"

"No," I said tersely.

"Why not?" Kiara asked, and I stalked toward her. She didn't back off as I stopped right in front of her.

"Because I don't fucking trust myself around her today, okay?"

Kiara nodded, a deep worry line forming between her brows. "Okay."

"I can bring her food up later," Fabiano suggested.

I slanted him a hard look. "Yeah, why not?" My voice rang with warning.

He held my gaze for a long time until he grabbed his phone from the pocket of his pants off the ground and brought it to his ear. I put my clothes back on, not giving a shit that I was sweaty. Kiara trailed after me as I sank down on the sofa. She didn't know what was good for her. Now that she wasn't completely terrified by my presence anymore, she was starting to annoy the fuck out of me.

"Is it because of Adamo?"

"What?"

"Your sour mood."

I smiled darkly. "You haven't seen me in a sour mood yet, and if I can help it, you won't."

She pursed her lips. "He's conflicted. He doesn't want to disappoint you, but he also doesn't want to kill and torture in your name."

I didn't say anything, only returned her gaze until she looked away. She had more trouble holding my eyes than Serafina did.

"He's killed before."

"And he feels guilty for it."

I braced myself on my thighs. "Nobody forced his hand back then. He could have hidden like all the other spectators of the fight. He could have run. He could have shot the asshole's leg or arm, but Adamo shot him in the head. Maybe Adamo doesn't want to be a killer, but he is. It's in our nature, Kiara. He can fight it as long as he wants, but eventually the darkness seeps through. It's what it is."

"Maybe," she agreed.

"Fabiano was a good boy once. Goldilocks with remorse and a squeaky clean white shirt, but now he's my Enforcer."

Fabiano snorted. "I was never good and definitely not goldilocks."

"I should get dinner ready. Can you help me with the mustard jar in the kitchen? I can't open it," Kiara said.

I nodded toward Fabiano. "He can help you."

Kiara shifted nervously, her eyes sliding to Fabiano then back to me. My eyebrows shot up. I got to my feet.

Fabiano gave a small shrug. "Leona will be here in five minutes."

I followed Kiara into the kitchen and took the mustard jar she held out to me. "I didn't think I'd live to see the day that someone was less scared of me than of Fabiano or anyone else for that matter."

Kiara flushed. "I know I'm safe with you," she said quietly.

Fuck, she was. I held out the open jar. "Here."

"Thank you."

"You're safe around Fabiano as well," I told her.

"I know," she said. "But it takes a bit longer for the message to get through to my brain."

"You should be wary of a brain that makes you love my brother and trust me, Kiara," I muttered.

She laughed. "It's not my brain, it's my heart."

I narrowed my eyes then turned on my heel and walked out, not in the mood for emotional nonsense.

NINE

Serafina

I WASN'T SURE IF IT WAS REMO'S PLAN TO BREAK ME BY LETTING ME STEW with my own thoughts all day. I had nothing to do except relive this afternoon's kiss, torn between guilt and a flicker of terrifying excitement, because that kiss had been unlike anything I'd ever felt before. And every time that realization hit me, my guilt doubled. I knew I wasn't supposed to enjoy it—not only because Danilo was the man I was supposed to be kissing, but also because Remo was the last man I was allowed to kiss.

Whenever Samuel had returned from a night out with friends while I was stuck at home, I'd be overwhelmed by a wave of longing and jealousy. I wanted to be free to party with him, but that would have been my ruin—even if Samuel had been at my side to protect my honor. I couldn't be seen in a club, dancing the night away. We'd had a few secret house parties, which had been exhilarating even if Samuel had been glued to my side every second so none of his friends got near me. Not that any of them would have dared. They were all Made Men or on their way to becoming one. My father was Underboss. My uncle was the boss of the Outfit. My fiancé as good as the underboss of Indianapolis and my brother a Made Man. No guy ever looked at me twice, at least not the guys allowed near me. I could have been naked and thrown myself at these guys and they wouldn't have batted an eye … from fear of losing it—and their life.

And I had been okay with it, had accepted it because we were bound by the rules of our world. It wasn't as if I wanted to sleep around like Samuel, even if the few stories he'd shared with me in the beginning when he was overexcited about losing his virginity had made me curious.

The lock clicked and I quickly sat up, bracing myself. I wouldn't allow Remo to catch me by surprise again.

My eyes widened when Fabiano stepped inside, carrying a plate. I stood. Why was he here? Would he help me after all?

Fabiano regarded my face then shook his head as if he could read my mind. "I'm bringing you dinner."

He came in but left the door ajar, and I wondered why he did it. I doubted it was so I could run. Was he worried of being alone in a room with me?

"Here," he held out the plate with steaming mac and cheese to me.

I glared. "Do you remember how you, Samuel and I played together? Do you remember how you and him pretended to be my protectors? Do you remember that?" For a moment we did nothing but stare at each other, but he didn't allow me to glimpse behind his emotionless mask.

With a sigh, he walked past me and put the plate down on my nightstand.

"You should eat," he said firmly.

I whirled around to face him. "Why? So I stay healthy just so Remo can break me?"

Fabiano glanced down at my arm and grabbed it, inspecting the wound closely. "That's Remo's doing?"

"Who else enjoys slicing up people?"

Fabiano's mouth switched into a wry smile. "Pretty much every man in the mob, Fina."

He touched the wound lightly. "It's not deep."

"I'm sorry that my wound doesn't fulfill your high standards. Next time maybe you should cut me."

Fabiano shook his head. "Remo cuts deep. Hits hard. Kills brutally. He doesn't do half-assed cuts like this."

I tugged my arm free. "So what? Maybe he wants to save the bloody fun for later."

Fabiano's blue eyes searched my face with a small frown. "Maybe."

For some reason, his scrutiny annoyed me. "When people said you were a traitor who ran off with his tail between his legs, I didn't want to believe them, but now I see they were right."

Fabiano leaned down, and the look was one I hadn't seen on his face before, one that reminded me that he was now Enforcer. "I didn't run. I'm loyal."

I huffed.

He took a step closer, and I backed off. "I am. My fucking father sent one of his men out to kill me. That man couldn't go through with it and dropped me off in Bratva territory so they could finish the job for him. Without Remo, they would have succeeded. I'm alive because of my Capo, because of those four Falcone brothers who stood together when the world was against them and against me."

I blinked, utterly shocked by his words. "Your father tried to kill you? Why didn't you tell Dante?"

He glared. "I'm not a fucking snitch. And the Cavallaros have stuck with my bastard of a father for too long. I don't give a fuck if your grandpa thinks highly of him. My father is a disgrace."

"My grandfather is very sick. He probably won't live much longer."

"Good," Fabiano said fiercely.

I swallowed. "Even if my grandfather doesn't hold a protective hand over your father anymore, Dante won't give him to the Camorra. He'll deal with him."

Fabiano smiled sadly. "Dante will hand my father over. Trust me." He took a step back. "I only wished you weren't the one who's going to make it happen."

I touched Fabiano's arm. "I know you can't help me escape, but at least let me talk to Samuel, Fabi. I miss him so terribly."

"That's not his decision," Remo said in a low voice as he stalked into the room. Fabiano gave a terse nod, exchanging a look with his Capo that I couldn't read. Then he walked out without another look at me.

"Trying to talk my Enforcer into betraying me?"

"Unfortunately, everyone I've met so far is loyal to you." It was true and they couldn't even blame it on fear. Despite his reputation, the people close to Remo seemed to tolerate him, maybe even liked him. Remo left the door open as well, and he kept a few arm lengths between us. Something about him was off, and it set my alarm bells off.

"Let me talk to my brother," I said. I couldn't bring myself to say please.

Remo tilted his head, his expression assessing. "What about Danilo? Don't you want a chat with your fiancé? After all, he'd be your husband by now if it weren't for me."

"Samuel. I want to talk to Samuel."

His eyes narrowed briefly before they traveled the length of me. "What do I get in return for allowing you to talk to him?"

"I'm not a whore," I snapped. "I won't give you *that* in return for a call."

Remo approached slowly, like a predator. "You will give it to me for free?"

"Hell will freeze over before that happens."

He backed me into the wall. The violent vibe he gave off was even stronger than usual, and it was starting to make me nervous. I wasn't sure what had him on edge like that, but I knew to be wary.

"Isn't your brother worth a kiss?" he taunted.

"My brother wouldn't want me to give away a kiss for him."

"You already gave away your first kiss, Angel. What do a few more matter?" His dark eyes raked over my face until they lingered on my lips.

I scowled. "One kiss and you'll let me talk to my brother? Tomorrow?"

"One kiss," he agreed with a dark smile.

I pushed to my tiptoes, gripped his neck to pull him further down, and smashed my lips against his for a second before drawing back. "There you go. One kiss."

Remo shook his head, his face still close to mine. "That wasn't a kiss."

"You didn't stipulate the details of the kiss. I kissed you. Now fulfill your part of the bargain."

Remo cupped my face, caging me in with his body. "I showed you what I consider a kiss. I won't settle for less."

I glowered, but trying to stare Remo down was a ridiculous notion.

"Not brave enough?" he murmured.

I shivered at the low vibrato of his voice. Gripping his shirt, I tugged him down violently. Our mouth clashed but Remo held himself still, waiting for me to make the next move, daring me to do it. With a burst of indignation, my tongue nudged his lips and despite the heat rising into my cheeks, I held his dark gaze. My moment of control was ripped from me the second Remo deepened the kiss. He took the lead, demanded with his mouth and tongue for me to surrender. I had trouble keeping up. His scent and heat sucked me in, made my body spring to life in the most terrifying way possible.

Remo's hand touched my waist and then it moved up, closer to my breast. My reaction was instinctual, instilled by defense training with Samuel; I jerked my knee up. Remo's reaction was quick, his hand shooting down, but the momentum still made my knee graze his groin. He growled and I stilled, frozen with fear because of the look in his eyes. He breathed harshly, his gaze burning me with its intensity. Yet a flicker of relief filled me because I doubted I'd have found the strength to end the kiss.

"You shouldn't touch someone without their explicit permission or they might try to defend themselves," I said, because obviously I didn't know when to shut up.

"I don't ask permission for anything," Remo said sharply.

Despite my hands trembling, I pressed my palms against Remo's chest and pushed. He didn't budge, cocking one dark eyebrow. I held his gaze, and he took a deliberate step back, finally letting me free. My eyes darted down to his hands, curled to white-knuckled fists at his side then back up to his face. I shivered at the harshness of his expression and without thinking about it, I looked away and walked toward the window, bringing space between us.

He followed and his breath fanned over my ear as he leaned down. "I'd better leave now. Tonight isn't a good time to be around you. Goodnight, Angel."

His fingers brushed my hair away, and he pressed a kiss to the side of my neck, the tender spot between my shoulder and throat, making me jump in surprise. I clapped a hand over the spot, stunned by the tingling.

The door closed with a soft click then the lock turned. I shuddered out a breath and braced myself against the windowsill. Would Remo allow me to talk to Sam now? I should have asked, but I had been too overwhelmed by Remo's presence.

This game was getting dangerous in more than one sense. The only question was who would lose control of it first?

Remo

I stayed in front of Serafina's door, fingers clutching the handle in a death grip. I had half a mind to walk back in and see how much else I could coerce from Serafina with her brother, but I resisted the urge. Taking a deep breath, I leaned my forehead against the wood. That was how Nino found me.

I saw his legs out of the corner of my eye, and even without looking up, I could imagine the analyzing expression he was giving me. "How did things go with Adamo and Harper?"

I straightened and as predicted, Nino was regarding me with that quiet scrutiny that drove me up the wall. "Dante called. He wants another word with you. He seems to be losing his patience," he said.

"He won't risk an attack, not if it means I could kill Serafina."

Nino inclined his head. "Still … we should start making demands."

"Maybe you're right. Think of some ridiculous demand he won't possibly agree to; I'm not done playing yet. Ask him for Indianapolis or Minneapolis. I don't care."

A muscle in Nino's jaw tightened, a clear sign of his annoyance with me. "Alright. I'll send him a message."

"Tell him that I'm allowing Serafina a video chat with her brother tomorrow. He better be ready at eight a.m."

"You're cutting it close. Adamo's initiation starts at eleven."

"Enough time," I said then frowned. "You didn't tell me what happened with Harper."

"As expected, she used Adamo to supply her with drugs. The moment he told her he couldn't give her anything, she dropped him and admitted to fucking around with that other guy. Adamo is crushed. He takes these things too personal."

"Is he angry?"

"Angry at Mason, not at the girl."

I smiled. "That's enough. We still need someone Adamo can deal with tomorrow. Tell Fabiano I want him to bring Mason to the initiation."

Nino looked thoughtful. "Maybe it'll work. Jealousy and a broken heart are good motivators for brutal acts."

"Where is he?"

"Outside, smoking. I allowed him one cigarette."

"I'll go talk to him."

"I'm not sure he's the best dialogue partner at the moment."

"Nor am I."

"That's the problem," Nino said with a twisted smile.

"Go fuck your wife and stop pissing me off."

"You haven't been to the Sugar Trap since you brought Serafina here."

I sighed. "Maybe I'm not in the mood for whore pussy. I'm taking a few celibate days."

"You haven't done that since you started fucking."

"Stop analyzing everything, Nino," I growled and stalked off before I punched him.

I found Adamo on a lounge chair beside the pool, scowling into the dark, the cigarette dangling from his mouth giving his face an eerie glow. He didn't look up when I sank down beside him.

He took a deep drag of his cigarette, and it took every ounce of my almost non-existent control to not rip the fucking thing out of his mouth.

"I hate it," he muttered.

"Hate what?"

"Hate that with our last name people always want something from us."

"You shouldn't have tried to make friends by giving them drugs," I said. "We're not Santa Claus. We're selling the shit, not handing it out for free, and we never fucking take the shit ourselves."

"When will people ever like me for myself and not for what I can give them? They only see my name. That's all they care about."

"You've got people who care about you," I said roughly.

Adamo glanced at me.

"You've cost me millions so far with the cars you crashed and the drugs you let disappear. What would I do to anyone who stole something from me?"

"You'd torture and kill them," Adamo said quietly.

"I would and have." I paused. "But here you are, safe and sound, and you know you will remain that way until the day I take my last fucking breath."

Adamo lowered his head.

"Tomorrow you're going to swear loyalty to the Camorra. You will take the oath and the tattoo," I ordered.

"I don't give a fuck about the Camorra," Adamo whispered, and my anger rose, but then he spoke up again. "But I will swear loyalty to you because even if I hate what you, Nino, and Savio do, you are my family."

I straightened up then looked down at my brother for another moment. "Don't waste your energy on another thought of that girl. She's worthless. There are many more girls out there. She used you. Maybe now you'll start using them as well."

Adamo frowned. "I can't help how I feel." He swallowed audibly. "She's been fucking him the entire time."

"So what? You fucked her. He fucked her. You move on."

"I didn't," he said quietly. "We didn't get that far."

"Please tell me she at least gave you head," I muttered.

Embarrassment flashed across Adamo's face. I sank back down.

"Can I ask you a question?" he said quietly.

I had a feeling this was turning into the sex talk I'd avoided with Savio by throwing him a freebie with two whores; he gladly accepted.

"How long does it take to get control?"

"Control?" I echoed. I didn't bother controlling myself during sex, but I had a feeling Adamo didn't mean that kind of control.

Adamo tossed his cigarette to the ground. "To hold back, you know? I kind of ... you know ..."

"Shot your cum the second she put her mouth on you," I provided.

Adamo grimaced and looked away. "Yeah."

I chuckled.

Adamo scowled. "Don't make fun of me."

"I'm not," I said. "You've never been with a girl, so it's pretty normal."

"Did it happen to you too?"

"No, but I fucked out of anger. That gave me better control."

"I bet Mason and Harper had a good laugh behind my back," he said miserably, then added in a low voice, "I want to kill him. Mason."

"I know."

Adamo's eyes widened. "You're going to make me kill him tomorrow."

"You will have to kill someone in front of our soldiers. It's either him or someone you don't hate. Mason is a dead man either way. He can die by your hand or Fabiano's."

I regarded my brother. He was biting his lip, staring down at the pool. "I'll do it." I touched his shoulder, and for once he didn't try to shake me off.

TEN

Serafina

I WAS STILL IN BED WHEN THE LOCK TURNED AND DIDN'T HAVE TIME TO sit up before Remo stepped inside the room.

Feeling vulnerable lying in the bed, I pushed into a sitting position. Remo regarded me with an intent expression. I was only in a chemise and shorts and was acutely aware of how little the fabric covered. Swallowing my nerves, I got out of bed, not wanting to show weakness. Remo's eyes followed my every move, lingering on my breasts. My body betrayed me as my nipples hardened in the cool air.

"I'm fairly sure God designed your body to drive men into insanity," Remo said darkly.

Stifling the excited thrill Remo's words sent through me, I retorted, "You believe in God?"

"No. I don't. But looking at you, I could turn into a believer."

I huffed. "There's a cozy warm place in Hell reserved just for you."

"I've burned before."

I slanted him a look. He'd said the same words before, and I wondered what exactly he meant by it.

"You have a video call with your brother in five minutes, so you better hurry."

I didn't have a bathrobe to pull over my clothes, so I reached for a dress but Remo shook his head. "Stay as you are." He grabbed my arm then paused, dark eyes roaming over me.

"I thought we were in a hurry?"

"You are. I'm not. I don't give a fuck if you talk to your brother or not."

Despite his words, he led me out of the room, through the hallway and downstairs.

"Again in your torture chamber?" I asked, shivering violently when my bare feet hit the first stone step leading down into the basement. I wasn't sure how the floor could be that cold when outside the sun was blazing.

I cried out when Remo lifted me in his arms. "Don't want you to catch a cold. That would be a shame. I'll have to ask Kiara to shop for clothes that fit you."

I was frozen in his hold. "You can send me back to Minneapolis. I have enough clothes there."

"I think Danilo wants you in Indianapolis, Angel, or have you forgotten?"

I realized I had. My wedding seemed so very far away, and it was the last thing on my mind.

Remo chuckled joylessly. His stupid manipulations were getting to me. How was he doing it?

I didn't answer his question because he knew. My traitorous body mourned the loss of his warmth when he set me down on my feet in the cell where he'd recorded the last message to my family. I wrapped my arms around myself, suddenly overwhelmed by the memories. My gaze flitted to my wound. With the Tylenol I barely noticed its existence and it was scabbing over. It wasn't the pain or the cut that bothered me. It was the memory of Samuel's and Dad's expressions when they'd seen me in Remo's hands. They were suffering more than I did, and that was the worst thing about all this.

Remo stepped up to me, his body a warm presence at my back, and he took my wrist, lifting it so he could inspect my wound. His thumb lightly traced my skin. He leaned in. "I won't cut you again, Angel. Don't be afraid."

That wasn't what I was scared of most. "You won't?" I asked curiously, tilting my head so I could evaluate his face. Why would Remo say something like that?

Remo cuts deep. Hits hard. Kills brutally.

Remo dropped my wrist, something in his expression shifting, his guard slipping in place. "Time for your call with Samuel."

He went to the screen on the table and turned it on followed by the loudspeakers. I moved closer when Samuel's face appeared. My heart clenched violently at the sight. His hair was a mess, his expression haunted, and dark circles spread under his eyes. He probably hadn't slept at all since my kidnapping.

Guilt crashed over me for not being as bad off as they all imagined. I could tell Samuel was struggling to keep his expression controlled. He wouldn't show weakness in front of his enemy.

"Sam," I said quietly, my voice shaking.

"Fina," he got out. His eyes scanned me and the skimpy outfit I was in. He swallowed, a muscle in his jaw flexing. "How are you?"

"I'm okay," I said. His brows drew together in disbelief.

"How much longer she stays that way depends on your Capo's willingness to answer my demands," Remo added.

What demands?

Samuel began shaking. I touched my palm to my chest, letting him know that he was in my heart. He mirrored the gesture then his eyes hardened as they settled on my forearm. "How bad is it?"

"Not bad," I said.

I could see he didn't believe me. He thought I was trying to protect him. I could feel Remo's eyes on us the entire time, but I tried to ignore him.

"How are Mom and Dad doing?"

Samuel's expression was cautious. He couldn't tell me everything with Remo close by. "They are worried about you."

"How's Sofia doing?" I whispered, fighting back the tears.

Samuel's eyes flitted to Remo, and I stiffened in turn. I shouldn't have mentioned my sister in front of him.

Remo made an impatient sound. "I don't kidnap children, don't worry."

"You only kidnap innocent women," Samuel snarled.

Remo pressed up behind me, and Samuel's expression switched from fury to dread. "Who says she's still innocent?"

Samuel jerked. Remo gripped my hip in warning, but I didn't care.

"It's not like that," I said fiercely.

Samuel's eyes found mine, searching, and a flicker of relief showed on his face.

Remo grasped my chin, turned my head, and gave me a harsh kiss. I froze in shock, not able to believe he was doing this in front of my brother.

He released me abruptly. "How innocent she returns to you depends on your cooperation. Tell your uncle that, Samuel."

I twisted out of Remo's hold and looked at Samuel, my cheeks heating up in embarrassment.

"Take me in her stead. I'll exchange myself for her."

"No!" I shouted desperately, but Samuel wasn't looking at me. I whirled around on Remo, wide eyed. A cruel smile played on his face. I caught his gaze. "No," I said forcefully. His eyes lingered on my lips then dipped lower before they locked on mine once more and relief coursed through me. Remo wouldn't exchange me for my twin. He wouldn't release me. Not before he got what he wanted. I wasn't sure what that was, but I had a horrible feeling it wasn't something my uncle could give him.

"Serafina is worth too much, I'm afraid. Time to say goodbye."

I turned back to my twin. "I love you, Sam," I whispered. Words I'd never said to him when other people were around because emotions didn't belong in public, but I didn't care anymore. Let Remo see how much I loved my family.

A haunted look passed Samuel's face, and he surprised me by rasping, "And I love you, Fina. I'll save you." For him to say those words in front of another man, his enemy, he must be even more worried for my life than I thought.

The tears spilled over then. Remo walked past me and switched the screen off. I didn't hold them back. I let the tears flow freely, not caring if Remo saw them. Remo watched me with narrowed eyes. Maybe my emotions annoyed him. I couldn't care less.

"I thought Danilo was the man who owned your heart, but now I see I was wrong."

I wiped at my eyes. "He's my twin. I've never been without him. I would walk through fire for him."

Remo nodded slowly. "I believe you."

Remo

Nino, Adamo, Savio, and I drove to the initiation together. My thoughts kept straying to Serafina. I'd locked her in the bedroom again, and Fabiano would keep an eye on her and Kiara while we were gone. I would have preferred to have him at the initiation as well, but someone needed to protect Kiara and make sure Serafina didn't do something stupid. I doubted she'd find a way out of the bedroom, but if anyone could do it, then it was her.

Nino was driving and Savio and Adamo sat in the back. It reminded me of the past, the months we'd spent on the run from the Russians, part of the Camorra, and the other mob families. We'd been on the road almost constantly, never staying anywhere for long, and still our pursuers almost got us a couple of times.

Nino slanted a look at me as if he, too, was remembering those days.

We pulled up in front of one of our casinos on the outskirts of Vegas, where the initiation would take place. The parking lot was crowded with limousines. My soldiers were already there. I got out first, not waiting for the bellhop to open my door, and stalked inside the casino with my brothers on my heels. The place had been closed since yesterday for the occasion. Inside familiar faces greeted me. Some of my men were nursing drinks at the bar. Others were engaged in conversation with each other. None of them were playing poker or roulette, even though the croupiers were there just in case. They knew it was a test.

An alcoholic shouldn't run a bar. And my underbosses and captains better not gamble or do drugs. Lower soldiers had more leeway.

Eleven Underbosses and their Consiglieres were invited for the initiation. Most of them were barely older than me. When I'd taken over power, I removed most of the old Underbosses and chose their young ambitious heirs or bastards. Similar to me and my relationship with my father, only a few of them had been sad to see their fathers gone. Only three cities fell under the rule of older Underbosses, who were loyal to the bone.

I shook their hands before we gathered in the center of the room. I put a hand on Adamo's shoulder. He stood tall, for once his expression not betraying his emotions, but I could feel his tension under my palm. "Today we've come here to initiate my brother Adamo."

The men nodded a greeting at him. They had all dressed in suits for the occasion, and my brothers and I had followed the tradition of dressing up. "As with every initiate, blood has to be paid."

Nino dragged a struggling Mason toward us. Fabiano had locked him in the utility closet. Adamo tensed under my hand, and I squeezed his shoulder lightly.

Nino threw the asshole to the ground. He wasn't in school anymore. A drop out, who'd managed to gather a posse of well-off, much younger kids around himself and introduced them to drugs. His father had been a Made Man before I disposed of him in my claim for power, but the son was even more useless than the father.

His mouth was covered by tape, and his eyes were wide with terror. I handed Adamo one of my guns. As an initiate, he wasn't allowed to bring his own guns. Adamo pointed the barrel at Mason's head. I was close enough to see the slight tremor of his hands. I squeezed his shoulder again, encouragement as much as a reminder not to show weakness, and then he pulled the trigger.

Mason slumped forward dead. Adamo shuddered under my hand and slowly lowered the gun, his expression hard, but in his eyes I could see the hint of conflict. It would get easier with time. The men nodded their heads in approval, and Adamo met my gaze.

"It's time to get the tattoo."

Nino came forward with the tattoo equipment, and Savio carried a chair over. Adamo sat down, rolled up his sleeve, and held out his forearm.

"I think it's time for some entertainment while we wait for Nino to finish the tattoo."

I clapped my hands, and one of the bartenders opened another door. A row of our most beautiful whores streamed into the room, half naked. Most of my men took me up on my offer, but a few chose drinks over female entertainment.

I stepped over to my brothers. Nino was still outlining the knife. He was quick and accurate. I wouldn't want anyone else do our tattoos. Even Savio stayed beside Adamo, but his eyes strayed through the room to look for a whore for later. Adamo's jaw was clenched as he watched Nino ink him. The kill bothered him more than it had Savio, Nino, or myself, but like all of us, he would get over it eventually.

"Do you want a drink, Adamo?" Savio asked.

Adamo looked up in surprise. "Sure."

"Whiskey, neat?"

Adamo gave a nod then winced when Nino started filling in the pupil of the eye. Savio came back with four glasses on a tray and handed one to each of us. I raised my glass. "Us against the world."

"Us against the world."

We downed the whiskey, and Adamo started coughing, not used to hard liquor. Nino lifted the needle with a frown. "I'll mess this up if you keep moving." He set his empty glass down and waited for Adamo to calm himself before he continued.

When the tattoo was done, Nino stood and I called my men over. The whores remained in the back. They knew they weren't welcome. Adamo stared down at his inked arm. I held out the arm with my tattoo. Adamo closed his fingers over it, and I closed mine over his, causing him to hiss with pain. "Will you be my eye?"

"I will."

"Will you be my knife?"

"I will."

"Will you bleed and die for our cause?"

"I will," Adamo said firmly.

"Today you give me your life. It's mine to decide over till death sets you free. Welcome to the Camorra, Adamo."

I released him and stepped back. Nino clapped his shoulder, and Savio did the same. Then my soldiers welcomed my brother into our world. Nobody paid any attention to the corpse lying in its own blood on the ground. The cleaners would remove it later.

Alcohol flowed more freely. Savio and Adamo sat together at the bar. A rare sight. Soon, two whores approached them, one latching on to Savio, the other pressed up to Adamo.

Adamo shook his head and after a moment, Savio disappeared with the two whores through the door behind the bar.

Nino joined me where I leaned against a roulette table. I'd exchanged a few words with each of my Underbosses. Most of them would return to their cities very soon, worried Dante might attack after all.

"I'm surprised you're not fucking a whore."

My eyes strayed to the gathered women, but none of them got my attention.

"I've fucked all of them before. It's getting boring."

Nino raised his eyebrows but didn't comment. "We should go to Adamo."

I nodded but we both stopped when one of the whores, C.J., sat down beside him at the bar and they began talking.

"Maybe she can talk him into losing his virginity," I muttered.

Nino shrugged. "She's a decent woman. He could do worse for his first time."

I gave him a look. "Can you cut the compassionate bullshit?"

He smirked. "It's got nothing to do with compassion. C.J. is a good, a logical choice for Adamo. She's skilled and will try to please him. Plus, she will pretend he's a good fuck. Pure logic."

"You enjoy pissing me off with your logic."

"It's quite satisfying, yes."

I shook my head at my brother. "One of these day, you, Savio, and Adamo will be my death."

"The only thing that will kill you is your lack of control."

My thoughts drifted back to Serafina, the sight of her in the skimpy night-clothes, the way her nipples had puckered in the cold. Fuck control. Fuck patience. I'd never wanted anything as much as Serafina, and yet I couldn't have her.

Nino shook his head. "Exchange the girl for Scuderi before you're in too deep."

"I'll exchange her the moment she lets me deep inside her."

"Telling you 'I told you so' one day will be as satisfying as annoying you with my logic."

"It's my game, Nino. I'm the best player on the field. I will win."

"There won't be any winners, Remo."

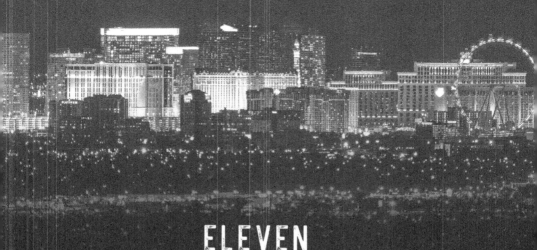

ELEVEN

Serafina

IT WAS AROUND LUNCHTIME WHEN SOMEONE KNOCKED. I HADN'T SEEN Remo since he'd brought me back to my room after my call with Samuel yesterday. Savio brought me breakfast in the morning without a word. He was probably still pissed.

Kiara opened the door with a shy smile and two bags in her hands. "I bought clothes for you. I hope they fit."

She stepped in followed by Nino. I hopped off the windowsill. My limbs were starting to feel sluggish from lack of use. I'd worked out almost daily before my kidnapping, and now all I did was sit around.

"I assume that means my stay won't be ending anytime soon," I said bitterly.

Kiara sighed. "I don't know."

My eyes moved over to Nino, who looked his usual stoic self, not that I had expected an answer from him.

Kiara held the bags out to me. "I got you sandals and a pair of sneakers. A few pairs of shorts, tops, and dresses. And underwear. I really hope I got the right size."

I took everything from her and went into the bathroom to change. The clothes fit, even if they weren't my usual style. I left the bathroom wearing shorts and a top as well as the sandals.

"And?" Kiara asked hopefully.

"It all fits."

"Why don't you join me in the gardens? It's beautiful outside, and I'm sure you can't stand these walls anymore."

I frowned. "I can't stand this city, but I'd love to join you." My eyes darted to her husband whose expression had tightened at her suggestion. "If he allows it."

Nino gave a quick nod, but it was obvious that he didn't approve.

I followed Kiara outside while Nino walked behind us to keep an eye on me.

"Let me get the salad I prepared so we can have lunch," Kiara said when we arrived on the ground floor. I made a move to follow her into the kitchen but Nino grabbed my wrist, stopping me. "You'll stay here."

I wrenched my wrist out of his grip, narrowing my eyes at him. "Don't touch me."

Nino didn't as much as twitch. "If you think about trying something, don't. I don't want to hurt you, but if you hurt Kiara, I'll make it very painful for you."

"It's not her I want to hurt. She can't help being married to you."

"Indeed," Nino agreed.

Kiara returned with what looked like a Cesar's salad, her gaze flitting between her husband and me. "Everything okay?"

"Yes," I said, because even if I hated the Falcones, Nino's protectiveness was something I could respect.

Soon we were seated around the garden table, eating salad. My eyes began wandering the premises once more, but I knew there was no easy way to escape. To my surprise, Nino gave us more space. He settled on a chair in the shadows with a laptop he'd grabbed on the way out.

"I can't imagine how horrified you must have been when you were told Nino Falcone was going to be your husband," I said.

Kiara chewed slowly then swallowed. "It's was a shock at first. The Camorra doesn't have the best reputation."

I huffed. "They are monsters."

"The monsters in my family hurt me. I haven't experienced any kind of humiliation or pain in Las Vegas," she said firmly.

"Still. I was already nervous on my wedding day. I can't imagine how it must have been for you."

Kiara shrugged. "What about your fiancé? What kind of man is he?"

"He's Underboss of Indianapolis."

"That doesn't answer my question ... or maybe it does."

"I didn't know him very well," I said when Remo stepped outside. "But I have every intention of getting to know Danilo better once I'm finally married to him."

Remo gave me a hard look. "I'm sure he'll be a delight."

I narrowed my eyes. "He is."

"I'm taking Serafina for a walk around the property," he said to Kiara. She nodded and he turned to me. "Come on."

Despite my annoyance at his commanding tone, I stood, glad to move my legs. Remo's eyes scanned me from head to toe as he led me past the pool. "Kiara got you clothes."

"I need to workout," I said, ignoring his comment. "I can't sit around all day. I'm going crazy. Unless that's what you want, you need to let me run on a treadmill."

Remo shook his head. "No need for a treadmill. I run every morning at seven. You can join me."

I allowed myself a quick scan of his body. Of course he worked out. His body was all muscle. I knew he and his brothers were into cage fighting and running was a good way to improve your stamina. "That sounds reasonable."

Remo's mouth twitched. "I'm glad you think so."

"What did you demand of my uncle for my freedom?" I asked him after a while.

"Minneapolis."

I jerked to a stop. "That's ridiculous. My uncle won't give you any part of his territory. Even my father wouldn't give up his city to save me."

Remo's smile darkened. "I think your father would gladly give me his city if it were up to him."

I swallowed. I didn't want to think of my family. Not when Remo was watching me closely. I'd cried enough in front of him yesterday. "You know Dante won't meet your demands."

Remo nodded.

"Then why make them?"

"This is a game of chess, Angel, like you said. I need to bring my pieces in position before I strike."

Remo sounded so awfully sure of himself, it made me worry that maybe he'd really win in the end.

I turned away from him and continued walking. "I'm surprised Luca Vitiello agreed to your plan. I used to think the Famiglia was honorable, but apparently they are stooping as low as the Camorra now."

Remo touched my shoulder and pulled me to a stop. "Tell me, Serafina, what's the difference between an arranged marriage with Danilo and being my captive?"

I stared at him incredulously, but before I could deliver a reply, he spoke again.

"You didn't choose Danilo. You will be given to him like an unwilling captive and the ring around your finger will be your shackle, the marriage your cage." His dark eyes held triumph as if I couldn't possibly argue my defense. My eyes darted to the ring around my finger. Its sight didn't hold the same pride and excitement it used to.

"You will have to surrender to his body, whether you desire him or not, and your body and soul are at his mercy. Tell me again, how is your arranged marriage different to being my captive?"

Remo leaned down, holding my gaze the entire time, and I didn't step back. His lips grazed my chin, then my cheek, and finally my mouth. "Your 'no' means nothing in a marriage. Do you call that freedom?"

Pressing my lips together, I glared at him, too proud to admit his words made sense. Remo had a way to twist things the way he wanted them until you believed they were the truth.

"Did you ever fantasize about Danilo? Do you desire him?"

I glared. "That's none of your business."

Remo shook his head as he stroked my throat, then my collarbone with his rough fingertips. "You didn't. Your mind said yes to him, and you hoped your body would follow." His fingers on my skin made thinking straight difficult, but I didn't want to give him the satisfaction of pulling back. "I wonder how long it'll take for your mind to say yes to me because your body has been screaming yes from the very first moment."

I ripped away from him. "You are insane. Neither my body nor my mind say yes to any part of you, Remo. I think being the undisputed ruler of Las Vegas has made you a megalomaniac."

Remo's dark eyes sent another shiver down my spine, and I stalked off, running as much from his terrifying expression as the weight of the truth. Despite my hate for the Camorra's Capo, his kisses and closeness wreaked havoc within me.

I suspected it was due to my captivity, a form of Stockholm Syndrome. I made sure to keep my distance as Remo led me back to my room, and he didn't try to touch me again. Before he locked me in, I asked, "What do you really want, Remo?"

He regarded me with unsettling intensity. "You know what I want."

"Body and soul," I muttered.

One corner of his mouth lifted. "Body and soul."

He closed the door and I was left with the whirlwind of thoughts in my head. I needed to figure out a way to get away. Maybe my family was already planning some insane hostage rescue. Samuel surely was. If not openly then definitely in his head. There was no way anyone would survive an attack on Camorra territory. And I didn't kid myself into thinking that Remo would release me any time soon. He was making demands, but he didn't want them to be fulfilled. Yet.

Remo

As promised, I picked Serafina up at seven so she could run with me. Usually I preferred to do my morning run alone, but I couldn't resist her presence.

Serafina had put on shorts, a T-shirt, and sneakers.

She followed me quietly through the house but stopped when I led her toward the driveway. "Where are we going?"

"We're going running, like I said. Did you think I do my laps in the garden?"

I opened the door to my Bugatti SUV for her, and she got in without another word. I got behind the wheel and pulled down the driveway, feeling her eyes on me. I enjoyed her confusion.

I took us to a trail in a nearby canyon where I'd run before. Soon it would be too warm, but this early in the morning the temperature was perfect for running. Serafina followed me out of the car and looked around the gravel parking lot. We were the only people around. Her eyes were assessing and attentive. She'd try something, and I had to admit I couldn't wait for it.

We jogged beside each other for a while before she spoke up. "Aren't you worried I'll run?"

"I caught you once before."

"I was stuck in my wedding dress, so I was too slow."

"I'll always catch you, Angel."

After thirty minutes, we stopped for a drinking break. I could tell that Serafina was scouting the terrain. Taking a deep gulp of water, I watched as she got down on her haunches and laced up her sneakers again. When she straightened, I knew from the tension in her limbs that she was about to do something. She threw sand at my face and actually managed to get some of it into my eyes. Through blurry vision, I saw her dashing off. Chuckling, despite my burning eyes, I took chase. I'd dealt with worse.

Serafina was quicker than last time, and she didn't stay on the trail, which was a huge risk on her part. If she got lost around here, she'd die of dehydration before she found her way back to civilization. I picked up my own pace. Serafina jumped to avoid rocks and practically flew over the ground. It was a beautiful sight. So much more beautiful than having her locked in a room.

Eventually, I caught up with her. Her legs were much shorter, and she was less muscular. When I was close enough, I slung my arm around her waist like last time. We both lost our balance from the impact and fell. I landed on my back with Serafina on top of me. She rammed her knee into my stomach and kicked to get out my hold. Before she could do real damage, I rolled over and pressed her into the ground with my weight, her wrists pushed up above her head.

"Gotcha," I murmured, panting, dripping sweat.

Serafina's chest heaved, her eyes indignant and furious. "You enjoy the chase."

"Actually, I don't," I said in a low voice, bringing our lips closer. "But with you I do."

"You knew I'd run," she muttered.

"Of course. You are meant to be free. Which makes me wonder why you allow someone like Danilo to cage you."

She wriggled under me. "Let me go."

"I'm enjoying being on top of you and between your lithe legs." I rocked my pelvis slightly.

She stiffened. "Don't."

I licked a droplet of sweat off her throat before I pushed off her and stood. Serafina ignored my outstretched hand and stumbled to her feet. Her hair had fallen out of her ponytail, and she was covered in dirt and sweat.

"I prefer you like this."

She frowned. "Dirty?"

"Untamed. Seeing you in that white atrocity can't compare. Too perfect, too groomed, too fake. I bet Danilo would have loved it, though."

She didn't say anything, and I knew part of my words got through to her. My eyes were drawn to her forearm, which she was rubbing absentmindedly. A small part of the cut had opened again and was bleeding.

A flicker of guilt caught me off guard. It wasn't an emotion I entertained very often. I took her arm and inspected the wound. Dirt had gotten in it. "We need to clean that to prevent infection."

Her blue eyes searched my face, but I had trouble reading the expression on hers. I led her back to the car. It was getting hotter and after the chase, we both needed a shower. I took a fresh bottle of water from the trunk and poured it over Serafina's wound, cleaning it carefully with my fingertips. She winced occasionally but didn't say anything. "The silent treatment isn't your usual style," I commented.

"You don't know me."

I smirked. "I know you better than most people. Better than Danilo."

She didn't contradict me.

"Hate can set you free," I said.

"So can love," she said. "But I doubt you'd understand."

Serafina was silent on the way back to the mansion, her gaze distant as she peered out of the side window.

I returned her to her room, knowing she had a lot to think about before I headed into my own room for a shower. When I came down into the game room later, Savio was lounging on the sofa, typing on his phone. Upon spotting me, he set it down and grinned.

"Nino isn't happy that you took the bitch running."

I sank down beside my brother. "It offends his logic."

Savio laughed. "But honestly, Remo, he has a point. That girl is unpredictable."

"That makes her all the more fun," I said.

Savio gave me a curious look. "You're enjoying this more than I thought. And you haven't even fucked her ... or have you?"

"No, I haven't. Serafina is a surprising challenge."

"Too much work for my taste," Savio said with a shrug. "I prefer girls who shut up when I tell them to, who suck my dick when I want it. Less hassle."

"Eventually, you've had it all. You've fucked in every position possible, have done all the kinky shit you can think of. It becomes more difficult to get the thrill from the beginning."

He leaned forward on his knees. "You're not thinking of keeping her ... are you?"

"No."

I called Dante in the afternoon. He picked up after the second ring, his voice cold and hard but with an underlying tension that gave me a thrill.

"Dante, I wanted to ask when you were going to fulfill my demand."

"I won't, just as you intended. I don't have time for your games, Remo. This is between us, between you and me. Why don't we meet in person, Capo to Capo, and settle this like men."

"You want to duel me? How archaic of you, Dante. You didn't strike me as the primitive type."

"I'll gladly convince you of the contrary."

I almost agreed because the idea of shoving my knife over and over into the cold fish was too fucking enticing. Fighting Dante would have been a high-light. Since cutting Luca into bite-sized pieces was out of the question for now,

Dante was the opponent I longed for. There was only one thing I wanted more than killing Dante: having Serafina in every way possible and destroy the Outfit through her.

"We will have to postpone our duel to a later point, Dante. For now, I have demands I want you to fulfill if you want to have your niece returned to her family in one piece."

"I won't negotiate with you, Remo. You won't get an inch of my territory. Now say what you really want. We both know what it is."

I doubted he knew what I really wanted. Maybe only Nino did. "And what do I want?"

"You want my Consigliere. Fabiano is your Enforcer and I assume the deal you struck with Vitiello entailed your promise to deliver Scuderi so you can all have him dismembered together."

"I doubt Luca will be part of Scuderi's disembodiment. He'd rather chop you into pieces, Dante."

"Vitiello isn't the ally you think he is. His Famiglia is prone to betrayal. It's unwise of you to make me your enemy."

"Dante, we've been enemies from the moment I claimed power. And the moment your fucking soldiers breached my territory, it got personal. I don't need Luca as an ally as long as I know his hatred for you trumps his hatred for me."

"One day his and your rashness will be your downfall."

"Very likely," I growled. "But until that happens, your conscience will have to live with Serafina's gradual downfall."

I hung up. With every day that Serafina was in my hands, my position got stronger.

TWELVE

Serafina

THE NEXT FEW DAYS AFTER MY ATTEMPT AT RUNNING AWAY, I FELL INTO A strange routine. Remo picked me up for a run in the morning. Sometimes I wondered if he wanted me to risk escaping again because the chase gave him a thrill, but I didn't waste my energy on it. Remo was too strong and fast. I had to beat him with wit. Unfortunately, he was as intelligent as he was cruel. He could twist my words faster than I thought possible, and I occasionally caught myself enjoying our strange debates.

I didn't have to hold back when I was around Remo. I didn't try to present my best side to him like I had done with Danilo because I didn't care about his approval. I was myself, unfiltered, careless, and strangely enough Remo seemed to get a sick kick out of it. The Capo was a mystery to me. He hadn't tried to torture me or force himself on me like I'd expected, and I couldn't help but be wary because Remo's motives were cruel.

"Once I set you free, you'll return to Danilo like a well-trained carrier pigeon." Remo said as we jogged along the canyon trail one day.

"Your bird analogies are starting to get old," I muttered. I was glad Remo didn't know Dad called me dove. He'd only use it to his advantage.

"But they are so very fitting, Angel."

I slanted a look at him. He had a strange smile on his face. His shirt clung to his body with sweat and showed the outline of his muscles and his gun holsters. "What are you in your ornithology scheme? The vulture waiting for the poor pigeon to drop out of the sky so you can tear into her?"

Remo let out a deep chuckle, which sent a shocking shiver down my spine. I sped up, trying to force my body into submission. "I don't think you'll ever fall from the sky. I'll have to snatch you out of the air like an eagle."

I snorted, not caring if it was an undignified sound. "You are insane."

He fell silent, easily following my faster pace. Remo was fit to the point of admiration, I had to give him that.

After we returned to the car, we shared a bottle of water. "Why are you doing this?"

He cocked one eyebrow. "Giving you water?"

"Treating me decently."

He smiled darkly. "Why do you sound almost disappointed?"

Part of me was because I knew the man in front of me was ruthless and cruel to the very core. More monster than man. The weaker part was relieved and didn't want to question his motives. "When will the torture begin?"

Remo propped his arm up against the roof of the car and stared down at me. "Who says the torture hasn't already begun? Just because I'm not torturing you doesn't mean I'm not torturing others through you."

I flinched. My family. They were suffering because they imagined the horrors I was going through, horrors that weren't taking place—yet.

"You are a monster," I bit out.

Remo leaned even closer, radiating heat and power, the scent of fresh sweat and his own forbidden aroma wrapping around me. I returned his gaze. Dark eyes. Monster eyes, but God help me, they always kept me frozen with their intensity.

"You know, Angel, I think you enjoy my monstrosity more than you want to admit."

I didn't have a chance for a comeback. Remo's lips crushed mine, his tongue sliding in, and my body reacted with a wave of heat. I clutched his shoulders, meeting his tongue with the same fervor.

Then realization struck me. I tried to shove him away, but Remo didn't budge. He wrapped his arms around me, molding our bodies together. Breathtaking, terrifying, intoxicating.

I bit down on his lower lip, but Remo didn't pull back. He growled into my mouth and tightened his hold, his kiss turning even harder. The taste of his blood swirled in my mouth, and I pulled away in equal disgust and sick fascination. Remo's mouth was covered with blood. He truly looked the monster then. A dark smile curled his lips, and I opened the door and got into the car, trying to catch my breath, trying to escape his overwhelming presence. I caught sight of my reflection in the rearview mirror and cringed. My lips, too, were red with Remo's blood. In that moment, I didn't look any less a monster than he did.

The moment Remo picked me up the next morning, I knew it wasn't for a run. For one, he was too early, and second he was only in his briefs. I tore my gaze away from his body.

"We need to record additional motivation for your uncle," Remo explained. "Come."

I perched on the bed, not moving an inch. Another recording?

When I didn't follow his command, Remo raised his eyebrows. "Come," he said with more force, and it took considerable effort to remain motionless. I stubbornly returned his gaze.

He stalked toward me and bent over me. "Maybe I'm being too lenient with you," he murmured, fingers nudging my chin up.

I smiled then gasped when Remo jerked me to my feet and threw me over his shoulder. His big warm hand rested on my butt as he carried me, and for a few moments I stilled in shock. More because of my body's reaction to the feel of Remo's palm than to my head hanging down over his shoulder. I started wiggling and Remo's squeezed my butt cheek in warning.

I rammed my elbow into his side, but apart from a sharp exhale, Remo didn't falter. "Let me down," I wheezed, horrified by the way my center tightened at the feel of Remo's hand on my backside. If he found out, I'd die on the spot.

Remo didn't set me down, however, until we were back in the cell. My head swam for a moment, but when my vision cleared I noticed the shackles hanging from a chain at the wall. Remo nudged me forward. "Arms up," he ordered.

"What?" I gasped out.

He didn't wait for me to comply. He grabbed my wrists and secured me. Confusion then terror shot through me. Maybe he was finally sick of torturing others when he had me to have fun with.

Remo leaned down and I shivered. His dark eyes roamed my face, and he gave a shake of his head. "Calm down. We need to give your family a show. I'll give that perfect throat a hickey for a few convincing photos, nothing else. Don't get your panties in a bunch over nothing, Angel."

"You want to make my family believe I'm shackled up in a cell?"

"Among other things," he murmured. His hands reached for the hem of my chemise and tugged hard. The fabric came apart until only the seam of the neckline held it together. My nipples hardened and Remo watched silently then released a harsh breath.

I swallowed. "These photos are fake. I'm not dangling from chains all day, and you're not ripping my clothes off," I muttered.

He smiled down at me. "Would you prefer if I didn't have to fake them, Angel?"

I swallowed again, goose bumps rising on my skin.

"I didn't think so," he said in a slightly rougher voice then carefully brushed my hair away from my throat. I held my breath when his lips were almost at my skin. "You smell so fucking sweet. Owning you one day will be the sweetest triumph of my life."

"You'll never own me."

Remo pressed his lips to my skin. Then his tongue darted out, licking along my pulse point. He sucked and nibbled on my throat, his fingers cupping my head, tilting it to the side. My eyes fluttered shut. The sensations were foreign and mesmerizing. Remo's mouth on my throat seemed to send shockwaves through my body, creating sensations I'd never experienced before. His warm body pressed into me, his scent flooding my nose.

I was motionless, stunned, confused by my body's reaction. How could my throat be such a sensitive spot of my body? How could it fill me with so much forbidden desire?

He pulled back but didn't straighten immediately, his face still close to my throat as he exhaled. When he finally stood, his dark eyes sent a new ripple through my body. His fingertips brushed over my tender throat, and my lips parted in a small exhale. Our eyes locked and one corner of his mouth lifted.

"Did you like that?"

"Of course not," I snapped.

"I thought you were a good liar."

My cheeks heated and I glared but didn't say anything because I wasn't sure if my next lie would be any more convincing.

"It's okay, Angel," Remo said in a low voice. "There are worse things than enjoying pleasure."

I wanted to lash out at him, but he wasn't even the main reason for my anger. I was furious at myself, enraged by my body for its reactions.

"I'm Danilo's," I said firmly.

Remo narrowed his eyes. "Are you reminding me or yourself?"

"I'm promised to him. I want him, not you."

"You can have an Underboss, someone who's learned to do another man's biding, or the Capo, a man who has men follow his command."

"I can have a monster or a man."

"Do you really think Danilo isn't a monster?"

"He isn't a monster like you."

Remo nodded. "He's a lesser monster. Who'd want to settle for less?"

"You don't even want me, Remo. All you want is to hold my fate over my family's head. Stop toying around."

He stepped back, turned around, and picked up his phone. "Look broken for a moment."

I glared.

"That's not the look we're going for." He waited. Then his jaw tightened, and he came toward me again, holding my chin. "I said it before, choose your battles wisely. I'm not a patient man nor a decent one."

He retreated and finally satisfied with my expression, he took a few photos. Guilt left a bitter taste in my mouth, but I wasn't sure how long it would take for my family to free me, if they succeeded at all, and I had to think of self-preservation even if I hated myself for it.

He unshackled me and I rubbed my wrists then touched my tender throat. Remo watched me. "I like seeing my mark on you."

I didn't say anything.

Later, I spent a long time staring at my reflection in the bathroom mirror. Remo had left his marks like he'd said. They were red and purple, and made me feel a wave of shame because of how my body had reacted. I wasn't sure what was wrong with me.

A knock drew me out of my reverie. Dragging myself away from the mirror, I went into the bedroom, where I found the youngest Falcone. He looked somewhat lost in the middle of my room.

"I have a few books and ice cream for you. It's one of the hottest days of the summer. I thought you could use cooling off," he said, holding up four books and a bowl filled with ice cream.

His gaze moved to my throat, and his brows drew together. He walked past me and put everything down on my nightstand before he shoved his hands into his pockets, looking awkward. My eyes lingered on the fresh tattoo on his forearm.

"You are a Made Man now."

He glanced down then nodded slowly. "I'm a Falcone."

I went over to the nightstand to take a look at everything.

"It's chocolate chip. It's all we got. Savio's got a sweet tooth. The rest of us not so much."

"So you gave me Savio's ice cream? He'll love that after the soup I threw at him."

Adamo burst out laughing. "I wish I could have been there. He's so full of himself. I bet his expression was hilarious." He sobered then cleared his throat.

I smiled. "He was shocked."

It was difficult to believe that Adamo was related to Remo. There was a slight resemblance, but Adamo's hair was curly and not as dark, and his eyes were a warmer brown. But the biggest difference was their personality. I picked up the bowl and pushed a spoonful of the sugary treat into my mouth before sinking down onto the bed.

Adamo came a bit closer and leaned against one of the posts. "I wasn't sure what kind of books you like, so I brought a memoir, a thriller, a romance, and a fantasy book. We don't have many new books. I don't think I'm allowed to give you my kindle. You could use it for other stuff."

I smiled. "It's okay." Despite my intention to hate on every Falcone, it was difficult not to like Adamo. "I think I'll pass on the thriller, though. I've had plenty of thrill in my life recently."

"I know," Adamo said quietly. He indicated my throat. "What happened there?"

Heat shot into my cheeks, and I allowed myself another taste of the ice cream to gather my thoughts.

Adamo watched me closely. "Did he hurt you?"

I considered lying, making up a brutal story to drive a wedge between the brothers, but for some reason I couldn't do it. "No. He's hurting my family by making them believe he's hurting me."

Relief flashed across Adamo's face, and for a second it annoyed me, but then I thought of Samuel and understood.

"You'll be united with them soon," he said.

I swallowed and nodded. Adamo touched my shoulder lightly then drew back. "Sorry I should have asked before touching you."

I shook my head. "How did you end up being so polite and kind when you are related to Remo? Were you raised by different parents?"

"Remo and Nino were raised by our parents, but Savio and I were mostly raised by Remo and Nino."

I stared. "They raised you?"

He nodded then rubbed the back of his head as if he realized he shouldn't have told me. "I should go."

I tried to imagine Remo raising a child. It blew my mind, especially since they all must have been on the run at the time.

Night had fallen and I was reading in bed, when suddenly the lights went out. I blinked into the unexpected darkness and climbed out of bed, putting the book down on the nightstand.

Following the trail of silvery moonlight, I glanced out of the window. The lights in the garden and every other window of the mansion that I could see were out as well. In the distance I could make out lights from other houses.

My pulse picked up. What was happening? My eyes searched the shadows of the perimeter, and then I saw two figures running across the lawn toward the house.

The Outfit. It had to be.

They had come to save me.

Euphoria pulsed through me, followed by fear. This was Remo's territory. The Falcones knew every inch of their property and the Outfit didn't. What if Samuel was among the attackers?

I clung to the windowsill, immobilized by terror at the thought. Dante and Dad would have never allowed my brother to come here. He was the heir to Minneapolis. He was too important for such a risky endeavor.

Maybe the dark gave the Outfit an advantage. Maybe it caught Remo and his brothers by surprise. Who knew how many of them were even in the mansion?

The lock of my room turned, and I faced the door. This was my chance to run. The Outfit didn't know where in the house I was being kept. They probably expected to find me in the basement. I needed to find them first. It would take too long for them to search every part of the mansion.

A tall figure stepped into the room. It was difficult to make out much, and it didn't matter who had entered. I attacked without hesitation, storming toward my opponent, hoping to ram my elbow into his stomach. Unfortunately, backlit by moonlight I was an easy target. My opponent sidestepped me then grabbed my shoulder and thrust me forward. I collided with the wall and a firm chest pressed against my back.

"No soup today?" Savio taunted, but his voice was filled with tension. I tried shoving away from the wall, but Savio didn't budge. "Do I have to knock you out or will you stop the fucking struggling?"

I jerked my head back, hoping to hit his nose, but he was taller than I remembered, and the back of my head collided with his chin.

"Fuck," he snarled. He lodged his arms around my chest and waist like Samuel had done in jest not too long ago, and despite my thrashing, he carried me through the room and shoved me into the bathroom. "I won't carry you into our panic room like that. Fuck it."

I whirled around to face him.

"Don't fucking move," he growled.

"The Outfit will kick your asses. I bet you shit your pants when the lights went out," I hissed.

Savio chuckled. "It was Nino who turned off the lights. We know every inch of this fucking house by heart. We don't need lights. By the way, our surveillance camera showed a guy with blond hair. I wonder who will kill him. Remo or Nino?"

I froze. Samuel?

Savio closed the bathroom door. I rushed forward and hammered my fists against the wood. "Let me out! Let me out!"

"Scream all you want," Savio said. "Maybe it attracts an Outfit fucker so I can have some fun as well."

I pressed my palms against the door and slowly sank down onto my knees. Savio had to be lying. Samuel wasn't here. If Remo or Nino got him in their hands ...

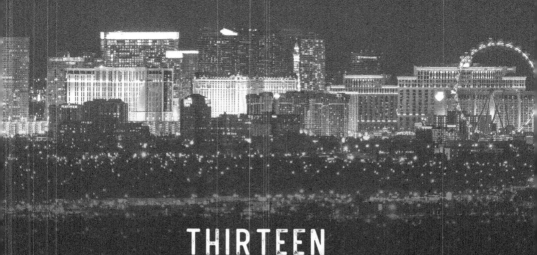

THIRTEEN

Remo

M Y BROTHERS AND I WERE WATCHING THE CAGE FIGHT OF SAVIO'S NEXT opponent. Kiara had already fallen asleep against Nino as usual. I doubted she ever watched more than a few seconds of a fight. Violence just wasn't in her nature.

"I can't wait to fight him," Savio said when his next opponent drop-kicked the other fighter into the cage. Not bad.

My phone lit up and so did the phones of my brothers. For a moment neither of us moved. I reached for it. An alarm had been raised. What the fuck? I opened the alert. Someone or something had touched the electric barbed wire at the top of the walls.

Nino was faster. He held up his phone with the live recording of the affected area. Four men had put a ladder over the fence, laid a wooden board over the electric wires, and climbed over the wall.

I stood, drawing my gun and a knife. Nino shook Kiara awake then turned to Adamo. "Take Kiara into the panic room. Shoot for the kill, no questions asked."

"What's the matter?" Kiara whispered. Nino shook his head, kissed her, then pushed her toward Adamo, who grabbed her hand and tugged her along, his own gun pulled.

"I'm going to turn off the lights on the premises," Nino said. "We can ambush them more easily that way."

I nodded. "Savio, go get Serafina. I want her in the panic room as well."

Savio frowned. "I want to kick Outfit asses."

"Savio," I snarled. I couldn't fucking believe the Outfit really dared to attack our mansion. It wasn't Dante's style. Way too risky.

With a glare, Savio ran up the stairs. Nino entered the code into his phone that was connected to our central control system and blackness fell upon us. It took my eyes a few seconds to adapt. Moonlight streamed in through the windows, and soon my brother and our surroundings became more than abstract shapes. I stepped up to Nino.

"They're heading toward the north wing," he said. The cameras had night vision, so we had no trouble following the attackers' progress. A blond head was among them, and I had a feeling I knew who it was. Samuel had come to save his twin, probably without his Capo's orders. If they were here on Dante's plan, they would have retreated the second the lights went out. That they still continued with it meant someone who didn't care about his life was the leader.

"Come on," I said. Nino and I crept into the garden, past the pool, in the direction where the attackers were headed. "Samuel is mine," I said quietly.

Nino didn't say anything, only shut down his phone so the glow of the screen wouldn't give us away. We reached the corner of the north wing and both crouched down. I peered around and found two men, one of them blond, working on the terrace door to Savio's domain while the other two scanned the area, guns pointed ahead. They had turned over the table and were half hidden behind it. It was massive wood. Maybe it would hold back the bullets.

"Two alive, Samuel and another," I ordered. Nino gave a terse nod. He'd give me a lecture later. He was pissed that we were being attacked because I'd brought Serafina here, that I'd put his wife in danger.

Nino and I raised our guns and began firing. Whoever our opponents were, they weren't the best shots. The first went down almost immediately. The two at the terrace door dropped behind the table and began firing as well. Eventually we ran out of bullets. The fun was about to begin. Nino pulled his knife. Clutching my own knife, I ran toward the remaining three attackers. Two went for me, one for Nino.

Samuel slashed his knife at me, and I blocked it with my own. The other Outfit fucker jabbed toward my stomach. I dodged that attack as well and rammed my blade into his thigh. He went down with a cry, but I grabbed him by the collar and jerked him up to block Samuel's next attack. His knife went straight into his companion's stomach. Before Samuel could attack again, Nino grabbed him from behind, one arm locked around his throat, the other over his arm with the knife. I dropped the Outfit bastard and jumped forward, hitting Samuel's wrist and breaking it so he would drop the knife.

He grunted but didn't drop the knife. He struggled like a madman, and Nino lost his balance. Fuck.

They both landed on the ground, Samuel on top of Nino. Grabbing my gun,

I lunged at Samuel, grasped him by the throat, and hit his temple with the butt of the gun. With a groan, he went slack. Nino shoved him off himself. I touched Samuel's throat to make sure he was alive.

"Did you keep your opponent alive?" I asked Nino, panting.

"Of course. I knew it was unlikely that you'd not kill at least one of them."

I chuckled. Nino stepped up to me. "If we torture him slowly, send pieces of him to his parents and Dante, the Outfit will do our biding. I can't imagine they'll risk losing both Serafina and Samuel."

"I don't think he acted on Dante's orders."

"Probably not. But Dante won't abandon his nephew because he tried saving his twin."

I nodded. "Take the other survivor into a cell and wake him. Find out everything he knows. I'll send Savio to join you or else he won't stop bitching."

"What about Samuel?"

"I'll take him to another cell. Then I'll have a word with Serafina."

"Are we going to deal with him together?"

I regarded the blond man on the ground. "Yes. If he's anything like Serafina, he'll be fun to break."

Serafina

The lights came back on. My eyes burned from the onslaught of brightness. I was still kneeling on the bathroom floor when Remo's voice rang out.

"Go into the basement and help Nino torture the Outfit asshole."

I could feel the color draining from my face. I'd heard the shooting, had prayed that the Outfit would win …

I forced myself to stand when the lock turned.

Remo came in covered in blood, and I started trembling, terrified my greatest horrors had come true.

For a couple of heartbeats, Remo regarded me. "Your brother tried to save you."

Terror gripped me like a vise. I could not breathe. I didn't want to believe it. "You're lying," I gasped out, voice broken and hollow.

A dark smile curled his lips. "He's a brave one."

I rushed toward Remo, clutched his bloody shirt.

Remo's dark eyes held mine. The predatory gleam in them made my heart thud even faster.

"No," I said again. "Samuel isn't here. He wouldn't risk it. Dante wouldn't allow it."

"I think your twin would gladly put his life down for you, Angel. I doubt he came on your uncle's orders. That means no reinforcement."

I swallowed. Oh Samuel. My protector. How could you be so stupid?

If Samuel was dead, I couldn't go on living, not with the knowledge that he'd died to save me. Tears burned a hot trail down my cheeks. "If you … if you …" I couldn't even say it. "Then kill me now."

"He's not dead yet," Remo murmured, dark eyes scanning my face. "We'll see how long he lasts, though."

Samuel wasn't dead. Not yet.

My eyes widened. "Let me see him."

Remo touched my throat, coming closer. "Why? So you can say goodbye?"

I bit my lip. "To see the truth."

Remo smiled. "I'm not lying." He grabbed my wrist and dragged me out of my room. He led me down into the basement, and holding me by the arm so I couldn't storm inside, he opened one of the cells. Inside lay Samuel, covered in blood and not moving except for the shallow rise and fall of his chest. His blond hair was matted with blood. My chest constricted so tightly I was sure to pass out any second.

"What did you do?"

"Not much yet," he said as he closed the door. "Hit him over the head. Once he wakes, Nino and I will tend to him." I knew what that meant.

A terrifying, agonized scream echoed through the basement. I flinched violently.

"That's Nino's doing. He's talking to the other survivor."

Soon those would be Samuel's cries. Soon he'd be submitted to the horrors he'd wanted to save me from. Horrors I'd been spared. Bile traveled up my throat.

My twin would suffer and die for me.

I grasped Remo's arm, my eyes begging with him, even though I knew he didn't have a heart I could soften. "Please don't. Torture me instead."

Remo smiled darkly, cupping my face. "I don't want to torture you. And I told you I won't ever cut you again, Angel."

Of course. I knew what he wanted, what he'd wanted from the start, and today he'd get it. Swallowing my pride because it wasn't worth Samuel's life, I lowered myself to my knees right in front of Remo. I tilted my face up, tears stinging in my eyes. "I'm on my knees. I'm begging you to spare him. Whatever you want, it's yours, Remo. Take it. Take everything."

His dark eyes flashed with an emotion I couldn't read. "You didn't beg for your own life. You didn't offer me your body to avoid pain, but you do for your brother?"

"I do. I'd do anything for him," I whispered. "I'm offering you everything. You can have it all. I'm giving it to you freely, willingly, if you spare my brother."

Remo grasped my arm and hoisted me to my feet. Without another word, he dragged me upstairs and into his bedroom. He released me and closed the door. His breathing was harsh.

My fingers shook as I reached for my dress and pulled it over my head. Remo's eyes scorched my skin as I reached for my bra and unhooked it, letting it drop to the floor. With a hard swallow, I pushed my panties down my hips until they joined my bra on the floor.

"It's yours," I said quietly. All I could think about was Samuel down in that basement, lying in his own blood and the torture that awaited him at the hands of Remo and Nino. I had heard the rumors of what they'd done to Kiara's uncle.

Not taking his eyes off my face, Remo advanced on me. His hands touched my waist and I trembled. "So strong," Remo murmured. "So very difficult to break."

"You won. You broke me. I begged you. I'm offering you my body. Please spare Samuel."

His eyes traveled the length of my body before they locked on mine once more. "You aren't broken, Angel. Sacrificing yourself for someone you love isn't weakness."

"Spare my brother, Remo." With shaking hands I reached for his belt, but he stopped me. And my world fell apart because if he didn't take me up on my offer, what else could I give him in return for my brother's life? What else did he want?

Remo leaned down to my ear. "Such a tantalizing offer." He exhaled. "You'd hate me fiercely."

"I would," I whispered.

"You would. So you don't hate me fiercely yet?"

I shuddered. I couldn't bear his mind games, not now, not when Samuel's life depended on it.

Remo kissed the spot below my ear. "I *will* spare your brother, Angel," he said in a low voice, and I froze because I couldn't believe it. "I will send him back to the Outfit with a message. It needs to be loud and clear so they understand I won't have my territory breached."

I nodded mutely. I'd agree to anything to save my brother. I didn't understand any of this.

"You will come down with me into the cell beside Samuel's. I will have a talk with him." I stiffened in Remo's hold. "*Just a talk* and tell him that his actions have consequences, and then I'll return to your cell and you're going to scream and beg as if I'm hurting you. You will make him believe it. Then I will release him so he can return home with the remains of the other Outfit soldier and the knowledge that you will suffer brutally for every single one of their mistakes."

I gave a nod. Samuel would hate himself for it. He would suffer worse than before, but it was better than the alternative. I needed to save him no matter the cost. I could tell him the truth once I was back home.

"Good," Remo said quietly. He gathered my clothes from the ground, his eyes level with my center for a moment before he straightened. "Now get dressed."

I didn't understand why he hadn't taken me when it was obvious how much he wanted me. He could have had me in every way he wanted. I wouldn't have fought him. He could have sent the warning message by recording Samuel's torture and my screams and sending the video to my family. He didn't have to keep Samuel alive to deliver it.

What else could he want?

Remo

Serafina had offered herself to me, but she'd done it out of despair, out of love for her brother. Not because she wanted to.

She loved her brother fiercely, wanted to protect him at any cost, like I would my brothers. I could respect that. I'd never admired a woman on her knees more than I did Serafina. She followed me quietly through the mansion. I could have asked anything of her, but that wasn't how I wanted things to go. Far from it.

I opened the door to the cell beside Samuel's, and Serafina stepped in.

The door to the third cell swung open, and Nino stepped out, covered in blood, his brows drawing together when he spotted Serafina. I closed the door and faced him.

"What's going on?" he asked. His eyes scanned my face. "Remo."

I smirked. "Change of plans."

He moved closer. "We're not letting him go."

"We will."

Savio joined us in the hallway, clothes drenched in blood as well. He didn't say anything, only regarded us carefully.

Nino shook his head. "You're losing yourself in your game."

"I'm not. I know exactly what I'm doing, Nino. Torturing and killing Samuel won't make the same impact as my plan does. He'd become a martyr. His death would forge Dante and his family closer together. They would unite in their loss. But shame and guilt will rip them apart."

"So this isn't about Serafina?"

"Of course it is. She's the center of my game."

Nino shook his head again. "We promised Fabiano his father, and I want this game over. I want her out of our mansion. Speed up the process."

"Some things take time."

"Your game has been evolving a lot since we kidnapped her. Are you sure it's because you think it necessary or is it because she's making you?"

"She's not making me do anything. You know me. I can't be coerced to do anything."

"I'm going to Kiara. Adamo took her back to our wing. I don't have the necessary patience for you tonight." Nino stalked off.

Savio raised his eyebrows.

"What did the Outfit bastard say?" I muttered.

"He was one of the younger soldiers. Made Men from Samuel's group. Apparently, the blond asshole has already quite the loyal following in the Minneapolis Outfit."

"I assume Dante and Pietro Mione didn't know?"

"They didn't."

"You can leave. I'll handle this alone."

Savio hesitated. "Are you really sure your plan is going to work? Nino is the logical genius."

"He doesn't take emotions into consideration. Emotional warfare is far more effective in this case than open violence."

"Not as much fun if you ask me."

I shook my head. "Oh, it's fun for me, trust me."

Savio snorted. "I'll go take a shower. You have whatever kind of fun you prefer."

He sauntered off and I stepped into Samuel's cell. His wrists and ankles were tied together, but his eyes were open in his bloody face and full of hatred. "You fucking bastard," he rasped.

I smiled. "I'd be careful with the insults if I were you."

"Fuck you," Samuel spat. "As if anything I say matters. You're going to torture me to death anyway."

I knelt beside him. "I don't think that's the right punishment for you, *Sam*."

Fear replaced the hatred in his eyes. He arched up. "Don't! Don't you dare touch her."

I straightened. "Someone will have to suffer for this. And I know you will suffer twice as much if I hurt your twin."

"No! Torture me. Kill me."

"Unfortunately, that's not an option. You will return to the Outfit with the memory of your sister's screams."

Samuel froze. "No," he gasped out.

I turned.

"Remo!" he roared, but I closed the cell door.

I stepped into Serafina's cell. She was pale and still so painstakingly proud and beautiful, I allowed myself a moment to admire her.

She tilted her head toward me, her blue eyes burning with emotion. "Samuel will be safe?"

"By my honor."

Her lips curled, but she didn't say anything.

"I hope you can be convincing. I want your best screams."

Her eyes narrowed briefly, giving me a fucking kick as usual. It was so much better than her desperate surrender.

She closed her eyes, chest heaving, elegant throat flexing.

I needed to own this woman. Body and soul and everything else she could offer. I fucking burned with the desire to possess her in every way possible.

Finally, Serafina screamed, and it was so fucking real that my body reacted to the sound, but not in a way it usually did, not with excitement and the thrill of the hunt. There was something close to revulsion filling my body, hearing her agonized cries and imagining they were real.

My hands curled to fists, my muscles tensing because a deeply buried instinct wanted me to protect her from whatever caused those screams. Unfortunately for her, nothing could protect her from me.

I couldn't fucking take it anymore. I stalked toward her, gripped her arm. "Enough," I growled, breathing harshly.

Serafina's eyes snapped open. They searched my face, and a second too late I realized she got deeper than anyone was allowed. "Enough," I repeated, my voice shaking with rage and confusion.

"Enough?" she whispered so softly. The sound was like a fucking caress.

Maybe I should end it now. Do what Nino said, end this fucking game. Get rid of Serafina and Samuel both.

I cupped her head and pressed my forehead to hers. She trembled, overwhelmed.

"Maybe I should kill you."

"Maybe," she breathed. "But you won't."

I should have contradicted her, but she was right and she knew it.

"You promised."

I pulled back from her. "And I will keep my promise. I'll release your brother now. I'll have one of my men fly him and the corpses to Kansas City. How he gets back to Outfit territory from there is his own problem."

She nodded.

"Come," I ordered.

I didn't touch her as I led her back to her bedroom. She moved toward the window and perched on the windowsill, pulling her legs against her chest. I stopped with my fingers against the light switch then lowered them, leaving the room in the dark.

Serafina twisted her head, staring at me. She was backlit by the silver moonlight as she perched in the window frame. She'd never looked more like an angel than in this fucking moment, and I realized I was on a precarious path.

Her whispered words broke the silence. "I wonder whose game is more dangerous, yours or mine, Remo?"

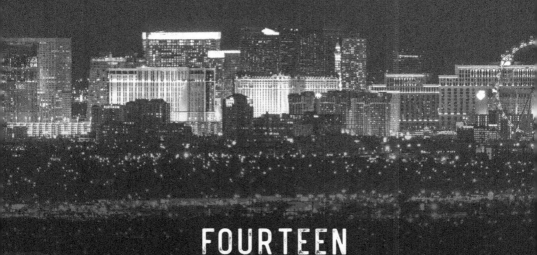

FOURTEEN

Serafina

Over the next couple of days, Remo kept his distance. We didn't go on runs, and Kiara or one of his brothers brought me food.

The look in his eyes when I'd screamed in the basement, it was difficult to describe, but I knew for some reason it had bothered him.

Nino had informed me this morning that Samuel was back in Minneapolis. I believed him. Remo had promised and despite my difficult feelings toward the Capo, I knew he'd keep this promise. I also knew that Samuel and my family were suffering every day I was here.

Nino treated me even colder than before—if that was even possible. I had a feeling things between Remo and him were strained because of Samuel. Nino probably would have killed my brother. It was the obvious solution, the one Dante would have chosen. But Remo … he was unpredictable. Cruel. Fierce.

I didn't understand him.

If he'd tortured and killed Samuel, I would have hated him with brutal abandon, would have done anything I could to kill him. But he hadn't. I was scared about his motives, but more than that … I was scared because a twisted part of me was grateful. I wasn't sure exactly why, but Remo had done this because of me.

It was way past midnight when I heard my door open. I couldn't sleep, my mind whirring with thoughts.

Lying on my side, I watched the tall figure step in. I knew it was Remo from the way he moved, from his tall frame, the shock of his black hair. "You're awake,"

He moved closer. His face lay in shadows, and my pulse picked up. He sank down on the edge of the bed, and I rolled onto my back.

"No," he said in a strange tone. "I prefer you awake."

He leaned over me, one of his arms braced beside my hip.

"What do you want?" I muttered.

"I want you gone."

My eyes widened. "Then let me go."

"I fear it's not that easy." He bent lower and then his palm touched my belly and slowly slid down. I held my breath, becoming still in a mix of shock and anticipation. He cupped me through the covers and my clothes. The touch was light, almost questioning, and I was completely frozen. My center tingled and that, more than Remo's touch, sent a fierce stab of fear through me. I wanted him to touch me without a barrier between us, wanted to get a taste of something utterly forbidden, something I wasn't allowed to want.

Neither of us said anything. I knew what paralyzed me, but what restrained Remo?

He exhaled slowly and stood. Without another word, he disappeared. Good Lord, what was happening? With him. With me. With the both of us.

That middle of the night visit seemed to have done something to Remo because he returned to our previous routine of taking me on runs and walks through the gardens. I wasn't sure if I should be relieved or worried. I'd almost missed our daily arguments because he took me seriously and was strangely excited about my comebacks. He didn't want me to be the restrained lady. Far from it. Remo thrived on chaos and conflict. His presence left me breathless and overwhelmed.

I slanted Remo a look as he walked beside me in silence. His expression was harsh, his dark eyes forbidding. I stopped and after a moment he did too. He narrowed his eyes.

"Why did you really let Samuel go? I want the truth."

Remo glared down at me. "I think you're forgetting what you are. I don't owe you the truth. I don't even owe you these fucking strolls through the gardens. You are my captive, Serafina."

Serafina? "What about 'Angel?'" I retorted.

Remo gripped my upper arms. "Careful. I think handling you with kid gloves gave you the wrong idea."

"I think I have exactly the right idea."

Remo's fingers tightened. I lifted my hands and pressed them to his chest.

The muscles flexed under my touch. Remo lowered his gaze to my hands then slowly looked back up. The expression on his face burned a fierce trail through my body. Fury and desire.

Remo jerked me against him, knocking the air out of me. One hand gripped my neck, and his mouth pressed against my ear. "I don't remember you pushing me away when I touched your pussy a few nights ago, *Angel*," he growled.

Shame washed over me from the memory, but worse, so much worse … longing.

"Every fucking day you want me a little more. I can see it in your eyes, can see the struggle in them. You aren't allowed to have me like I'm not allowed to have you."

"You are Remo Falcone. You are Capo. You rule over the West. Who could stop you from having me?" I murmured. My God. What was wrong with me?

His fingers shifted on my neck, loosening, and he pulled back to meet my gaze, and I wished he hadn't because the fierceness in his eyes was like the first breath of air after holding your breath for too long.

"The only force on this earth that can stop me is *you*. You're the only one I'd allow to do so," he said in a dark voice. He kissed me, a slide of his lips over mine. "How much longer will you?"

I wanted to deepen the kiss. My fingers trembled against Remo's chest. I wanted to look away from his dark eyes and at the same time I wanted to drown in their power. I wanted so many things when he was around. Things I'd always be forbidden to want.

A man of unparalleled cruelty. My captor. My enemy.

I stumbled back, wheezing.

"Do you want to run again?" The dark amusement in his voice wasn't as convincing as it usually was. He sounded strained.

I didn't want to run, and that was the problem because I should want to run from the desire. I took another step back.

Remo smiled darkly. "I don't think I've ever seen you as scared of me as you are now."

Terrified. I was completely terrified. I turned and ran back to the mansion. On the terrace I collided with Kiara, and we had to grip each other to keep our balance. My eyes met Nino's—he was standing behind her as always—and for a moment I was sure he'd attack me, but Kiara pulled away from me.

"Hey, are you alright?" she asked, touching my arm, looking concerned.

I nodded jerkily.

"You sure? Did Remo do something?"

Did he? Or did I? The lines were getting blurry. Remo was right. Every day

I was here things got more complicated. Captivity broke me, only not in the way I thought it would.

Nino's gaze moved past us. I knew whom he was seeking.

"No," I whispered in reply to her question.

Kiara frowned. "Come on. Let's go inside."

"Kiara," Nino warned.

"No," she said firmly. "This is getting ridiculous. Serafina won't hurt me."

She took my hand and led me inside where she pushed me down on the sofa. Remo and Nino remained outside. I could hear the low rumble of their voices. It sounded as if they were in an argument.

Kiara handed me a glass of water then sat down beside me. "Is it because of your brother? Nino said they allowed him to return to the Outfit. That's good, isn't it?"

I nodded. It was. My brother. My family. The Outfit. My fiancé. I owed all of them loyalty. I owed them resistance and a fight.

"Serafina?" Kiara touched my thigh.

I met her compassionate gaze and touched her hand. "I'm losing myself."

Her eyes widened then flitted to the French windows. "You know, I was completely terrified of Remo in the beginning. But I saw sides of him that made me realize he's more than brutality and cruelty."

"Remo is the cruelest man I know. He is beyond redemption."

She smiled sadly. "Maybe he just needs someone who will show him the path to redemption."

I laughed harshly. "I hope you don't think that's going to be me. The only path I'll show him is the road to Hell. I hate him."

Kiara squeezed my thigh but didn't say anything. I was relieved when Nino took me up to my room, not Remo.

I traced the line of the healed cut on my forearm, wishing it were still fresh, wishing Remo would hurt me again. More than that, I wished I didn't need that kind of reminder because Remo Falcone was beyond redemption. I shouldn't need reminding.

The next day Remo and I did our longest run so far despite the exceptionally hot late August sun. We both needed to relieve pent up energy it seemed. We hardly spoke. I tried to keep my mind blank, tried not to think of my family who was suffering because Remo refused to make a new demand. Guilt became harder to bear every day. The guilt over not suffering the way I should be.

My eyes registered a shadow above our heads. A large black and white bird of prey with a red head. "Look," I panted. "There's your spirit animal. A vulture."

Remo stopped and laughed. A real laugh. Not dark, taunting, or cruel. "Good to know you find me that repulsive."

I wished. He took a bottle of water from the small running backpack and handed it to me. God, how I wished I found Remo's body repulsive. I took a sip of water then handed him the bottle back.

"When are you going to ask my uncle for Rocco Scuderi?" I asked to distract myself and him.

Remo's expression hardened, his eyes returning to the sky. "Vultures wait for their prey to drop dead. I think the Outfit's almost there."

"You can't win this game. The moment you return me, the Outfit will rise and strike back. An endless spiral of violence will start."

"Why would you say that, Angel? Don't you want to be returned? Danilo is waiting eagerly to wed and bed you."

I followed the large bird's flight, wondering how it would feel to be free like that. A marriage to Danilo seemed so unreal in that moment, so far away, when I had already been less than forty minutes away from being married to him. That girl in the beautiful white wedding dress, she felt like more of a stranger every day. My eyes were drawn to my hand, but the ring wasn't there. For the first time since my engagement to Danilo, I'd forgotten to put the ring on in the morning.

"One month," Remo reminded me as he led me through the garden.

It took me a moment to understand what he meant. "Since you captured me," I said quietly.

One month. Sometimes it felt so much longer, sometimes like only yesterday. I had never thought I'd survive a single day in the hands of the Camorra, in Remo Falcone's hands, and now I'd survived so many more. Remo was more patient than I'd thought. I was fairly sure my family and the Outfit was at a point by now that they'd hand Scuderi over, even if my grandfather disapproved. He was an old man close to death.

I stared down at my bare feet in the grass. As a child I'd loved to run around barefoot, but eventually I had stopped because I was told it was undignified. Ice Princess. I'd enjoyed being her in public, even if she wasn't a reflection of my true self. It was who I was supposed to be as Dante's niece, as Danilo's wife. Controlled. Dignified. Graceful.

I caught Remo watching me. No control. Unbridled emotion. Furious passion.

One month.

I averted my eyes. Remo led me closer to the mansion.

"I want to know what's going on in your head," Remo said.

I was glad he couldn't. "Maybe I'll tell you if you tell me what's going on in yours."

Remo stopped. "Right now I'm imagining how it would feel to bury my face between your legs, Angel."

I froze. Remo obviously enjoyed my shock if his smirk was an indication. I didn't get a chance to retort because a low moan sounded above us. My eyes darted to the open window, my brows pulling together. Remo moved behind my back, standing very close and leaning forward slightly so his face was beside mine. He nodded up to the window. "That's Nino and Kiara's bedroom."

A woman moaned again, an abandoned, uncontrolled sound full of pleasure.

I took a step back but bumped into Remo, who didn't budge. "That's the sound a woman makes when a man is eating her out."

"You are disgusting," I gritted out, trying to get away, but Remo's arms wrapped around me from behind, keeping me in place.

"Please," Kiara gasped out. "Please, more."

"Do you want to know why I know Nino is currently licking pussy? It's because you don't hear him. His face is buried in it."

Kiara's moans turned louder, desperate, and then she cried out.

I wanted to be disgusted, but my body reacted hearing these sounds. Heat gathered between my legs.

"Have you ever made this sound, Angel?" he murmured. "No, you haven't. But don't you wonder how it would feel to be overwhelmed with so much pleasure to force these kinds of moans from your lips?"

I stopped struggling, but Remo didn't loosen his hold on me. His firm chest, warm and strong, still pressed up against my back. "A tongue between your thighs, licking, sucking. Don't you want to know how that would feel?"

I pressed my lips together, but I could do nothing about the trickle of wetness between my thighs. Above us new moans rang out. Kiara, followed by deeper, more restrained grunts.

"You are a grown woman, and yet you've never come so hard you lost yourself. You've never had a man buried between your thighs, eating you out." Remo's mouth brushed my ear. Then his tongue slid along the outer rim until it reached my earlobe. He circled it then drew it between his lips and sucked lightly, and I felt it all the way between my legs. He released my earlobe and exhaled.

Something hard dug into my lower back. I should have drawn back in disgust, but I was utterly frozen.

"Are you wet, Serafina? Wet for me?" Remo rasped in my ear, and a small shiver passed through my traitorous body upon hearing his voice.

"I won't ever bow to your will, Remo," I whispered harshly.

"Who says I want you to bow, Angel? I want you to give me yourself freely because you want to, because you choose to. Have you ever chosen anything only because you wanted to? Without heeding the consequences? Without regard to what's expected of you? All your life you've bowed to your parents' will, your uncle's will, the Outfit's will, and once I'll release you, you'll bow to Danilo's will."

I hated Remo, hated him for making sense, hated him for getting under my skin. And I hated myself for letting him.

"One day you will realize that you were never freer than in your time with me. Whatever you do, no one from the Outfit must know, and even if they find out, they won't blame you, Angel."

I closed my eyes, trying to ignore how good Remo's body felt against mine, trying to block the moans growing in crescendo, but my throbbing center was difficult to forget. Remo's arms around me shifted until his thumb brushed the underside of my breast. I stilled but didn't push him away, didn't utter a word of protest. His mouth found my throat, nibbling, licking, biting, and his hand slipped under my shirt. Rough fingertips slid over my skin, higher and higher until they reached my nipple through the lace of my bra.

My lips parted from the sensation.

"Won't you tell me to stop?" Remo murmured in my ear before his tongue led a wet trail down my throat. His free hand cupped my cheek and twisted my face around so he could assault my mouth with an all-consuming kiss. His tongue licked every crevice of my mouth, tasting, consuming, owning my lips.

"You better tell me to stop, Angel, because if I don't stop now, I fear I won't stop at all."

I barely listened to his words, too caught up in the sensation his fingers on my nipple created, too overwhelmed by the moans ringing out above us. Remo released my face and nipple, gripped my hips in a bruising hold, and got down on his knees. Glancing over my shoulder, shock washed over me to see the Capo kneeling before me.

He pushed up my skirt and bit into my ass cheek then slid his tongue over the spot. His palm cupped my other cheek, hard, kneading possessively before he slid up and wedged his fingers under the strap of my thong. He tugged hard and the drenched fabric jerked against my center and clit. I gasped in surprise and pleasure.

Remo chuckled against my ass cheek then circled his tongue over the soft skin while his fingers kept tugging at my thong. How could this feel so good, so overpoweringly perfect? How could the sensation of fabric rubbing against my sensitive flesh bring me down like that?

Remo tugged harder and I arched, biting down on my lip to keep the sounds in. He sucked the skin of my ass cheek into his mouth as he gave my thong a few hard tugs. Waves of heat and tingling spread from my center to every nerve ending in my body. I was getting closer to something impossible, wondrous, mind-blowing. Something I'd never felt, not even close. Then Remo dropped his hand and released my skin from his mouth. I had to hold back a sound of protest. Gripping my hips, Remo turned me around. I stared down at him. He knelt before me, his eyes dark and possessive, a dangerous smile playing around his lips.

Even kneeling at my feet, Remo oozed dominance, control, power. Looking down at him I still felt like the one he brought to her knees.

I narrowed my eyes, wanting to step away from him. Away from his violence and darkness that seemed to draw me in like an undercurrent.

As if he could feel my resistance, Remo tightened his hold on my hips and leaned forward, pressing a soft kiss to my white panties, right over my throbbing nub. My hand flew forward, gripping his muscular shoulders to steady myself. His eyes pierced me to the core with their intensity as he leaned his rough cheek against my thigh, his mouth close to my center. "I can smell your arousal, Angel," he said in a raw voice that traveled through my body like a jolt of electricity.

As I watched, he smirked, parted his mouth, stuck his tongue out, and traced the small valley where my panties clung to my folds. I began to tremble.

"Will you let me pull down your panties and taste your pussy?"

I didn't say anything. Not yes, but worse. Worse ... I didn't say no. Because I didn't want to. I wanted Remo, had never wanted anything more.

Remo

Serafina stared down at me with hatred, but she didn't fight when I hooked my fingers in the waistband of her thong. I waited a couple of heartbeats, relishing in her silence, bathing in her surrender. I pulled down her panties. She shuddered but lifted her feet so she could step out of her panties. I pushed her skirt up. "Hold it up, Angel."

Her elegant fingers curled around the hem of her skirt, and she pressed it up against her flat stomach.

I was at eye level with her pussy. The trimmed hair above her clit glistened with her juice, and her lips were swollen with arousal. I leaned forward, breathing in her heady scent. Before I'd kidnapped Serafina, I'd entertained different scenarios of how I would conquer her, break her, but this hadn't been among them. I had to admit I enjoyed it tremendously.

I ran my rough palms up her smooth thighs. She trembled, but not from fear, and fuck … with Serafina I preferred any emotion but fear.

My thumbs stroked her soft folds and parted them, revealing her small nub. She released a shaky breath, face half terrified, half expectant. "My mouth being the first to taste your pussy, I'll be very thorough, Angel."

I leaned forward and licked her clit lightly. She bit down on her lip, stifling a sound. She closed her eyes, her cheeks blazing. I pulled back a couple of inches. "Yes, don't watch, my little angel. Maybe you'll manage to pretend I'm someone else."

Her eyes flew open, furious, and she returned my gaze. She wouldn't look away again.

I dove in with small, gentle licks, testing how she'd react. A flood of her juice was my reward. I'd never been with a virgin or someone inexperienced, and I hadn't gone down on a woman in ages, much less ever been gentle with one. This was a new experience but one I found myself enjoying. My cock throbbed every time my tongue delved between her lips, from her opening up to her clit. I tasted every part of her sweet pussy, traced the smooth inside of her lips, her opening, knowing my cock would soon claim that part of her.

Serafina shook, her legs starting to give in.

"Hold on to the wall," I ordered, and she complied without protest, leaning forward, her forearms braced against the rough façade, golden hair curtaining her face as she glared down at me while I ate her pussy. My teeth grazed her clit lightly, and she jerked, a small moan slipping out.

I brushed the inside of her knee and pushed. She parted for me until she stood with her legs in a V over me. I tilted my head up, my hands curling over her hips and firmly pulled her down on my mouth and sucked each fold lightly before I closed my lips around her clit. She started rocking against my face almost desperately, and I complied with her silent demand by practically burying myself in her pussy, lapping at her, diving into her tightness, sucking. Then her lips parted, her brows pulling together in shock and astonishment, and she tensed.

My eyes drank in the expression on her face, the wild abandon of passion on her perfect features, the shock, the resignation, the delight. Possessiveness wasn't one of my character traits, because I owned everything that mattered, but seeing Serafina in the throes of her orgasm and knowing I was the first man to give it to her, I felt fucking possessive. She was mine, body and soul, and would be until I decided to set her free.

I smirked against her as her pussy throbbed. After another long lick, I leaned my head back against the rough stone and licked my lips. Realization filled Serafina's eyes, and her face twisted with horror and shame.

I smiled darkly. She shook her head, stepping back, tugging at her skirt until it covered her pussy again.

I stayed on the ground, my cock throbbing in my pants, my chin coated with her juices, and my body swelled with sweet triumph. "Run, *Angel*. Run from what you've done," I murmured with a dark smile, and Serafina did. She whirled around, blond hair whipping through the air, and stormed away.

No one knew better than I did that you couldn't run from what you've done.

I pushed to my feet, wiped my chin with the back of my hand, and set out to find my angel. She'd received pleasure; now it was time she gave something back.

I wanted nothing less than every last part of her. Her innocence, her heart, her soul, her body. Her purity and her darkness.

I would take everything.

FIFTEEN

Serafina

I'D NEVER EXPERIENCED THIS ACUTE SENSE OF SHAME BEFORE. I DIDN'T stop running until I reached the bedroom and shut the door, but even then I continued into the bathroom, snatching at my clothes, needing them gone. I dropped them on the floor, everything except for my thong, which was still with Remo.

What had I done?

I turned on the shower and slipped under the spray of warm water, rubbing myself clean, rubbing between my legs, but the warm, wet, throbbing sensation remained. It wouldn't go away. I slumped against the wall. I had let Remo put his mouth on me, his tongue inside me, and I had enjoyed it.

My body hummed with the remnants of pleasure, a distant memory my body was eager to refresh. I'd never experienced sensations like that. But worse, Remo's words had been proven true. I'd never felt freer than in that moment with Remo between my legs, showing me pleasure. It had felt amazing, freeing, and utterly wrong. All my life I had been taught to be honorable, to do what was expected of me, and today I'd gone against it all.

Dark and tall, Remo appeared in the doorway, come to claim his prize. His eyes roamed over my naked body, and mine did the same.

He was cruel and twisted. *Beyond redemption.*

Brutal attractiveness, forbidden pleasure, promised pain. I should have been disgusted by him, but I wasn't. Not by his body and not always by his nature.

I shut off the water, scared of what he wanted, completely terrified of what I wanted. This was his game of chess; he was the king and I was the trapped queen that the Outfit needed to protect. He moved me into position for his last move: the kill. Check.

He began unbuttoning his shirt then shrugged it off. He moved closer, stopping right before me. "You always watch me like something you want to touch but aren't allowed to. Who's holding you back, *Angel?*"

"Nothing's holding me back. I don't want to," I muttered with false bravado, the lie ringing loud and clear.

"Is that so?" Remo asked quietly. He reached for my hand, and I let him. Let him put my palm against his strong chest, let him slide it lower, over the hard lines of muscles, over the rough scars. He placed my palm over his belt then released me. "Don't you want to be free of society's shackles for once? To do something forbidden?"

What I wanted more than anything was his twisted smile gone. I gripped his belt and tugged him toward me, angrily, desperately, because I was falling, already lost, content to lose myself. His lips crashed down on mine, tongue domineering my mouth, hands rough against my ass. He jerked me up and against him so his erection pressed against my center.

I gasped, which he swallowed with his lips.

My fingers hooked in his waistband, scared and curious. Remo caught my gaze, his full of hunger and harshness. He ripped his mouth away from mine, backing me into the wall. "Be brave, Angel."

I curled my fingers in his belt and held his gaze as I opened the buckle. The clink was the sound of my last wall crumbling. Gripping his zipper, I pulled it slowly down, terrified and aroused. Then I paused.

Remo bent low, his mouth brushing my ear. "I'm not a patient man. You are playing with fire."

Forcing down my nerves, I turned my face, bringing my own lips to his ear. "Oh, Remo, I will be your first angel. Patience is a virtue, and you will be rewarded for it." I kissed his ear then trailed my tongue over the rim.

He exhaled and pulled back so he could look at my face, and the look in his eyes, it almost made my knees buckle. For a second, I had him. I held the reins on the cruelest, most powerful man in the west, and it was thrilling. But Remo wouldn't be Remo, wouldn't be Capo, if he didn't know how to take his power back.

He grabbed his pants and pulled them down together with his boxers. His erection sprang free, and Remo braced himself against the wall with his hands on either side of my head.

I stared down at him and sank back against the wall. He was long and thick and impossibly hard. I tore my gaze away, only to be hit with Remo's penetrating stare.

My cheeks blazed with heat, and Remo smiled as he leaned forward, trailing his tongue over my heated cheekbone. "Tell me, Angel, what will be my reward for my patience?"

I stood on my tiptoes, curling my fingers over Remo's neck, pulling myself up and against him. His hardness rubbed against my naked stomach, and he groaned a low, dangerous sound. "Something forbidden. Something you aren't meant to be gifted."

Remo's body became taut, eager, and he tipped my head back, his lips brushing mine. "Something you promised to someone else?"

My throat tightened, but Remo kissed me hard, not allowing me to dwell on it. He hooked one of my legs up over his hip, opening me up. His fingers brushed my center, and then two fingers breached my opening. Pain shot through me. I ripped myself from his mouth, tensing, a choked sound bursting from my throat.

Remo stilled, his fingers deep inside of me. He pulled back, a hint of surprise on his face, then it was gone. He regarded me intently, almost curiously. My chest heaved as I tried to grow used to the stretched sensation of having his fingers in me. Remo touched his forehead to mine. "I think you were right, Angel, my reward will be worth it."

Anger flooded me. "Did you enjoy hurting me?" I whispered.

Remo kissed my lips. "This isn't me hurting you. This is me trying not to hurt you. You will know when I want to hurt you." He pulled his fingers out then slid them back in. My muscles clung to him, and I exhaled. He held my gaze as he established a slow rhythm. I leaned my head back against the wall, never averting my eyes.

Remo's dark eyes dragged me deeper and deeper down into their abyss. Pleasure slowly replaced the feeling of being stretched. I began rocking my hips, causing Remo's erection to rub over my belly. His breathing deepened, but he kept up pumping his fingers into me at a slow pace, watching me, his other hand clinging to my outer thigh. A deep throbbing spread from my center, and I gasped, and not from pain this time. Remo's thumb flicked over my nub, and I splintered from the inside out, into thousands of particles filled with sensation.

Remo watched me hungrily, almost reverently, and I smiled, not even sure why. I was still reeling from my high when Remo pulled his fingers out and grabbed my other thigh, lifting me up, my back against the wall, my body trapped between it and his chest. And I knew what he wanted. My hands flew up to his chest, resisting. When his erection brushed my inner thigh, I gasped out, "No!"

Remo's dark eyes flew up to mine, angry, incredulous … but he did pause. "Not like this," I said quietly. "Not against a wall." This would happen on my terms, not his.

The anger lessened. "You are right," he said darkly. He hoisted me higher so my legs wrapped around his middle, and my center pressed up against his six-pack.

Then he walked with me out of the bathroom and into the bedroom. "I will fuck you on the bed, Angel. I put white sheets on for the occasion. What a pity it would have been if I didn't stain them with your blood."

Shock and indignation shot through me because I realized my sheets had been white for a few days now, but then Remo kissed me. I dug my nails into his shoulders angrily and battled his tongue.

We tugged and kissed and suddenly we were on the bed. Remo knelt between my legs, shoving them further apart, his mouth harsh against my throat, and I became still, soft, scared. This was it.

Remo stilled above me and raised his head. Our eyes met. I don't know what he saw in mine, but he cupped my cheek, startling me. His kisses became light, gentle, almost caring. So wrong. That wasn't Remo. That was a lie. "Shh, Angel. I'll be gentle."

His fingers stroked my breasts, my side, oh so gently, and his mouth … his mouth dusted me with loving kisses. Even though I knew them to be false, knew I was supposed to shove him away, to put up a fight, I kissed him back. Lost, lost, lost.

Remo molded our bodies together, shifting, and then I felt a light pressure against my opening.

I gasped and tensed. Remo watched my face, full of intent, and his eyes … they quieted my hesitation, my fear, any protest I might have come up with.

He slid into me slowly, inch by inch, never taking more than my body could give, but still he seemed to tear me apart. A slow conquest but a conquest nevertheless. I'd expected brutality and cruelty. I wished for it. But this gentle Remo, he terrified me the most. He didn't let me escape, not even the only way I could. He wanted to consume me with his eyes. He sunk all the way into me, and then he paused as I shivered under the force of the intrusion. His dark eyes said what I'd known all along.

He possessed me. He *owned* me.

I was the queen.

He was the king.

Checkmate.

Remo

This was the ultimate victory over the Outfit. They didn't know it yet, but they would soon. Serafina trembled under me, her marble cheeks flushed, lips parted. She was in pain, and somehow it didn't please me because I had tried not to hurt her. I gave pain willingly, deliberately, freely. Not by accident.

I held myself still, content in the feeling of her tight walls squeezing my cock mercilessly. I was fucking ecstatic feeling the slickness around me and knowing it was her virgin blood. The sweetest reward for my patience I could imagine.

My eyes roamed Serafina's perfect features, and her blue eyes met mine, searching, wondering. I pulled out of her slowly, recognizing the signs of pain in her expression, then pushed back in even slower.

I rocked my hips slowly, keeping my movements as controlled as possible. Her face twisted with pain and pleasure, and I angled my hips to increase the latter. She gasped, surprised. I kept up the slow rhythm. Patience wasn't my forte, but I knew this prize would be worth it too.

She gasped again. Her pale blue eyes rose to mine, questioning and confused and scared. Scared of my consideration, of my gentleness. She hadn't expected it from me, had accepted her fate. She had braced herself for me fucking her like an animal. She had expected agony and bruises, humiliation and cruel words. She had prepared herself for it, had promised herself to fight me.

This was something she hadn't prepared for, something she couldn't fight because she was too desperate for it. She was proud and noble, but she was still only a sheltered woman. Showing her kindness was like giving her water in a time of drought.

It was something new to me. I fucked hard. Women were pleasure and money. Bargain and burden. They weren't allowed to be more than that.

She moaned, her marble-like cheeks flushing. She was getting closer. I lowered my mouth to her lips, slid my tongue in, tasting that unblemished sweetness.

My fingers slid up her side, over her slender ribs to the swell of her breast. She gasped again. I brushed her nipple with my thumb, the touch feather soft because that was how she liked it, as inexperienced as she was. She'd soon enough see that pain and pleasure worked well together. I reached between us and slid two fingers over her clit. She shuddered and I repeated the motion and thrust my hips faster, forcing one astonished gasp after another from her lips.

I lifted her leg up over my back, changing the angle and sliding a bit deeper into her.

She cried out and threw her head back, baring that elegant neck. Pain and pleasure. I couldn't take my eyes off her face as she gasped and whimpered and moaned. Her gaze sought mine again. She hardly ever looked away. She was the first woman who dared to hold my gaze while I fucked her, the first woman I allowed to do so. My fingers slid over her clit as I sunk into her in deep controlled strokes over and over again.

I wanted my prize, wanted to force it from her quivering body, wanted her complete surrender.

Her tight walls clamped around my cock as she came under me. I closed my lips over the perfect skin at her throat and bit down, wanting to leave my mark. My angel. She tensed and shuddered even harder.

I leaned down. "And you thought I wouldn't own you, Angel," I said softly then kissed her ear.

She glared up at me, shame and hate mingling on her perfect features. Her cold, proud eyes blazed with emotions I had summoned.

"Now that we got this out the way, why don't I fuck you like I wanted to from the start?" I said in a low voice. Serafina was a chess piece.

There was a flash of fear, but I didn't give her time to consider my words. She was slick around my cock. I slid all the way out of her and thrust back into her in one hard push. She gasped from pain this time. I hummed my approval. I soon found a pace that was fast enough to be painful but not so overwhelming that she'd not feel the dark promise of pleasure behind it.

She closed her eyes. "No," I snarled, giving her a far less restrained thrust, showing her that I was still holding back. She looked at me with hate and disgust. I claimed her mouth, growing even harder under the intensity of her emotions. Hate was good.

I sucked her nipple into my mouth, and she tensed. Oh yes. Fucking Serafina was better than my imagination had promised. "I can't wait to send these sheets to Danilo and your family," I rasped against her wet skin.

She clawed at my back, and I groaned, my cock twitching.

She fought against the pleasure, clung to the pain, even preferring it. I reached between us, found her nub, and flicked my finger over it. She squeezed harder around my cock, causing my eyes to close under the blinding pleasure. "If you stop fighting the pleasure, it'll be less painful, Angel," I murmured against her pink nipple before I sucked it back into my mouth. I hit deeper than before, still not as hard and deep as I wanted, but Serafina whimpered.

I lifted my head. She bit her lip, holding back the sound. "Surrender to the pleasure. It'll be worth it."

She hit me with a hateful gaze but didn't pull back when I kissed her mouth and slipped my tongue inside. She'd rather suffer through the pain than stop fighting the pleasure. Proud and strong. Determined not to give me another one of her sweet releases. I claimed her mouth, hard and fast, like my cock did her tight center.

I decided to allow her that small victory. I'd already won the prize and the war. I let loose, submitted to the pressure in my balls. I thrust into her one last time then shot my cum into her with a violent shudder.

I stared into her eyes as I claimed her body. She was mine. I couldn't wait for Cavallaro and her fiancé to find out.

SIXTEEN

Serafina

REMO PULLED OUT OF ME, AND I WINCED, SUCKING IN A SHARP BREATH. I rolled over to my side, away from him, but the shame stayed with me. Remo brushed my hair away and kissed my neck then lightly bit down, and I shivered. "You are mine now, Angel. I own you. Even if I ever let you go, I'll still own you. You will always remember this day and deep down you will always know that you are mine and mine alone."

I closed my eyes, trying to hold back tears, fighting them, holding on to my composure with sheer force of will. The sheets rustled as Remo got out of bed, and I didn't look over my shoulder to see what he was doing. I heard the water running in the bathroom.

He returned moments later and ran his fingers down my spine then back up before he grabbed my shoulder and rolled me onto my back. My eyes found his. He parted my legs, his eyes taking in my thighs covered in my blood.

Not taking his eyes off my face, he knelt between my legs. I tensed, confused but too stunned and overwhelmed to act. With a dark smile, he leaned forward and ran his tongue over my thigh, licking up the blood. I was frozen. He traced a finger up my leg and circled my opening with it. I stiffened. I was sore but Remo slid his finger inside of me very slowly. His dark eyes held mine and after a moment, he gently pulled his finger back out, now slick with my blood. A horrible suspicion wormed its way into my head, and he proved it right. Remo put his blood-coated finger in his mouth with a twisted smile. "The taste of blood never disgusted me, and your virgin blood is sweeter than anything else."

My nose wrinkled in disgust, and shame warmed my cheeks.

Remo assessed me calmly as he released his finger from his mouth. He stroked my inner thighs as he lowered himself to his stomach between my legs.

"What are you doing?" I asked.

Remo pressed a kiss to my center. "Claiming my missing prize."

My hand shot out, wanting to shove him away, but he caught my wrist and pressed it to my thigh.

His mouth gently moved over me, followed by his tongue. He was so gentle, my body responded despite my soreness. He held my gaze as he traced his tongue along my slit over and over again. Then he closed his lips over my clit and began sucking softly.

I moaned, unable to hold it in. Remo smiled against my flesh. I stopped fighting it and sank into the mattress, my legs parting further. Remo kept up the soft touch of his tongue and mouth but pulled back slightly. "There you go. Let me make you forget the pain."

And he did. There was still an undercurrent of a dull ache, but somehow it heightened every spike of pleasure Remo's tongue brought me.

"Look at me," Remo ordered, his lips brushing against my folds. I met his gaze and started trembling as my core tightened. Pain and pleasure mingled as Remo's tongue worked my nub. My lips parted and I cried out, unable to contain it. Remo's eyes flashed with triumph, and he pressed closer to my center, devouring me. I thrashed under him, gasping. It was painful and mind-bendingly pleasurable. I was torn apart and put back together, miss-matched and wrong but back together.

I slumped against the bed, resigned, exhausted, my body throbbing with pain and the remnants of my orgasm. Remo stayed between my legs, but his tongue had slowed. His fingers pulled me apart, and he lapped at my opening. I moaned as it caused another aftershock. Everything about this was wrong and filthy. With a last kiss to my clit, Remo climbed over me and claimed my mouth. The taste of blood and my own juices made me shudder.

Remo pulled back. "Pain and pleasure," he rasped. "What do you prefer, Angel?"

Shame crashed down on me hard and fast. "I hate you."

Remo smiled darkly and pushed off me. "There is a washcloth on the nightstand." His erection and upper thighs were smeared with my blood, but he didn't bother covering himself as he walked out of the room, leaving me alone.

The door clicked shut.

I sat up, wincing again. My eyes were drawn to the sheets, and I closed my eyes again. This was supposed to happen on my wedding night. It was supposed to be Danilo's privilege, and I had given it away because that was exactly what it was: giving not taking. I got up and moved slowly toward the bathroom. The soreness wasn't even the worst part. Not even close. That was the shame, the guilt over what I let happen.

I stepped into the shower and turned it on. The water was hot, on the verge of being painful but it felt good. I leaned back against the wall and slowly sank down. Pulling my legs up against my chest, I cried because Remo was right: what I'd done today, I'd never forget. Even if I returned to the Outfit, how could I face my family again? How could I face Danilo, my fiancé, the man I had promised myself to?

I wasn't sure how long I sat like this when Remo stepped into the bathroom. I didn't look up, only saw his legs in my peripheral vision. He moved closer and then the water stopped. He crouched before me. I still didn't look up. My throat and nose were clogged from crying and I started to shiver without the warmth of the water.

"Look at me," Remo ordered. "Look at me, Serafina."

When I refused to do as he asked, he reached for my chin and nudged it up until my gaze met his. His dark eyes searched my face. I couldn't read the emotions in his eyes. "If it helps, try telling yourself I raped you," he whispered in a low voice. "Maybe you will start believing it."

Nothing had ever cut deeper than Remo's words. He didn't need a knife to make me bleed. I glared at him, wanting to hate him with every part of my being, but a tiny, horrible part of me didn't, and it was that part of me I despised more than I could ever hate Remo.

Remo

After claiming Serafina, I left her in the bed. I needed time to gather my fucking thoughts. I went to my bedroom and put on briefs but didn't bother cleaning my thighs or face. It was late in the evening, so Kiara should still be in her bedroom with Nino.

I could still taste Serafina, sweet and metallic.

The sweetest triumph of my life.

Fuck. This woman …

I fixed myself a drink, a bourbon, then leaned against the bar, swirling the liquid in the glass, fucking averse to washing away her taste. The memory still burned bright.

This was the moment I'd worked toward, had been patient for. For once in my life I'd been patient.

Your reward will be worth it.

I will be your first angel.

Serafina was so much more than I'd hoped for. She was magnificently gorgeous, ruinously breathtaking. Even lesser men would kill to have someone as regal as her in their bed only once. I almost got a fucking boner thinking about how Danilo would feel seeing the sheets with Serafina's virgin blood on them, how acutely he'd feel the loss of something he had desired from afar for years, something that had almost been in his reach only to be painfully ripped from him. It was enough to drive even the most controlled man into a rampage.

And her father and brother … for them it would be a painting of their greatest failure.

"That smile on your face creeps me the fuck out," Savio muttered as he came in, smelling of perfume and sex.

"Thinking of my next message for Dante," I said, setting the glass down without taking a single sip. I couldn't bear the idea of getting rid of Serafina's taste just yet.

Savio's eyes flitted down to my upper thighs coated in Serafina's blood then up to my face.

He crossed his arms. "Either you mauled a kitten and rubbed your face and groin all over the spoils or you had a disturbing meeting with virgin pussy."

Something dark and possessive burned my chest hearing him talk like that about Serafina. I shoved it down. "Not a virgin anymore."

Savio regarded me curiously then shook his head with a disbelieving laugh. "You really got her to come willingly into your bed. Fuck, Remo, you must have twisted that girl's mind."

I grinned. "And tomorrow I'll bathe in my triumph and send Dante the sheets."

Savio laughed, came toward me, and downed the drink I'd poured for myself. "To your twisted mind and all the twisted shit it comes up with. You wanted to break her and you broke her."

I left him standing there, not in the mood to talk about Serafina anymore. My body yearned for her, for more. For everything. When I entered the bedroom, I found the bed empty, except for the stained sheets. I followed the sound of running water into the bathroom.

Serafina was huddled in the shower and the sight caused an unpleasant twinge in my chest. I turned off the water then knelt before her. "Look at me," I said. "Look at me, Serafina."

Her blue eyes held anguish and guilt when I forced her face up.

"If it helps, try telling yourself I raped you," I murmured. "Maybe you will start believing it."

Hatred flared in her eyes, and for once it didn't give me a thrill.

I got up, frustrated by my body's reaction. I stalked back into the bedroom and stripped the bed of its sheets, not wanting them ruined. Serafina would probably try to burn them to destroy any proof of what we'd done, but she couldn't burn the memory. I threw them into the hallway before I returned to Serafina. She stood now, her fingers clutching the edge of the shower stall, her other hand pressed against her stomach. She took a step, wincing.

I moved closer and her eyes darted down to my bloody thighs. She grimaced. "Why don't you clean up?"

"Because I want to remember."

"And I want to forget," she bit out.

"You need to own up to your actions, Angel. You can't run from them," I said, stopping in front of her.

Hatred swirled in her blue eyes, but not all of it was directed at me. "Leave."

I narrowed my eyes.

"Leave!" she rasped.

"The Tylenol will help with your soreness." I turned and walked toward the door.

"I don't want the pain gone. I deserve it," she muttered. I paused in the doorway and tossed a glance over my shoulder, but Serafina wasn't looking at me. She was glaring at the floor.

I left the bathroom, took new sheets from the wardrobe and threw them on the bed before I headed out and locked the bedroom door. Stuffing the discarded sheets under my arm, I hesitated. I couldn't pinpoint exactly what, but something didn't sit well with me. Ignoring the sensation, I went downstairs.

Nino crossed my path as I headed into the game room. He, too, was only in his briefs. His eyes flitted down to the stained sheets then lower to my thighs before he raised his eyebrows. "I don't suppose it's menstrual blood."

"It isn't. It's Dante's downfall."

Nino trailed after me in that annoying, brooding way he had when he disapproved of something I did. "Not only his downfall."

I moved on into the office. Our father's office. It was one of the few rooms we'd left mostly as it was, but neither of us worked out of it. I narrowed my eyes at him. "Are you referring to Serafina?"

"She will be ruined in her family's eyes, in her circles. Some might even consider her actions betrayal. She is a woman and Dante won't kill her for it, but she will be shunned ... if she's allowed to return to her home at all. I assume you intend to send her back now that you got what you wanted."

Something in his voice set me off. "I haven't gotten everything I wanted from her yet. Not even close. And she will stay until she gives me every little thing I desire."

Nino stepped in front of me. "Is this even still about revenge?"

"It has never been only about revenge. It's about obliterating the Outfit from within, not mere revenge." I sidestepped him and went in search for something I could wrap the sheets in. Finally, I found a box and stuffed them inside.

"Don't lose yourself in a game you don't have full control over, Remo."

The worry in his voice made me look up. I touched his shoulder. "When have I ever been in control? Losing control is my favorite pastime."

Nino's mouth twitched. "As if I don't know it." His expression turned serious again. "In these last few weeks you've spent a lot of time with Serafina. We need you, Remo. The Camorra can't risk an endless conflict with the Outfit. Go in for the kill."

"These sheets are the point of my knife. Are you going to help me with that note to Dante and her family?"

Nino sighed. "If it puts an end to this, then yes."

I rummaged around for a fancy piece of stationery in the old wood desk then took out a pen.

"Now let's figure out the best words to crush them. I thought we could start with a reference to the bloody sheets tradition of the Famiglia for an additional kick."

Nino shook his head. "I'm glad you are my brother and not my enemy."

SEVENTEEN

Serafina

I HOVERED BESIDE THE BED, UNABLE TO MOVE. THE WHITE SHEETS WERE gone, sheets covered in my blood. Remo had taken them, and I knew why.

I closed my eyes for a moment. He would send them to my family. They would find out what had happened. What would they think?

Would they hate me? Banish me?

This wasn't rape. I could not defend my actions. There was no force, no torture, no violence. Samuel had risked his life for me. Men had died because of me, and I had betrayed them all.

I turned away from the bed, unable to bear its presence, and headed toward the window. I climbed on the windowsill, wincing at the sharp twinge between my legs. A painful reminder I didn't need. Every moment of what I'd done was burned into my memory, blazing fiercely when I closed my eyes.

I slept with Remo Falcone.

Capo of the Camorra.

My enemy.

Not Danilo. Not my fiancé. My eyes found my engagement ring discarded on the nightstand. I hadn't worn it today, and now I could never wear it again without feeling like a fraud. I swallowed. He would see the sheets as well. I had given away what had been promised to him for five years. What was worse was I had wanted to give it away.

I could still feel Remo's body on mine, the way he moved in me.

It was … wondrous. Freeing. Intoxicating.

Sin.

Betrayal.

My ruin.

What I did couldn't be undone. A kiss could be denied. A touch could be concealed. This? This had left scars. There was tangible proof, and Remo would flaunt it in my family's faces.

You have to own up to your actions, Angel.

I knew I needed to, but I wasn't sure if I could.

Remo

The next morning I found Serafina perched in her usual spot on the windowsill. The sheets weren't rumpled. She must have slept leaning against the window or not at all.

"You sent out the sheets," Serafina said quietly, not looking my way. Of course, she knew. She was not only beautiful, she was stunningly intelligent. A lethal combination.

"I did. Express delivery. They should arrive at your family's home tomorrow morning or maybe even tonight."

She didn't turn, didn't react. Only looked out of the window. Her hair was brushed over her other shoulder, her slender neck bared to my view. My teeth marks marred her unblemished skin. Her shoulders gave a small twitch. Then she stiffened her spine. "What did you tell them? I assume you sent them a note with your gift." There was the slightest waver in her tone, a chink in her cool voice.

I stalked closer. "What would you have wanted the note to say?"

She peered over her shoulder at me, a beautifully hateful expression perfectly frozen on her face.

"Who knew hatred could be this beautiful?" I said as my fingertips slid over the soft bumps of her spine through her thin satin robe.

She jumped up, whirled around, and slapped my hand away. "Don't touch me."

I pressed her into the wall, one hand curled around her wrists as I shoved them into the wall above her head. "Yesterday you let me touch you, let me eat your pussy, let me fuck you. You gave me yourself, willingly, desperately, *wantonly.*"

The last word broke through her mask. "You would have forced me eventually."

My eyes locked on hers, my grip on her wrists tightening. "I thought you were brave, Angel. I thought you wouldn't choose the easy way, but now I see you can't even stand down the truth of what you did."

She didn't look away.

"Now tell me again, why did you give yourself to me yesterday? And be brave. Was it because you feared I'd take your gift without asking or because you wanted to be the one who decided to whom you wanted to gift it to?"

She swallowed hard. "I wanted to gift it to Danilo. It was his privilege."

"Did you really? Or did you feel obligated to gift it to him because someone promised that gift to him without your consent."

"Don't you dare talk about consent."

I moved closer. "Why did you give it to me?"

Her eyes flashed and tears sprang into her eyes. "Because I wanted to!" She snapped her lips shut and finally looked away. A tear slid down her perfect cheek, and she took a shuddering breath. "They won't forgive me for it. They will hate me fiercely, but never as much as I hate myself, never enough."

I leaned down and grazed my nose over her pulse point, my hand cupping her face.

"Do it," she whispered, begged, and I drew back, looking into the blue pools of despair.

"Do what?" I nuzzled the soft spot behind her ear.

"Hurt me."

My mouth brushed her chin and higher over her lips.

"Hurt me." She said it harsher this time. I gripped her waist and turned her around, pressing her into the wall, her wrists still above her head, my body caging her. I was already painfully hard. The hand that wasn't holding her wrists moved under her satin robe, and I found her bare beneath. I exhaled against her neck then bit down lightly, causing her to shudder. My fingers moved to her flat belly then lower to the trimmed curls until I dipped between her folds. "Hurt me, Remo!"

"I will, Angel. Patience is a virtue. Don't you remember?" My fingers slid deeper.

She wasn't wet like she'd been yesterday, just barely aroused, mostly broken and desperate to exchange one form of pain for another. I unbuckled my belt and took out my cock before easing it between her beautiful firm ass cheeks. Her breath caught but I dipped lower to her pussy. She was tense as a fist against my tip, sore, braced for the pain.

I didn't push in. Instead my fingers started playing with her pussy, light, teasing, coaxing touches. Nothing like what she wanted.

"Why can't you just hurt me?" she whispered, tilting her face sideways and upward.

Yes, why? My hands always gave pain readily.

I held her in place, arms raised above her head, her front pressed to the wall, my cock wedged between her thighs, and watched her cry. I claimed her mouth for a kiss, tasting her tears as my fingers stroked between her pussy lips. Soon I could feel her surrender. My fingers slipped through her wetness, and her pussy loosened against my tip. Using my foot I shifted her legs further apart then looked into her teary blue eyes as I eased into her. She winced and I kissed her mouth again, slow and languid, until I was sheathed in her up to my balls, my cock buried deep inside her.

"Now *your* patience will be rewarded, Angel."

She smiled joylessly against my mouth, and I pulled all the way out of her then slammed back in. She gasped, her body coiling tight, trapped between my chest and the wall. Her pussy clenched mercilessly around me. I stroked her clit as I drove into her again. My body longed to go even harder, and so did she, but I held back not wanting to do any lasting damage.

Fuck.

What the fuck was Serafina doing to me?

Her eyes held mine as if she could find salvation there, but we were both damned, and I was dragging her closer to damnation every day.

My balls slapped against her with every thrust, and I was losing control, not just of my fucking dick but also of everything else. Serafina was still tight and her moans hesitant, pain stronger than pleasure. Claiming her mouth for a kiss, I abandoned control and came with a violent shudder.

She shivered in my hold as my cock twitched inside her. I pressed my forehead to hers, staying inside for a few moments. Her warm breath fanned over my lips, and finally I pulled out of her. Her whimper made me kiss her shoulder blade. Then I lifted her into my arms.

I carried her over to her bed and laid her down then pressed up to her back, and she let me. She was quiet. I ran my fingertips over her smooth arm. Her sweet scent mingled with mine and the muskiness of sex. The perfect mixture.

"And do you feel better? Did the pain help?" I murmured against her shoulder blade as I kissed it again. I wasn't sure why I felt the urge to kiss her like that, but I simply could not stop.

"No," she said quietly.

"I could have told you that."

"You know all about pain and its effects, don't you?"

"I don't think one person can ever know everything about pain. Everyone feels pain differently, reacts differently. It's a curious thing."

Serafina's body loosened further in my embrace. "I think I prefer pain. It doesn't make me feel as guilty as pleasure does."

I buried my nose in her hair. "You have no reason to feel guilty."

She didn't say anything and eventually her breathing evened out. I lifted my head carefully and found her asleep. Her pale lashes fluttered, her face peaceful. I'd never understood the appeal of watching someone sleep, had always found it dull, lacking. I had been so fucking wrong.

I kept stroking her arm then kissed her skin again. Fuck. How was I going to give her back?

I rested my head back on the pillow. I wasn't tired despite the long night I'd had, but I couldn't bring myself to get up with Serafina in my arms.

Closing my eyes, I allowed myself to relax. I had fallen into a light slumber when Serafina stirred, jerking me awake. She stiffened in my hold.

"It's strange when your nightmares are less horrendous than reality," she whispered.

"I've lived it, Angel. It makes you stronger."

"I wished you had taken me on the first day, back in that basement on that dirty mattress like the whore that I am."

The words ripped from her throat as if every syllable was pure agony.

I tensed, turning her around to me, feeling so fucking angry. For an instant, Serafina shrank back from the force of my fury, but then she met my gaze. She lay unmoving on her side, eyes full of anguish.

"You aren't a whore. Is your fucking virginity all that matters to your family?"

"It's not just that I'm not a virgin anymore," she whispered. "It's to whom I lost it to. They won't understand. They won't forgive. They will hate me for what I've done."

"Shouldn't they be relieved that you didn't suffer through pain and humiliation? You succumbed to pleasure. So what? All of them have sinned worse than that, even your brother, particularly your fiancé. What right do they have to judge you?"

She blinked slowly. Then she surprised me by leaning forward and kissing me. A soft kiss. A soft nothing that felt like fucking everything. My brows drew together, trying to gauge her mood.

"I'm lost, Remo."

I cradled her head and kissed her again before I rasped, "My note said that I ripped your innocence from you, that you fought me like a spitfire and that I enjoyed every second of breaking you."

She held her breath, searching my eyes. "You made it sound like you raped me." She swallowed. "Why did you lie? Was it because it would hurt my family worse?"

I smiled darkly. "I fear your family would have been more crushed if they knew you gave yourself to me freely."

"They'd hate me."

"Now you can decide what you tell them when I return you to them."

"You will?" she asked quietly.

I drew back and sat up then turned my back to her. "You were never meant to be a captive forever."

Her fingertips traced my tattoo. "Now that you got what you wanted from me, you'll ask for Scuderi." There was a strange note to her voice, but I didn't turn around to see her face because then she would have seen mine as well.

"Do you think they'll still want me now that I'm ruined?"

Serafina was many things, but ruined wasn't one of them, and anyone who declared her as such was a fucking fool. "Your family loves you. They will do anything to save you, even now. Especially now."

I rose to my feet and left without another look at her.

It was nearing midnight when my phone rang. I turned away from the screen where Savio and Adamo were playing a racing game. Nino and Kiara had already retired to their room to fuck. Without looking at the screen, I knew who it was. I picked up.

"Dante?"

My brothers slanted me curious looks. "I got your message," Dante gritted out. I could practically feel his fury. It wasn't as exhilarating as I'd expected.

"I know you don't follow the Famiglia's bloody sheets tradition, but I thought it was a nice touch."

Adamo grimaced and his car crashed into the wall. Savio had stopped playing altogether.

There was silence on the other end. "There are rules in our world. We don't attack children and women."

"Funny that you say that. When your soldiers attacked my territory, they fired at my thirteen-year-old brother. You broke those fucking rules first, so stop the bullshit."

Adamo's eyes widened, and he glanced down at his tattoo.

"You know as well as I do that I didn't give the order to kill your brother, and he's alive and well."

"If he weren't, we wouldn't be having this conversation, Dante. I would have killed every fucking person you care about, and we both know there are so many to choose from."

"You have people you don't want to lose either, Remo. Don't forget that."

Savio and Adamo watched me, and it took considerable effort to keep my fury at bay. "I thought the sheets might have made you see reason, but I see that you want Serafina to suffer a bit more."

I hung up. After a couple of heartbeats, my phone rang again, but I ignored it.

"I take it Dante isn't willing to cooperate yet," Savio said with a grin.

Adamo shook his head, pushed to his feet, and stormed upstairs.

Savio rolled his eyes. "For a few days he's been almost tolerable. I suppose that's over now."

I stood, switched the phone to silent mode, and shoved it into my pocket. "I'll have a word with him."

"Good luck," Savio muttered.

I didn't bother knocking before I stepped into Adamo's room. My eyes scanned the floor, which was littered with dirty clothes and pizza boxes. I walked toward the window and flung it open to get rid of the horrid stench.

"Why don't you clean your room?"

Adamo hunched over in front of the computer at his desk. "It's my room and I don't mind. I didn't invite you to come in."

I walked up to him and tapped against his tattoo. "You'd do well to show me respect."

"As my older brother or my Capo?" Adamo muttered, jutting his chin out.

"Both."

"For what you did to Serafina, you don't deserve my respect."

"What did I do?"

He frowned. "You forced her?"

I brought our faces closer. "Did I?"

"You didn't?"

"Are we going to keep exchanging questions? Because it's getting annoying."

"But you slept with her," Adamo said in confusion.

"I did," I said. "But she wanted it."

"Why?"

I laughed. "Ask her."

"Do you think she's in love with you?"

My muscles tautened. "Of course not." Love was a delirious game for fools, and Serafina was many things but not a fool.

"I like her." Adamo regarded me almost hopefully. I wondered when our world would rid him of the last shreds of his innocence.

"Adamo," I said sharply. "I kidnapped her so she could serve the purpose of getting revenge on the Outfit. She won't stay so don't get attached." He shrugged. Sighing, I touched his head then left.

Oh, Serafina.

I headed toward my wing, but instead of continuing to my room, I stopped in front of Serafina's door. I knew Dante would agree to give me Scuderi any day now. I unlocked the door and entered. Serafina was curled up on her side, reading a book. She put it down when I closed the door and walked toward her.

She frowned. "Just because I slept with you once—"

"Twice," I corrected.

"Just because I've slept with you *twice* doesn't mean I'll sleep with you whenever you feel like it."

I sank down beside her. "Is that so?" I trailed my fingertips over her exposed arm. Goose bumps rose on her skin.

"I'm too sore. I think last time was too much," she admitted, her cheeks turning pink.

My fingers halted on her collarbone. "Do you need to see a doctor?"

"It's not that bad." She narrowed her eyes a tad. "Are you concerned for me?"

Ignoring her question, I said, "I didn't come for sex anyway."

"What did you come for, then?"

If only I knew. I removed my gun and knife holster and dropped it to the floor beside the bed before I stretched out next to her and propped my head up on my hand.

"Don't tell me you've come to cuddle," she said.

My mouth twitched. "I've never cuddled with a woman."

"You did today."

I considered that. I'd held her in bed after sex, had watched her sleep in my arms. "I was only there to make sure you didn't drown in self-pity."

"Sure," she muttered. "You said you never cuddled with a woman. Do you make a habit of cuddling with men, then?"

I chuckled and slid my hand into her hair. She leaned into the touch ever so slightly. I wasn't sure she noticed. "I don't anymore." At the questioning lift of her eyebrow, I continued. "I used to cuddle with Adamo and Savio when they were really small."

Her nose wrinkled. "Sorry. I can't see it. Considering how exhausting small kids can be, I'm surprised you didn't end up killing them."

My fingers twitched but I restrained my anger. "They are my brothers, my flesh and blood. I'd die before I ever hurt them." I fell silent.

Serafina was quiet too. "I don't understand you, Remo Falcone."

"You aren't supposed to."

"I'm perceptive. Before you know it, you'll reveal more to me than you want."

I feared she was right. A chess piece. A means to an end. That was all Serafina could ever be. Nothing more.

My smile turned cruel. "Serafina, I know losing your virginity to me makes you think we share a special bond. But two fucks don't make you anything special to me. I've fucked so many women. One pussy is like any other. I took something from you, and now you want to justify it with fucking emotional bullshit."

She stiffened but then gave me a cunning smile of her own. Her fingers curled over my neck, and she pressed her forehead against mine like I had done before. "You took something from me, true, but you're not the only one doing the taking. Maybe you don't see it yet, but with every bit you take from me, you're giving me a bit of yourself in return, Remo, and you will never get it back."

I harshly claimed her mouth and rolled on top of her, pressing her into the mattress with my weight. "Don't," I snarled into her ear. "Don't think you know me, Angel. You know nothing. You think you've seen my darkness, but the things you haven't seen are so pitch black no fucking light on this earth can penetrate them."

"Who's not brave now?" she whispered.

I shook with anger. I wanted to fuck my rage out of my system. Wanted to hurt. Wanted to break something. I moved down her body and shoved her nightgown up then ripped her thong down her legs.

"I told you I'm sore," she said softly.

Fuck, why did she have to sound so vulnerable in that moment? What the fuck was she doing to me? I pushed her legs apart. She didn't stop me despite the tension in her limbs. Taking a deep breath, I lowered myself to my stomach, resting between her thighs.

Her body softened immediately when she realized I wasn't going to hurt her. I jerked her toward my mouth, and she winced. I softened my lips against her folds, and soon she was writhing and moaning, her legs falling open, trusting, and fuck, it was better than any rage fucking had ever been. I took my time, enjoying the way she allowed herself to surrender to pleasure. My fingertips traced the soft flesh of her inner thigh, the relaxed muscles there. No sign of tension or fear.

She came with a beautiful cry, her body arching up, giving me a prime view of her gorgeous nipples. I trailed kisses up her body until I reached her lips. "You're all about giving and taking. I gave you my mouth. How about you giving me yours now?"

"You can have my hand, no more," she said firmly.

"I want to come down your throat, not in your hand."

She held my gaze. "You can have my hand or nothing."

"The last time a woman gave me a hand job, I was fourteen. After that I came in a mouth, pussy, or ass."

"I'm not like them, Remo."

No, she wasn't. Serafina was everything. Cunning and strong. Loyal and fierce. She could have been Capo if women were allowed that place in our world.

I rolled on to my back and crossed my arms behind my head. Serafina sat up. She tried to mask her inexperience, but her nerves shone through when she fumbled with my belt. I didn't help her. My cock was already painfully hard when she pulled it out of my briefs. Her touch was too soft as she stroked me, but I enjoyed watching her. Soon she found the right pressure and tempo, and I reached down between her legs and drew small figure eights along her clit and folds. When Serafina began shaking with the force of her orgasm, and her hand tightened around my dick, my own release overwhelmed me, and I came like a fucking teenager all over my stomach.

I used her thong to clean my stomach despite her frown. Then I pulled her down against me. She was stiff but eventually she put her head down on my shoulder.

"That wasn't so bad," I drawled. "But if you want to bring me to my knees, you'll have to use your mouth."

She huffed. "I'll figure out another way to bring you to your knees, Remo."

If anyone could, then it would be her.

EIGHTEEN

Serafina

I WOKE WITH SOMEONE PRESSED UP AGAINST MY BACK, A WARM BREATH fanning over my shoulder.

I didn't pull away, only stared at my hand, which rested atop his on the bed. The skin on my ring finger was lighter from wearing my engagement ring for five years, and now it lay on my nightstand abandoned. And how could I ever wear it again? How could I ever face my fiancé again after everything I had done? Everything I still wanted to do.

Deep down I knew I didn't want to marry Danilo anymore, but it was my duty, even now. I ran my fingertips over Remo's hand, and he woke with a current of tension radiating through his body. I assumed he wasn't a man used to sharing a bed with someone.

He exhaled and relaxed but didn't say anything. I turned his hand over until his palm was up then traced the burn scars there, wondering how they'd come to be. My touch followed the scars up to his wrists, where crisscross scars fought for dominance with his burn marks. Remo's breathing changed, became cautious, dangerous.

"Will you ever tell me how you got those?"

He bit the nape of my neck. "Why should I?"

Yes, why should he spill his guts to me? I turned around in his hold. His expression was forbidding, but his eyes held a hint of something even darker. "You're right," I whispered, holding his gaze. "I'm only your captive. The queen in your game of chess. Something meaningless, easy to forget the moment you give me back." Even as I spoke the words, I couldn't imagine Remo really letting me go, not with the way he looked at me, and I wasn't sure if the realization terrified or relieved me.

"Oh, Angel, forgetting you will be impossible."

And I smiled. God help me, I smiled.

Remo shook his head slowly. "This is madness."

"It is." It was and worse … betrayal. Dad. Mom. Sofia. Sam. Guilt gripped me in its choking hold. I swallowed. "My family …" I didn't say more.

Remo's face hardened and he untangled himself from me and stood. My eyes took him in, the harshness of his expression, those cruel eyes, the scars and muscles.

Remo was the enemy. He was trying to destroy the people I loved by using me as his weapon. I couldn't forget that. He put on his clothes and gun holster. Then he nodded grimly. "That's the look you're supposed to give me, Angel. Hold on to your hatred if you can."

"Can you?"

He didn't say anything, only smiled darkly. He turned around and left. The fallen angel tattooed to his back seemed to mock me because every day I felt a bit more like an angel falling.

Kiara picked me up around lunchtime. I could tell from the way she was looking at me that she knew I'd slept with Remo. Nino had probably told her, and Remo had told him and probably everyone else. I hadn't dared to ask him if the sheets had arrived yet. The mere idea that my family and fiancé saw them drove bile up my throat.

We settled on the sofa. She'd ordered vegetarian Sushi, which was set up on the table in front of us. I didn't see Nino anywhere, but I knew he was close and would storm in at the slightest sound of distress from Kiara.

We ate in silence for a while, but eventually Kiara couldn't contain her concern anymore. She touched my shoulder, her eyes flitting to the bite marks on my throat. "Are you okay?"

I set down the sticks and met her gaze. "I'm a captive in these walls, and I betrayed my family. I let Remo dishonor me. I'm ruined. So what do you think?"

She pursed her lips. "You're only ruined if you allow others to make you feel that way."

"You don't understand." I snapped my lips shut, shame washing over me because everyone knew the stories about her. "I'm sorry."

Kiara shook her head, a flicker of pain in her eyes but she straightened her shoulders with a smile. "I felt ruined for years … until I didn't anymore, and then I was free."

"If my family and fiancé find out Remo didn't force me, they won't forgive me."

"Do you want to return to your fiancé?"

"Do you think I want to stay with Remo?" I muttered. "He kidnapped me. He keeps me locked in a room. He is my enemy. Sex won't change that."

Kiara regarded me closely. "Maybe there's a chance for peace between the Outfit and the Camorra. You could be that chance. Something good can be born from an act of brutality."

"But there won't be. My dad, my uncle, my fiancé, my *brother* won't ever agree to any kind of peace. They are proud men, Kiara. You know how Made Men are. Remo took me from them, stole my ... stole my innocence."

"It's either stolen or given."

I looked away. "They won't see it that way. He ripped something from them, took something they considered their possession. He insulted my family, my fiancé. They won't forget or forgive. They'll retaliate. They'll avenge me with brutal intent."

"Do you want to be avenged?"

"Remo kidnapped me. He took everything from me."

"Everything?" Kiara said curiously.

"Everything that used to matter." I took my chopsticks again and continued eating, hoping Kiara got the hint that I didn't want to talk anymore.

Remo came to my bedroom again that night. I had expected him and didn't say anything as he dropped his gun holster on the ground then lay down beside me. I only regarded him, trying to understand him, myself, us. But I saw the same confusion in his eyes that I felt every time he was close.

We were both caught in an undercurrent, dragging us down into its unforgiving depth, unable to swim to the surface on our own. The only people who could save us only wanted to save one of us and see the other drown, but we were entangled. One of us would have to let go first to reach the surface.

And just like the night before, Remo's mouth forced me into submission, lips and tongue and teeth, harsh one moment, gentle the next. He didn't try to sleep with me, and for some reason it made things worse because I didn't want him to hold back. I wanted him to take without consideration, without mercy. Because when he was something more than the monster I knew him to be, he took something I was even less willing to give.

He pressed against my back, breathing harshly, his erection a demanding presence pushing into me.

"When will you set me free?" I asked.

"Soon," Remo murmured but didn't elaborate. For some reason I heard the echo of the word "never."

Never. Never. Never.

And it didn't scare me as much as it should.

I considered asking about the sheets. Dante must have contacted Remo by now. But I was too scared, didn't want to know their reaction. Remo's lips brushed my shoulder blade.

"You always do that."

Tension shot through his body as if I'd caught him committing a horrendous crime. "I think Danilo ruined your uncle's plan to keep it cool."

I stiffened as well. "What?"

Remo's hold tightened, not allowing me to turn around. "Dante tried to pretend the sheets didn't have the desired effect, but this afternoon Danilo called me, and he wasn't as controlled as the cold fish wanted me to believe."

I sucked in a shaky breath. "You talked to Danilo?"

"He was furious, murderous. He told me he'd cut my balls and dick off and feed them to me." Remo paused and I tensed further. "And I told him that he could try but that it wouldn't change the fact that I was the first man inside you."

I wrenched myself out of his embrace, whirled around on him, kneeling on the bed.

Remo smiled darkly. My eyes caught the holster on the floor. I lunged, ripped the gun from the holster, released the safety, and pointed it at Remo's head.

He rolled on his back, arms stretched out in surrender. There was no fear, no apprehension in his eyes.

I straightened on my knees beside him. "If you think I can't go through with pulling the trigger, Remo, you are wrong. I'm not the girl from before who couldn't cut your throat."

Remo held my gaze. "I don't doubt you can kill me, Angel."

"Then why aren't you scared?" I asked fiercely.

"Because," he murmured, gripping my hips. I tightened my hold on the gun, but I allowed him to keep his hands on my skin. "I'm not scared of death or pain."

Without lowering the gun, I straddled his stomach, and my core clenched at the feel of his muscles.

Remo's eyes flashed with desire. I leaned forward, resting the barrel against his forehead. "If I kill you now, I'm free."

"There are still my brothers and hundreds of loyal men who will hunt you down," Remo said, his thumbs stroking my belly in a distracting way. I had already been wet from Remo's earlier ministrations, but a new wave of arousal pooled between my legs now.

"But I'd still be free of you and that's all I care about."

Remo smiled darkly again. He lifted one arm and I tightened my finger on the trigger. "You can't be free of me. Because I'm in there." He touched my temple lightly, though it was another spot he should have touched because it was his presence in another place that scared me far more. "You will always remember that I'm the one you gifted yourself to for the very first time."

I gave him the cruel smile he used on me whenever I got too close. "The memory will fade. Two times don't matter after a while. I'll sleep with Danilo for the rest of my life, and I'll forget that there ever was a man before him."

Remo jerked into a sitting position, his eyes flashing with fury. The gun dug into his forehead, but he didn't care. His grip on my hip tightened, and his other hand cupped my head. "Oh, Angel, trust me when I say you'll remember me for the rest of your existence."

I lifted up and positioned myself over Remo's erection. I touched my palm to his cheek, causing his eyes to flash with an emotion that scared him and me equally. I released the trigger but didn't drop the gun. I lowered myself on Remo's length slowly, despite the fierce twinge. My head fell back when he was buried all the way inside me.

"Devastating."

I lowered my head, locking gazes with Remo.

"Devastatingly beautiful," he murmured. I lowered the gun and pressed it to his chest.

"There's nothing in there for you to shoot."

I engaged the safety, wrapped my arms around his neck, and rocked my hips, the gun dangling loosely in my hand. Pain and pleasure shot through me. Remo groaned. I moved faster, lifting and falling. Remo held me tightly, his eyes dark and possessive as he let me be in control.

Remo's teeth scraped my throat, leaving marks, and my nails raked over his back, leaving my own marks in turn. It was painful but I rode him hard and fast, relishing in the burning sensation. Remo sucked my nipple into his mouth, and his thumb rubbed my clit. Pleasure spiked fiercely, mingling with the pain in a delicious dance.

Both were spiraling higher and higher, and I knew one of them would eventually shatter me, and I longed for it. Needed it. Remo flicked my nub and pleasure overpowered all else. I cried out, dropping the gun as I desperately held on to Remo's shoulders, my nails digging in. Remo held my gaze with fierceness and hunger, and I felt alive and free and weightless.

I was still shuddering from the force of my orgasm when Remo flipped us around, locking my knees under his arms, parting me wide and thrusting into me in one hard push, going so much deeper than before. I arched up, lips parting in a choked sound, half moan, half whimper. Remo didn't pause. He slammed into me, hard and fast, shoving me into the mattress over and over again, ripping every last shred of innocence from me. The gun lay beside us on the bed.

Remo had been right. A bullet to his head wouldn't free me of him. At this point, I wasn't sure if anything could.

Remo

Sitting on the sofa in the game room, I stared down at my phone. Two missed calls from Dante. The last from yesterday. Three days since my entertaining call with Danilo. I couldn't bring myself to talk to Dante, knowing I had him right where I wanted him.

"It's time to end this. Dante called me today. He'll exchange Scuderi for Serafina."

"I'm Capo. I decide when and how to set her free."

Nino leaned forward, arms braced on his thighs. "Remo, if you have feelings for her—"

I cut him off. "I'm not like you. One woman won't turn me into an emotional mess."

He narrowed his eyes but his expression remained calm. "Then send her back. Fabiano is getting impatient and so am I. There's nothing else to gain from this. Dante won't give us more than Scuderi. You already made them believe you tortured and raped Serafina. They are on their knees, but Dante is Capo. He won't give up more than his Consigliere."

"Next time he calls, I'll take his call," I said with a shrug.

Nino assessed me. "I told you there would be no winners in this game."

"We are the winners."

He shook his head but didn't say anything.

I stood and went over to the boxing bag. Kicking and punching it didn't help with my fucking inner turmoil, and Nino's judgmental presence didn't help either.

I kicked the bag once more then stalked upstairs and burst into Serafina's bedroom. She was reading on the windowsill. By now, Adamo must have brought her half of our library. She put the book down and stood. In the last few days, a gradual power shift had started and I couldn't allow it.

Serafina moved closer, scanning my face cautiously. She stopped in front of me. Instead of dealing out harshness like I'd intended to, my eyes took in her soft lips, lips I couldn't get enough of, lips that drove me insane with desire.

"You have a very strange look on your face."

"I can't think about anything else than having you on your knees in front of me with those perfect lips around my cock." It was a half-truth, the only truth she'd ever get.

"I was on my knees once," she hissed.

I shook my head. "That doesn't count. You can be on your knees and still be in control."

"I won't kneel."

"That's a shame considering there's no better way to bring a man to his knees than to kneel in front of him while you suck his cock. Didn't you want to bring me to my knees?"

She pushed me back and I sank down on the edge of the bed. I pulled her between my legs so her knees pressed up against my erection. I slipped my palm between her closed thighs and rubbed her through the fabric of her panties. "I wake with a fucking boner every morning, dreaming about your lips and your tongue, Angel. How it would feel to fuck your sweet mouth."

She was burned into my fucking mind, not just the feel of her body …

Her brows drew together, but her mouth opened as her breathing deepened. Using my thumb, I grazed her clit while my other finger slid along her slit. Her panties soon stuck to her folds with her juices. "I eat your pussy almost every day. Don't you ever wonder how it would be to return the favor? To control me with your mouth?"

Her eyes flashed and she moaned when I pressed my hand harder against her center. Slowly, I withdrew my hand and smiled darkly. I gripped her hips and pressed down, not enough to make her knees buckle but to show her what I wanted. She resisted so I loosened the pressure and finally she lowered herself to her knees, head held high. My cock hardened further at the sight of Serafina before me. I unbuckled my belt and unzipped my pants before I took my cock out. I began stroking myself, swirling my thumb over my slick tip.

Serafina watched with parted lips but narrowed her eyes when she noticed my smirk. After another swirl of my thumb, gathering my pre-cum, I brushed her lips and pushed into her mouth. Her tongue tasted me hesitantly, and my fucking dick twitched. Serafina noticed, of course, and smiled in triumph.

I pulled my finger out and placed my hand over her neck, but I didn't push her toward my waiting cock, knowing she'd resist again if I tried to coax her into doing what I wanted.

Finally, she reached out, curling those elegant fingers around the base of my cock. She squeezed experimentally, and I stifled a groan. And then Serafina leaned forward and slid my tip into her mouth. She licked the tip then sucked, unpracticed moves that drove me insane with desire. I began thrusting into her mouth, driving my cock deeper into her, but not all the way in, still holding back when I'd never held back for a woman in my entire life.

My balls clenched every time she hollowed her cheeks, and the sight would have brought me to my knees if I weren't already sitting. Kneeling before me, challenge and triumph in her blue eyes, Serafina owned me. Body ... and whatever black soul was left.

My phone rang and I tightened my hold on her neck when I took the call. "Dante, what a pleasure," I got out.

Serafina tried pulling back, her eyes going wide, but my hand on her neck kept her in place as I thrust into her mouth. She glared and scraped her teeth over my dick, which made my eyes roll back and my cock twitch. I smirked. She'd have to bite down much harder for me to release her. Pain only turned me on more.

"I'm not calling to exchange pleasantries," Dante said coldly.

I turned the loud speaker on and loosened my hold on her neck. Serafina jerked back, but I grabbed her arm and hoisted her up. Then I pulled her onto my lap, her back against my chest, one of my arms wrapped around her chest. My feet shoved her legs apart and kept them spread eagle. Serafina scowled but couldn't say anything. I brushed two fingers over her folds, finding her fucking dripping with arousal. I grinned and shame flashed across her face. "That's a pity," I said to Dante.

I slid two fingers into her and began fucking her while my other hand cupped her breast.

"We should come to a solution," Dante said. I could hear the barely restrained fury in his voice.

"I'm sure we will," I said as I slid my fingers in and out of Serafina's pussy and swirled my thumb over her clit. "You know I want Scuderi. I want you to hand him to me in person."

Serafina's muscles clenched around my fingers as I fucked her slowly. She twisted her head back and bit into the side of my neck. My hold loosened, and she wrenched free of my grip and stormed into the bathroom, slamming the door shut.

"In two days. In my city. I want you to bring him all the way to Vegas. You get Serafina. I get Scuderi. I want her fiancé there as well. I'd like to meet him in person."

Dante was silent. "We will be there."

"Nino will send you the details. I'm looking forward to meeting you." I hung up, but the triumph I felt lasted only a moment. My eyes found the door behind which Serafina was hiding.

Two more days.

Then I'd set her free.

It would be up to her if she flew straight into Danilo's cage …

My chest constricted but I pushed past the sensation. Serafina was never meant to be mine.

I stood, and tearing my gaze away from the door, I left.

NINETEEN

Serafina

■■ WEAR THIS," REMO ORDERED, THROWING MY WEDDING DRESS DOWN ON
the bed. I stared at the white layers of tulle, at the blood stains and the
tears. I hadn't seen it in almost two months. It didn't feel like something I'd
ever owned. Nothing I was meant to wear ever again.

"Why?" I asked.

Remo turned toward me, his dark eyes hard. "Because I told you to do it,
Serafina."

Not *Angel*. Serafina. What was going on? I narrowed my eyes. "Why?"

He moved closer, glaring down at me. "Do as I say."

"Or what?" I said harshly. "What could you possibly do to me? You have
taken everything from me that mattered. There's nothing left for you to take, to
break."

Remo's mouth turned cruel. "If you really think that's true, then you are
weaker than I thought."

I swallowed hard, but I didn't put on the dress. We both knew I was so
much stronger than he'd ever imagined. Maybe that was why he kept doing this,
pushing me away.

Remo reached for his knife and pulled it out with a bone-chilling clink
of the blade against the sheath. Goose bumps rose on my skin, but I stood my
ground because if I knew one thing it was that Remo wouldn't hurt me. Not
anymore, not ever again.

Whatever twisted bond had formed between us, it prevented him from
causing me pain.

Gripping the neckline of my nightgown, he sliced through the fabric with a sharp slash of the knife. The shreds pooled at my feet, leaving me in only my panties.

His dark eyes roamed over my body, the knife still clutched in his hand, and my core tightened with need. He gripped my hip and wrenched me toward him, his lips crushing down on mine. I gasped as his tongue conquered my mouth, teeth clanking. He backed me up against the bed until I fell back. He slashed through my panties with his knife, and the closeness of the blade caused a shiver to pass down my spine. Remo towered over me and freed his erection, his eyes furious and hungry and terrifying.

Holding his gaze, I opened my legs for him because I was lost, had been lost from the moment Remo had laid eyes on me, and as I looked up at him, I knew without a doubt that he, too, was lost.

The corners of his mouth lifted as he lowered his gaze to my center. He got down on his knees, pushing my legs even further apart. Remo buried his face in my lap. I arched up, my nails digging into the crisp sheets, my gaze finding my torn wedding dress. Remo's mouth claimed me relentlessly, with tongue and lips, bites and licks. There was no escaping. He wouldn't let me. He made me surrender, not with force, not with violence … He dove in, swirling until I was a slave to the sensations he created. My orgasm crashed over me like an avalanche, but my eyes remained locked on the stained white fabric of my dress—a sign for my honor, my purity.

Both lost.

Both taken … No. *Given.*

Remo's mouth traveled up my stomach, licking and nibbling, tongue flicking my nipple. He bit down lightly then soothed the spot with an open-mouthed kiss. His body covered mine, his palms pressed into the bed beside my head, the knife still clutched in his grasp. For a moment our eyes locked, and I hated him, hated myself, hated us both, because hate became harder to hold on to each day that I spent with him.

We both needed our hate, and yet it was slipping through our fingers like sand. There was no way to contain it. Lost. His dark eyes reflected my inner turmoil. Losing ourselves to each other.

My gaze returned to my dress when Remo thrust into me in one all-consuming merciless stroke. His mouth pressed up to my ear as he slammed into me angrily. "When I saw you in that dress, I knew I needed to be the one to rip your innocence from you. I knew I needed to be the one to make you bleed. Who knew you'd make me bleed in return?"

I shuddered, my throat tightening even as my body throbbed with traitorous pleasure. Finally I tore my gaze from the dress to glare up at Remo—my captor, my nemesis, my ruin … and yet, despite what he'd taken from me, hatred wasn't the only thing my weak, idiotic heart felt. But that was a truth I would take to my grave.

"I hate you," I whispered as if saying the words aloud would make them true.

Remo's eyes bore into mine, filled with emotions, his mouth twisting in a dark smile because he *knew*. He moved closer, tongue sliding along the seam of my lips. "Nothing tastes sweeter than your lips, even when they're spewing lies, Angel."

His next thrust hit deep, and I could not hold back. Blinding pleasure rushed through my body. My lips parted but I swallowed my cry. I wouldn't give it to Remo. Not today. He bit down on my throat, and the force of my orgasm doubled. The moan clawed itself out of my throat. He couldn't even allow me that small victory. His own face twisted with strain as he kept thrusting, shoulders flexing. He kissed my mouth softly then my ear, and I knew he would deliver words meant to break, words worse than any torture could ever be. I'd known it from the moment I'd seen his cold face this morning.

"You wanted to know why I need you to put on your wedding dress," he rasped as his thrusts became less controlled.

My chest tightened with dread.

Remo kissed my ear again. "You see, I arranged a meeting with Dante for tonight, and I promised to give you back. Danilo will be there as well, and I thought he'd appreciate finally seeing you in your wedding dress. Even if I stole what you promised to him."

Shock and fury crashed down on me, and I slapped Remo hard. He gripped my wrist and pressed it into the mattress over my head as he thrust into me again, eyes staking claim on me over and over again, taking more with every thrust. But he couldn't lock me out anymore, because I, too, had laid claim to a part of him.

· His body tightened, coiling tight with pleasure, and as always, my own traitorous body submitted to him again. I cried out. Remo linked our fingers, pressing them deeper into the mattress as his mouth found mine for a kiss full of anger and dominance. When he finally stilled on top of me, my eyes moved up to my dress.

"You are mine, Angel. Body and soul," he rasped. And God help me, he spoke the truth.

When I put the dress back on, it felt like a sacrilege wearing something so pure and white. Goose bumps rippled across my skin when the heavy fabric settled around my legs. I stared down at the layers of tulle, the blood stains and tears. Had I really chosen this dress? Had I ever felt comfortable wearing it?

Remo regarded me with a hard expression. "I still remember the first time I saw you in it."

I didn't say anything.

Remo reached for my engagement ring on the nightstand, and the little hairs on my neck rose. He stopped right in front of me and took my hand then slid the ring on with a twisted smile. "This marks you as Danilo's, doesn't it?"

I stared at him fiercely, unyieldingly because he knew the mark he had left went deeper than an expensive ring. Something in Remo's eyes shifted, a flicker in his harsh mask, yet he still held my hand. He released me abruptly and stepped back. "Danilo will be delighted to get you back."

"I'm not the girl I used to be."

Remo's gaze hit me like a sledgehammer, but he didn't say anything, even though I wanted … needed him to.

Up until the very end, I was convinced Remo would keep me. I kept denying the truth until I was faced with the result of my sins: the exhausted faces of my family and fiancé.

They waited in the abandoned parking lot. Dad, Dante, Danilo. Samuel wasn't there, and I knew it was because he would have lost it. Behind them on the ground lay a tied up man, probably Fabiano's father. His back was turned to me so I couldn't be sure.

Their eyes were drawn upward toward one of the buildings, and when Remo pulled me out of the car, I found the reason why. Nino was perched on the roof as a sniper. Fabiano got out of the car as well, his own gun drawn.

Remo led me a few steps away from the car. Then he stopped. "You were very ill-advised attacking our territory, Dante," he said pleasantly, his grip on my hip tight as he held me against his body. My eyes lingered on the ground because my guilt sat so heavily on my shoulders I couldn't find the courage to meet the gazes of the men who'd come to save me. The white fabric of my dress seemed to mock me, and I focused on the bloodstains.

Bracing myself, I finally raised my head and wished I hadn't.

Nothing had ever hurt worse than the look on Dad's face. He took in my bloody dress, the bruises on my throat where Remo had marked me over and over again. Remo had made his claiming of me as apparent as possible, flaunted it in front of everyone, and it had the desired effect. Uncle Dante, my fiancé Danilo, and my father regarded me as if they had been gutted. Remo's ultimate triumph.

I wanted to scream at them that I hadn't suffered the way they thought I had, wished they would hate me, but I wasn't brave enough for the truth.

"Next time you consider fucking with us, look at your niece, Dante, and remember how you failed her."

Dante's face was stone, but there was a flicker of something dark in his eyes.

I couldn't meet their eyes. Burning shame sliced through me at what I had let Remo do, at what I had done. What I had wanted to do, what I still wanted to do.

Remo leaned closer, his lips brushing my ear. "I own you, Angel. Remember that. You gave me a part of yourself and you'll never get it back. It's mine no matter what happens next."

Dante, Danilo, and my father looked on the verge of attacking, their body's tense, expressions twisted with hatred and fury. They wanted to protect me when I no longer wanted saving, couldn't be saved because I was irrevocably lost.

I turned my head slightly, meeting Remo's cold gaze. "I'm not the only one who lost something," I whispered. "You gave me part of your cruel black heart, Remo, and one day you will realize it."

Something flashed in Remo's eyes. Those cruel eyes that haunted his victims' nightmares ... how long would they haunt me? Especially all the times they hadn't looked upon me with cruelty or hatred but with a far more terrifying emotion.

Then he tore his gaze away from me to stare at my uncle. All I could think was that he hadn't denied my words. I had Remo's cruel black heart and maybe that was the most painful realization of all.

"Hand over Scuderi," he said.

Dante gripped the rope that coiled tightly around a struggling Scuderi and dragged him toward us. I'd known my uncle all my life, but I'd never seen that look on his face. Utter fury and regret. He thrust Scuderi to the ground halfway toward us. "Release my niece, *now*," he ordered.

Remo chuckled. This was a trick. This had to be a trick. Remo had said it himself: I was his. He owned me. Body and soul. He wouldn't let me go. The worst was that deep down I hoped he wouldn't—and not just because I didn't want to live among the family I'd betrayed so horribly, but also because the idea that he could give me up so easily tore at me.

His dark eyes locked on mine, possessive and triumphant, and he leaned down. For a heart stopping moment I was sure he'd kiss me right in front of everyone, but his lips lightly grazed my cheek before they stopped at my ear. "I never thought you'd give me this look on the day I released you—as if giving you freedom is the worst betrayal of all. You shouldn't want someone to cage you in. You should long for freedom." He exhaled, his hot breath against my skin making me shiver. "Goodbye, Serafina."

Remo released me then shoved me away from him. I stumbled forward, away from him, my heart thundering in my chest. Strong hands grabbed me and quickly ushered me away from Remo. I walked toward my family, my fiancé—freedom—but it didn't feel anything like being free.

Dante was beside me and Danilo stepped toward me, *reached for me*, and I flinched, feeling unworthy of his touch after I'd betrayed him, betrayed the Outfit with Remo. Dante and my father both tensed, and Danilo lowered his arm and stepped back from me with a look full of utter hatred toward Remo. But Remo's expression was the worst because when I met his gaze I knew what it said.

I own you.

I half fell into my father's arms, and he hugged me tightly, whispering words of consolation that I didn't catch, pulling me away toward their car. My eyes weren't on him.

Fabiano loaded his father into the back of the car before he got in. With another glance at me, Remo followed and drove away. *Drove away.*

And again I shivered because part of me, the part that terrified me most, missed Remo.

I own you.

He did.

Dad got into the back of the car with me, still hugging me to his chest and stroking my hair, and a new wave of guilt overcame me. Dante got behind the wheel, and Danilo sat beside him. My fiancé glanced at me through the rearview mirror, and I ducked my head, my cheeks flaming with shame.

"You are safe now, Fina. Nothing will ever happen to you again. I'm sorry, dove. I'm so sorry," Dad whispered against my hair, and I realized he was crying. My father. A Made Man since his teenage days. Underboss of Minneapolis. He was crying into my hair, right in front of his Capo and my fiancé, and I fell apart. I clutched his jacket and cried, ugly cried, for the first time since I could remember, and my father hugged me even tighter.

"I'm sorry," I gasped out, broken words full of despair. Words weren't enough to convey the extent of my sins. Of my betrayal.

"No," he growled. "No, Fina, no." He shook, his grip painful.

"Remo … he … I."

Dad cupped my head. "It's over. It's over now, Fina. I swear, one day I'll hunt him down. I will kill him for what he did to you … for … for hurting you."

I swallowed. He thought Remo had raped me. They all did, and I couldn't tell him the truth, was too cowardly to tell him. Closing my eyes, I rested my cheek against his chest. Dad held me tightly, rocking me like a little girl, like he could restore my innocence by doing so.

Would the truth set him free? Set them all free or would it break them worse? I wasn't sure of anything anymore.

Remo

Fabiano kept tossing glances at his father resting on the backrest of the car, looking fucking eager to tear into the man.

"Your plan really worked. You crushed the fucking Outfit," Fabiano said, turning to me. I stared at the road. The triumph I'd been working toward, destroying the Outfit from within, I held it in my hands. I'd seen it on the faces of my enemies. I knew they'd keep suffering.

Fabiano shifted in his seat. "Remo, you realize we won, right? We got my father. Your insane plan worked."

"Yeah, my plan worked …"

"Then why—" Fabiano's eyes widened.

My grip on the steering wheel tightened.

"We can try kidnapping her again. It worked once, who's to say it won't work again," he said almost incredulously.

"No," I said harshly. "Serafina doesn't belong in captivity."

Fabiano shook his head. "They will marry her off to Danilo. Even if you spoiled the goods, she's still Cavallaro's niece, and Danilo would be foolish to refuse a marriage because she isn't a virgin anymore."

I wanted to kill someone, wanted to spill blood. "She won't marry him."

"Remo—"

"Not another word, Fabiano, or I swear you won't get a chance to rip your father to shreds because I will and then maybe do the same to you."

He sank back into the seat with a frown. "Should I call Nino?"

"We'll see him in five fucking minutes," I growled. "Now shut the fuck up."

We met at the Sugar Trap. Fabiano dragged his father down into the basement while I sat down at the bar. Jerry put a bottle of brandy and a glass down in front of me without a word.

Nino joined me after a couple of minutes. "Matteo and Romero's plane arrived thirty minutes ago. They'll be here soon."

"Good. A sign of goodwill for Luca."

"He still isn't happy about the kidnapping. But now that we gave Serafina back and give his brother and Captain a chance to partake in the torture, he'll probably come back around. We don't need a conflict with the Famiglia. The Outfit will start attacking viciously soon enough."

"Set up a cage fight for me. Two opponents. Death match. Tomorrow. The day after at the latest."

Nino grasped my shoulder. "Remo. We can't have you play with your life now. We need you strong."

I stood and gave him a twisted smile. "If you want me strong, give me someone to kill. I want blood. I want to maim and kill. And I'm not risking my life. I will fucking obliterate every fucking person who enters the fucking cage as my opponent."

"It won't make you miss her any less."

I lunged at him in blinding rage. For the first time in my fucking life, I attacked my brother. Nino blocked my fist and took a step back, and I jerked to a halt, stopping myself after realizing what I was doing. My chest heaved as I stared into my brother's cautious gray eyes.

Jerry had run off and a moment later Fabiano stormed inside but froze when he saw me and Nino facing each other, standing almost chest to chest.

"Fuck," I rasped, taking a step back. I held out my arm, tattoo on display, my palm up. A silent apology, the only one I was capable of. Fabiano turned back around, leaving us alone. Nino linked our arms, my hand on his tattoo, on his scars, and his palm on mine.

"You walked through fire for me, Remo," he said quietly, imploringly, "but you should know, I'd do the same for you. I wouldn't have asked you to send her back if I'd known … And I'll walk straight into Outfit territory for you and get her back if that's what you want."

"That's not what I want."

"She won't return to you of her own free will."

"Then so be it. Now find someone I can kill and set up the fucking death match."

Nino squeezed my arm then released me.

"I think for the first time in my life I envy you your lack of emotions."

TWENTY

Remo

"I F THEY DON'T ARRIVE SOON, I'LL START WITHOUT THEM. I DON'T GIVE
a fuck if it offends Luca fucking Vitiello or not," Fabiano growled as he
stood over his father, who lay on his side on the ground, mouth taped,
arms and legs bound together. He stared up at his son with terror-widened eyes.

"They'll be here any second," I muttered.

I could tell Fabiano was barely listening. He was too focused on his father.
He'd waited a long time for this moment. Fuck, I got it. I'd do anything for a
chance to torture my father to death. I still remembered the fucking day I found
out my traitorous half-brother had killed the asshole, something I'd dreamed of
since I understood our father wasn't the invincible god he made himself out to be.
That he could, in fact, be killed. Since I was a fucking kid, I'd dreamed of erasing
our father from our lives …

If there were a Hell, I'd walk straight down into it to make a deal with the
Devil so he'd give me the chance to kill the man just once. Maybe twice.

"Not the scrawny boy you can torture for your own amusement anymore,
am I?" Fabiano murmured as he crouched in front of the other man. I prided
myself on my scary smile, but Fabiano's expression surpassed everything. He'd
enjoy today.

The door creaked open, and Fabiano straightened. Nino came in, followed by
Matteo and Romero. I had been surprised when Luca had told me he'd send them
but not come himself. I supposed he had less reason to tear into Scuderi than the
others. He had been gifted Aria because Scuderi sold his daughters off like cattle,
and anyone could admit Aria was a very nice gift. An image of another woman
with blond hair and blue eyes entered my mind, uninvited. I shoved it down.

I'd set her free.

"Nothing better than bonding over shared torture," Matteo said with a grin as he sauntered into the cell in the basement of the Sugar Trap. That asshole always looked as if he'd walked straight out of a photo shoot for a fashion magazine. One day I'd fuck up his pretty face. Romero gave me and Fabiano a curt nod before his eyes, too, fell on Scuderi.

I pushed off the wall and extended my hand to Matteo, who took it after a moment.

"I still can't stand your fucking face, Remo," he said with a smirk. "But for this I might hesitate a millisecond before cutting your throat once we're back to being enemies."

"That millisecond will be the moment I'll cut your head off, Matteo," I said with a twisted smile of my own.

He released my hand. "May the craziest fucker win."

My smile widened and I caught Nino's gaze across the room. We both knew who that would be because when it came to crazy fuckery I was the undisputed master.

I turned to Romero, who didn't display the careless attitude of Vitiello. He obviously was wary about being in a basement in Vegas. I didn't have the slightest intention to attack either of them today. War with the Famiglia would have to wait until the Outfit was crushed and its territory split between us.

He briefly shook my hand. "Your methods are dishonorable," he said tersely.

"You disapprove of them and yet here you are … benefiting from them."

Romero pulled his hand away, his brown eyes returning to Scuderi and his expression filling with hate.

I went over to Scuderi and smiled down at him. His eyes flickered with terror. "I must say you've gathered many enemies over time, and we've all come together to tear you apart."

I reached down and ripped the tape from his face then straightened and returned to my spot at the wall. Maybe his agonized screams would drown out the voice of regret in my head.

Serafina walking away in that fucking white dress and that last look she gave me. Fuck it all.

Fabiano circled his father. "Father, I've been waiting for this chance for a very long time, and I have every intention of making it last for as long as possible. Lucky for me, Nino is a master at prolonging torture. With a little luck we can keep you alive for two or three days. That way we can all get the fun we deserve."

Scuderi tried to push himself into a sitting position but failed. His expression became pleading. If he thought that would warm Fabiano's heart, he didn't understand what Fabiano did on a daily basis as my Enforcer. "I'm your father, Fabi. You already lost your mother. Do you want to lose me as well?"

Fabiano lunged, smashing his fist into the man's face. Bones crunched. I watched from my spot against the wall. This wasn't my moment. Despite my need to maim and kill, I'd hold back. Matteo, Fabiano, and Romero had more reason to spill Scuderi's blood.

"Shut up," Fabiano snarled.

Matteo had begun twisting a Karambit knife in his fingers, an eager gleam in his eyes I knew all too well.

"I've got small kids who need me," Scuderi tried in a hoarse voice.

Fabiano lifted him by the collar and jerked him up against the wall, getting in his face. "They'll be better off without you. My sisters and I would have that's for sure."

Nino put a chair down in the center of the room, and Matteo helped Fabiano drag Scuderi over to it. They tied him up despite his struggling.

His beady eyes found me. "Remo, you are Capo. I could be of use to you. I know everything about the Outfit and Dante. If you let me live, I'll tell you everything."

Fabiano scoffed as he pulled his knife from the holster around his chest.

I smiled cruelly at the disgusting bastard before me. "You will reveal everything I want to know. I know you're in very capable hands that will coerce every truth out of you."

"Oh we will," Matteo said with his fucking shark grin. He stepped up to Fabiano, and they exchanged a look. Then Matteo leaned over Scuderi and brought the knife down on his chest. "Gianna sends her regards. I told her I'd let you suffer, and I will."

Matteo left a long cut across Scuderi's chest, making the bastard scream like a fucking coward.

Romero moved up to Scuderi after that. He wasn't holding a knife in his hand. He smashed his fist into Scuderi side twice then into his stomach. Some men preferred to dish out pain with their fists, others with a cold blade. I enjoyed either, depending on my mood and what my opponent feared more.

"You gave Lily to a fucking old bastard so you could get a child bride for yourself. You're a disgrace of a father." He punched the man again.

Fabiano took over. "I hope you will spend your last hours considering that not a fucking soul on this planet will be sorry you're gone. If you find time for sane thoughts between the agony." He inflicted a long cut on the man's arm. The sight of the red rivulets trailing enticingly over bare skin made my body hum with excitement. Fuck, I wanted to spill blood, dish out agony. I wanted to fucking destroy someone.

Nino leaned beside me. It wasn't time for him to help yet, and his attention was on me, not the scene in the center of the cell.

"Stop the assessment," I said in a low voice.

Nino narrowed his eyes slightly but complied and finally turned toward the torture. Matteo, Romero, and Fabiano took turns beating and cutting Scuderi until his screams and begging filled the cell.

After a few hours, Fabiano, covered in blood and sweat, indicated for Nino to get involved. My brother rolled up his sleeves and after another lingering glance at me, he moved toward the medical kit that would ensure Scuderi didn't die too soon.

Romero leaned against the wall. Matteo and Fabiano had taken turns torturing Scuderi over the last hour, and I had a feeling they'd be the ones to deal with him in the remaining hours of his life. My own body hummed with the need to destroy, the need to give pain and feel pain, to fill the fucking void in my chest.

My body screamed for sleep, but except for a few toilet breaks, I stayed in the cell while Fabiano dealt with his bastard of a father. It wouldn't be much longer.

Fabiano's shoulders heaved as he stared down at his father. The man was breathing shallowly.

Fabiano turned to me, blood splatters dotting his face. His naked chest was completely coated with it. Our eyes met. "Remo...will you...?" His voice was hoarse.

I pushed away from the wall and walked up to him, not sure what he was asking of me. Fabiano clutched the bloody knife in a death grip, the look in his eyes reminding me of the boy I'd found in Bratva territory many years ago—a boy desperate for death because his father had taken everything from him.

Nino motioned for Matteo and Romero to leave, and with a last look at me, he closed the door. Fabiano swallowed before he held out his forearm with the Camorra tattoo. "You gave me a home. A purpose. You treated me like a brother..." He glanced down at his father. "Like family. I know you wanted nothing more than to kill your father and had that taken from you. I know it's not the same, but...will you help me kill my father?"

I linked arms with Fabiano, clutching his forearm tightly. "We aren't blood but we are brothers, Fabiano. I'll walk through fire for you." I stared down at the fucker who'd wanted his own son dead then back up to Fabiano. "And there's nothing I'd rather do than kill him with you. It's an honor."

Fabiano nodded, then got down on his knees beside his father. I did the same. Fabiano raised the knife above his father's chest then looked at me. I closed my fingers over his and together we jabbed the blade down, right into Scuderi's fucking heart.

Fabiano's shoulders sagged and he released a harsh breath as if the man's death finally set him free. I wondered if anything would ever do the same for Nino and me?

Serafina

Outside of Las Vegas we traded in the car for the private jet belonging to the Outfit. I huddled in my seat, my cheek pressed to the window, watching the city grow smaller in the distance. Dad sat across from me, looking and not looking at me, caught somewhere between utter relief and hopeless despair.

I knew what a pitiful sight I was. Bloody and torn dress. Bite marks all over my throat. Dante was talking quietly on the phone, but he, too, slanted the occasional look at me. The only one who hadn't looked at me after I flinched from his touch was Danilo. He leaned forward, forearms braced on his knees, staring blankly at the floor.

Guilt and a flicker of sadness washed over me. For him. For us. For what could have been and never would.

I swallowed and looked away. I met Dad's gaze. He forced a small smile and reached for me as if to touch my legs over the tulle of my dress, but then he hesitated as if he was worried about my reaction. I snatched his hand and squeezed. His eyes were still glassy and haunted. *I'm a sinner, Dad. Don't cry for me.*

He lifted his other hand with the phone. "Do you want to call Samuel? I sent him a message that we got you."

I nodded fiercely, my throat clogging. Dad's eyes darted to my throat once more, and the hint of something cruel and harsh flared in them. Something he had never showed at home. He gave me his phone, and I hit speed dial with shaking fingers.

"Yes?"

For a second, hearing Samuel's voice immobilized me. "Sam," I croaked.

There was silence. "Fina?"

The word was a broken exclamation that splintered me apart. Tears trailed down my cheeks, and I could feel all eyes on me. I closed my own. "I'm sorry."

Samuel sucked in a sharp breath. "Don't … don't apologize. Not ever again, Fina."

I couldn't promise that. One day I'd have to deliver the apology that would make Sam hate me. A higher voice rang out in the background. "It's okay, Mom," Samuel soothed. "I'll give her to you." He addressed me again. "I'll give you Mom now. I can't wait to hold you in my arms, Fina."

I sniffled. "Me too."

"Fina," Mom said softly, trying but failing at sounding composed and not like she was sobbing.

So many broken hearts. So much pain and despair.

Remo Falcone was indeed the cruelest man I knew, and I had to be the coldest bitch on this planet, because even still my stupid heart thudded faster when I thought of him.

"I'll be home soon," I whispered.

"Yes … yes," Mom agreed. We hung up eventually because it got to be too much, the silence of suppressed crying and the distance we couldn't bridge.

"Where are we going?" I hadn't asked before because I'd just assumed we'd go back to Minneapolis … but I was as good as Danilo's wife. Would they take me to Indianapolis? Or maybe to Chicago because Dante needed to question me about every little detail of my captivity?

Dad leaned forward and cupped my cheek. "Home, Fina. Home."

I nodded. My eyes found Danilo, who was watching me. Our gazes locked briefly, but then guilt forced me to look away. I'd have to face him eventually. I wasn't sure what to tell him.

The rest of the plane ride passed in utter silence. I knew they all had so many questions to ask but held back for my sake, and I was glad because I still wasn't sure what to say to any of them.

With every second that passed, my skin crawled more and more trapped in my wedding dress. It felt so utterly wrong, like being wrapped in lies and deceit.

Mom and Samuel waited in front of our house when we pulled up with the car. I didn't see Sofia anywhere, probably to protect her from the sight, and I was glad. She didn't need to see me like this.

I trembled when Dad helped me out of the car, his fingers tight around my forearm as if he worried I might faint. Dante and Danilo stayed back as we walked toward the house. Samuel staggered toward me. My twin. My confidante. My partner in crime.

He froze when his eyes registered my state, the marks on my throat, and his expression became one I'd seen the first time shortly after he'd become a Made Man five years ago. Cold, cruel, out for blood. He caught himself, bridged the remaining distance between us, and hugged me to his body, lifting me off the ground in a crushing embrace. I buried my face in the crook of his neck, shivering.

"I thought I'd never see you again," he rasped.

I wasn't the person he knew. She was gone. If he knew what I'd become, if they all knew, they'd hate me. And rightfully so.

Can you un-lose yourself?

I clung to Samuel for a long time, just breathing in his comforting scent, relishing in the feel of him. Eventually, he set me down and my eyes fell on Mom, who stood behind Samuel, her hand covering her mouth, tears running down her face. Dad had wrapped his arm around her, steadying her. Their anguish cut me deeply.

They thought Remo had raped me. I looked like I had been raped with my ripped and bloody dress. Mom rushed forward and embraced me so tightly I could barely breathe and she sobbed into my hair, and my heart … it just broke hearing it. And not for the first time, I wished Remo had done what everyone thought so I could cry rightfully with my mother and with all of them.

I should have told her the truth, but the words didn't pass my lips. Soon. Dad and Samuel joined us, and I sighed, because right then I allowed myself a moment of contentment being united with them. Samuel wrapped his arm around my shoulders as he led me inside our home.

"Where's Sofia?" I asked.

"She's with Valentina and the kids in a safe house close by. They'll come over soon," Dante explained from behind me.

I nodded.

"I need to shower," I said and regretted my words when I saw the look my family exchanged. I quickly moved away and headed upstairs into my room, starting to tear at my dress, but the thing clung to me. Angry, desperate tears gathered in my eyes.

"Sam!" I called, and in a blink he was there. "Can you … can you help me with the dress?"

He nodded and pushed my hair to the side to reach the zipper. He froze, releasing a shuddering breath. I knew what he saw: the bite mark on the nape of my neck. He leaned forward, burying his face in my hair. I allowed him a moment to gather himself even as my own heart broke and broke and broke. "I will kill him."

A threat. A promise. Not my salvation as he hoped it could be.

He pulled down the zipper. I stumbled into the bathroom, not looking at him, and closed the door. The warm water didn't wash away my shame and guilt. How could I remain among the people I had betrayed? How could I look into their faces knowing they had suffered more than I had?

I closed my eyes. They were happy to have me back. I had to focus on that. But why, why wasn't I happy? I stepped out of the shower, dried myself, then wrapped a towel around my body. I stepped back out to grab clothes.

Samuel perched on the edge of my bed, his expression tight. His eyes flitted to my throat then to my thighs. My gaze followed his and I saw the hand-shaped bruises on my inner thighs where Remo had held me in place when he'd buried his face in my lap.

I felt the color drain from my face, grabbed some clothes, and returned to the bathroom. Shaking, I quickly dressed in a soft dress and tights. With a deep breath, I emerged and approached Samuel hesitantly. He was staring down at his hand on the bed, tightly curled into a fist.

I sat beside him, curling my legs under my body. Samuel raised his eyes and the look in them was like a wrecking ball of guilt. His gaze darted to my throat again, to Remo's marks, and utter despair filled his face.

"Oh, Fina," he said in a broken murmur. "I won't ever forgive myself. I failed you. I should have protected you. These last two months I almost went crazy. I can't stop thinking that I had to sit back while you went through hell. That I'm the reason why you suffered worse." He swallowed. "When Remo sent us those sheets …" His voice broke.

I threw myself at Samuel, wrapping my arms around his neck and burying my nose against his neck. "Don't. Please don't blame yourself. You did nothing wrong."

I did. I wronged you all.

His arms came around me, and he shuddered. "You were supposed to be protected, to be safe from the horrors of our life. I never wanted you to find out how cruel the mafia could be. No one will ever touch you again, Fina. I won't leave your side. And one day Dad and I will get our hands on Remo, and then we'll show him that we can be as cruel and merciless as the Camorra. He will be begging for mercy."

"It's over," I whispered. "It's over, Sam. Let's not talk about it ever again. Please." I knew Remo better than he did, and nothing they could do would make Remo beg for mercy.

He nodded against me, and we stayed like that for a while. "When I heard your screams in the basement, I thought I'd go insane," he said darkly.

I pressed my face into the crook of his neck, not able to look at him when

I delivered the truth. "Remo didn't torture me. He wanted you to believe he did. He wanted me to make you believe you hurt me so you'd suffer. I ... I ... only wanted to save you."

Samuel cupped my head and pulled back, his eyes softer than before. "It was my job to save you and I couldn't. Even if those screams weren't real, I can see what he did to you ..." Samuel swallowed, his eyes lowering to the bite marks once more. "You were meant to be treated like a princess, cared for and cherished ... not ... not ..." He shook his head and buried his face in his palms. "I can't get the image of those sheets out of my head, can't forget Mom's sobs or the way she fell to her knees in front of Dante and begged him to save you, or how Danilo destroyed Dad's entire office. I can't forget Dad crying. He's never cried, Fina. Dad and I have done and seen so much, but we both fucking cried like fucking babies that day. I swear by my honor, by everything I love, that I won't rest until I've rammed my fucking knife into Remo Falcone."

I kissed the top of his head and held him because despite being the one who had been kidnapped, Remo hadn't broken me, and I realized it had never been his intention. He'd done worse.

"Sam," I said, gathering my courage because I needed to save him, needed to save them all with the truth even if it ruined me. "I didn't suffer like you all think. Remo didn't rape me, he didn't torture me."

Samuel pulled back and I braced myself for the inevitable, for the disgust and hatred, resigned myself to it, but his eyes held pity and sadness.

He stroked my throat then touched the faded cut on my forearm. Something dark swirled in the depth of his blue eyes when they locked on mine. "You were innocent. You've never been alone with a man and then you were at the mercy of a monster like Remo Falcone. You had nothing to protect yourself. You did what you had to, to survive. The brain is a powerful tool. It can survive the cruelest horrors by creating alternative realities."

I shook my head. He didn't understand. "Sam," I tried again. "I wasn't raped."

Sam swallowed and kissed my forehead as if I was a small kid. "You'll realize it eventually, Fina. Once you've healed, once the brainwashing ceases, you'll see the truth. I'll be there for you when that happens. I won't ever leave your side again."

And I realized then that he'd never believe the truth because he couldn't. The sister he knew and loved wouldn't have slept with Remo, and if I wanted to return to him, to my family, I needed to become her again.

I wasn't sure if she was still inside of me somewhere or if Remo had ripped her from me, just like he did my innocence, and kept her for himself.

TWENTY-ONE

Serafina

AFTER COVERING THE BITE MARKS WITH CONCEALER, I LEFT MY ROOM with Samuel at my side. Mom was in the dining room, setting plates up for dinner. Usually the maids did it, but I got the impression she needed to keep busy. She'd lost weight. She had always been tall and thin, but now she was willowy.

Samuel's words flashed through my mind, that she'd fallen to her knees and begged Dante to save me. My mother was a proud woman. I don't think she'd ever begged for anything in her life nor knelt. But kneeling for the ones we loved … that was something she and I would always do. I walked over to her. She smiled but her eyes held questions and fears.

"Can I help you?"

Her eyes flitted down to my throat. "No, Fina. Just rest."

I didn't feel like resting. "Where are the others?"

"Your father and uncle are talking to Danilo in the office. Sofia will be here soon. She'll be so happy to see you again."

I smiled but my thoughts strayed to Danilo. My fiancé. My gaze fell to the engagement ring around my finger, and I shivered, remembering the look in Remo's eyes when he'd slipped it on.

"I need to talk to Danilo," I said quietly.

Mom put the plates down, searching my face. She didn't ask why. Maybe she knew and could see it on my face. "Do that, sweetheart."

I nodded and turned to head for Dad's office. Samuel followed at my heel. "You're not going to marry him, are you?"

I stopped in the hallway and peered up at my twin. There was no judgment in his voice, but there was relief. "I can't."

He touched my shoulder. "I'm here for you."

"Won't you have to go to Chicago to work with Dante?"

He shook his head, mouth thinning. "We decided against sending me away. Dad needs me here. We need to protect our territory."

Me. They needed to protect me … and Sofia.

"I want to talk to Danilo alone, Sam."

He frowned, protectiveness flashing in his eyes.

"Sam," I said firmly. "I can handle it."

I'd handled Remo for months. Nothing could scare me anymore. Maybe the same thought crossed Samuel's mind because he nodded with a grimace.

"I'll wait in the hallway," he said, leaning against the wall beside the wooden door.

I knocked twice then walked in, not waiting for a reply.

My breath caught in my throat at the mess. Someone had thrown two book cases over. Ripped books and broken glasses. Dad's beloved collection of whisky tumblers scattered the floor. The leather sofa was slashed, filling poking out everywhere.

Danilo had done this and nobody bothered to clean up afterward.

My eyes found my fiancé. He was controlled, so much like Dante that he probably couldn't stand being compared to him anymore. I couldn't imagine him doing this. His brown eyes latched onto mine, full of regret and anger.

"Dove?" Dad asked.

I cleared my throat, realizing he and Dante were staring at me as well.

"I'm sorry for disturbing you," I said. "But I need to have a word with Danilo."

Dad hesitated, his eyes flitting between my fiancé and me. Dante put a hand on his shoulder and eventually they both left. Danilo faced the window, his hands pressed into the wall on both sides.

The door closed with a soft click, and silence reigned in the room.

Danilo's shoulders heaved. He was tall and muscular, but not quite like Remo.

"I …" I began but then didn't know how to go on, how to explain that I was lost to him.

Danilo turned around slowly, a haunted expression on his face. He smiled but it was strained, tired, and behind it lurked something dark and broken. "Serafina," he murmured. He took a step closer but stopped when I tensed. "I still want to marry you. If you want me."

I regarded Danilo's handsome face. He knew to hide his violence better than Remo. He was elegantly handsome, not brutally attractive like Remo. Remo. Always Remo. *I own you.*

"I'm not the girl you were promised anymore," I whispered. "I'm ... lost."

He shook his head and came closer, but still not close enough to touch. "He will pay. In these last two months, I've spent every waking moment thinking about you, going crazy with worry and rage. Your family and I ... we wanted to get you back ... We failed ..."

"It's okay," I said softly.

"And I don't care that he ... that you aren't ..." His face twisted with guilt and fury. "I still want to marry you, and you don't have to be scared, Serafina. I won't touch you until you've healed, until you want me to, I swear."

I moved toward Danilo. We could have been happy. He would have been kind to me, as good a husband as a Made Man could be. I didn't kid myself into thinking he wasn't a monster, but he was a restrained one. I touched my palms to his chest and looked into his eyes. Something in them had changed from our last encounter two months ago. They were harsher, darker. My captivity had left its mark on him too.

"I can't. I'm sorry," I whispered. "You deserve someone else. Please find someone who deserves you."

He regarded me, his jaw flexing. "From the moment I saw you the first time, I only wanted you."

I lowered my eyes because from the moment Remo had laid eyes upon me, I had been his.

"I'm sorry," I repeated.

He nodded slowly. I dropped my hands from his chest and stepped back. "Falcone got what he wanted, didn't he?" he said hoarsely. "But your family and I will bring him down. We will destroy him."

I shivered. I slid my engagement ring off my finger and handed it to Danilo. "Don't waste your time on revenge, Danilo. Move on. Find someone else. Be happy."

He shook his head, obviously fighting for control. "Revenge is all I want, and I won't stop until I get it. Remo will curse the day he took you from me."

Remo already did, but not for the reason Danilo wanted him to.

He left without another word. Swallowing hard, I leaned against the windowsill. This was it. I was no longer engaged ... I was nothing. I was ... ruined. In our circles, I was ruined. If I'd married Danilo, things might have been different, but now ...

There was a soft knock and Mom entered, looking worried. I gave her a small smile, wanting to banish the hard line between her brows. "Danilo told me you don't want to marry him."

As if it was as easy as that. Wanting had little to do with it. I couldn't because deep down I knew I needed to loosen Remo's hold on my stupid heart before I could ever consider moving on.

I knew the rules of our world, even now they still bound me, bound my family. We had promised the Mancinis Dante's niece, and now they wouldn't get what they wanted, what they expected as the ruling family of Indianapolis. Maybe Danilo had accepted my decision but his father was still alive, sick and bedridden, but alive. He pulled the strings in the background. The Mancinis wouldn't settle for just anyone as my replacement.

"I can't," I said quietly. "I can't ever marry, Mom. Don't make me."

Mom rushed toward me and embraced me. "We won't. Not me, not your father, not Dante. We all failed you horribly. You don't ever have to marry, sweetheart, you can live with your father and me for as long as you wish."

"Thank you, Mom," I said, and even as I said it I knew it wasn't what I wanted.

She pulled back, frowning. "Your uncle would like a word with you. I told him it's still too soon, but he insists it's necessary. Still, if you aren't ready, I will stand up to him."

Dread filled me but I shook my head. "It's fine. I'll talk to him."

She gave a terse nod. "I'll get him. He needs to return to Chicago tomorrow morning. He's been gone for too long these last two months."

She kissed my cheek before she left.

Dante stepped in a moment later, tall and controlled as always. He closed the door then paused, his cool blue eyes flickering to my throat where Remo's marks had been—no longer visible, covered by layers of concealer, just like my traitorous feelings for him were covered up by stacks of lies. I flushed and touched my skin in shame.

"Don't," he said firmly.

I frowned. He moved toward me slowly, cautiously, as if he thought I might bolt. I lowered my hand from my throat when he came to a stop in front of me. "Don't be ashamed for something forced upon you," Dante said quietly, but his voice was off. It had a note to it I had never heard before. I searched my uncle's eyes, but it was difficult to read him. He exuded control and power. But there was a flicker of regret and sadness in his gaze. "I don't want to open up painful wounds, Serafina, but as the Boss of the Outfit, I need to know everything you know about the Camorra so I can bring them down and kill Remo Falcone."

I swallowed, looking away. This war would become so much bloodier and crueler soon. As if that would undo my kidnapping. As if Remo's death could change anything. But my family and Danilo needed to make amends for their guilt. Nothing I could say would change that.

"I don't think I know anything that will help you."

"Every small detail helps. Habits. The dynamic between the brothers. Remo's weaknesses. The layout of the mansion."

Remo's weakness. His brothers. Remo's biggest weakness may be his only one.

"Remo doesn't trust anyone but his brothers and Fabiano. He would die for them," I whispered.

For some reason I felt almost guilty for revealing that to my uncle, as if I owed Remo loyalty, as if I owed him anything at all. He had kidnapped me and then let me go. I wasn't sure what made me hate him more.

"Apart from the family, only Fabiano and Leona are allowed inside the mansion, and occasionally cleaners. Remo keeps a knife and a gun close at all times. He's a light sleeper ..." I froze, falling silent.

My skin burned at what I'd just revealed, but Dante only regarded me calmly. No judgment or anger. I still had to lower my gaze from his because his understanding made me feel even worse. He didn't know I'd come freely into Remo's bed, enjoyed not only the sex but also the tenderness afterwards. It was a side of Remo no one knew and that he had showed it to me meant more to me than it should.

Could I reclaim what was lost? I began shaking, overwhelmed with the situation, with my feelings.

"Serafina," Dante said firmly, touching my shoulder. I raised my eyes to his and shook even worse, overcome with the need to spill everything but not brave enough. I pressed myself against my uncle, and he touched the back of my head in comfort.

"What am I going to do? How will I belong again? Everyone will look at me with disgust."

Dante's body coiled tighter. "If anyone does, you'll let me know, and I'll deal with them."

I nodded.

"And you never stopped belonging. You are part of the Outfit, part of this family, nothing changed."

Everything did. Worst of all, I had.

When we finally emerged, Samuel took his place as my shadow again. We were on our way into the dining room when the front door opened. One of our bodyguards stepped in, and then Sofia shot inside. Her wide eyes landed on me, and she stormed off in my direction. She collided with me, and I would have fallen backward if Samuel hadn't steadied me.

"You're back!" Sofia hugged my middle tightly, and I rested my chin on top of her head, smiling. When I pulled back, her eyes were alight with happiness despite the tears in them. "I missed you so much."

"I missed you too, ladybug."

I wondered how much she knew, how much my parents and Samuel had divulged or had been unable to hide from her.

Valentina entered with her two kids, Anna and Leonas. Anna was around Sofia's age, and they loved each other dearly. They were not just cousins but best friends despite the distance between them. Leonas was almost eight and the spitting image of Dante, except for the eyes. Anna and Leonas gave their mother a questioning look, and she nodded before they came toward me as well. I hugged them, though it proved difficult because Sofia continued to cling to my arm. Anna and Sofia sometimes were mistaken for sisters because their hair color was similar.

Valentina was the last to greet me. Her embrace was gentle as if I was breakable but I gave her a firm smile.

"We can have dinner," Mom said with a brave smile of her own. With the kids around, she wouldn't burst into tears again nor would anyone else.

Conversation flowed easily at the dining table. Too easily. I could tell everyone was trying to create normalcy for my sake and their own. Danilo wasn't there. I assumed he wanted to be alone after I'd broken off our engagement, and he wasn't part of the family and now he'd never be.

It was strange being surrounded by my family again. I sat between my siblings, both of them eager to be close to me, but my thoughts kept straying to Las Vegas, to Remo.

"How was Las Vegas?" Leonas blurted when we were done with dessert, a decadent chocolate cake, my favorite.

"Leonas," Dante said sharply.

My cousin flushed, realizing his mistake.

I took a sip from my water then shrugged. "Not worth visiting if you ask me."

Leonas giggled, and my family relaxed again. Samuel squeezed my hand under the table. Maybe I could find my way back to them.

It felt strange being back in my own bed. I had trouble falling asleep. Too much had happened. This morning I'd woken in Las Vegas with Remo, and now I was here.

The door opened and Samuel slipped in. I made room for him in the bed.

"Awake?" he asked quietly.

"Yeah." I didn't elaborate. He lay down on the covers on his back. "What about you?"

Samuel was quiet for a couple of heartbeats. "I was in a late night meeting with Dante and Dad."

"Oh," I said. "About your plans to get revenge on the Camorra?"

Samuel swallowed audibly. "No. Not that. It was about Danilo. His father isn't happy about the state of things."

Worry overcame me. What if they married me off to him despite everything? What if his family insisted on being given Dante's niece?

"Sam," I whispered, and he reached for me in the dark, his hand covering mine.

"Dad promised Sofia to him."

I froze. "She's a child."

Samuel sighed. "They will marry the day after her eighteenth birthday."

"That's still six and a half years away."

I could feel Samuel nod. "They think Danilo is still young and busy taking control over Indianapolis and taking care of his father. He can wait." He paused. "And it's not like he can't keep himself busy with other women until then."

I closed my eyes. "What will Sofia say? It's my fault. I should just marry him."

"No," Samuel growled. "We won't let you. That's a point we all agree on, Fina. You won't be given in marriage to anyone. You've gone through enough. You'll stay here until you feel better."

"And then?"

"I don't know," he admitted. I couldn't live on my own. As a woman that wasn't an option. They'd have to marry me off or I'd have to stay with Mom and Dad forever.

"You come live with me eventually."

I laughed. "Yeah right. I'm sure your future wife will be ecstatic to have me under the same roof."

"She'll do as I say," he murmured.

I fell silent. "Once you marry, it's your duty to protect her, to be good to her, Sam. I won't be your responsibility anymore."

"I'm not going to marry anytime soon, not with the way things are developing with the Camorra."

"When will Sofia find out?"

"Dad will talk to her tomorrow first thing in the morning. Danilo insists on it. He also insists we up the number of guards."

"He doesn't want history to repeat itself, I suppose," I said softly.

Samuel stiffened. I pinched him lightly. "Stop it."

"Why did you do that?"

"Because you were feeling guilty again, and I want you to stop. I want things to go back to how they were before."

"I want that too," Samuel said. We both knew it wouldn't be that easy.

Samuel was already gone when I woke the next morning. He'd always been a late riser, but that, too, seemed to have changed. I slipped out of bed and dressed before I left my room. Instead of heading downstairs, I moved down the hallway to Sofia's room and knocked. My stomach tightened painfully.

"Come in!" she called.

Frowning at her chipper tone, I slipped in. Sofia lay on her stomach, her ankles crossed. She was drawing. When she spotted me, she flushed. I walked toward her and perched on the edge of the bed. Her arms covered her drawing, and I tilted my head.

"I wanted to talk to you about Danilo. I assume Dad already talked to you?"

She gave a tentative nod, biting her lip. "Are you mad at me?"

"Mad?" I echoed, confused.

"Because Danilo wants to marry me now and not you."

The tightness left my chest. That was what they told Sofia. Good. I regarded her closely. "No. I'm not. I want you to be happy. Are you okay?"

She bit her lip again and gave a small nod. With an embarrassed smile, she pulled her hand away from her drawing. It was her name and Danilo's over and over again.

Surprise washed over me. "You like him?"

Her cheeks blasted with heat. "I'm sorry. I liked him even when you were promised to him. He's cute and chivalrous."

I kissed the top of her head. Was I this innocent once? This hopeful and clueless?

I pulled back and gave her a stern look. "He's a grown man, Sofia. It'll be many years before you'll marry him. He won't come anywhere near you until then."

She nodded. "I know. Dad told me." She sounded disappointed. So beautifully innocent. I stroked her hair.

"So we're okay?" she asked.

"Better than okay," I said then stood and left my little sister to her daydreaming. I missed the days when I thought a knight in shining armor riding a white stallion would steal my first kiss.

Instead a monster had claimed me, body and soul.

My stomach led me downstairs, but I paused when I spotted Danilo in the foyer. I assumed he'd gone over the details of his engagement to my sister with my parents and Dante. For some reason, I was furious. Sofia might be happy, but she didn't know the extent of her promise. Of course she would have been promised to someone eventually but not as a consolation prize because the Mancinis wanted Dante's niece.

I walked straight toward him. His face flickered with regret and self-hatred as he looked at me. "Sofia is a girl. How could you agree to that bond, Danilo?"

His expression flashed with anger. "She is a child. Too young for me. She's my sister's age for God's sake. But you know what's expected. And we won't marry until she's of age. I never touched you and I won't touch her."

"You should have chosen someone else. Not Sofia."

Tension shot through his body. "I didn't choose her. I chose you. But you were taken from me, and now I have no choice but to marry your sister even though it's you I want!"

A sharp intake of breath made us both look up at Sofia, who was standing on the highest stair, watching us with wide hurt eyes. Her chin wobbled and she whirled around, storming off.

"Damn it," Danilo muttered. He made a move as if to follow, but I grabbed his arm.

"What are you doing?"

"I should talk to her."

"I don't think that's a good idea."

Danilo pulled back, his expression back to being controlled, calm, poised. "I should apologize."

"I'm not sure she'll talk to you. But we can try," I said quietly. I led him upstairs, trying to ignore the way his eyes lingered on my throat. I hadn't covered the marks this morning.

I pointed at Sofia's door, and Danilo knocked firmly.

"Go away!"

"Sofia," Danilo said calmly. "Can I talk to you?"

It was silent behind the door for a long time. Danilo's brows drew together.

"She's probably trying to clean up her face so you don't see her tears."

He gave a small nod and again glanced at my throat. I sighed and looked away.

"I will protect her. I won't fail her like I failed you," Danilo muttered.

My eyes shot up but the door opened in that moment. Sofia stood in the doorway, looking shy and embarrassed. Her eyes moved from Danilo to me, and I gave her a smile.

She flushed when she raised her eyes to Danilo.

"Can I talk to you for a moment?" he asked.

Sofia looked at me for permission.

"Sure," I said. I knew custom forbade girls from being alone with men, but Sofia was eleven and Danilo had always been a perfect gentleman with me.

Sofia walked back into her room and perched on her plush pink sofa. Danilo followed her inside, leaving the door open. His eyes took in her pink girly room, and I could see how uncomfortable he was. He sank down on the sofa with as much distance between them as the piece of furniture allowed. He looked out of place in the room, like a giant beside her. The contrast couldn't have been bigger: Sofia in her pink dress with her boisterous nature, and Danilo in his black pants and black dress shirt with his cool demeanor. He had already seemed so much older to me, but in comparison to Sofia?

Not that she seemed to mind. She was peering up at him with so much childish adoration that even my crushed heart sang with joy. I hoped she could hold on to it for a long time. I took a few steps back and gave them a moment of privacy. Two minutes later, Danilo stepped back out. He ran a hand through his dark hair. His eyes met mine, and again I saw the flash of longing and fury.

"And?"

He gave a terse nod. "I think I managed to convince her I said those things to make it easier for you."

"Good," I said.

Danilo shook his head, his brows drawing together. "Nothing is good about this situation, Serafina, and I'm surprised that from all of us you are the one who seems to be dealing with it the best."

I stiffened. "I just want things to return to normal. That's all."

He nodded tiredly. "They won't, but I understand. I need to go now." He left without another word. I waited until his tall form had disappeared before I stepped into Sofia's room. "Everything okay?"

She was still sitting on the sofa, staring down at her hands. "I think so," she said thoughtfully.

"You will be the most beautiful bride, I just know it."

Her eyes lit up. "You think?"

"I know it." My chest ached for what I'd lost, for what I could never have, especially not with the man who had my heart.

TWENTY-TWO

Remo

ROGER'S ARENA WAS PACKED FOR MY FIGHT AS I STRODE IN. NINO followed close behind as we walked toward the booth where Adamo, Savio, Kiara, Leona, and Fabiano were waiting. I was already in my fight shorts, and my body thrummed with barely contained bloodlust.

Roger helped behind the bar for once and gave me a nod in greeting, which I returned. The audience was throwing glances my way, eager, curious, terrified. My fights were always particularly popular—for those who could stomach them. Griffin looked fucking ecstatic as he noted the bets down.

"Who are the unlucky souls you'll fight?" Savio asked curiously.

"Ask Nino." I didn't care who they were. I'd rip them to shreds either way.

"Two ex-cons. Both on the run. Both in desperate need of money and new identities. Out of options," Nino said matter-of-factly. "One of them kicked his pregnant wife half to death and she lost the baby. Already served a sentence because of manslaughter. The other spent half of his life in jail for child molestation."

"Sounds like they deserve their death sentence," Fabiano said with a grin, his arm wrapped around Leona and she smiled up at him in adoration. The sight spiked my fury, and I focused on the cage. "They will wish for the death penalty when I'm done with them."

The ref called out my name, and I walked through the parting crowd toward the cage and the two dead men waiting for me inside.

The crowd roared and clapped, ecstatic. I swung myself into the cage and assessed my opponents. One of them was taller and broader than me. Maybe I could imagine it was Luca. It would add a nice thrill. The other was short but bull-like, and his stance suggested he was a boxer. Both looked like they knew how to pack a punch. Good.

The moment the fight began, they attacked together. I gripped the short one and rammed my knee into his side but was grabbed from behind by the giant. Short guy scrambled toward me and landed a punch in my stomach. I jerked my head forward and smashed it against his. He staggered and I kicked out against his chest, catapulting myself and the fucker who held me from behind. We crashed into the cage, and I jumped out of Big Guy's hold. Whirling around, I pushed off the ground and flying-kicked his fucking face, breaking nose, chin, and cheekbone. Blood splattered everywhere, and he fell backward, holding his face. That would keep him busy for a while.

I turned toward Short Guy and smiled. The audience roared. They knew that smile. The look in my opponent's eyes was familiar: panic and horrified realization. I stalked toward him, and he raised his fists. I feigned an attack, causing him to stumble back. I chuckled. This was going to be fun. I lunged at him, kicking and punching hard without mercy. The cries of the crowd and the fucking whimpers of my opponent spurred me on, but the fucking hollowness in my chest remained. I kicked him over and over again until everything was red. When he didn't even twitch anymore, I let up.

The other guy had his back turned to me and was shaking the cage door, wanting out.

"No one's going to open that door. If you want out of this cage, you'll have to kill me."

Big Guy turned, face swollen and bloody. He tried his best. Soon I had him in a choke hold, and then I smashed his face against the cage. Once. Twice, and then over and over again. I couldn't fucking stop. I needed to crush something.

"Remo."

Smash.

"Remo!"

Smash.

A hand gripped my shoulder and ripped me backward. I released the bloody pulp and stared at Nino. His face was splattered with small red dots. Blood.

I glanced down at myself then at the floor. It was silent in the arena and everyone was staring at me in open horror.

"I won," I muttered.

Nino shook his head. "Come."

I followed him out of the cage and toward the changing room. The crowd parted even wider. The stench of vomit hung heavy in the air. Griffin was pressing a fucking tissue over his mouth.

Inside the changing room, I stripped off my drenched fight shorts, leaving a red trail on the ground as I stepped inside the shower. The hot water remained red for a long while, and Nino watched me the entire time from his spot on the bench, his elbows propped up on his thighs.

"Like what you see?"

He didn't say anything, and it was starting to piss me off.

Grabbing a towel, I stepped out of the shower and dried myself off. "Say what you've got to say."

Nino regarded me with a small frown. "Is this because of Serafina? Do I have to worry?"

My lips pulled wide. "I don't have a heart that can be broken, Nino. Stop the fucking hovering."

"She won't come back to you, Remo. She'll try to find her way back into the Outfit where she thinks she belongs. If you wait for her to come to you freely, you'll be met with disappointment."

I bent low, meeting his eyes. "I don't care if she comes back or not. There are whores to fuck, Outfit bastards to kill, and the fucking Bratva to piss off."

I got dressed in the pants Nino handed me. Then we left. Part of the crowd had already left, the others were whispering quietly. Nino led me toward the booth, but only Savio was there, and he regarded me like I had risen straight from Hell. "Where is everyone?"

"Well," Savio muttered. "Kiara and Adamo are probably busy throwing up, and Fabiano and Leona went outside with them to keep watch."

Nino's frown deepened at the mentioning of Kiara. We headed outside and found them all in the parking lot beside our cars. Adamo sat on the hood of Nino's car, smoking. Kiara was bent over behind the trunk, heaving, and Fabiano had his arm wrapped around Leona's shoulder, who looked a little faint.

Nino went over to his wife and rubbed her back.

Fabiano shook his head. "What the hell, Remo?"

I rolled my eyes. "You've seen me do worse. We tortured together." And after what he'd done to his father, he really had no business being shocked by me losing control.

Savio snorted. "We've all seen you torture, but you never lost control like that. Take a look at the video footage and if your expression doesn't scare even you shitless then I don't know what to say." He went over to Adamo and took the cigarette from him, taking a deep pull.

"You don't smoke," Adamo grumbled.

"I need to get rid of the vomit taste in my mouth."

"Don't tell me you threw up as well," I said.

Savio cocked his eyebrow. "No. But when people around me started ejecting their food, I could practically taste it in my mouth."

I felt Fabiano's eyes on me and met his gaze, daring him to say something. He didn't. Adamo couldn't meet my eyes, and I didn't have the necessary patience tonight to deal with him. Maybe tomorrow. Nino finally managed to calm Kiara, who leaned into him, pale and sweaty. She locked eyes with me. It wasn't disgust or fear I saw in her gaze but compassion and understanding, and it sent a new wave of rage through me.

"Keys," I ordered, holding out my hands to Nino.

He shook his head. "You're not driving anywhere right now."

"Give me the fucking keys," I growled.

"No."

"I can drive you," Adamo quipped.

I slanted a look at him. Of course he'd come with his new car, and of course he wasn't sitting on its hood. Nino nodded, as if I needed his fucking permission to get into Adamo's car.

"Then let's go, kiddo," I muttered.

Adamo hopped off Nino's car, threw away his stub, and got into his Mustang. The moment I sank down into the passenger seat and closed the door, Adamo shot out of the parking lot. "Where do you want to go?"

I rubbed my temple. "I want to kill and maim but now that I have you to keep an eye on, that won't fucking happen."

"I think I'm meant to babysit you tonight. Nino's worried," Adamo said.

I shook my head. "Fucking nuisances, all of you."

"You scared the shit out of me tonight."

"I hope that wasn't the first time or I'm doing something wrong."

"I've been scared of you before. When you sent Fabiano after me because of the cocaine. But today I was kind of scared for you."

"Trust me, Adamo, you have absolutely no reason to be scared for me."

Adamo frowned. "Is it because of her?"

My brothers seemed intent to test the limit of my patience. "Shut up and drive."

"Where?"

"Home. Just take us home."

Serafina

Mom and I sat in the garden on a swing, enjoying a warm fall day. I'd been back for only two days, and it was the first time Mom and I were really alone. Our feet gently kicked the ground to keep the swing in motion. Mom held my hand, peering up at the sky.

I knew she had questions but couldn't ask them, and I wasn't sure if I could give her answers.

"Why did you give Sofia to Danilo?" I asked eventually to say something.

"It's not what we wanted, not what Danilo wanted, but we need to bind our families. It's what's expected," Mom said. "And he's a decent man."

"You said the same words to me on my wedding day."

Mom paled but managed a small nod. "I wanted to take away your fears."

"I know."

Her blue eyes held mine, filling with anguish. She touched my cheek. "I wanted only the best for you. I wanted happiness. I wanted a man who would carry you on his hands, who showed you kindness like your father did to me." She looked away briefly, gathering herself. "I can't imagine the horrors you lived, Fina, but I wish I could have suffered them in your stead."

"Mom," I whispered. "It's not like you all think. I didn't suffer the way you believe. Remo didn't force me."

"Your father didn't allow me to see the video where *he* cut you, but I saw the sheets. I see the marks on your throat. Don't make light of your suffering to make me feel better, love. Don't."

She cradled my face, her eyes fierce, determined. She, too, would never understand the extent of my betrayal. My family needed me to be the victim in this.

I wanted to belong, wanted to be part of the Outfit again, but every passing day, it became more obvious that part of me had stayed in Vegas with Remo. People were talking. They did it behind closed doors mostly, but I caught the pitying glances of the bodyguards and maids. All my life people had regarded me with admiration and respect, and now I was someone to pity. They didn't know I wasn't the victim, not in the sense they all thought.

And I had been shielded from attention so far. I hadn't left the house, hadn't attended any social gatherings, but eventually I'd have to make an appearance or the speculations would rise even higher. I needed to show them that I wasn't hiding, that I had no reason to hide.

More than three months since Remo had kidnapped me. More than four weeks since he'd set me free—body *not* soul. Sometimes I managed to forget him for a few minutes, only to be reminded with a crushing force, but it was getting better. Maybe Sam was right. Maybe Remo's brainwashing was ceasing. Maybe I could be free one day.

Today my family would return to the public, would show strength, would show that we weren't broken, that I wasn't. It was Dad's fiftieth birthday, and the party had been planned for almost a year, a splendid feast with family and friends, with Underbosses and Captains.

My parents had considered calling the party off, but I had convinced them to celebrate. Life had to go on.

Dante, Valentina, and the kids were staying with us as well, and I was excited to see them again. I busied myself helping Mom prepare for the party these last few weeks, needing to distract myself, trying to ignore the nagging fear at the back of my head that grew louder every day.

I stared up at the ceiling in my room. It was already late, and I needed to choose a dress, get ready, and help Mom, but I couldn't move. For the last two hours I lay motionless, except for my shallow breathing.

I'd got my period the last week of August. It was the end of October now. My fingers traced my belly, terrified, immobilized.

Slowly, I got out of bed and perched on its edge for a long time, letting a horrible realization fill my bones. Two months since my last period. Closing my eyes, I swallowed. I'd never taken the pill during my time with Remo, and he had never used protection, wanting to claim me without that barrier between us. I stared up at the ceiling, praying that it wasn't true. It would be the end of all my hopes, of everything.

I swallowed again. A knock sounded. "Fina, are you awake?"

Samuel. It was already late and what he was really asking was if I was okay. I wasn't. I should be getting ready, should play my part, be strong for appearance's sake.

"Come in," I said.

He opened the door and stepped in, already dressed in dark pants and a royal blue dress shirt. His eyes took in my rumpled state. He moved toward me and crouched down in front of me. "What's wrong?"

I considered keeping my suspicion to myself, but it was a truth I wouldn't be able to hide from them. If it really was true …

I met his gaze. "I think I'm pregnant."

Samuel froze, eyes widening in shock. "You mean …" He swallowed, staring at my flat stomach. His expression twisted with anger, sadness and worse … disgust.

Disgust, because this was Remo's baby. He leaned his forehead against my thigh and released a shuddering breath.

"I will kill him. I swear it. One day I'm going to kill Remo Falcone in the cruelest way possible."

I touched his head. "Can you ... can you get Mom? I need a pregnancy test. I need to know for sure."

Samuel straightened and stood. With a last glance at me, he left. I couldn't move. If I was pregnant with Remo's child ... I couldn't even finish the thought. I didn't want to, not yet, not before I had certainty.

A few minutes later, Mom stepped in, her face pale. We looked at each other before she walked toward me and touched my cheek. "Whatever happens, we'll get through this, Fina. We will get through this."

"I know," I said. "Can you get a test for me?"

"I will ask Valentina. Maybe she's got a spare test. She and Dante are trying for another child."

Mom dropped her hand and left the room. I stood, taking a deep breath. Maybe there was another explanation, but deep down I knew the truth.

Mom returned with a test. I took it from her with shaking hands. "Can you leave me alone? I'll come downstairs once I'm ready."

Mom hesitated but then she kissed my cheek. I watched the closed door for a while before I forced myself to get up from the bed and move to the bathroom. My heart beat in my throat when I unpackaged the test.

Fifteen minutes later I stared down at the test in my hands, at the truth that shattered the last shred of hope I'd held. Hope that I could ever find my way back into the Outfit. Hope that I could forget Remo. As if there was a way I could have ever forgotten him. I stared at the two lines on the test.

Pregnant.

With Remo Falcone's child.

A man of unparalleled cruelty and mercilessness.

The man who'd robbed me of my innocence, of my future ... of my heart.

Body and soul.

I own you.

Oh, Remo, if you knew what you gave away ...

I set the test down and touched my stomach. It seemed unreal, impossible.

Pregnant.

My heart was a war-torn land: two conflicting emotions battling for dominance, leaving nothing but devastation in their wake. Unbridled happiness that a small human was growing inside of me. A small part of Remo that would always remain with me. And raw fear of the future, of my—of *our* future. Our world was cruel to women who got pregnant out of wedlock; it was even crueler to children born out of wedlock.

Damned to be called bastards. A child of Remo Falcone couldn't hope for a kinder name. I'd protect my child, but I wouldn't always be there to fend off the attacks. It would be strong enough to defend itself, no doubt, but the idea that my baby would have to grow strong out of necessity, because the world forced it into a corner, made me furious. I tried to calm my raging emotions. I was getting ahead of myself. I came from a good family, maybe things would be different for my child, no matter who their father was.

Taking a deep breath, I headed downstairs. My family was gathered in the dining room, and when I entered they all fell silent. Mom. Dad. Valentina. Dante. Samuel. Dante's kids. Anna, Leonas, my sister Sofia. The room was already decorated for the event, and in the garden a white tent had been set up, which held the dance floor. The caterer would arrive in about two hours, the guests in three. A day of celebration.

Mom motioned at Sofia, Anna, and Leonas. "Out. Go to your rooms for now." They did, no protests. In passing Sofia gave me a small smile.

I looked at Samuel. He got up, slowly, hesitantly, and our eyes met. His expression fell, turning desperate.

"I'm pregnant."

Mom covered her mouth with her hand, and Dad closed his eyes. Valentina regarded me with sympathy, and Dante gave a terse nod. No celebrations. No happiness.

Samuel slowly sank back down onto his chair. From hundreds of miles away and not knowing it, Remo had landed another hit.

"It's still early. We can call the doc and he will get rid of it," Dad said, face pale and worried when he finally met my gaze.

My stomach tightened and something angry and protective reared its head in my chest. *My child.*

Mom nodded slowly. "You don't have to keep it."

Samuel only looked at me. He knew me. Until recently better than anyone else, but Remo had seen parts of me nobody knew, my darkest parts. "You want to keep it," he said quietly, uncomprehending.

I touched my stomach. "I will keep this child. I will take care of it and love it and protect it. It's mine." And the moment the words left my mouth, I knew it with certainty. This child would be born, and whoever tried to take it from me would see how strong I was.

Silence greeted me. Then Dante nodded once. "It's your decision."

"It is," I said firmly.

Mom got up. It was obvious that she was fighting with herself. I walked up to her because she couldn't move and touched her shoulders. "We will get through this, right? This baby is innocent. It's my baby."

Mom smiled shakily. "You are right, sweetheart."

Dad got up and touched my cheek. "We will stand by your side." I could see how much these words cost him. I wasn't sure if my family could get past the fact that my child was Remo's child. Would they love it because it was mine or hate it because it was his?

TWENTY-THREE

Serafina

I SAT IN FRONT OF MY VANITY AND BRUSHED MY HAIR, STROKE AFTER stroke, trying to find calm. I could hear the first guests downstairs, could hear laughter and music.

I needed to go down. Taking a deep breath, I stood. I'd chosen a floor-length form-fitting dark blue dress matching the color of Samuel's shirt. I touched my stomach, still flat, but I knew in a few months I couldn't wear dresses like this anymore.

Remo's baby. I closed my eyes. I was happy and sad, terrified and hopeful. What would Remo say if he knew? Would he care at all? I had been a means to an end, a queen in his chess game, and he'd won.

He had let me go as if I was nothing.

I'd heard the rumors of his cage fights. He was back to fighting, back to living his life. I wondered if he'd already moved on to one of the many whores at his disposal? Probably.

I had been stupid.

Sam was right. Remo had twisted my mind so he could control me, and I had let him.

A familiar knock sounded and Samuel stepped in. We hadn't talked since I'd revealed my pregnancy to my family. It had become obvious that they needed time to let it sink in, time to put on their public masks so our guests wouldn't find out the truth. Not yet.

He stopped near the door, watching me like I was breaking apart right before his eyes. I turned around myself, showing him my dress. "We match." I wanted to see his smile, anything but the soul-crushing darkness.

"You are beautiful," he said, but he didn't smile. I walked toward him, and as I did his eyes were drawn to my stomach. "Fina, get rid of it."

I froze. Sam stepped up to me and gripped my arms. "Please, get rid of it. I can't bear the idea that something belonging to him is growing inside of you."

"Sam," I whispered. "This is a baby. It's innocent. Whatever Remo did, this baby won't suffer for it."

Samuel ripped away from me. "But you will! What do you think people will say if you give birth to his spawn? And the thing will remind you of the asshole every fucking day. How will you ever forget if you see the result of Remo's fucking sins every day?"

I turned away and moved toward the window, clutching the windowsill in an iron grip, trying to hold on to my composure. If I wanted to show up at Dad's party, I couldn't lose it now.

Samuel came up behind me and touched my shoulders. "I shouldn't have said that."

"It's okay," I said. I put my hand over Samuel's. "I need you at my side, Sam. The baby and I … we both need you. Please."

Samuel put his chin down on my head and sighed. "I'll always be there for you."

We stood like that for a while until I turned and gave Samuel a firm smile. "Let's go down there and show people that we are strong together."

Samuel held out his hand, and I took it. We moved downstairs together, and Samuel's grip on me tightened when the attention shifted to me. People were trying to be discreet about it but failing miserably. Every Underboss was there, even Danilo. He stood off to the side, next to the bar, nursing an amber colored drink. Our eyes met briefly, but then I looked away.

Samuel remained glued to my side. My shadow, my protector, but even his harsh gaze couldn't stop the pitying looks or the whispers, and people didn't even know about my pregnancy yet. I could imagine how much worse the gossip would become then.

I'd been known as the Ice Princess, meant to become the Ice Queen at Danilo's side.

Now I was the woman whom Remo had defiled. The men could hardly look at me. Somehow I had become all of their failures.

Samuel's hand on my lower back twitched, and one look at his face told me he was close to losing control.

"Dance with me," I pleaded.

Samuel nodded with a small, tight smile and wrapped me in his embrace then stiffened when my still flat stomach pressed up to him. His eyes darted down and anguish flashed across his expression before he could mask it. As if he could already see my pregnancy when it was still safely hidden. I tightened my hold on him briefly, and finally he met my gaze. We began to dance. All eyes were on us.

Samuel held my gaze because he was on the verge of losing control. One look at the others and he'd snap. I smiled up at him and he relaxed. I, too, felt the glances. Could practically hear the whispers. A few women my age who'd always resented me for my status looked almost … triumphant, happy to witness my fall from grace.

I lifted my chin higher, angry and then worried … because how would all these people treat my child?

After three dances, Dad took over and Samuel moved over to the side to watch.

"You are beautiful, dove," he said quietly. His expression was controlled, calm. His public face. Mom, too, looked poised and elegant as she stood beside Sofia, Anna, and Valentina.

"Thanks, Dad," I said then added, "I'm sorry I don't have a present for you."

I hadn't left the house since my return, and to be honest, I'd completely forgotten to get a present. My mind had been occupied with too many others things.

"I got my present already," he said, and for a moment I thought he meant my child but then I realized he meant my freedom. He didn't mention my pregnancy.

Dante danced with me next.

I met his eyes, wondering what he thought of my pregnancy, wondering what kind of future lay ahead for my child, if it was a boy. Would he be allowed in the Outfit? Or would his father's identity close every door before it could ever be opened? I didn't dare ask my uncle. Not in public, not on my father's birthday party.

After the dance, I headed back to Samuel, who was talking to one of his oldest friends. He gave me a nod, but he, too, had trouble meeting my eyes. Samuel noticed and his jaw flexed. He excused himself, touched my back, and led me away.

Samuel and I walked into the entrance hall. I had a feeling Samuel needed to be away from the festivities for a couple of minutes. A few younger Made Men I didn't know had gathered there, and when we passed them, their words managed to reach us.

"I don't understand why they don't keep her hidden. It's a fucking disgrace to have her walk around as if Falcone hasn't defiled her."

My shock had barely registered when Samuel attacked. He broke the first guy's nose with a sickening crunch then shoved the second to the ground, pressing his knife against the man's throat.

"Sam," I said firmly, clutching his shoulder.

He leaned down, bringing his face close to the other man's. "I should cut your throat for insulting my sister. Apologize."

The man glanced at his friends. One was nursing his broken nose, the other obviously unsure if he should interfere, considering our Dad was their fathers' boss.

"Apologize!" Samuel snarled.

"I'm sorry," the guy blurted.

I tightened my hold on Sam's shoulder. He jerked back, took my hand, and dragged me outside, not into the garden but into the driveway where we were alone. He released me, turning his back to me. He sucked in a deep breath. I pressed my palms up to his shoulder blades then rested my forehead against his back. "Don't let their words get to you. I don't care about them and neither should you."

"How can you not care about them? You are a mafia princess. I should cut their tongues out for daring to whisper his name in one sentence with yours."

His name.

Remo Falcone. The father of my unborn child.

And worse, the man who filled my nights not with nightmares but with longing.

The next morning, Dad, Samuel, and Dante wanted to talk to me.

When I walked into Dad's office, I knew from their expressions that it wouldn't be an easy conversation and definitely not one I'd like. Dad sat behind his desk, Sam perched on its edge, and Dante stood with his hands in his slacks beside the window. I made a beeline for the sofa and sank down. My brain felt sluggish from lack of sleep. I'd spent all night trying to come to terms with the fact that I was carrying a baby, Remo's baby.

"What do you want to talk about?"

Three sets of eyes darted to my belly, and my hand automatically—*protectively*—pressed to the spot.

"If you keep this child," Dante began.

"I *will* keep the child."

Dad looked away and then at the picture frame on his desk. A photo of our family taken shortly before I'd been kidnapped.

"You will have to keep it hidden," Dad said.

I blinked at them. "What?"

"Once you start showing, we'll have to keep you out of the public eye, Serafina," Dante said, his voice resolute. "I doubt Remo Falcone has the slightest interest in his offspring, but he might use it against us. The Outfit needs to be strong. This child might cause tension within the Outfit, and we can't have that at the current time."

"Or we could arrange a quick marriage with someone who agrees to a fake marriage and pretend it's his child," Dad suggested gently.

I stared between them. Samuel looked at the floor, his brows snapped together.

"I'm not going to marry anyone, and I'm not going to lie about the baby's father. People wouldn't believe it anyway."

Now I was the woman pregnant with Remo's bastard child. Soon my protruding belly would carry the guilt and shame of the Outfit.

"Eventually people will realize I have a child. Once it grows older, it'll be difficult to keep it hidden. And what if he's a boy? Won't he be part of the Outfit?"

They exchanged a look.

"You haven't even given birth yet. It's still early," Dante said tersely. I searched their faces, and as I did it was difficult to hold on to my indignation and anger. My kidnapping had left its marks. They were still shaken up. Maybe over time things would get better. I'd give them the time they needed to accept the situation. I owed it to them. I owed them more than I owed Remo.

This baby and I belonged in the Outfit. This was my family, my home.

Still, part of me wondered if I was lying to myself, if it wasn't better to return to Las Vegas.

But Remo had sent me away. I'd served my purpose. How much did I really know about him? And how could I be sure if everything he'd done hadn't been part of a show, his masterful manipulation. It had worked, hadn't it? And how could I even be sure what I was feeling was real? Could feelings like that be born in captivity?

My pregnancy became the pink elephant in the room, an ever growing presence that everyone tried to ignore, and I did my best to make it easy for them. I wore loose-fitting clothes, glad for the cold winter days that allowed for thick sweaters and even thicker coats. I think my family often managed to forget I was even pregnant.

Only when I was alone in my room did I allow myself to admire my bump. It wasn't big yet. I had even managed to take part in Dante and Val's Christmas party because in my seventeenth week, if my calculations were accurate, an A-line dress still hid everything it should. If people suspected something, they kept it to themselves. It was a possible shame the Outfit didn't want to voice aloud.

It was early January when Samuel and Mom accompanied me to my first doctor's appointment. So far I hadn't asked for one, but Mom had surprised me a few days ago by asking if we should check on the baby. It was her silent apology, her attempt to accept what was so very difficult for all of them to accept.

The doctor had been working with the Outfit for years. She treated most of the pregnant Outfit women and would keep the secret I carried.

Fear filled me as I stretched out on the examination couch. I wasn't even sure what exactly scared me. It wasn't as if I didn't know I was pregnant. It was unmistakable at this point.

The doctor was on one side of me with the ultrasound while Samuel and Mom stood on the other. I swallowed when I pushed up my sweater, revealing the bump for the first time in front of others.

Samuel's face became still, and Mom swallowed before she managed an encouraging smile and squeezed my hand.

"This will be cold for a moment," the doctor warned me.

I nodded distractedly, my eyes fixed on the ultrasound.

The doctor started frowning, moving the ultrasound around on my belly. The thud-thud of a heartbeat filled the room and my own heart sped up, swelling with love and wonder. But the thud-thud was off, as if it was off-beat, two out-of-sync rhythms.

Mom's eyes widened, but I wasn't sure why, and fear filled me. I stared at her, then the doctor, then Samuel, but he looked as confused as I felt.

"Oh God," Mom whispered.

"What? What's going on?"

Mom's eyes filled with tears. "Twins."

The doctor nodded, and my eyes jerked toward Samuel.

"Like us," I said in wonder.

He managed a small smile, but his eyes held worry.

The knowledge that I carried twins changed things for Mom. It was as if she could finally see the babies as mine, not as something alien.

Samuel seemed to be coming around as well. He painted the nursery and set up the furniture for me. And Sofia? She was ecstatic about the prospect of being an aunt. But Dad … Dad had a harder time. He didn't mention the pregnancy and never looked anywhere below my chin. I understood him, couldn't possibly be angry because his eyes reflected his conflict.

I often managed to feel like I belonged once more, managed to pretend I wasn't forced to hide in our home so no one found out I was pregnant. What I didn't manage was to stop thinking about the man who was the reason for everything.

Every night I lay awake in bed. Every time I stroked my bump I saw him before my eyes. And every time I was torn between anger and longing. Sometimes I wondered if I should find a way to let him know, but then I thought of my family, of their slow healing process, of what my kidnapping had done to them, and I couldn't do it. What did you owe the man who kidnapped you? Who tried to destroy the people you cared about? The man who took your heart, only to push you away?

Nothing.

I owed Remo Falcone nothing.

These were my children, and they'd grow up as part of my family, as part of the Outfit. I'd hide the truth from them as long as I could. They would not find out who their father was until they had to. If I wanted them to have a chance in the Outfit, they couldn't be Falcones. They couldn't be associated with Remo at all.

In mid-May I gave birth to the most beautiful creations I could imagine and knew with absolute certainty that everything I'd wished for them would never become reality.

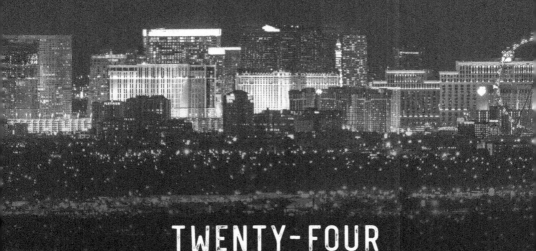

TWENTY-FOUR

Serafina

I LOVED MY FAMILY WITH ALL MY HEART. AND THEY LOVED ME. BUT THE moment I held my children in my arms, I knew I could not stay with them forever, knew it with soul-crushing certainty.

Nevio and Greta were Remo. Dark eyes, thick black hair.

For everyone in the Outfit they'd always be Falcones, always the result of something horrid, born out of something shameful, something dark. But for me they were the most beautiful creation I could imagine. They were utter perfection. Twins like Samuel and me. They would lift each other up, make each other stronger like Samuel and I had done when we were younger and still did. It would be us against the world. It couldn't be any other way.

Samuel stayed with me in the hospital after the birth while Mom went home for a few hours of sleep after twenty hours at my side during labor. Samuel's eyes were kind and loving as they looked down at me, but these tender emotions vanished as soon as he turned toward my children sleeping in their cradle. He wasn't doing it on purpose, but my children reminded him of something he and everyone else were desperate to forget.

And how could he not be reminded when my twins looked like Falcones?

My heart ached fiercely when I looked at them, throbbing with a longing I'd tried to bury with the memories of Remo, but Remo wasn't a man that could be

Two days after giving birth, Mom and Samuel carried my twins into the house because I still had trouble lifting anything heavier than a glass of water. The family had come together for the occasion, but I knew it wasn't to celebrate. Dad and Dante probably needed to discuss how to keep my children a secret. The Underbosses knew. They had to for the sake of the Outfit. Danilo did, but I hadn't talked to him since the day Sofia had been promised to him.

Samuel held my arm while his other carried the baby carrier. Walking the stairs was more than a little uncomfortable, and I was glad when I finally arrived inside our house.

Valentina came toward me and hugged me gently. She and Dante were still trying for child number three, but so far it wasn't working. She peered down at my babies with a soft smile. "They are beautiful, Serafina."

"They are," I agreed.

Sam and Dad exchanged a look, and it felt like a stab in the heart because when they looked at my children they saw the black hair and dark eyes and nothing more. They saw Falcones. They saw shame and guilt. Would they ever allow my babies to be more than the greatest failure in the history of the Outfit?

Sofia rushed down the staircase followed by Anna. Leonas showed less enthusiasm than the girls as he sauntered down the steps, rolling his eyes.

Sofia stopped beside me and Samuel, looking down at Greta sleeping soundly in the carrier. I'd noticed that Samuel had insisted on carrying Greta, not Nevio, but I tried not to put too much meaning into it. Sofia hadn't been allowed in the hospital because we didn't want to draw too much attention to us, and her eyes were wide in surprise.

"Wow," she breathed. "I've never seen hair that black."

She'd never seen Remo.

Anna nodded as she lightly brushed a finger over Nevio's head. His eyes peeled open and as always when they did, my breath lodged in my throat. Dark eyes. Remo's eyes. Even at two days old, my boy was his father.

Dad averted his eyes, brows pulling tight, and looked at Dante with an expression that tore me cleanly in half.

Valentina squeezed my shoulder and leaned in. "It takes time, Serafina. Give them time. One day they will see your babies as what they are: only yours."

I nodded, but deep down I knew Greta and Nevio would never only be mine because they were also Remo's, and nothing could change that. And I didn't want it to.

The next day, I was cradling Greta in my arm while Nevio rested on the sofa beside me, deep asleep when Dante came in. He strode toward us, his eyes flickering over my children. His expression didn't give anything away, and I wondered if it was because he didn't resent my twins like everyone else or if he was too good at hiding his true feelings.

He sank down in the armchair across from me, opening his jacket so it didn't wrinkle. He gave me a tense smile. "How are you?"

I stroked Greta's cheek before I looked up again. "Good."

He nodded. "I know things aren't easy for you, Serafina. It was never meant to be like this. I've wanted to talk to you for a while ..." He trailed off, his expression tightening. "But I'm not in the habit of justifying my actions, nor apologizing."

I frowned. "You are Capo."

"I am, but that doesn't make me infallible." He paused. "I think you should know that when Remo kidnapped you, your father would have handed over his territory to save you. I didn't allow it. And Samuel attacked the mansion without my permission because I wouldn't have allowed it. I'm not a man who answers to another's demands. I refuse to be blackmailed. I have to think of the Outfit."

"I know and I understand, Uncle." Then I paused. "But in the end you gave Scuderi to Remo."

Something dark and furious flashed in Dante's eyes. "I did. Because I'm not only Capo. I'm a father. I'm your uncle. This is my family, and I owe it protection. I owed you protection and I failed." He lowered his gaze to my children. "You'll have to live with the consequences of my decisions."

I shook my head. "Those decisions gave me my children, and that's not something I could ever regret."

Dante got up and touched my shoulder. Then he traced his index finger over Greta's head before he turned. Like Samuel and Dad, he had a harder time looking at Nevio than at my daughter. I peered down at my son and took his little hand in mine, and not for the first time I wondered what Remo would see when he saw them.

A high pitched wail sounded.

Samuel and I jerked up at the same time from where we'd fallen asleep on the sofa in the nursery. We didn't bother going into our beds most of the time because Nevio and Greta woke every two hours. He and Mom took turns helping me, and during the day Sofia changed diapers and helped feed them as well.

I couldn't remember the last time I'd slept more than two hours in the last six months.

Samuel rubbed his face. I knew he didn't sleep much on the nights he wasn't helping either. The Outfit was planning something. He had only hinted to it, but it could only be an attack on the Camorra. It scared me, *terrified* me because I wasn't only scared for Samuel and Dad but also for the man I couldn't forget.

I stood and so did Samuel. He reached for Greta like usual and I took Nevio. This was our routine, one I didn't question anymore. I was glad for Samuel's support, even if he couldn't bear being near my son.

Thirty minutes later, Samuel and I sat shoulder to shoulder, Greta sound asleep in his arm and Nevio wide awake in mine. He snatched at my hair and yanked. I loosened his hold, wincing, and pushed the strand out of reach. Nevio let out a happy yowl, eyes zooming in on Samuel.

I followed his gaze. My brother sighed and put his head back. "Don't give me that look, Fina."

"What look?"

"Like I'm breaking your heart."

"Why do you have such a hard time looking at Nevio but have no trouble holding Greta?"

"Because with her I can overlook the similarities, but with Nevio ..." Samuel shook his head, lowering his gaze to my boy who was happily chewing on his own fingers. "With him all I can see is Remo fucking Falcone."

"Shh," I shushed him. I stroked Nevio's head but he was oblivious to what was being said. One day he would understand, though. One day he would realize what the looks he got meant.

"You'll never be free of him because of them, Fina. Maybe without those kids people would have eventually forgotten what happened and moved on, but they are living breathing reminders. Once people find out they are Falcone's kids, and trust me everyone will know they are his, things will get really ugly."

I rocked Nevio and his eyes began drooping. "If anyone tries to hurt my children by making them feel less than, they'll have to go through me."

Samuel smiled sadly. "I'll be at your side. I'll always protect you."

Me. Not my kids. Never them.

Falcone. Falcone.
One look.
Falcone.

The same cruel eyes.

Pitch black.

Falcones through and through.

Shame. Sin. Dishonor. Bastards.

Why did she ruin herself by having his children? Why didn't she get rid of them?

Falcones.

So far the words were only whispered in the Outfit, but soon they would be screamed because every day my children looked more like Remo, like Falcones. In a week my twins would be seven months old, and I hadn't even left the house with them yet. The only fresh air they got was when I was in the garden with them. The midwife and doctors had made home visits. Despite these precautions word about them was spreading among our circles. Maybe the maids let something slip. Maybe it was one of the bodyguards or maybe one of the Underbosses trusted his gossipy wife too much.

I'd attended two events with Samuel, and the whispers had followed me everywhere. The pity and curiosity. The incomprehension and even anger that I had chosen these children and not disposed of them, as if that would erase the kidnapping.

When we arrived home after one of these social gatherings, the birthday party of Dad's second-in-command, I lost it right in the middle of the lobby.

"I can't stand it," I said harshly. "Can't stand how everyone whispers their names as if they are something sinful. I don't want them to grow up ashamed of who they are."

Mom who'd stayed with the kids because she didn't feel well enough to attend an event appeared on the landing, looking concerned at my outburst.

Dad sighed, his expression reflecting pain. "Everyone knows what happened. Everyone knows what they are and that won't ever change."

"*What* they are ..." I stared at my father.

Samuel touched my shoulder, but I shook him off.

"They are mine! They are your blood too. They are part of the Outfit! When will you accept that? Will it take Nevio taking the oath for you to come to terms with it?"

Dad and Samuel exchanged a look, and I took a step back. "He'll become part of the Outfit, right? He'll become Underboss of a city one day? It's his birthright."

His birthright is to become Capo of the Camorra.

Dad gave me a sad smile. "Dove," he murmured.

"No," I whispered. "Don't tell me you won't let Nevio amount to anything because of who his father is."

Samuel gave me a look as if I was being unreasonable. "Fina, he looks like a fucking Falcone. They are all fucking insane. Remo's twisted blood runs through his veins. And just look at him. He's already got an impossible temper at only seven months."

"Our soldiers will never accept him, not after what his father did. We've still barely recovered from the attack. Every wedding is heavily guarded, every woman protected by twice the number of guards. That shame lingers and your children are a constant reminder of it," Dad said quietly.

I turned around and left them standing there. Rushing past Mom without a word, I stormed into the nursery and closed the door, breathing harshly.

Nevio and Greta were asleep in the crib they shared, both sprawled out on their backs. Greta's hand rested on Nevio's chest. They always ended up touching when they slept.

My children weren't something shameful.

I wouldn't allow anyone to make them feel that way. Not even the family I loved.

Remo

Kiara was in full-blown Christmas mode. She'd decorated every area of the house she was allowed into. I knew she would have loved to wield her magic in my wing as well, but she wasn't that daring yet. Good for her, because I was in a fucking foul mood, had been for days, and today was the worst of all.

The scent of freshly baked cookies wafted through the house as I read the email from Rick, the organizer of our races. Everything had been set up for the biggest race we'd ever held. Nino wasn't happy I decided to end it in Kansas City after the last incident, but I wanted to make a fucking point. The Outfit had been surprisingly careful in their attacks. An ambush here and there, a few dismembered soldiers, but nothing major. Until three days ago when they killed my fucking Underboss in Kansas City. A warning not to get so close to their territory. Maybe the beginning of more. Ending the race anywhere else would have sent the wrong message.

Kiara came in carrying a plate with what looked like small half-moons dusted in sugar. She held it out to me. "Kipferl."

"I'm not in the mood for something sweet." I was in the mood to blast something to smithereens, for blood and death, and more than that … Dante's fucking demise.

She frowned. "They're delicious." Her eyes moved to the screen. "Kansas?"

I nodded then grabbed one of the cookies and took a bite. Sweet and soft. I put half of it back down on the plate. Kiara took it and ate the rest.

I didn't like the way she regarded me as if she *knew*.

"I've been thinking about your offer."

I had no clue what she was talking about.

"About training with you."

"I made that offer more than a year ago," I said.

She bit her lip. "I wasn't ready then."

I knew another reason why I hadn't been part of her defense training in the last few months. Nino was wary of my emotional state, but he was out visiting a few of our drug labs. He was interested in the chemical processes, but I only in the end result. The only times I visited our labs were when they needed reminding to work more efficiently.

"And you think today's a good time to fight me?" I asked in a low voice.

"Not fight. Train," she corrected.

I pushed off the sofa, towering over her. She didn't flinch. "Now?"

She put the plate down and indicated the boxing ring. I shook my head. "In real life you won't be in a boxing ring when you're being attacked. It'll be in a dark alley, when you're on your way home. Your attacker will have been following and watching you for a while. He'll be behind you."

We both knew that it would never come to that. Kiara was never alone anymore, and the stupid bastard daring to look at her the wrong way would lose his eyes.

"Run."

She blinked. "What?"

I leaned down, invading her personal space, trying to get her pulse up. "Run."

Understanding filled her eyes. She took a step back and then she turned and began running.

I took another cookie and bit half of it off before putting it back down on the plate. Then I chased her. Running after Kiara brought back memories I didn't fucking need today or ever. Anger surged through me. I took the steps two at a time and caught up with her in the connecting hallway to their wing. I gripped her hand and jerked her back. Kiara gasped but acted immediately, whirling on me before I could press her to the ground. She knew she couldn't allow me to press her onto her stomach. Once my weight rested on her back, she wouldn't have a chance to defend herself anymore. She was good, but I was angry and not in the mood to take it too easy on her.

The second I straddled her hips with her arms pressed above her head, the flickers of panic filled her eyes.

"Snap out of it," I ordered.

I saw the struggle in her eyes, the memories threatening to burst forth even after all this time.

"Snap the fuck out of it," I snarled. I wouldn't release her if she didn't.

Indignation flashed in her eyes, and she bucked her hips, but I was too heavy. She was small and lithe, and managed to jerk her leg up in a way that her knee smashed right into my balls.

Every fiber in my body, every muscle, every fucking blood cell, acted on instinct, wanting to lash out. I shoved off her and sank back against the wall, chest heaving, trying to calm the rage in my veins.

"Sorry," Kiara said, sitting up and watching me worriedly.

I smiled darkly. "No need. You did what Nino taught you."

"But you didn't pull back because I hurt you ... only to stop yourself from hurting me in response."

I raised my eyebrows. She was perceptive. I wasn't sure if I liked it. "It doesn't matter. The average man isn't as familiar with pain as I am. A kick to the balls would distract them."

She nodded then she surprised me by sitting beside me against the wall. "Today's Serafina's birthday, right?"

"Kiara," I said in warning.

She tilted her head. "She didn't marry, did she?"

"I don't have spies in the Outfit, so I wouldn't know."

"It would have been in the news."

I had stopped searching for news on Serafina a few days after I'd released her. She was a thing of the past.

"I thought she was falling for you ..."

I stood, glaring down at her. "You women always need to turn everything into a fairy tale, even a kidnapping. Serafina was my captive. The only falling she did was her fall from grace."

She pushed off the ground as well. "You can pretend all you want, but I saw the way you looked at her."

I backed her into the wall. "You didn't see anything because there wasn't anything. I fucked Serafina and enjoyed every moment of it. I wanted to possess her, wanted to rip her innocence from her, and I did. That's it."

"If that were all, you would have bathed in your triumph afterward. But you hardly even mentioned her since you let her go ... as if you can't bear saying her name."

"Kiara," I growled. "Don't push me too far. Not right now."

She pushed against my shoulder, and I stepped back. Without another word, she left, but her eyes had said more than enough.

When I came back down into the game room to kick the punching bag, Savio and Adamo were on the sofa, playing some fucking shooting game. As if we didn't have enough bloodshed in real life. The plate with the cookies was empty.

"Are there more cookies in the kitchen?" Savio asked without looking up.

"How would I know? Ask Kiara."

Savio slanted a curious glance my way. "What crawled up your ass?"

I sank down across from them. "Right this moment? You. In general? Kansas."

"That race is going to be spectacular," Adamo said.

"Don't sound so fucking excited. You don't really believe Remo will allow you to race again after last time, do you?" Savio muttered, throwing his feet up on the table.

"That wasn't my fault," Adamo snapped.

"Sure. When you crash a car it's never your fault."

"I won't crash this time. I'm much better. I'll win."

Savio didn't look convinced. "It's the longest race. Eight hours minimum. That gives you plenty of time to fuck up."

"I won't fuck up. And the long distance is the best part. It's a cool layout," Adamo said.

"You won't drive," I said finally. "The race ends in Kansas City. I don't want you that close to Outfit territory."

"Nobody has to know that I'm there. I'm in a car. I can use another name."

"No. And that's final."

Adamo frowned and sank deeper into the sofa. "You promised me I could race more often if I didn't skip school and did my Camorra duties."

"And that promise stands, Adamo, but not this race."

"But Luke will be there again with a new car. He rammed me last time. I want to kick his ass and make him crash his car."

I leaned forward. "You won't go anywhere near that race, Adamo."

"Fine," he mumbled. "But next race I'm allowed?"

I nodded. I'd thought Adamo's fascination with races would wane with time, but it hadn't. He still lived for the occasional race, and I had started rewarding him with them for tasks well done. He was still a reluctant Made Man, but he'd improved, not just his fighting skills but also his guilt over what we did. Sometimes I wondered if I should just let him become the organizer for our races and have him race cars instead of trying to force him into another role, but we needed him. Open war with the Outfit required every Made Man we had.

TWENTY-FIVE

Serafina

DAD WAS ANTSY. HE KEPT CHECKING HIS PHONE, WHICH RESTED BESIDE his plate. He usually didn't have his phone on display when we had dinner. It was our family time.

Mom brought a spoon with pureed sweet potato in an arch to Greta's waiting mouth; she smacked her lips happily around the food. I, on the other hand, tried to stop Nevio from throwing his food around. He didn't like being fed and preferred to shove food into his mouth by himself, but he was still too small for that and made too much of a mess. I held his small hands so he couldn't grab the spoon and brought it to his mouth. It took three attempts before he accepted the food.

"They are cute but watching them eat is a bit disgusting," Sofia said, her nose wrinkled. "And since they started eating normal food as well, their diapers stink."

Dad frowned, obviously unhappy about the topic. He could eat dinner while someone was tortured right in front of him but a stinky diaper bothered him. Men.

Nevio let out an indignant howl when I tried for another spoonful of puree. He jerked in his seat.

Dad's eyes held disapproval. Seven months, and he still couldn't bear Nevio's sight. At least he'd held Greta a few times, but I didn't think he could ever look past their DNA.

The front door banged open, and Samuel rushed into the dining room, looking ecstatic and a bit unhinged. Dad rose slowly and Samuel smiled. I shivered because there was something dark and awfully eager in my twin's expression. "We got him," he said. "We got the bastard."

"Where is he?" Dad asked, knowing exactly whom Samuel was referring to. I set down the spoon. Mom and I exchanged a look.

"Danilo and I took him to our safety house as discussed." Danilo? A horrid suspicion overcame me.

Mom began cleaning Greta.

Dad's eyes moved to me, and finally Samuel turned to me as well. I approached them. "Who did you catch?"

Samuel touched my shoulders lightly, his eyes bright, but in their depths something was lurking that scared me. "We got our hands on Adamo Falcone. He was taking part in a street race close to our borders and we caught him."

My insides turned to stone. "Why did you catch him?" I had a feeling I knew exactly why.

"To torture the little pisser and send Remo a video of it like he sent us a video of you. And maybe we will send him each part of his brother that we'll cut off, wrapped in a white ribbon."

"Sam, Adamo is only fifteen. He is a boy. It's not right."

Samuel's face hardened. "He is a member of the Camorra, the fucking tattoo and all. And Remo Falcone didn't give a fuck about right and wrong when he kidnapped an innocent woman on her wedding day and tortured and raped her."

The color drained from my face. "It wasn't like that," I whispered.

I glanced over my shoulder at my children, but Mom was already picking up Greta. I took Nevio out of the seat and handed him to her as well. She left quickly. I turned back to Samuel, shaking because he'd said a name I hadn't heard in a while. I still felt incredibly guilty because my family didn't understand that Remo hadn't forced me, didn't understand that he had only taken what I had given.

Dad stepped up beside Samuel. He still had a hard time meeting my gaze when this topic was addressed, too ashamed for not having been able to protect me. "Your brother is right. The Falcones get what they deserve. We will destroy their crazy family like they destroyed ours."

I swallowed. That's what he thought? That our family was destroyed? I saw it every time he looked at my children and his expression flashed with guilt and disgust.

"Remo won't stand back and let you torture his brother. He won't care about the danger. He will walk into our city and tear everything down that's in his way."

Samuel dropped his hand, face twisting with self-hatred. "Like we should have marched into Vegas and saved you."

Dad ran a hand through his hair. "You know we couldn't. Remo would have killed Fina the second we got close. We were lucky he didn't do so when you went there on your own. We couldn't risk it after that."

Remo would have never killed me, but they didn't know that, couldn't possibly understand, and how could I ever explain to them when I didn't understand it myself?

"Instead we sat back and waited for him to make demands while he was busy forcing himself on her and getting her pregnant."

"I'm here! Stop talking about me like I'm not here."

"Sorry, dove," Dad said with a sigh. My heart fluttered. He seldom called me 'dove' anymore, not because he loved me less but because he felt responsible for my broken wings.

"I'm not blaming either of you," I said firmly, looking first at my father then at Samuel. "But I know Remo and he will do anything to save his brother. Anything."

"We will see. We're going to do a live recording for the fucker today. He can watch his brother getting tortured live on the Darknet." Samuel grinned.

I took a step back. "You're joking."

"No," Samuel said. "I only came to pick up Dad. Danilo is already preparing everything, and Dante is supposed to arrive any moment as well."

"You planned this?"

"Not Adamo, no," Samuel said. "We wanted to attack the race. It was pure luck that the little bastard enjoys racing cars."

Dad nodded. "We should leave now. Let's go."

I gripped Samuel's arm. "Let me go with you."

He exchanged a look with Dad who said, "No, dove. That's nothing you should see."

"Why not? I've been a captive of the Camorra for months. Do you really think torture or blood still bother me? Do you think anything can bring me to my knees anymore? I'm not the innocent girl of the past. I have a right to be there. I was the one they kidnapped. You owe it to me to let me go with you."

They both stared at me like I'd punched them, and I felt a flicker of guilt, but playing the guilt card was my only chance to convince them, and I needed to see Adamo.

Dad closed his eyes briefly then gave a small nod. "Come on."

He went ahead. Samuel wrapped his arm around my shoulder and squeezed. "We will make them pay for what they did to you. Remo will regret the day he laid a finger on you."

I averted my eyes and followed Samuel out of our house, a place that felt less like home every day. Every day that Nevio looked more like his father.

The house they took me to was a shabby three-story building close to the tracks, located in the industrial part of Minneapolis. When we stepped inside, my eyes registered Danilo first. He had his arms crossed and was staring at a screen on a table against one wall. Beside him stood my uncle Dante, as usual dressed in a suit, but his jacket was already slung over a chair that sat in front of the screen, and he had rolled up his sleeves.

My stomach turned. I'd never seen him with rolled up sleeves, and I knew why. I had never been around when he'd tortured someone. There was another man, one of Dad's soldiers, who was working at a laptop, probably establishing the Darknet connection. They turned when we entered, and all eyes zeroed in on me. I wasn't supposed to be here.

Dante frowned and came toward us. Danilo stayed where he was, but he, too, watched me. I wasn't his fiancé anymore. I was nothing to him. My sister was promised to him, and now she was as precious as I had been. And yet he would be part in the Outfit's revenge because Remo had insulted Danilo in the worst way possible: he had taken me from him.

Dante stopped before us, his cool eyes resting on me. "Serafina, this is Outfit business. You shouldn't be here."

"It is my business, Uncle. The Falcones held me captive." I met his gaze head-on. After months in Remo's company, I didn't feel the urge to lower my gaze despite my uncle's own scary vibe, especially today. There was something predator-like about him, about them all. Eager to tear into their victim, to hear its screams and taste its blood.

He inclined his head. "It will be brutal and bloody. You are free to watch on the screen."

He turned and walked back to Danilo, followed by Dad. Samuel squeezed my shoulder. "If it's too much, go sit there." He pointed at a sofa behind the table with the screen. "You shouldn't leave the building. I don't want you outside without me or Dad."

I nodded. Samuel released me and joined the other men. Slowly, I moved closer and when I reached the table, I caught sight of the screen. My breath caught in my throat. It showed Adamo in an empty room, bound to a chair, his head hanging down.

"Ready?" Dante asked. Danilo, Dad, and Samuel nodded. Dante turned to the man at the screen. "Are we live?"

"All set. The camera in the torture room is sending."

"Good," Dante said coldly. With a last glance at me, the men disappeared through a door. A few minutes later they appeared on the screen, entering the room. I sank down on the chair beside my father's soldier, who gave me a quick curious glance. I could imagine what he thought, what they all thought. Since I had been kidnapped, I was only known as the woman Remo Falcone sullied. The broken one.

Samuel held something under Adamo's nose so he jerked upright, eyes flying up in shock. He had changed since I'd last seen him. His face had become harder, older, and he had grown and become more muscular. He wasn't wearing a shirt, and a few scars littered his chest but not nearly as many as Remo had. The distant resemblance to Remo sent a stab through my heart.

Adamo's gaze wandered over my dad, Samuel, Danilo, and Dante, and for a second fear flashed across his face. Then he controlled his features.

Dante stepped forward, and the look on his face sent a chill down my spine. "Adamo Falcone. Welcome to Outfit territory."

Adamo smiled bitterly. "I would have won the race if you hadn't shot out my tires."

My eyes grew wide. Provoking my family in a situation like that was madness.

Dante's expression became harder. Samuel had already taken his knife out, and Danilo looked ready to plunge his dagger into Adamo as well. Only Dad remained back. He was a restrained man but his stance was off.

"You share the same arrogant disposition as your brother Remo, I see," Dante said pleasantly. "It's only fair that he gets to watch you pay for his sins."

Adamo shook his head. "No matter what you do, Remo won't care. Remo is crueler than all of you combined."

Dante tilted his head. "We will see." He took a knife from a table to the side and moved back toward Adamo, who tensed and leaned back. Dante reached down and cut Adamo's right arm loose.

Confusion drew my brows together. Dante grabbed Adamo's arm and turned it over, displaying the Camorra tattoo. "How long have you been a Made Man?"

"One year and four months," Adamo muttered, glaring up at my uncle.

"You will be judged as a Made Man, not a boy, Adamo Falcone."

Adamo grimaced. "I don't give a shit about all this. Do what you have to do. It won't change a thing."

Dante stepped back and gestured at the other men. "Who wants to go first? You are the ones who are closer to Serafina."

Adamo winced and looked at Samuel, who took a step forward. "I want to go first."

Tears stung in my eyes. Please don't, Sam.

Samuel moved toward Adamo and punched him hard. Adamo's head fell back, blood spraying out of his nose as it broke. I rose slowly from my chair, ignoring the stare from the man beside me. Samuel brought his knife down on Adamo's stomach and left a long cut. Adamo cried and lashed out with his free hand, but Samuel grabbed it and twisted the hand back, breaking it. I took a step back, my hand covering my mouth. I had never seen Samuel like this. I knew what he was, what they all were. This wasn't right. I had to stop them somehow.

"See, Remo, your brother will bleed in your stead. We'll tear him apart piece by piece for what you did to my sister. He will suffer for you," Samuel snarled. In that moment, little of my twin was left. A Made Man, a monster. Just because I never saw his monstrous side didn't mean Samuel was less of a monster than any other of the men in our world.

Dad pushed away from the wall, gripped Adamo's free arm, and jerked it back with a sickening crunch. He had a look on his face I had never seen. Adamo's screams blared through the speakers, and I began running.

Adamo didn't deserve this. And with their actions, they would make everything worse because Remo would seek retribution. He would attack viciously, would maim and kill, would leave nothing in his wake, and whatever the outcome, I would lose someone I cared about. Either my family members or the father of my children.

I followed the screams to the last door and burst through it then froze as the smell of burning flesh filled my nose. Adamo was screaming as Danilo was holding a lighter to his forearm, burning away the Camorra tattoo.

"Enough!" I cried. I stormed forward and pushed him aside before either of them could grab me. Danilo's eyes flashed with fury, and all the men stared at me. "Enough!" I screamed. "Enough!"

Adamo groaned and I turned to him, kneeling before him. Only a small part of his tattoo had been burned away, and the skin was blistered and red. I touched his shoulder and he flinched. "Adamo," I whispered.

He raised his head a few inches, teary eyes meeting mine. A weak smile pulled at his lips. "Serafina." How he could still sound friendly after what had been done to him was a mystery to me.

A shadow fell over me and I looked up. Samuel. "Fina, you should leave. He gets what he deserves."

"He is a boy," I said. "And he always treated me with kindness."

"He is a Falcone," Danilo said, stepping forward with the lighter still in his hand. His eyes were hard and merciless. "You were punished for something Outfit soldiers did. Adamo will pay for something his brother did."

"I suffered for your sins," I spat at them. "And he suffers for Remo's. I'm sick of it. This ends here. Adamo won't suffer any more pain under your hands."

"That isn't your call to make," Dante said firmly.

I looked back at Adamo, who looked resigned and had begun shaking. A phone rang and Dante picked it up. "Remo."

I jerked, my eyes widening.

Remo

Kiara was asleep with her head in Nino's lap. It was early afternoon, so I didn't understand how she could be tired. Maybe Nino kept her awake all night. I frowned then drew my gaze back to the screen where the race was playing out. The number of participants was staggering. They had to start from different spots, all the same distance from Kansas City, to divert the attention of the police. A few of them would be arrested like usual, but that was part of the game. Eventually the different routes would merge to one for the last 100 miles before the end.

Car racing brought in good money, but I didn't really care for it. I preferred cage fighting.

Savio ate another bite of the cake Kiara had baked. "Do you think Adamo has a crush on that whore?"

"C.J.," Nino said.

"Whatever. He's been in the Sugar Trap an awful lot. They're definitely fucking. And come on, he spent the night with her again. What is he doing with her? Cuddling? He can't fuck her for hours. I'm surprised he gets one up at all. If he had to pay for her, he'd be broke by now."

I shrugged. I didn't care if Adamo fucked a whore or not. I'd never seen him talk to any of the other whores, though. It worried me, not to mention that it wasn't the first night he'd spent with the whore at the Sugar Trap. Fucking her was okay, but spending so much time with her could definitely prove to be a problem.

"Trust Adamo to fall in love with a whore and be monogamous when she's got about a dozen dicks up her pussy every day," Savio said.

Nino made an impatient sound, obviously keen on watching the race in peace. One of the participants was currently being chased by three police cars. Bets if the fucker managed to escape or not were probably burying us already.

"You don't know what's going on. Maybe he only enjoys her skills."

Savio scoffed. "She's not bad but there are better whores out there."

"It's not like he has many to compare her to," I said, growing tired of the discussion.

"One of these days he's going to bring her over here and keep her," Savio said.

The perspective switched to another drone camera, and my brows drew together. It briefly showed a few burning cars, some of them black limousines. The others were race cars. Then it changed back to the police chase.

"What the fuck was that?"

The front door swung open with a bang, steps thundered toward us. Nino put an arm over Kiara and pulled his gun. I rose with my own gun raised. Fabiano stormed into the living room, panting. "The Outfit attacked our territory!"

I froze. Savio jerked to his feet.

"What?" I growled. If Dante had set a single foot on Vegas ground, I'd walk into Chicago tomorrow. Then another thought struck me. "The race."

Fabiano nodded. "The organizer from the Kansas race called a few minutes ago. There was an attack on the race. I think he called me because he thought it would stop you from killing him."

Tough luck. I'd deal with him once I was done with the Outfit. "How long ago did they attack?"

"About an hour ago. There's chaos over there. But the race is going on with the remaining cars."

"Why didn't they alert us sooner?"

"They didn't know what was going on at first. When they realized it was the Outfit, they tried to divert the other race cars first so they could keep the race going."

Kiara stirred. "What's wrong?"

I pulled my knife, shaking, furious that Dante had attacked again. Nino stood, pulling Kiara to her feet. "Go to our bedroom."

She looked at me, eyes widening, then nodded quickly and hurried away.

My phone rang. I picked it up and brought it to my ear. "Remo," said a man. The voice was distantly familiar, but I couldn't place it. The background noise suggested he was in a helicopter or small airplane. "This is Danilo Mancini. I'm calling to tell you we have your brother and we're going to enjoy his screams like you enjoyed Serafina's. Tell Nino to set up a Darknet connection for later so you can watch as we tear him apart. I will enjoy slicing him into tiny pieces." He hung up.

It took my brain a few moments to process the information. "Call the Sugar Trap and ask if Adamo's there," I ordered.

Fabiano frowned but did as he was told. "Is Adamo there?" he asked without a greeting. "Then ask her."

"Remo, what's going on?" Nino asked carefully.

My phone beeped with an incoming message with detailed instructions for the connection.

I held it out to Nino, who took it from me, frowning. His mouth tightened when he read what the message said.

"He's not there. Apparently he left last night. C.J. said he asked her to pretend she was with him because he wanted to join the race."

I nodded, trying to ignore the way my chest kept constricting.

Savio didn't say anything, only stared at me. Fabiano had fixed himself a drink and downed it in one gulp.

Eventually Nino looked up from the phone. "We won't be quick enough to save him."

"There won't be anything left of him to save when they're done with him," I got out, fury and a weaker emotion burning through my veins. Why couldn't the kid have listened for once? Fuck it.

"Call Grigory. Tell him he can have Kansas if he attacks the Outfit."

Nino nodded, and pressed the phone back to his ear as he walked back and forth in the room.

Savio ran a hand through his hair. "Fuck. We have to do something."

From the words I caught, Grigory had no intention of getting involved. I flung my knife at the heavy bag. "Fuck!" I snarled before Nino had uttered a single word.

"He says this isn't his fight."

"Bastard," Fabiano muttered.

"I will soon make it his fucking fight. For this, I will declare war on him and the fucking Bratva in Outfit territory."

"Do you want me to set up the connection?" Nino asked quietly.

"Of course," I growled. "If Adamo has to suffer, we will watch. We will suffer with him. Fuck it all!"

Nino didn't move for a moment. Then he nodded slowly.

"We need to figure out where they are taking him," I told Fabiano. He knew the Outfit better than any of us.

"I assume honor dictates that they take him to Minneapolis because that's where her family lives. She wasn't married to Danilo yet or they would have taken Adamo to his city to dish out punishment there," he said.

It would take us at least three hours to reach Minneapolis and probably several more hours to figure out where they kept Adamo. The Darknet connection would begin in fifty minutes. I took my phone again and dialed Dante's number. He rejected the call.

"Fuck him," I rasped. "Call our pilot. The plane better be ready in twenty minutes or I'll kill him."

Nino made the call and we set out toward the airport. Fabiano stayed with Kiara, whom he was taking to a safe house with Leona. I'd alerted every fucking soldier in Las Vegas to be vigilant.

The plane was ready on time, and we started almost immediately. I tried to call Dante again, but he didn't pick up.

"It's his game this time," Nino murmured after a while.

Savio had his face buried in his hands.

"It is," I agreed. "And he'll win."

Nino raised his eyebrows.

"I'll allow him to put me checkmate."

"Remo," he began, but I smiled grimly and indicated the laptop. "It's time to turn this on."

I pressed the blade against my palm when Adamo appeared on the screen. He was slumped forward on a chair.

When they started cutting him, Adamo's scream filled the airplane, blaring from the speakers mercilessly, and fuck, they were the first screams in forever that got under my skin. The first since *her* screams. I cut into my palm, deep, drawing blood. Savio gripped the armrest of the seat, his arms shaking. Nino was behind me, one hand digging into my shoulder.

Danilo was next and took out a lighter. I jumped to my feet, shaking with rage ... so much rage, it threatened to rip me apart. Adamo's eyes widened. Fuck, he was a kid. He wasn't like us. This was supposed to be me. I was supposed to burn for them.

Danilo touched the flame to Adamo's skin, and his screams got louder. I reached for my phone again, knowing that Dante would reject my call like before and hating this fucking sense of helplessness. I was supposed to burn for them, for him, and I would.

"Enough!" a female voice rang out, and my eyes snapped back to the screen as Serafina threw herself in front of my brother, protecting him. I froze, unable to trust my eyes, to believe that the woman who haunted my nights was really in front of me.

Nino and Savio stared at me, as if they waited for me to lose my shit completely.

"Fuck," Savio murmured, shaking his head.

She hadn't returned to me like I'd thought she would.

She hated me more than I'd expected, and yet she protected Adamo. Because he wasn't the one she wanted to see suffer. She wanted to see me bleed. She would get her wish.

"Remo?" Nino said in a cautious voice.

I raised the phone to my ear, waiting for the inevitable, but this time it didn't come. He finally answered my call. "Dante, I'll give you what you really want. Tomorrow morning I'll be in Minneapolis and exchange myself for Adamo." He didn't need to know we were already on our way, but maybe he did.

"Remo," he said coolly. His eyes focused on the camera for a moment before the screen turned black and Serafina and my brother disappeared from view.

"It's me you want to see burn, not my brother, and you will get your chance."

"Tomorrow morning, at eight. If you're late, your brother won't be recognizable as your brother anymore, understood?"

"Understood."

"I'll have someone send you the details, Remo. I'm looking forward to meeting you again," he said coldly.

I hung up.

"They will kill you, Remo," Savio said.

"They will cut me, skin me, burn me, cut off my dick, and then maybe they'll kill me," I said quietly. And all I could wonder was if Serafina would watch them do it.

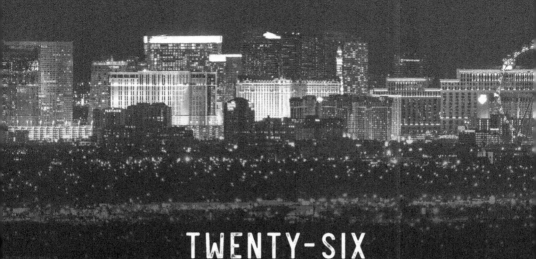

TWENTY-SIX

Serafina

THEY ALLOWED ME TO STAY WITH ADAMO, AND I CROUCHED AT HIS FEET, feeling sick to my stomach from what I'd witnessed and even worse thinking about what was to come.

"Remo will exchange himself for you," I whispered. "Tomorrow, you will be back in Vegas, and Nino will treat your wounds."

Adamo tilted his head, dark eyes bleak. "Remo is Capo. He won't die because I've been stupid enough to get myself captured. I've been a disappointment to him since I was born. He will use this chance and kill Dante instead of handing himself over."

I lifted soaked fabric from his burn, and he groaned deeply. His wrist and nose were broken and his shoulder dislocated. He must have been in horrible pain, and there was nothing I could do to help him. Playing the guilt card forced my family give me this small freedom. It didn't convince them to call a doctor though. They would have probably kept torturing Adamo if I hadn't refused to move away from his side.

"You're wrong, Adamo. Remo will protect you. He doesn't fear death or pain. He will take your place because you are his brother and he cares for you. He'd do anything for you."

Adamo let out a choked laugh. "Why do you speak about him as if you don't hate him? He kidnapped you. He ruined your life."

I looked away. I wouldn't tell him about Nevio and Greta and certainly not about my twisted feelings for his brother either.

Adamo leaned forward, wincing, and brought our faces closer together, a risk because we were undoubtedly being watched, and my family was still eager to spill Falcone blood. His or Remo's, it didn't matter, as long as it was a Falcone. I met Adamo's gaze, and realization settled on his face.

"Fuck," he whispered hoarsely. He leaned even closer, despite the rope binding his unharmed arm to the chair. "You're giving me the same look Remo has whenever someone mentions you."

My chest constricted. "I need to go now." I stood and took a step back. Adamo Falcone. Falcone, the name my children were supposed to carry.

"Goodbye," I whispered, but deep down I wondered if this was really the last time I would see him.

I turned quickly and left the room. Samuel waited right in front of the door. He regarded me, incomprehension in his features. "Why do you take care of a fucking Falcone bastard?"

"He never hurt me. He's a boy."

Samuel shook his head. "He is a Made Man, Fina. You should let us handle him and Remo. We are capable of doing what needs to be done."

We walked into the main hall where Dad, Danilo, and Dante were talking in hushed tones. They turned to us the moment we entered.

I faced Samuel. "And what is that?"

"Bring Remo to his knees. Make him beg for mercy. Beg for death. I will cut his dick off myself. Danilo will take care of his balls, and then we will keep them in a nice bag with ice so he can see them while we tear him apart. Then we'll shove them down his throat."

Danilo smiled grimly, and even Dad looked like he could imagine nothing better than committing the most brutal murder he could think of.

I swallowed. "He is the father of my children."

Samuel grabbed my shoulders hard, desperately. "He broke you, Fina," he said softly. None of them had ever asked if I considered myself broken. They had declared me as such, and all four of them made me feel like I was.

"He is a monster," Samuel added.

"He is not the only one," I whispered, my eyes wandering over the gathered men.

Samuel dropped his hands, face twisting as if I'd stabbed him. "I'm doing this for you. To avenge you."

"Did any of you ever ask what I wanted? If I wanted more blood spilled? If I wanted to be avenged?" I shouted.

Dante came forward, expression tight. "Don't you want to see Remo Falcone on his knees? Don't you want to see him broken?"

I did, but not in the same way they wanted. "I want nothing more," I said quietly, because they could never, would never understand.

Samuel wrapped an arm around me and kissed my temple. "Fina, let's go home."

"Yes, let's go home," I said quietly. I peered up at Samuel, realizing that for the first time in my life, we didn't mean the same place.

Remo

Nino, Savio, and I linked arms, pressing over the tattoo of the other. "You will be a better Capo than me, Nino. You won't kill people who might be useful to us. Your logic will make the Camorra even stronger."

Nino didn't say anything, only stared at me.

Savio shook his head. "Remo, let's attack them. I'd rather die fighting than have you in their fucking hands."

I smiled darkly. "You will have to die another day. I will pay for my sins."

Nino made a low sound. "She didn't return, Remo. She stayed in Minneapolis. They won't let you anywhere near her. You will die for nothing."

"No, I will die so she gets what she wants."

Nino pulled away. "Damn it. Be reasonable for once."

"I made my decision and you will accept it."

Cars pulled up, and I moved away from my brothers who took shelter inside the car. Nino and Savio raised their guns through the open windows. I wasn't armed as I walked toward the parked cars, my arms raised over my head. I didn't think Dante would attack Nino or Savio. Once he'd dismembered me in the cruelest way possible, he'd send my brothers the recording and probably to Luca as well. He'd try to break my family like I had broken his, killing us all just wouldn't do. Not yet.

Dante got out, followed by Samuel, Pietro, and Danilo, and more men I didn't know and didn't give a fuck about. Samuel walked around to the back of the car and pulled Adamo out.

Adamo could hardly stand as Samuel dragged him behind himself toward me. Rage boiled under my skin. Samuel shoved Adamo to the ground in front of my feet, and Adamo looked up at me with his blood covered face, cradling his broken and burned arm against his chest.

"Don't," he whispered. "Don't do this. Don't let them kill you because of me. I'm a fucking failure."

I moved toward him and touched his head briefly. "You are the one from all of us who deserves death the least, Adamo." I removed my hand from his head, but before I could move on, he grasped my forearm, his fingers curling over my Camorra tattoo. "It's us against the world," he croaked.

"Us against the world," I said.

Samuel gripped my arm, and I shoved down the instinct to smash his face. I saw his fist coming toward my face and smiled. The first punch only blurred my vision. His kick to my balls brought me to my knees. And his gun to the back of my head finally pulled me into blackness.

Serafina

Samuel and Danilo dragged Remo into the safe house, his arms and legs bound, his nose busted and dripping blood, his hair sticking to the back of his head with more blood. I slowly rose from the sofa where I had been waiting for almost one hour with two bodyguards.

Dad moved toward me, trying to shield Remo from my view—or me from his. I wasn't sure and didn't care. "Dove, you shouldn't be here." His eyes narrowed on my bodyguards, harshly, cruelly. I touched his arm.

"I will stay," I said firmly, my voice resolute.

Dante was the last to enter.

The men exchanged a look. Their word was law, not mine, but their guilt gave me power over them, more power than they'd ever held over me. I hated using it against them, but they would never allow me to possess power for any other reason.

I walked past my father, toward Danilo and Samuel holding Remo between them. His head hung down, body was slack. I tried to hide the tremor that had taken hold of me the moment I'd spotted him.

Remo Falcone.

Danilo's expression twisted like it always did when he saw me. With guilt and a flicker of humiliation because something had been taken from him, because Remo had taken it from him. He was a strong, powerful man, and having lost me haunted him like it haunted every man in the room. I was their failure. Their pride a tattered sullied rag. Every time they had to peer into my eyes, and worse the eyes of my children, they were reminded.

They'd never let me be anything but the dove with broken wings. They couldn't. But I wanted to fly.

"Have you come to watch the bastard die, Fina?" Samuel asked, his face cruel, eager, brutal as his blue eyes settled on Remo, who still hadn't moved, but I noticed the almost imperceptible shift in his shoulders, his muscles twitching. He was waking up.

My heart beat faster, my palms becoming sweaty.

"I know you deserve your revenge, dove, but this is going to be more than you can stomach, trust me," Dad said, coming up behind me and putting a hand on my shoulder. His voice was soft, compelling, but his face held terrifying eagerness and cruelty as he regarded the father of my children.

"What are your plans for him?" I asked my uncle, because he was the man who would have the last word on the matter.

His cool blue eyes weren't as controlled as usual. He, too, wanted to tear into Remo. They had waited a long time for this moment. "We will prolong his torture as long as possible without risking an attack from the Camorra."

"He won't die today?"

"Oh, he won't die today," Samuel muttered. "But he might wish for it."

I gave a nod. It was what I had expected. Remo wouldn't experience any mercy at the hands of the Outfit, not that he'd ever ask for it.

"He'll *beg* for death," Dad said harshly.

"I don't beg for anything, Pietro."

I shivered at the familiar timbre, at the underlying threat, the undercurrent of power. How did he do it?

Remo lifted his head, and my brother and Danilo tightened their hold, but they blended into the background when Remo's eyes finally met mine. Fourteen months.

The force of his gaze hit me like a tidal wave. In the time since he'd released me, I'd often wondered if I could ever forget him, if I could move on and live a new life, but now as I looked at him, I realized I had been foolish to consider that an option.

The corners of his mouth lifted in a twisted smile. "Angel."

My brother punched Remo's face, but he only laughed darkly as blood spattered on the ground.

"This is your chance to ask for forgiveness," Dad said.

Remo looked from each of them until his eyes finally settled on me. "Do you want me to beg for forgiveness?"

His eyes dragged me down fiercely, mercilessly, irrevocably as they'd always done. As they always would. "I won't give you my forgiveness," I said quietly.

Something flickered in Remo's eyes, but Samuel and Danilo wrenched him away from my view, down the corridor into their torture chamber.

Dad kissed my temple. "We will avenge you, make him pay for what he did."

He walked away, leaving me with Dante, who regarded me with calm scrutiny. He touched my shoulder lightly, and I met his gaze. "He will ask for forgiveness in the end," he promised.

I briefly touched his hand. "I don't want him to because it would be false."

Remo did everything with unbridled passion, with ferocious rage, without an ounce of regret.

He consumed, obliterated, ruined.

He took everything and left nothing in his wake. He was an unrepentant sinner. He was a destroyer, a murderer, a torturer.

A monster.

The father of my children.

The man who held my heart in his cruel, brutal hand.

"You will castrate him?" It was an unnecessary question. I knew they would, and it was only one of the many atrocities they'd planned. All I needed to know was when.

Dante gave a terse nod. "Tomorrow. Not today. It would speed up his death too much. Danilo and Samuel will do it. I'm not sure you should watch any of this, but maybe you need to. Today will be easier to stomach than tomorrow, so stay if it's what you want."

"Thanks," I whispered. Slowly I made my way toward the screen on the table and turned it on.

My brother and Danilo were kicking Remo in the stomach, in the side, and Remo made no move to defend himself. When they finally let up, because Dante had entered, Remo rolled onto his back and looked directly into the camera, knowing I was watching.

He didn't look away when my father took out his knife and cut his chest. Not when it was Samuel's turn. Not when it was Danilo's turn. Not when it was Dante's turn.

I'd spent so many hours, day and night, wondering how it would feel to see Remo broken, to see him on his knees.

This wasn't how I imagined things to be, my heart clenching in my chest so tightly I could hardly breathe, the tears pressing against my eyelids so fiercely I had to bite the inside of my cheek to hold them back. And even through the torture, Remo didn't look broken because he couldn't be broken, not with violence and pain. Maybe not at all.

I turned away from the screen and walked away. My bodyguards followed close behind, their steps slow and measured. Shadows meant to protect and save me. But I was beyond saving. My family tried to mend me, but I didn't need it because I wasn't broken.

Slipping behind the steering wheel of the Mercedes limousine, I revved the engine the second my bodyguards were inside. My foot pressed down on the gas. They slanted looks my way but didn't comment. They were meant to protect not judge.

I was allowed this freedom because my family's guilt had paid for it. They couldn't bear keeping the dove with broken wings in a gilded cage.

The second I had the car parked in front of my family's home, I killed the engine and got out, not waiting for them. I stepped inside and hurried upstairs, didn't stop until I entered the nursery. Both Nevio and Greta were asleep in their shared crib, looking peaceful and painstakingly beautiful.

I stroked their heads, the thick black hair like their father's. When my fingers brushed Nevio's temple, his eyes peeled open with those dark brown, almost black eyes. I leaned down and pressed a kiss to his forehead then to Greta's, breathed in their scent, then sank down in a chair and watched them sleep.

I wasn't sure how long I stayed like that when the door opened. Familiar steps sounded behind me, steps that had accompanied me almost all my life. A warm hand came down on my shoulder, and I covered it with mine.

Samuel pressed a kiss to the crown of my head then rested his forehead against it for a couple of moments. So gentle and caring, so very different from the man I'd seen torturing Remo. He straightened and I tilted my head back, peering up at him. His gaze rested on Greta and Nevio, but for him there was nothing beautiful about them. As always, his eyes shone with guilt and aversion when he regarded them before he noticed my scrutiny and lowered his gaze to me.

Warmth filled his expression. I wished he could spare some of it for the children I loved more than life itself. Samuel was my blood. He would always be. He was part of me as I was part of him, and I didn't resent him for his feelings toward my children. I knew he hated their father, not them, but more than that he hated himself.

I stood, grabbed his neck, and pulled him down until his forehead rested against mine. "Please, Sam, stop blaming yourself. Please, I beg you. I'm not broken. You have no reason to feel guilty."

He returned my gaze but I realized his guilt ran too deep. Maybe tomorrow he'd finally be free. Maybe he could let go of his guilt when he had to let go of me. "I love you," I said, knowing it was the last time.

Samuel wrapped his arms around me. "And I love you, Fina."

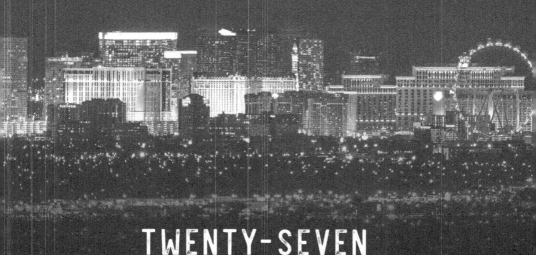

TWENTY-SEVEN

Serafina

D AD AND DANTE DIDN'T COME HOME THAT EVENING. THEY WOULD spend the night in the safe house. Safe house. What a name for a house to torture enemies.

After Samuel had made sure I was okay, he drove back there as well. Maybe they were worried Remo might manage to escape or maybe they wanted to keep torturing him throughout the night. Probably the latter.

I grabbed a bag and packed a few things for Greta and Nevio. Then I walked down into the basement where we kept our weapons as well as other necessities in case of an attack. I perused the display of guns and knives. I strapped a gun holster to my chest over my T-shirt. It allowed me to strap a gun and a knife to my sides as well as another gun to my back. Just to be on the safe side, I added a knife holster to my calf. I had chosen loose linen pants for the occasion just for that purpose. After that I rummaged through the medical supplies. Samuel had explained everything to me so I was prepared if something happened, not so I could use it against them. I grabbed a syringe with adrenaline and one with a sedative. After I'd put on my thick cardigan, I stuffed the syringes into its pockets and returned upstairs.

It was quiet in the house. Sofia was probably reading in her room before bed, and Mom was most likely doing the same.

The bodyguards were in their quarters in the back of the house, and two were guarding the fence surrounding the garden. I put on comfortable sneakers then headed for the nursery.

I considered going to my mother, saying goodbye, apologizing for what I was about to do, but words would never be enough to explain my betrayal.

Words were too insignificant. They would never understand. I'd try to call her later, once we were safe.

Lifting the bag over one shoulder, I grabbed Nevio and Greta before I made my way out of the nursery, moving quietly.

I froze when I spotted Sofia standing in her doorway in her pink nightgown, brown hair disheveled. Her eyes took in everything and a small frown drew her brows together. "Where are you going?"

I considered what to tell her, how to explain to a twelve-year-old what I had done and was about to do. "I'm leaving. I have to."

Sofia's eyes widened, and she padded toward me with bare feet. "Because of Greta and Nevio?"

I nodded. She was young but she wasn't as oblivious as we all wanted to believe. She stopped right in front of me. "You're leaving us."

I swallowed hard. "I have to, ladybug. For my babies. I want them to be safe and happy. I need to protect them from the whispers."

Sofia regarded my twins. She leaned forward and kissed each of them on the cheek, her eyes filling with tears as she peered up at me. My heart clenched tightly. "I know what people say about them, and I hate it. But I don't want you to go ..." Her voice broke.

"I know." I tried to hold back my emotions. "Give me a hug."

She wrapped her arms around me and the twins, and we remained like that for a moment. "Don't tell anyone, please."

She pulled back with a knowing look. "You're going to return to their father?"

I nodded, a half-truth, but Sofia didn't need to know that our family and her future husband were currently torturing the man she was referring to.

"Do you love him?"

"I don't know," I admitted. Sofia looked confused for a moment, but then she nodded, biting her lip, more tears gathering in her eyes. "Dad won't allow me to see you anymore, will he?"

I swallowed. "I hope one day he'll understand."

"I'll miss you."

"I'll miss you too. I'll try to contact you. Remember I love you."

She nodded, tears trailing down her cheeks. I quickly turned before I lost it. I could feel Sofia's eyes on me as I walked downstairs. The light from upstairs illuminated my path as I headed into the garage. I put Nevio and Greta into their car seats then slipped behind the steering wheel. The guns were digging uncomfortably into my back and side. The garage door slid up, and I pulled out and steered the car down the long driveway. I pressed the button for the gate and it opened.

A guard stepped in front of the gate, and I had to pull to a stop or run him over.

The windows were tinted, so he couldn't see the kids on the backseat. I let down the window a gap.

"Miss Mione, nobody informed us you'd be leaving."

"I'm informing you now," I said firmly.

He frowned. "I'll have to ask the boss."

I scowled. "Get out of my way. I'm driving over to the safe house to kill the man who raped and tortured me."

His eyes grew wide, and he lowered his gaze, the shame of all Outfit soldiers reflecting clearly on his face. "I'll have to make a quick call."

He lifted his phone to his ear, and I considered hitting the gas. He lowered the phone, touched the screen again then lifted it once more. "Samuel, I can't reach your father. Your sister is at the gate, trying to leave."

He held the phone out to me. I took it with a glare.

"Fina, what's going on?"

"Tell him to let me leave."

"Fina."

"I'm coming over. I need to … I need to see what you're doing. You owe it to me, Sam."

Guilt sliced through me, but I shoved it back.

"You should take a bodyguard with you."

"Sam," I whispered harshly. "Let me leave. Do you want me to beg? I've done enough of that, trust me." A lie, one I'd never wanted to use on Samuel.

He sighed. "Okay. But right now we're not doing anything. Dad, Danilo, and Dante are catching some shut-eye. It's been a long day."

"I'll be there in fifteen minutes. Let them sleep for now. They don't need to know I'm coming over yet. You know how Dad can be."

I handed the phone back to the guard and after an order from my brother, he finally let me through.

Samuel was waiting for me outside the safe house when I pulled up. I programmed the heating so it would keep the car warm for my babies before I exited. Samuel regarded me with a deep frown. He was wearing a different shirt than last time I saw him, and as I got closer, I noticed the red under his fingernails. He wrapped an arm around my shoulders, and for a moment I tensed because I worried he could feel the holster, but his arm was too high up and my cardigan too thick. He led me inside. My eyes searched the main area.

"They're in the sleep area upstairs. Do you want me to wake them?"

"No," I said quickly. My eyes were drawn to the screen. It showed Remo lying on the floor, not moving. I tried to gauge the angle. Samuel followed my gaze. "We'll continue in about an hour."

I raised my eyes to his. Dark shadows spread under his eyes. "You look like you should get some sleep."

"Someone's got to keep watch."

"He doesn't look like he can do anything."

Samuel's lips curled. "He's a tough fucker." His expression softened. "But we'll get him to beg. At some point, even he will break."

I doubted it but we'd never find out. "Do you have something to drink for me?"

Samuel nodded and walked over to the table in the corner. I took out the syringe before I followed him. "Water okay?" he asked as I stopped close beside him.

I touched his chest. "I'm sorry, Sam." His brows snapped together in confusion, and I shoved the needle into his thigh.

Sam jerked. "Fina? What?" But he was already staggering, his eyelids drooping. I clung to him, trying to stop him from falling and injuring himself, but he was too heavy. He sank to the ground. His eyes began to lose focus. I bent over him and kissed his forehead. "I hope you'll forgive me one day."

I stepped into the torture room, my eyes landing on Remo. He was sprawled out on the floor, lying in his own blood, naked except for black briefs, his arms and legs tied to hooks in the ground with rope. Bruises and cuts littered almost every inch of him. On the table to the right, I could see torture tools. The knives covered in blood, but some of the others were still pristine and untouched, waiting for their purpose.

Remo's eyes peeled open in his blood-covered face, and they knocked the breath out of me again.

A dark smile twisted his mouth, but there was an emotion in his eyes that tightened my stomach. "Angel, have you come to watch your family cut off my dick? I hear that's scheduled for today."

I crept closer to him, my sneakers trudging through his blood covering the rough floor. My steps didn't falter. Blood did nothing to me. Not anymore.

Remo regarded me quietly. His eyes slid down my arm to the tip of the knife peeking out from my long cardigan sleeve. "Or have you come to do it yourself?"

I stopped right above Remo. Even though he was on his back, cut and bruised, covered in his own blood, he appeared powerful. Remo couldn't be broken because he didn't fear pain or death.

Was this love? Or madness?

I sank down to my knees beside him, kneeling on the sticky floor, my white linen pants soaking up the blood greedily. My pants soon stuck to my skin with Remo's blood. "No," I whispered, finally answering him.

Remo's eyes traced my face. He looked almost at peace. "To kill me?"

I tilted my head, regarding him. Remo was Nevio. Nevio was Remo. As if they had been carved from the same template. My children were the spitting image of their father. Even if I didn't have feelings for the man before me, I could never kill him because the faces of Greta and Nevio would remind me of him every day of my life.

"I always thought it was meant to be that way. Your hand ending my life."

I shook my head. "I won't kill you." I leaned over Remo, my fingers spreading through his blood on the ground, my hair dipping in it. So much blood.

"You didn't marry Danilo," Remo murmured.

"How could I?" I whispered, bending low until Remo and I were almost touching. "How could I marry him when I was pregnant with your children?"

Remo stiffened. I'd wondered how he would react if I ever told him about Greta and Nevio, but nothing came close to the look on his face. Complete and utter shock, and more than that … wonder.

"When you gave me up, I carried your babies in me, Remo. You gave us up."

"I thought you'd return to me," he rasped.

"You pushed me away."

"I set you free."

"I wasn't free," I hissed. How could I ever be free when his name was etched into my heart?

"You were pregnant," he said quietly.

"I was pregnant, a living breathing reminder of the greatest failure of the Outfit, a living breathing reminder of something dark and shameful. A reminder that you took something from the Outfit, took something from me. That's what everyone thought. My family and everyone else in the Outfit. I knew giving birth to a child of yours would ruin any chance I had to find my way back into the Outfit, back into my family. I knew I'd seal my fate if I had your child. I'd be damned to live a life of pity stares and disgusted expressions."

Something flickered in Remo's eyes. Dread, maybe even fear. "You got rid of the babies." And his voice wavered ever so slightly.

A cruel, unbreakable man.

My nemesis, my captor, the man who took everything from me and without knowing it gave me the greatest gift of all.

I'd always wondered what it would take to break Remo, and I realized I held the power to do it, to crush the cruelest, strongest man I knew in my hand, held it on the tip of my tongue. One word would shatter him. The knowledge filled me with unparalleled joy, not because I could break the man before me. *No*, because our children even without knowing them meant so much to him that their death would destroy him.

"Oh, Angel, have they sent you to deliver the ultimate blow? Tell Dante he wins."

I shook my head. "No," I said quietly, then fiercer, "No. I didn't get rid of the babies even though everyone wanted me to do it."

Remo held my gaze.

"How could I get rid of the most beautiful creation I can imagine? Greta and Nevio are pure perfection, Remo."

He exhaled, and the look in his eyes … God, that look. This cruel man had stolen my heart, and I had let him.

"They look like you. Nevio is you. Everyone who sees him knows he's yours."

Remo smiled the darkest, saddest smile I have ever seen. "Have you come to tell me before my death that I'll never see them? Angel, I must say you are crueler than I could ever be."

I linked my fingers with his bloody ones, the blade cupped between our palms. "Our children are perfection but here, in the Outfit, they represent shame and dishonor. People whisper behind their backs, call them Falcones as if it is something sinful, something dirty. Our children are beautiful." My voice became fiercer with every word. "They are meant to hold their heads high, not be ashamed for who they are. They aren't meant to bow, aren't meant to live in the shadows. They are meant to *rule*. They are Falcones. They belong in Las Vegas where their names carry power and respect. They are meant to rule at the side of the cruelest, bravest man I know. Their father."

Remo didn't say anything but his expression set me aflame with emotion.

"How badly injured are you?" I whispered in his ear.

"Badly," he admitted.

I nodded, my throat tightening. I reached for the syringe in my pocket and pulled it out. "Adrenaline."

Remo's mouth pulled wider. I injected him with the liquid and he shuddered. His pupils were dilated when he met my gaze again.

My lips brushed his lightly. "How strong are you, Remo Falcone?"

"Strong enough to take you and our children home where you all belong, Angel."

I smiled. I wedged the blade under the rope. "Swear not to kill my family. Not my brother, not my father, not my uncle. Swear it on our children, Remo."

"I swear it," he murmured. I cut through the rope when I heard the creak of the door. I dropped the knife in Remo's now free hand.

"Serafina, get the fuck away from the asshole!" Danilo growled, gripping me by the shoulders and pulling me to my feet. I whirled around on him, getting in his face. "Don't tell me what to do. I have a right to be here."

Danilo was breathing harshly, his chest heaving. I took a step back, closer to Remo again. Dante and my father stepped in. I shielded Remo mostly from their view but that wouldn't last long.

"You shouldn't be here, dove. This isn't something for a woman," Dad said gently.

He still believed in my innocence, but Dante and Danilo regarded me more cautiously. "Where's Samuel?" Dante asked.

I wrapped my arms around my body and slid my hands beneath my cardigan, my fingers curling around the gun strapped to the holster there.

"I'm sorry," I whispered and pulled the gun on them.

Dante put his hand on his gun at his waist but didn't pull it. My father and Danilo were completely frozen.

"Samuel's going to be okay. He's knocked out behind the sofa."

"Fina," Dad said in a soothing voice. "You've been through a lot. Put down the gun."

I took another step back, releasing the safety catch. "I'm sorry," I said again, biting back tears, thinking of Samuel, of what he would think once he woke up. In my peripheral vision, Remo cut through the last rope around his ankle.

Dante pulled his gun and so did Danilo, but I barred their view of Remo. They wouldn't shoot me, not even now that I was holding them at gunpoint. I was a woman, someone to protect. I was their responsibility and their failure. Remo staggered to his feet behind me, and Danilo aimed. I shot at him, nicking the outside of his upper arm. He gasped, his eyes flashing at me.

"Not a single move," I warned. Remo pressed up behind me, as usual not heeding any safety measures, towering a head over me. "We only want to leave. No one has to get hurt," I whispered.

Remo reached for my gun but I shook my head. "My back," I told him. His hand slid under my cardigan and pulled the gun from there.

"Dove," Dad croaked. "You don't owe this man anything. He raped you. I know emotions can get confused in a situation like this, but we have people who can help you."

I smiled sadly at him and then Samuel stumbled inside, holding on to the doorframe. I hadn't dared use a higher dose on him than was absolutely necessary; obviously it wasn't enough. He stared at me uncomprehendingly, his arm with his gun hanging limply at his side. My twin, my confidante. For most of my life I had been sure my love for Samuel, for my twin, could never be challenged, and I still loved him, loved him so much the look of betrayal on his face splintered me in half, but now there were my children and the man behind me.

Remo's gaze moved from me to him, and he touched my hip. I swallowed the rising emotion.

"Please let us leave, Uncle," I addressed Dante. "This war is because of me, and I can tell you I don't want it. I don't want to be avenged. Don't rob my children of their father. I'll go to Las Vegas with Remo where I belong, where my kids belong. Please, if you feel guilty for what happened to me, if you want to save me, then do this. Let me return to Vegas with Remo. This doesn't have to be an endless spiral of bloodshed. It can end today. For your children, for mine. Let us leave."

Dante's cold eyes were on Remo, not me. "Is she speaking in the name of the Camorra?"

Remo's grip on my hip tightened. "She does. You breached my territory, and I breached yours. We're even."

"We're not!" Samuel roared, stepping forward, swaying. Remo lifted his gun a couple of inches. "You kidnapped my sister and broke her. You twisted her into your fucking marionette. We won't be done until I'm standing over your disemboweled corpse so my sister is finally free of you."

"Sam," I choked. "Don't do this. I know you don't understand, but I need to return to Vegas with Remo, for myself, but more importantly for my children."

"I knew you should have gotten rid of them," Samuel rasped, his eyes glassy. Remo's hand on my hip jerked and I knew without the promise he'd given me, he would have killed my brother for his words.

Dad came up behind Samuel and put his hand on his shoulder. "Send them with him to Las Vegas. They are Falcones, but you aren't Fina. Be free of them and him. You can start a new life."

"Where my children go, I will go," I said. "Don't you think I've suffered enough for all of your sins? Don't turn me into another pawn in your chess game. Set me free."

Realization settled in Sam's eyes, and it broke my heart. I ached, ached for my family who would never understand. I could only hope they'd come to hate me one day so they didn't miss me anymore. Remo's grip on my hip loosened. Even the adrenaline wouldn't keep him on his feet for an endless amount of time. He was too injured for that.

"Let us leave. You failed me once, and now I'm lost to you. But please allow me to bring my children to a family that will love them. Allow me to bring my children home. You owe it to me."

Danilo made a disbelieving sound, his hand around his gun tightening.

I hated myself for playing the guilt card, but I knew it was our only chance. For Remo to get out of here alive, I had to hurt the family I loved.

Dante's cold eyes met mine. "If I allow you to leave today, you are a traitor. You won't be part of the Outfit. You will be the enemy. You won't see your family again. There won't be peace with the Camorra. This war has only begun."

Samuel heaved a deep breath, his eyes begging me to reconsider. Could I live without him?

"When will this war ever end, Uncle?" I asked quietly. He looked at Remo, and I knew what he would say. "Never," I whispered the answer.

Dante inclined his head. Dad looked at me as if this was the final goodbye, a daughter lost for good.

"Leave," Dante said coldly.

Danilo shook his head incredulously. "You can't be serious, Dante. You can't let them go."

Dante glanced at my ex-fiancé, looking tired.

"Set me free," I said softly.

"Leave."

Relief and wistfulness slammed into me hearing that word. "Thank you."

Dante shook his head. "Don't thank me. Not for that."

Remo nudged me lightly, and I walked closer to the door, keeping my body between him and the others. I walked backward to keep an eye on my family. They didn't attack. They didn't stop us. Dad and Samuel looked broken. I had landed the ultimate hit, had broken them. I wondered how Mom would react when she found out. She'd be crushed. My heart was heavy as I led Remo to the parked car. He sank down on the passenger seat, passing out immediately. I closed the door and got behind the steering wheel. Greta and Nevio were still fast asleep in their seats.

I hit the gas and sent the car flying down the long gravel road. I quickly connected to Bluetooth and called the Sugar Trap. It was the only number I'd found on the Internet.

It took a while before the guy I talked to agreed to call Nino and to give him my number. I was starting to go crazy.

Remo wouldn't survive if I had to drive all the way to Vegas with him, and I couldn't take him to a hospital in Outfit territory. What if my family got over their initial shock and decided to get rid of us after all? I needed to reach Camorra territory.

My pulse spiked when my phone finally rang. I picked up after the second ring.

"Is he dead?" Nino asked at once.

I glanced at Remo who was slumped against the passenger door, breathing shallowly.

"Not yet," I got out.

Nino was quiet for a moment. "Did you call to gloat? To let me hear my brother's last screams?"

That's what he thought?

"I'm in a car with him. We got out. We're on our way."

"You got him out?" Nino asked sharply. "Where are you? We're taking a helicopter and meeting you halfway. We're in Kansas City. I'll calculate the best spot now."

I told him where I was heading, and we agreed on a meeting place eighty miles from where I was.

"He's badly injured," I said quietly.

"Remo is too strong to die," Nino said.

Tears stung in my eyes. "I'm driving as quickly as I can."

"Serafina," Nino began. "He thought you'd come back. He wanted you to come back on your own free will."

I swallowed. This wasn't about Remo and me. This was about my children, and yet my chest ached with emotions as I regarded the man beside me. His dark hair sticking to his bloody forehead. "I need to drive," I said and hung up.

About one hour later I steered the car toward a deserted parking lot where a helicopter was already waiting. Nino and Savio stood beside it. I'd hoped Fabiano would be there. I trusted him more than these two.

I came to a stop. They had their guns out, not trusting me. And I didn't trust them either, but Remo was barely breathing. I gripped my gun and pushed out of the car. Nino approached, as usual a blank expression on his face. I had my gun pointed at him like he had his pointed at me. Of course, with his skills I'd be dead before my finger as much as twitched on the trigger.

I lowered my gun and walked toward the passenger door, opening it. Nino still regarded me cautiously. Savio came up behind him, his gun at his side, not pointed at me. "Will you help me? Or do you want Remo to die?"

Nino moved forward and the second he saw his brother, he shoved the gun into his holster and rushed to my side. He quickly checked Remo then gripped him under the arms. Remo groaned. Savio took his legs and they were about to lift him out when Greta woke and let out an earsplitting cry upon seeing two men she didn't know. Nino and Savio both jerked their heads back then froze. Nevio had also awoken and his dark eyes stared back at them. My small Remo.

"Holy fuck," Savio gasped. His brown eyes flew up to me. "They are Remo's."

It wasn't a question because one look at Nevio and they knew he was their brother's. "They are and he passed out before he could see them." My throat constricted.

Nino held my gaze for a moment and I knew then that I wouldn't regret my decision because already now I could see that my kids would be Falcones.

"Quick," Nino muttered, and he and Savio carried Remo over to the helicopter.

My heart thundering in my chest, I walked to the back door and opened it to unbuckle Nevio and Greta. "Shh," I soothed my daughter. Nevio looked merely curious and a little sleepy.

"Do you need help?" Savio asked close behind me, surprising me.

I looked over my shoulder, hesitating, my protectiveness rearing its head.

"Don't give me that look. Your kids are safe. They will always be safe, and not just because Remo would kill me if something happened to them."

I nodded. "Can you take Nevio? Greta doesn't like to be held by anyone but me."

Savio moved to the other door, opened it, and bent over Nevio, who regarded him with big dark eyes. "I've never held a baby," Savio said reluctantly.

"Speak to him soothingly and lift him against your chest. He can support his head by himself."

"Hey, Nevio," Savio said as he slid his hands under Nevio's armpits and carefully lifted him. It looked as if was holding a bomb about to detonate, but I was glad he was being careful. I hadn't thought Savio could be like that.

I turned to Greta and quickly lifted her as well then straightened to keep an eye on Savio. He held Nevio against his chest, and my son seemed content to be held by the unknown man. Savio's eyes were curious and fascinated as he looked down at my boy. No resentment, no associated shame.

Together we walked toward the helicopter. Greta pressed herself against me from the noise of the rotor blades. Nino was bent over Remo inside the helicopter. Remo was already getting a blood transfusion and another IV with a clear liquid while Nino felt his body.

A man I didn't know was in the cockpit.

Nino turned to us when Savio held Nevio out to him. He grabbed my boy immediately, a strange look on his face as he regarded him. Savio climbed in and held out his hand for me. I awkwardly got in with Greta still clinging to me for dear life.

I sank down on the bench, and Savio helped me buckle up. Nino handed Nevio back to him and Savio sat beside me. Nino's eyes kept darting between Nevio and Greta, as if he couldn't comprehend what he was seeing. The moment the helicopter lifted off, Nino returned to Remo's side.

Nevio stared down at his father, then at me, and I swallowed the emotion. What if Remo died before he could see his kids? What if my children never met their father?

I'd never expected Remo to want his children, but now that I knew he did, guilt washed over me. I thought I protected them by keeping them from him, by staying in the Outfit, but I had been wrong. Las Vegas was their home because it was Remo's home.

TWENTY-EIGHT

Serafina

AFTER WE LANDED IN LAS VEGAS, NINO IMMEDIATELY RUSHED REMO off to a hospital the Camorra worked with, and Savio stayed with me. I was exhausted and emotionally drained. "What happens with us now?" I asked tiredly.

Savio gave me a surprised look. "I will take you to the mansion. Remo will want to have you and his kids around when he returns."

"You think he will survive?"

Savio nodded. "Remo won't die."

I followed Savio to a car and sank down on the backseat with my children.

When I jerked awake, we had arrived and Fabiano was staring through the window as if he was seeing a ghost. He opened the door. "What the fuck?"

"Remo's got kids," Savio explained.

"I see that," Fabiano said.

Savio took Nevio again, and I got out with Greta, who had her face buried in my neck. Fabiano couldn't stop staring at Nevio, then finally he met my gaze. "You saved Remo?"

I nodded. Fabiano searched my eyes, and I wasn't sure what he was looking for. "It's too cold for Nevio and Greta to stay outside. Can you get my bag from the trunk?"

Fabiano nodded and walked to the back of the car. I followed Savio inside the house, a strange sense of familiarity washing over me. This place didn't feel like home. I'd only experienced it as a captive, and I wondered how things would be now that I had come here freely.

Could this become a home for me and my children?

Savio had said Remo would want me to live here with them, but I wasn't sure. It felt surreal being here, but there was no going back now.

The realization sank in slowly, and for a moment I felt immobilized by the weight of it. Holding Greta seemed to ground me. "You can give Nevio to me," I managed, offering my free arm.

Savio's brows drew together, but he gave me my son without hesitation, and I hugged him to me. Savio and Fabiano watched me for a moment, as if they weren't sure what to do with me.

"How is he?" Kiara asked, hurrying into the entrance hall. She jerked to a stop when she spotted me with the kids. Her eyes widened.

"Nino took him to hospital," Savio said.

Kiara only stared at me. Her eyes darted down to Nevio and Greta, and she shook her head in disbelief. A girl with freckles and brown hair followed Kiara and also stopped in her tracks.

Kiara was the first to move. She came toward me, her eyes alight with warmth. "How did Remo react?"

Tears sprang into my eyes, and her smile fell.

"He passed out before he saw them," I whispered.

"Nothing kills Remo," Fabiano said firmly.

I nodded.

Greta began crying, and Nevio, too, was becoming increasingly cranky. "I need to feed them and change their diapers. Then they need a place to sleep."

Savio glanced at Fabiano, who shrugged.

Kiara rolled her eyes. "Would it be okay if I took you to the bedroom you were in … last time? I don't want to open the other rooms in Remo's wing. Or would you prefer to stay in my and Nino's wing?"

I choked out a laugh. "I'll stay in Remo's wing."

The other girl smiled hesitantly.

"I'm Serafina. And this is Nevio and Greta."

"Leona," she said. "Nice to meet you." Fabiano stepped up to her and put his hand on her waist in a possessive gesture. So she was his girl.

Kiara took my bag from Fabiano and led me upstairs into Remo's wing. I knew the way by heart, but her company felt good. When we stepped into my old room, my breath caught in my throat at the rush of memories that overwhelmed me, but another loud wail from Greta snapped me out of it. I moved over to the bed and carefully lowered them on it.

Kiara kept throwing glances at my twins, longing in her gaze. "How can I help you?"

I opened the bag and held out the baby formula. In the evening, they always needed the bottle to calm down. "Could you prepare two bottles?"

Kiara returned fifteen minutes later with the bottles and settled beside me on the bed. "Why don't you feed Nevio while I take care of Greta," I suggested.

Her eyes lit up. "Thank you."

I laughed. "You're helping me. I should thank you."

She grinned as she took Nevio and settled him on her lap.

"I should warn you. He's a bit of a wrestler."

Kiara brought the bottle to Nevio's mouth, and as expected his little hands reached for the bottle, trying to snatch it out of her hand. She laughed.

I blinked back tears as I focused on Greta, who was happily drinking, her big dark eyes peering up at me sleepily. Emotions painfully tightened in my chest.

Remo had to survive. I couldn't believe fate would be so cruel to rip him from me before he could see his children. Maybe Remo deserved death, but I didn't care. He needed to live for Greta and Nevio.

"He'll love and protect them," Kiara murmured.

Remo would protect them. Was he capable of love? I wasn't sure.

After Kiara left, I lay down beside my babies, who were already asleep after their feeding. I didn't have beds for them or anything else except for the few things I'd stuffed into the backpack.

I closed my eyes. The image of Remo in his blood flashed into my mind, and I shuddered.

I must have fallen asleep because Greta's wail woke me shortly after. It was the first night without the help of Samuel or my mother, and a heavy weight settled in the pit of my stomach thinking about my family. I wasn't sure how my future nights would be. Would I handle everything on my own?

I was up early the next morning and blinked against the soft light streaming in through the window. I had barely slept, and not just because of my twin's erratic schedule. Worry for Remo had haunted my sleep. I got myself and my babies ready before I headed downstairs, carrying them on my hips.

Following the scent of coffee and bacon, I made my way into the kitchen but stopped in the doorway. Adamo, Savio, and Nino were sitting around the kitchen table while Kiara was stirring something in a big pot. All eyes turned to me, and I swayed on my feet. I'd always been the enemy, the captive, and now I was what? A guest? An intruder?

"Good morning," I said then turned to Nino, fear clogging my throat. "How is he?"

"Stable. A few broken bones, bruises, rupture of the spleen. He's upstairs, knocked out with pain meds."

"He won't like that one bit," Savio said grinning. "You know he prefers pain to being helpless."

I still hadn't moved from the doorway.

"I'm preparing a pumpkin puree for the babies. I hope that's okay?" Kiara chimed in.

I nodded. Nino grabbed a chair and pulled it back for me. With a small smile, I approached the table and sank down. Nevio knocked Nino's glass over, spilling water over him.

"Sorry," I said, leaning back so Nevio's sneaky arms wouldn't get into more trouble. He still made grabby motions.

Nino regarded him intently as he dried himself with a dishtowel that Kiara had handed him.

Adamo shook his head. His arm was bandaged and his face was swollen. "I can't believe Remo's got kids."

"I bet the Outfit hated seeing them. I mean, there's no way they couldn't be Falcones," Savio said with a grin.

I stiffened, pain slicing through me. I looked away, swallowing.

"Is that why you're here?" Nino asked mildly. "To give them a chance?"

"I want them to be proud of who they are," I said. I didn't want to explain everything.

"They will be. They are Falcones," Nino said.

I looked into his emotionless gray eyes. "Just like that? My family tortured Adamo and nearly killed Remo and I'm technically the enemy."

"Just like that. You are Remo's and they are his too. You are family."

I frowned. "I'm not Remo's."

Nino gave me a twisted smile. "You are."

Kiara put a plate piled with eggs and bacon and toast in front of me.

"Do you have a blanket?"

She hurried off and returned with one a few minutes later, spreading it on the ground. I put Greta and Nevio down on their backs so I could eat. I smiled when Nevio rolled onto his stomach and raised his head curiously.

"This is too weird," Adamo said. I gave him a smile.

Savio shook his head. "I'm not going to change diapers. I don't give a fuck if Remo gives the order or not. I'm not going anywhere near someone else's shit, baby or not."

I huffed. "I'm pretty sure you come into contact with more disgusting things on a daily basis."

Adamo laughed. "He's full of shit anyway."

Savio punched Adamo's unharmed arm.

Some of the weight I'd felt since yesterday lifted from my shoulders.

Remo

I felt like shit, cotton mouth and a full-body ache. Peeling my eyes open, I found Nino staring at me. "You asshole. You gave me pain meds and some kind of fucking sedative."

"Your body needed it."

I tried to sit up but my body was very averse to the idea. I struggled and shot Nino a death glare when he tried to help me. Eventually, I managed to sit against the headboard, every fucking inch of my body throbbing fiercely. Most of my upper body and arms were covered with bandages.

Nino sat on the edge of my bed. "You looked like shit when Serafina brought you to us."

Serafina had saved my life. The woman I'd kidnapped, she'd saved my fucking life. "For a second I thought I dreamed up the whole shit, but the way my body screams with agony tells me it's true," I got out.

"They almost killed you, and they would have if Serafina hadn't gotten you out."

"Where is she?" I asked, ignoring the way my chest hollowed at the thought that she wasn't in Las Vegas after all.

"Downstairs," Nino said slowly, his eyes searching mine. "With your children."

"My children," I repeated, trying to make sense of the words, trying to fucking understand that I was a father. Greta and Nevio. "Fuck," I breathed.

"It's like looking at a baby version of you," Nino said with a disbelieving look.

"Make sure they have everything they need. No matter what Serafina says she needs, you get it for her."

Nino nodded. "She's here to protect her children because the Outfit didn't accept them. Not because of you."

I narrowed my eyes at him. "I don't care why she's here. All that matters is that she is. I told you before, I don't have a fucking heart that can be broken, or have you forgotten?"

Nino touched my shoulder lightly. "I know you better than anyone else, Remo. Or have *you* forgotten?"

"That's why you're so good at pissing me off."

"Do you want me to get her?"

I nodded. I didn't think I'd ever wanted anything more. I would have gone through days of torture, through weeks of it, to see Serafina. That she saved me? Fuck, I'd never considered it an option.

After she'd told me she wouldn't give me her forgiveness, I'd resigned myself to the fact that she wanted me dead, that she wanted to see me suffer. I deserved it. There was no fucking question about it. I knew what I was.

There wasn't anything white about me, very little gray, and a ton of black. And yet she was here.

She was here with our children.

I tried to imagine them, but I couldn't. I'd never wanted kids, because I was certain I'd never find a woman who wouldn't prove to be the same fucking failure my mother had been. I'd been certain that I'd break any woman, but Serafina was strong. She'd proven me wrong, had twisted my game until I felt like the loser, like the one who'd been checkmated.

Serafina

Nino walked into the living room where Kiara and I were sitting on a blanket with Nevio and Greta. Kiara was a natural with kids, and it was obvious how much she loved them. She held Nevio in her lap as she showed him a picture book. Greta sat in my lap, her tiny hand wrapped around my thumb and looking down at the book in my free hand.

I looked up at Nino but his eyes were on Kiara, who was smiling down at my son, practically glowing with happiness.

Slowly, he dragged his gaze up. "Remo just woke up."

Without thinking, I got up with Greta clinging to me. I didn't want my kids there when I first talked to Remo after he'd woken. I felt like we needed a moment before I could allow that.

I untangled Greta gently and laid her down on the blanket, then hesitated. Kiara looked up with a smile. "Nino and I can watch them while you talk to Remo."

Nino moved closer but I stayed where I was. I couldn't help it. This would be the first time I let them out of sight since our arrival. "Each of us would lay our life down for these kids," Nino said. "You brought them here. They are Falcones. They are Remo's kids. He burned for us. We will burn for them."

I gave a small nod and took a step back. Greta's eyes followed me. "Kiara, can you take Greta. She's very shy around people she doesn't know, especially men."

Nino lowered himself beside Kiara and took Nevio from her. I tensed when Kiara reached for my daughter, expecting a crying fit, but Greta's face scrunched up only briefly then smoothed when Kiara sang softly. I took another step back. Kiara beamed at Nino as he put Nevio down on his lap and pointed at the picture book. Nino oozed calmness, which was perfect for my kids.

Nevio ignored the picture book that Nino held up and stared at the colorful tattoos on Nino's arm, touching them with his small hands as if he thought they'd come alive under his fingertips. My heart swelled once more, and I turned quickly before I got too emotional.

I took a deep breath before I slipped into Remo's bedroom. He was sitting back against the headboard, elevated by pillows. His upper body was naked, except for the many bandages covering his skin—the cuts my family had inflicted to avenge me.

He looked up from his iPad, and I took a hesitant step closer as I let the door shut.

His face pulled into a strange smile. "I'd never have thought that you would be the one to save me."

I moved closer, half terrified, half excited, and stopped beside him. Remo's dark eyes burned with emotions that set my heart aflame, but I shoved the sensations back. "I saved the father of my children so they would be safe."

"My brothers would have protected them even if your family had killed me."

I put a hand down beside him on the headboard, hovering over him. "Nobody will protect them like you will. You'll go through fire for them."

I didn't ask. I *knew* it.

He raised his hand stiffly, most of his arm bandaged, and cupped the back of my head. I let him pull me down. "For them. For you," he murmured, fiercely, harshly, angrily. His lips brushed mine, and my entire being melted. I fell as I had the first time he kissed. Shuddering, I drew back and straightened. This was too soon. I needed to figure things out between us.

He watched me with a bitter smile. For some reason, the sight tore at me. I leaned down and briefly brushed his lips with mine to show him that my with-drawal didn't mean "never" only "later."

I quickly stepped back and turned.

"Will you show them to me?" he asked quietly.

I looked over my shoulder. "Of course."

I held Greta and Nevio tightly against my body as I nudged the door open. Then I stepped in. I was inexplicably nervous. My family had never looked at my chil-dren the way I regarded them, like they were something precious, a gift I wanted to cherish every single day. Remo's eyes zeroed in on our babies as I moved closer, and he didn't look away again, appearing almost stunned. I sat down beside him and carefully put Nevio down on his back next to Remo. Greta still clung to me tightly.

Remo's expression held wonder, and when he raised his eyes to mine, they were softer than I'd ever seen them. He stretched out his bandaged arm and stroked his fingertip over Nevio's chest reverently. Nevio being Nevio snatched up Remo's finger and brought it to his mouth to chew on it with a toothless grin. Remo's lips twitched. Then he raised his gaze to Greta, who'd turned her head to watch him curiously.

"She's shy around most people," I said. She'd always been like that, even when she was a tiny newborn.

I took his hand so she saw me doing it then brought it toward her. When she didn't protest, I released Remo's hand, and he caressed her back with his fin-gertips. He was so gentle and careful with her, I could feel a mix of happiness and wistfulness rise up in my throat. Greta watched him silently. Did she know he was her dad?

Tears ran down my cheeks. Remo stroking Greta's back and having his fin-ger chewed off by Nevio was the most beautiful sight I could imagine. "I don't think I've ever been this happy," I admitted, not caring that I was being emo-tional in front of Remo. This was no longer a battle of wills, a twisted game of chess. These stakes were too high.

Remo locked his gaze with mine. "I *know* I've never been happier."

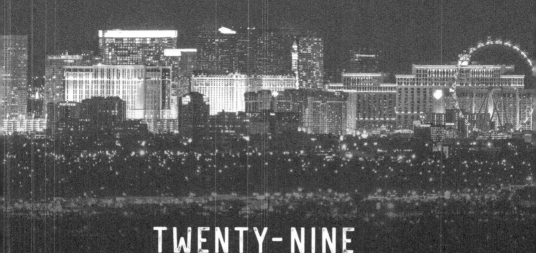

TWENTY-NINE

Serafina

As far as patients went, Remo was a nightmare. He was a nightmare in many other regards as well, but giving his body time to heal wasn't on his agenda.

Nino wasn't happy about it. "You need to rest, Remo. It's been only three days and you're already running around."

"I've had worse. Now stop the fucking fussing. I'm not a child."

"Maybe not. But I'm obviously the only one of the two of us capable of sane decisions."

"Neither of you is sane. Now help me with this fucking crib," Savio muttered.

I leaned in the doorway of the future nursery. Nino and Kiara had gone shopping this morning, and now the four Falcone brothers were trying to put together the furniture. Though Nino and Savio were doing all the work because Adamo's arm was in a cast and most of Remo's body was bandaged, not to mention the many broken bones in his body.

Adamo sat on a plush baby blue armchair, which sat close to the window. Sometimes when he thought no one was looking, his eyes twisted with something dark, something haunted. Some wounds would take a long time to heal. Remo leaned against the windowsill, wearing only low cut sweatpants, barking orders.

A smile tugged at my lips.

"The instructions are quite clear, Remo," Nino drawled. "I don't need your orders on top of that."

Savio scoffed. "As if that'll stop him."

It was still difficult to grasp what had happened these last three days. I'd left my family, *Samuel*, to live in Las Vegas with the man who kidnapped me and his family who helped him do it. But with every passing hour, I realized it had been the right decision for my children and maybe even for me. The moment Remo saw his babies, a knot in my chest loosened, a knot that had strangled me since he released me, only to be pulled tighter when Greta and Nevio were born. They belonged here.

I had tried to keep my distance from Remo so far, only visited him twice so our twins could get used to his presence, and I knew he wasn't happy with it.

Remo spotted me in the doorway, his eyes becoming more eager and intent. My pulse picked up, and I turned around to return to Nevio and Greta who were waiting downstairs with Kiara.

Remo cornered me in the hallway. For someone with his injuries, he was annoyingly fast. "Are you running from me, Angel?" He backed me into the wall, his palms on either side of me.

"I've learned that doesn't work. You always catch me," I said, leaning back because with him so close I was having trouble focusing.

"I often imagined how it would be to see you again," he said in a low voice. "But this wasn't one of the scenarios I came up with."

I regarded him. "When you sent me off like a thing easy to dispose of, it didn't seem like you wanted to see me again."

He shook his head, anger flashing on his face. "I gave you a choice, one you didn't have before … and you chose to stay with the Outfit."

I huffed. "That's ridiculous. You traded me like a piece of cattle. Why would I return to you? I'm not in the habit of thrusting myself upon someone who obviously couldn't wait to get rid of me."

Remo leaned even closer. "Did you really believe that I didn't want you? Or did you tell yourself that because you didn't want to leave your family?"

I frowned. "You could have …"

"What?" he growled. "I could have what? Kidnapped you again? Asked Dante to send you back?"

He had a point and it annoyed me.

"When were you planning on telling me about our babies? Would you have told me at all if Adamo hadn't gotten himself captured?"

"You sent me away, back to my fiancé. I didn't think you'd care what happened with me, much less wanted kids," I muttered, but something in his eyes made me continue. "I wanted to tell you. The moment I saw them, I knew I needed to tell you, but I didn't know how. I was … a coward."

His hand came up, cupping my cheek, his dark eyes impossibly possessive.

"I was sure you'd return to me." His lips brushed mine. "You aren't a coward. You saved me. You went against your family to protect our children. You gave up everything for them … and for me."

I deepened the kiss, couldn't keep the distance I so desperately wanted to keep. Remo's lips, his tongue, the feel of his rough palm against my cheek awakened a deep longing, a desperate need I'd kept buried since he'd set me free.

My core tightened as his familiar manly scent flooded my nose, and memories of how Remo's hands, his mouth, his cock had felt came to the surface …

I drew back, coming to my senses, and slipped out from under Remo's arm. He gave me a knowing smile before I hurried away. But I had seen the proof of his body's reaction to me in the bulge of his sweatpants.

Only one week until Christmas. The mansion was decorated beautifully with red baubles, golden tinsel, and sprigs of mistletoe. Luckily Greta and Nevio weren't mobile yet or the greenery would have had to go. I'd sent Samuel a few messages, telling him I was safe and asking if he was okay. He hadn't replied yet but I knew he'd read the messages. Maybe his hurt was still too fresh. Five days weren't enough to come to terms with the fact that your sister betrayed you for a man you hated more than anything in the world. My messages to Mom and Sofia hadn't even been received. I suspected Dad had gotten new phones for them so I couldn't contact them.

I approached Kiara as she stirred a new batch of baby food, a sweet potato puree. "Do you get Christmas presents for each other?"

Nino had given me a credit card from one of the Falcone bank accounts yesterday, and while I'd wanted to decline at first, I took the card. Remo seemed determined to make sure I had everything I needed. Still, it felt a bit odd to use their own money to buy them presents, but it wasn't as if I could access my family's accounts anymore.

"Well, last year was still a bit of a Christmas trial. Nino and his brothers still need to get used to a female touch in their life, but I got them gifts, and a few days after Christmas I got gifts from them as well." She laughed. "I think this year they might have gifts on time."

"I don't know what to get any of them. I don't know them well enough, and I don't really feel like part of this family yet …"

She touched my shoulder. "But you are, Serafina. It's a strange situation for all of us, but it's the best thing that could have happened, especially for Remo."

"You think?" I whispered.

"I know it," she said firmly. "How are things between you?"

"I'm trying to keep my distance. I'm scared of allowing too much closeness too fast."

"But you want to be with him?"

I laughed. "I don't think I have a choice."

"He won't force you."

"That's not what I mean," I said quietly. "I don't think my heart or my body will leave me a choice."

She nodded, understanding filling her face. "I'm so happy for the both of you, the four of you."

"Do you think Remo's capable of … love?"

Kiara looked thoughtful. "He and Nino went through horrible things as children. It formed them into the men they are today. It still affects them. I'm not sure what it did to Remo. If parts of him were irrevocably destroyed …"

I didn't ask what kind of horrors lay in Remo's past. Kiara would have told me if she thought it was her place to share. If I wanted to find out, I'd have to ask him.

"If you want to go Christmas shopping, we can go together tomorrow. Fabiano could guard us."

"That would be nice," I said.

Despite Nino's words of protest, Remo came down for dinner that evening, and we all settled around the dining room table. Greta and Nevio were in their new high chairs between Kiara and me. I had taken over the job of trying to wrangle food into Nevio's mouth since Greta seemed to do well around Kiara. I could feel Remo's eyes on us the entire time with an expression I could only describe as longing. My food was getting cold anyway, so I decided to give him a chance to be a real dad.

"Why don't you give this a try?" I asked Remo. I wasn't sure if he was interested in feeding or if he was like some fathers whose interest in their children ended when it required them to do something.

Everyone paused what they were doing for a moment. Remo put down his fork and stood. His movements were still stiff, not just because of the bandages; it would take some time for his broken bones and bruises to heal. I gave him my chair, took my plate, and settled into the place he'd vacated. Nevio was making grabby motions, but the spoon and bowl were out of his reach. I could tell that he was getting frustrated with the situation and a hissy fit was fast approaching.

Remo took the spoon and lifted it toward Nevio's face, but he didn't restrain his arms. Before I could warn him, Nevio snatched at the spoon and catapulted sweet potato puree through the room. Most of it landed square on Remo's shirt. The rest in Nino's face.

I bit the inside of my cheek to stop laughter.

Kiara didn't show the same restraint. She burst out laughing. Nino wiped his face with a napkin, his eyes on his laughing wife—and softer than I'd ever seen them.

Nevio rocked excitedly in his chair, a toothless grin on his face. Remo glanced down at himself, then at his son, and his lips twitched. This time he took Nevio's hands in his big one before he brought the spoon toward his mouth. Nevio pressed his lips together, obviously unhappy about the situation.

"This reminds me of you, Adamo," Remo said.

Adamo grimaced.

Nino nodded. "You always made a mess during feeding as well."

"If we start exchanging baby stories, I'm out," Savio muttered.

Remo turned back to Nevio and nudged his lips with the spoon. "Come on, Nevio."

I stood and got on my haunches beside Nevio's high chair. "Come on, Nevio, show your dad how well you can eat."

Remo looked down at me, his expression stilling when I called him 'dad.' After a moment of hesitation, Nevio finally allowed Remo to put the spoon in his mouth.

I smiled, straightened to my feet, and pressed a kiss on Nevio's head. Then I leaned over Greta and did the same. She smiled at me with the spoon in her mouth, and my heart just exploded with gratefulness. I caught Remo's eyes but quickly glanced away because the look in his threatened to crush my resolve to keep my distance.

After bringing the twins to bed, I grabbed my phone and headed for Remo's bedroom. Nino had practically dragged him there so he could lie down and rest.

I knocked.

"Come in, Angel."

Frowning, I entered. "How did you know?"

He regarded me with an expression that sent a little shiver down my spine. "Because my brothers don't knock, they barge in, and Kiara usually stays away from my bedroom."

I nodded, my hand still on the door, debating if I should leave it open just to be safe.

Remo smiled knowingly. "I'm practically bedridden. No reason to be worried. I won't attack you."

Bedridden. As if. That man couldn't be broken easily. I closed the door. I wasn't worried about Remo making a move. I was worried I'd throw caution in the wind and do what I'd been dreaming of forever. "As if that would stop you."

Remo didn't say anything.

I held up my phone. "I thought you'd like to see photos of Nevio and Greta."

"I'd like that," Remo said, moving to the side so there was room beside him on the bed. I eyed the spot then Remo leaning against the headrest with his naked upper body. Even the bandages didn't make Remo any less attractive.

Trying to hide my thoughts, I strolled over to him casually and sank down beside him, legs stretched out before me. Remo's eyes lingered on them. I was wearing a dress and no tights because it was surprisingly warm in the house. Goose bumps rippled across my skin. I cleared my throat and clicked on the first photo, which Mom had taken shortly after I'd given birth to the twins. I held them in my arms and looked down at them with an exhausted yet adoring expression.

Remo leaned in and his arm brushed mine. Despite the material of my dress between us, a tingle shot through me at the brief contact.

"You look pale in the photo," he said quietly.

"After twenty-two hours of labor everyone does."

Remo's dark eyes flickered with a hint of wistfulness.

"I wish you could have been there...if I'd known what I know today, I would have come to Vegas sooner. I'm sorry I took that away from you."

Remo cupped my chin and I tensed because he looked like he was going to kiss me. "Regret over the past is wasted energy. We can't change the past, no matter how much we want to do it."

"What would you want to change?" I asked, trying to ignore the feel of Remo's touch.

He shook his head with a dark smile. "Not your kidnapping. I don't feel an ounce of regret about stealing you."

"You don't?" I frowned, pulling back slightly but Remo leaned in, fingers still on my chin.

"Not one fucking bit. I'd kidnap you again to be the one you gift yourself to. You could have never been mine if I hadn't stolen you."

I didn't argue, neither about me being his, nor about the fact that without the kidnapping we would have never found together.

"What about you?" Remo murmured. "Do you regret becoming mine?"

"No," I admitted, and finally drew back from his touch. "Not that. I just wish it wouldn't have cost my family so much."

Remo nodded and settled back against the headrest. "Hardly anything worth having can be gained without loss and pain and sacrifice."

My eyes trailed over his wounds and bruises. He'd sacrificed himself for his brother. But I had a feeling it wasn't the only reason why he'd allowed my family to capture and torture him. He'd accepted pain, maybe even losing his life, for a chance to see me again.

I cleared my throat and clicked on the next photo. The first photo of Nevio and Greta lying in a crib beside each other.

I showed him photo after photo, neither of us saying anything. It was difficult to focus on anything but Remo's warmth, his scent, the strength and power he oozed.

When I finally shut off my phone, my body was humming with need. I met his gaze, which rested unabashedly on me. Remo regarded me with an expression I knew too well. Hunger and dominance. He touched my bare knee.

I exhaled.

His hand slipped slowly up between my legs. "Remo," I warned, but he held my gaze, his lips pulling wider.

"Have you let anyone touch what's mine?"

I glared, but my body screamed for more. For Remo's touch, for his lips.

He knew the answer, could see it on my face. "No," he said quietly. "All of you is only mine."

"You set me free, remember? I belong to myself."

We both knew it was a lie. I'd never been free of his hold on me, but he, too, had lost his freedom. His hand slipped higher until finally he brushed over the fabric of my panties. They were drenched, just from being in his presence.

Remo groaned, low and dark, and my resolve crumpled. His thumb drew small circles on my crotch, and I could feel myself growing even more aroused. Remo's dark eyes held mine, and as usual I couldn't look away. His thumb pushed under my panties and between my folds, spreading my wetness. I whimpered from the contact, skin on skin. So good, so desperately needed. He drew small circles on my clit, round and round and round. I parted my legs a bit more and gripped the sheets, needing something to hold on to as I stared at Remo. His gaze possessed me like it always did.

"Are you going to come, Angel?"

I gave a small nod. It had been too long. I was falling apart so quickly. He didn't speed up the pace as his other hand pushed up my dress so he could see his finger working me. Round and round. "Part your legs more," he growled, and I did.

He slipped between my folds again, spreading my wetness some more. "I want to fuck you so badly."

"You're still healing," I rasped. His broken bones needed to mend. One of us needed to be the voice of reason, even if my body hated me for it.

He sat up stiffly. "Straddle me with your ass facing me."

"What?"

"Do it," he ordered.

I didn't question him, could barely think straight from the throbbing between my legs. I pushed up and climbed over Remo, careful not to ram my knees into his ribs. My palms rested beside his knees as I knelt over him, my ass pushing out. Remo lifted up my dress until I was exposed and my core tightened in anticipation. "Fuck," Remo murmured, causing me to shiver again.

I gasped when he pushed two fingers into me, my back arching at the delicious sensation of my walls gripping him. Remo let out a low groan, and I almost came hearing it. I could see the proof of his own need straining against his sweatpants.

"The sight of your pussy taking my fingers is the fucking best."

I whimpered in response and began to meet his thrusts, needing his fingers deeper, faster, harder.

"Yes, Angel, take them," he rasped.

More wetness pooled between my legs. I threw a glance over my shoulder. Remo was focused on his fingers as they fucked me, his dark eyes burning with so much desire it stole my breath. I shuddered with pleasure. He glanced up, his lips curling in a pleased smile.

"Come on, Angel. Fuck my fingers." Remo added a third finger and my eyes rolled back in my head at the sensation.

I ground myself against Remo's hand, driving his fingers deeper into me. He watched me intently and his other hand began massaging my butt. I wanted to grasp his erection, but I could hardly support myself with two arms, already spinning out of control. He gathered my wetness with the fingers of his other hand, and then I felt one finger against my back entrance. I tensed but didn't stop riding Remo's fingers.

"Relax," Remo ordered, his eyes compelling. "It'll be good."

Anxious and excited, I gave a small nod. Slowly he pushed a finger into me. "Oh God," I gasped as I felt his fingers in both my openings. There was a slight discomfort, but it didn't stand a chance against the pleasure Remo's fingers in my center caused.

Remo established a gentle rhythm with his finger while I kept grinding myself against his other hand. He didn't take his eyes off me as he worked my body, and I could feel the first traitorous spasm of my orgasm. My pussy clenched around his fingers. I moaned, the sensations overwhelming. I felt a second finger at my back entrance and tensed again. Remo stroked my butt cheek, and as I drove his fingers deep into me he curled them and hit my g-spot. I came hard, crying out desperately, and he pushed the second finger into my back entrance. I gasped from the pain and my orgasm heightened in force. I shuddered, caught between intense pleasure and dull pain. My arms gave way, and I braced myself on my forearms. Remo kept thrusting.

"Yes, Angel, I told you I'd show you pain and pleasure."

Half lowered onto him, I could feel his erection digging into my belly. He groaned again, almost in agony. I was completely overwhelmed, stunned, and a little embarrassed. I'd never considered allowing someone to go anywhere near my ass. Of course Remo wanted that part of me as well.

Remo pulled out of me slowly, and I gasped. His hands came down on my ass cheeks, and he massaged me gently. "If I died now, it would be worth it."

I huffed. "You won't die today. I won't explain that to Nino. No thank you."

Remo chuckled and the sound sent a different kind of shiver through my body. I loved the sound of Remo laughing, especially if it was earnest.

I pushed myself up then knelt beside Remo. He curled his hand over my neck and pulled me toward him for a slow kiss. When he drew back, his eyes searched my face. I knew my cheeks were flushed, not just from my orgasm but also from embarrassment.

"There's so much pleasure I still want to show you," Remo murmured, tracing his lips over my jaw and cheek.

He dropped his head back against the headboard, sighing as he reached for a glass filled with dark liquid on his nightstand.

I recognized the scent immediately. "Scotch, really?"

"It'll help with the healing, trust me. I've done a lot of research in the past."

I shook my head.

"And," he added, with a challenging smile, "it seems to be the only pleasure I'm allowed today." He took a sip.

My eyes darted down to the impressive bulge in his pants. I knew what I wanted to do. I wanted to render him into a helpless mess of desire as he did with me.

"Trying to decide if you're brave enough?"

I glowered. "I've given you a blowjob before."

His mouth twitched. "You tried, but you didn't finish, so it doesn't count."

I knew he was trying to goad me. Unfortunately, it was working.

I moved down until I knelt beside his groin. Remo reached for his pants and pulled them down, wincing as he did so.

"Quite eager, aren't you?" I teased.

He smiled but it was dark and hungry, and his body was tense. I lowered my head and took his tip into my mouth. Remo moaned, his fingers tangling in my hair. I swirled my tongue around him, and my own core tightened with renewed need. Remo's breathing deepened, his muscles tensing as he watched me.

"Take more of me," Remo ordered quietly, and I did. I let him claim my mouth until he hit the back of my throat. He thrust into me slowly, his hand in my hair keeping me in place. He held my gaze as I let him claim my mouth. His other hand cupped my cheek. Remo. Brutality and tenderness. I still didn't understand him or us.

Remo's body coiled tighter, his hips jerking up with less control, lips parting in a low moan.

"I'm going to come," he rasped. I saw the question in his expression, and my heart swelled with affection … and God help me … love.

I gave a small nod around his head before he drove deeper into my mouth again, and his grip on my neck became firmer. His face twisted with passion, his eyes almost harsh with lust as he tensed and came with a sharp exhale. I had trouble swallowing around his length, and Remo loosened his hold on my neck so I could pull back slightly. He kept rocking his hips, his breathing harsh.

Remo's gaze laid claim to another part of me, possessive and warm, as he stroked my cheek. I slowly released his cock from my lips and swallowed, frowning at the taste. Remo drew me toward him, brushed my lips with his, and handed me his glass with scotch. I took a sip and coughed. That tasted even worse.

"You'll get used to the taste," he said with a small laugh.

"The scotch or your …?"

He gripped my arms and wrenched me against him so I was cradled against his chest. I caught the wince but then it was gone. "My cum," he murmured as he licked my lips then dove into my mouth. Our kiss was slow, almost teasing, until it wasn't. It became needy and eager.

He positioned me so one of my legs was thrown over his groin, my head against his shoulder. His hand parted me then his fingers slid over my drenched panties. He pushed the fabric aside and slowly pushed two fingers into me. His other hand began pinching and twirling my nipple. He played me masterfully with his fingers as I lay draped over him. We kissed softly, our eyes locked the entire time, until a new wave of pleasure shot through me.

I'd barely caught my breath when Greta's cry rang out.

I sighed with a small smile.

"Perfect timing," he murmured, giving me another lingering kiss. I quickly slid out of bed and rushed into the bathroom to wash my hands before I returned to the bedroom. Remo stood beside the door, waiting for me.

"You should stay in bed and rest," I said.

"I should help you with our children."

His voice didn't allow any objections, and I had to stifle a pleased smile. By the time we arrived in the nursery, Nevio had started crying as well. I took Greta because she didn't know Remo well enough. Remo lifted Nevio out of the crib without hesitation and pressed him to his chest. It was obvious that he'd held a baby before, that he knew how to handle them. I took a whiff. "New diapers."

Remo carried Nevio over to the changing table and began his work. I watched him for a moment longer, my body flooding with so many hormones, I could feel the waterworks beginning. I blinked and looked away. "I'll go into the kitchen and prepare their bottles."

Remo glanced up, his gaze lingering on my eyes, then nodded.

When I returned ten minutes later, Nevio was already dressed and resting in Remo's arm. I handed him a bottle, and he sank down in the armchair, wincing again. He was moving more stiffly than before, probably from overexertion.

I changed Greta's diaper before I settled on the armrest beside Remo and started feeding her. "This is strange," I whispered after a moment.

Remo frowned. "It's not what I imagined when I kidnapped you."

I searched his face, trying to figure out what this meant to him, what I really meant to him, but I didn't dare ask. I knew it was futile to stay away from Remo, not only because my body was already calling for his touch again but also because my heart yearned for his closeness.

After they had fallen back asleep, I was on my way toward my room when Remo gripped my wrist, stopping me. "Stay with me."

I nodded and allowed Remo to pull me back to his bedroom, where I put one of his shirts on before slipping under the covers. Remo pulled me against him, wincing as I touched his bruises. "You're in pain," I protested, trying to put distance between us, but Remo tightened his hold on me.

"Fuck the pain. I want you in my arms."

I stilled and finally relaxed against him, my cheek pressed up to his strong chest. This felt too good to be true.

THIRTY

Serafina

CHRISTMAS ROLLED AROUND. THE FIRST CHRISTMAS FOR NEVIO AND Greta. The first Christmas as a part of the Falcone clan. After wishing Samuel a merry Christmas and not hearing anything in return, I went downstairs with Nevio and Greta. Remo was already in the living room with his brothers, discussing their plans for future races. After the Outfit attack, safety measures would have to be doubled. I was supposed to help Kiara in the kitchen but still needed to figure out what to do with the kids.

Remo looked up when I entered. As usual, his expression stilled when he saw me with our twins, almost as if he still had a hard time trusting his eyes. "Can you watch them?" I asked as I headed toward them.

Nino sat beside Remo. Adamo and Savio were on the couch across from them. "Will you take Nevio?" I asked Nino who rose at once and took my son from me. Nevio didn't mind, too fascinated by the tattoos on Nino's arms. I moved closer to Remo. Greta was clinging to me, still shy around others. Remo gave me a questioning look. He hadn't held his daughter yet. The only person except for me who didn't make Greta wail was Kiara.

He gently stroked her black tuft of hair then ran his hand down her back. His voice was low and soft as he spoke to her. "Greta, mia cara."

My heart seemed to skip a beat. It was the first time I heard Remo speak Italian. My family and I had only ever spoken Italian when we were surrounded by outsiders, and I knew many families handled it the same way. I carefully un-tangled her from my neck and gave her to Remo. Her big dark eyes blinked up at him, and her face began to twist. Remo rocked her gently in the crook of his arm then lowered his face and kissed the top of her head. She let out a hesitant cry, as if she wasn't sure if she wanted to wail or not. I handed him her favorite rattle, and he showed it to her.

She reached for it, eyes already brightening, and he helped her shake it. I took a step back then another as Remo rocked her. Remo sank down, still rattling and whispering words of consolation. Greta's expression made it clear that she wasn't convinced yet but that she wasn't wailing was a good sign.

Savio and Adamo looked as if they were having a stroke. I got it. Remo was one of the most feared men of the country, and here he cradled his baby girl in his arms, patient and careful. Nino was rocking Nevio on his thigh, and my son let out delighted screeches.

"I suppose that's the end of my whoring days in the house," Savio muttered.

Remo looked up from Greta, his eyes narrowing. "I don't want a fucking whore anywhere near my children."

Greta cried at the harshness in his voice, and Remo's lips tightened. He shook her gently then murmured something I didn't catch. The moment she stopped crying, I turned and left. My babies were cared for.

I finally went to help Kiara in the kitchen. Kiara was taking care of the vegetarian appetizers and the vegetarian main course, while I tried my hand at a roast beef and a chocolate cake. I didn't have much experience preparing any kind of food except for the occasional baby puree, so this proved to be a challenge.

Later we all settled around the table with a well-done roast beef, not medium rare as intended, and a slightly burnt chocolate cake, but nobody minded. During my captivity I'd only caught glimpses of the brotherly bond Remo and his brothers shared, but now as I became a part of their family, I realized just how strongly they cared for each other. Remo had traded himself for Adamo, had signed his death sentence so Adamo could live. There was no greater sign of love than that. It gave me hope that Remo was capable of that kind of emotion.

When Remo and I returned to our bedroom that night, I risked another glance at my phone, and my shoulders slumped. No messages.

Remo came up behind me, his hands on my waist, his lips hot on my throat. "Do you regret leaving the Outfit?"

I leaned back against him. His chest was bare and he'd removed most of the bandages despite Nino's protests. "No. Greta and Nevio will be happier here."

He bit down on my throat gently. "And you?"

I turned in his hold and kissed him. "I think I'll be happy too."

Remo pulled my dress over my head before he backed me up toward the bed, and we both fell down. We kissed for a long time until I was desperate and hot. Remo moved down my body and removed my panties then stretched out between my legs. His lips and tongue pushed me over the edge within a couple of minutes, then he climbed back up, his body covering mine, his weight braced on his forearms. His eyes held mine when he slammed into me, claiming me fully for the first time in fourteen months. "Remo," I gasped out.

Despite the flashes of pain on his face, Remo's thrusts didn't falter. He hit deep and hard, his eyes owning me. When he reached between us and stroked my clit, I cried out, clenching around him and gripping his shoulders tightly. Remo growled in pain and pleasure but kept thrusting as I rode out my orgasm. He kissed me fiercely, possessively, then pulled out.

He turned me on my stomach before he kissed my ear as he settled between my thighs. I felt a firm presence at my ass and stiffened in surprise and fear. Remo stroked my back, massaged my butt.

"I want to own every part of you," he murmured, kissing my shoulder. He turned my head so I met his gaze and kissed me slowly. Remo had put his fingers into me a couple of times, but his erection was so much bigger.

"Say something," he urged.

I swallowed, nervous. "I'm yours. All of me."

Remo's eyes softened. "Relax, Angel. I'll be careful."

For a moment his weight lifted, and I heard him take something from the drawer. Over my shoulder I saw him covering his cock with lube then he was back over me. He bit down on my shoulder blade lightly as he pushed forward, and I arched up when the stretching got too bad. Remo stopped, kissed my shoulder, my cheek. His hands slid under my body, found my nipple and my clit. He tugged at my nipple while his fingers stroked my clit and opening. Soon, I loosened around him as pain and pleasure mixed. He pushed two fingers into me and groaned roughly, the sound so primal and erotic my core clenched with arousal. "I feel my cock inside you. It's perfect."

I moaned as he moved his fingers slowly while his other hand kept twisting my nipple. Despite the pain, I felt a release approaching. My lips parted and my muscles tightened as pleasure overcame me. Remo pushed his cock into me all the way, and I moaned and whimpered, caught up between pain and pleasure. I'd never felt more stretched, teetering on the edge of overwhelming pain and yet happy that Remo had claimed this part of me as well.

I shivered, overcome with sensations.

Remo kissed my cheek. "Can I?"

I gave a nod and he pulled almost all the way out. I trembled as he pushed back in. He kept working my pussy as he thrust into me slowly.

"It'll get better, Angel," he murmured.

His movements became faster, and I bit down on my lip. Pain and pleasure mingled, almost becoming one. Remo's body pressed me into the mattress as his cock and fingers claimed me.

With a guttural groan, Remo slammed into me one more time, and I felt his release. I shuddered desperately under him. Remo stayed inside of me for a couple of heartbeats, his breath hot on my shoulder, his fingers gentle, almost soothing on my clit.

He pulled out of me carefully then turned me on my side and pressed up behind me, kissing my shoulder. I couldn't move, overwhelmed, stunned. Every time I thought Remo had taken everything, he took another part of me.

"Angel?" he asked in a low voice.

I turned around in his embrace and nestled close to him, my nose buried in the crook of his neck. Remo tensed and gripped my chin, nudging my face up. I could see a hint of hesitation on his face as he evaluated my expression.

"You will never surrender to my will because you think I want you to. Was it too painful?"

I glanced up, swallowing hard. Remo was concerned for me. Cruel, merciless, brutal to the very core, and yet *concerned for me*. "I wanted to surrender to you, to give myself to you like that. You already own every other part of me."

His brows pulled together even further. He traced my face with his finger. "I don't enjoy hurting you unless it heightens your pleasure."

I tilted my head. "You sound surprised."

"I enjoy hurting people, but not you, never you."

I fell silent, wondering what it meant. Remo pushed up and reached over me and into the drawer of his nightstand. He pulled out a small parcel then set it down between us. "For you," he said.

My eyebrows rose. He hadn't given me a present earlier, but I had assumed the gifts for Greta and Nevio had been meant for me as well. It had been difficult enough to get something for Remo. Eventually I'd opted for a guide of running trails of the region as well as a quickly assembled photo book from our twin's first seven months.

"What is it?"

"Open it," Remo demanded, fingertips tracing my side and hip.

I lifted the lid and my breath stilled as my eyes registered the necklace with the pendant in the shape of wings. It was a beautiful piece of finely worked gold-smithing. Intricately gorgeous. I took it out carefully.

"Where did you get it? You didn't leave the house."

"I had it handcrafted by a local goldsmith shortly after I released you."

My lips fell open in surprise. Remo helped me put the necklace on, and the cool gold settled in the valley between my breasts. "Ruinously gorgeous," Remo murmured as he traced my skin.

I gave him a curious look.

"You ruined me for all other women."

A wave of possessiveness overcame me. Remo was mine.

Remo

I watched Serafina as she stroked the heads of our children, patient, loving, even though they both had been crying on and off for hours. She sang to them, whispered words of sweet nothings to them. She had left her family for them so they would be safe, so they would get the life they deserved, the life they were destined for. I had seen the look in her eyes when she'd said goodbye to her twin. Serafina had given up so much for our children.

Her body was weaker than mine. She wasn't as harsh or cruel or fearless.

But God she was strong.

When Nevio and Greta had finally fallen asleep, she straightened from where she'd been bent over their crib and when she noticed me, she tensed slightly but came toward me. She'd been oddly quiet today, and I knew something was bothering her, but I didn't talk emotions if I could help it.

Serafina stopped in the hallway. "I've been here for three weeks, but I still don't know what we are."

I braced myself beside her shoulders, peering down at her. "You are an angel, and I'm your ruin." My lips pulled into a wry smile.

She shook her head almost angrily. "What am I to you? Your lover? Your girlfriend? A nice change from your usual whores?"

My own anger spiked. "What do you want me to say?"

"Nothing," she said quietly. "I want the truth. I need to know what to expect from you."

"I love death. I love spilling blood and causing pain. I love to see terror in people's eyes, and that won't ever change," I whispered harshly because it was true.

She looked up at me. "You are the cruelest man I know. You took everything from me."

I nodded because that was true as well. "Few women can bear the darkness. I can't ... I won't force you to be with me. You are free."

"Free to do as I please," she murmured, warm and soft against me. Tantalizing. "Even take another man into my bed?"

A burst of rage filled me. I wanted her for myself, wanted to remain the only man who'd ever tasted those perfect lips, who'd ever claimed her, but more than that I wanted her to want it too. I swallowed my fury. "Even that," I said then continued in a harsh whisper, "I won't stop you. I won't punish you for it."

She smiled a knowing smile. "But you will kill anyone who touches me."

I brought our lips close. "Not just kill them, *obliterate them* in the cruelest way possible for touching something they are unworthy of."

Challenge flickered in her eyes. "Are you worthy?"

I claimed her mouth, hard and desperate, before pulling back. "Oh no, Angel. From the day I saw you, I knew I was the least worthy of them all." I should have never laid a hand on her, but I was a fucking bastard and had taken everything she was willing to give.

She tilted her head up, regarding me. She opened my shirt slowly, one button after the other, and it gave way under those elegant fingers. She rested her palm against my chest, over my heart. "Is there something in there capable of love?"

My fucking chest constricted. "Whatever's in there, it's yours. Whatever love I'm capable of, it's yours too."

She cupped my face, her eyes fierce, almost brutal in their intensity. "You are beyond redemption, Remo," she whispered, and I smiled bitterly because I knew it.

She shook her head. "But so am I because even free to do as I please, I choose you. I'm no angel. An angel wouldn't love a man like you, but I do. I love you." And she kissed me harshly, brutally, all rage and love, and I kissed her back with the same love, the same rage.

This woman had stolen my black heart. From the first moment I saw her, I wanted to own her. At first to destroy the Outfit and Dante then later because it became an irresistible need, a voracious longing. And in the end, Serafina was the one who owned me, black heart, condemned soul, scarred body.

Every fucking part of me was hers, and if she'd let me, I'd be hers till my last day.

Serafina

My heart burned with emotions. Fiercely. Remo had declared his love for me. Something I'd never considered a possibility.

This cruel man owned my heart, and I didn't want it any other way.

Remo's kiss was violent, harsh. Then he pulled back. "Marry me."

I froze. It had been an order. Remo wasn't a man who asked for anything. I leaned back against the wall slowly, searching his eyes.

He didn't let me retreat. He kissed me again but gentler. "Marry me, *Angel*."

It still wasn't a question, but his voice wasn't dominant anymore. It was soft, compelling, raw. "Become a Falcone?" I murmured against his lips.

"Become a Falcone. Become mine."

I smiled. "I have been yours for a long time."

"Is that a yes?" he asked, his hand sliding over my outer thigh, stroking, distracting me.

"Yes," I whispered.

"Serafina Falcone," he murmured. "I like the sound of it."

I smiled because this name sounded right, more right than Mancini ever had.

Was this love? Was this madness? I didn't care. It was perfection either way.

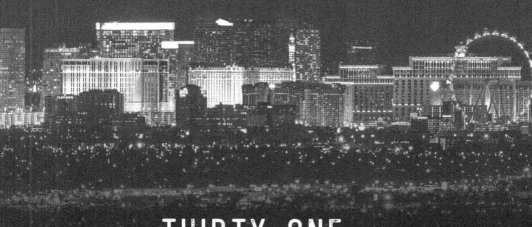

THIRTY-ONE

Serafina

I was inexplicably nervous when Remo told me he wanted to announce our wedding to his brothers and Kiara the next day. We'd all gathered in the kitchen for breakfast, Nevio on Kiara's lap and Greta on mine.

"You have a new wedding to look forward to," Remo said without warning.

Every pair of eyes darted from him then to me. My cheeks flushed. I wasn't sure what Savio and Nino thought of the situation. Adamo and Kiara liked me, but the other two …

"Will we be allowed to kidnap someone? Or at least spill some blood? Since you sampled the goods before, bloody sheets won't happen after all," Savio drawled, grinning.

Remo reached over the table and hit him over the head. Savio only chuckled.

"Be careful I don't spill your blood."

Adamo smiled at me then rolled his eyes at Savio.

Kiara got up, handing Nevio to Remo so she could hug me. "I'm so happy."

Savio and Nino definitely didn't look unhappy, but their reaction wasn't as enthusiastic as Kiara's or Adamo's, not that I had expected it to be.

When Savio got up to take a call, I followed after him but waited until he was done before I approached him. He eyed me curiously when he noticed me. He didn't look like a teenager anymore, especially now that he was sporting stubble.

"Are we good?" I asked.

"If you're talking about the soup incident, that's forgotten. Trust me, most people want to do worse to me, especially women, so I've learned not to hold grudges." He shrugged. "And we were the ones who held you captive, so you have more reason to be pissed."

"True. But my family kidnapped your younger brother and almost killed your oldest, so I guess we're even?"

Savio's expression tightened briefly at the mention of my family and my own stomach churned painfully. "You are part of our family now. I don't give a fuck about the past. Just make sure you don't break Remo's fucking heart."

"Do you think that's a possibility?" I teased.

His dark brows drew together. "Before you, I'd have bet my balls against it. To be honest, I wasn't sure if Remo had something resembling a heart."

"He loves you."

Savio looked away, obviously uncomfortable. "We are brothers. We'll die for each other."

I smiled.

"We should return," Savio muttered. "I don't want Remo to think we're getting it on behind his back."

I snorted. "Sorry, Savio, nothing against you, but you don't stand a chance."

Savio gave me an arrogant smile. "You like what you see, admit it." He sauntered back into the kitchen before I could shoot something back. But for some reason his insufferable ego was almost endearing. It reminded me a bit of Samuel, which was consoling and painful at the same time.

After my conversation with Savio, I felt better. Now I only needed to straighten out things with Nino. He and I had never really warmed up to each other, and I wasn't sure if it was because Nino didn't like me or if it was because of his nature.

Remo leaned in when I sat down beside him. "Did he behave?"

Savio rolled his eyes at his brother.

"He tried," I said.

"That's all I can hope for. Maybe they'll try your patience as they do mine."

"Raising twins will teach you the patience of a saint. I doubt your brothers can test me."

"We'll see," Savio said with a chuckle. "And don't hold your breath. Remo won't reach sainthood anytime soon."

"I don't want him to be a saint," I said, looking at Nevio and Remo, both watching me with those impossibly dark eyes.

After breakfast, I asked Nino if we could talk. We headed into the garden despite Remo's suspicious expression.

"Do you disapprove of our wedding?"

Nino assessed me without a flicker of emotion. "No. I never considered marriage an option for Remo, but that doesn't mean I don't think it's a good thing. It was for me despite my own reluctance in regards to marriage."

I nodded. "You never seemed to like me much."

"It was never a matter of dislike, Serafina. You were our captive, the enemy, and I didn't want Remo to lose himself in his game. I thought it wouldn't work. But I was wrong. You saved him."

"I couldn't let my family kill him."

Nino shook his head. "That's not what I mean."

I waited, watching Nino's profile as he stared off into the distance.

"Remo and I, we are messed up in ways that can't be fixed, not really. For someone to accept us despite what we are, it takes a lot of forgiveness and love. Our past … it broke certain parts of us."

"Remo never talks about the past."

Nino nodded. "He'll tell you eventually. Give him time."

"We have all our lives."

Remo

I held Serafina in my arms after sex, my chest pressed up to her back, my nose buried in her soft hair, relishing in her sweet scent. She traced the scars on my palm. She did it often. In the beginning it had bothered me because it was a part of me I didn't share with anyone except for Nino.

"I was nine," I began then stopped because even with Nino I'd never discussed what had happened. Words had always seemed lacking to convey our shared horrors. The smell of blood filled my nose as it always did when I remembered that day. Soon the stench of burning fabric and skin joined the metallic tang.

Serafina's fingers on my palm had stilled. "I love you no matter what. I've heard of every horror you committed, and I'm still here."

She was. I could imagine what kinds of stories were whispered in the Outfit and they were all true. And Serafina had experienced a small part of our nature when I'd captured her, when I'd cut her. Looking at the faded white scar, I still felt a fucking twinge in my chest. I brushed aside her hair and kissed the nape of her neck. That she found it in her heart to love me despite it all, that she trusted me with our children, it seemed impossible.

"I know what I am. But my father, he was monstrous in a different way. He enjoyed torturing the people he was meant to protect, just as much as he did his enemies, maybe even more. My mother loved and feared him equally, and she allowed him to humiliate and torture her because of it. Allowed him to do the same to us. Love made her weak."

Serafina gave a small shake of her head. "Real love doesn't make you weak. Love how it's meant to be makes you stronger. But there's no room for fear where there's love."

I tightened my hold around her. "Don't you fear me?"

"I used to, but not anymore and never again."

I rested my forehead against her hair. Very few people didn't fear me. My brothers and maybe Kiara, and that was what I wanted, what I worked for. "Eventually she hated my father more than she loved him, and she decided to punish him in the only way she thought she could."

I closed my eyes, remembering that day.

Mother came into my bedroom in her long nightgown, which was straining over her belly. She never brought us to bed or said goodnight, so I tensed when I saw her in the doorway. I'd gotten me and my brothers ready for bed while she lay on the sofa, staring at nothing.

"Remo, my boy, can you come with me?"

I narrowed my eyes. She sounded too caring, too loving. My boy? She sounded like a mother. She smiled and I took a hesitant step forward, more hopeful than suspicious.

"Nino and Savio are already in my room."

That convinced me. I followed her toward her bedroom. For a second I considered slipping my hand in hers, but she had never held my hand like that and I was too old now. The moment I stepped inside the bedroom, she threw the door shut and closed us in. My eyes registered Nino kneeling on the floor, cradling his arm. Everything was red. Rivulets of red trailed down his arms, his wrists gaping open. His eyes locked on mine. He wasn't making a sound, only crying as he bled. Blood. Everywhere. It clogged my nose.

I frantically looked for Savio and found him motionless on the bed. A cry wedged itself into my throat until I noticed the rise and fall of his chest. Not gone.

Mother stepped in front of me and grabbed my arm. Silver flashed before my eyes and I jerked. My hands and face burned as the blade cut me. I hit and clawed and roared, fighting her off. And then she stopped and the smell of smoke filled the room. The curtains were burning. We'd burn. We'd all burn. Nino began to hum, rocking back and forth, pale and sweaty.

I rushed toward the window. Outside I heard the shouts of my father's men.

I ripped at the curtains and flames licked at my palms and neck and arms, snatching hungrily at my skin. I screamed as I broke the window. I helped Nino out then grabbed Savio and jumped out of the window with him in my arms. Bones broke and I burned all over. Agony, pure and overwhelming. Staring up at the window, I saw our mother's crying desperate face amidst the smoke and flame. Crying because I'd taken her revenge from her, because I hadn't died with my brothers as we were supposed to. I wanted her to burn, wanted her gone from our life. I wanted her dead.

Serafina was quiet when I finished. She swallowed. "How can a mother do that to their children? I'd die for Greta and Nevio. I'd never hurt them. And if you ever hurt them, Remo, I'll kill you. That's a promise."

"I hope you will because if I hurt them, I deserve nothing less than a knife to the fucking heart."

Serafina turned around in my arms, her blue eyes fierce and trusting. "But you won't ever hurt them. I know you won't and you protect the people you love."

I nodded. "I won't and nobody else will either." I'd fucking destroy anyone who tried.

She traced the scar over my eyebrow. "I know it's wrong but I wish I could have killed your mother for what she did to you."

My chest tightened. I didn't tell her that my mother was still very much alive. I brought Serafina's hand up to my face and kissed her palm then the scar I had created. "I won't allow you to be dragged down into my darkness."

I was going to kill my mother one day.

One day, Nino and I would be strong enough to do it.

"That's not your choice alone."

"I rule over hundreds of men. I can be very convincing if I try."

She smiled a slow, fierce smile. "Believe me, I know. You convinced me to fall in love with my captor. But I can be very stubborn."

I pulled her closer. "That's true. You almost brought me to my knees."

She raised one perfect blond eyebrow. "Almost?"

"You had me lying in my own blood at your feet, isn't that enough?" I asked in a low voice.

"Don't do that ever again."

"I won't. The next blood I'll bathe in won't be my own."

Realization flickered in her eyes. She sighed then kissed me. "You swore not to kill my family."

"Angel, I swore not to kill them that day. The men in your family are high-ranking Outfit members. Your uncle is Dante fucking Cavallaro. If I want to win this war, I'll have to kill him, and I *will* win this fucking war. Because if I don't, Cavallaro will and that means Nevio and Greta, you, my brothers... won't be safe. And I don't care how many I'll have to kill to guarantee your fucking safety. I will kill everyone who threatens the people under my protection." I touched her throat, stroking the soft skin there. "You can't have it all. You have to make a choice."

She shook her head. "I made my choice, Remo. I chose you and I'll choose you over and over again."

Fuck. I didn't deserve this woman.

Serafina

We'd been living in Las Vegas for two months now. I was starting to feel at home, more at home than I'd felt in Minneapolis since I'd given birth to my twins. I kept sending Samuel messages, but they became less frequent because of his lack of reaction. Every week I'd send him a short note telling him I was well and a photo of the twins and me. He hadn't replied so far, but I knew he'd read them and even that was a small victory. He hadn't blocked me. He still wanted to know how I was doing even though I was practically the enemy now. The war between the Camorra and the Outfit wouldn't end anytime soon, even if things had calmed down for the moment. Dante was probably planning something, and I was fairly certain Nino and Remo wouldn't ease down on the Outfit either.

Remo's birthday was tomorrow and even if he didn't celebrate it, I wanted to give him something special. It was difficult to come up with a present for someone who ruled over the West Coast and could buy anything he wanted because money wasn't an issue.

It had taken me a long time to come up with something that held meaning and showed Remo what he meant to me. Early in the morning, after another sleepless night with the twins, I approached Nino who was swimming his usual laps in the pool. Kiara was keeping watch over the babies since they were both rather needy at the moment due to their teething.

Nino noticed me standing beside the pool and swam toward the edge. "Is something the matter?"

"I have a favor to ask of you."

Nino hoisted himself out of the water. My eyes scanned the myriad of tattoos on his upper body and thighs. Nino regarded me curiously, and I realized I'd been staring. "Sorry. I didn't mean to gawk, but I was wondering where you've had your tattoos done."

Nino walked over to the lounge chair and picked up his towel. "Some of them I did myself. The ones in places I can't reach I had done in a tattoo studio not too far away."

"You do tattoos?"

"I can do them, yes," he said. "Why?"

I hesitated. "Because I want to get a tattoo. Can you do it for me?"

"That depends what exactly you want."

"I want angel wings on the back of my neck," I said, a flush spreading on my cheeks under Nino's scrutiny. I wasn't sure if he knew Remo's nickname for me, but it felt like something personal I was sharing.

"Wings, I can do … if you have a design in mind. Can you show me where exactly you want the tattoo?"

He came up to me and I pushed my hair to the side, baring the nape of my neck and touching the spot. "Here."

"It will be painful," Nino warned.

I sent him a look. "I gave birth to twins. I think I can handle a needle."

Nino inclined his head. "That is true. While I can't assess the force of labor pain since I've never experienced it, I assume it's excruciating."

"It is," I said. "So you will do it?"

"If it's your wish, then yes. When?"

"As soon as possible. The tattoo is Remo's birthday present."

Again Nino gave me a mildly curious look. "We can do it later in the afternoon. I can set up everything in one of the guestrooms."

"Thank you," I said.

"Thank me once it's done and you're happy with the outcome." He paused. "I assume you don't want Remo to find out for now."

I nodded. "If possible."

"It's a secret I don't mind keeping from my brother."

As promised, Nino had set up everything in a guest bedroom in his wing. I was nervous despite my best intentions not to be.

Nino oozed calm as I stretched out on my stomach on the bed. He disinfected my neck before he touched the tattoo needle to the skin, and I winced at the first sting. I soon got used to the burning sensation. Nino moved quickly, meticulously, and I didn't speak as he worked, not wanting to distract him. When he was finally done, I sat up and accepted the mirror Nino held out to me. He held a second mirror behind my neck.

The outcome was more stunning than I could have ever imagined. I didn't know it was possible to paint such intricate artwork with a needle. The feathers of the wings looked so real I expected them to flutter in the wind.

"It's beautiful," I admitted.

Nino nodded. "Remo will appreciate the message."

"You know that he calls me Angel?"

"I overheard him saying it, yes, and you are the counterpart to his fallen angel on his back."

"Did you tattoo it as well?"

"I did," Nino murmured.

"Why the broken, singed wings? The fallen angel is kneeling, and the tips of the feathers are crooked and burning."

Nino regarded me closely. "What did Remo tell you about our past?"

"He told me your mother tried to kill you and that you almost burned to death."

Nino's face tightened and he nodded. "Remo burned to save us. I never asked Remo about the details why he wanted to get the tattoo, but I think it has something to do with that day."

"Thank you, Nino."

Nino gave a small shake of his head. "No, thank you."

Hiding my tattoo from Remo proved difficult. I had it covered with my hair, but when I moved my head, I often had to stop myself from wincing.

That evening, after bringing the twins to bed, Remo pulled me against him in our bedroom, his hands squeezing my butt before they moved higher. He kissed me and touched my neck. I drew back with a wince before I could stop myself. His eyes narrowed.

"What's wrong?"

I considered making up something, but Remo was too good at detecting lies, and his birthday was only two more hours away. "This was supposed to be your birthday present," I said softly as I lifted my hair and turned so he could see my neck.

Remo was quiet and I risked a look at him over my shoulder.

Slowly he raised his eyes from my wings with a strange smile. "Wings."

I smiled. "Because you gave me wings."

He shook his head, his dark eyes softening. "Angel," he said quietly, brushing his fingers over my tender skin. "You had wings all along. You only needed a little push to spread them and fly."

I turned back to face him. "Maybe, but I wouldn't have done it on my own."

We kissed slowly at first, but Remo quickly deepened our kiss, and suddenly we were on the bed tugging at our clothes and stroking every inch of naked skin we could reach. I pushed Remo onto his back, smiling, and his answering smile, all desire and dominance, sent a stab of arousal through me. Leaning forward to claim his mouth for a kiss, I lowered myself on his erection, groaning at the feeling of fullness. Remo pushed up into a sitting position, bringing us chest to chest, racing heartbeat to racing heartbeat. I gasped at the shift of him inside of me, at the feel of his strength as his arms slung around my back. I rolled my hips, driving him deeply into me as we kissed.

We held each other's gaze as we always did, and those dark eyes captivated me as they'd done from the very start. So often cruel and merciless but passionate and reverent when they rested on me, tender and caring when they regarded our twins.

When we'd both found our release, we stayed wrapped up in each other like that, our breathing ragged, bodies slick with sweat. I ran my fingertips over Remo's back, tracing the spot where the wings of his fallen angel spread out. He trailed his own fingertips upwards, along my spine until he reached my new tattoo. I winced slightly and Remo's touch turned even softer. My heart was ready to burst out of my ribcage from the look in his eyes.

Remo scanned my expression, his brows drawing together.

I sighed. "Sorry. Since my pregnancy I'm more emotional. I hope it'll go away soon." I cleared my throat then rested my palm over his shoulder blade. "What's the meaning of your tattoo? You know why I got mine, but I wonder why you got yours."

A hint of wariness flashed in Remo's eyes, the walls he was used to keeping up wanting to lock back in place. "Nino did it. About seven years ago."

I nodded to show him I was listening.

"It's a fallen angel, like you said. It represents the fall Nino and I took on the day our mother tried to kill us."

My brows snapped together. "Fall? You saved your brothers. How's that falling?"

Remo's expression was dark and twisted, his eyes far away, haunted, angry. "Until that day Nino and I were innocent. After that we weren't. We'd already experienced our fair share of violence from our father, but it never affected us like that day did. The flames of that day they singed our wings and our fall into darkness began. We became who we are today. That's why the fallen angel is kneeling in pools of blood."

I'd noticed that the fallen angel knelt in pools of some kind of liquid, that a few of its singed feathered dipped into it, but I hadn't realized it was blood. For a moment I wasn't sure what to say, how to console Remo. Could words ever be enough to make the horrors of his past better?

"I'm sorry," I said quietly.

Remo's gaze focused on me, tore away from the images of the past. "You aren't the one who should be sorry. And I won't forgive her no matter how often she'd apologize. Not that she ever did."

I froze. "Your mother didn't die that day?"

"No. Even though I wanted her dead, I'm glad she survived that day or Adamo wouldn't be here. She was heavily pregnant with him."

I shook my head, completely at a loss over what Remo's mother had done. "Where is she?"

"In a mental facility." Remo's voice dipped and turned vicious. "We are paying for it so she can live and breathe and exist, when she shouldn't be doing either."

"Why haven't you killed her?" With anyone else I would have never asked something like that, but this was Remo. Killing was in his nature, and his words made it clear that he hated his mother.

Remo pressed his mouth to the crook of my neck. "Because," he growled. "For some fucking messed up reason Nino and I are too weak to kill her. We haven't seen her in over five years …"

"Do Savio and Adamo know what happened?"

"Savio has known for a while. And we talked to Adamo a few months after he got initiated."

I stroked Remo's neck. "Have you thought about visiting her again to try and find closure?"

Remo looked up, his expression harsh. "There won't be any closure until she's dead. I don't want to waste another second of my life on her. She's already fucking dead to me. You and Greta and Nevio are what matters now. My brothers are what matters. That's it."

I kissed him to show him I understood. I didn't think it was as easy as that. Their mother still dominated part of their existence, but I respected that Remo wasn't ready to seek a solution now. It wasn't my place to meddle. He and his brothers would have to face their mother one day, and maybe then they could move past their demons.

All I could do was show Remo a better future. A future with a family that loved him. He'd always only had his brothers, but now he had us as well.

THIRTY-TWO

Remo

SERAFINA, LEONA, AND KIARA WERE BUSY IN THE KITCHEN, BAKING birthday cakes for the twins whose first birthday was today. It was already close to noon. I doubted they'd get the cake ready in time for the afternoon, but I didn't say anything.

"It seems like a waste of effort to create elaborate cakes in the shape of a unicorn and a car when their only purpose is to be eaten," Nino commented as we left the kitchen to give the women their space. They'd found images of complicated cakes on the Internet, and were determined to recreate them for Greta and Nevio.

"I don't give a fuck, but Serafina is so damn excited about the cakes, so I guess it's worth the work. I doubt the kids will care much. They'll only smash their hands into the cake and stuff their faces," I said, peering down at Greta whom I cradled in the crook of my arm. She felt completely comfortable in my presence now, and it felt like one of the biggest triumphs in my life to have her big dark eyes look up at me with trust. And by my fucking honor and everything else that mattered, I'd never do anything to betray that trust. When she'd been wary of me in the beginning, it had felt like a knife to the heart. I'd always relished the fear in the eyes of others, with the exception of my brothers, but with my children and Serafina I never wanted to see it again.

"I never considered marriage an option for the two of us," Nino said thoughtfully as we stopped beside the pool.

"I never thought I'd find a woman I wouldn't want to kill after a few hours."

Greta gave me a toothy grin, and I stroked her hair back. It had grown quite long and curled slightly like Adamo's hair did.

"Hmm, *mia cara*, ready for your first swim?"

Nevio was nestled in Nino's arm and as usual making grabby hands at the colorful tattoos. I could already guess what he wanted to get once he was older.

Fabiano was already lounging on the pink flamingo float Savio had used before I'd banned any kind of whoring in the mansion. I rolled my eyes at him. "That's a disturbing sight."

Fabiano shrugged. "It's comfortable."

Savio and Adamo were playing water ball close to the waterfall in the pool and bickering as usual.

It was the first swim for the babies since we didn't have a heated pool before and only had it installed now that the babies were part of our household. Nino slowly stepped into the pool with Nevio.

Nevio let out a screech, smiling at me. My fucking heart swelled with pride. That boy didn't fear anything. Sometimes it almost worried me how similar to me he was. He'd get himself in trouble as soon as he could walk better.

Nino moved over to Fabiano on the float, and Nevio made his grabby hands, wanting to ride on the flamingo with Fabiano. Fabiano raised his eyes to mine, asking for permission. I nodded, twisting my forearm with the tattoo. Between us it meant more than just an oath to the Camorra, more than being a Made Man. The day Fabiano had sworn himself to me, to the Camorra, he'd become family, and I trusted him with my kids. I'd never told him, but I got why he'd acted the way he did when I tried to drive a wedge between Leona and him. He wanted to protect her, wanted to protect someone who could see past the fucking darkness, who loved him despite it all.

Serafina had changed my view on things, and if it was in my nature I might have apologized to Fabiano for how I'd acted.

Fabiano held out his arms, and Nino handed him Nevio, who kicked happily with his legs until he sat in the front of the float, holding on to the neck of the flamingo.

"I hope you gave that thing a good scrub," I called over to Savio who gave me the finger.

I went down the steps into the pool. The moment Greta's feet touched the water her face twisted, but I made a low soothing sound and she relaxed. Shifting her so her head was level with mine, I lowered us further into the warm water. Greta held on to me, eying the water critically. After a while she smiled and hit the water with her palm. I went over to the flamingo float, but Greta tightened her hold on me when I tried to put her on it.

Nevio babbled, his tiny legs wiggling as Fabiano held him by the waist. Both Greta and Nevio were big on the babbling, but they both hadn't said any word except for 'Mom,' and while Nevio was already making his first steps, Greta only crawled. She was a cautious kid and reminded me a lot of Nino.

Nevio grinned at me, squeezing the neck of the flamingo before he extended his arms with his grabby hands. "Dad. Daaad."

For a moment, I froze, my expression stilling. Fabiano grinned and Nino squeezed my shoulder. I wrapped my arm around Nevio and pressed him to my chest. Greta pressed her wet palm against Nevio's cheek, giggling. I waded through the water with the two, dipping lower, causing them to scream with joy.

Serafina headed toward us in a heart-stoppingly sexy white bikini, Kiara and Leona close behind her.

She lowered herself to the edge of the pool.

"Mom!" Greta called, and I handed our daughter over to Serafina. I stayed close and touched Serafina's thigh. She raised her eyebrows. "Something the matter? You have a strange expression."

"Nevio said Dad," I told her.

She leaned down and kissed me, her expression so full of happiness it filled even my cruel heart with warmth.

"Dad," Nevio confirmed, hitting the surface with his palm again and sending water everywhere.

Serafina shook her head with a soft smile as she slid into the water with Greta pressed to her chest.

"This is close to perfection," I said, indicating the people gathered around us. "Everyone who matters is here."

And I'd fucking protect them all with my life.

A shadow passed over Serafina's face, and she averted her gaze, blinking. I curled my hand over her neck, bringing our faces closer together. She locked gazes with mine. "I know you miss them, especially your brother."

She nodded. "I do, and I wish you could meet Sofia and my mom. I wish they could see you as I see you."

Serafina saw me in a way most people never would because I'd never allow them to do so. "I can't promise you peace. It's not only my call to make, and there's a lot of bad blood between the Camorra and the Outfit. I won't back down, not when Cavallaro was the first to breach my territory."

I still wanted to bathe in Cavallaro's blood and I knew he shared the sentiment. Peace would never happen.

"I know, and I can deal with it. This is my new family now, and I'm happy that the babies and I are here where we belong." She paused, sighing. "I can't help missing my family, especially Samuel. We've always been so close, and now I haven't heard from him in so long. It's hard."

I was used to handling things, used to things going my way, but this was one thing I couldn't change for her. I wasn't going to make a peace offering toward Cavallaro, even when the attack on Roger's Arena was orchestrated by Scuderi, but the attack on our race in Kansas definitely wasn't. He'd tortured my brother. That was another thing I couldn't easily forget. I wanted them to bleed. At least Dante fucking Cavallaro.

Greta giggled again and Nevio fell in. Serafina's expression brightened, and she smiled at me. Fuck. That smile got me every time.

Serafina

Nevio was a small whirlwind, and it had only gotten worse since he started to walk. It was the day before our wedding and only four days since the twin's birthday, and Kiara was busy with last minutes preparation, even though it was going to be a small affair. Adamo had babysitter duty for Nevio, which mainly consisted in running after him and making sure he didn't break his neck or got his hands on anything breakable.

Every time Adamo lifted Nevio into his arms, he began wailing in protest. I gave Adamo an understanding smile when he let out a sigh. "I can take over if you want?"

Adamo smiled sheepishly. "I need a break."

Chuckling, I took Nevio from him and hoisted him up on my hip despite his loud protest. "Mom, no. No. No. No!"

"I was so looking forward to them speaking," Remo said from his spot on a blanket where he played with Greta while trying to get work done on his iPad simultaneously. "But Nevio enjoys the word 'no' a bit too much for my taste."

"No," "Mom," and "Dad" were the only words that Nevio had mastered so far.

"No!" Nevio bellowed.

I laughed.

Remo shook his head. "Nevio, that's enough."

Nevio frowned, his lips turning into a pout. "No?"

Remo's mouth twitched.

"If you're being quiet, I'll set you back down," I said. Nevio regarded me, then Remo, obviously unsure if our offer was worth it.

Greta crawled closer to Remo, and he looked back down to her. She pressed her hands to his legs and slowly pushed up, her butt raised, then she stumbled to her feet. Remo reached out, and she curled her tiny hand around his index finger and Remo's other fingers covered hers, steadying her, and my eyes began to water.

"Good," Remo encouraged.

She looked at him, surprised, and still a bit unsure.

She took a hesitant step, and he smiled. "Very good, *mia cara.*" Her smile widened and she took a few uncoordinated, shaky steps and stumbled into him. He became still as she clung to his shirt and finger, peering up at him with absolute trust.

I set Nevio down because I could tell he wanted to join them. The second his tiny feet hit the ground, he wobbled toward Greta and his dad. Remo wrapped an arm around him as well.

Greta released Remo's shirt and made the grabby motion when she wanted to be picked up. She still preferred to be carried. Remo put one hand under her backside while the other steadied her back and pressed her to his chest. He held out his hand to Nevio. "Arm?"

Nevio nodded for once, and Remo bent down to lift him up as well. He straightened with a kid on each hip and pressed a kiss to the top of their heads. His eyes found mine, and I didn't care that he saw my tears. Today I gladly gave them to him.

Remo was beyond redemption in the eyes of so many.

He was the cruelest man I knew.

But with every atom in my body, I knew that he would never hurt our children. He would protect them. They were Falcones. They were his. *Ours.*

We would both die for them, for each other.

Tomorrow I'd officially become a Falcone, and so would my kids. I knew we'd all carry the name with pride.

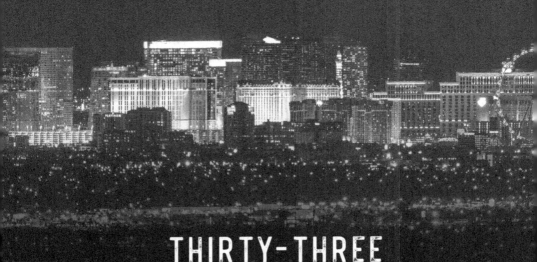

THIRTY-THREE

Serafina

THE WEDDING WAS SCHEDULED FOR LATE AFTERNOON. I CHOSE A BOHO-style dress without pearls or a bodice. The top was knitted with a V-neckline, and the skirt flowed freely around my body, touching the ground in soft waves. My hair was down and fell in untamed curls around my shoulders.

I allowed myself another moment to regard my reflection. This day felt so very different to my last wedding day. Back then I'd been scared of the unknown but determined to do what was expected of me, content to marry a man I hardly knew and definitely wasn't in love with. Today I was absolutely certain of my love for my future husband. Remo held my heart in an iron grip, and I wouldn't have wanted it any other way.

Love can bloom in the darkest place, and ours did wildly, freely, untamable.

I hadn't thought it possible to feel that way for someone; occasionally I'd dreamed of it or foolishly hoped for it, but I knew it to be a rare gift in our circles.

I left our bedroom and walked through the silent hallways of the mansion, a place that had become my home and a safe haven for Greta and Nevio. Falcone. A name we all would carry with pride. A name that our kids would always be able to speak with their heads held high.

Adamo waited for me in the game room and smiled when he spotted me. The French windows were open and a gentle breeze carried in, warm and soothing. Adamo was dressed in slacks and a white shirt and had gotten a haircut to tame his wild curls for the occasion. Tears sprang into my eyes, and my chest constricted painfully. This was supposed to be Samuel. I wanted him at my side in one of the most important moments of my life. He was meant to walk me down the aisle. It had always been meant to be him, but he wasn't here.

Adamo extended his hand and I put mine in it. He squeezed. "One day your family will understand. One day there will be peace."

I peered up at him, at his kind smile and warm eyes, then lowered my gaze to the burn mark on his forearm, on the healed cuts. Occasionally, I still saw the haunted look in his eyes and I wondered if he hid the worst of his struggle from us. He was barely home anymore. So much pain and suffering in the name of revenge and honor. "You want peace after what my family did to you?"

"You're going to marry the man who kidnapped you."

I laughed. He had me there. If someone had told me on the day of my almost wedding to Danilo that I'd ever consider becoming a Falcone, I would have laughed in their face. So much had changed since then. I hardly knew the girl from back then anymore. She had been replaced by someone stronger.

Adamo lightly tugged at my hand and indicated toward the gardens. "Come. They're all waiting, and you know how Remo is. Patience isn't his strength."

No, it wasn't, but he'd waited for me more than once.

Adamo led me out of the mansion and past the pool toward the small congregation down the lawn.

My bare feet touched the warm grass, and then I spotted Remo at the end of the aisle below a white wood arc, and a sense of rightness filled me. Blood-red roses trailed around the arc, contrasting beautifully with the white. Kiara had arranged everything with Leona's help.

It wasn't a big feast with hundreds of guests, most of whom neither of us would have cared about. It was just us, Remo's brothers, Fabiano, Kiara, Leona, and the twins, and it felt perfect that way. By not inviting every Underboss of the Camorra, Remo had risked insulting a lot of people, but knowing him he didn't give a damn and his soldiers probably knew better than to voice their displeasure should they feel it.

In his dark slacks, black dress shirt, and blood-red vest, Remo was a sight to behold. Tall and dark and brutally handsome. His eyes scorched me even from afar, and one corner of his mouth pulled up in that twisted smile, always on the verge of darkness, that I'd come to love.

"Ready?" Adamo asked when we arrived at the starting point of the long aisle of white petals. I didn't even want to know how long Kiara and Leona had spent arranging them neatly in a pathway, but they had insisted on doing it.

"Yes," I could say it without doubt, without hesitation.

Everyone had gathered to both sides of the arc. Kiara held Greta in her arms and Nino held Nevio. I couldn't wait for them to be parents as well. And then I caught sight of a blond head off to the side, away from the rest, at the very fringes, and my throat tightened up. My gaze locked with Samuel's. He stood with his hands shoved inside his pockets, his expression unreadable. For a moment I was completely immobilized by my emotions. Pure joy and a flicker of worry, because there definitely wasn't peace between the Camorra and the Outfit. I pushed the last sentiment aside, focusing on the fact that my twin, my Samuel was here on one of the most important days of my life.

Adamo and I started walking down the aisle. I still wished Sam was the one walking beside me, but I understood why he couldn't, why his pride didn't allow him to hand me over to Remo.

My gaze drew away from Samuel toward the man who had captured my heart with wild abandon. Remo's dark eyes held mine as I headed toward him. When we arrived in the front, Greta spotted me and gave me a huge grin. A single petal stuck to the corner of her mouth. That was why Kiara had only bought edible flowers. She was just perfect with kids.

My heart overflowed with love for all of them. Nevio stood beside Nino, or rather held onto his leg, but I could tell that he was growing tired of standing still. He'd soon roam the gardens on unsteady legs.

I let go of Adamo and took Remo's outstretched hand. Smiling up at Remo, I whispered. "How? How did you get Samuel to come?" My eyes darted to my twin for a moment, disbelieving, incredulous, and so impossibly happy.

I looked back up to Remo, trying to hold back my emotions.

Remo ran his thumb over the back of my hand, his dark eyes filled with warmth he didn't bestow on many.

"I swore he'd be safe if he came. I used your phone to call him. It was a difficult process."

I swallowed. I could imagine how much time and effort it had cost to convince Samuel to come here, to risk so much. And I knew that Remo would have to let go of some of his pride to make a step toward my brother, the enemy. He'd done it for me. "He tortured you, almost killed you…"

Remo squeezed my hand. "I did worse. I took you from him. If I was him, I wouldn't forgive me either."

"Thank you for bringing him here, Remo." I touched his chest, hoping he could see just how fiercely I loved him.

"Whatever's in there, it's yours," he said with a dark smile.

"And I love every part of it, *of you*, the good, the bad, the light, the dark, even your blackest corners."

Remo's eyes flashed with fierce affection.

Nino did the ceremony since we didn't want any outsiders around for our special day. He'd gotten the license to do so only recently, which didn't pose a big problem in Las Vegas.

We kept the ceremony short, foregoing a long-winded traditional speech before we spoke our vows. We each had chosen rings for the other that we hadn't seen yet.

I took Remo's hand and slipped the ring on. It was a black tungsten carbide ring with an ebony wood inlay. Remo raised his eyebrows in surprise. "Carbide is twice as strong as steel," I whispered. "Because you are the strongest man I know." I smiled at the flicker of adoration in his eyes. "And ebony because wood is enduring and because you gave not only me roots but also our children and your brothers."

The look on Remo's face made it clear that I had made the right choice and relief filled me. He took my hand and slipped on a ring in the shape of two entwining wings, one dotted with white diamonds, the other with black gemstones.

"The white wing represents you," Remo said in a low voice, leaning closer so only I could hear him. "Because you are pure perfection, my *angel*. And the black wing with the black sapphires represents me, my darkness, that you manage to accept."

Remo kissed me, his fingers touching the tattoo on my neck.

"You set me free," I said, my voice thick with emotion.

He shook his head and our lips brushed, his eyes dark and intent. "I was the one who needed to be freed."

I kissed him fiercely. Free of the shackles of his past. When we pulled away, I realized everyone had taken a few steps back to give us privacy. My eyes were drawn to Samuel whose expression was like stone.

I needed to talk to him, to embrace him. Remo squeezed my hand to show me it was okay.

I headed for Samuel and Remo released my hand, but my fingers clung to him, pulling him along.

"Angel, you had one ruined wedding. Do you want to add a bloody one to your list?"

I glanced at him. "You won't attack my brother."

His eyes went past me. "*I* won't."

"And Samuel won't attack you either," I said firmly.

Samuel stood tall, expression harsh as it settled on Remo. I finally let go of Remo's hand, and he stayed a few steps back as I bridged the remaining distance between Sam and me. I stopped right in front of my twin. I peered up at Samuel, and he lowered his gaze to mine, and despite everything I had done, everything he knew, his expression softened with love and tenderness.

I started crying because I hadn't realized how much I'd missed him, how much I longed for his forgiveness. "You came."

I wrapped my arms around his middle, and he hugged me back. "I'd do anything for you Fina, even stare into the eyes of the man I want to kill more than anything in this world." We stayed in each other's embrace for a few moments, trying to make every second last a lifetime because we knew there would be few chances like this in the future.

I pulled back, searching his blue eyes. "They don't know you're here."

"Nobody knows. If they did ... it would be considered betrayal. We're at war."

"You're risking too much for me," I whispered.

"I didn't risk enough. That's why we're standing here today." He sighed. "I got all of your messages. I read them and I considered replying so often, but I was an idiot. I was angry and hurt."

I touched his cheek. "Forgive me."

"Fina, I'd forgive you of anything. But him..." Samuel indicated Remo "...him I won't ever forgive for taking you from us, from me. Not in one million years."

I swallowed. "I love him. He's the father of my children."

Samuel kissed my forehead. "That's why I won't put a bullet in his head today, even if I considered doing it on the way here."

Samuel's love for me stopped him from killing Remo, and Remo's love for me stopped him from killing my twin. I wished their love could also make them see past the feud, past the old hatred. "Will you be safe?"

"Don't worry about me, Fina." He raised his gaze to the man behind me. "I don't have to ask if you'll be safe because his eyes tell me all I need to know. He's a fucking murderous bastard, but a bastard who will kill anyone daring to look at you the wrong way."

I glanced over my shoulder at Remo, who was regarding us with intent. He looked relaxed to someone who didn't know him very well, but I caught the subtle tension in his muscles, the vigilance in his eyes. He didn't trust Samuel. Further down beside the arc, Nino kept throwing evaluating looks our way as well. "Remo will go through fire for me and our children," I whispered.

Samuel nodded. I could tell that he needed to go. He was surrounded by his enemies, and even if I knew he was safe because Remo had declared him as such, he felt uncomfortable.

"Will I see you again? I can't lose you, Sam."

Samuel rested his forehead against mine. "You won't lose me. I don't know how, but I'll try to talk to you on the phone and reply to your messages. But I can't come here again. And you can't come to Outfit territory."

"Thank you for being here."

He kissed my forehead again. Then with another hard look toward Remo, he walked away, sideways, never fully turning his back because he didn't trust Remo's promise. When he finally disappeared from view, I released a sharp breath. A bittersweet happiness filled me.

Remo came up behind me, his arms wrapping around my chest, pulling me against him. "You'll see him again. He won't give you up. He's as stubborn as you."

I gave him an indignant look. "I'm not stubborn."

"Of course not." He kissed my shoulder blade then lightly bit down on the crook of my neck, making me shiver with desire. I couldn't wait to be alone with him.

Remo

Serafina was practically shaking with arousal as I led her to our bedroom after the wedding feast. She was a beautiful bride, free and untamed and glowing with happiness. She was everything she was meant to be.

When we arrived in our bedroom, she pushed me against the door, shutting it in the process. Standing on her tiptoes, she pressed her body against mine, her fingers raking through my hair as her mouth tasted mine. Fuck. I met her tongue with hunger and need as my hands cupped her ass through her dress, squeezing hard. She moaned into my mouth, rubbing her breasts against my chest. One of her hands slid down my chest and closed over my cock, which was already painfully hard.

I rocked my hips, driving myself against her palm.

Snatching up Serafina's hand, I turned us around, trapping her between the door and my body, her arm raised above her head, pressed into the wood. "So dominant," she teased, and I silenced her with a harsher kiss, thrusting against her to show her what awaited her. I gathered her long skirt. "Hold it up, Angel," I ordered.

She bit her lip, stifling a smile. Her fingers curled over the fabric, and she held it up, revealing a flimsy lace thong.

I got down on one knee, smiling darkly as I slid the thin piece of clothing down her legs, laying her pussy bare to me. "Remember the first time I tasted your pussy?"

She widened her stance slightly, making a small impatient rocking motion with her pelvis. "How could I ever forget? It was the best thing I'd ever felt." Her voice was heavy with arousal.

"I'm going to make today even better," I promised.

"Please, Remo, just taste me already."

I hooked my palm under her knee and opened her up as I pressed her leg up against the door. Finally, I leaned forward and took a long lick. Pulling back, I rasped. "Oh, Angel, you're already so fucking ready for my cock."

Her eyes narrowed. "I don't care. I want your tongue first. Now stop talking."

I chuckled, ridiculously turned on by her desire and bossiness. Thrusting two fingers into her, I began sucking her clit. She cried out, one of her hands clutching my head as I alternated between sucking her nub and her soft lips while my fingers worked her deeply. Her wetness and the heady scent of her arousal drove me insane with desire, my cock close to combusting. I just wanted to fuck her, but she'd get what she wanted first. Her moans and whimpers turned more desperate as I drove her close to the brink only to release her clit and suckle the inside of her thigh, my fingers stilling.

"Remo," she said, half angry, half desperate.

I closed my mouth over her clit as I slammed my fingers into her, and Serafina arched up, crying out my name as her release shook her body. I kept thrusting and suckling until she began jerking, overwhelmed by the sensation. Sliding my fingers out of her channel, I dipped my tongue in, causing her to let out another low moan. I pushed to my feet, shoving down my pants and crashing my lips down against hers so she could taste herself. "Ready to be fucked now?" I growled.

"Oh yes," she groaned, her marble cheeks flushed with desire.

I hoisted her up against the door, her dress bunched between our bodies as Serafina wrapped her legs around my hips. Locking gazes, I drove into her in one hard thrust. Her walls clamped down around my cock, and she tilted her head back with a gasp, baring that perfect throat. I marked her unblemished skin, my fingers digging into her soft thighs as I slammed into her again and again. She clung to my shoulders, her lips parted, lids hooded with pleasure. Her grip turned painful as she got closer, her heels digging into my ass. I groaned, my balls tightening, but I kept thrusting into her, pushing her up against the wall, and then she froze with a beautiful cry. It took all my fucking self-control not to be swept away with her. Grunting, I kept rocking my hips until she softened, and her head fell forward for an uncoordinated kiss.

"Don't get too comfortable. I'm not done with you," I said roughly.

She smiled against my mouth, her blond hair sticking to her and my forehead as I carried her over to our bed. I dropped her down on the mattress, and she let out an indignant huff, her legs already parting in invitation.

I shook my head with a dark smile. "On your knees."

She rolled over, presenting her round ass cheeks then knelt on the bed. The sight of her waiting for me like that made my cock twitch. I leaned over her and bit her ass cheek before I pulled her toward my waiting cock. I caught the slight tensing of her muscles, the way she braced herself but she loosened, turned soft when I slid into her pussy not her ass.

We'd tried it a few times. It had always been my favorite before her, but I could tell Serafina only did it for me. She didn't enjoy it and in turn it had lost its appeal to me. I wanted Serafina crazy with lust not tense with discomfort.

I established a hard, fast rhythm, my balls slapping against her pussy. Serafina reached under her body and began stroking her clit, brushing my dick with her nails in the process, driving me completely crazy. Leaning forward, I brushed her hair aside so I could see her inked wings. I had already been close, and as I slammed into Serafina deeper than before, I finally let loose. Serafina got caught by my climax as well and bucked up, her arms giving out as her own release hit her. I kept pumping into her until I was completely spent. I gave her ass a clap before I pulled out and dropped down beside her. She snuggled against me, our breathing ragged, bodies slick with sweat. We shared a slow, lingering kiss.

I wrapped an arm around her shoulder, and Serafina linked our hands, holding them up. The winged ring with the diamonds and black sapphires looked perfect on her long finger. I had it made for her, and it had taken the jeweler several tries to get it exactly how I wanted it. His forehead was always slick with perspiration the moment I'd paid him a visit.

Serafina had caught me by surprise with her choice for me, but she couldn't have chosen better. The black carbide with the ebony center didn't feel foreign on my hand like I'd feared it would. I'd never worn any kind of jewelry, and I had thought I never would. Marriage had been out of the question. I'd never understood its appeal. I had companionship with my brothers, and I had enough women at my disposal for sex.

I'd never cared for any woman, except for Kiara maybe, but that was a different kind of caring. And then came Serafina, my angel, the woman meant to be my greatest triumph, and she was—only not in the way I'd thought she'd be.

"What are you thinking?" Serafina murmured, her voice slow and relaxed.

"That you are my greatest triumph."

She peered up at me. "I'm the queen. You are the king. And you used me to put the Outfit in checkmate."

Her voice was soft and teasing because she knew I didn't mean it like that, not anymore.

"If anyone's been checkmated, then it's me," I murmured. "You knocked me over, wiped away my resolve, captured my cruel black heart."

She raised her head. "Neither of us has been checkmated. We both won the game. We got each other. We got Nevio and Greta."

"You had to lose something to win."

She nodded but her eyes weren't sad. "I did. But losing something makes you appreciate the things you have so much more. I don't regret a thing because it brought me here. I love you with every fiber of my being."

I pulled her in for a kiss, still stunned that she could ever love me after what I'd done. I lightly traced the almost invisible scar on her forearm. "And I love you," I murmured harshly. I never thought I'd utter those words to anyone, even though I'd admitted my feelings to Serafina before. "Because you brave my darkness every day, because you should run but you don't, because you gave me the greatest gift of all, our children and yourself."

"I brave your darkness gladly because your light shines all the brighter against it," she said. I kissed her fiercely.

This woman had my cruel heart. She'd always have it.

I was cruel.

I was beyond redemption, but I didn't care as long as Serafina … as long as Nevio and Greta saw something redeeming when they looked at me. I'd make sure I'd never betray their love and trust. And if anyone ever dared to take them away from me, I'd show those unfortunate bastards what I was to those I didn't give a fuck about: the cruelest man of the west.

THE END

OTHER BOOKS

The Camorra Chronicles:

Twisted Loyalties (#1)
Fabiano

Twisted Emotions (#2)
Nino

Twisted Pride (#3)
Remo

Twisted Bonds (#4)
Nino

Twisted Hearts (#5)
Savio

March 2021:
Twisted Cravings (#6)
Adamo

Mafia Standalones

Sweet Temptation

Fragile Longing

Born in Blood Mafia Chronicles:

Bound by Honor
(Aria & Luca)

Bound by Duty
(Valentina & Dante)

Bound by Hatred
(Gianna & Matteo)

Bound By Temptation
(Liliana & Romero)

Bound By Vengeance
(Growl & Cara)

Bound By Love
(Luca & Aria)

Bound By The Past
(Dante & Valentina)

Bound By Blood Anthology
(various couples)

ABOUT THE AUTHOR

Cora Reilly is the *USA Today* Bestselling author of the Born in Blood Mafia Series, the Camorra Chronicles and many other books, most of them featuring dangerously sexy bad boys.

Cora lives in Germany with a cute but crazy Bearded Collie, as well as the cute but crazy man at her side. When she doesn't spend her days dreaming up sexy books, she plans her next travel adventure or cooks too spicy dishes from all over the world.

Made in the USA
Las Vegas, NV
26 June 2023

73941755R00431